BONE BY BONE

Also by Peter Matthiessen

Fiction

RACE ROCK

RADITZER

PARTISANS

AT PLAY IN THE FIELDS OF THE LORD

FAR TORTUGA

ON THE RIVER STYX AND OTHER STORIES

KILLING MISTER WATSON

LOST MAN'S RIVER

Non-Fiction

WILDLIFE IN AMERICA

THE CLOUD FOREST

UNDER THE MOUNTAIN WALL

THE SHOREBIRDS OF NORTH AMERICA

SAL SI PUEDES

THE WIND BIRDS

BLUE MERIDIAN

THE TREE WHERE MAN WAS BORN
(Also an illustrated edition with photographs by Eliot Porter)

THE SNOW LEOPARD

SAND RIVERS

IN THE SPIRIT OF CRAZY HORSE

INDIAN COUNTRY

NINE-HEADED DRAGON RIVER

MEN'S LIVES

AFRICAN SILENCES

EAST OF LO MONTHANG

Peter Matthiessen

BONE BY BONE

THE HARVILL PRESS
LONDON

First published in 1999 by Random House, New York

First published in Great Britain in 1999 by
The Harvill Press
2 Aztec Row, Berners Road
London N1 0PW

1 3 5 7 9 8 6 4 2

Copyright © Peter Matthiessen, 1999

Peter Matthiessen asserts the moral right
to be identified as the author of this work

A CIP catalogue record is available from the British Library

ISBN 1 86046 667 2 (hbk)
ISBN 1 86046 668 0 (pbk)

Printed and bound by Butler & Tanner Ltd
at Selwood Printing, Burgess Hill

To my old friends (and agents) Candida Donadio and Neil Olson
and my new friend (and editor) Deb Futter (and Becky and Lee, and Beth
and Benjamin, and many other friends at Random House)
with sincere gratitude for their great patience and support in the long throes
of what can only be called a twenty-year obsession

There is a pain—so utter—it swallows substance up—
Then covers the Abyss with Trance so Memory can step
Around—across—upon it
As one within a Swoon—goes safely—where an open eye—
Would drop Him—Bone by Bone

—Emily Dickinson

Good and evil we know in the field of this world grow up
almost inseparably.

—John Milton, *Paradise Lost*

A man's life of any worth is a continual allegory, and few eyes
can see [its] mystery.

—John Keats

Sir, what is it that constitutes character, popularity, and power
in the United States? Sir, it is property, and that only!

—Governor John Hammond of South Carolina

Author's Note
and Acknowledgments

A man still known in his community as E. J. Watson has been reimagined from the few hard "facts"—census and marriage records, dates on gravestones, and the like. All the rest of the popular record is a mix of rumor, gossip, tale, and legend that has evolved over eight decades into myth.

This book reflects my own instincts and intuitions about Watson. It is fiction, and the great majority of the episodes and accounts are my own creation. The book is in no way "historical," since almost nothing here is history. On the other hand, there is nothing that could *not* have happened—nothing inconsistent, that is, with the very little that is actually on record. It is my hope and strong belief that this reimagined life contains much more of the truth of Mr. Watson than the lurid and popularly accepted "facts" of the Watson legend.

—from the Author's Note for *Killing Mister Watson* (1990)

Bone by Bone is the third volume of a trilogy. Like *Killing Mister Watson* and *Lost Man's River*, it is a work of fiction. Certain historical names are used for the sake of continuity with the first two volumes, and certain situations and anecdotes were inspired in part by real-life incidents, but no character is intended to depict an actual person, and all episodes and dialogues be-tween the characters are products of the author's imagination.

Once again, I am grateful for the kind assistance of the pioneer families of southwest Florida, who supplied much local information, both historical and anecdotal. None of these friends and informants are responsible for the author's use of that material, or for his fictional renditions of the life and times of these families and others.

—Peter Matthiessen

E. J. WATSON

His ancestors:

John and William, sons of Lucius Watson of Virginia, moved to Edgefield District, South Carolina, in the middle of the eighteenth century. John's son Michael, who became a renowned Indian fighter and great hero of the Revolutionary War, married William's daughter Martha, his first cousin. Their only son was Elijah Julian (1775–1850), who consolidated the large family holdings and left a plantation at Clouds Creek to every one of his eleven children, including Sophia, Tillman, Artemas, Elijah Junior, Michael, Ann.

His paternal grandparents:

Artemas Watson (1800–1841) and Mary Lucretia (Daniel) Watson (1807–1838)

His parents:

Elijah Daniel Watson ("Ring-Eye Lige")
    b. Clouds Creek, S.C., 1834
    d. Columbia, S.C., 1895
Ellen Catherine (Addison) Watson
    b. Edgefield Court House, S.C., 1832
    d. Fort White, Fla., 1910

Edgar Artemas* Watson
    b. Clouds Creek, S.C., November 7, 1855
    d. Chokoloskee, Fla., October 24, 1910
1st wife (1878): Ann Mary "Charlie" (Collins) Watson, 1862–1879
    Rob Watson, b. Fort White, Fla., 1879–?
2nd wife (1884): Jane S. "Mandy" (Dyal) Watson, 1864–1901
    Carrie Watson Langford, b. Fort White, Fla., 1885–?

*Apparently he changed his second initial to J in later life.

Edward Elijah "Eddie" Watson, b. Fort White, Fla., 1887–?
Lucius Hampton Watson, b. Oklahoma Territory, 1889–?
3rd wife (1904): Catherine Edna "Kate" (Bethea) Watson, 1889–?
Ruth Ellen Watson,† b. Fort White, Fla., 1905–?
Addison Tilghman Watson,† b. Fort White, Fla., 1907–?
Amy May Watson,† b. Key West, Fla., 1910–?
Common-law wife: Henrietta "Netta" Daniels, ca. 1875–?
Minnie Daniels, ca. 1895–?
Common-law wife: Mary Josephine "Josie" Jenkins, ca. 1879–?
Pearl Watson, ca. 1900–?
Infant male, b. May 1910; perished in hurricane, October 1910

EJW's sister: Mary Lucretia "Minnie" Watson, b. Clouds Creek, S.C., 1857–?
Married William "Billy" Collins of Fort White, Fla., ca. 1880
Billy Collins died in 1907 at Fort White
The Collins children:
Julian Edgar, 1880–?
William Henry "Willie," 1886–?
Maria Antoinett "May," 1892–?

ALSO: EJW's Great-Aunt Tabitha (Wyches) Watson (1813–1905), 3rd wife
and widow of Artemas Watson's brother Michael: instrumental in
marriage of Elijah D. Watson and Ellen Addison.
Her daughter Laura (1830–1895), childhood friend of Ellen Addison.
Married William Myers ca. 1867
Married Samuel Tolen ca. 1890

†Not real name.

BONE BY BONE

Chapter 1

Oh Mercy, cries the Reader. What? Old Edgefield again?
It must be Pandemonium itself, a very District of Devils!

—Parson Mason L. Weems

Edgefield Court House

Edgefield Court House, which gave its name to the settlement which grew from a small crossroads east of the Savannah River, is a white-windowed brick edifice upon a hill approached by highroads from the four directions, as if drawing the landscape all around to a point of harmony and concord. The building is faced with magisterial broad steps on which those in pursuit of justice may ascend from Court House Square to the brick terrace. White columns serve as portals to the second-story courtroom, and an arched sunrise window over the door fills that room with austere light, permitting the magistrate to freshen his perspective by gazing away over the village roofs to the open countryside and the far hills, blue upon blue.

Early in the War, a boy of six, I was borne lightly up those steps on the strong arm of my father. On the courthouse terrace, I gazed with joy at this tall man in Confederate uniform who stood with his hand shielding his eyes, enjoying the fine prospect of the Piedmont, bearing away toward the northwest and the Great Smoky Mountains. In those nearer distances lay the Ridge, where a clear spring appeared out of the earth to commence its peaceful slow descent through woodland and plantation to the Edisto River. This tributary was Clouds Creek, where I was born.

On that sunny day when we climbed to the terrace, my father, Elijah Daniel Watson, rode away to war and childhood ended. As a "Daughter of Edgefield," his wife Ellen, with me and my little sister, waved prettily from the courthouse steps as the First Edgefield Volunteers assembled on the square.

Her handsome Lige, wheeling his big roan and flourishing a crimson pennant on his saber, pranced in formation in the company of cavalry formed and captained by his uncle Tillman Watson. Governor Andrew Pickens saluted the new company from the terrace, and so did Mama's cousin Selden Tilghman, the first volunteer from our Old Edgefield District and its first casualty. Called to the top step to inspire his townsmen, the young cavalry officer used one crutch to wave the blue flag of the Confederacy.

Hurrah, hurrah, for Southern rights, hurrah! Hurrah for the bonnie blue flag that flies the single star!

Governor Pickens roared, "May the brave boys of Edgefield defend to the death the honor and glory of our beloved South Carolina, the first great sovereign state of the Confederacy to secede from the Yankee Union!" And Cousin Selden, on some mad contrary impulse, dared answer the Governor's exhortation by crying out oddly in high tenor voice, "May the brave boys of Edgefield defend to their deaths our sovereign right to enslave the darker members of our human species."

The cheering faltered, then died swiftly to a low hard groan like an ill wind. Voices catcalled rudely in the autumn silence. Most citizens gave the wounded lieutenant the benefit of the doubt, concluding that he must have been dead drunk. He had fought bravely and endured a grievous wound, and he soon rode off to war again, half-mended.

Clouds Creek

When the War was nearly at an end, and many slaves were escaping to the North, a runaway was slain by Overseer Claxton on my great-uncle's plantation at Clouds Creek.

Word had passed the day before that Dock and Joseph were missing. At the racketing echo of shots from the creek bottoms, I yelped in dismay and dropped my hoe and lit out across the furrows toward the wood edge, trailing the moaning of the hounds down into swamp shadows and along wet black mud margins, dragged at by thorns and scratched by tentacles of old and evil trees.

I saw Dock first—dull stubborn Dock, lashed to a tree—then the overseer whipping back his hounds, then two of my great-uncles, tall and rawboned on rawboned black horses. The overseer's pony shifted in the shadows. Behind the boots and milling legs, the heavy hoof stamp and horse shivers, bit jangle and creak of leather, lay a lumped thing in earth-colored homespun. I was panting so hard that my wet eyes could scarcely make out the broken shoes, the legs hard-twisted in the bloody pants, the queer gray thing stuck out askew from beneath the chest—how could that thing be the limber hand that had offered nuts or berries, caught my mistossed balls, set young "Mast' Edguh" on his feet after a fall? All in a bunch, the fingers had contracted like the toes of a stunned bird, closing on nothing.

*

At daybreak Mr. Claxton, on the lookout, had seen a small smoke rising from a far corner of the swamp. His horse was saddled and he did not wait for help, just loosed his hounds and rode on down there. The runaways had fled his dogs, obliging him to shoot and wound them both—that was his story. He was marching them home when this damned Joseph sagged down like a croker sack, pissing his pants. "I told that other'n over yonder, Shut up your damn moanin. Told him, Stand that son-bitch on his feet, I ain't got all day. Done my duty, Major, but it weren't no use."

Major Tillman Watson and Elijah Junior sat their horses, never once dismounted. My great-uncles chewed on Claxton's story. The dead boy's wet homespun was patched dark and stuck with dirt, and a faint piss stink mixed with dog smell and the sweet musk of horses. "Wet his damn pants," the overseer repeated to no one in particular, awaiting the judgment of those mounted men. He was a closed-face man, as hard as wire.

"You have no business here," Great-Uncle Elijah Junior told me, not because night was coming on or because I was too young to witness this grim sight but because I was certainly neglecting whichever chore I had abandoned without leave. To the overseer he never spoke, confining his exasperation to muttered asides in the direction of his older brother concerning "the waste of a perfectly good nigger."

Major Tillman Watson, home from war, seemed more disturbed by Claxton's viciousness. "Dammit, Z.P., you trying to tell us these boys was aiming to outrun them hounds of yours? How come you had to go and pull the trigger?" He was backing his big horse, reining its wild-eyed head away toward home. "Close his eyes, goddamnit." He was utterly fed up. "Go fetch a cart."

"I reckon he'll keep till mornin," Claxton muttered, sullen.

Major Tillman frowned down on me, in somber temper. "What do you want here, boy?" (*Badly enough to run out here barefoot,* that's what he meant.) "It's almost dark," he called, half-turned in the saddle. "You're not afraid out here? All by yourself?"

"Yessir. I mean, nosir."

"*Nosir.*" The Major grunted. "You're a Watson anyways, I'll say that much. All the same, you best go on home while there's still light, and don't go worrying your poor mama." The old soldier rode away through the dark trees.

"Tell them niggers bring the wagon if they want him!" the overseer bawled, not wishing to be heard. Receiving no answer, he swore foully. "Niggers'll come fetch him or they won't—that sure ain't *my* job." He did not bother to shut the black boy's eyes. "Too bad it weren't this monkey here," he rasped, stripping the bonds from the wounded Dock, who yelped with each rough jerk of the hemp line.

Though Claxton had grumped in my direction, he had paid me no attention until this moment. "What in the name of hell you want? Ain't never seen a dead nigger before?" He climbed gracelessly onto his horse, cracked his hide whip like a mule skinner. "Nosir, I ain't goin to no damn court, cause I ain't broke no law. Just done my job." The slave stumbled forward, with the man on horseback and lean hounds behind. In single file against the silver water of the swamp, they moved away into the dusk. "You aim to leave him here alone?" I called. *Out in the swamp all night? All by himself? With the owls and snakes and varmints?*—that's what I meant. It sounded absurd, and Claxton snorted, cursing his fate because he dared not curse a Watson, even a Watson as young and poor as me.

In the dusk, the forest gathered and drew close. Behind me, the body lay in wait. Alone with a woodland corpse at nightfall, I was scared. I peered at the earthen lump between my fingers, retreating from its great loneliness. In the dusk he seemed to withdraw, as if already rotting down amongst the roots and ferns, skin melding with the black humus of the swamp, as if over the night this bloodied earth must take him back—as if all of his race were doomed to be buried here in darkness, while white folks were laid in sunny meadows in the light of Heaven.

*

On long-gone sunny Sabbath mornings of those years before the War, before the restless and ungrateful Africans were banished from our churches, I would run with the black children into the bare-earth yards back in the quarters, scattering dusty pigs and scraggy roosters to make room for hide-and-seek and tag and jump-rope games, or go crowding into Aunt Cindy's cramped dark cabin to be lifted and hugged and fed molasses biscuits, fatback or clabber, hominy, sometimes wild greens. And in those slave cabins on a Sunday morning I was always looked after by this sweet-voiced Joseph, who went out of his way to make the white child welcome.

Now that shining face had thickened like a mask with its stopped blood, and bloodied humus crusted its smooth cheek. I stood transfixed by the glare in those brown eyes. The dead I had seen before, even as a child, but not the killed. Until Mama protested, our cousin Selden, home from war, had related philosophically that the corpse of a human being slain in violence and left broken where it fell looked nothing at all like the sedate family cadaver, eyes closed and pale hands folded in its bed or coffin, scrubbed and perfumed, combed and suited up in Sunday best for the great occasion. Only those, said he, who touched their lips to the cool forehead one last time knew that faint odor of cold meat left too long.

In violent death, Cousin Selden said, even one's beloved—and here he looked sardonically at Mama, whose husband he "cordially" disliked—looked like a strange thing hurled down out of Heaven. Cousin Selden was well-read and liked to talk in that peculiar manner. Not that black Joseph had been my "beloved," I don't mean that. Joseph was guilty and the laws were strict, and had he lived, he would have been flogged half to death, as Dock would be. But Joseph had been kind to me, he had been kind. I was still young and could not help my unmanly feelings.

*

Damn you, Joseph—that yell impelled me forward, for in a moment I was kneeling by his side, trying to pull him straight, trying to fold his arms across his chest. The dead are heavy, as I learned that day, and balky, too. He would not lay still the way I wanted him. The brown eyes, wide in the alarm of dying, were no longer moist with life but dry and dull. I was terrified of his company, I had to go.

The forehead was drained of blood and life, like the cool and heavy skin of a smooth toadstool. Drawing the eyelids down, my finger flinched, so startled was it by how delicate they were, and how naturally and easily they closed. Where the shock lay was not in the strange temperature but in the protruding firmness of the orb beneath, under thin petals—I had never imagined that human eyes were so hard. A moment later, one lid rose—only a little, very very slowly—in a kind of squint.

I don't recall how I reached my feet, that's how quick I jumped and ran. *Joseph! I'm sorry!* To the horseman, I hollered, *Wait!*

"Just goes to show you," the overseer was muttering as I caught up. "There is such a thing as too much nigger spirit." I did not ask what that might mean, and anyway, I doubted if he knew.

As for my fear, it was nothing more than common dread of swamps and labyrinths, of dusk, of death—the shadow places. Yet poor black Joseph sprawled unburied in the roots, losing all shape and semblance to the coming night, was an image etched in my mind's eye all my life.

*

My grandfather Artemas Watson had died in 1841 at the age of forty. His second wife, Lucretia Daniel, had predeceased him three years earlier, at age thirty, and my father—Elijah Daniel Watson—born in 1834, was therefore an orphan at an early age. However, the family held considerable wealth.

Grandfather Artemas had owned sixty-nine slaves, with like numbers distributed among his brothers. Upon his death, his estate was mostly left to his eldest son, my uncle James, who became my father's keeper. In 1850, at age fifteen, Papa still held real estate and property in the amount of $15,000, by no means a negligible sum, but he seems to have squandered most of his inheritance by the time he married Mama five years later, mostly on gambling and horses.

The marriage of a Clouds Creek Watson was duly recorded in the Edgefield Marriage Records: *Elijah D. Watson and Ellen C. Addison, daughter of the late John A. Addison, January 25, 1855.* My maternal grandfather, Colonel Addison, had commissioned the construction of the courthouse from which the village took its name (and in which his unlucky daughter's husband, in the years to come, would make regular appearances as a defendant). His pretty Ellen was an orphan, her mother having died at age twenty-five, but she had been a ward in a rich household—she was given her own slave girl, and piano lessons—until the day she was married off to young Elijah. They had little in common other than the fact that their fathers had died in 1841, and both were orphans.

*

Four years after his bugled glory on the courthouse square, Private Lige Watson, having lost his horse, walked home from war. Papa told us of the sack and burning of Columbia by General Sherman, evoking the capital's lone chimneys, the black skeletons of its noble oaks. Astonished that Clouds Creek and Edgefield Court House had been left untouched, he said, "You folks at home know nothing of real war."

We had known something of real war, of course, having scoured bare sustenance from our poor remnant of the Artemas Plantation. The rest had been bought or otherwise acquired by Great-Uncle Elijah Junior, who early in the War had assumed our mortgage, extending modest help to the absent soldier's wife and children. As a precaution against his nephew's famous temper, he let our family remain in the dilapidated house and raise such food and cotton as we might.

However, my mother, burdened with little Minnie, could not manage alone, not even with my eight-year-old hard labor, so my great-uncle sent over the sullen Dock, knowing Dock would run off at the first chance, which he did, this time for good. Next, he sent us old Tap Watson, who had grown up on the Artemas Plantation, since Tap was going to be lost to him in any case, the way the War was going. As the father of the slain boy Joseph, Tap no longer worked well under Overseer Claxton, who had been too quick on the trigger, all agreed. *That feller could never see eye to eye with niggers, just can't tolerate 'em,* sighed Great-Uncle Tillman, *but he scares some work out of 'em, I'll give him that.*

Tap Watson was a small blue-black man of taciturn and truculent disposition, but he had not forgotten the kindness received from his late Master Artemas, that vague and gentle farmer who had owned Tap's parents and from his deathbed had set this old man free. Unlike his boy, Tap preferred slavery to Freedom—*If Freedom never comes, we has our jobs, y'know, somethin to eat*—and when it came, he had cashed it in by selling himself to Elijah Junior for cold coin. Slave or freedman, Tap had never missed a day of work—such was his boast and pride—not even the day after Joseph died down in the swamp. Earlier, Tap had warned his boy that runaways deserved dire punishment, but hearing the news, Tap had stopped dead in his tracks and fixed his son's slayer with a baleful yellow eye, only turning away when the overseer hitched his whip by way of warning.

Ordered to leave that old man be, Claxton folded his arms and remained right where he was, to make sure Tap finished slopping the hogs before taking time off to hitch a mule to the wagon and go fetch the body. Never again would Tap acknowledge the overseer's presence. Even when the shouting Claxton pointed at his eyes, those yellowed eyes out of Africa looked past him. For these reasons, Great-Uncle Elijah Junior was happy to be rid of that old man.

Besides Joseph, Tap had a second child, this one with Cinderella, Mama's slave girl, now the grown woman whom we called Aunt Cindy. Since all of the Watson plantations at Clouds Creek adjoined one another, these darkies had no need to change dwellings when Tap came back to us. Even so, Mama ordered them to marry.

*

When I told Papa how Mr. Claxton had killed Joseph, Papa said roughly, "Damn nigger runaway. Deserved no better." He was turning bitter, he was very restless. Returned from the War impoverished, now close to thirty, Papa had been obliged to start all over as a poor relation of stern prosperous kin who prided themselves on self-sufficiency and independence. A tenant farmer on the Artemas Plantation, he was paying a third of all crops raised to his uncle Elijah Junior. But in the lean aftermath of war, struggling to grow cotton with his wife and children, he slid into heavy debt to his own clan. As a war veteran, disarmed and disenfranchised, he would rail against the injustice of his fate, yet he would not tolerate Mama's criticisms of Elijah Junior. Indeed he acclaimed his uncle's "Watson thrift" even when this dour trait caused his own household to go hungry. (It was all very well about Watson thrift, his wife would say, but how did that differ from hard-hearted stinginess?) With a genuine and gallant optimism, my father pledged that one day, with God on his right hand and his strong son on his left, he would reclaim his family land, restoring the line of Artemas Watson to Clouds Creek. Carried away, he roughed my hair with vigor. Though my eyes watered, I wanted my soldier daddy to be proud of his son, and I did not whine.

For a time Lige Watson enjoyed oratorical support from his aunt Sophia, eldest daughter of the late patriarch, Elijah Senior, "the Old Squire," whom she liked to refer to in her brothers' presence as "the ramrod of this family." Sophia Boatright was a big top-heavy woman with a baying voice, and her favorite topic—indeed, her *only* topic, Mama whispered—was the Watson clan, all the way back to the English Watsons (or Welsh or Scots or perhaps Ulstermen, sniffed Mama), those staunch landowners and men of means who had sailed in the sixteenth century to New York City, then traveled on to Olde Virginia to claim their tract of unfettered, free, and fertile land. The first New World patriarch was Lucius Watson Esquire of Amelia County in Virginia, whose sons would move on to South Carolina as early as 1735, when their first land grants were registered at Charleston—well before the arrival of these Edgefield Court House clans who gave themselves such airs today, Aunt Sophia assured us.

A son of those forefathers was Michael Watson, a famous Indian-fighter who chastised the Cherokees and later led a citizens' militia against highwaymen and outlaws who had foully murdered his father and a brother. Meanwhile, he acquired a tract of six thousand acres on Clouds Creek, which was consolidated as clan property when he married Martha Watson, his first cousin. (Here Mama dared roll her eyes for her children's benefit, screwing her forefinger into her temple to convey the lunacy caused by inbreeding, and sending our little Min into terrified giggles.)

During the Revolutionary War, Michael Watson had served as a field captain of Pickens's Brigade, a mounted company armed with rifles and muskets for the mortal fight against the "King-Lovers" or Tories. At one point, he was captured and imprisoned at Columbia, where according to one reputable account—which Aunt Sophia enjoyed reading out loud to the clan— Martha Watson Watson, who was "small and beautiful, with wonderfully thick long hair . . . wound a rope around her body and carried files in her hair for the use of Captain Watson, [who] made his escape." (Here my mother might pretend to yank and struggle desperately with her own hair, risking what she called "the Great Wrath of the Watsons" with her sly whisperings: *Captain Michael, darlin? Mah handsome he-ro? I have brought you this nice li'l ol' file so you can saw those bars in twain and make good your escape! So hold your horses, Captain dear, whilst I unsnarl this pesky thing from mah gloerious hay-uh!*)

In an early history of South Carolina, our famous ancestor had been described as "a determined and resentful man who consulted too much the counsels which these feelings suggested." From Tory gaol, the choleric Captain had rushed straight back into battle, and was fatally wounded in the forest swamps on a branch of the south Edisto. Having turned over his command to Lieutenant Billy Butler, our ancestor composed himself and "died for Liberty."

"Those Edgefield families prate about their 'aristocracy'!" Sophia Boatright scoffed one day. "How about our Clouds Creek aristocracy? The first Watsons held royal grants for two decades before Andrew Pickens came down out of the hills, and they owned more land. It's just that our land is farther from the Court House."

("Nevertheless," Mama might murmur to my flustered father, who could not hush her forcefully in a family gathering, "it was called Pickens's Brigade, not Watson's Brigade, isn't that true, dear? And that handsome young lieutenant became General Butler, father of General Matthew Calbraith Butler, who married the exquisite Maria Pickens, whose father was a general, too. Has there ever been a General *Watson*, dear?" Such remarks would be made just loud enough to stiffen the black whiskers of Aunt Sophia.)

Captain Michael's only son, Elijah Julian, would become the landed patriarch of the Watson clan. Through industry and force of character, the Old Squire acquired eleven plantations, one for each of his eleven children. However, "his favorite was always his first daughter, Sophia," declared Aunt Sophia. Among his seven sons, besides Tillman and Artemas and Elijah Junior, was another Michael, whose meddling widow, Great-Aunt Tabitha, was held responsible by both my parents for their unhappy marriage.

"I do declay-uh, I've been bred up on ouah family traditions," Aunt Sophia liked to say, with the shuffle and shift of bombazine and feathers that signaled the onset of another anecdote which celebrated her own insights and accomplishments. One day when the Yankees ordered their black militia to drill on her broad lawn, the Ramrod's gallant eldest daughter had strode forth shouting, "Now you monkeys just stop all that darn foolishness and go on home!" which of course they did.

We are no Eire-ish nor Sco-atch, nor are we Enga-lish—thus would the Old Squire tease his proud Sophia whenever she put on English airs, according to the recollections of her siblings. With Border folk, he would point out, who could determine who was what, since none had agreed for seven hundred years where the Borders lay? *No,* the Old Squire had mused, rapping his pipe. *We belong to none of those benighted races. We are sons of Watt, we are*

Border Watsons, nothing more and nothing else. But when pressed, the Old Squire would concede that the clan was Welsh.

*

Mama's cousin Selden Tilghman, a young bachelor and scholar who lived alone on his family plantation, known as Deepwood, held the opinion that those early New World Watsons had probably turned up first in the port of Philadelphia, in the shiploads of Highland refugees from seven centuries of war and famine in the Border counties. These clannish and unruly Celts (as Cousin Selden delighted in portraying them) had horrified the Quakers with their outlandish speech and uncouth disrespect for all authority. Their women were infamous for short-cropped skirts, bare legs, and loose bodices, while the men mixed unabashed poverty and filth with a raw arrogance and a furious pride which hastened to avenge the smallest offense, denigration, or injustice. Worse, they did this in the name of "honor," a virtue which more mannerly colonials would never concede to such rough persons. They were urged westward toward the back country of the Pennsylvania Colony, in the hope that wild peoples as barbaric as themselves might do away with them.

The Borderers were a suspicious breed of feuders and avengers, cold-eyed and mistrustful of all strangers, or any who interfered with them in the smallest way. They fought their way through Indian territory with fatalistic indifference to hard faring and danger, spreading south like a contagion along the Appalachians into western Virginia and the Carolina uplands. Many were drovers of cattle and hogs, throwing up low cabins of wood or stones packed tight with earth, hunting and gathering the abounding game and fish, trading meat where possible for grain and iron, boozing and bragging and breeding, ever breeding. Scattering homesteads and ragged settlements south and west to the Great Smokies, massacring Cherokees wherever fortune smiled, they strengthened and perpetuated their headstrong clans without relinquishing one dour trait or archaic custom. When times were hard, not a few would resort to traditional Border occupations—reivers and cattle rustlers, highwaymen and common bushwhackers.

Or so, at least, Celtic life was represented by Cousin Selden, whose mother had come from the Cavalier gentry of Maryland, and whose amused, ironic views, spiced up by Mama, she passed on to her children in their father's presence. The Border Watsons were essentially of this same breed, Selden implied—quarrelsome fighters disrespectful of all authority, obstreperous rebels against Church and Crown, and as careless of good manners as of hardship and rude weather, not to speak of all the finer sentiments of the human heart.

Papa detested Cousin Selden's casual disparagement of the Clouds Creek Watsons. Though no match for his tart Ellen, he defended his family with a heartfelt rage. If the Watsons were mere Border rabble, he might bellow, then how would "precious Selden" explain their early prosperity in the New World? For whether by grant from the South Carolina Colony or Crown patent from King George, enlarged by land purchase, the first Carolina Watsons had acquired sixteen square miles—*sixteen square miles!*—of the best land in the Clouds Creek country on the north fork of the Edisto River even before that mud crossroads—not known until a century later as Edgefield Court House—would arise. What was more, my grandmother Mary Lucretia Daniel had been a descendant of Martha Jefferson, President Jefferson's great-aunt. "You have a long proud heritage to uphold," Papa exclaimed with passion, tossing his head dismissively in his wife's direction.

For his violent abuse and abysmal failure as a father and provider—for her own exhaustion and privation—the former Miss Ellen Catherine Addison repaid her husband with sly laughter at those "darned old Watsons," as she called them. The Addison family, she would imply, was better educated, more refined, and in every way more suitable than the Watsons to consort with the aristocracy at Edgefield Court House, not to speak of Charleston, far less England.

Lige Watson, in turn, would refer to his wife's "traitorous" Tory antecedents and their "lily-livered longing," as he called it, to be accepted by the Pickenses and Butlers, the Brookses and the Hammondses. "Spare your poor children these vulgarities, I beseech you," his wife might protest, to hone her point that he was not a gentleman. Ellen Catherine Addison, she would remind us, had been born into aristocratic circumstances, however straitened and reduced. It was scarcely her fault that her feckless husband had sold off all of her inheritance excepting her mother's set of the Waverley novels, which was missing her own favorite, *Ivanhoe*. "To think," she would sigh, cocking her pretty head, "that I once thought of Elijah Watson as my Ivanhoe!" Gladly would she play the piano for her husband—"to soothe your savage breast, dear," she might add with a girlish peal—if such an instrument were to be found in a Watson house, or fit into a Watson house, for that matter, since for all their prosperity those Clouds Creek farmers, foregoing the large white-columned mansions of the Edgefield gentry, were mainly content with large two-story versions of the rough-sawed timber cabins of their yeomen forebears.

"*Yeomen?*"

Thus would my mother prattle for our benefit. We scarcely heard her, so intent were our wide eyes on the enraged and dangerous father in the chimney corner.

*

Increasingly, Papa would jeer at the emancipated Negroes, who could find no work around the towns and villages. In this past year of 1867, under the Reconstruction Act, all blacks had become wards of the Union government, to be protected henceforth as citizens and voters, and a Yankee detachment had been sent to Edgefield to enforce their rights. In a district where blacks outnumbered whites, and where white soldiers had been disenfranchised, the terrible hatred of Reconstruction would find its scapegoat in black freedmen, especially those "woods niggers" or "road walkers" who wandered the mud roads between settlements, awaiting fulfillment of the Union's promise of "forty Confederate acres and a mule." These ragged hordes were perceived by the ex-soldiers as a menace to white womanhood and were commonly terrorized and beaten, sometimes worse.

Colonel Selden Tilghman, waving a copy of a Freedmen's Bureau report that murdered blacks were being found along the road or in the woods or swamps, had spoken publicly in favor of federal relocation of all freedmen from our Edgefield District, though he knew well that our local planters were counting on near-slave labor to survive. The crowd heard him out only because he had been a war hero with battlefield promotions, but finally the more bellicose began to shout that Tilghman was a traitor, war hero or no. Wasn't it true that he had freed his slaves before the War in defiance of Carolina laws against manumission, and openly endorsed Damn Yankee Abolition? Wasn't he the officer who had interfered with the execution of black Union soldiers imprisoned at Fort Pillow before General Nathan Bedford Forrest rode up and commanded the killing to resume? ("Blood and Honor, sir! In Virginia they take no nigger prisoners, and nor shall we!")

Tilghman's proposal never reached a vote, and Tilghman, never to be forgiven, was "hated out" of the community, in that hoary Celtic custom of assailing the outcast with hisses, blows, abuse, or stony silence. Next came the theft and slaughter of his stock, the burning barn, the threat of death, until at last the poor man fled the region or destroyed himself, "all because he had spoken out for Christian decency," said Mama, very upset that, for her children's safety, she dared not speak herself.

Cousin Selden had the courage of his isolation. Refusing to abandon the old family manse, he remained at Deepwood as a recluse even after the Regulators passed word that no one, white or black, should be seen going there or entering its lane. Within a few years, its roads and fields were sadly overgrown and the house had withdrawn and shrunk down like a dying creature behind the climbing shrouds of vine and creeper.

Deepwood

Lige Watson rode with a rifle in a saddle scabbard, a revolver in his belt, a hidden Bowie knife. Mostly, said he, the Regulators made their patrols on Saturday nights of the full moon—Major Will Coulter, Z. P. Claxton, Lige Watson, and two younger men, Toney and Lott, were the regulars. Other men would join when needed, and an indifferent nigger on a mule to tend the horses.

On what I thought must surely be the happiest day in all my life, Papa swung me up behind him on his big horse. "Come along and you will see something," he promised, grinning. From time to time, he would teach me those arts which Mama disapproved of—how to manage and race horses, how to shoot and use a knife. Sometimes he let me taste his whiskey, and when he was drinking, he might show me "just for fun" how to cheat a bit at cards or conceal weapons. But as I would learn, he was barely competent in most of these attainments, which he confused with some ideal of manhood. I did, too, of course, for I was twelve.

We rode toward Edgefield. At the Tilghman place, called Deepwood, a slight fair man came out onto the highroad in his linen shirtsleeves, stretching his arms wide to bar our progress as the big horse danced and whinnied, backing around in its own dust.

"Not one word, boy," Papa growled over his shoulder.

Cousin Selden murmured to the roan, slipping his hand onto the bridle so that Papa could not wheel into him, knock him away. The easy movement was so sure of horse and rider that the muscles stiffened in my father's back. "Let go," he grunted, shifting his quirt to his right hand as if set to strike our kinsman in the face.

With his fair hair and shy expression, Cousin Selden looked and sounded less like a bold cavalry officer and Edgefield hero than like my sister's young piano teacher (paid for by our uncle John Addison). Because of his high tenor voice—and because he had never married—Papa called him a sissy out of Mama's hearing. However, that voice was very calm and cold. "There's three young nigras back up yonder in the branch. Wrists bound, shot like dogs. Dumped there like offal." His pale fury and contempt seemed just as scary as Papa's red eruptive violence. "Since today is the Sabbath, Private Watson, I thought you might assist me with a Christian burial."

To call a man "Private" who was known as a captain of the Regulators was proof enough of Selden Tilghman's craziness. "It was done last night," Tilghman persisted. "These murder gangs ride at night, isn't that true?" He had a fever in his eyes. "Since you claim to be his kinsman, Private Watson, you cannot have forgotten the immortal words of Jefferson of Virginia: *I tremble for my country when I reflect that God is just!*

Papa had raised his arm but that shout stopped him. He could not bring himself to horsewhip the man down. "I'll have nothing to do with traitors!" he yelled. "Now stand aside!" Lashing the reins, digging his spurs, my father fought violently to ride free with his son clinging to his sweaty back. The struggle amused Cousin Selden, who smiled just a little, catching my eye. (I smiled, too, before I caught myself.) All the while, Tilghman braced his back against the horse's neck. Talking to it, fist clenched on the reins under the bit, he brought the wheeling beast under control.

Heavy in the saddle, his big shoulders slumped, Papa appeared deflated and subdued. "Road walkers," he growled.

" 'Road walkers.' " Tilghman mimicked him with wry distaste. "How do you know that, Private? How do you damned vigilantes know about these murdered boys back in my branch?"

"Because if they were home niggers, sir, a Radical Scalawag and traitor like yourself would know their names. Now stand aside!" Whistling like a pigeon's wing, the quirt struck Selden Tilghman on the side of the head, knocking him off balance, and still he kept a tight grip on the reins. The horse screeched and snorted, dancing sideways, and Papa struck Tilghman heavily again. This time he fell. Papa shouted "You can thank your honorable record in the War, sir, that you have your life!"

Tilghman rose unhurriedly, brushed himself off. " 'My honorable record,' " he repeated. Lifting his pale bleeding face, he contemplated mine. "What would Lige Watson know about such matters?" he inquired, looking straight at me.

"I served four years, sir, Edgefield to Appomattox. Are you challenging my honor, sir, before my son?" But when I hollered, "You damned nigger-loving traitor!" Papa shot an elbow back, bloodied my nose. "You'll show some respect for a Confederate officer, even this one!" I was astonished by his need to prove to Cousin Selden that Elijah D. Watson was a gentleman and a fierce guardian of Southern honor.

Amused that he and I were wiping bloody noses, Tilghman ignored him. Once again I had to scowl not to grin back. "Send her cousin's fond respects to your dear mother," he said courteously, as Papa wheeled and booted his horse into a canter. Hand on the hard-haired dusty rump, I turned for a last look at the figure in the road, and Cousin Selden raised his hand in a kind of half salute, calling out cheerfully, "God keep you, Cousin Edgar!"

"Face around, damn you!" Papa shouted, cocking his elbow. I hugged up close, out of harm's way, in his rank smell. "Damned sissy," he muttered. He galloped back the way that we had come.

"Papa? What was it you were going to show me?"

"Face around, I say!"

The Traitor

The day after our ride to Deepwood, the Traitor (as my father now referred to him) appeared at our door in full dress uniform, hands and face charred like a minstrel in blackface, gray tunic rent by black and ragged holes. Having long since sold his horse, he had come on foot. On the sill he set down a heavy sack containing his volumes of Greek literature—all he had saved from his burning house. "For your boy," he told Mama, who disobeyed her husband's edict and implored him to come in. He accepted a cup of water but would not enter the house nor even talk with us, lest that bring trouble.

Filled with dread, heart pounding, I followed the Traitor down the road toward the square. Already word had circulated that Colonel Tilghman meant to defy a warning from the Regulators to leave these parts on pain of death and never show his face again at Edgefield Court House. At his appearance, a great moan, then a wildfire whispering, foretold an evil end.

My kinsman addressed the market crowd from the courthouse steps. Though all could see the black smoke rising from Deepwood, to the eastward, he made no mention of night riders, but only denounced the senseless murder of three Negro youths. The refusal of a lawless few to accept the freedmen as new citizens, he cried, would not only imperil their mortal souls but cripple the recovery of South Carolina. "Before the War, our colored people were gentle, harmless folk who lived among us and worshiped with us in our congregations. Most remained loyal and many fought beside us!" He paused, looking around him. "Now there are those who would revile these faithful friends, and castigate them. Treat them as dangerous animals, and kill them. Every day black men are terrorized, not by outlaws and criminals but by so-called Christian men, including many who stand here today before this Court of Justice."

He glared about him, in a dangerous silence.

"Have not these poor souls suffered enough? What fault of theirs that they were enslaved and then turned free? Was it they who imposed these Reconstruction laws? Friends, it was *not!*" He raised both arms toward Heaven. "In taking revenge on innocent people for the calamity we brought down upon ourselves, we only worsen a dishonorable lie. We lost the War not because we were beaten by a greater force of arms. The North had more men and guns, more industry, more railways—that is true. But that was also our excuse, as we soldiers knew." He paused, lowering his arms in the awful hush. "More than half our eastern armies—and the bravest, too—put their arms down and went home of their own accord. We did that because in our hearts we knew that human bondage had never had—and could *never* have—the blessing of the Lord God who made us all."

When the first rock flew and yells of "Traitor!" started up and the crowd barged forward, the boyish colonel raised his hands, not to protect himself but seeking time to finish. "Our officers will tell you—those who are honest—that we only fought on so that the lives of the best and bravest of our young men should not have been sacrificed in vain. We fought for some notion of our Southern honor, and thousands died for it, to no good purpose, and now our dear land lies ruined on all sides.

"Where is that honor now? In taking a dishonorable revenge in cowardly acts of terror in the night, do we not dishonor those who died? Neighbors, hear me, I beseech you. Our 'Great Lost Cause' was never 'great,' as we pretended. It had no greatness and no honor in it, no nobility. It was merely wrong!"

He yelled this into my father's face as the Regulators seized him. He was dragged down the steps and beaten bloody and left in a poor heap in the public dust. There Major Coulter, hair raked back in black wings beneath his cap, stalked round and round him, stiff-legged and gawky as a crow. I had an impulse to rush out, perhaps others did, too, but nobody dared to breach the emptiness and isolation which had formed around him.

When Selden Tilghman regained consciousness, he lay a minute, then rolled over very slowly. Visage ghostly from the dust, he got up painfully, reeled, and fell. Next, he pushed himself onto all fours and crawled on hands and knees all the way across the square to the picket fence in front of the veranda of the United States Hotel, as Coulter and his men, jeering, watched him come. He used the fence to haul himself upright. Swaying, he blinked and then he shouted, "You are cowards! Betrayers of the South! You are cowards! Betrayers of the South!" With each *cowards!* he brought both fists down hard on the sharp points of the white pickets, and with each blow he howled in agony and despair, until the wet meat sounds of his broken hands caused the onlookers to turn away in horror. Even Z. P. Claxton had stopped grinning. It was my father, Captain Elijah D. Watson of the Regulators, who strode forth on a sign from Coulter and cracked our kinsman's jaw with one legendary blow, leaving him crumpled in the dust.

Cousin Selden's body was slung into a cotton wagon and trundled away on the Augusta Road. In the next fortnight rumors would come that the traitor had been dumped off at the gates of the Radical headquarters at Hamburg, but nobody could say what had become of him. The District heard no more of Selden Tilghman. When Mama finally confronted him about it, Papa blustered, "If the traitor is dead, the Regulators never killed him, that is all I know."

My pride in my father's prominence that day was edged with deep confusion and misgiving. Hoping and dreading Cousin Selden might reappear, I was drawn back to Deepwood over and over. Others in our district felt uneasy about "Tilghman's Ghost," which was said to come and go in that black ruin, and so I had Deepwood to myself, a private domain for hunting and trapping. Wild rose thorn and poverty grass returned to the fields and the woods edged forward, even as vines entwined the blackened house. *God keep you, Cousin Edgar!* When wind stirred the leaves, I imagined that I heard my kinsman's voice and its sad whispered warning.

*

In a voice pitched toward her husband, outside on the stoop, Mama said that before the War, his own family had belittled Cousin Selden. In adopting the New Light Baptist faith, he had disgraced his Anglican upbringing. The New Lights had not only advocated Abolition but had sought—and here she smiled—"a more liberal attitude toward the rights of women. These days, Negro men are allowed to vote, but not white women."

"Nor white men either," bawled her husband from the porch. "Not those who fought."

"Addisons being Episcopalians like most of our good families, I had no real acquaintance with the New Light Church, nor with your father's Baptist congregation, for that matter." Rising above the growls and spitting out of doors, she invited us to pity those poor women whose husbands were not God-fearing citizens—steadfast men who would abstain from the grog shops and gambling and sinful license to which the weak seemed so addicted, to the great suffering and deprivation of their families. Her tone was now edged with such contempt that Papa appeared in the door, though he held his tongue. "And throwing away their wages on mulatta women. Of course harlots have never been tolerated in Edgefield District. It is the bordellos across the Georgia line which beckon our local sinners to Damnation."

Mama bent to her knitting with the martyred smile of the good churchwoman whose mission on earth was to purify the immortal soul of her crude lump of a man and keep him from the Devil's handiwork. "In our church, of course, a man may be excommunicated for wife beating, or even," she added, brightly, "for adultery. With white or black. Or perhaps," she inquired directly of her husband, "you Baptists feel that mulatta women don't count?"

And still he held his tongue, mouth open, breathing like a man with a stuffed-up nose. As always, the son would reap the whipping, not the mother, and my heart sank slowly as a stone into wet mud. "Please, Mama," I whispered. "Oh please, Mama." And this time, with her quiver empty and her arrows all well-placed, our mama nodded. "Yes, Mr. Watson, we are still your slaves," she sighed, offering her children a sweet rueful smile. " 'Wives, submit yourselves unto your own husbands as unto the Lord. For the husband is head of the wife, even as Christ is head of the Church.' " Braving his glare, she added cheerfully, "Ephesians, dear."

Ellen Addison blamed nothing on cruel providence. She kept up her merciless good cheer in the worst of circumstances, as if aware that otherwise our wretched family must go under.

"Precisely because our soldiers cannot vote, South Carolina remains prostrate, at the mercy of damn Scalawags and their pet niggers!" Papa shouted. "That's Radical Reconstruction for you! Just what your mother's precious cousin wanted! And do you know who forced Reconstruction through the U.S. Senate? Charles Sumner of Massachusetts! And do you know why?"

"Oh we do, indeed we do," sighed Mama. "And since we know the story well, then surely our Merciful Savior will spare us another recounting—"

"*Yes,* boy! Because Congressman Preston Brooks of Edgefield caned Sumner on the Senate floor for having insulted Brooks's kinsman Andrew Pickens Butler! And Senator Butler—*do you hear me, boy?*—was the son of that same Billy Butler to whom your great-great-grandfather turned over the command of his brigade when fatally wounded by the Tories near Clouds Creek!"

Mama lured him off the subject of our Watson hero. "Now which Mr. Brooks shot that black legislator the other day, dear? While he knelt in prayer?"

"No Brooks shot that damned Coker, but Nat Butler."

"Well, Congressman Brooks was my father's commanding officer," she reflected. "In the Mexican War, children. Unlike Clouds Creek, Edgefield Court House was strongly represented in that Mexican War." Before Papa could protest, she exclaimed, "Think of it, children! The Brooks house has four acres of flowers! In the *front!*"

But Papa was not to be deterred. The caning of Sumner had occurred on May 22 of 1856, in the year after my own birth, and once again he brandished the event to imbue his son with the fierce and forthright spirit of Southern honor. He also invoked President Jackson's vice-president, John C. Calhoun, grandson of Squire Calhoun of Long Cane Creek, whose family lost twenty-three members to Indian massacres in a single year. "One day I saw the great Calhoun right here in Edgefield. Had the same lean leather face and deep hawk eyes as Old Hickory, Andy Jackson, and he was that same breed of fearless leader, unrelenting towards his enemies."

"Cruelty and vengeance. Are these the virtues you would inspire in your son?"

Papa, in full cry, paid her no attention. Before the War, said he, patriotic Carolinians had served in the Patrol, and in these dark days of Yankee Reconstruction, the Patrol's place had been taken by that honorable company of men known as the Regulators, among whom he himself was proud to ride.

"Honorable company!" Mama rolled her eyes over her knitting, the needles speeding with an incensed clicking noise, like feeding insects. Behind his broad back, she shook her head. Her lips said, *No.* She slapped her knitting down. "Is it considered honorable in this company of men to terrify and harm defenseless darkies?" Braving his glare, she quoted Cousin Selden's opinion that the vigilantes who terrorized the freedmen were mostly those weak vessels cracked by war. And she dared to cite Papa's "superior officer," Major Coulter, who kept the cropped ears of lynched black men in his saddlebags. "No act perpetrated by that man, however barbarous and vile, seems to shake your father's high opinion of him," Mama sighed.

I caught the nice distinction Mama made here—the implication that her husband, not being warped or cracked like Major Coulter, had been weak to start with. She would even hint that he had joined the vigilantes less because of his own convictions than because he knew no better way to be accepted or at least tolerated by the night riders.

Ring-Eye Lige

Late in 1868, "the Bad Elijah" (Papa's nickname at Clouds Creek) sold his share of what was left of the Artemas Plantation to Elijah Junior's son Colonel Robert Briggs Watson. Forsaking his ancestral home was a fatal uprooting that worsened the tumult of his disposition and hastened the dissolution of our family.

For a few years we lived at Edgefield Court House, in a poor section off the Augusta Road. Our neighbors on both sides were freedmen whom Lige Watson scarcely deigned to speak with, although one was old Tap, whose progenitors had been black Watsons for a hundred years. Papa felt humiliated when his wife asked Tap's assistance in finding him a place as a common laborer, a job he would lose in a matter of days for the same drunken insubordination which had held him to a private's rank during the War.

Eventually, beset by debt, Papa found work at the factory of Captain Gregg, whose father, in the first half of the century, had imported Europe's industrial revolution to the Carolinas, constructing textile mills at Vaucluse and Graniteville, southwest of Edgefield. In these dark times when so many begged for work, Papa took such pride as he could muster in his new employment, which favored veterans from Captain Gregg's old regiment and was "closed to niggers." At Graniteville he earned nineteen dollars a month, which he mostly spent in support of his own drinking habit and occasionally in the brothels of Augusta. Or so his scrimping wife suspected, outraged by the pittance he brought home when he happened to turn up of a Sunday morning.

Papa would remind me how fortunate I was to be laboring out in the fresh air rather than in those "dark, Satanic mills" where children as young as eight or nine worked fourteen-hour days beside the adults. He described the cold, grim aspect and pervasive darkness in that deep Horse Creek ravine, a gloomy place that had scarcely changed since the time of the eighteenth-century outlaws and highwaymen who had murdered those pioneer Watsons before the Revolution and were finally destroyed by our illustrious ancestor—

"For pity's sake, let us hear no more of Colonel Michael!"

For the fabled captain of the American Revolution, Mama had perversely substituted that inconsequential colonel whose Widow Tabitha had hurried young Ellen Addison into the brawny arms of young Lige Watson. In their early days, as a kind of wry flirtation, it had amused them to blame their fractious marriage on Aunt Tabitha, but now it was Mama's unforgiving view that Auntie Tab with her intolerable meddling had ruined a young girl's life. She would state this grievance as plain fact, not in self-pity—for Mama found no solace in complaint—but merely to torment her husband, whom she chased with words and pecked upon the head like a blackbird harrying a crow.

As his fortunes diminished and his reputation ebbed, Papa's need for conviviality increased. Wild-eyed and boisterous, he laughed ever more loudly, even as his face betrayed his deepening confusion and anxiety. On Sundays he wandered the still town, invading church meetings and even funerals, in flight from solitude.

At crossroads taverns, he would declaim loudly on such topics as fine horseflesh, Republican Scalawags and carpetbaggers, insolent niggers, weapons, Southern honor, and the Great Lost Cause. Vaingloriously would he extol the warrior society of Edgefield, boasting of Edgefieldians of yore who fought in the Indian Wars and the American Revolution, not to mention those gallant volunteers, Watsons among them, who rode away to the War of 1812, to the Seminole Wars, and to the War with Mexico. Modestly would he include a mention of their obedient servant Captain Elijah D. Watson, and also Major Tillman Watson and Colonel Robert Briggs Watson of Clouds Creek, whose gallant service in the War of Northern Aggression had done honor to the sovereign state of South Carolina.

Occasionally Papa's rhetoric was challenged by veterans with different memories of Watson's war years, dyspeptic men who refused to recall his field commission and derided his current captaincy, declaring that he was better known for delinquency and courts-martial than for deeds of battle. A willing brawler, at least when in his cups, my father dealt forcefully with these naysayers until that fell evening he was parted from his wits by the earnest application of a horseshoe, and was left groaning in the sawdust with a hand-carved knife wound encircling one eye. The raw ring made him look bug-eyed, as if he were glaring out of a red peephole at impending doom, and its livid scar, which caused him to be known as Ring-Eye Lige, became a badge of disrepute for our forlorn family.

When Papa was elsewhere, and then only—for the smallest reflection on his tender honor would propel him at once into a fury—our household was modestly assisted by Mama's brother, who served as an attorney at the Court House. Uncle John Addison found part-time employment for his sister as a clerk and paid the school fees for her children. For a brief period I was enrolled in Edgefield's Male Academy, but was shortly dismissed for wrenching a hickory switch from the frightened pedant and backing the man into a corner—"menacing the schoolmaster" was the formal charge in my report. Neither teacher nor pupil cared to explain that this episode was caused by the victim's reference to "Ring-Eye Lige," which his student, in an "ominous and silent manner," had warned him never to repeat.

Far from flogging me, Papa hooted in triumph at this news, having always resented the schooling paid for by John Addison as a personal insult to himself. "Pity you didn't cane him, boy, the way Senator Brooks caned Sumner of Massachusetts—" He was stopped only by his wife's blighted expression. He welcomed his son back to the ranks of honest working men and ridiculed Mama's distress that my first chance at a formal education had been ruined. Yet when he discovered that the humiliated teacher was a Butler kinsman, he stripped off his belt and flogged me unmercifully as a young ruffian who had spoiled our family's chance of gaining its rightful place in the society of Edgefield Court House.

When Papa left to go to work in Graniteville, I took his place as a plantation hand, another blow to Mama's hopes which intensified her bitterness toward her husband. She increased her effort to tutor her young Edgar, whom the school had judged "intelligent and thoughtful" before getting rid of me. "You were born the same year that dearest Charlotte Brontë was taken from this cruel world," she sighed, for she had literary aspirations, even for me. She stuffed my brain with the English literature she so loved, and plied me with those doom-ridden Greek classics from Cousin Selden's Deepwood library. Alas, I was too young to do chores at dawn and dusk and field labor all day, then apply myself to reading in the evening. I fell asleep in Ancient Greece night after night.

Mama, although not yet forty, was looking pinched and aged from overwork, but she made time to play with my sister Mary Lucretia, known as Minnie, in the slave-made toy box in which she herself had rummaged as a little girl. Humming songs of childhood as she sorted tops and marbles, she recalled for her daughter her own antebellum memories of fairs and berry-picking parties, birthdays and spelling bees, of fine silver service and the Addison piano and the beautiful china fired from Edgefield clay by an English visitor, Mr. Josiah Wedgwood. On the backrest of her last good chair she embroidered a line from Keats: *"Beauty is truth, truth beauty,"—that is all ye know on earth, and all ye need to know.* (To Papa she cried, "Now surely, Mr. Watson, you have no quarrel with that?" She invited "the head of the household" to be first to use the chair, watching his wary approach to it with strange soft desperate laughter that her uneasy children did not understand, having no previous acquaintance with hysteria.)

Although adept with the floral patterns of embroidery, Mama knew nothing about mending, far less cooking meals or keeping house. She depended on frequent visits from Aunt Cindy, the tall Indian-boned black woman in the next cabin, who had been her slave during their girlhood and was now her neighbor and unaccredited true friend. Aunt Cindy regularly brought sorghum, boiled potatoes and corn bread, sometimes greens or peas. In summer she made sarsaparilla and in winter parched-corn coffee. In the evenings, when flax was to be had, she wove homespun for both families, linens in summer, linsey-woolsey in the winter.

Cinderella Myers had helped her Miss Ellen faithfully throughout the War, and Tap Watson, in his sour way, had continued to look out for the Artemas descendants when the War was over. For all his grumbling, he accompanied his wife and child when they followed Miss Ellen to Edgefield Court House, where, unlike my father, he soon found a job, being both hardworking and dependable. As for their young daughter, the apple-hipped and nut-colored Lulalie, she cheered and helped us, too. Due to a certain strange, stirring aroma, Lulalie seemed to me almost as edible as a baked candied yam. Her accidental touch tingled my skin, inspiring a yearning in my belly to caress her. Being scarcely ten, Lalie never noticed my eleven-year-old interest in her person.

In truth, Lalie loved another, namely our little Minnie, whom she strove mightily to bring to life with her own high spirits. She would drag her pale and shrinking heroine out into the sun, then race back inside to fetch my sister's toys. "Gone be back with mo' fun in a minute now, Mis Minnie!" she would promise, shining her sudden smile, already having fun enough for both of them. She showed my sister how to use small thorns to pin leaves into her dress and hair, thereby creating fanciful frocks and bonnets they might play in. But out of doors, that sickly dark-haired child was forever fretting, peering fearfully over her shoulder. Trailing Lulalie through the whortleberry patch, she wept over what Aunt Cindy called "brambledy fingers." She soiled her Sunday frock while weeding vegetables and suffered a spurring by the rooster while trying to help Lulalie feed the chickens.

However, our timid Mary Lucretia did well at the Edgefield Female School and soon became what the teachers called "a happy little scholar"—"happy because safe from her father," Mama sniffed, in reference to Papa's habit of baring Minnie's behind over his knee when she was punished and gazing down upon it as if reconsidering, even taking a long breath, before clearing his throat and spanking it rose pink.

After Papa went to Graniteville, Mama would join me when she could in the sharecropped cotton, yanking or whacking down the tough old stalks in the late autumn, digging and manuring the new furrows through the winter, planting in April, thinning the new growth in May. We cultivated and hoed in June and July, when the plants blossomed, and picked the opened bolls from mid-August late into the fall, hauling the cotton in burlap sacking to the gin, where it was processed and packed and sent to market. All the while Mama's small fingers that had danced and fluttered light as butterflies over ivory keys of the Addison piano became ever more knobby, red, and swollen as her hands turned coarse, but if this loss dismayed her, she refused to show it.

Disrespectful of her lord and master, Mama revered her Lord and Maker, He Who Abideth in Trinity Episcopal, with its severe facade and glinting steeple pointing our way toward the Firmament. She looked forward to Heaven. "This World Is Not My Home, I Have No Mansions Here" was her favorite hymn. Aunt Cindy hummed "In My Father's House Are Many Mansions." Like most of the old-time darkies at Silver Bluff Baptist, Aunt Cindy preferred the New Testament's Sweet Lord of Love and Mercy in this life on Earth to her white folks' punishing Old Testament Jehovah, glaring down from Heaven.

*

From the first year of the War, when I was five, until the age of fifteen, when I fled Edgefield for good, I had very little to show for life besides the calluses and grime of endless seasons of hard labor, lice, mosquitos, dirt, and poverty. Every hour of every day not spent hacking a crop, I was trapping and snaring, fishing and gathering, and scavenging from other people's gardens for our hungry family. Mostly we subsisted on clabber, a pasty mix of thin milk, curds, and whey.

Black Tap Watson, not my father, taught me how to hunt and gather, how to set fine horsehair snares and sturdy rabbit gums, where to find wild tubers and the gopher tortoise, when to fish the creeks. In the wake of war, the bear, deer, rabbit, coon and turkey, dove, quail, and wild duck—formerly common fare on the poorest table—had all but vanished from South Carolina. Only fugitive squirrels and foolish possums, with a few rabbits and robins, fell to my slingshot. In summer, I gigged frogs and skinned out snakes, to eke out the clabber and dandelion greens, the hardtack biscuits, dusty beans, and mouse-stained grits left in our meager larder.

Occasionally, in winter dusk, returning from my trap line out at Deep-wood, I would wrench a few collards and cold muddy turnips from Tap's patch next door. It was no sin to borrow a few vegetables from these nigger folks "who had welcomed the bluecoats, then presumed to lord it over their former benefactors," as my father put it. (Proudly would Papa have us know that Elijah D. Watson would never accept the smallest charity from niggers, while Mama, for her part, made certain that he knew that his black neighbors provided more sustenance than he did to his needy family, helping us faithfully and with no hope of reward almost every day.)

One afternoon Black Tap appeared from behind his cabin in the twilight gloom. I straightened, putting a bold face on it, bringing my hands out from behind my back. Tap lowered his stave. "You gettin so big, I took you for your daddy." He was embarrassed for the ragged culprit and resentful of the stolen greens that drooped from my cold mud hands.

That the irascible old man said nothing worse made it clear that I had never fooled him, that he had ignored my raiding for some time. On the other hand, I had not told anyone that I had seen him taking food packets sent secretly by Mama to our cousin Selden out at Deepwood. I hollered after him, "You raising that stick to a white man?" And his rasp came back out of the dark. "Take what you be needin, white man, jus' so's you recollect that black ones gots to eat somethin, too." When I yelled out that we aimed to pay him, there came a derisive whoop from the twilight shadows.

"We don't need charity from damn niggers!" I shouted. "Tap?" I called. "Don't tell, all right? I was aiming to bring you folks a rabbit."

"*Rabbit?*" Tap's whoop came from the far side of his cabin. "Some ol' nigger must teached you purty good, you been cotchin *rabbits*!"

*

I tossed those greens onto our table, telling Mama they had come from "the Black Watsons." Though this was true, my sullen way of speaking told her they were stolen, for she banged her heavy pot lid on the iron stove. For my rags, rough manners, and my "thievery," I was always hard chastised, but she never failed to help eat up my ill-gotten gleanings. "Just nigger greens," I taunted her. "Just toss 'em out if you don't want 'em, Mama."

In our poverty, such an idea disturbed her more than theft. "Hush," she said, stoking the fire to boil water. "Our Lord provideth in our hour of need. To waste His bounty would be sinful." She would set aside my sin until the greens were eaten, and this made me furious.

Coldly I said, " 'And the thought of eating came to her when she was wearied of her tears.' "

She turned to look at me. "A line from Cousin Selden's books," I said. "The *Iliad*," I said. She held my eye a moment longer, then turned back to the stove. "Good," she murmured—a remark that made me nervous, since I had never been insolent before. "Tap better watch his step, not get caught by the Regulators," I blustered gruffly.

"Regulators!" She gave the stove another wallop with the pot, startling me and scaring weak-eyed Minnie, who was bent deep into her primer as if to inhale the lesson through her nose. At supper, Mama reminded us that Tap had known us all our lives. For all his gall and sour temper, that old man had remained loyal to the family. Therefore he deserved forgiveness for enrolling himself in the Republican Party and forgetting his place in certain minor matters. Old-time darkies, after all, sometimes adopted habits of familiarity, even impertinence, for want of a better way to express affection. Being so well taken care of by their white folks, they had lost the fear that made most of their people mumble and shuffle and play dumb to get along.

Tap Watson was the old kind of church Negro, Mama said, proud as could be that Silver Bluff Baptist, founded before the Revolutionary War, "was de oldes' nigger church in de whole of de whole country." True, its first minister had been a white man, but back in those days, black and white worshiped together. Tap had attended "white folks' church" without much spiritual reward. "All dere preacher speakin about is niggers mindin Marster and 'beyin Missus cause dey is de kin'ly folks dat's feedin you for Christ sweet sake, Amen."

Neither Emancipation nor Reconstruction had changed things very much, she said. The evil hostility between the races had begun in the first year of the War when the black faithful were notified that henceforth they must sit up in the church balcony. "Since the War, the poor things are no longer welcome, but mercifully they have their own nice church, and their own Book of Genesis, too." Tap Watson preached that Adam and Eve had started out as darkies, but after they sinned, they turned so pale out of fear of the Lord's wrath that they had passed for white folks ever since.

The Negro churches were still harassed by the Ku Klux Klan, founded in recent years by that General Forrest who approved the ferocious slaughter of unarmed black Union soldiers in the last year of the War. (As Major Coulter's commanding officer, General Forrest had given Coulter his inspiration for the Regulators, Papa claimed.) Tap had been present that great day when the Negro preacher Paris Simkins, holding his baby in his arms, preached a sermon to the whites who had come to lynch him and actually shamed them into departing. Having put aside his skepticism about Freedom, Tap was proud of his citizenship, proud of his vote, yet he was still cautious, believing that progress must be nurtured slowly lest it perish. He had kept silent when Joseph was killed by Z. P. Claxton, and he had not protested the Black Codes, which restored near-slavery conditions and flouted Reconstruction by discouraging blacks from leaving their plantations or owning land or even leasing it. Tap understood that for the black man, this was a time of terrible danger as well as hope. Like most of his people, he had little interest in emigration to Liberia or Arkansas. Edgefield was where he was born a slave and Edgefield was where he meant to end his days as a free man.

White folks pointed to Tap Watson as a fine representative of the Negro race, and because they trusted him to know his place, he was usually forgiven his abrasive tongue. True, he was sour about whites, but he was just as sour about blacks, "Negroes" especially. Asked for his sage opinion by the Edgefield *Advertiser*, he would neither repudiate nor praise a black man whose "genteel manner" and "good sense" had won high praise before the War but was now denounced in the same newspaper for "swagger and bad character" in urging the new Negro citizens to vote. Tap had intoned without a smile, "Them 'Negroes' gone to get us niggers killed."

District of Devils

These days Papa was drinking worse than ever, until I became frightened he might kill me. Early in my life I learned that in trying to dissuade this man, I only fed the fury of the drunkard. Maddened by what he saw as his son's defiance, he would punch or clout me in the face or whip me raw with a green switch across the back and legs. Afterwards that wet flushed face of his would look misshapen, and the red-ringed eye barbarous and greedy.

I knew better than to expect help from Mama, and I despised Minnie, who wet herself at the first banged door or drunken shout, and whose fear and panic when the time came to run had so often caused me to be caught and beaten. Even worse, she betrayed me to Papa every time we quarreled, complaining that Edgar had been mean. Both mother and daughter used the threat of Papa's violence on the only one who was beaten black and beaten blue, and this injustice, more than the terror and humiliation and the burning pain, would raise tears to my eyes, although tears never fell. My one confidant was a secret brother I called Jack, whom I confided in and raged and wept with throughout most of childhood.

After childhood, I never let Papa see me weep, I never hollered, I never wet my pants again. I learned how to set my teeth and bite down hard on pain the way a dog clamps its jaws on another's throat. Swearing furiously to Jack Watson, I held myself like some fanatic in the center of hell's fire until his mad demons wore out and his arm, too.

"Edgar? Are you all right, dear?" But Mama's whisperings came much too late to spare me, and I never answered. My silence frightened her so that her eyes got jumpy and veered off, the way a dog's will. "Please, Edgar," she begged, "it scares me so when your eyes shiver that way!" Strange eyes, the threat of craziness, were not much of a revenge but I had no other. She could not know that my voice would have broken if I'd said one word.

I soon realized that those eyes she saw, that was Jack Watson. Sometimes he appeared unbidden, but I would know that he was there from the uneasiness of others. In a dream my mother's small slight figure pressed against a wall. Slowly she raised a fingertip to seal her lips, keeping God's secret, bearing witness to His acts, not intervening.

The first time I was beaten to unconsciousness (perhaps I fainted from the pain), Mama ran across the yard to seek comfort on the bosom of Aunt Cindy. It never occurred to her to offer comfort to her son. It was her little girl who crawled out of her cranny and found her brother, his whole body shaking, clutching the bedpost with both arms, intent on the man with dogshit on his boots sprawled across the mattress. Lost in a realm from which sunlight and color and all past and future had been struck away, I never noticed the girl until she whimpered. When I turned, that whimper became a whine of fear. It was not my bloody face. The child was cringing back as from the Devil, when the true Devil lay snoring swinish on the bed.

Though not foolish, as some might suppose, Minnie was crippled by her fear. Like certain blind folk, she perceived what commonly escaped others, and she was the first to recognize Jack Watson. Finding her voice, she begged, "Oh please, Edgar, I don't know who you are." Her voice seemed to be calling from far off. Then a black bubble around my brain burst with a soft silent *pop*, and time and space and sound and colors rushed back in—Minnie's weeping and the broken cabin and the reek of bad old broken boots and the big thick carcass on the bed in its fume of moonshine.

Ring-Eye coughed once and came thrashing off the bed. He rolled too quickly to his feet and fell again, groping through the murk of drink like a man emerging from his root cellar after a tornado, staring around as if scared that someone in the family had been destroyed. Relieved to see me still among the living, he ventured a loose wave and grin. "Well, damn if my son don't stand straight up and take his punishment." Incredibly—pathetically—his praise healed me a little, just as Great-Uncle Tillman's words bucked up my nerve long ago down in that twilight swamp with Joseph's corpse. It never occurred to me that one day soon I would vow to blow that red-faced curly head clean off its shoulders.

*

The night that old Tap caught me in his truck patch, Mama finished her supper, dabbed her lips, and said, "I must tell your father." She had scarcely spoken when the man of the house barged through the door, the big red-eyed, unshaven man in soiled silk neckerchief and muddy boots and cavalry greatcoat of soiled darkened gray which stank of booze and horses when it rained. Minnie gave that tiny shriek that sounded like a rabbit pierced by the quick teeth of a fox. I shouted at her, waving her outside. Dark eyes round, the little girl was off her chair and scurrying for the door, which the man had left wide open to cold blowing rain. When she hesitated, whining at the darkness, I shoved her out into the wind, and she tumbled and blew like a rag doll across the muddy yard toward Aunt Cindy's cabin.

Inside, Papa was glaring at the door as if I had closed it on some guilty secret we had kept from him. When Mama said coldly, "What is it, Mr. Watson?" he stared at his wife and son in stupefaction.

"Please, Mama," I said in a low voice. But she scarcely saw me, so intent was she upon her quarry. Like Papa, she was getting worse. What had formerly been sly baiting had become a practiced dance. She would poke her husband, nip at him, dance back with a delighted cry of fear when he surged suddenly toward rage, trip forth once more in trembling suspense, prolonging her delight, as if this were the sole ecstasy her life had left to her. No longer able to restrain herself, she always dared too much, exposing us to a careening din and wild-eyed violence that would leave the cabin shattered, deathly still. And always she insinuated the idea that the son was the true head of the family, with responsibility to protect it from the drunk rogue father.

"Have some turnips, Mr. Watson," Mama said, spooning them up out of the pot and dumping them smartly into our large bowl. "Nice fresh turnips stolen from our neighbors' garden." In his drunkenness and life discouragement, he scarcely heard her. "In order to feed your family," she concluded nicely.

Papa lurched to his feet, overturning his chair. She clenched her cotton-pricked hard hands, then folded them resignedly beneath her apron—prim little Miss Addison with her small waist and pretty primrose face.

"You stole? From niggers?"

"We are so famished in your household that your son was reduced to stealing—"

"Be still!" he roared.

"Run," Mama whispered. I refused. When he caught hold of my arm, I put my other arm around him, trying to slip in under the blows, hugging the thick trunk of him with all my might. Hurling me off, he swung me around so violently that my boots came off the floor. I actually flew backwards, Mama said later, and my head struck on a log butt in the wall, and all was obliterated by the sharp explosion in my brain. People talk about seeing stars. I did. One star is all I saw, bursting forth in blades of pain flashing outward through a blackness, then oblivion.

*

Ghost voices faraway. Surrounding darkness and dark apparitions. Had night come? I did not know who or where I was, or why. My head was transfixed in an iron vise of pain and nausea. Unable to clear a misting in the eyes, unable to move a muscle lest I vomit, I wondered if my brain might not be bleeding.

The shadow figures did not know I had returned. For a long time I halfwatched, half-listened, inert behind slack eyelids.

The shrouded woman sat holding a hand. My hand? I could not feel it. The man—a grainy silhouette in profile—staring out his one small window into darkness. His voice: *Why does he never save himself? He is too hard-headed. There is no discipline he will submit to.* For once the woman neglected to point out that if the son was ungovernable, the father he adored was the one to blame, having encouraged a rebellious nature by these beatings. This time she said none of that. This time she was content to say, *I see. It was his fault, then.* She sighed wearily. *What a low brute you are, Lige Watson. The boy works like a darkie to support your family, he has never done you harm—quite the contrary. It is you who have done the harm, over and over.*

Hearing Mama speak up for me at last, I had to fight tears back so as not to weep. *You may have harmed him seriously,* her voice continued. If Mama regretted her incitement of this drunkard, or letting her own perverse game get out of hand, she gave no sign. *Are you so depraved with all your grog and fornication that you would do injury to your own son?*

Papa's voice mumbled that it was an accident, he did not know for the life of him why that boy always put him in a fury. He was lachrymose, contrite, enraged, and baffled. He had scared himself this time as well as me, for both of us had realized now that Lige Watson, drunk, was drawn toward the murder of his son. From now on I must defend myself, and since he could not be overpowered, I must carry a weapon. I would give fair warning. I would say—and now, in disbelief, I heard a voice, dull, slow, and swollen: *If you ever lay hands on me again—or on Mama or on Minnie—I will kill you.*

Mama rushed to hush me. *Just you rest, son. Edgar? Just you rest.* Well, then. Had I spoken aloud or had I imagined it? Either way, my threat made my heart pound, it made my fingers twitch and my saliva flow and sent strange ecstatic shivers through my neck and arms. But the power of it was instantly overtaken by a bursting in my brain, and blackness, as I sank into oblivion.

My father was back into his bottle within the fortnight. I suffered fainting spells and severe headaches. When Minnie entreated me not to be so stubborn but to beg for mercy, I swore I would never beg for anything, not if he broke my head like a frozen pumpkin. Clenching my teeth, I would force air hard against my stomach wall to fire my resolve and keep my head from splitting.

*

When sober enough to sit up in the saddle, Lige Watson rode with the Edgefield Rifle and Sabre Club—a detachment of the Regulators—having earned a reputation as a man who was good with horses and would "do the necessary" to protect the honor of the South and Southern womanhood. He went about his duties of an officer with a grim fervor. But even Papa, who when sober could be generous and not always insensitive or unkind, was disturbed by the fanaticism of his commander. On one occasion, advised by Captain Watson that a certain Tap on the Regulators' list was actually "a pretty good ol' nigger," Major Coulter gave my father a long look of warning. "Sometimes—even when there's been no trouble—sometimes it gets so us ol' boys might feel like killing us a nigger," Coulter told him in his low dead voice. "At such times it don't matter much if that nigger has done something or not."

"Us ol' boys" included Coulter's henchman, Sergeant Z. P. Claxton. Papa mentioned that it had been Claxton who wanted Tap punished, accusing Tap of hostile looks toward a white man. Papa would boast that, thanks to his own efforts, old Tap had been spared without ever knowing he had been in danger. Papa was hoping that my response would make him proud of his good deed, but all I envisioned was Joseph's body in the swamp. "If I was Tap," I muttered, "I would probably disrespect ol' Z.P., too."

Unlike my father, I understood what Major Coulter meant. Afterwards I brooded some about this. *Us ol' boys might feel like killing*—wasn't that the point? The remark continued to disturb me, less because it sounded so cold-blooded than because it stirred something powerful in my own nature— some secret self I had to fear without quite knowing what it was, only that it was related to an ire as imminent and cold as that chill breath of wind which shivered the birches before a coming storm.

*

Even in Reconstruction days, most men of Edgefield refused to tolerate any foolish niggers who failed to make way for them on the plank sidewalks. Ring-Eye Lige Watson demanded more respect from them than most. But one day as I led him home, his careening gait made it impossible for a black wench to get out of his way. The nervous girl dodged to and fro, teetering along one edge so as not to be forced off into deep mud, until this dance of black and white struck her suddenly as so absurd that she had to clap her hand over her mouth to quell her giggles.

Humiliated, I drove her into the mud. General M. C. Butler, rounding the corner in frock coat and shining boots, had missed the first part of this charade, so that all he saw was a roughly dressed young man shoving a nigger wench off the sidewalk for no reason. Blood rushed to my face as he extended a gloved hand and handed her back onto the boards—*hauled* her would be closer to the spirit of it—with a distaste impartially extended to all parties. The woman babbled, "I'se sorry, genlemans, dat itched my funnybone." She was ignored by General Butler, who ignored us, too, striding onward as she hurried off in her muddied dress.

Because his son had witnessed his humiliation, Lige Watson bawled hoarsely at the young general, claiming he had been insulted. For want of a better plan, he went plunging after him and challenged him to a duel. The other turned and chastised him for drunken imposition on a general officer. Mustached, with curved sideburns to the jaw like a peregrine falcon, the handsome Butler declared that Elijah D. Watson was not privileged to fight a duel, since he had never been an officer and was no longer a gentleman. What he was, said Butler, was a disgrace to a good family as well as to that filthied uniform which he still wore.

Matthew Calbraith Butler had commanded a cavalry regiment under General J. E. B. Stuart at the battle at Brandy Station, in Virginia. He had lost a leg leading a charge and returned to his command not long thereafter. When Ring-Eye Lige staggered after such a hero, shouting out that the early Watsons had preceded his family into the Piedmont, and that Captain Michael Watson had been Butler's grandfather's superior in the fabled Pickens's Brigade, Calbraith Butler smiled. As the street idlers hooted gleefully, he checked the drunkard's pitching onrush by placing the point of his cane against his chest, just hard enough to redirect him off the boards.

Shamed beyond endurance, I cried out, "Duel with the son, then, if you are not a coward!" But my voice broke grotesquely in its adolescent croak, and again Butler permitted himself a narrow smile. "When it comes to dueling with boys," he told me quietly, "I am indeed a coward, Master Watson." With a slight bow, he turned and kept on going in strong limping stride and shortly disappeared around the corner.

The idlers hailed "Ring-Eye" by that name. Turning on me, my muddied father declared himself outraged that an unschooled boy "good for nothing but nigger labor in the field" should insult an Edgefield hero and a leading citizen. "Challenge General Butler? *You?*" Jeering loudly for the public benefit, my father swore that his useless son would be flogged at once for bringing such ignominy upon his family. With that, he seized me by the ear and reeled toward home, so roughly that the shock of pain tore at my head.

Aunt Cindy, out watering her hens, straightened slowly as we drew near. Young Lalie ran to her and peered from behind her skirts at poor ear-twisted Edgar. Tap came outside. My maddened father bellowed at them to mind their nigger business.

From the door, I waved to the dark witnesses, as still as oaken figures in the sad spring light. Then the door closed and the wheezing man seized the hickory stick behind it, and Mama and Minnie cried out in fear as I was slung into the corner. My ear, my wrenched and twisted arm, were fiery with pain and rage flowed through me. Slowly I stood, letting my breath go in a kind of ragged sigh as he drew near. Commanded to lean forward, hands spread on the log wall, I turned a little, pretending to obey, then whipped around and sprang and grasped the stick, wrenching it from him with a violent twist.

"Give it back," he said, not understanding my intent.

In the kitchen corner my mother stood as formal as a mourner. "Edgar?" she said—a kind of query. That one word signified *Are you certain you know what this means? That he may kill you?* Hearing her uncommon concern, Minnie moaned with terror from inside her cupboard.

The man turned his ring-eyed glare upon his wife as if this unholy insurrection was her fault. I muttered thickly, "Don't you touch her." Panting like a cornered animal, I circled out into the center of the room. "Don't you touch us anymore." I wept with nerves. Sensing weakness, he made a rush and a chair crashed and poor Minnie shrieked.

When I leapt aside, he pitched forward onto hands and knees. Hollering my terror, I brought the stick down across his shoulders—*whack!* I struck again with all my might, for my life depended on it—*whack!* Knowing I must not let him rise, frantic to disable him, afraid that his heavy coat might dull the blows, I went after the head and neck, then the broad back, the stout stick biting into the thick meat of him—*whack!*—and another—*whack!*—another and another, hardly conscious anymore that this thing to be obliterated was my father, no longer hollering but somber, silent, stepping lightly around the yelping hulk which was still struggling to flounder to its feet, only to be struck off balance and crash down again. That hickory whistled as I beat and beat and beat and beat him, leaning into the blows with every last thorn and rock and splinter of old fear and fury, leaping out sideways to avoid his lunges, teeth grinding in my passion. I bent that stick with savage cuts—a-*gain*, a-*gain*, a-*gain!*—until at last this stinking brute brayed in woe and wrapped its arms around its head and rolled away bloody-eared into the corner.

The little house was swollen with harsh groans and gasping.

Ring-Eye Lige lay quaking by the wall, a mound of boots and rags. Minnie crept out but remained crouched behind the chair. Across the yard, Aunt Cindy would be covering Lulalie's ears, hearing nothing but the death of Master Edgar in those dreadful blows. And my mother? Why was it that I felt ashamed to face my mother?

I lowered the stick, starting to tremble.

"Oh, how dare you, Edgar." It was not a question. My mother quieted her heart, pressing her fingers to her chest. She was very pale but her eyes glittered. "How dare you." She drew back her hand as if to fly at me. I watched coldly. The tip of the extended stick tapped lightly on the floor between us, marking the boundary she was never to cross again. I suppose she was looking straight into Jack's eyes, and his expression scared her in a way her husband never had, even when violent. "Your own parent," she finished weakly.

" 'How *dare* you.' " I repeated it in disbelief. But in the next moment I was overcome by fears of abandonment, of banishment, of final solitude in the great turning world. "You think it's *me* who should be beaten, Mama?"

Not once had she tried to intervene. Even while belaboring her spouse, I had glimpsed her transport, her clenched exultation. Her protest now was a mere twitch of old instinct, like the tiny spasms in the hard tail tip that a rat snake once left in my hand, escaping into a rock crevice on a boyhood morning. For a long time that tail tip writhed as soundless as a nerve between my thumb and finger, still trying to hum its warning on dry leaves.

I thrust the stick at her. "Your turn," I told her with a harsh dislike I could no longer conceal. "Might do you good." She stared at the stick, then at the man, still coughing and moaning. The stick fell to the floor.

I pushed my few things into a sack and shoved his stick through this poor bindle and departed from my parents' house without good-byes. For their own safety—for I had grown up all of a sudden, and I knew who my father was—I passed those black folks standing in the yard without a word. Having heard those terrible blows and cries, they were astonished when I emerged alive. Even that flinty old Tap seemed to be crying, but except for an awed groan, they kept silent. When Minnie ran after me down the road, sobbing her pleas that I not forsake her, I lifted her and hugged her but I could not answer.

*

I walked all night to reach Clouds Creek, where I fell down in my grandfather's house and slept in a dry corner. That afternoon, I called upon Robert Briggs Watson, who lived just east of the Ridge spring. Colonel Robert's large house under pecans and magnolias, built early in the century by the Old Squire, was set off from the road and the farm fields all around by a wall of crenellated brick which let a humid breeze pass through in summer. The old wood house was quaking with the hound rumpus inside, so eager were they to inspect a stranger.

Colonel Robert came out onto his vine-shaded veranda in his shirtsleeves. An imposing man with a comfortable kind of heft, he was less handsome than steadfast in his appearance, being calm and courtly and well-tempered by all weathers. Uncommon among men of Edgefield District, he kept his silvered hair cropped short, and his clothes looked fresh even with dirt on them (unlike those of his first cousin Lige, whose ingrained greasy stains were born of unclean habits rather than good earth and honest labor. Whatever grime that man got into, as Aunt Cindy once complained to her Mis Ellen, its trace could not be ousted from his clothes "with lye nor dynamite").

Colonel Robert was a decorated soldier who had ridden home from Appomattox Court House to manage the family properties around Clouds Creek. Like his father and grandfather before him, he raised timber and tobacco, cotton, corn, and rice. He had also made a reputation for fine hogs and cattle. In the year of my return, he was trying grain crops—oats, wheat, rye, and barley. Taciturn, he listened as I asked permission to live in the old Artemas house and sharecrop its fallow land. He nodded vaguely but he gave no answer. Instead he invited me inside for a drink of water, asking how my mother might be getting on. "You remember Cousin Edgar, don't you, Lucy?" he inquired of his wife. "I do," she answered with a smile, not pleased to see me and a bit suspicious. *What do you want here?* her expression said.

We did not discuss my troubles with my father. I told them about my earnest hope to restore the Artemas lineage to Clouds Creek, to show my serious intention and resolve. In the end, after working with me for a fortnight, the Colonel put aside the doubts and warnings of his kinsmen. He gave "Cousin Ellen's boy" permission to sharecrop the Artemas Tract and patch up that old house as best he could.

As a Clouds Creek Watson, Colonel Robert had faith that whatever satisfaction might be found in life was of a man's own making, and that no good would ever come from coddling. On the other hand (though he revered his father), he seemed to suffer some uneasiness that his family had acquired the Artemas Tract through plain hard dealing, and was anxious to atone for this by helping this young cousin to restore his grandfather's succession. He warned me that I would be held to his own standards, but he also looked for small ways to encourage me, sending me "home" with old blankets, a Bible, a new kerosene lantern, also fundamental tools and rough provisions. As I left, he invited me to come for Sunday dinner. "After church," my cousin Lucy called—a warning that church attendance was required to receive the blessing of her ham and sweet pudding.

And so, on most Sundays after church, I dined at Colonel Robert's house, where I enjoyed browsing in the Carolina histories and the family Bible with its list of births and deaths, and also in the browned warm-smelling pages in the Shakespeare folios brought into the family by my great-grandmother, the former Chloe Wimberley, daughter of James Wimberley, one of George Washington's generals in the Revolution; these leather volumes, sadly soiled by mold and mice, had turned up in her son Artemas's falling house. "Those may be yours one day," said the Colonel, offering more oil for my lamp so that I could study in the evenings.

*

Colonel Robert, a farmer to the heart, was happy to answer any questions about agriculture. Seeming to enjoy my company, he spoke of the advent of the cotton gin after the Revolutionary War, which drastically increased the need for labor, and how the white indentured servants of the old days had been replaced by slaves from Africa and the Caribbean, who were not only less troublesome but were owned in perpetuity like real estate and bred like domestic stock, according to their methods. He also evoked the antebellum days of the Old Squire, when even the rich Tidewater planters had been attracted to the short-staple cotton industry of Edgefield District. Before the War, Edgefield had shipped more cotton bales than any district in the state, but even in the Old Squire's time, erosion was leaching the clay soil, and problems grew with fluctuations in the cotton prices and rising competition from the west. With the onset of the War, he said, "King Cotton" was deposed for good.

Despite Reconstruction, said the Colonel—who was gracious enough to speak to a young cousin as one farmer to another—Clouds Creek was stirring back to life. The Watsons were planting all their former crops except for cotton, and he himself was putting in small orchards. This year, in fact, he would become the first Carolina planter ever to ship peaches from the state.

Listening proudly to my kinsman, I dared speculate that my fortunes had turned, that the worst part of my life was behind me, and that there was a future at Clouds Creek for Edgar Watson.

*

Something in the cold dusk of early spring—the naked light and the ringing of tree peepers—twists at the heart. I was lonely all that April in that silent house. Even so, the return to Clouds Creek had bathed my battered spirit in the warmth of my own belonging, and on Sundays at the Colonel's house, when the clan met, I listened eagerly to the same old Watson history which had stunned me with boredom in my childhood. These fertile meadows, the clear creek softening the loamy air, filled my heart with well-being, as if the old roots torn and exposed in the loss of our plantation had been covered over once again and were feeling their way back into the earth.

That first spring I renewed acquaintance with those old trees climbed in childhood, stirring in that aching light which pierced the branches as the sun rose higher in the Southern sky. Soon the twigs came into their fresh leaf, with redbud and dogwood and the mountain laurel opening cool blossoms in the understory. Though not much drawn to nature in the past, my eye rejoiced in the wild azaleas and the songs of unknown birds from the soft woodlands. Then bird silence descended and the birds hid in thick greens which would dry in late summer to the fire colors of the Piedmont autumn—the blood red of the swamp maples, the oak russets, the hickory yellows and pale golds which once hid the Cherokees of these broad uplands.

Day after day, alone out in the fields, I drifted into reveries and dreams of my home earth, feeling mortally homesick although I had returned. I had always thought that Clouds Creek had been named for the reflections in its pools of the soft cumulus that passed across the Appalachian blue. However, Colonel Robert told me that the name commemorated a trader, Isaac Cloud, whose wife had survived to tell their bloody tale. In May of 1751, she wrote, two Cherokees came to their cabin just at dark. Given supper and tobacco, the Indians engaged the trader in friendly banter until near midnight, when all "dropt into Sleep. And when the Cocks began to Crow, they came to the Bed and shot my Husband through the Head. And a young Man lying upon the Floor was shot in the same Minute. And thinking the Bullet had gone through [my head], too, struck me with a Tomahawk under my right Arm . . . I lying still, they supposed I was dead, and one of them went and killed both my Children; and then they came and took the Blankets from us & plunder'd the House of all that was valuable and went off. And in that bad condition I have lain two days amongst my dead."

I have lain two days amongst my dead—that phrase troubled my mind then, and it does today. Oddly, it brought to mind Jack Watson, who had not appeared since my return to Clouds Creek. Now it struck me as astonishing that I treated his presence as real and yet not there. All these years, quite unaware of it, I had been talking to myself, or *my* self, rather. It was lucky I was not overheard and dismissed as crazy.

*

Robert Watson was a modern farmer who had outlived most of the old Celtic sorceries—charms, potions, and secret incantations for the good husbandry of crops and animals. He taught me all the latest methods of raising hogs and cattle, mules and horses—all but sheep, which our up-country settlers had detested since old drover days when the immigrants moved south along the Appalachians. With the canny brain of the wild ancestor long since bred out of them, these dim creatures fell prey to wolves and panthers and even to the berry-grubbing bears. Suffocating in their filthy wool, they died prodigiously in the damp heat of summer.

The merry hogs, on the other hand, took joyfully to the wild, rooting through the woodlands as if born to it. Also, they resisted predators, having quickly reverted to the razor-backed pugnacity of the wild boar—huge, black, and hard-bristled, with curled tusks. "Some of our ridge runners turn feral, too, only they get meaner," the Colonel winked, aware of my prejudice against Z. P. Claxton. Unlike feral humans, he continued, wild hogs could be baited in and tamed in pens, rounding off their rangy lines and turning pink beneath their bristles, until only the snouts and squinty little eyes remained the same. "Ridge runners have those eyes, have you ever noticed?" The Colonel gave me a keen look. "First time I ever saw you smile," he said. "Does your face good."

That first year, when a sow farrowed toward Christmas, I helped with the deliveries, tugging each piglet by the shoulders to work it free. Quickly the Colonel cleaned off the shining membranes which enclosed the heads, then pumped the small legs to get them going. Finally the sow heaved a sigh and pushed her runt out in a bloody blurt of afterbirth. The Colonel grinned to see my face so overjoyed.

Ordinarily, each piglet would choose a teat and stick to it till weaned (even the hind tit, which provided the least milk), but since he could not trust this sow not to eat her litter, he made me a present of a half dozen shoats in exchange for hand-rearing the whole lot. "For a little while you'll have to cook their feed, raise them by hand."

"If I can catch them!" Senselessly I laughed out loud, startling us both with my new happiness, and the Colonel chuckled kindly along with me. "You don't 'catch' a pig. You 'fetch' it, Edgar. And fetching is no problem at all, not when there's food." Well-kept piglets tended to be sociable, nudging their keeper with their rooters just like pups and kittens. In a few weeks, my gang of shoats should be racing around in a din of grunts and squeals, playing tag and mauling one another. Without affectionate attention, he explained, they grew poorly and became sluggish, and their curly tails would droop like dying flowers. As he spoke, Colonel Robert petted the six shoats. He had almost forgotten how much he enjoyed them. "Give 'em plenty of water, Edgar. Helps 'em gobble up their food so they can grow. Any pig under one hundred pounds can't call itself a hog, so they're in a hurry."

*

One day after I knew the Colonel better and dared confide in him a little more, I asked about my father's comportment as a soldier. Taken aback by this abrupt question but realizing I wished to hear the truth, the Colonel gave me a terse answer—that while Elijah D. had never hesitated to seek privilege or favor from his higher-ranking relatives, he seemed to shun constraints of any kind. Early in the War, Captain Selden Tilghman had dismissed him from the Edgefield Volunteers—that helped explain why my father always hated him—and within the year, Major Tillman Watson had transferred his nephew from the Nineteenth Cavalry to an infantry company of half-trained soldiers, on account of chronic and grievous absence without leave and general dereliction of his duties. The alternative had been courts-martial and imprisonment.

The Honorable Tillman Watson, state senator and a vice-president of the Edgefield Agricultural Society, was an old Borderer in his appearance, like Andrew Jackson and John C. Calhoun, being tall and rangy, with an imposing forehead and strong eyes sunk back beneath heavy black brows which commanded his severe and bony face. Though he had been kind enough during my childhood, he now avoided me, perhaps to escape the effort of concealing his distaste for my father or possibly because, as my grandfather's brother and a man who had farmed a thousand acres and owned nearly a thousand slaves, he was troubled to see this ragged great-nephew working so hard on that overgrown plantation in the desperate hope that he might earn it back.

As for the other Clouds Creek kinsmen, they were civil but not hospitable, being anxious to keep their distance from "the Bad Elijah." Though I never complained, the Colonel worried that living alone in that damp and decrepit house, I might well perish or go mad. He could never know how much I preferred solitude at Clouds Creek to existence under the roof of Ring-Eye Lige.

"I am truly sorry to relate these things," Colonel Robert was saying, gazing out over the land, avoiding my eye so as not to embarrass us. "I wish you had known your grandfather—such a kind and gentle man, and a respected farmer. And a drinker. In the end, his whiskey sickened him and he died young." The Colonel saw no need to mention my father. "It has been left to you, boy, to restore your line. I shall assist you if you deserve help, not otherwise."

These last words were said bluntly, a bit harshly. Thanks were not expected. I kept still.

Another day, I asked the Colonel if he knew what had become of Selden Tilghman. He considered the hands clasped on his knee before muttering what he had heard, that "men without authority" had given Colonel Tilghman one hundred strokes of an overseer's lash, then tarred and feathered him. To a discordant clamor of tin pots, catcalls, and chaotic drumming, he had been ridden backwards on a pole in an old-fashioned "rogue's march," after which he'd been dumped into a hog wallow at Hamburg, the Republican stronghold across the Savannah River from Augusta. Apparently he regained consciousness and crawled away, but nothing had been heard about him since.

"So he is dead, then?"

"I pray that he is dead."

Colonel Robert's ruddy hide had thickened in its color. His detestation of the martyrdom inflicted on a Confederate hero by "that half-mad Coulter and his gang of bullies" was quite clear, but he avoided any allusion to my father's role, or any mention of him. "They cannot dignify unlawful violence by calling themselves 'Regulators.' 'Regulation' occurred a century ago, in Michael Watson's day, when there was need of a citizens' militia to control the outlaws and highwaymen who ruled the up-country. These night riders of today are not a citizens' militia, and certainly they are not patriots, but only a gang of vigilantes making their own law. The cruelties they perpetrate would be diabolical even in war." He had agreed with Selden Tilghman that the violence of these men kept the old wounds open, and that their actions would isolate the South, making it a backwater of the Republic.

While not in sympathy with Tilghman's New Light heresies, Colonel Robert respected the integrity and courage of that God-stunned man, repeating fervently how much he hoped that my cousin had died quickly. Even if Tilghman had survived, he would certainly be hunted down and killed should he ever wander back to Edgefield District, not because he had been punished insufficiently but because of the bad conscience of his neighbors, to whom he would be a figure of horror and reproach.

"Selden Tilghman was abominated because he warned the public—publicly—about what had become monstrous in themselves—ourselves. To enrich ourselves, we good Christians permitted human bondage, so what are we to say now? The enslavement of our fellow men, a great many of them new Christians—Lord! How did good churchmen justify this for so long?" He shook his head. "My father owned a hundred slaves, Uncle Tillman many more, Uncle Artemas and the others, too. The Watsons were slaveholders until the end, saw nothing wrong with it. We went to war for it. And many thousands of our best young men never returned."

I was astonished by these words from a Southern officer, wounded at Frayser's Farm and again at Gettysburg, decorated for gallantry in the Great Lost Cause, then deprived of the free man's right to vote.

*

With the Colonel's help, I castrated four young boars for barrows. While they were small, all six of my frisky shoats kept me good company in my empty house. I constructed a snug pen in an unused room, which I mucked out faithfully and bedded with dry straw. Rejoicing in their progress and my own, I hauled slops and mash and gallons of fresh water to this roisterous gang, talking back to them in their own squeal language, with suitable *choughs* and a few explosive *harfs* of false alarm. I even moved my bedroll to a place next to the pen where I could revel in so much well-fed contentment. Catching myself smiling in the dark, I laughed out loud, drawing forth sweet earnest sounds from their ear-twitching sleep. Those shoats were my children and my family, too, forever nudging at my boots in greeting. I would give them treats out of my pockets, and bend and rub the bristle tuft between their pale blue eyes.

When spring came, I built an outside pen and cut a doorway. Sometimes I led my sturdy band on an outing across country, where they would hurtle off in all directions, wider and wider in their circles until they tired and came trotting in, heeding my call, to follow close behind all the way home. *SooEEEEEEE*, I sang across the meadows, *Pig, pig, pig!* I only called to celebrate being a pig man, there was no real need. Only later did Colonel Robert tell me that hearing me in the distance and taking those mournful calls for cries of solitude was sorely troubling to certain relatives. I believe that good man—though he knew better—was probably the most troubled of all.

My Sunday dinner at the Colonel's house had been changed to one Sunday every month, and before long, Aunt Lucy put a stop to it entirely. So inhospitable did my aunt become that I wondered if she was punishing the son out of her churchly disapproval of the father. In my wretched need of human company, I longed to whine about how I had been hurled against a wall, how I had lain unconscious for hours, how ever since that day I had endured sudden violent headaches that sometimes brought me to my knees. But in the end, I could not solicit sympathy which involved such disloyalty to my father. Showing weakness before these Clouds Creek Watsons would convince them that the son was made of the same poor stuff as the Bad Elijah, and they might lose faith in my resolve.

*

The final pronouncement on my character was reserved for Great-Aunt Sophia Boatright, who made regular rounds of the Watson households in her buggy. Aunt Sophia wished to assure herself that the Old Squire's standards for the clan had been maintained, with prayer meetings duly attended and morals up to snuff. One day, careless of the fact that Bad Elijah's boy was reading in the sun outside the window, she held forth to the Colonel's lady on the weakness of "poor dear Artemas" that had led to the fatal dissolution of his son. She also blamed that spoiled Addison girl whom Elijah D. had married for the ragged look and sour smell of "that somber hard-faced boy who scarcely speaks." As for "that Minnie or whatever they call her," she was dismissed as "rather a pretty thing for a near half-wit." Aunt Lucy assured Aunt Sophia that poor peaked little Minnie was not half-witted but simply scared out of her wits—"Let's pray she gets some back," sniffed Aunt Sophia—but Aunt Lucy confessed that she no longer tolerated that Edgar in this house due to his odor. Her voice died as she realized I might be within earshot. Young Edgar—this sudden voice was Colonel Robert, who had just come in—had toiled hard since early childhood, and had been deprived of a proper upbringing and formal education or even decent clothes. What did the family expect? And they might care to know that having had to spend so much time alone, that boy was better read than any Watson in Clouds Creek. "Well, that's not saying much," Aunt Sophia snorted. "Dear old Tillman can scarcely read a word!"

Such a pity, she continued, that this boy had not been orphaned like his father so that Tillman, with no heirs to all his money, might have adopted such a promising young farmer. Reminded that Tillman had a wife, she nodded grimly—"Yes, a barren wife, who will outlast him and inherit everything!" And a good woman, Colonel Robert rebuked her, whom Uncle Tillman loves. With affection, he quoted my great-uncle, who favored country accents: "I never had but the one wife, but she done me all my life."

Edgar was bright and industrious, the Colonel finished, and was bound to do well. "That is doubtless to his credit," the old lady retorted, "but I cannot help it, I don't like the look of him. Possibly he has read too much and taxed his brain. Even *talks* like a book, like that cousin of Ellen, what's-his-name, the one who—"

"Aunt Sophia? Very likely the boy is acquainted with your interesting opinions, but you might lower your voice in case he's not." Colonel Robert must have pointed toward the window, for there was a stiff silence in the room as I ducked down to slink away around the house. "Oh? An eaves-dropper?" Aunt Sophia's voice flew out into the sunlight, as if hunting me. "Are you out there, boy?"

Yes, ma'am, no, ma'am—the fire of humiliation, the Indian summer sun on the sad goldenrod, the dread of loss. I hadn't known I had offended them, nor that my great-aunt disliked my looks, and the knowing scared me. When they went into the dining room, I slipped through the door and peered into the mirror. I can see that image to this day, a stiff portrait of an ordinary boy, rather husky for fourteen and roughly dressed, mostly in sacking, a freckled blue-eyed boy of level gaze, straight nose, strong chin, nothing out of the way except, perhaps, the set cast of the expression, hard-fired by ire and loss, ingrown and solitary. His hair was not a common red but a dark auburn, the color of old rust or dried blood.

Yes, a hard face and somber-looking, as she'd said, and dirt-streaked, too. I liked the stubborn cast of it no more than she did, and being indoors, I was shocked by my strong smell. Confronting myself—and having been found wanting—I suddenly detested the name Edgar. *"Edgar,"* I whispered, consid-ering the image with real hatred. "You stink, boy," I said. However, I had no idea how to escape myself.

*

At Christmas, which I spent alone, pretending illness, I was given a tooth-brush, a bar of brown octagon soap, and a hand-me-down set of clothes, in-cluding a warm jacket from the Colonel. As winter passed, I grew ever more removed from my Clouds Creek kin. Perhaps it was my own self-disgust that made me see disgust and unfriendliness in all their faces. In certain weath-ers, out of loneliness, I piled up straw and slept under the stars beside the hog pen.

That year I helped the Colonel with spring planting. The other field hands were all niggers, all but a newcomer who turned up one day in the next row. We were planting peas and he kept looking at me. Distracted, I worked care-lessly, until finally the other straightened and pointed at my "crookedy" rows, saying I had better do them over. He didn't intend to share the blame for such poor work, he said. I asked him who he thought he was, giving or-ders to Colonel Robert's kin.

The boy laughed, saying, I'm family, too. Rudely I said, Well, you're no kin to me, I have never seen you around here. No? he said. My father is Old Man Ring-Eye Lige. You any kin to *him?* Angered, I called him a liar. Elijah D. Wat-son had one son, I said, and that son's name is Edgar. He laughed at me, hav-ing known who I was right from the start.

"He has two sons. Two handsome blue-eyed boys," he added slyly. "One has a bit more color to his skin, that's all." And he pinched the skin of his own cheek so hard that it went white. I had noticed his use of *crookedy*, a nigger word, and now I knew.

"You're a damn nigger, then? That what you're saying?"

"Yassuh, massuh." He laughed angrily into my face. He had blue eyes and chestnut hair, but now I saw the shadow in his skin. "Nigguh to de bone." He leered, shooting his face too close to mine and laughing at me when I raised my hoe. I could scarcely believe he dared speak to me this way.

"You better watch out, telling lies on white people. You better shut up your damn nigger mouth and stay well clear of me."

Seeing my eyes, he stopped smiling. "Mind you don't go threatenin American citizens, Brother Edgar. Just you plant them fuckin peas straight like I told you." He spat those bad words at my eyes like venom.

I threw the hoe aside and went for him. He was ready for me and as furious as I was. His muscles shivered as he forced me to the ground. In our struggle, rolling in the dust, we did not see Colonel Robert at the field edge. The stranger hissed a warning to let go or take the consequences. I said, "Not until you tell me your damned name." He cursed me, saying, "Jacob Watson of Augusta."

For the first time I truly understood Mama's bitter reproaches to my father. Fuming and sweating, we went back to our peas, but he had not relented. "Start that row again, you hear?"

Within the fortnight, the Colonel sent Jacob away "for his own safety. He's very bitter, he's much too outspoken—"

"Jacob doesn't know his place, sir. That what you mean?"

The Colonel shot a warning look but took a moment to compose himself and give me time to rue my own impertinence. I was stupidly jealous of his concern for this Jacob Watson, and I felt afraid. "That is what *you* mean," he said quietly at last. "What *I* mean is, he's so bitter and so angry that he's crazy. He won't bend. *I have full rights as a citizen,* he says. *The law is the law.* But unfortunately, the law is not the law in Edgefield District." Colonel Robert measured me from beneath his thick brows. "He is hunting for trouble, and sooner or later it will come. It will come from those who speak as you just did, and think that way. I sent him away because sooner or later they are going to hear about him."

"The Regulators?" I stood up. "You think I am some sort of coward who can't take care of his own business?"

"I saw you and Jack fighting." He shrugged, letting it go. "Forgive me, Edgar."

My heart was pounding. *"Jack?"*

"That's what he calls himself. Jake or Jack. Hates the name Jacob, perhaps because he hates the man who gave it to him." Noticing the opened window, he led me aside to avoid being overheard. We sat in the magnolia shade on his brick wall, where he explained that Jacob's mother was a light-skinned slave who had worked in this house until she became pregnant. After she was sold away, it was put about that she had been raped by some poor white, but the family knew that young Elijah D. had been the father.

I nodded and got up and went away.

A few months later, Colonel Robert let me know that Jacob Watson had gone west to Texas to join a black regiment fighting the Comanches. Earnestly, he read aloud from Jacob's letter. " 'Buffalo soldiers,' the Indians call this rough-and-ready bunch, on account of their dark hides and woolly hair. Those redskins are in for a surprise when they see Black Jack Watson— that's what these nigger conscripts call me for a joke. I reckon I make everybody somewhat nervous."

*

By 1870, when Elijah D. Watson and his son were listed in the census as "farm laborers," my father had sold off everything but those few bits of hidden jewelry that were Mama's last claim upon the past—all he could lay hands on save his horse and rifle. His wife was no longer "Mrs." but plain Ellen Watson, which signified in our community that she was no longer a gentlewoman but a common person. For a Daughter of Edgefield, that humiliating listing confirmed the ruin of our reputation.

One Sunday Tap rode to Clouds Creek on a mule, bringing word that Mama wished to see me. I rode back with the black man up behind me, clinging like a tree frog to my back and grumbling about his crotch when that mule trotted. At Edgefield, Mama came running out to meet me, scarcely able to contain the news of our adventure.

The previous year, Great-Aunt Tabitha Watson and her daughter Laura—Mama's childhood friend—had journeyed to Florida to see to the plantation of Laura's deceased husband, William Myers. In a letter to Laura, Mama had described the unhappy marriage to Lige Watson which Aunt Tabitha—though Mama did not mention it—had advocated and supported. Requesting shelter, she took pains to mention that Colonel R. B. Watson held her strong and willing son in high esteem. Surely such a promising young man could be put to good use on the Myers Plantation.

In fear of her husband, she told no one what she'd done, not even Aunt Cindy. A few months later, when her prayers were answered in a return letter sent in care of her brother John, she made her secret preparations to depart. We were to leave in the next days on a cotton wagon bound for

Augusta, where we would join some Florida pioneers in a wagon train on the old Woodpecker Trail south across Georgia. Asked how she would manage without Aunt Cindy, Mama looked surprised. "Cindy will come, too, of course." And Lulalie? And Tap? Curtly, she waved away these questions. The black woman's domestic arrangements were her own affair, No doubt her people would follow when they could.

In her excitement about her escape, Mama had never considered my situation but blithely assumed I would be delighted to abandon Clouds Creek and escort my family on this journey. I was silent awhile, not knowing what to say. I felt vaguely homesick for some reason, but whether for Mama's household or Clouds Creek, I was not sure. Soon my young pigs would be sold as hogs, and I was excited by my plan to slaughter one and bring the first ham to Edgefield as a Christmas present.

Abruptly I told my mother I would not be going. She was upset, exceptionally vexed. She cried out, "But I promised them! They may not want us there if you don't come!" When I stood unmoved, she added bitterly, "This is a long and dangerous journey. Who will protect us, Edgar?" Next, she said, "Edgar, you are my dear son! And your sister loves you!"

But Mama was sensible, and seeing my expression, she gave up at once, she did not cling. With me or without me, she would make good her escape, there was no stopping her. She even mustered up a smile, patting my arm. "I understand, dear. Your heart lies at Clouds Creek," she said in a sincere manner. "We shall miss you, dear, of course we shall," she continued briskly, eyes already straying as the next thing to be taken care of came to mind, "but no doubt your womenfolk will get along just fine."

I nodded my assent, yet could not help wishing that she had entreated me to go. It was my choice to remain behind, and yet, ridiculously, I felt abandoned—and offended, too, that my family would leave Carolina forever without even a taste of my Christmas ham! I had to laugh at myself then, it was so pathetic. And walking home that afternoon I cheered up a good deal, as my dank emotions turned to admiration. "Well, now, Aunt Sophia," I would say to that old blunderbuss, "it looks like 'that spoiled Addison girl' has some grit and spirit!"

At Clouds Creek, I confided my mixed feelings to the Colonel, who assured me I had made the right decision. Robert Watson awarded me a rare smile of fond pride that his young cousin knew where duty lay and had the character to make this sacrifice. The good man took me by both shoulders, saying, "Edgar, I have sincere faith that one day you will regain your family property." And he quoted that notable Edgefieldian, the former Governor James Hammond: "Sir, what is it that constitutes character, popularity, and power in the United States? Sir, it is property, and that only!"

48

All my life, I would remember those ringing words, having never found reason to doubt that they were true.

The Owl-Man

Not yet at peace with their departure, I wanted to make my womenfolk some sort of present, and since I was penniless, and my pigs too young to slaughter, I was anxious to trap one or two rabbits or a squirrel or possum. Because it had a curse on it and was still avoided, the old Tilghman place was still my best hunting ground. I would run a trap line through its ancient forest, where I knew the dim passages through glades and hollows as a nesting bird knows every point throughout its territory.

One late November morning I entered the drive which opened out in the dim greening ring of the old carriage circle. The Deepwood manor house, charred and hollowed out by fire, lay half-hidden in a copse of oak and juniper and vine-shrouded magnolia. On iron earth of gullied oldfields all around, hard brambles and thin poverty grass choked the spent cotton. Over the black hole of the doorway, the high dormer was bound in creeper and wild grape, and the shingled roof peak, ragged now, sagged swaybacked in an ever-failing line along the sky. Overtaken by the woods, the ruin had the mournful aspect of an old harrow left in the corner of a field or a broken-wheeled wagon load of dark rain-rotted hay, but on that day as I drew near, its aspect shifted. The gutted habitation squatted there in the tree shadows seemed to come to life.

In those hungry day, any abandoned roof might shelter outlaws or deserters, or desperate black men without means or destination. This day I sensed an imbalance in the air—a sign that someone watched or something waited. I went on past the house, not breaking step, looking for boot prints or fresh horse dung, fire smoke, straining ear and nose and eye for anything untoward or out of place. I was prepared. Even so, what I saw stopped my heart and snapped my breath away.

I kept my head, let my gaze skip past, walking on a ways before slipping my jackknife from my pocket, letting it fall. Turning and stooping to retrieve it, I scanned that little window porch under the peak, scanned a second time as I straightened, turned, and kept on going. Beneath the wild bees' nest under the dormer, a dark shape crouched behind the leafy rail. Its eyes were burning holes into my back.

Whatever it was had kept dead still but was by no means dead. That imbalance in the air was the withheld breath of it. It was too bulky for a human being, not dark enough for a black bear, even if a bear would climb up in there—I groaned, longing to run, but I seized hold of my panic and walked on and did not look back. I remember the great helplessness I felt, crossing the dead cotton fields toward the woods.

*

When I returned to run my traps a few days later, I thought at first that I must have imagined that dark thing. The same gray weather lay upon the land, the same stark light, but there was a shift of atmosphere, a balance and a lightness in the air, and only a clear emptiness behind the frost-bronzed vine on the porch balcony—so clear that I knew I had not imagined the dark shape under the eaves which was now missing.

What was it, then? Why had I been so certain it was not a man? It seemed too bulky and too dark, wasn't that true? The enigma frightened me so badly that even now, with the mystery long resolved, my heart frets every time I think of it. Yes, it is resolved, and yet I fear it still.

I tried to remain calm. Probably the thing had fled the region, knowing it had been seen. I had scarcely reassured myself when, at the wood edge, I came across a trail of dirtied feathers—not dove or quail killed by hawk or bobcat but wisps of white feathers from a pilfered leghorn, beckoning sadly from the thorns and twigs in the browning woodland air.

I stared about me. Mute ranks of hickory and tupelo gathered behind as I moved into the forest, peering through the skein of bare black twigs and branches, in the chill gloom that at this time of year persisted in the deeper woods even in day. Nearing my trap, I sensed something, as if a rabbit struggled—not a sound, exactly, but a kind of shift, then that imbalance in the air and a kind of ringing. Feeling too weak to walk upright, I sank low and moved forward in a crouch, then on hands and knees.

In a hickory hollow where low ivory sunlight fired the shagbark, the big rough shape mantled my trap like a great diurnal owl. It had detected my approach, for it appeared to be transfixed, in a deep listening. Minutely, the tattered head turned in my direction, crest burning in cold rays of autumn light. When the thing rose soundlessly, clutching my rabbit, I rose, too, in backwards retreat—*Git away!*

Scared by my own squawk, turning to run, I fell over a dead limb—*Git away!* That screech tore the silence of the trees, and when it died away, the wood was empty. The great owl-thing, risen on man's legs, had vanished with the echo.

Picking myself up, I wiped my nose, regained my breath, cursed mightily, to summon outrage from the theft of the lost rabbit. I fled the woods and lit out across the open fields toward Deepwood, where it must have its den. It would keep to the shelter of the woods, circling the long way around the fields and approaching the west wall of the ruin, which was half-fallen and wide open to the weather.

Nearing the house, gasping noisily from the run, I crept in through the shaggy boxwood to an east wall window. Peering and listening, I shivered in the twilight shade, fighting my fear. I was losing my resolve, on the point of flight, when the shape loomed in silhouette in that jagged opening in the west wall, in failing light. Passing through without a sound, it sank into the blackness, slow as any cat. It listened as I fought to still my breath. The frozen rabbit thumped onto a board, the tinder scratched, a small blaze flickered, jumped to life, casting weird shadows. The fire caught at the creature's red eyes, lit grotesque matted arms and chest and neck, the rough head of stubbled feathers. When I gasped, the Owl-Man rose and vanished through the wall.

I scrambled backwards, slashed by the hard briar. It was circling the old house, rushing soundless through the dusk to strike me to the ground. It would hunch upon me as it had my rabbit in the woods, shifting bloody talons, beak glinting in low wintry moonrise.

Git away! Footfalls pursued me down the lane toward the highroad. *You git away from me!*

*

Elijah Watson lurched and staggered back when I burst in, his forearm raised in self-defense, eyes squinted in malevolence. "Damn you, don't bang the hinges off my door!" Confused by drink, he would not sit down to his thin gruel and stale biscuit but simply swayed there, wheezing where he was beside the table, casting huge shadows. Standing by the stove, hands in her apron, Mama ignored me. Though neither had laid eyes on me since I had left two years before, they seemed unsurprised by my return.

"*Our* door," Mama corrected him. Waving away his malignant wife, Papa lost his balance, staggered again. He frowned at my frightened face. "What's the matter with you?"

In her place of hiding in the cupboard, my sister whined. By now, poor Ninny Minny would have wet her drawers.

"I need the rifle," I said, gruff and sullen.

My father roared, stamping the earth floor like a bee-stung horse. Banging through our door that way? Was that how Elijah Watson's son had been taught to respect his mother? And now this wretch dared to demand his father's rifle as if he had some bounden right? The man's head loomed over me, huge and wild, broad shining brow and gold-red locks matted with sweat.

"Welcome back to our little household, Edgar." Mama smiled in her sprightly way. "Our breadwinner has been dismissed again, from Graniteville."

I hated the excitement in my mother's face. Since leaving home, I had never been sure which parent I despised more, the red-faced violent male or this pale vindictive female who teased his violence like a child picking a scab, until it bled. But this day, Lige Watson was too sick with failure, too rotted by bad moonshine, to assault anybody. Shaking his head over his wife's queer satisfaction in their straits, he responded only with an oath and a hacking cough, dragging a chair to the pine table. There he sat down hard and blinked and squinched his nose, trying to focus. Forgetting his thought, he drew his Bowie knife from his scuffed boot and hacked at the stale bread. Soon he gave that up, too. "We ate better on the battlefield." Lige Watson glared into his bowl, as if in the bottom of this cracked clay vessel of insipid soup he might descry every last sad little gobbet of his hopeless life. "She can't even cook an egg," he told his son.

"Papa? Please. I need it," I said.

"Please?" He nodded with heavy irony. "Well, mind you don't get caught by Yanks—" He heaved around but seeing my expression, thought better of a threat to inflict punishment. "What scared you so bad? You have never been the scairdy kind."

Mama moved past the man's show of concern. "Well, Mr. Watson? Who will provide for us? Is your son to be the head of his father's household?"

"He don't live in his father's household, last I heard." Papa scowled in sudden memory of the beating. "I asked you a question."

"Need to take care of some business.

"What sort of business?" Mama said, afraid.

My defiance faltered. I blurted out what I had seen—a strange man-thing, inhabiting the Deepwood ruin.

"The old Tilghman place? Ah Godamighty!"

The woman told me I'd imagined things, but the man kicked the chair back, lurched to his feet. He dragged his musket from between the beam and eaves, as its oily sacking fell to the earth floor. He did not give it to me, only cursed and slammed out of the door. His horse, left saddled, snorted as it wheeled, and the carom of its hooves on frozen clay came back out of the night.

"Deepwood?" she inquired, turning from the door. "Is that where he's going?"

Still standing, I was wolfing Papa's soup. She told me to sit down while I was eating. I paid no attention. "No," I said. "He'll go to Major Coulter."

"Of course. Where else?"

With Papa gone, her eyes had softened. Relieved to see me in some way, she tried to smile. A moment later, she chastised me for wiping my mouth with the back of my hand. I raised my gaze to hers over the bowl rim, then wiped my mouth and belched, to see her shudder. She feared me a little now, I saw, which made me feel even more lonesome than before.

"And how are things going at Clouds Creek?"

Knowing she did not care, I did not answer.

Mama told me everything was ready. She and Minnie and Aunt Cindy would leave for Florida at the first opportunity, she only hoped I might have changed my mind. When I said I had not, and wished her well, she took my hands across the table and held my gaze for a long time, to make sure I was a witness to a mother's tears. Had this strange mother ever realized how she had risked her children?

Perhaps she saw the coldness in my face, for almost instantly she straightened up, released my hands, blew her nose smartly. "Never mind," she said.

Toward midnight, he came home just long enough to wrap his musket in the sacking and return it to its place of hiding in the rafters. I could watch him now with some detachment. He appeared clumsy and shaken and he reeked of spirits, his red brow glistening with sickly sweat despite the cold, red ring-eye pulsing. "I was here all evening, and I slept here. Don't forget it." Frowning ferociously, Ring-Eye Lige lurched out into the night and rode away.

Deepwood

I set off at daylight and I took the musket. I had not slept well or long enough, and turning into the narrow lane at Deepwood, I was racked by dread. I had no idea what had happened here the night before nor what I might stumble into, nor any clear idea what I aimed to do besides threaten it, drive it away. I could not ignore it and go home, that was all I knew.

At the edge of the green carriage circle, my eye picked up a trail. I tracked dark spots to an old boxwood where something had lain wounded. Still bleeding, it had crawled toward the ruin, then along a shaded wall where an old lilac had been overgrown and choked by honeysuckle. The trail led around the corner and on down the west wall where that fire hole made a black wound in the house. I paused at the corner to get my breath and muster up some courage.

It was not hard to imagine what had happened. Torches, blowing horses, and wild shots, angry orders to stop shooting and listen. In the dark, they could not track the blood because they were drunk and had rushed off without their dogs, and because they were ignorant and superstitious and afraid. When the Owl-Man crawled under the dense boxwood, they had lost him.

The wounded creature was alive inside that hole a few yards away. Though I heard nothing, I could sense its life. I checked my load. Then I cleared my throat, took a deep breath—"Come out," I demanded, my voice thin and scared. There was no response. From behind the wall came the slight shift of something stirring. I crept along toward the hole, picking my way through the gaunt winter briars, lifting long thorny rose stems from my leg, struggling to keep the musket disentangled. I heard a hard hurt breathing and a dry ratcheting cough like a raccoon sneeze.

Inside the charred wall, on a rough board by the fire, lay my hoarfrost rabbit, stiff and unnatural as furred wood. Behind it, taking shape in the cold shadows, were ragged legs and broken boots, also a sinuous dark stain where blood had probed and found a passage back into burned earth. I could just make out the crusted head, last tufts twisted askew, and a swollen black hand like a talon, clutched to the heavy bloodstain on the stomach.

I straightened, still outside the wall, shaking with horror. It must be some old nigger, I thought, unless that skin between the crust patches was ingrained with filth. This creature was neither black nor white but only some frightful effigy of a human being. It was close to death, there was nothing I could do. I only wanted to get out of there, and to forget it.

"The Coward . . . Watson."

I forced myself to bend and peer inside. The Owl-Man watched through raw slits in the crust. I could scarcely make out nostrils or mouth, only the owl mask, worn to a leprous stubble. A rude line showed where the head had been half-scalped, then sealed with boiling tar, then crowned with feathers. When the mouth opened slowly, strings of dry slime stretched between dry broken teeth. It had no expression, yet the mouth uttered a choked gasp.

"Finish it. I entreat you."

Such agony was horrifying beyond anything I had imagined, unbearable—*not bearable!*—as if all past and future misery of mankind had been distilled here in this ruin, with no relief but the ultimate mercy of annihilation. But when I raised the musket barrel and put my finger to the trigger, I was blind with tears and sagged down weakly, trying not to vomit.

In a sudden thrash, the Owl-Man seized the barrel, twisting it in his black claw with the force of spasm, yanking the muzzle to his throat as I fought to pull away. My wrist was clasped in a horny hand, my cry obliterated by explosion. The gun came free with the recoil, and I fell backwards through the hole in a roil of smoke. A voice—my own?—cried out as the echo died and the thinning smoke wandered away into the deafened woods.

*

My boot heels rang on the frozen earth, echoing off the rigid trees like rifle shots. *Why did you?* I cried, *Why did you? I never*—never what? Even years later I would not know the true question, never mind the answer.

I stood yelling on the county road to drive the present from my brain, fall back into the past, into *before*.

Yesterday, a young farmer named Edgar Watson with good prospects and high hopes had turned up this same lane, only to wander out of life into dark dream. He had awakened now and he must hurry to Clouds Creek to feed his hogs, wasn't that true? What had happened—*had* it happened?—in the Deepwood ruin, what did such nightmare have to do with prime hogs waiting to be fed? Hogs rooting and grunting and *harfing*, waiting for slops?

I howled at the high heavens, but to whom?

Alone on the highroad in the leaden light, I knew my life had lost its purchase. The future was flying away forever, like a dark bird crossing distant woods. Not knowing where to turn, with no one to confide in, I hurried onward. Burdened with the heavy gun, I could not even run—and run and run—all the way home.

*

A hard wind searched the roadside trees, cracking cold limbs. Over the rushing of dead leaves, scraps of voice were coming hard behind. When I whirled, the weight of the heavy musket swung me off balance, and I fell to the frozen road.

The hand that set down the water bucket and retrieved the musket was hard-veined, burnished black. I scowled, got to my knees. Tap Watson backed away a little, brushing the dirt off the gun, inspecting the breech. "What you runnin from? What's them tears for?" He squinted in the direction of the ruin. "You know somethin 'bout dat shootin over yonder?" I shook my head, but he persisted. "Las' evenin, and again dis mornin?"

"Never heard it. Not that it's any of your nigger business."

He took his hat off, bent his head. "O Lordy Lordy!" Then he wept, and his cheeks shone like dark wet wood in the cold sunrise. "Been leavin these few greens for him since he come home," he muttered finally, face hardening. "You people needin any?" He tossed his old croker sack at my chest, contemptuous. I made no attempt to catch it. It flopped onto the frozen dust between us.

The old man raised the gun, waving the muzzle in the direction of the ruin. "You and me, we's goin back up yonder."

"You raising that gun to a white man, Tap? You threatening me?"

"I b'lieve that you is threatenin *me*, Mist' Edguh." He waved the gun again. "Le's go now."

"Supposing I refuse? You aim to shoot me?"

"Nosuh. I aim to tell dem Union officers over to de Court House where dat gunfire come from late last evenin, and another shot again dis mornin. After dat, I tell 'em how I seen dis boy Mist' Edguh runnin away from dere totin his daddy's shootin iron, which his daddy ain't allowed to have back in de firs' place."

I went ahead of him up the red road. "Very dangerous, messing into white men's business. Your word against mine."

He uttered a woeful groan. "Dis gun barrel still *warm*, Mist' Edguh. Sposin I telled 'em dat?"

"It won't be warm by the time you reach the bluecoats."

There was no answer, only the slow scuff of boots on the frozen clay. What would the Regulators say about a nigger who raised a weapon to a white man? I asked next. Slung greens at that white man as if tossing slops to some ol' hog? Threatened to report him to the bluecoats? If Major Coulter got wind of such behavior, Tap Watson would be a stone dead nigger before nightfall.

But of course Tap's story would be told before the Regulators could get to him and shut him up. He was a "good home nigger" and a deacon, swearing his oath on the Bible—who would doubt him? Who would believe Old Ring-Eye's ragged boy even if I told the truth—that the traitor had been stealing from my trap line, that the traitor had already been shot—

Is that true, boy? Shot by whom?

Start again: he had gone to demand his rabbit back, taking along an old gun to protect himself in case the traitor attacked him. Instead he had found the man mortally wounded, dying in agony. The traitor had begged the boy to take mercy on him, to finish him. He had grabbed the gun barrel, and the old gun went off. It was an accident.

You hold on right there. You say "mortally wounded"—how do you know that? Wounded by whom? You have no idea? You'd better get your story straight. Was your father with you? Isn't it true that Lige Watson hated Colonel Tilghman?

The Coward Watson. There was no way I could tell them the whole truth.

For defending my trap line against raids by a fugitive traitor, I might escape judicial punishment, but Colonel Robert would arrive at a harsh judgment. *A pilfered rabbit—was that good cause to kill a starving man? An Edgefieldian, a gentleman? A Confederate cavalry officer and hero? Your own kinsman?* He would call it murder.

Didn't I tell you?—I could hear Aunt Sophia now. Those iron-eyed sky-crazed Celts out at Clouds Creek (as Cousin Selden had once called them) would seize this excellent excuse to cast out Bad Elijah's seed, deny my birthright. In the imminence of such injustice came a pounding ache so violent and so sudden that I never even realized I was falling.

A black face inset in the gray heavens. The eyes were wide and the mouth working, but there came no sound. Then darkness passed and I came clear of it, at a distance from my self. Jack Watson had awakened in grim mood as panic and indecision gave way to a resolve as clear as when, with the wind's dying, shattered moonlight on the surface of rough water regathers its shards into one reflection, one single gleaming blade. I rolled up onto my feet so easily and swiftly that the only witness actually drew back. I led him toward the fire-hollowed house.

How simple it would be. No one lived near.

Entering the Deepwood lane, I felt an immense spring in my step, and every breath I took deepened my strength. Over my shoulder, I teased Tap, laughing, saying he only wanted me along because niggers were scared to be alone with corpses. With his contempt for darkie superstitions, Tap would be caustic in response. But he remained silent, and when I turned to laugh at him, the old man stopped short in the road. He was staring bald-eyed, as if he'd never seen me in his life.

"Nosuh, dis sho'ly ain't no nigguh business, nosuh, it sho ain't." Distressed, he took out a blue bandanna, wiping his neck in the cold air as he might have done in the hot cotton fields in the midsummer.

When I reached for the musket, he returned it. I motioned him ahead. "You have come here before, isn't that true?"

"Yassuh. Las' evenin. Come mos' ever' evenin after dark."

He had slowed, and after a few more steps, he stopped. He took a deep breath and sighed, putting his neckerchief away. "You too young to be mixed up in dis, Mist' Edguh."

"I'm not mixed up in it. Unless you mix me."

"Ain't gone mix nobody." When I waved him toward the hole in the west wall he went ahead, then sank to his knees in prayer, summoning courage. When he saw what lay inside, he placed his hands over his eyes. "Oh Godamercy!"

When Papa's gun had gone off, I had tumbled out and fled. I had not seen the body through the smoke. The head was missing. Having no tool to chip a grave in the frozen ground, we piled half-burned timbers on the trunk, which I could not look at. Afterwards, the black man, on his knees, croaked a Baptist hymn, but being too upset to sing, he mumbled prayers instead. "You was a *good* man, Cop'n Selden, suh," he finished, bowing his head. "We ain' nevuh gone fo'get you in our prayers."

Behind him, I had raised the rifle and sighted down the barrel at the grayfrizzed scalp, the bare skin of the crown, the ears, the twitching skin and throbbing pulse, the skull from Africa—how fragile and transient this bent figure seemed. How caught in death as well as life, death as close as the impulse of my forefinger, so numb with cold and clumsy on the frozen metal.

Stiffening, he turned his head and looked straight into the rifle muzzle from a foot away. "Lo'd he'p us," he gasped, seeing the blue eye behind the hammer.

At the base of my tongue was a quick metallic taste—not the taste of death but the taste of an unholy power to take life. I held my breath as, with great care, I lifted that numb finger from the worn and shiny lever of the trigger.

Departure

Even as I hurried home toward Clouds Creek, my criminal parent, Ring-Eye Lige, was hitching his roan to Major Coulter's cart. Roaring with drink, he drove it like a chariot, careening around the courthouse square, scaring old ladies and scattering dogs and children. When one wheel was struck off by the wood sidewalk and the buggy pitched him out into the dust, my father was seized and haled forthwith up the courthouse steps and straight back through the courtroom to the cells behind. Next morning he was charged with endangering life and limb, disturbing the peace, inciting to riot, resisting arrest, and whipping his poor beast bloody—everything and anything the constable could think of to hold him without bail until the next session of the circuit court.

Early Sunday, before church, I went to collect my wage and let the Colonel know my plan to go to Edgefield Court House to see to the care and feeding of my father's horse. From the stoop, I called good morning to his wife as she crossed the corridor, but Aunt Lucy only shook her head and did not answer. Then her husband came, more to bar the door than to welcome me within. He did not offer his hand, as was his custom, but looked me in the eye and told me that a hunter's dog had sniffed out a charred corpse at the Deepwood ruin.

"Deepwood?"

He awaited me. Perhaps I flushed, or perhaps he hoped I would explain this matter of my own accord. Still watching me closely, he said next that someone had seen me near Deepwood a few days ago, in the early morning. "You were carrying a rifle. And a shot was heard."

I was struck dumb. I had been betrayed.

"You must leave here," Colonel Robert's voice was saying, far away now.

"Sir? If my work—"

"It has nothing to do with your work, Edgar. You are an exceptional young farmer." He sighed mightily, handing me a money packet. "Fair payment for your hogs. Now go at once. You have no future at Clouds Creek. You are in danger here."

I searched his face as a crippled bird follows the hand which stoops to wring its neck. There was no absolution in that gaze. I wanted to howl, *It is not just! It was not me!* Then that inner screaming came, a ringing like crazed bells, and this time I went straight over backwards. Later I imagined I had heard the faraway *whump* made by my head and shoulders as I struck the ground.

Cousin Edgar?

"Cousin Edgar?"

Muffled hog grunts and the croon of chickens. Cold white winter sun.

"He fainted, did he? Wily as a snake, just like the father!"

"He has these spells, woman. Look at the color of him. Now kindly fetch that blanket here as you were told."

A close warm smell. Horse tack and burned tobacco. My kinsman, taking pains, was tucking me under the coarse blanket. I turned my head away. Eventually he helped me up off the cold earth, taking me under the arm, intending to lower me onto the steps. Wrenching my arm away, shaking off his help, made me dizzy and unsteady, and again that darkness passed across my vision as a small cumulus blots the sun. I sat down hard. "It was not my doing. I wished him no harm."

The Colonel nodded. "Yet you know what was done. You know who did it." He paused a moment. "And you will not betray the guilty, even though they have not hesitated to cast suspicion upon you."

"Who has accused me?"

He shook his head. "People are filled with shame about Colonel Tilghman. To absolve themselves—to absolve *all* of us—another scapegoat must be found. And since you won't defend yourself—" He put his big hands on my shoulders, squeezing hard to make sure I understood. "Travel quickly across country to the Georgia line. Now hear me, boy! You could be shot or hung."

He had led me around behind the house, out of sight of the main road. "You think I exaggerate? They are already looking for you." Colonel Robert offered his hand. "You have had a hard road for one so young. You were set a very poor example. I am truly sorry."

"It is not just," I stated in a stony voice, as my kinsman's face blurred and began to shimmer. When his face came clear again, his hand was still extended. It dropped to his side at just the moment I resolved to take it.

"Very well," my kinsman said, resolute and patient, scanning the countryside. "Go quickly. And may God be with you." He crossed the yard to the back stoop and closed the door behind him. On the blank face of the house, the windows had curtains of white lace. The glass was clean and clear and empty, with a shine in winter that reflected the black walnut trees behind.

All my life I have recalled the proffered hand of Colonel R. B. Watson, the grained and weathered hide of it, the wrist hairs like finespun golden threads in the coldest sunlight I ever remembered.

Flight

I fled across the frozen fields. At Grandfather's house, I flung the hog pen gate clean off its hinge and drove out my dear burly hogs with kicks and curses. Their snouts would lead them to the Colonel's troughs—if not, then let them run hog wild. I tossed my few rags and books into some sacking, along with cold grub and a knife and slung this meager bindle from the musket barrel. I left the split door wide. For a last time I headed out across the fields to Clouds Creek and followed it upstream through the home woods to the Ridge spring behind the church. Seeing no dust or other sign of riders on the highroad, I walked on west toward Edgefield Court House. Near Deepwood, hearing oncoming hoofbeats, I peered from the wood edge as armed riders passed at a fast trot and slow canter.

Crossing lots, I climbed the back fence of the livery stable, where I paid my father's bill and reclaimed the roan. Realizing I was a fugitive, the blacksmith sidled up too close, but something in my eye made him think better of an attempt to take me prisoner. "Heard you had trouble." He was sneering. "Same as your old man."

The dirt lanes between dwellings held a Sunday silence. In the distance I saw Tap, gleaning in the field. Otherwise, there was nobody in sight. At my mother's cabin, I returned the rifle to the rafters. A note on the bare table advised me that Mama had departed the day before with Minnie and Aunt Cindy while "Mr. Watson" was safely lodged in jail. She hoped that one day I might join them in north Florida, but if not, why then, good-bye, my son, and God be with you.

I don't imagine He was with me as I rode to the courthouse to finish up my business. The jail cells were upstairs back of the courtroom. I fiddled the old lock and slipped in quietly and listened—not a sound. No deputy, no guard. The single prisoner was sprawled upon his bunk.

Ring-Eye Lige rolled over, squinted, asked me what I wanted. Challenged that way, I realized I had meant to kill him. But he was safely behind bars and I had not brought the rifle. To save face, I lied. "I want to notify you I have changed my name."

"You walked all the way here from Clouds Creek to tell me *that?*" My father hooted, rolling over on his side, facing the wall.

"Edgar Addison Watson. Uncle John took care of all the legal papers."

"God *damn* that woman!" he shouted, sitting up. "The eldest son carries the name of the paternal grandfather unless he wants to be disowned!"

I wanted to jeer at him—*Disowned from what?*—but in the light of what had happened to my life, I had no heart for it.

He ordered me to make sure Job was getting plenty of oats down at the stable. I told him the account was settled and the roan outside.

"Job? You damn well take good care of my roan horse."

"I will. Better than you did." I blurted, "Mama has left home. Sister, too. I aim to follow 'em. And not on foot."

"You're not taking my horse, you sonofabitch." Shaking off news of wife and daughter as brusquely as his roan shivered off flies, he lay back again, his arm over his eyes, boots on the blanket. "I'll get the law on you," he said.

"Looks like you did that already," I said. If he heard, he gave no sign.

From out on the square came the shout of a young boy. Afraid that boy had recognized the tethered horse, raised the alarm, I turned to leave. My father said, all tired out, "Take the rifle, then. Leave me my horse. I guess I don't amount to much without that horse."

When I kept going, he yelled, "Edgar!" and I paused. He said pitifully, "They aim to hang me, son."

"No," I said. "It's me they're looking for."

When he realized what I'd said, he loosed a loud whoop of relief.

I watched him laughing. He grew wary, tried to muster up some outrage. "Don't go looking at me that way, son. It wasn't *me*. Know who put it all on you? My goddamn partners!" He lowered his voice to a gravelly hard scrape, conspiratorial, as if inviting me to help him plot the Terrible Retribution of the Watsons. "Can you believe it? Do that to the son of Captain Watson?"

The blackness swirled so thick before my eyes that I had to grasp the bars. "I almost shot that poor old man," I muttered, as the truth fell into place. "I nearly took his life."

"Tap, you mean? Tap knows the truth?" Slowly he rose and came over to the bars, his blanket like a hood around his head and shoulders. We considered each other, son and father. Having come off the drink the hard way, all alone in his cold cell, he looked puffy and haggard. As if sick of life, he came out with it all. They had meant to ride to Deepwood in the daytime and hunt the Owl-Man down and finish him. But when he went home to fetch his rifle and learned I had already left, taking the weapon, he consulted with his cronies, who decided they would follow me out there, wait to see what happened. Hearing the shot and seeing me run out, they rode away. But he had felt guilty about me and got drunk and whipped his horse around the square, got himself jailed.

"You scared I might come gunning for you? You thought you might be better off in here?"

Croaking, he backed away from the cell bars. "For the love of Jesus, boy, don't show that devil face to your mortal father!"

He blurted out the rest. The Regulators had reported shooting to the Union garrison and volunteered as deputies and "found" the body. As the only person in Edgefield District known to frequent Deepwood, young Edgar Watson was the natural suspect, all the more so because he had been seen headed out that way that morning, armed with a musket.

"The Coward Watson." Eyes closed, I pressed my forehead to the cold iron of his bars. "The Coward Watson. You have destroyed me, Papa."

"You're very pale, boy. Are you all right?" He hadn't wished to hear what I had said and so he hadn't. Reaching through the bars, he cupped my nape almost gently in his sweaty hand. I stiffened. *He fears that I will bring the gun and shoot him through the bars, so he will break my neck right now while he has his chance.* But his fear was justified and his intent was harmless. "You have grown up too fast," he said sadly, letting go.

"Yessir," I said. "I have grown up some."

My voice broke. I had to fight back tears. With all of Edgefield District on my trail—even the jailer was out looking for me—I had come to see my father one last time, not to take his life as I imagined, not to tell him that his family had forsaken him, nor even that I meant to take his horse. After all those dark and violent years of terror and humiliation, I had come here to receive my Papa's praise for having cleaned up after the botched lynching, to receive the credit due for covering the Coward Watson's bloody tracks and saving the Watson honor.

He said, "You hate me, don't you? First your mama and the girl. And now my son." His eyes glistened in self-pity when I nodded. He whispered, "I am forsaken, then." And I said, "You are."

I was at the door when he called after me a last time. "Tap Watson knows the truth? That what you meant?" He gave me a bad smile. "Son? Will you take care of that before you go?" When I was silent, he said quickly, "Never mind, boy. You save your own skin." I hated him for that. "Come back and see me someday, will you do that, son? Come back and see your papa? Will you promise?"

"Yessir, I will. I aim to kill you, Papa." Going out, I heard Ring-Eye's howl of fear as the truth of his lost life fell down upon him. From the courthouse terrace, I stared at my home country—the first time I had beheld that view since Private E. D. Watson of the First Edgefield Volunteers bore me up these steps in the first year of the War. The terrace was not nearly so high as I had imagined as a child, and its noble views appeared sadly diminished. The countryside looked commonplace and the world small because my heart had grown small, too.

People in the square were pointing at me as I ran down the steps and mounted. I rode home and returned with the rifle, but my father's cry had raised the alarm. I wheeled and fled.

I found Tap still gleaning cabbages, way out in the middle of a field. He must have seen the long rifle across the pommel. Having no place to run, he straightened slowly as the horse came toward him. Slowly he laid down hoe and sack, then removed his lumpy hat to await the rider.

He could not look at the long gun. "Nosuh, Mist' Edguh, I sho' ain't spoked to nobody about *nothin.*" His voice was dull and dead. "I done jus' like you tole me, Mist' Edguh." His eyes were shivering.

Men were running toward the clamor in the square. A shroud of winter dust arose from the hooves of horses. I said, "You know too much. You have to hide. They will be coming." I told him he must find Lulalie, then they must go. I handed him the Colonel's packet. "Buy a mule," I said. They should leave at dark, head for Augusta, follow the women south to Fort White, Florida.

He refused the money.

"Dis yere dis'rict is mah home, Mist' Edguh. I ain't done nothin wrong, so I ain't goin. Trus' in de Lord! Dass what Preacher Simkins tole 'em at our church when dem white men come for him. Dem white men listened, and dey went on home."

"These men won't listen, Tap. They won't even ask."

He was watching the dust over the town. "You best go, Mist' Edguh. Dey be comin. Tell dat woman dat Lalie and me be waitin on her here at home."

I rode away. Avoiding the main roads, I headed south and west down through Horse Valley and forded the Savannah River near the fall line. When the roan clambered up on the Georgia bank, I turned in the saddle to gaze back. This was the first time I had ever left my native Carolina, and everywhere ahead was unknown country.

Chapter 2

On Echo River

I caught up with the women on a warm afternoon on the old Woodpecker Trail, down west of the Great Okefenokee—rode up alongside the cargo wagons taciturn, untalkative, as if this had been my plan right from the start. Those poor females were delighted and relieved, Aunt Cindy, too, but seeing that roan horse made them uneasy. They never asked about old Job nor his owner, either, and I never offered to explain, not then, not later. I didn't want to talk about that ring-eyed bastard, nor open the hurt of my lost hopes at Clouds Creek. I hitched the roan to the tailgate of the wagon and crawled inside amongst their bedding and slept straight through until early the next morning.

Seeing my head poke out, Aunt Cindy whooped over how well I looked, fixed me a big breakfast, and finally got around to her little family. How was her Lalie getting on, and had that Tap sent word? Remembering how close I came to killing her old man, I could scarcely look her in the eye. Nor could I assure her that Tap and Lulalie were on their way to join us, since the cause of their sudden departure would worry this good woman half to death. I lied, saying that living at Clouds Creek, I had scarcely seen them.

That woman gave me a queer look—she didn't miss much. She saw that my heart was crippled, my smile false, but it was not her place to question me and so she didn't. In my gut, I knew that Tap Watson was done for, and as for Lulalie, who could say what would become of her?

On the twelfth of March of 1871, we crossed over into Florida. With two state lines behind me, I was breathing easier. Only now did I introduce my-self to other pioneers—E. A. Watson, overseer of the Artemas Plantation at Clouds Creek, South Carolina, at your service, sir. Nobody knew quite what to make of this husky youth who was no boy but not a man yet either. I was a homesick greenhorn in a strange new country, but also a fugitive, angry and dangerous as a gut-shot bear.

*

The last leg of the journey took us by slow barge south to Branford Landing on the Suwannee River, "far, far away, that's where my heart is turning ever, that's where the old folks stay." That song stirred me, bringing on misty-eyed upwellings—ridiculous, since my old folks were on Clouds Creek, not the Suwannee. Sprawled in the sunshine and warm tar smell of the hemp hawsers on the bow, I wallowed in tender emotions, maintaining an austere silence with the others.

Try as I would to enjoy my escape from the cold rain and mud of Pied-mont winter, with its coarse meager food and numbing drudgery and lone-liness, nothing seemed to ease the ache of longing. The farther I traveled, the more senseless my exile seemed. From my *Iliad*—the one frayed heirloom I had brought with me in my sack—I had memorized a passage about the great rage of revenge which "swirls like smoke within our heart, and be-comes in our madness a thing more sweet than the dripping of honey." That fury had not abated, nor the will to vengeance, which chewed like a black rat at my lungs. My one consolation was my determination that justice would be done, that one day I would reclaim my Clouds Creek land. And "in my madness" I would take Ring-Eye Lige Watson's raw red life.

*

Before my eyes as we sailed farther downriver—"way down upon the Suwannee River"—were visions of spring furrows opening behind the plow, of wildflowered meadows, cool and verdant, and airy open woods along the shaded creeks, winding southeast to the Edisto. That spring landscape turned forever and away in my mind's eye, changing softly with the seasons into the warm golden greens of upland summer in that lost land where I was born, the country of my forefathers, the heart of home. Clouds Creek—my earth—was the wellspring and the source of Edgar Watson, the lost Eden, all the garden he might ever hope to find.

Then reverie dissolved, leaving cold sweat like a dank swamp mist on my skin—like the dead sweat on that young slave's corpse, long ago in the Clouds Creek swamps. I stared around in disbelief at the undiscovered coun-try on both sides of the river, a howling waste of dark riverine forest and rank coarse savanna where the seasons scarcely changed. When I wasn't gasping in black rage, I was suffocated by melancholy. When I wasn't mourning my well-built pens bursting with sprightly hogs, I cursed the weeds, vines, and hard briar that would creep over my crops, returning my farmland to the desolation of choked thorny oldfields. The neglected land might languish for years as evidence of the failure of our lineage—the weak seed of the grandfather, the violent coward son, the distempered grandson already embarked upon his misadventures.

A sudden squawk of pain and anger silenced every soul on that slow barge. My mother and sister, pretending they were deaf, went on about their business. Not knowing what had happened back at Edgefield, they were afraid of my darkness and silence. Only Aunt Cindy seemed mostly unconcerned. She was awaiting me, sure I would spit it up when I was ready. Unable to meet her skeptical cool eye, I set my jaw and glared fixedly at the forests of the wild Suwannee (Creek Indian for "Echo River," so the bargeman said). That song was an infection on the barge; everyone hummed, whistled, and sang it, and just when it seemed it might die out, I'd hum it inadvertently myself, unable to drive its dreary plaint out of my head.

> *All up and down the whole Creation*
> *Sadly I roam*
> *Still longing for the old plantation*
> *And for the old folks at home.*

But finally I sickened of that song, and of self-pity, and of Sad Edgar, too. Day after day, the mysterious smells and voices of this wilderness had called to me unheeded, seeking to draw me back into my life. And one fresh morning, as if touched by a wand, the world came clear again, the whole Creation. The new country presented itself simply, in exciting light, and daybreak turned the earth as dark withdrew, and sunrise leaves spun and cavorted on the fresh wind from the Gulf of Mexico which filled my lungs. I sat suddenly upright, startling poor Minnie. I was young and strong, said to be very able, and one day I would go home to Carolina. This year a virgin land was opening before me and April had drawn near. We would reach our destination at Fort White in time for the spring planting.

*

Here and there, rounding a bend, the barge surprised dark people on the banks, crouched back like wildcats caught out in the open. We saw them only in remote regions, because even before the War their tribes had been rounded up and shipped away west of the Mississippi to the Indian Territories. The women and young would rush into the reeds or flee through the shadows of the great live oaks which spread their mossy limbs over the clearings, but the grown men and older boys, drifting out of gun range, would turn to watch the intruders over their shoulders, in the way of deer. Their calm was feigned—they were set to jump, they had to be. Barge travelers, bored and sullen, often drunk, blazed away at every furred and feathered thing along the river, and sometimes shot at the earth near the Indians' feet, the bargeman said, "to see them redskins dance." On the lookout for the glint of a raised gun barrel, these people would slip away as graceful and slick as snakes, until the invaders disappeared behind the trees on the next bend and the ancient forest silences regathered.

The Cherokees chastised by my ancestors were almost gone from upland Carolina. These were the first wild men I had ever seen. I was awed by the stillness in them even when they moved. We never greeted them. We learned our lesson well the first time, when even the smallest child among them refused to notice Minnie, though she waved and waved until they disappeared around the bend.

"Why don't they wave back?" she cried, desperately hurt and disappointed. I said roughly, "Why should they? They despise us." I saw the world "through a glass darkly," Mama said.

"Them wild ones come down from Muskogee Creeks that Ol' Hickory chased south out of Georgia," the bargeman told us. Most were never seen at all, easing down into hiding at the noise of our approach, watching us pass. But in long days and months alone on my lost farm, my senses had learned to sift out every sound and shift of atmosphere. I imagined I knew when they were there, and more often than not I was proved right. Though I thought nothing of it at the time, this faculty was to serve me well later in life.

*

These hinterlands, so distant from the settlements, remained uncultivated and unhunted. The bargeman said that in Spanish times, when a road was opened from St. Augustine on the Atlantic coast to Pensacola on the Gulf, there were still buffalo in these savannas, and also the great jaguar, called *tigre*, and panther, bear, and red wolf were still common. At night, shrill screams scared Mama and poor Ninny half to death—panthers mating, the bargeman assured Mama, who backed away a step in disapproval. Big bull gators coughed and roared back in the swamps, and once there came a lonely howl that the bargeman identified as wolf. Bronze-back turkeys were dark flocks among the live oaks, and everywhere wood ducks and mallards jumped up from the reeds shedding sparkling drops of water. I shot big drakes and gobblers for provisions and hooked all the fresh catfish we could eat. I never saw such plenty in my life. Pairs of black woodpeckers, larger than crows, white flashing on the wing and ivory bills and crimson crests which caught the sun, crossed the river in deep bounding flight, and small hurtling companies of long-tailed parrots, green as emeralds in the morning light—Carolina parakeets, these birds were called down in the Tidewater. Every wild creature was bursting with spring colors and fresh sap, and I was, too. I wanted to seize and devour this morning land like a fresh peach.

*

The river barge was warped ashore where a tributary, the Santa Fe, joined the Suwannee—the confluence of the Echo and the Holy Faith. De Soto and his men, more discouraged by the heat and insects than by Indian attacks, had called it the River of Discord. (That's those Spaniards for you, Mama sniffed, worn out by her journey and on the lookout for the smallest cause to be indignant.) This stream is a great mystery, since it vanishes quite suddenly beneath the earth—no swirl, just gone away under the ground. Because the red-skinned devils had made life Hell with their unholy shrieks, early travelers imagined they had stumbled on the River Styx into the Underworld, and very few lingered long enough to learn that the water surfaced a few miles downstream as a beautiful blue spring in a deep wood.

While the barge continued on to Branford Landing, I wanted to investigate this fabled place, then head cross-country to Ichetucknee Plantation. Hollering good-bye to the pilot, I rode the big roan off that barge before she touched the shore—a horseshoe clatter sharp as rifle fire, a gathering of haunches, a huge jump and splash and heave up onto the bank. Alas, the heroics of our leap were spoiled by the hydraulics of my stallion, which instantly lowered its great nozzle to release a stream of horse piss even while it rid itself of gas. We hightailed off in a grand salute of horse farts and manure as the womenfolk's alarmed cries of admiration turned to galling laughter.

The river trail ran north along the "Santa Fee" (as local people call it), a clear blackwater stream which descends from a dry sandy country of piney woods and scrub oak to the cypress sink where it is drawn beneath the earth. Farther upstream, the trail turned north along a forest creek called Ichetucknee—not a warm gold amber like the Santa Fe but a crystal stream with blue water so clear that the underwater weeds swam over white sand like schools of turquoise eels.

Ichetucknee

The Ichetucknee post office and trading post (and blacksmith shop and grist-mill) was six miles up this woodland stream, on the east bank of the Mill Pond spring and only a few miles from Fort White, in Columbia County. The proprietor, a small quick man named Collins, was eager to relate how Fort White had been built back in '37, during the Second Seminole War, only to be abandoned to the savages a few years later. The first Collinses had come pioneers in '42, twenty years before the last Indian attack in the Third Seminole War. Soon after came the War Between the States, when this blacksmith-miller-trader-postmaster had rushed over to Lake City—known as Alligator at that time—eager to join the Columbia Rifles and go fight the Yankees. (I did not ask him if he'd got his wish, knowing he hadn't. Otherwise I would have heard about that, too.)

This lively little Edgar Collins would later become my sister's father-in-law, and because we shared a detestation of our given name, we got on fine. After his wife had packed me with good grub, Mr. Collins pointed me northeast through the woods toward the plantation, but not before warning me to watch my step around the new foreman and his boys, a bunch of Georgia ridge runners by the name of Tolen.

Back home in Carolina our roads are iron red, but here in the forests of north Florida the trails were white, a cool white clay, wandering off like ghost paths through the trees. I dismounted and took some in my hand. In summer this stuff would powder to fine dust, but in this damp season the clay felt smooth and fine as bonemeal, beaten hard by wheels and hooves and rain. Peering about me in these silent woods with no idea what I was looking for, I was overtaken by that morbid despair which I'd hoped I'd put behind me. I remounted and rode on, anxious to reach the plantation before nightfall.

*

Aunt Tabitha Watson and her daughter Laura lived in "the Plantation House"—nothing at all like a plantation house in Edgefield. The grand manor that poor Mama had set her heart on was no more than a big log house with rooms on both sides of a center passage. The outside was framed over with pine boards, and a stoop was tacked onto both ends of the rough corridor. Otherwise it differed not at all from what the old folks used to call a dogtrot cabin, through which any stray hound—or coon, hog, rooster, or rummaging bear—could travel from the front door to the back without so much as a how-d'ye-do to the rightful inhabitants on either side. With five rooms, it was the biggest cabin in the county, said our kinfolks, well-situated on the rich soil of a former cow pen, now a fenced-in grove of bearing pecans and black walnut and persimmon.

Great-Aunt Tabitha (she pronounced her name Ta-*bye*-a-tha, throwing in that extra *a* for her own reasons) was sneaking up on sixty years of age, and her daughter Laura wasn't far from forty. Cousin Laura habitually stood one dutiful step behind her mother, where both of them (this was clear at once) thought she belonged. They were lanky, horse-faced females in high collars and white aprons, neither plain nor pretty, but the daughter was only a dim copy of the mother, who had saved for herself every last dab of brains and character.

Cousin Laura, Mama had warned me, was exceptionally kindhearted but not bright. As a girl, Laura had passed for pretty, with her large eyes and soft brown hair and creamy skin, but that wide mouth (as Mama remarked charitably) "lacked the chin needed to control those flying teeth."

I said, "Aunt, I am E. A. Watson—your great-nephew—at your service."

"*A* for Artemas, I take it." The old lady smiled. "You don't much resemble my late brother-in-law. Such a kind good man, for all his little foibles. We called him Bird because he sang with such sweet voice."

"If you please, ma'am, Addison is my name. Edgar Addison."

"*Artemas*," she admonished firmly. "After your grandfather. An old tradition in this family. That is the name inscribed for you in our family Bible, so that is that."

I saw that Mama and this haughty personage were doomed to tangle, but I held my tongue, holding my hat over my heart in evidence of my sincerity as Mama taught me.

A black man named Cobber Banks fetched our family from Branford Landing in a wagon. How threadbare those poor things looked as they came in! I glanced at Aunt Tabitha, who shared that opinion and did not trouble to hide it. I was glad of what Minnie had confided, that Mama had hidden her jewelry from her husband from the very first day of her marriage, and had brought along her few small diamonds, "enough to start us out down here in Florida." She had always worn her hair in a big old rat's nest perfectly suited for hiding diamond rings—two beautiful rings, according to our Ninny, "not just little chips stuck onto something."

Cobber Banks—or Calvin, as he dubbed himself, now that he was a full-fledged citizen of the Republic—told me all there was to know about the Myers Plantation, which consisted of four or five square miles of good flat land. Originally called Ichetucknee, it had been bought by William Myers of Columbia, South Carolina, who had fled south in 1861 to start all over in north Florida, having settled his women in Atlanta until a few primitive comforts could be provided. When he first arrived, he had set his men to girdling the trees, to deaden the pine forest all around, and before long, three square miles had been cleared and fenced. By the time I came there, in the spring of '71, five hundred acres had been planted in corn—"twenty-five acres per nigger and mule" was the way they figured, Calvin said—and three hundred and fifty in Sea Island cotton, which had been the cash crop around here since the War.

"What corn we grow, dass mostly for hog and home. Bale up de shucks in de place of winter hay, fodder de stock dat way, keep de niggers in cornmeal and hominy. Hog food, corn bread, hominy, sometimes sourins—you Carolina folks know about sourins? Turn cornmeal sour by sun-cookin it? Pretty good to eat with chicken. Gopher, too. You folks like gopher?" Calvin hummed a little, his mouth working, savoring those tortoise feeds of yore.

After the War when Abolition came, Colonel Myers sold his field hands their own mules on credit and rented them land at $2.50 an acre, figuring he'd get his money back out of the share crop. Next, he set up a gin and processed cotton for small farmers all around the county. The ginning lasted from September until Christmas except in years when a sharp frost killed the plants down. The crop was several thousand pounds, and four pounds made one pound of ginned cotton at $1.00 a pound.

Cousin Laura said that Colonel Myers had returned each year to his old home in South Carolina, leaving the management of Ichetucknee to his overseers. Most of his slaves had stayed on here as freedmen, having neither the wherewithal nor sense to find their way back home. The only one with sense was Calvin Banks, who had served some years as Myers's coachman and remained loyal to the family. During the War, when the Yankees reached Olustee, thirty miles to the northeast, Colonel Myers buried his gold in a secret place back in the woods. A few months later, he was struck dead by lightning while standing beneath an oak during a rainstorm (just when he was drawing up his plans for the first real manor house in Columbia County). Meanwhile he had let the coachman sharecrop his own hundred-acre piece, and after his employer's death, Calvin Banks, now thirty-five, bought this piece from Cousin Laura, paying $450 in cash money. After the War, this land had gone for $6 an acre, so he got it cheap, but even so, nobody could figure how that darn nigger saved so much so fast. Naturally the rumors spread that he had been with Myers when the Colonel buried his gold out in the woods and that this rascal must have gone out there and dug it up. Aunt Tabitha believed that Calvin was a thief, Cousin Laura did not— a clue to the philosophical differences between those women.

Because Laura had no head for business—nor much else, observed her old loyal friend, my mother—the poor widow had been left out of her husband's will. Myers specified that Aunt Tabitha would inherit his plantation, which upon her death should be turned over to his nephews, who were Watson cousins on their mother's side. After Myers's death in 1869, Cousin Laura and her mother came here seeking to break the will, and because conditions at home were so uncertain, Aunt Tabitha decided to stay on in Florida and manage this huge, remote plantation which nobody in Reconstruction times could afford to buy. Not long after our arrival, the Widow Laura was awarded a "child part" of the plantation by the county commission, a Reconstruction body which included a black farmer, Simeon Watson—Tap's half brother—and also Aunt Tabitha's kinsman and neighbor, Captain Thomas Getzen. Ex-slave and Confederate officer alike were daunted by Aunt Tabitha, and did her bidding.

The Watson ladies soon discovered that cultivated or even educated people were very uncommon in this frontier county, and very soon they came to hate their isolation. Since Ellen Addison had been Laura's friend and schoolmate, and since Aunt Tabitha regretted her failed marriage, my mother's plea for refuge in Florida had been granted. "The family at Clouds Creek informs me that you have done all you could to save the soul of my afflicted nephew," read Aunt Tab's letter, which Mama had shown us on those days on the Suwannee, "and suffered no end of violence and sorrow for your pains. Forsake him, then, as God is your witness, and flee to us in Florida, for your children's sake as well as for your own."

And for Aunt Tabitha's sake, too, Mama had sniffed. The plantation would need the experienced help that her strong young Edgar could provide.

My very first day, I jumped right in and joined in the spring planting, making sure that Aunt Tabitha understood I was not a poor relation but a farmer, and that just because we had accepted her hospitality did not mean we were there to accept charity. Anyway, I enjoyed work and was excited by the possibilities of this plantation. Eager to understand its economics, I was up early and rode till late, helping out wherever I could learn something. I was confident that I could run this place as overseer, though it might take a year or so to prove it. Meanwhile, there was plenty to eat and a clean warm place to sleep—I could not get over such prosperity.

In my spare time, out hunting and exploring, I rode all over the south county. The forest all around was fairly trembling with deer and turkey, an abundance not to be believed after the worn-out woods of home. As for robins, redbirds, orioles—those larger songbirds which I hunted for the table in the War years—their choruses arose each morning from the oak trees near the house, and I never paid them the least bit of attention. What I listened to contentedly instead was an ax chopping or the cheerful tinking of an anvil, or hammers banging on some new construction. Every shack had roosters crowing and hogs grunting and darkies crooning in the evenings, which made Mama homesick for "the good old days," by which she meant the antebellum days of wealth and slavery. All that was lacking here, she whispered, with a wry glance at our benefactors, was witty company. Oh how she missed her poor lost Cousin Selden, Mama sighed.

*

Because I was close kin to the owners, I was already disliked by the overseer, Woodson Tolen, who was hired originally to run the place in those months of the year when Colonel Myers was away. I soon saw that this man's designs on the plantation had been born on the very day Myers was killed. He knew that the old woman could not live forever no matter how hard she might try, and that once Aunt Tabitha was out of the way, Cousin Laura would cheerfully sign almost any piece of paper a conniving and ambitious skunk like Woodson Tolen might set in front of her. He was already training his oldest boy, the shifty James, to take over any year now as plantation overseer.

A redneck from the Flint River country in the Georgia hills, this Woodson Tolen was a wiry small weasel with mean red eyes pinched too close to his nose and traces of ancient grime in every seam. From his vantage point close to the ground, this feller spied on my hard work, which he perceived as a sinister attempt to thwart his ambitions for his sons. Right from the start, these ridge runners did all they could to make me look as bad as possible.

*

In those windless days in the long Florida summer, the earth seemed to slow and the air died, under a sky as thick and white as a boiled egg. The woodland trees along those white clay roads stood still as mourners. Even the dust-shrouded leaves appeared exhausted.

On such a day in that first summer, hoeing cotton, I feared I might faint unless I stripped off my wet shirt, as all the niggers had sense enough to do. Back then, a white man of good family would never strip his shirt off in the field, because even in Reconstruction times, deep in the country out of sight of Yankee law, our new black citizens were still treated like slaves, never mind what they might call themselves back in their cabins.

That day the snooping overseer W. Tolen came along on his woods pony with his second son, Fat Sammy, up behind him. Seeing me shining with sweat from my hard work, Sam jeered and stuck his tongue out. I ignored this—I'd have done the same for him. Trying to get along, I had let him be my friend, although he was younger and not much of a friend, having been tutored by his daddy in every meanness he had not been born with.

However, he was the only white boy close to my own age for a mile around, and I enjoyed his comical and dirty mind.

Woodson squinted across the fence, grinning that dog grin of his that had no fun in it. In his redneck whine he said, "I reckon Mis Ta-*bye*-a-tha mightn't care to hear her neph-yew was workin half-naked like a nigger." And he pointed his bony index finger at my eyes, which amongst such backwards mountain folk sends evil luck. A bird flown through an open window brings in fortune. Some even wear a little bag around the neck with a piece of their own shit in it, to keep evil at bay and decent people, too.

Calvin Banks was the one nigger in that field who knew his nigra rights under Reconstruction. Hearing Woodson's words, he straightened slowly, and the rest copied him. Those boys might not know too much about Reconstruction, but they sure knew every last damn way there was to leave off working.

A threat to tell tales on me the way Mama and Minnie used to do made my blood boil and it always will. To tickle the niggers, I mimicked his shit-eating grin, and his own boy giggled. Spitting mad, Woodson hollered at the hands, *Get back to work!* And right then I heard my own voice say, "Why don't you send your fat kid over here to help out in the field, instead of riding him around on that poor horse, giving stupid orders?" That gave the niggers a bad fit of nervous glee. They were whimpering so hard that they had to turn their backs on Woodson so's he wouldn't see.

"You talkin to *me*, boy?" Woodson hollered. "I already told you onct, put that damn shirt on!"

I had gone too far and the hands knew it, and Sam knew it, too. And I will say this for Fat Sammy, he tried a comical distraction, to help me ease my way off of the hook. "Damn you, Edgar!" he yelled, shaking his fist over his pa's shoulder. "You don't put that shirt on right this minute, I'm comin over there and beat you to a jelly." Well, I busted out laughing, and Sammy, too, he was quaking like—well, like jelly. He nearly shook his pap out of the saddle.

But Woodson was screwed a lot too tight to laugh with the rest of us and let the whole thing go. He yanked that pony's head around and rode right out from under his own son, dumping him onto that hard road like a sack of feed. For a moment there, I do believe, he meant to take his whip to his smart-mouth son. To take his mind off Sam, I yelled, "Too *hot* to wear a shirt!" Then I turned my back and went back hoeing as if the whole thing had blown over, and Calvin and the other boys jumped to do the same.

"Never you mind how hot it is!" our overseer hollered at my back. "Just you put that shirt on like I told you!" And he rode on a ways as if that settled it, leaving his boy still moping in the dust. When his order was ignored, he walked his pony back real slow, reined in, and sat there with one knee propped up on the saddle horn. "Jus' sposin," he drawled, after a silence. "Sposin I was to let on to Mis Ta-*bye*-a-tha how you never paid her overseer no mind? Sposin I was to tell your mama about them blast-phemies you spoke, cussin out that self-same overseer while he was doin his rightful job of overseein?"

When I paid him no attention, never even turned around, he nodded awhile, then spoke more softly, to let me know I was in real bad trouble. "Sposin she was to send you back to Carolina?" Woodson Tolen said. Right then I knew that some way, somehow, this man had heard something he aimed to use against me, something that might spoil my hopes of a new start in life at Ichetucknee.

My sister had described to me that "horrible Edgar mask" I sometimes wore stuck to my face. "Like the *real* Edgar," Minnie whispered, "but blank and dead." At such times, I was beside myself, so to speak. Edgar Watson was *beside* that other one, Jack Watson, whom I came to think of as the "somber hard-faced boy" disliked by Great-Aunt Sophia. For some time now, Jack Watson seemed to have replaced that rush of pain and vertigo which once blackened my brain until I fell. I had never admitted that to anybody, for fear of being called crazy.

Well, I was never crazy, and neither was Jack Watson. He was always cool, swift, and efficient. He knew when to appear and when to go, knew what he was after, and would never let anyone get in his way. That is why I, too, feared him a little, thinking he might one day do me harm.

*

Jack Watson spat his words at Tolen like cold bullets. "You want my shirt on so damn bad, you get both halves of your dirty ass down off that horse and come across that fence and put it on me."

It's a very good thing there was fifty yards and that split-rail fence between us, or Jack might have run and jumped and hauled that spavined cracker down out of the saddle and slit his stringy throat, and maybe slashed his frogmouth son right along with him. As it was, he challenged Tolen clear and loud so there could be no mistake. "Trouble is, you sonofabitch," Jack Watson called, "you are not nearly man enough to do that."

Fat Sam shut off his moaning and picked himself up out of the road, and the field hands hurried back to work like bald-eyed demons.

Mr. Woodson P. Tolen climbed down off his woods pony and yanked his rawhide whip from beneath the pommel. Seeing that plaited cracker whip uncoil across the rail like a blue racer, the pony shied and the niggers moaned low. I had come clear again and Jack Watson was gone, but it was too late to undo all that damage. I did say I was sorry I had lost my temper, but even if he believed such a poor lie, the overseer did not aim to miss this chance. Expecting me to beg for mercy, he curled that whip back in a coil and climbed the rail, and when he jumped down and kept on coming, I warned him loudly, "Put that thing down!" But fear had rotted out my voice, and he had heard that. On he came with stiff, small steps, bristled up like one of his mean hounds.

"Beg fo' yo' life, Mist' Edguh, beg him," Calvin pleaded.

I took a deep breath and drew my knife out of my boot, turning the blade up to the sun so the man could appreciate that quick glint off the tip. "Come on, then," I whispered, and I crouched and circled the way Ring-Eyed Lige had taught me.

Tolen was good with that long whip; he could sit in the saddle and snap the raised-up head right off a rattler. Unless I caught hold of it, yanked him off balance, he would strip me to fish bait before I got in close enough to cut him. But this feller had noticed more than once how handy I was with my old Bowie, playing at mumbledy-peg with Sam, and he never got ten yards from the fence before he wavered. He said, "A man don't knife-fight with no boy"—the same thing General Butler had said, except that it had no honor and no truth in it. He backed away and crossed that fence and clambered up onto his horse, dragging Sam after him. "I will take care of this, I promise," he gasped, all out of breath, before he rode away.

For this breed of dirt-floor redneck, that promise to "take care of this" was an oath more sacred than three swears on the family Bible. A boy had backed him down, and the niggers had witnessed it, and his son, too. No cracker could set aside that kind of insult, nor could he forgive that dog name I had called him. These Tolens might lie low awhile, but revenge was the age-old way of mountain honor, and they would never rest until they got it. If it wasn't Woodson, it would be one of his boys, probably shifty James.

I worked my hoe a little while, to simmer down the field hands while I thought things over. Calvin was the driver on this crew when I was absent, and pretty soon he had worked his way up alongside, anxious to be seen imparting to the white boy the wisdom of his long years at Ichetucknee. And it was true that Calvin knew the overseer's low ways and habits better than anyone. He whispered, "Scuse me, Mist' Edguh, but from dis day on, doan you nevuh turn yo' back on one dem Tolens!"

Calvin was not disrespectful, not exactly. Because he had brains and got things done, he had been spoiled by William Myers even before he was a freedman, Aunt Tab told us. He knew his place but he put too much importance on it. I didn't want to punish him for disrespect toward the overseer because what he said took loyalty to our family and some courage, too. Even so, he could not be allowed to speak that way about a white clan, even miserable po' whites like Woodson Tolen.

"Calvin," I growled, for the rest to hear, "you mind your nigger business." The other boys all whooped and laughed, to ease their nerves at the boss nigger's expense. I wasn't laughing. I was remembering Clouds Creek and how I'd lost my chance due to ill fortune I could not control, and how if I wasn't very careful, I might lose it here.

*

Leaving the field, I went straight to the house to make my own case to Aunt Tabitha. Woodson got there well ahead of me, of course; I saw him slipping off the stoop, sly as a tomcat. I darkened the door and called for Aunt Tab's attention, and when she asked querulously what the heck I wanted, I declared I would not work another day with that white-trash rascal who had just told her a pack of lies behind my back. Furthermore, I could not tolerate the way the overseer and his shiftless sons were letting this fine plantation go to rack and ruin. It was him or me, said I in manly tones.

Her silence lasted longer than I cared for. Aunt Tab knew Woodson Tolen's nature and had seen trouble coming a long time before I did, but clearly she was disappointed after hearing Tolen's story—how he had caught that young troublemaker, *beggin yer pardon, ma'am,* working near naked with the nigras, how this boy, refusing to obey her overseer, had vilely cursed him and threatened him with a knife while the overseer was going about his bounden duties.

If she needed time to think, I said, as she finally came out onto the stoop, would she mind if I offered my services to Captain Getzen?—a bluff, of course, since she valued my unpaid labor much too much to let me go. Without thinking it over even for a moment, this irascible old woman waved me away toward Getzen's with her fan. In fact, she sat down in her rocking chair and fanned herself, taking no further notice of me whatsoever.

What a pity, she told Mama later, that such a capable and strong young man should be so pigheaded and insubordinate. "*Like his father*—that's what she meant," Mama complained. Mama was "heartbroken" that my "vicious temper and unruly attitude" was spoiling all our prospects. *This is a Watson plantation, Edgar!*—that's actually the way she saw it, and perhaps I did, too. I said, Well, I'm sorry, Mama. I'll work hard for Captain Tom, make a good name for myself, and when the smoke clears a little, I will come back.

"Is that what you told Colonel Robert, too?" Mama was bitterly disappointed. Aunt Tab had told her that she'd had great plans to make me the plantation overseer, having heard from Clouds Creek (Colonel Robert, that is) that Cousin Edgar was hard-working, resourceful, and an excellent young farmer altogether. The Colonel had said not a single word against me, which put me forever in his debt and reawakened my old hopes, besides. Well, said I, if she thinks me so capable, why don't she give that job to her own kin and get it over with? *Doesn't,* said Mama (who would never relent in her lifelong effort to raise me as a "well-spoken young gentleman").

Mama was deathly afraid that Auntie Tab might "hear something about Edgefield" from other sources. I did not dare ask what she meant, but plainly she had heard something herself. She said, "Please stay a moment, Edgar." She sat me down and told me that in late afternoon of the same day I rode away from Edgefield Court House, poor Tap Watson had been murdered in the field by an unknown hand.

Holding my eye, Mama said she was relieved that her spouse had been locked away in jail and that her son had departed earlier that day for Florida. "That's true, isn't it, Edgar?" I nodded. It was true. And she said, uneasy, "Then why would folks suspect a boy who had been so close to that old darkie all his life?" Powerfully upset, I rose, but before I could storm out of there, she answered her own question, looking out the window. "Somebody reported that they saw you in the field with Tap where he was gleaning. You were the last to be seen with him before he was found dead."

Though not astonished by Tap's murder—I had warned him, after all—I was stunned that the true murderers had taken advantage of my flight to make me the suspect. And I would not tell my mother my side of the story, though she asked. To have to defend myself to my own family—that wrenched my gut and started up all the old bile. I refused to speak, and in the next minute, I left. Because when I demanded to know who was spreading such vicious rumors, she would not tell me, only hunched over her needle-work, shaking her head.

*

In my boyhood, desperate to please Papa, I once told Mama how much I despised Selden Tilghman, calling him "a fair-haired little sissy." (This was after my first visit to Deepwood, riding up behind on Papa's horse.) Mama boxed my ears, reminding me that he was a war hero, my own cousin, reminding me how Cousin Selden had given me all those books, to compensate me for my lack of schooling. To be so ungrateful about someone so concerned about me was a sin!

Hearing that he had cared about me was very upsetting for some reason. To cover a surge of feeling, I yelled out, *Who cares about those darned old stupid books?* This was dishonest. It was I who cared about them, more than anybody. I felt ashamed.

When I let Mama know that her cousin was dead, she became very upset, then sentimental, declaring at once that she had always shared Cousin Selden's abolitionist convictions and had only kept her views a secret out of loyalty to her soldier husband and the Great Lost Cause. Of course, she added hastily, she had also been obliged to protect her children. However, she said one interesting thing. One day she had asked him why he had risked his life, and fought heroically, in a cause he did not believe in—why had he not refused to go to war? And Selden said simply, "I was not brave enough."

*

On the roan horse, I rode four miles each day to the Getzen Plantation, at the crossroads where the old Spanish Road from Jacksonville west to Tallahassee was transected by the north-south road from Lake City to Fort White. I told Captain Tom what he knew anyway, that I hoped one day to be the overseer at Ichetucknee, but meanwhile I would do my best to be of help to him. Those words made a good impression, I worked hard, and the next spring Getzen leased me my own piece to sharecrop.

Captain Tom furnished fertilizer and common stores, and we split the crops halfway. He took his croppers—he had black as well as white—over to Frazee's in Fort White, told Josh Frazee, Now these boys get a hundred dollars' worth of groceries this year. So Old Man Frazee would set up the page: *Edgar Watson for One Year*—he'd write it down. We bought only coffee, flour, and such things, because all our meat and meal came from the farm, and there was plenty of wild game, besides.

Fort White was the county's second largest town after Lake City. Phosphate, cotton, timber, mostly yellow pine, and turpentine and resin from the pine sap. The pine gum ran from April to November, and after two or three years that tree was cut for timber. Anyway, the town had well-stocked stores, a sawmill, gristmills, cotton gins, and a cottonseed oil mill, too. Dirt streets and a boardwalk, hitching posts and water troughs, kerosene lampposts and saloons—looked like the Wild West frontier we saw in pictures. A couple of fine eateries and a three-story hotel, the Sparkman Hotel, where in later years, when I grew prosperous and liked to talk, I would go to eat my lunch almost every Saturday.

*

I always rode home by different routes over those pale roads through the woods, and I carried a pistol and kept a hawk eye out for any Tolens. Those ridge runners were too smart to bushwhack Edgar Watson, since every man in the south county would know who pulled the trigger, but I could not assume they were that smart when drunk. And they were drunk one autumn day when our paths crossed at the Collins store at Ichetucknee Springs. Old

Man Woodson, swaying in the saddle, pointed his bony finger at my eyes like he was sighting down a musket barrel—his way of reminding me how he had promised to take care of me in his own good time.

Mike Tolen was only a small boy back then, and as for his brothers, they still acted friendly, pretending their daddy's threats were all in fun. Sometimes we drank a little shine together, and one night—for the fun of it, of course—I told those boys that the day I decided their old man was serious about his threats—and here I paused to give 'em a hard squint—that day might be his last on earth, and maybe their last, too.

Jim Tolen had cockeyed ears and a rodent mouth way up under high nostrils, and he had a sniffing manner to go with it, as if he were scenting some nice rotted food. Jim sniffed, then spat. "Pa ain't botherin his head none about no damn bullshit such as that, but I wouldn't go to stirrin up no trouble if I was you." Mikey had tried spitting, too, and dribbled up his chin, and Fat Sam spat to make fun of his two brothers. "Your turn," he told me with a wink. I winked back, then spat into Jim's eye. He jumped like a mink, in slit-eyed fury. When Mikey laughed, Jim held his tongue, pretending this was Edgar's joke, though a drunk and stupid one. He scowled and left and Sam said, worried, "This here mess ain't none of my doin, Ed, ain't nothin in the world to do with me." Nosir, we were bosom friends so far as Sam Frank Tolen was concerned. But from the day I'd backed his daddy down, Fat Sam and I could never be true friends, and we both knew it.

Not long after that, Woodson's wife moved in with another man who had four boys of his own, and before the smoke cleared, every one of those seven white-trash stepbrothers was my sworn enemy. Old Man Woodson slunk on home to Georgia, leaving his older boys in charge, and once he was gone, the tension around those woods eased up a little. Shifty Jim ran the plantation, making a worse job of it than his old man, and Sammy and I fooled around some as before, bird-hunted and fished and drank together, mostly. I enjoyed teasing him and he enjoyed being teased, that was about it. (One day that damn fool got drunk and took a swig of kerosene out of a lantern, told me this was the de luxe beverage back where he hailed from in Bainbridge, Georgia. As any man with sense would know, said Sam when he got through vomiting, this magical stuff from the bowels of the earth which had replaced whale oil was bound to contain all sorts of healthful properties.)

Sam never let me forget that the Tolen boys, not Edgar Watson, were running the plantation. Where they were running it, I told him, was straight into the ground. But mostly I just played along, convinced it was only a matter of time before Aunt Tab got fed up with these corn rats and asked me to come back and take over. Before that happened, Jim Tolen left for Georgia to avoid a shotgun wedding, leaving Fat Sammy as the overseer. Sam got drunk, to celebrate, and came to see me. He said, "Too bad you ain't some-what smarter, Ed. Might get you a good job overseein, the same as I got." And I grinned back at him and said, "Sam, I may get there yet, you never know."

I believed that, too. According to age, experience, and bone ability, not to mention the blood ties of kin, that job should have been mine. Auntie Tab knew that as well as I did, but that old woman would not lift a crooked fin-ger. Mama believed that my checkered reputation, as she called it, might have come here with the Dan Herlongs, lately arrived from Edgefield Court House, who were clearing the woodlands south of the plantation. The Her-longs were Methodists, Mama said, strict and judgmental, and maybe the darkies they brought with them had told Edgefield rumors to Simeon Wat-son, Tap's half brother, or even to Aunt Cindy. In recent months, that woman had been giving me the evil eye, and scarcely spoke.

*

One fine evening, dough-faced Minnie was waiting for me in the road when I came home. She raised her arms and I swooped her up at a full canter, sat her up behind on the old roan as she screeched and shrilled in that elation of young girls who don't know what to do with all their juices. In her uneventful little life, she loved to be the first with news of others, and this day she had news indeed, simpering in my ear as we rode home.

For some time now, Miss Ninny giggled, Sam Tolen had missed no chance to tickle her—his loutish way of reconnoitering a young girl's person. Cousin Laura, though twenty-nine years his senior, was anxious to be tick-led, too, and sure enough, she got overexcited. "Oh, you horrid boy!" she'd shriek, rassling Sam right to the ground and seating herself on what would have been his lap if he'd sat up. The evening previous, Ninny said (daring such topics only because her blush was well-hidden behind me), Aunt Tab, hearing peculiar sounds out behind the sheds, had caught the Widow Laura seated on Sammy with her nightshirt up and naked as a tulip all the rest of the way down. This morning our spry old aunt had whipped these cringing sinners into the buggy and carted them north to Lake City, where they were duly united in holy wedlock.

Truly angry, I burst out, "Oh Christ sweet Jesus!" Misunderstanding (but thrilled anyway), my sister cried, "Edgar, that's blasphemy! A mortal sin!" I brooded in silence the rest of the way home. "This was Jim's idea," I explained finally. "He had Sam make all that rumpus and get caught screwing that old simpleton because Tolens want some kind of claim to our plantation, can't you see that, Ninny?" Ninny was shocked, protesting that Aunt Laura was *not* a simpleton and that she loved Aunt Laura very, very much and that I was being vile and unkind, and anyway, it wasn't "our" plantation. She had understood nothing, as usual. At the house, I swung her down roughly off the horse, and she ran away in tears.

Sammy ate with us that evening, having already moved in. His table manners were just plain disgusting. Nobody spoke, not knowing where to look or what to say. "Well, folks might call you lots of names, but nobody could call you a cradle robber," I sneered finally, to break the silence. And damned if this manure-flecked feller—sitting right beside that sweet coy fool too old to be his mother—damned if he didn't wink at me, as if this mess were the best joke in the world. *I am the Master of Ichetucknee*, that wink said. *And you?*

Sam offered me a cheap cigar, and when the ladies protested, we went outside. He belched heavily and coughed, spitting something up. "Looks like you're fucked pretty good now, don't it, Edgar? You and my hot old lady." Sam had always enjoyed an ugly way of talking.

Charlie Is My Darling

From the Getzen place, the old Spanish Road led west through Ichetucknee Springs past the Collins trading post. Mr. Collins's gristmill turned so slow that his son Lem claimed you could top its hoppers full of grain and go home and eat dinner and get back to the mill in good time for a smoke before it finished grinding. Lem Collins was my age and my best friend, and his brother Billy was courting our Miss Mary L. Watson. What Billy saw in that crushed girl I will never know. I suppose Minnie was beautiful in her way, but she had no spirit. All her life she would speak in a childish voice and keep her head flinched over to one side, and her pale underchin pulsed with trepidation, like a spring peeper.

One Sunday, on a cold clear afternoon, Lem and I were hard at work on a half jug of moonshine out behind the store when his cousin Miss Ann Mary Collins happened by with Billy and Minnie. From the first moment, I could not take my eyes off her heart-shaped face. She had fair skin and a small nose light and pretty as a petal and a bright smile in a fresh and shining mouth, but what one noticed at once were her beautiful black eyes like the wondering round eyes of some night creature. She was neither beautiful nor plain and yet not merely pretty.

Yes, I was pierced clean through the heart, love at first sight. So stricken was I (and inebriated, too) that I reeled backwards, throwing my arms wide, crying out senselessly, "Charlie Is My Darling!" Having read so much, I was articulate enough, but my life had been so solitary, with so much silence, that I had few graces. All I had really wanted to cry out was *I love you.* I said the rest to cover my confusion. Naturally, this angelical Miss Collins, unacquainted with my Scots ballad, thought me rude, crude, and dead drunk, besides. Minnie cried, "Oh Edgar!" and Ann Mary went pink and turned haughty, reproving her cousins for keeping "such rough company."

I flushed hot with shame but did not falter. I jumped forward, striking both knees into the dirt, and seized and kissed her hand, which was cool and clean and warm at the same time. *Oh please, oh please, Charlie my Darling.* When she snatched back her hand, I lay down prostrate and banged my forehead in the dust, groaning for forgiveness. I could scarcely believe what I was doing, I had never behaved so idiotically in all my life, but at last Ann Mary had to hide her smile. She thought me a brave idiot, she told me later. Finally she relented, saying, "Well, Mr. Watson, you have guessed my secret. I purely hate the name Ann Mary. You may call me Charlie." And after that, we all sat in the grass, leaning back against the sun-warmed slats of the old mill, and told our stories and jokes there by the water. From that time on, while her life lasted, Miss Ann Mary Collins was called Charlie.

Of course Charlie was right, I was "rough company," but also such an overjoyed poor fool that she forgave me. In all my twenty-two hard years, I had known nothing to compare with such blissful feelings, and by some miracle, Charlie my Darling Collins loved me, too. From the first minute, we were delightedly in love, smiling and smiling for no reason every time we met, holding each other's smiling eyes and passing through into the other's smiling heart. In this unimaginable moment, nothing needed to be said or thought or doubted or considered but was perfect and complete, with nothing missing.

Until that day, when it came to love, I had been as lifeless as the white clay in these woods lanes. My life had been breathed into me at last by this graceful creature. On a day of new spring rain lilies and a first pale haze of dogwood, she brought me the first true happiness I ever knew, as if all these years I had crept about in some dark painting, and only now had escaped into the air and light of precious morning.

*

On an autumn day, I borrowed Aunt Tabitha's buggy and took Charlie Collins on a picnic to Ichetucknee. We left the buggy at the store and walked barefoot down along the edge of the blue springs and turquoise water of this small woodland river, and she started to sing as we passed beneath our royal canopy of crimson maples, old gold yellow hickories, and russet oaks. I pointed out the mysterious weeds like a school of bright green eels swimming upstream, and the pristine white limestone sand where the current turned clear blue, and she showed me duckweed and watercress, used for wild lettuce, and a sort of blueberry with reddish stems, called sparkleberry, used in these parts for tanning and carving pipes, and pointed out the silent woodland birds of fall. My darling knew all their brown names—hermit thrush, creeper and nuthatch, winter wren.

Charlie gave me her hand on the way home, and after that—every free Sunday, when she would permit—I loitered around her father's place and helped out where I could with barnyard chores. Before her mother was finished with me, I burned hickory and boiled ash resin for lye soap, worked flax for linen, parched goobers for coffee, ground homespun dyes from sweet gum and red oak, stuffed Spanish moss and feathers into mattress casings. Happy that Sam was not there to jeer at my humiliation, I even helped out with the washing, which I'd always hated. We built a fire in the yard, stirred flour for starch into cold rainwater before heating up the tub, then shaved a soap cake into the water. Like a barefoot sprite, Charlie made a dance of sorting the wash, casting the clothes into three piles, one white, one colored, one confined to dirty britches and old rags. We rubbed the spots out on a rough board before boiling them—never *never* boil the dyed things, Mr. Watson, Charlie warned, waggling her finger under my nose and blushing when it touched my lips.

Afterwards we fished everything out with a broom handle and spread the fresh wash on towels and flung the rags onto the fence to dry. The old soapy water was applied to the privy seats and floor, and I denounced myself for conjuring up my beloved's adorable behind perched neat as a pear on that wood seat—I could not help it. At last we turned the tin tubs upside down. She slipped indoors and washed herself, and of course I imagined her ablutions, too. She came out in a fresh dress, combing out her hair, and brewed some tea. Those round black eyes drinking me in over her teacup, she said, "We must rest now, and count our blessings, Mr. Watson." We were already lost in each other's awe, and as her mother came and went at the edge of earshot, Charlie whispered, "May I ask how many blessings you have counted so far, Mr. Watson? Will you pity me if I tell you I can find but one?" We were still deep in each other's eyes, and so I knew, but my silence unnerved her, and she murmured, "A certain Mr. E. Addison Watson is the greatest blessing ever to befall this poor fond female creature."

*

As a middle-aged bachelor, William Curry Collins had married the Widow Robarts, mother of my friend John C. Calhoun Robarts, called J.C. Ann Mary was their late and only child. Mr. Curry hired me to accompany him down the Santa Fe and the Suwannee all the way to the Gulf at Cedar Key, where we hired a nigger and boiled down half the Gulf of Mexico for a few barrels of salt. After that expedition, Mr. Curry thought the world of me, informing his daughter that Edgar Watson was a hard worker, an up-and-comer, and altogether an exceptional young man. "Don't I know it!" said the pert Miss Collins.

Mama and Minnie loved Charlie, too, for what she'd wrought. Suddenly the son and brother who had always been so abrupt and sullen was orating nonsense to make them smile and reeling off Greek quotations and Romantic poetry or bursting into song at peculiar moments. "I thought you'd *never* learn to laugh!" Mama exclaimed.

For once, I gave Mama a real hug, and Minnie, too, and Minnie cried, "This is the first time our poor family has ever hugged and smiled together!" She wailed at the great pity of it all, she wept and wept in her unaccustomed happiness, quite inconsolable.

I was astonished, too. I had discovered that beneath my melancholic moods, beneath the rage, I was in my deeper nature a merry and irreverent rascal who liked nothing better than to laugh, and to startle others into laughter with some outrageous turn of irony or grotesque humor. Far from being reserved, I loved to talk elaborately in the elegant English found in books, and I loved to tell stories—funny, beautiful, and dirty—so long as they stripped the bric-a-brac of pretense from hard truth. Being unsophisticated, I did not see that sometimes I bullied people with my talk, and sometimes was not as humorous as I thought but merely cynical and cruel.

*

With my scrimped pay, I leased an old cabin on Robarts land down west of the plantation. The front door was missing and the back door, too, while the single window was boarded over, and even those boards were loose and all awry. Nobody had cleared the moss and fallen limbs from the old cedar shakes so the roof had rotted, and the tin sheets which patched the rot had gone dark copper red with scaling rust. But with credit from Mr. Collins at the Ichetucknee store, I mended the roof and plastered over the damp black-blotched walls inside.

Charlie came along one day and peered up at the big hole under the peak. Her elegant small head turned upward brought to mind a beautiful green tree snake on a sunlit branch, serene, quick, and mysterious, with those depthless black eyes catching the light. I was silhouetted on the sun, "in a wild halo," she cried. "My hero! The man who patches the blue sky!"

I couldn't bear so much feeling any longer. I climbed down and took her hand and asked her to marry. When tears came to her eyes, I feared I'd been abrupt again, and implored her to forgive me and to think it over. "Mister, I will marry you," she said, taking my hand. "I have given it too much thought already." We dined in the oak shade out of her napkined basket. Afterwards we lay together, and we kissed. This was to occur on any number of desperate occasions.

One day we gave in and turned our backs and clambered out of our cumbersome farm clothes. When I said, One-two-three, we turned around, not knowing where to look, starting to laugh. Still not looking, I stuck out my hands, and at last she took them and we kneeled, still facing, on the sun-warmed linen, on those fragrant summer grasses. Excepting the burned copper of our arms and faces, we were milky white. I drew her close and knew at once that our grand pure love had nothing to do with spidery old ideas of sin, whether or not we fathomed His commandments. Even our dread of discovery and disgrace was a precious secret to be shared with the dear other.

We were brave virgins, scared and clumsy, but we trusted each other with all our hearts, and nothing else could matter. Still trembling, I laid her down and held her a long while before venturing to kiss her hair, her cheek and lips. But very soon, my monkey hand was exploring the small breasts and taut nipples, the silken skin of her inner thigh. When it touched her wetness, she gasped and closed her eyes in a last farewell to her doomed maidenhood. Her knee rose and her leg slid over mine, and those places touched each other.

I eased her over on her back and lay between her legs for near a minute, thanking my lucky stars. When I realized that, awaiting me, the poor thing had held her breath almost all that time, I ran my hands under her hips to raise her gently, and she bent her knees as her legs rose so that the round of her formed a strange upside-down heart. With a groan of abandon, I went home into the pearly glisten.

I was awkward and too urgent and too quick. I know I hurt her. That first time, pain was the reason she cried out, and a moment later, I cried out, too, as heat and moisture, grass and birdsong, and a fly stitching the soft skin of my hips came together in waves of sun-warmed delirium and light. Afterwards I lay astonished, home at last.

Shyness had returned but not too much—not until I remarked on a stupid impulse, "You know what Woodson Tolen would have said if his son brought you home, and Woodson had learned that you were still a virgin?"

She raised her head to look into my eyes, then shifted a little and reached for her blouse and held it in front of her as she sat up, her eyes still searching mine.

I knew I should stop right there. I didn't. I said, "Woodson would have shouted, '*Vir-gin?* Why, hell, no, boy! Don't matter *how* purty she is, no virgins ain't allowed, not in our Tolen family! If she ain't good enough for her own menfolk, she sure ain't good enough for our'n!' "

That accursed bent to outrage and do harm! How could she never understand the impulse to joke crudely on this vulnerable occasion? "Please turn away," she whispered. Covering my loins (which were suddenly my shame), I did so, and she dressed behind me. I pled for forgiveness, tried to walk her home. "I know the way," she said.

*

One day she let me apologize. "You are very peculiar, do you know that, Mr. Watson?" She had been less offended by my joke than by my insensitivity at such a moment. But the first time our path crossed Sam Tolen's, and she heard how he spoke, she remembered the joke and smiled a secret smile.

As the months passed, I learned her body better than my own; I know it still. I hear her small cries as we became one heart and fell back, awed. "Who are you, Mister?" she would whisper, holding my eyes with hers, tracing my face with her light fingertip.

"Jack Watson," I said, feeling hemmed in. She raised her brows, expectant, questioning. I shook my head. "Charlie my Darling," I whispered, kissing her until finally she abandoned her question. "Mister my Darling," Charlie sighed.

*

She heard the bad stories soon enough. Her Collins cousins, who got them straight from Herlongs, warned her parents. Lem warned me. Charlie refused to repeat what she'd been told. There's so much *good* in you, she whispered. She only hoped that her love was so strong that no matter what I'd done, God would redeem me.

"How do you know I've done anything at all? Why don't you tell me what they said and I'll tell you the truth."

"I believe in you, Mister. You don't need to hear their wicked gossip, and I don't need to hear your truth. Whoever you are, I believe in you, don't you know that?"

Charlie Collins. Eventually her tenderness dissolved the crust of rage that I had brought with me from Edgefield, and she set me free. Over time, I confided to her most of what had befallen me, and the burden I had carried, even the longing for the lost plantation at Clouds Creek.

In a dream I introduced her to Colonel R. B. Watson. In Confederate grays, the Colonel gave his blessing as another hero in dress uniform strolled toward us. Drawing near, he turned into Selden Tilghman. I hollered and woke up. That day I told Charlie all about the Owl-Man, and how Cousin Selden died. She was silent a very long time, and my heart pounded, but finally she took my hand. "I think God will forgive you such an act of mercy. Let's never talk about it anymore."

*

She turned fifteen before we wed. Gaily she sang out "Miss Charlie Collins" when giving her name for the marriage record at Lake City. It is there still. November 24, 1877. Thanksgiving. We were married by her half brother, J. C. Robarts.

Baptist by birth, raised an Episcopalian, I attended the Methodist chapel services which Lem Collins's family had started with the Herlongs in a small house on what was now called Herlong Lane. I prayed on my knees up in the front where those tale-bearers from Edgefield could all see me—could bear witness that Ring-Eye Lige's son (a sinner redeemed, they whispered) was worshiping the Lord. This was quite true. I gave fervent thanks to Whoever among gods had bestowed my dear wife and our unborn child on this wretched, blessed sinner.

*

She was scarcely sixteen on the day she died, not ten months after we had wed, on the thirteenth day of a windy cold September. Her parents stood withdrawn and stoic by the doorway. Her mother murmured in my hearing, That child was wed too young. She meant, My beloved daughter was destroyed by his lust.

Thrust squalling in my face was the red life expelled by her dear body—a boy! they cried. I could not look at it.

My darling's lips were parted, her gaze fixed, the black strands of sweat-bedraggled hair across the pillow in the mortal scents of perspiration, blood, and urine. The awful stains on her last sheets, soaked into the moss mattress we had sewn together, our bed of life and death where we had created this red and squalling death-in-life.

I was on my knees. I had been there for some time. I took the cool hand, rested my head. Charlie my Darling. The loveliness of her dear face shone through the mist of tears.

Edgar? Son? My mother's voice. *Son, she is gone.*
What will you name him? Mr. Curry Collins.
No name. The voices hushed me.
Ellen Catherine—Ellen Addison again. *I mean, of course, if the child had been a girl . . .*
Go away. You, too, Mama. Everybody. Him, too.

In my own corpse I lay down beside hers. Holding cold hands, we gazed at the low rafters. The roof dissolved where one bright morning I had patched up the blue sky, and stars seemed to appear through the black firmament. I clung to her hand, longing to go wherever she might be going. I did not stir. Night fell. I turned cold, too.

At first light, troubled faces watched from the cabin door. *Son? Get away from there. Don't you go acting crazy.* Shouting, I drove them all away.

Still shouting at the sky, I made her coffin. I would bury her in our field beside our cabin, carve her cross, take leave of her in a ceremony of my own. But in the end they took her, the blue-gray remains of her, my blue-gray wife, her face sucked in, and that first odor of the tomb. They seemed distressed that nobody had washed her, nor closed her eyes nor crossed her arms nor laid her in that coffin. My friend, her stepbrother, our minister J.C. twisted her wayward arm to force it in—It's not a chicken wing, I told him angrily. His face went red, then mushy with tears. It weren't like I was tryin to hurt Ann Mary, J.C. protested.

And so the remains of young Mrs. Charlie Watson were nailed up in my pine box, were carted off under black crepe, were bounced and thrown about in a black wagon. I went outside, unshaven and half naked. Though they beckoned, I did not join the mourners.

Ann Mary went away with her grim kinsmen. May she disintegrate in peace beneath her stone. Charlie my Darling lies with me, rests in my heart.

In a dream her coffin was lowered into a deep pit in Bethel churchyard. It was left uncovered, I could see inside. Night after night, the dream returned. The fair skin which had shivered at my touch purpled and softened. Eyes sunk and teeth thrusting, dead hair creeping forth, the skull emerging, putrefaction—I yelled, backing away.

Cousin Selden stood among the mourners. He was rotting, too. I cried, *What do you want here? Where are you going?*

Roaming the white woods roads in October, under sleepless stars, I howled and cursed, I swore terrible revenge, but upon whom?

Charlie my Darling had taken with her my last hope of Heaven.

Miss SueBelle Parkins

I moved unseeing through the ache of days, banging and wrenching with loud careless tools and doing myself harm in violent labor. In the evening, in my shack back of Getzen's pasture, I drank rotgut for the pain until I sank onto the floor, only to come to and drink more in the dark hours. I reeled into the sun at noon and boiled off my poisons in a frenzy of head pain and sickness, yet I was durable, and by nightfall had regained the strength to drink again.

On the Sabbaths I rode out to the crossroads taverns. I started out friendly, drew a crowd of men and made 'em laugh, and usually I was laughing when

I picked a sudden fight which nobody could understand. Pretty soon, no man would drink with the quarrelsome Ed Watson, and no good woman either. One after another, the grog shops would not serve me, until I was riding out so far that I rarely returned in time for work on Monday. By this time, poor old Job had pulled up lame. All across the northern counties, I earned a bad name as a hothead and a crazy-wild mean skunk, quick to pull a knife. Knowing Watson might turn up, the taverns warned clients not to mix with a brawny drunkard of such ugly reputation. When Watson barged into the room, the fun was over. When he refused to leave, he was waylaid and dragged into the road and kicked bloody and broken in the public mud.

All this while I was feverish with longing. By early spring, I was visiting the nigger whores up in Lake City. These girls had plump soft lips and candied tongues, sly gentle fingertips and round high rumps. Out of respect for my lost bride, I never took one from the front but rode her hard behind, slamming her cool rubbery hind end against my hipbones, riding her till her back bowed and her neck twisted as her head was jammed against the wall. At the end, I rammed with all my strength—A-*gain*, a-*gain*, a-*gain!*—until she yelped in faked abandon or fear or honest pain—what difference did it make? For me, obliteration never came, I could not escape. I was always right there, detached, observing, numb. A shadow of pleasures might drift over my skin, as light as a transparent cloud crossing high sun, but when it had passed, I fell off in despair, gasping as if I might never find an easy breath again.

*

The one whore I was less rough with was "Sweet Miss SueBelle Parkins," a young newcomer to the Lake City whorehouse. In some way, this mulatta girl had got under my skin, until I inevitably chose her for the evening. The first time I accosted her downstairs, she had seemed startled and upset, even waved her hand before her face to ward me off. I told her sharply that I was not so drunk and useless as I might appear. In the end, I overcame her doubts by dragging her upstairs. She was so terrified that she said no more but numbly permitted me to complete our carnal dealings before blurting out in honest tears, "Lo'd God fo'give me, Mist' Edguh!"

Disguised beneath a brassy wig and enough rouge paint and powder to doll up every blossom of the night in Gay Paree was my childhood neighbor, Miss Lulalie Watson, the sweet-potato daughter of Tap Watson and Aunt Cindy Myers. She clothed herself before she wailed that the day I left Edgefield, her daddy had been shot dead by two white men on horseback. Black folks knew them as Major Will and Overseer Claxton, but no one dared report them to the bluecoats. Lulalie had sense enough to flee, walking all night and the next day to reach Augusta. She knew she must try to find her mother, who had left behind a Florida address, but having no friends along the way, and finding no work in the fields, she was finally reduced to selling herself here and there in order to pay for her travels farther south.

Somehow years passed before she reached Lake City. Being so ashamed of what she had become, and so afraid of the wound and sorrow she would cause her strict, religious mother, she did not dare present herself at the plantation. (It never occurred to the poor girl that Aunt Cindy's joy at seeing her child alive would certainly outweigh her disappointment.) Instead, she took a position, so to speak, at the Lake City cathouse where I'd found her. In tears once more, poor Lalie implored me to keep the dreadful secret of "Sweet Miss SueBelle Parkins." I said I would do so, on my honor, upon which she rewarded me with another crack at her sweet person.

I visited Lalie soon again, and then again. From the first, this brown girl had a hook in me—nostalgia, I suppose, or the generous healing nature that had made her so precious to my sister. All true, all true, but it was also true that in the nude this girl did great credit to her Creator. The seed of hunger for Lulalie Watson had been well-planted in boyhood and needed no encouragement to sprout.

However, I could not escape my grief, nor even separate it from carnal bliss. It was like a spring rain in the sunshine. The groan of pleasure and relief would end in a low moan of woe, and I hated this girl for knowing that I wept, and that I needed her tenderness and warmth as much as her brown body—for knowing that, no matter what, I would be back. Nigger or no, she was quite aware of my self-disgust, and finally begged me to forget poor Lalie and deal with her by her professional name of SueBelle Parkins—and fuck her under that name, too, is what she meant. I felt injured for some reason but agreed. Banging through SueBelle Parkins's door stupid with drink, needing to shame her because so ashamed myself, I'd holler, *Sooee-belle, Sooee-belle,* as I used to call my hogs, back at Clouds Creek. Pitying me in my grief, she always understood, even laughed out loud at all my fancy rantings. And finally her good heart got me laughing, too, heartbreak and all.

When SueBelle got accustomed to me, or less afraid, she called me Wild Man. *You bes' come on upstairs with yo' sweet Sooee-belle, cause you my Wil' Man.* Undressed, she lay back like a banquet, breasts smooth and sweet as mangoes and thighs warm as fine smoked hams. But in my soiled grief, I wanted no real intimacy, no face to face. "Why won't you learn?" I snarled. She would sigh as I flipped her and yanked her up onto her knees and took her like an animal, just as before. Because I denied her the dignity of real intimacy, she would not or could not join in my abandon but simply knelt on all fours and endured it.

One night there came hard pounding on the walls—*Shut up that crazy racket, Mister! Ain't you got no manners?* And another displeased customer was hollering at the boss whore, *You hear them two acrost the hall? How come I ain't gettin laid as good as that?*

Collapsed in mirth, I increased our uproar, rolling off the bed on purpose in a grand finale, dragging the underdog right down on top of me. Sure enough, one of the plaintiffs came banging on the door. I jumped up buck naked and yanked it open, attacking at once the way I had been taught at my father's knee. Knocked down, well-mauled, the intruder apologized while still upon his knees to that magnificent specimen of negritude, Miss Sooee Parkins, swathed with all due modesty in our used sheets. As naked as myself, this gent mopped dolefully at a bloody nose. "Beggin yer pardon, Miss," he sniffed. "I don't mind if I do," said the demure Miss Parkins, with a little curtsy. I banged the door on him, went back for more.

Hard drinking and hard fucking were my oblivion and sole forgetting. But rolling off, spent and sticky on her sheets, I would fill again with that deep slow-seeping rage. Screwing Sooee from behind was a lonely business, and to awaken vile-breathed in her whore's bed, head splitting from bad rotgut, was still worse. Dragging my stinking carcass into crumpled clothes, lurching out of that rickety room, I was reviled by lowlifes and their black Jezebels for making so much noise at such an hour.

I felt rancorous and poisoned to my soul. Outside, I was struck sightless by the sun like a bear blundering out of hibernation. Sometimes I found myself assailed by slop jars flung from the upper windows by the religious element among the whorehouse couples, then scourged by the cold stares of upright churchgoers whom I had offended beyond all Christian endurance by defiling the Sabbath morn. "Go get saved," I snarled, to offend them further. "Leave me the hell alone."

Oh Charlie my Darling, oh my Dearest. How do you like your filthy Mister now?

*

Billy Collins married Minnie Watson that same year. Their first child was Julian Edgar Collins. The Edgar honored Billy's father, but our poor Minnie, frantic to please her disgraceful, distempered brother, tried to hint that he was named for me. I knew, of course, that no Methodist Collins would name his firstborn after Edgar Watson, and anyway, Billy feared and disliked me. Hadn't Edgar sent poor Cousin Ann Mary to an early grave? Hadn't he insulted her memory by refusing to attend her funeral or take any responsibility for that poor child? And of course Ann Mary's brothers felt the same.

When Lem and Billy's father died at Ichetucknee, I paid his estate fifty-five dollars for a beautiful gray filly, long-legged and delicate, with big dark eyes. I named her Charlie. For ten and a half dollars more, I acquired the old man's .12 gauge double-barrel, which back in those days was a fancy gun, not used by common people. The right barrel threw a broken pattern, but I soon learned to compensate for that. I would use that old firearm all my life and never heard any complaints about its accuracy from what I fired at.

*

That spring, though shaky, I gave up my night wanderings and made a good crop for Tom Getzen, who had been patient. With my debts paid, I tried to heal things in the family and invited the Collins boys to celebrate. Entreated by my sister, Billy accepted. And so, one Saturday, we rode to the O'Brien tavern in Suwannee County, the only place for thirty miles around that would still serve me. I had promised Minnie I would pick no fights, even in fun, and that evening, we all got along just fine. Lem and Billy got liquored up and in fact uproarious for such good Methodists, and Lem toasted me over and over, yelling, "See that, Billy? Ed ain't near so bad as what you thought!" I got feeling so kindly toward my fellow men, even my brother-in-law, that finally I paid for drinks all around, then jumped up on a table to lead my new friends and former enemies in a grand old song of the Confederacy, to which every man present knew the rousing chorus:

> *Hurrah! Hurrah! For Southern rights, Hurrah!*
> *Hurrah for the Bonnie Blue Flag that flies the single star!*

When I sang out the cornet part (*buppa-ba-buppa-ba-boo, ba-buppa-ba-buppa ba-buppa ba-boo*), Lem hollered to the crowd that the singing voice of this man Watson was an insult and gree-vious dishonor to the Great Lost Cause. So saying, the Collins boys did their best to catch my legs and haul me off that table, with the whole room catcalling and laughing fit to kill, including me. Getting into the spirit, I caught Lem with a good boot in the mouth, but when he grabbed my heel, my momentum spun me off that table. A scary whirl of yells and smoke, then my knees struck hard on that oaken floor. I tried to jump up, cursing and laughing, but collapsed at once and nearly fainted in the rush of pain. I was carted home in a cotton wagon, both knees broken.

For half a year, while my leased fields went to hell, I lay at the mercy of the women. When I could concentrate, I read a little, but most of the day I listened to mouse scratch and crickets in the quiet house, the far crows in the hot woods, and suffered the tuneless whistling of Sam Frank Tolen, who would grin in at the door when he happened by.

*

Though my injury had been Lem's doing, that was the end of it for me and Billy, and I didn't give a good goddamn because what came next was worse. I had hardly recovered and resumed work at Getzens when Lem murdered the farrier in the blacksmith shop in back of his daddy's store at Ichetucknee. This man thought Lem was fooling with his wife and he was right. When Lem was clambering out of his cabin window, John Hayes yelled that his one aim in life was to tear Lem's head off. Lem being kind of small and slight, he reasoned that a feller twice his size who could rassle a plow horse to a standstill would fulfill that aim with no trouble at all. And because of my "checkered reputation," he came straight to Ed Watson for advice.

I knew this man Hayes. John Hayes meant business. I said, Lem, you better leave this county. Hell, no! Lem said. I love her! Well then, I said, your only choice is to get to that feller first. Lem said, Jesus! You mean, *kill* him? I put up my hands, shaking my head. I would never advise any such thing. But Lem, you better start thinking along the lines of self-defense. I mean to say, a lot of us have heard John swear he aims to kill you, so he only has himself to blame if you defend yourself.

I never meant to stoke him up, only to cool him down. I told him he should leave the county and lay low until Hayes came to his senses, because I never thought Lem Collins was cut out for mayhem. But the Lem who pulled me off the table at O'Brien and broke my knees all up, the Lem who had fallen in love with little Mrs. Hayes and refused to give her up— that Lem, without further consultation, got himself dead drunk to get his courage up and went on over to Hayes's place at suppertime, waving that double-barreled gun I'd bought from his dad's estate. He hollered from the yard that he had come for the woman of the house, and the man of the house never wiped his mouth but kicked his chair over and came roaring out and was met by a hail of lead as he came off his stoop and that was that. A clear case of self-defense except to those who did not see it quite that way. One of these was the county sheriff and another was Lem's beloved, Mrs. Prudence Hayes.

Now Lem truly adored that little Prudence, and expected her kind blessing in his deed. Instead his lovebird in her perky bonnet told the grand jury she had no idea why Lemuel P. Collins would murder her dear departed in cold blood after climbing through her window with intent to rape her. If the Sheriff wanted her opinion, sobbed this little widow, looking the defendant straight in the eye, what this man deserved was a good hanging. Said those cruel words with her hand on the Bible and her sweet little honeypot keeping its own counsel under that dimity dress. Told the court, I aim to see justice done and who can blame me?

This widow had overplayed her hand. The Sheriff got suspicious, got to thinking he might prosecute two for the price of one. In fact, he stood ready to reward Lem for his testimony with a nice plea bargain. But even though his darling had betrayed him, Lem remained a stiff and starchy Collins, too gallant to testify against the tiny widow or betray her role in all his difficulties. It therefore being generally agreed that there was motivation—not only the romantic complication but the death threats made against the accused by the deceased—Lem Collins was indicted for murder in the first degree.

Being as cash poor as most families in our section, the Collinses needed hundreds of acres of Collins land and a large loan from Cousin Laura to make the $20,000 bond to pay Lem's bail. Because he had no case to speak of, Lem jumped his bail and lit out for Georgia, as he should have done right after he killed John Hayes. Some of the bail debt was paid off by the Sheriff's auction sale of Collins land, but Laura Myers would never recover a penny. Kind Laura forgave this cheerfully enough but her husband and mother did not, and the situation created difficulties between the families which were very hard on the newlyweds, Billy and Minnie.

In short, Lem Collins ruined his family, causing a fatal downturn in its fortunes, since it lost most of its land trying to pay his debt. Naturally anxious to ease his guilt before departing by evading full responsibility, he mentioned to his brother the advice he claimed Ed Watson had given him about John Hayes. I don't know just what he said or what Billy repeated, but pretty soon the whole mess was blamed on me. There was even a story that Ed Watson went along with Lem and did the shooting.

Even my own family gave me funny looks, although only Sam Tolen had the gall to bring it up. "Some fellers been tellin me just lately, Ed, how it might been you who killed that farrier. So I says, 'Why hell, no, boys! There weren't no money in it! Ed never had no damn motive at all!' " Sam gave me that big dirty wink of his, but seeing my expression, he stopped chuckling.

I was still in my twenties, with my good name in the mud, and my prospects, too. I believe it was about this time that my whole way of growing up began to change, as a shrub battered by constant wind grows gnarled and woody. A man might as well be hung for a sheep as for a goat—that about describes it. I grew hard, having no choice about it.

It's a good thing there was some bad luck around, because otherwise I'd have had no luck at all. As someone said, I would have to make my own luck now.

Rob

I was going on thirty when, in 1884, I married a schoolteacher out of Deland, Florida, named Jane S. Dyal. A minister's daughter, she was a lady even
by my mother's standards, well-educated and soft-spoken, though no longer
young. A sensible person, glad of my attentions, she was not in the least offended by coarse, manly needs, having missed a maiden lady's fate by a cunt
whisker.

Soon Goodwife Jane (I called her Mandy) presented me with a lovely baby
girl. We named her Carrie. Two years later we had a boy, Edward Elijah. As
if these two dear little smellers weren't enough, Mandy was worrying her
head about poor Son Born, as I referred to Charlie's child on those rare occasions when I referred to him at all. (Since no one had bothered to go eight
miles to Lake City just to provide an official Christian name, he was still listed
as "Son Born" in the county register.) I had not laid eyes on him since the
dark hour of his birth eight years before, when his mother's parents took
him, and now those folks were pretty well worn-out and growing older.
Lately Charlie's mother had been poorly, and Curry Collins had trouble
enough tending his wife and keeping up his farm without taking care of a
little grandson, too.

Or so Mandy murmured in my ear. I told her it was not her business, she
was not to mention him again. But that brave woman dared to mention him
over and over, calming me by stroking my head and rubbing my neck and
whispering how wonderful it might be, not only for the little boy but for his
father. From Minnie she knew something of our family past, and she dared
to hint that the direful act of banishing my firstborn from my sight might
have widened the great wound inflicted by those long dark years of my own
father's irresponsible behavior—*"Irresponsible?"* I interrupted. I was trying
to bluff her back into her corner before she said what in fact she said next,
that my refusal to acknowledge Charlie's only child might have bred guilt in
regard to my late wife. This made me furious, since it was true.

As soon as I stopped shouting, she continued. If the first Mrs. Watson had
indeed been the perfect angel I described so often to the second Mrs. Watson
(here she smiled gently), she surely watched over her loved ones from her
golden throne and was grieving that her innocent child had been abandoned. (That idea gave me a start, and not because of Son Born. If Charlie
and the Lord were in cahoots up there and had witnessed all my dirty doings
with Miss SueBelle Parkins, I would have to rethink any idea I had of joining
her one day up in Heaven.)

On a Sunday I rode over to the house of Curry Collins and found him on the stoop whittling a toy. As I entered his yard, old Job, half warhorse and half mule, gave me the walleyed look he doubtless showed my father when they first heard Yankee guns fired in anger. Job stamped and snorted, moving sideways and in circles.

"Been a bear around," Mr. Curry advised me. Charlie's brother Lee came out and looked me over, hands in hip pockets, before returning inside. Lee Collins did not like me. I was nervous and did not know why. I told the old man I had come there for my son, having heard that Mrs. Collins was feeling poorly. No doubt the boy had become a burden, and anyway, it was high time he came home.

Collins stood up slowly but did not come down the steps, and he never invited me into his house. "This is his home," he said. "It's up to him."

I never got down off my old roan, which chose this moment to drop a big steaming load square in the dooryard. "No sir," said I. "It is not his home and it is *not* up to him. I never rode all the way over here to be told that. You advise that young feller to pack up and walk on out here unless you want me to go in there and fetch him."

Curry Collins had been hearing the bad stories, that was plain. He was concerned about the child and didn't try to hide it. "We tended little Elton these eight years while you decided you was ready, Edgar. I reckon that gives us some say about it."

"Nosir, it does not," I said. "You have my thanks for your hospitality to your own grandson. Now let's get a move on."

Already I was talking past him to the small boy in the doorway, who held my eye with a gaze as cool and steady as my own. Well, you weedy little shit, I thought, you're sure not much to show for so much love of life and joyous mating. A moment later, he disappeared inside, but that brief glimpse scared me. I couldn't fool myself. With his young mama's black hair and black eyes and pale rose-pointed skin, he was bound to stir a squall of that hard grief which I dearly hoped I had left behind for good.

"I am his daddy, after all," I said to Curry Collins.

"First time you acted like it." He was getting peevish. "You never even took the time to give Elton a name."

"His name is Robert," I decreed right then and there. "After my distinguished kinsman, Colonel Robert Briggs Watson, Esquire, of Clouds Creek, South Carolina."

A wail of woe rose from the ill woman within. "Elton!" she cried. Then the boy was standing in the door, his thin arms wrapped around a little bindle of his clothing.

"Whatever happened to you, Edgar?" Curry Collins said, very sharp and cold. "You were a pretty nice young feller when you first come around these parts, as I recall."

"Say good-bye," I told the boy.

He stuck his hand out, saying, Good-bye, Grandpa. He winced and shifted when his grandfather leaned down to peck him on the head. Good-bye, Elton, Curry Collins told him in a muffled voice. He straightened as the boy ran forward. He looked defeated by his life but kept some dignity and did not speak again.

I swung the child up behind me on the horse. His grandfather lifted a slow hand, which he did not notice. "Your name is Robert now," I notified him. "You will likely be called Rob."

"Yessir," he said. He put his arms around me, and I led his small bony fingers to my belt loops, feeling his pale face against my shirt. We rode off with Curry Collins growing smaller in his doorway, gazing after us. Hanging on hard, the boy said in a muffled voice, "I knowed you'd come." And in a little while he said, "Papa? I been waiting so long. Waiting and waiting." I didn't know how to answer that, so I said shortly, "Don't set so far back on his withers, boy. Makes the old fool buck."

*

Even before we arrived home, I knew this boy had brought along the ghost of Charlie, just as I had feared. Upset and angry, I blamed it all on Mandy, who came running out to Rob with a big smile. "You wanted him so bad, goddamnit, you take care of him," I said harshly. I never dismounted, but swung him off and galloped away down the woods roads and crossed the county line into Suwannee, headed nowhere.

In the next days, I drank worse than ever before. Morning after morning, sick to death and surly, I woke up lying on some sawdust floor or in a shed or even in the ditch. Finally I wound up in jail, jaw swollen, bilious, mean down to the bone. The last dollar was gone. I was in Live Oak. I rode south through Lake City, distempered through and through. At the saloon, nobody came near me, not even the barkeep. I went out thirsty, sour-stomached, in a filthy temper, and who should I see tilting down the sidewalk but sweet Miss Sue-Belle Parkins, feeling no pain. I came up behind her, betting she had a flask on her and studying how best to work a drink or two. I whispered, *Sooee, Sooee,* kind of soft and sweet, and watched that big sappy grin of hers inch clear around under her ears. She might be just drunk enough to take me on for nothing.

Even drunk, Sooee knew better than to show any acquaintance with this white man who was trying to pass, but to tease me, she murmured in a little song, "Bes' not go whisperin Sooee to Miss SueBelle, cause this Sooee gal ain' no white man's li'l shoat." All the while she sashayed in front of me, and her smoky hips shifting along in that white dress fixed me hard as an ol' bird dog up on point. Sooee knew this, too, she never had to look. She was having such fun stoking the fire in her Wil' Man that she clean forgot to move off that sidewalk, let the white man through.

Folks were stopping now and grinning. Recalling that bad day on the square at Edgefield Court House when his neighbors laughed at Ring-Eye Lige for challenging General Butler to a duel, my brain pounded, heat swelled my face, I seemed to choke, and in the next moment, Jack Watson banged the heel of his hand between her shoulder blades—*Out of my way!* The shove pitched her forward and she almost fell. Finding her balance, she stopped short, her head hunched low, then turned around with a drunken smile of cunning. "Wil' Man? Dat *you*, honey?" Hollered that right out for all to hear.

Thinking herself safe in the bright sunlight of a Sunday morning, Sue-Belle grinned saucily, waving her perfumed lace whore hankie as she pirouetted. "How come," she cried out loud and clear, "you never come around no mo' to visit SueBelle?" Right then she saw Jack in my place, and her step faltered and she gave a whoop, skedaddling sideways like a startled partridge in her haste to flutter off that sidewalk.

She was too late. His hand flew from behind and cupped her forehead, pulling her back against his chest. The other hand held the knife blade to her throat. Her eyes and mouth popped open as her head was bent all the way back onto her shoulder blades—a terrified face seen upside down, with the nose and mouth above the staring eyes. That grotesque mask startled him and brought him to his senses, but not before he had guided the blade between his forefingers like a long razor so that it barely slit the skin.

SueBelle remained motionless, trying to breathe, head still cocked back. The knife edge rested lightly on the skin. There was a minute trickle and she felt it—felt what she thought must surely be the first drops of a fatal spurt of her lifeblood. Her eyes begged but she could not get a word out.

Church bells. Figures drifted in the morning street. There was no voice nor any sound, only a dog barking and the fading bells. No one drew near. The stiff figures waited. All was a dream, with that bright knife blade at the heart of it, set to lay open her throat in a red smile.

Slowly the hand relaxed on SueBelle's brow, and she sagged slowly, slowly to the ground. Slowly her hands drifted up under her chin, fingertips touching her cheap tinsel earrings, thumbs pressing up under her chin to hold her life in. But her throat was not slit, she had only imagined it. She groaned dolefully and coughed, then sobbed and vomited at the same time, soiling her dress.

In those old days of Redemption in the South, even before the Jim Crow laws were nailed up on the walls, a man had the lawful right and duty to punish any colored wench who forgot her place. A drunken whore had sassed a white man, refusing to make way for him on the main street. To teach her a lesson, he had threatened her and scared her. That was all. But having always liked Lulalie, I was thankful that no harm had come to her. I left her there.

The figures turned to watch me go, and no voice sought to stop me. A silence followed me down that street and around the corner. Inevitably I would be blamed for an unpleasant episode perpetrated in broad daylight on a Sunday in front of an assembly of churchly citizens hell-bent on worship. Taking care of troublemaking darkies—that was seen to after sundown, somewhere out of town.

He had no call to give the ladies such a fright, where were his manners? Why, that man came within an inch of nastying up our brand-new hard pine sidewalk! Gave God-fearing folks such dreadful indigestion that they belched on their hog and hominy all through the service.

SueBelle vanished that same day, scared I might come hunting for her at the whorehouse, and word soon spread that the prostitute had disappeared, no one knew where, though all agreed that E. A. Watson knew more than he should have. Next, word got around that this young Watson had killed another nigger back in Carolina. Every time I went up to Lake City, the coloreds would shy across the street to get out of my way, causing embarrassment to me and to my family. The truth was, I got along with niggers, treated 'em like people, whereas most men of my time didn't know one from another, couldn't be bothered.

Our Watson women at Fort White, and Mandy, too, heard all the stories thanks to Sam Frank Tolen, who spared the ladies not a single gory detail, not even those he had thought up. However, in my star-crossed mood, nobody dared to question me, not even Mandy. Perhaps she didn't care to learn more than she had to. But Aunt Tabitha passed the word to Captain Getzen, who knew no way but to ride straight out and face me in my field.

Captain Tom was a small, fierce, feisty feller, a war hero and presently the deacon of Elim Baptist Church on the Bellamy Road. He did not touch his hat when he rode up, which was not like him, but stayed stiff in the saddle whacking his peg leg smartly with his crop. While he prepared what he had come to say, that crop rapped that hardwood like the snap of rifle fire. When I rested my hoe and asked what I could do for him, he cleared his throat and said it might be best if I cleared out of the south county for a while.

"Best for who?" I didn't like the way he said "cleared out," as if I were some kind of riffraff. I reckon he saw that, for he danced his horse back as I came forward, raising his crop just enough to give me warning. This good man to whom I owed so much no longer trusted me not to attack him—that hurt, too. To calm myself, I bowed my head as if to pray, making sure Jack had withdrawn before I spoke. Then I said that Edgar Watson was the man who should determine Edgar Watson's future. I had been driven unjustly from my home in South Carolina, and did not intend to leave home a second time, having done no wrong.

"No wrong, you say." Captain Tom shook his head. "Come over to the house, pick up your pay." He rode away. At the house he would not explain his reasons, much less name my accusers. I tossed his money at his feet and left there before something worse could happen.

*

Cornered, Billy Collins said "the family" agreed with Captain Tom. I should leave the county. Which family do you speak for, Billy? I demanded. You weren't a Watson, the last time I heard. He shrugged that off, telling me I could come back when things blew over. It's not up to you to give me that permission, I told him. And don't you act like I'm the only one who has gotten into trouble around here. At this, Minnie fled the room.

"The reason my brother killed a man," said Billy, "if Lem *was* the killer"— and he stepped back as I moved toward him, but only to set himself, for he was nerved up now and meant to finish it—"was self-defense."

"*If* Lem was the killer? Because otherwise, the murderer was Edgar Watson—that what you're saying?"

From the other room, our Minnie screeched, "Billy Collins, how can you suggest such an evil thing! You tell Edgar you're sorry!" That was the boldest thing I ever heard my sister say to anybody, which shows how terrified she was.

Billy said, "How about that nigra man in South Carolina?" I raised my hand to stop him. I hadn't killed any such man, I said. Minnie seemed overjoyed to hear this, but her husband appeared shocked by such a barefaced lie. He said, "How about knife fights with strangers, over in those taverns in Suwannee?"

"Honor," I said drily.

"One of those men died later on to pay for your damned drunken crazy honor. And that woman in Lake City? What became of *her*? Never mind she was a darkie and a whore. She was a woman!"

"Still is, far as I know. Course you might know better." I took out my clasp knife and opened it and tested the fine blade with the ball of my thumb. "Billy? Maybe I should kill *you* out of my honor, because you are insulting me every time you open your damned mouth." When I raised my eyes to his,

his nerve ran out and his voice went shrill. "You'd murder your own sister's husband? A man half your size?"

The fear had taken him a little quicker than I had expected. An opened knife will do that to a man. I pared my nails with it. Billy was a Collins, he was proud, and I was content to let those shameful words ring in his ears. Then I said, "I have no idea where that whore went. She is not my responsibility." I closed the knife, put it away. "As for your brother, I advised him before John Hayes's death to leave this county, because otherwise it would be kill-or-be-killed."

That fool admission was all it took to get me implicated in the Hayes killing. Within a day or two, somebody took that to the County Sheriff. It wasn't even evidence, just hearsay, but in the public uproar over the fact that the prime suspect was safe across the Georgia line, the Sheriff decided to make do with a confederate. He issued a warrant for the arrest of E. A. Watson as an accessory before the fact in the unlawful murder of John Hayes. Knowing he had no real case, he leaked word of the warrant, hoping I would flee the county or get lynched, leave him in peace.

*

Poor old Job, the strong-hearted roan which had carried me south out of Carolina, was spavined from long months of wild hard riding. Since it looked like I might need a sound horse in a hurry, I replaced him with another roan of the same mulish temperament. I named him Job as well.

Sam came to warn me. "You might be havin you a necktie party," said pig-eyed Sam, who was all read up on the Wild West, knew all the lingo. "You better light out for the Territory," he said. Sam's little brain was working fast, I could hear it sizzle. He thought he could get my prime hogs cheap, because after these hints about a lynching party, he made me an exceptionally insulting offer.

I said, "Hell, no. Those hogs are the county's best."

"That's why I'm buyin 'em." He fingered his greasy wad. "You're runnin out of time, boy. Better take it."

"I'll remember this good turn," I said, counting the money. Sammy burst out in a guffaw. "Don't forget to write!" he yelled, and clapped me on the back.

I told him not to laugh too hard, he just might hurt himself. But Sam didn't scare as easy as his daddy. He was always a nervy sonofabitch, or just bone stupid, maybe a lack of imagination or a fatty brain. In his view, fate had nothing disagreeable in store for such a fine fat feller. And his attitude on this point was so foolish that I had to laugh, too. We laughed along together a good while, for our own reasons.

Finally I said, "Tell my mama good-bye, and tell her not to get her hopes up, cause she hasn't seen the last of her loving boy. You either. I won't forget your kindness in my time of need."

Sammy hooted, breaking wind in a carefree manner as he departed. "I aim to make my fortune off them hogs of yours!"

*

Anger and rotgut burned a bad hole in my lungs. Every breath hurt. Hurling my farm tools into the wagon, I threw back another snort. By now I had decided that Billy Collins had brought this down on me by repeating my words to the Sheriff. Seeing my expression, Mandy seemed scared. "Mr. Watson," she said, raising her hands almost in prayer, "we have each other and we have our children. We will make a clean start somewhere else."

"*Clean start,*" I repeated with disgust, turning my back on her. But remembering how she had forgiven me for wasting all our savings, and seeing anew the honest goodness in her face, I relented and took my dear wife in my arms. "You don't have to go with me, Mandy sweetheart," I whispered. "Oh, I *do*, my dearest," she whispered back, wiping a tear. "Oh, I do, I do." And she hurried to pack up food and our few possessions.

I rode over to my sister's house to settle my account with Billy Collins. My brother-in-law knew I would be coming because even before I swung out of the saddle, Minnie ran out and got down on her knees. Clutching little Julian, she begged her dear, dear brother to have mercy for the love of God and not cause more harm to a family which loved him dearly and hoped and prayed for his salvation and safe journey wherever he might go.

"So long as I go far enough and don't come back."

I pushed past her and sat down on the porch in Billy's rocker. The darkness seeped in slowly from the woods. Sitting hunched up in the cold, nodding off a little from the whiskey, I suffered a kind of rigor mortis of the spirit. Here I was, past thirty years of age and on the move again, still broke, still looking for a farm where I could prosper. Finally I knew that Billy wasn't going to come home, not while he saw that big horse in the road. Maybe I was relieved, I just don't know. He would tell people he had been off somewhere when Watson came, but he and I would always know he had been hiding, even if his wife had made him do it.

I rose stiffly and went in to Minnie where she was sniveling amongst the crockery, and she snatched her baby from the floor, fearing I might step on it. By now the anger was all gone, I could scarcely recall why I had come. I told her to let my friend Will Cox have my little cabin because Will was the one man I could trust to give it back. However, I was feeling doomed and homesick. I took my scared sister in my arms and gave her a gentle hug and kissed her brow for about the first time ever, and she burst into tears and hugged me back, and kissed me, too, got my face all wet and sticky with the baby's clabber, which she had been nibbling for her own poor supper.

Her clabber breath was sour from these tense scared hours. "Please, Edgar," she whispered. "Don't do my Billy harm. You are such a *good* man, deep in your heart. We won't forget you." Feeling me go remote and cold, she shrank back, clutching her mouth. "Oh please, I beg of you, don't look at me that way!"

"You won't forget me, that is true," I told her, "because I will be back. So you tell that tale-bearing husband of yours not to sleep too soundly."

I rode toward home. Dismounting at some distance, I circled through the pines on foot, making no sound on the needle ground, to be certain there was no sign of any ambush. Seeing that Mandy had everything well-packed, I came in to help load. I backed the horse into the traces, piled my wife and kids in under blankets, and hitched Charlie the filly on a tether out behind. Loading the shotgun and sliding it under my seat, I climbed up and snapped the reins—*Gid 'yap!* I said—and big Job kicked the wagon boards a lick that rang off through the winter trees sharp as a rifle shot. I talked Job down and got him going at a good fast-farting trot, the woman murmuring to calm her little ones, the pale-faced Son Born sitting up straight, by himself as usual, staring back down the long and ghostly lanes.

Under the moon, the white road through the pines flowed like a silver creek under black trees, the hooves so quiet on the clay that an owl might have heard little Carrie's pretty sighs and the suckling of Elijah Edward at his mother's breast.

Rob cried suddenly, What will become of us? as if he had awakened from a bad dream. I growled at him over my shoulder and Mandy hushed him. My wife looked drawn and fearful, which she was. She thought she was leaving her whole life behind her, which she was. She thought that armed men might come after us—quite likely, too—and that our children might be badly frightened, even harmed. But never once did she complain, nor ease her nerves by fraying mine with foolish questions, as the boy did. "Miss Jane S. Dyal from Deland," as she had bravely dubbed herself the first time we met, was a very good young woman who forgave her husband, though she knew he would never put away his grief for his dead Charlie, and though he was on the run again, with no destination.

At the Fort White Road I turned the wagon north. A solitary light was burning when the wagon passed the Herlong place, where dogs were barking. Through the trees, I saw a man's silhouette come to a window—the righteous Methodist Dan Herlong, who had blackened my name with the tales he'd brought from South Carolina. *I'll be back,* I promised, and just then, the figure drew back from the window and the light was snuffed. To this day I believe that Herlong sensed something out there in the dark, something that frightened him.

I took the night roads north and west, under cold stars which shone on the unknown land where we were going.

Chapter 3

Indian Nations

Toward dawn, I pulled the wagon off into the woods and picketed the horse beside a branch. We slept all day, taking turns on watch, and at dusk we ate up a pot of cold hominy, hitched the roan, and crossed into Suwannee County, traveling all night and the next night, too, clearing Live Oak and Suwannee Springs. North and west of the Suwannee River was new country, but taking no chances with my evil luck, I moved by night until the Georgia border was behind us.

From Valdosta, the way west crossed the Flint River and the Chattahoochee, and finally the great Mississippi at Vicksburg, where the Confederate Army came to so much grief. From Vicksburg we went on across to Monroe, Louisiana, and from there northwest again to the Arkansas Territory, where a man pestered by the law might pause to catch his breath. Already the weather had turned cold, numbing our spirits. The Indian Nations was no place to arrive as winter was setting in, with its promise of hunger and misery for our little children. There was harvest work for a man with horse and wagon on a late cotton crop in Franklin County, Arkansas. That's where we wintered. I rented a small farm, figuring to make a pea crop before heading west after harvest the next summer. That worked out about as well as could be expected, and in early autumn of '88, I headed over to Fort Smith and on west into Oklahoma Territory.

This hill country of plateaus and river buttes had been turned over to the Cherokees and Creeks, with a few Seminoles from Florida thrown in. Some of these Indians still had the slaves they took along with 'em back in the thirties, when Andy Jackson ran these tribes out of the East. Quite a few stray niggers had drifted out this way after the War, and a lot more showed up after '76, when Reconstruction was finally put a stop to. There were plenty of Southern cracker boys and some hard Yankees, too, because the local government was Northern, even if most folks were Southern—Texas, Missouri, Mississippi. In short, all colors of humankind were mingled in various shades of mud, like the watercolors in my sister's paint box back in Edgefield, and every last one—every redskin and nigger, every halfbreed, including those kinky-haired Seminole breeds they called *mascogos*—every man with a cock between his legs, no matter what his breed or general hue, considered himself your equal if not somewhat better, since you were a stranger and likely on the dodge and maybe worse.

The most arrogant of all were the buffalo soldiers with their Comanche scalps strung on their belts. I kept a wary eye out for my would-be brother, asked casual questions here and there, but these boys told me Jacob Watson was in Texas, taking care of the local white ladies as best he could. When they saw I disapproved of that, they laughed at me. I saw their point and elected to hold my tongue.

Under the bluffs out of the prairie winds, that Canadian River country had some good alluvial soil in the river bottoms. In those days, neither whites nor blacks could own Indian land, but I leased a good piece off a Cherokee named Milo Hoyt who was married to a Choctaw woman and farmed her land. I made a good crop of corn and cotton but could not renew my lease, due to complications. However, a white female who was hitched up to an Indian leased me some land across the river in Cherokee territory.

For a time this Mrs. Maybelle Reed was Mandy's best friend in the Nations. Mandy never forgot how generous she was and how kind to our small children—this was when we first arrived and didn't know a soul amongst our neighbors—and I will grant that she was big-hearted in her way, with a door wide open to people in need, including strangers. But man and woman, she was the most shameless liar and show-off I have ever come across, bar none.

This Maybelle, by her own account, preferred the company of men to that of the ignorant rough women of the Territory, but she made an exception of my Mandy, who was well-educated and soft-spoken and a lady, and whose friendship elevated her own standing in the community, which had fallen low due to a bedtime preference for Indians and breeds.

Maybelle's first husband was Jim Reed, who rode with Will Quantrill and his guerrillas, including the James boys and the Youngers, during the Border Wars between Kansas and Missouri. Like a lot of armed riders who passed themselves off as irregulars, Reed was a killer by inclination and by trade who only joined up with Quantrill when those men turned outlaw. After the War, he gambled and raced horses for some years around Fort Smith, took part in armed robberies, held up the Austin–San Antonio stage, shot and killed a bystander, and generally made a nuisance of himself before a former partner with an eye to the reward deprived him of his life in the early seventies.

The Younger boys sometimes hid out in an old cabin about six miles west of Briartown, on a rocky bench facing south across the Canadian River. The land was part of a large spread belonging to Tom Starr, a huge bloodthirsty Cherokee who rustled cattle all the way south to the Red River. Tom Starr called this place Younger's Bend, having taken a liking to the Younger boys for no good reason. Pretty soon, maybe 1880, the Widow Reed moved in there with Sam Starr, one of Tom's sons, and in no time at all, "boys" on the run were infesting this hideout, including the famous Jesse James, whom she introduced into her social circle as Mr. Williams from Texas. Pretty soon, the U.S. marshals in the Territory got wind of this place, too, but Maybelle—or Belle Starr, as she now called herself—told the newspaper that her hospitality to outlaws had been much exaggerated by "the low-down class of shoddy whites who have made the Indian Territory their home to evade paying taxes on their dogs." This female preened herself on her local reputation for "moxie" or "old fire," and was often obnoxious whether the situation called for it or not.

The Younger boys weren't rednecks like her neighbors. They were the wild seed of the richest slave owner in Jackson County, Missouri, who happened to be a family friend of Maybelle's daddy, Judge John Shirley. Belle was never Cole Younger's lady friend the way she claimed, but later in life, her daughter Rosie Reed took the name Pearl Younger for professional purposes. Her son Eddie, a chip off the old block, was faithful to his daddy's name and his profession and his early death by bullet, too, as shall be seen.

A few years before our arrival, Miss Maybelle and her Injun Sam had been hauled up for horse theft in the Fort Smith federal court and received short sentences from the well-known "hanging judge" Isaac Parker. This was Maybelle's first and last conviction, not because she was hard to catch but because she never committed a real crime. Her popular repute as Queen of the Outlaws was born of her own bare-assed lies, since the closest that female ever came to the outlaw life was screwing every outlaw she could lay her hands on. When her Sam was shot to death over in Whitefield, Maybelle soon replaced him in her bed with Tom Starr's adopted son, Jim July, adding Starr to his name to shore up her claim on that property.

Belle's haughty airs and gaudy style and even the big pearl-handled .45 shoved pirate-style into her belt did not distract much from her poor appearance. She was a long-nosed thin-mouthed woman, hard-pocked and plainer'n stale bread, also wide of waist and slack of hip from too much time spent on her back with her feet flat to the ceiling. Her dark skin, leathered by the sun, and the coarse black hair she pinned under big hats when it wasn't down behind like an old horse tail, made her look more mixed-blood than her halfbreed husband.

However, my kind Mandy felt that this old squaw must have some good in her. Needing a woman to trust and confide in, my wife let it slip to her new friend that her own husband, Mr. Watson, had been unjustly accused of murder in the state of Florida and obliged to flee. Since Belle was the widow of two killers and domiciled with a third, the news that I might be such a man only enhanced me in her eyes. Being a man-eater, she pursued me, and when I ignored her wiles and blandishments, she became furious. Tearing up my lease and flinging my payment down into the mud, she claimed she'd been warned by the Indian agent at Muskogee to harbor no more fugitives from justice lest she forfeit her precarious claim on Indian land. Refusing to pick up the money, I told her my lease was duly paid. I rode away, leaving her squalling in her yard, loud and mean as a horny raccoon. A few days later Belle sent a formal letter stating that her land had been rented to another sharecropper, Joe Tate.

When I questioned Mandy about Belle's sly reference to "fugitive from justice," my wife confessed her indiscretion. I chastised her severely and forbade her to associate with a treacherous female who had not only broken her word on the lease but might well turn me in. In late November, I persuaded Tate to have no dealings with this woman, who would only drag him into her own troubles with the law. Once Tate had backed out of his lease, I rode over to Younger's Bend to smooth things over.

The discussion ended before I could dismount. Hearing that Tate aimed to break his lease, Maybelle snarled, "Maybe the U.S. marshals won't come after you, but the Florida authorities just might." Saying nothing, I just looked her over once before departing. Later I learned from her son Eddie Reed that his sister Rosie Lee had seen my expression from the doorway and had warned her mother to make no more threats.

In January of 1889, with Mrs. Starr still evading her obligation, I moved my family into a cabin on the land of Jackson Rowe, whose claim adjoined the land of Milo Hoyt. Another resident was Eddie Reed, who had left home at Christmas after a humiliating public horsewhipping from his mother, inflicted at Whitefield in the presence of the postmaster, W. S. Hall. It seems Belle was punishing him for taking her black horse without permission and returning it lathered and abused. Then and there, Eddie vowed publicly that he would kill his mother.

Murder in the Indian Country

On February third of 1889, on the eve of her forty-third birthday, one of the many people who had it in for Mrs. Starr took care of that troublous bitch once and for all. She was shot out of the saddle on the muddy river road south of my cabin.

A telegram caught Jim July Starr at Fort Smith, where he had been detained for another horse theft. Released for his wife's funeral, he arrived on Tuesday, and the burial took place at Younger's Bend at noon on Wednesday. Because of that scrape over the lease, it seemed best to attend, and Mandy insisted upon going with me, leaving our hired hand, Ansel Terry, to mind the children. We crossed on the ferry and rode up the ridge to Belle's place.

Cherokee relatives and a few outlaw friends were standing silently before the cabin, squinting hard at every rider who appeared. There was a stir when I trotted in but no one spoke. Jim Starr stalked me, red-eyed and suspicious. The casket lay inside the one-room cabin, attended by stone-faced Indian women sitting in tight rows on rough benches. There was no service, no Indian chanting, only the strange silence of unfinished business.

Armed men carried the coffin from the cabin and set it down near the rough grave. The lid was removed, and the Starr clan and other Cherokees dropped ceremonial corn bread on Belle's tight-lipped remains, after which the box was lowered into the pit. I stepped forward with a shovel to help Jim Cates—he had built the coffin—bank the grave, but had hardly started when Starr and his sidekick Charley Acton drew their guns and yelled at me to put my hands up. This horse thief pointed the gun between my eyes, accusing me of murdering his woman, as the other Indians and breeds grunted beady-eyed assent, without expression.

Having anticipated something of the kind, I remained steady and my wife did, too, despite the likelihood that her husband would be gunned down before her eyes. I did not trust Starr, who was drunk, to keep his head. Instead of raising my hands as ordered, I grabbed hold of Cates and yanked him between me and the guns. Cates implored me to raise my hands or else we'd both be killed, and I finally did so, but not before remarking to Jim Starr, "If you kill me, Jim, you will be killing the wrong man." My assurance and calm demeanor persuaded those present that I deserved a trial, and eventually Starr, still growling, put his gun away. For the moment, we were free to go. That evening, however, he came to my house with other Indians and put me under citizen's arrest, intending to take me to the U.S. District Court at Fort Smith. He finally agreed to my demand that Jack Rowe and others be permitted to accompany our party rather than leave me to their mercies with no witnesses. We left for Fort Smith that very evening, stopping for the night at a farm along the way.

Next day, February 8, I was marched before the Commissioner in the U.S. District Court, where Starr would claim at a preliminary hearing that during our journey I had attempted to bribe my way out of trouble, promising him five thousand dollars in exchange for my release. Why would I do that, I answered, when I didn't even have enough to pay my bail? Starr filed a formal affidavit "that Edgar A. Watson, did in the Indian Country . . . feloniously, willfully, premeditatedly and of his malice aforethought kill and murder Belle Starr, against the peace and dignity of the United States." Deputized, he was given two weeks to assemble witnesses and evidence for a second hearing before the circuit court to determine whether Watson should go to trial. With my lease still unsettled and spring planting near, I cooled my heels in jail, but crop or no crop, this was fine by me. I felt a lot safer behind bars than alone out in the Cherokee Nation, with Tom Starr and his outlaws on the loose.

Interviewed in jail by the publisher of the Van Buren (Arkansas) *Press Argus,* I said (I have the clipping): "I know nothing about the murder and will have no trouble establishing my innocence. I know very little of Belle Starr, though she for some reason, I know not what, has been prejudiced against me. I am thirty-three years old and have a wife who is living with me. Two years ago I came from Florida to Franklin County, Arkansas, and from there moved about a year ago to where I now live, and I have never had any trouble with anyone. I was at Rowe's on Sunday when Belle Starr came along, and soon afterward my wife came by and I left and went home with her, and Belle Starr was shot by someone soon afterward. I have no idea who killed her but know that I did not, and had no reason to feel even hard toward her."

Jim Starr was quoted in the same edition: "I knew enough to satisfy me that Watson was the murderer. We buried Belle at Younger's Bend, and I went after Watson and got him. He showed no fight or I would have killed him." This was all lies, of course. And Farmer Watson made a better impression than Horse Thief Starr. The interviewer described the accused as a man of "fair complexion, light sunburnt whiskers, and blue eyes" and reported that he "was decidedly good-looking and talked well." Furthermore, he appeared to be "the very opposite of a man who would be supposed to commit such a crime." (The Fort Smith *Weekly Elevator* for February 15 was of similar opinion, describing the defendant as "a white man of good appearance.")

On the twenty-first, Starr returned to Fort Smith with Belle's two offspring and ten other witnesses, and the hearing commenced on February 22 and ended the next day. Having a passing interest in the case, I took some notes.

*

The hearing began badly. The Prosecutor established at once that three closely spaced buckshot in Belle Starr's back had caused her death; that according to Watson's neighbor William England, who had shot Watson's .12 gauge gun at target paper—"It throws three shot close together and scattered the others right smart around"; that a few days before the killing, Watson had refused to lend bird shot to the witness, claiming he had only the one load and he might need it; that Watson had left Rowe's house an hour before Mrs. Starr, in good time to set up an ambush where she would have to pass; that the killer's tracks led to a point within one hundred yards of Watson's house; that Watson wore a size 7 shoe that fitted the footprints; and that ill feeling existed between victim and defendant.

Jim Starr also testified to this ill feeling, and so did Turner England. "Belle came to me where I was splitting rails and wanted to know why Mr. Tate did not move onto her place as he had agreed. I knew why but did not tell her and she said it was that long-tongued Watson. Says, Tell Watson he need not be afraid of the Cherokee officers but he might look out for the Creek officers. When I told him this, the defendant said they had better look out what they was telling on him."

Some background to the killing was now established. On February 2, 1889, a Saturday, Maybelle Reed had accompanied her common-law husband Jim July Starr as far as San Bois Creek, spending the night at the cabin of a Mrs. Nail. Next morning they went on to Fort Smith, Arkansas, where he was charged with horse theft before Judge Parker. She returned alone next day and stopped off at the Sunday gathering at Jackson Rowe's. According to witnesses, her son Eddie had been there earlier but left not long before she came; they also stated that Ed Watson, who was sitting on the porch, got up soon after she rode in and walked away in the direction of his cabin. Jack Rowe would testify that Mrs. Starr did not speak to Mr. Watson when they saw each other at his house that afternoon.

Mrs. Starr soon departed, too, taking a trail that led past the Hoyt property. At a point less than a quarter mile from the Watson cabin, where she had to pass a rail fence corner by the lane, she was shot out of the saddle with a charge of buckshot. Then her unknown assailant or another crossed the fence and discharged a second charge of turkey shot into her shoulder and face, leaving her to die there in the water puddles.

Galloping homeward, Belle's horse was seen by Frog Hoyt at the bank of the South Canadian, where the frightened animal leapt into the flood and crossed to the Cherokee shore. Riding in the direction it had come from, Frog Hoyt found Belle "lying on her face stretched out across the road." Assuming she had been thrown and injured, he turned back toward the ferry, seeking help. There he met her daughter Rosie Lee, who had been alarmed when the riderless horse came galloping into the yard at Younger's Bend.

Frog Hoyt, somewhat dim and shy, had memorized his testimony. "I went to the body alone. It was almost dark when I got to her. She was not quite dead. She never spoke. She was lying on her side and face, kind of across the road. Her whip was in her hand. She was shot in the back with buckshot and left side of face and arm with fine shot. . . . There were three buckshots in her back close together."

The defendant was now called to the stand. Asked if my shotgun fired such a pattern, I confirmed that this was true. However, I swore upon my oath that I had never fired at the victim.

Though several witnesses claimed to have heard two shots, only Ray England had been curious enough to go investigate. "They were about a mile from me at the time. When I got within one hundred yards of Watson's house I heard someone calling hogs. He called his hogs for a good while . . . he calls them every morning and evening. Belle had been gone from Rowe's some little bit when I heard him calling hogs. When I got past the house someone hallooed to me and I took it to be Watson. It was muddy at the fence corner . . . which was about twenty steps from where Belle Starr fell. The man that shot her crossed over the fence and went across toward Watsons. The sun was near down. He would have had time to have done the shooting and return from the time I heard shots until I seen him at his house."

However, my hired hand, Ansel Terry, would testify that he saw me in the corncrib getting corn for my hogs. "I unsaddled my horse and went to the spring for water. When the two shots were fired, the defendant was at the fence calling his hogs."

When cross-examined, I backed up Ansel, saying I had heard two shots when I went out to call my hogs, at which time I saw Ansel Terry at the woodpile. I also took this opportunity to repeat that I'd heard the deceased was angry with me but that we'd never had any difficulty. "She never said one cross word to me. I had nothing to do with the killing and know nothing about it."

The body was removed to Alf White's house, where it was visited by Ray England and Jack Rowe. Ray testified that he "sat up all night with her and in the morning me, Jim Cates and Ed Reed went down to where she had been shot and found tracks where someone had stood in the fence corner." Soon Turner England joined the tracking party. "I seen blood in the road, seen tracks of the man that I thought done the shooting . . . followed these tracks two or three hundred yards. . . . Watson's house was about 150 yards from where we quit.

"Watson and his work hand came to my house on Monday morning before I started off . . . came to grind their axes. I told him about the killing and he said he heard it too, away in the night. I told him I was going over and he had better come along. He came with me as far as Mr. Tate's. I left him there but seen him up at White's house when I came back from tracking."

Jack Rowe also investigated those small boot prints. "One hundred yards from where the body lay . . . That track was going towards where the dead woman was and coming from the direction of Watson's field. It was about a size 7 track. The track went over leaves which kept us from getting the exact measure." However, Rowe never crossed the fence into my field and admitted he did not know if there were tracks there.

Ed Reed told the court he had turned up at Rowe's about nine next morning. Claimed he'd spent the evening with a friend a mile and a half away upriver. Hearing the news, he said, "I got on my horse and went to Alf White's. She was lying on the bed dead and I got Jim Cates to show me where she was killed. I found where tracks had come into the field and come up to the fence. Stood on their toes right by the fence corner. She fell about thirty feet from there and these tracks had got over the fence and went up close to her and then they left there and went right opposite through the woods. Those tracks kept winding around, looked like they were trying to stay on the leaves for almost two hundred yards. Then I lost the track."

Never once did Eddie Reed mention my name, nor did he suggest that any evidence pointed to me.

My attorney, Bill Mellette of Fort Smith, dismissed all of Jim Starr's so-called evidence as circumstantial, an opinion shared by the Fort Smith *Era*. There was no proof that those small footprints belonged to this "quiet, hard-working man whose local reputation is good," nor one iota of evidence that this good citizen fired his own gun, whether or not it was the murder weapon. Starr was granted an extension while he sought more witnesses, but very little new evidence was forthcoming. On March 4, the plaintiff's case was judged too weak to merit an indictment. Essentially it was a horse thief's word against that of an honest farmer.

*

Jim Starr was so disgusted by my release that he jumped bond on the horse-stealing charge and joined an outlaw band. He died less than a year later, shot down in the Chickasaw Nation by a sheriff's deputy, who reported that the dying Starr had confessed to killing his own wife with Watson's gun. By that time, a rumor was going around that Tom Starr had killed her to avenge the death of his beloved son Sam, whom she had led into bad company. Pony Starr declared that a white rancher, threatened by Belle the previous year, had hired one of his cowhands to dispose of her. Others suspected an outlaw named John Middleton. True, I was the only one ever arrested, but many other names were soon put forward.

On that Sunday, the victim's son had left Jack Rowe's not long before his mother's arrival, just as I had. Since Eddie had sworn publicly that he would "slaughter that old sow," it seems curious that no one wondered if the hot-tempered young Reed and the threatened Mr. Watson, who were neighbors at Jack Rowe's, had not been partners in the killing.

*

With her death, Maybelle was transformed by the newspapers from the ill-favored consort of rustlers and thieves to the beautiful Civil War spy, border hellion, and Queen of the Outlaws whose bloodthirsty lovers had terrorized the West. The legend got off to a flying start on the day of her funeral, in a brief item in the local *Press Argus*, which made four mistakes in its single sentence: "It is reported that the notorious Indian [*sic*] woman Bell [*sic*] Starr was shot dead on Monday [*sic*], at Eufaula [*sic*], Indian Territory." I suppose the "woman" part was accurate, but only barely.

A Fort Smith editor filed the following dispatch, duly printed on the front page of *The New York Times*. Every sentence after the first one is untrue.

> *Word has been received from Eufala, Indian Territory, that Belle Starr was killed there Sunday night. Belle was the wife of Cole Younger . . . the most desperate woman that ever fig- ured on the borders. She married Cole Younger directly after the war, but left him and joined a band of outlaws that oper- ated in the Indian Territory. She had been arrested for mur- der and robbery a score of times, but always managed to escape.*

A few years later, a juryman in Judge Parker's federal court would fertil- ize Belle's myth in a book called *Hell on the Border*—the first account but by no means the last to attribute Belle Starr's death to a man named Watson, despite the finding of the federal court that there was insufficient evidence to indict him.

Dr. Jesse Mooney, who had tended Eddie after the savage beating from his mother, arrived at Alf White's house a few minutes after Belle died. He con- cluded that her son had been her killer. Dr. Mooney was told this in so many words by Rosie Lee Reed, alias Pearl Younger, who had covered for her brother by pointing her finger at me. Rosie Lee related to Dr. Mooney that when she found Belle dying in the road, she lifted her head from the bloody puddle and held her in her arms, at which point Belle opened her eyes and whispered, "Baby, your darned brother shot me. I turned and seen him across the fence before he cracked down on me."

Mercifully she seemed unaware that Eddie Reed then climbed the fence and walked over to his mother and fired a second shot into her face. Otherwise, Belle's account was pretty accurate. I know that because I saw him do it. I was there.

*

On account of hard feelings, I could not settle there in Tom Starr country, so I leased a farm in Crawford County, Arkansas. Having lost a month in jail, I got my seed in late and watched the weak sprouts wither in that summer's drought. By the start of winter I was in bad debt, with three hungry kids and a new baby. Rob was eleven now and helped some with the chores, but Carrie and Edward were still toddlers who were most helpful when they stayed out of the way.

We called our newborn Lucius Hampton Watson, after the family patriarch Luke Watson of Virginia, and also General (later Governor and Senator) Wade Hampton, our great Carolina hero. Despite his proud name, I was not glad to see this little feller, who looked like he had come into this world to pule and die. Once winter set in, there were times—and I hope God will forgive me, though I do not count on it—when I thought that Lucius might be better off in Heaven. He brought no joy to our meager hearth but only plagued us down those cold dark days with his fret and yawling. Mandy was shocked when I spoke this way about the baby, and reproved me for my "brutal way of talking." I told her that the world was brutal and man's lot was, too, so she might as well face hard truth. "That is your truth and not mine, Mr. Watson," Mandy said.

We had no Christmas that year, none at all. We had no friends nor relatives in that section, nor near neighbors, either. Huddling with our offspring in a damp and dirty shack, doing our utmost to forget our stomachs and stay warm, we passed our days in the nightmare sleep that famine brings, a kind of fitful hibernation, with no fat to tide us over. The dull cold misery, the endless days—dark winter days all but inseparable from night—were worse than Carolina in the War, as if somehow I were losing ground and falling back into that hellish period.

By midwinter I could scarcely bear the children's hollow eyes, the coughing and mute suffering. Day by day those pinched and staring faces shrank against the bone. Trapped by my own helplessness, I lay there stunned, my breath cold and slow as the breath of a reptile in deep winter mud. "Better not lay too long without breathing, Mr. Watson. We wouldn't want rigor mortis to set in." Poor Mandy did her gallant best to poke up my dead ashes, but her eyes had gone dull, too, and in the dim light from the one pane, she looked haunted.

Enough, I thought. When bellies are full, it is easy to be law-abiding, but with cold and hunger in the house, a man with wife and children may be forced to break the law, and may God condemn those who would condemn him.

One day three strangers with closed faces showed up at my place with a string of ponies, offering to pay me twenty dollars in advance if I would keep them over the winter. Two did the talking while the third stayed with the ponies. If nobody claimed 'em by the spring, they said, then I could sell 'em. That told me that these animals might be stolen, but I was in no place to ask hard questions.

While those two put their heads together, counting out the money, the buffalo soldier eased up alongside. He was a halfbreed and half out of uniform, a deserter. "Friends of Belle," he said in a low voice. "They won't be back. Best run this string into the Nations quick and sell 'em to the Injuns— either that or run 'em off your place." He touched his hat brim, moved away.

I had no chance to sell those ponies, because the deputies rode in at daybreak the next morning. They had been tipped off, they even took the twenty dollars. Lashed my wrists behind my back and heaved me up into the saddle and rode me away as my poor family wept. With winter coming hard behind that iron sky to northward, and no man on the place and no food, either, even poor Mandy finally lost heart and sank down with a moan of woe.

Rob in his thin outgrown jacket and split soggy boots came running and hollering alongside the horses, socking at the deputies' stirrups until he got knocked sprawling in the muddy tracks. Poor Son Born thought the world of me and I don't know why, because even then my face grew stiff at the sight of him and my manner hard and cold. I could not help myself. "Get away!" I barked at him, heaving around to stare at my huddled family a last time. Being bound tight, I could not even wave.

In the Territories, stealing horses was a crime far worse than murder, which was very common and often well-deserved. I could count my lucky stars, the deputies told me, grinning like coyotes, that they hadn't strung me from the nearest cottonwood. Perhaps these men felt merciful because they were in on the whole frame-up, which they hardly bothered to deny. The horse thieves were friends of Belle, they said. On January fourth of 1890, in the county circuit court there in Van Buren, I was given fifteen years at hard labor and carted off to Arkansas State Prison.

I will say this for Eddie Reed, he knew what he owed me for my friendly counsel, and moved my family to a good ranch in Broken Bow, in the Choctaw Nation, where Mandy could earn their room and board as housekeeper. Reed did not live long after that, being even wilder than his father. A drunk at twelve, a moonshiner and bootlegger by age fourteen, he was a robber, gunslinger, and killer all of his short life. He slew his mother at age seventeen, and the following year was convicted of horse theft and sentenced to five years in prison. Paroled in 1893, he was rearrested for bootlegging whiskey into the Indian Country. The story goes that his sister Rosie Lee pled with Judge Parker before sentencing to give that poor, remorseful boy another chance, and the Hanging Judge told her it would do no good. Said, That young feller was born ornery, and he won't quit. He's better off right where he is. If I let him out, he'll be dead within the year.

Rosie Lee bet the Judge a hundred dollars that he was mistaken, and he took the bet. Eddie received a suspended sentence on the condition that he quit drinking and go straight. He took a job as a railway guard, serving as deputy U.S. marshal when needed. Eddie was always a crack shot, and in a brief gunfight in the line of duty, he killed Luke and Zeke Crittenden, halfbreed Cherokee brothers, who had resisted a routine arrest for shooting up the streets. The Crittenden boys were also deputy marshals, having never been criminals and drunken troublemakers except in their spare time. But Reed himself would be slain within the year under similar circumstances, and so his little sister lost her bet. Owing money to the Hanging Judge and to her brother's lawyers, Rosie Lee embarked upon her own lifelong career in "show business." Under her professional name, Pearl Younger, she showed it all nightly at the Pea Green House in Fort Smith, a gorgeous whorehouse celebrated far and wide as the "pride and joy of the Southwest."

Frank Reese

I'd been in prison close to a year when a work gang captain at Little Rock said he'd sure be sorry, Jack—I used Jack's name in prison—if Florida claimed you before you boys go out in March to bust the sod, because for a horse thief you're a real good worker and an inspiring example to these other criminals. When no word came from Florida by spring, I was sent out with the chain gangs. The leg chains were removed while we worked, and the guards rode up and down the fields with rawhide whips and rifles. The farmers worked the gangs like slaves, gave us rotten grub and very little of it. Worried about my family, I was desperate to escape. The fields were mostly in the river bottoms, with no bridge nor ferry for many, many miles, so any man who could swim to the far side would have a day's head start on the guns and bloodhounds.

The day came when I saw my chance and ran through the cornstalks and down the bank and struck out across the current, along with a bull nigger named Frank and a skinny halfbreed, Curly. We had a good jump before the first guard yelled and started shooting. Halfway across, Curly took a bullet in the shoulder, but his vicious streak gave him a kicking spurt that carried him as far as the shallows, from where we hauled him out of range.

Curly was goose-bump blue with cold and bleeding badly, in no shape to go further. "Should of left me drown in peace," he whined. His eyes darted, following our expressions like a dealer. The man was certain to betray our destinations as soon as they twisted that bad shoulder up behind him. Curly's life luck had run out, with nothing good headed his way—he knew that, too. We would have to silence him, as he would have done with much less hesitation in our place. And so he jeered at what we must be thinking, and cursed us vilely while he had the chance. He wanted to provoke us, get it over with. "Fuckin idiots," he complained bitterly. He jerked his chin toward the shouts across the river, but he meant us, too, and all of humankind. He had some grit.

Out of respect for Curly's feelings, we went off a ways to discuss what to do, and Frank said, Boss, we got to kill him. I said, Okay by me, Frank, go ahead. It was going to be hard to finish him without a knife or club, and I did not have the character required to hold under the current the head of a man who had risked his life with us only a few minutes before. What we decided was, we would duck the whole damned problem, we would just keep going. We yelled good-bye, but not before pumping up a lot of jabber about heading west for Oregon, which never fooled ol' Curly for a minute.

*

Our first job was to hunt up two good horses and some common clothing. That afternoon we scouted a big farm, waiting till dusk for our chance to jump the homesteader when he went out back of the barn to feed his hens. That German told us he was tickled pink to saddle up his two nags for his visitors. When I inquired about firearms, he presented me with a fine German revolver, also a canvas kit with all his bullet molds and makings, observing mournfully that without the gun, he had no use for 'em. When Frank frowned evilly, feeling left out, the farmer asked how "your nigra" would like a packet of smoked venison with some nice baked grits thrown in. My partner growled, "I ain't nobody's nigra," but after all that bad food we'd been given by tight-fisted farmers, his stomach told him to shut up, take the damn packet. "Like I say, I ain't nobody's nigger." I reckon Frank knew what he meant, and perhaps the German, too, because he uttered a nervous bray, so desperate was he to get rid of us.

In the days to come, we were to hear that while attempting an escape, we had been struck by bullets in the head and drowned, according to "the wounded and recaptured convict, an accomplice of Watson and the Negro." Maybe that's what Curly told 'em (breeds can't be counted on even to lie, Frank said), but what was more likely—since the guards had seen us crawling out on the far shore—was that Curly had snitched and the warden was playing possum, making us think nobody was after us while alerting lawmen all over the Nations, east and west.

There was no way to get word to my family. I regretted Mandy's grief over my death but could not help it.

We cautioned our benefactor not to leave his farm until next day, or things would not go his way when we returned his horses. At nightfall, we rode out toward the west so that the German might support our Oregon story. We hid our hoofprints in a stream and circled wide behind a pinewood before turning east toward the Tennessee state line.

Mostly Frank was silent as a knothole. When I asked him finally why he talked so much, he grinned, a little sheepish, and said he was grieving in advance for the faithless woman whom he aimed to murder. He had tracked her "sweet man" to Arkansas—that was how he ended up in the local prison—and now he was headed home to Memphis to finish up the job. "I got my good name to think about, Mist' Jack," he said.

"To err is human, to forgive divine," I told him. I saw no sense in mentioning I was on my way to South Carolina to kill my father. Instead I described the Christian way I had forgiven SueBelle Parkins, not mentioning how strange that girl had looked with her upside-down face and that red line on her throat that had come so close to parting in a bloody smile. At the last moment, I told him fervently, the Good Lord had stayed my hand. I was moved by my own parable but Black Frank only scowled. "Nigger bitch, you said? Well, after I got her dead and buried, maybe I'll forgive that bitch of mine, but I ain't promisin." We chuckled for a good while over that one.

We rode toward Memphis, where Frank claimed he could get us lost indefinitely. I concluded he had no real plan for Memphis or anyplace else. We were wanted men, and one of us was white, and in any niggertown in this part of the country, I would draw too much attention right away. A nigger in a white man's company was one thing, but a white man in niggertown was quite another.

We parted company at the Black River. Not that I didn't trust Frank Reese. I did. Frank had his own code of honor. All the same, my destination and my plans were my own business. If he got caught in some mistake, and knew where Jack Watson might be headed, the law was duty bound to whip it out of him.

"Well, so long then, Frank," I said abruptly at the fork, turning my horse off toward the north. That took him by surprise, I reckon. I always thought Frank was pretty hard, and still do, but plainly I had offended him or hurt his feelings, if he had any. He didn't answer me, nor did he wave, just sat his horse in the deep shadow of the river woods and watched me go. He wasn't sulking, either. As he often said, very matter-of-fact, "I ain't nothin but a nigger." He expected no better out of life.

This man and I had often talked about black men and whites. If a nigger won't take his hat off, or he sasses me, speaks out too loud—well, I won't tolerate it, I told Frank. But as far as joking with you people, passing the time of day, making sure you get your feed and some fair treatment, I believe I can say I have done better by the niggers—or coloreds or darkies, or whatever my Mandy wants to call 'em—than a lot of these carpetbaggers and damn-Yankee hypocrites who used to agitate so hard for so-called nigra rights.

That detachment of Union soldiers quartered at Edgefield, back in Reconstruction—hell, those bluecoats were uneasy around niggers, had no feel for 'em. Besides that, being few in number, they were scared by the hating faces of our home folks, and they had to stay right there and live with it. They wanted so bad to get along that they jeered harder than the town folks at those dressed-up black monkeys who had the vote and dared to call themselves Americans, and they never raised a hand to stop the Regulators. Soon after they first arrived, a sniper shot a bluecoat, left him screeching and kicking in the dust on Court House Square. The Union officer in charge never appeared, and those scared bluecoats made no move to find the sniper. My father hinted in his cups that the sniper had been William Coulter, and it might be true.

For all their talk, the Yankees never knew black people and never liked 'em, not the way we did. Our niggers learned that truth real quick when Redemption came in '76 and they were sold out by the Radical Republicans, who turned their backs on their new black friends. The quiet ones lived along as best they could, but the smart-mouthed ones were paid off for their swagger with the rope and bullet. Slavery was gone for good, but the Black Codes and Jim Crow law, the KKK—life hadn't changed much for the black man. There was far more burning and lynching during Redemption than before the War.

Back in '76, General Wade Hampton had become governor, then U.S. senator. The people voted for him although he spoke against Jim Crow law on the new railroads. I didn't go along with that, but I had to admire that rare public man who stood up for his principles, which was why I named my youngest in his honor. I had considered Lucius Selden Watson, after Cousin Selden, but with all my dark memories of Deepwood, I decided that name might curse my little boy with evil luck. Recently Senator Hampton had been run out of office by Ben Tillman's noisy bunch, and it looked like Calbraith Butler might be next. Pitchfork Ben would go far in life with his ranting about black rapists and the sacred honor of our Southern womanhood. No Southerner could disagree with that, but his platform had a lot more noise than thought behind it. As Frank pointed out, we had no black rapists in Arkansas Prison, only white ones, because black ones never got that far alive.

Anyway, this man and I had escaped together, we had swum the river. He wasn't just any old nigger, he was my partner. I rode back over there and stuck my hand out, wished him luck. First time in my whole damned life I ever offered to shake hands with a black man, and he didn't take it—or not until he looked me over, and even then there was a very awkward pause. When he finally stuck out that limp cool hand, he let me do the shaking, and that riled me.

The tension between us as I rode away finally turned me like a ranging dog at the end of a long rope. I had to see if that black man was still there under the trees. He was. He hadn't moved a muscle. I tried a wave and his arm never twitched, not even to touch his hat brim. I rode back there a second time, aiming to warn him how that kind of insolence might get him into bad trouble in Memphis. He regarded me for one more moment, then lifted his hat the same way he had put out his hand. His face looked like a block of hard dark wood.

Controlling myself, I reminded Frank that in Memphis, the law would be on the lookout for a fugitive, it was only a matter of time before they got him. If he really wanted a fresh start in life, he could ride southeast to Columbia County, Florida, where my friend Will Cox, who was now using my cabin, would oblige me by finding him some work. I was very careful not to say that I might turn up there myself before the year was out.

He nodded but he didn't thank me, didn't even answer. I had nothing more to say, yet I didn't go. We sat our horses by the river in the cool spring wind, watching long strings of sandhill cranes coming up across the country from the south. I reckon we were awaiting something that might mend our mood. Finally, I said, Well, so long, and turned my horse away. I never looked back. Maybe Frank Reese lifted his hat, maybe he didn't.

The Shadow Cousin

I rode across the backlands of America, tracing the south border of Tennessee. Hunting my supper from the saddle, I could not afford to waste my loads, and I'm proud to say that, by the end, I hardly ever missed with that revolver. I took squirrel, turkey, and one fawn, a red grouse, here and there a rabbit.

Torn and filthy in the German's baggy clothes, I rode over the Great Smokies into Carolina. The mountain people were suspicious of lone riders, and I had to shoot more than one mean hound along the way. After twenty years of exile, I was restless and excited, and very clear about what I had come for. I would honor my vow and settle my account with Ring-Eye Lige.

Years ago, when they first arrived in Florida, those Herlongs had brought word that Elijah D. Watson was still kicking up trouble around Edgefield Court House. Before tracking him down, I was curious to learn what that trouble was. Dismounting at the horse trough near the hotel, I crossed the small fenced park among the China trees and went into the Archives Library, which kept records of our prominent county families. In these close quarters, in the stuffy air, I was offended by my own badgerish stink and beggar's clothes, but the elderly librarian, Miss Mims, quiet and courteous, pretended to take no notice of my condition as she came and went, fetching me documents.

From census information in the Watson file, I discovered that my grandfather had been wealthy and that my father had wasted more inheritance than we ever knew. I had scarcely learned this when a large old lady came barging through the door, waving her cane at me even as she entered. From the librarian's resigned expression, it was plain to see that this personage accosted every visitor she chanced to spot coming through the Archives door.

My great-aunt Sophia Boatright—for that is who it was—was elderly now, the last of my grandfather's generation. In pink bonnet and raspberry gown, she looked and smelled like a giant peony, and her perfume was no doubt powerful enough to block my scent. "It's always gratifying to see manners, my good man," said she, as I hunched down among my documents, "but please don't get up on my account." Laying her hand upon my shoulder, she pressed me down like a jack-in-the-box, the better to scan my reading matter. "Aha!" she said. "Since you, no doubt"—she leaned back to inspect me closer—"are a stranger in these parts, you might not know all that you should about some of our great Edgefield heroes, the earliest of whom was said to be my grandfather." She tapped the page and there he was, the deathless Captain Michael. "Do you know who else was born in Edgefield? William Travis, hero of the Alamo, and Lewis Wigfall, who led South Carolina's secession—we were the flagship of the Confederacy—and almost every governor our state has had!" She drew from her large reticule a worn copy of an editorial from the Charleston *News and Courier,* which she spread on top of my reading matter on the table.

> Edgefield had more dashing, brilliant, romantic figures,
> statesmen, orators, soldiers, adventurers, daredevils than
> any county of South Carolina, if not any rural county of
> America . . .

"Think of that! Right there in the Charleston newspaper! And General Martin W. Gary, 'the Bald Eagle of the Confederacy,' came from Edgefield, too. Rallied the Redshirts from his balcony up the street at Oakley Park—

'The Redshirt Shrine.' General Gary and General M. C. Butler and Miss Douschka Pickens, 'South Carolina's Joan of Arc.' August 12, 1876! Yes, indeed! Redemption Day! They put on red shirts and marched with fifteen hundred volunteers down to the Court House."

Dutifully I followed her strong finger, which was pointed at the door onto the square. "The Heroes of 1876! Centennial of the American Revolution! Put Wade Hampton in as governor and cleaned the rascals out! So much for so-called Yankee Reconstruction!" She slapped a leaflet down upon my documents. "There," she said. "This nice paper we got up for visitors tells all about it."

> *In that dark period when South Carolina was prostrate, the honor of womanhood was imperiled, brutal insults forced upon citizens by foulmouthed freedmen were more than flesh and blood could endure, and civilization itself hung in the balance . . .*

"See that?" Aunt Sophia tapped the page. "Honor of womanhood!" Dutifully I read around that tapping finger.

> *All over the State men organized Saber Clubs and Rifle Clubs in utmost secrecy. Even as Paul Revere had ridden for freedom's sake a century before, South Carolina Red Shirts rode in grim determination, daring all for liberty . . . Danger lurked in ambush, shots rang out from the forests, and a riderless horse might go on its way alone, but the Red Shirts rode on . . .*

"The Red Shirts rode on!" cried my kinswoman with real emotion, standing erect and straight as any soldier. Her eyes shone bright, and the feather in her cocked hat fairly bristled. No longer a giant peony, she resembled a very fierce old leghorn chicken.

Mildly the librarian remarked that Edgefield's Red Shirts were "just fine" but that elsewhere, red-shirted vigilantes had burned out houses and murdered defenseless Negroes. Edgefield's own Rifle and Sabre Club had terrorized not only black folks but the Radical Republicans who supported them. On July fourth of '76, in the black community at Hamburg, Independence Day had been celebrated with the murder of five unarmed black militiamen. In the presence of their terrified families, they were hauled into the street and told to run, whereupon the Sabre Club shot them to pieces. Finally General Butler shouted a warning that the next "patriot" to shoot a Negro would be executed. General Butler had behaved responsibly, if a bit late, but elsewhere "the Red Shirts had quite a violent reputation," the librarian suggested.

Aunt Sophia glared hard at this nigger lover. Although genteel Miss Mims came from an old Edgefield family related to our own, my great-aunt wished to know if perchance she had been born someplace up North? "Personally, I'm proud of our violent reputation," she declared, not waiting for an answer but turning her broad raspberry back on this fainthearted naysayer. "The United States of America, as some are calling it, could use a little more of our Old Edgefield spirit. This country has gone softer than milk toast. Why, all around the world we just take *anything* these days, and from any color!"

"In that case," I said to her then, "you'll be sure to know where I might locate a relative of yours, Captain Michael's great-great-grandson." "Of course!" she cried. "Yes! Which one?" And I said, "Mr. E. D. Watson." I raised my brows as if perplexed by her consternation. "Better known, I'm told, as Ring-Eye Lige."

Objecting to my stink for the first time, Aunt Sophia recoiled and coughed and put her hand up to her throat. "Sir, this is an archives library, not a poorhouse or some low saloon!" And firing a last furious glare of blame at poor Miss Mims, she swept out the door in a great waft of funereal perfume.

*

When I told Miss Mims that the Watson file contained no recent record of Elijah D., whom I was anxious to locate, she hesitated before advising me that his name had been dropped from the county census after 1870. "He was not dead, but his place in the community—" Here she stopped to confess that she had withheld an 1878 document entitled "Trial of the Booth and Toney Homicides," which turned out to be a trial transcript of an infamous local episode in which four men had died.

In 1878, on the two-year anniversary of Redemption Day, with the entire county gathered to hear rousing speeches by Governor Hampton and other dignitaries, a shoot-out occurred inside and outside Clisby's Store just down the street. Three men died, with several others seriously wounded. According to one account, Elijah D. Watson had been in the crowd at Clisby's and had probably fired, after which he apparently took to his heels.

> Burrell Abney called for the defense, sworn and examined by General
> Butler.
> Were you at Edgefield Court House on the twelfth of August, 1878?
> Yes, sir.
> Did you see any of the difficulty that occurred there on that day?

Yes, sir.

Will you please state to the court and jury what you saw that day?

I saw Elijah Watson running toward where I was from Clisby's Store with a pistol in his hand.

Had the firing stopped when you saw him running off?

It was just before the firing stopped, for I think there were three or four shots fired afterwards.

Was he running from the fray before it ended? Very likely. Had he fired fatally, then made an expedient departure? Was he a coward? I had never been certain of my father's courage.

Elijah Watson and William Coulter were among four men indicted for murder. My father's attorneys were "Gary & Gary" and also John L. Addison, his brother-in-law. In his summation, General Gary called these homicides "the most desperately fought combat that ever transpired in this dark and bloody region." The Bald Eagle of the Confederacy would discount the testimony that placed Elijah Watson at the scene, whereas Ring-Eye's old nemesis, General M. C. Butler, passionately argued the reverse.

Despite a threat by the prosecution, denounced by the Judge, that if the jury "let loose a criminal upon the community, the people of Edgefield may rise up in their might and do justice themselves, and in such an event, some harm may come to you," the primary defendant was acquitted in just twenty minutes. Since none of the attorneys saw any point in repeating the testimony with the other defendants, the same jury was resworn next morning and rendered an immediate verdict of "not guilty" in each case. On October fourteenth of 1879, it was ordered by the court that all defendants be permitted to go home.

The trial transcript had established that within a few years after his family had abandoned him, the fallen Lige had wandered into dissolution, sharing a disreputable roof with "the Widow Autrey." Miss Mims confessed that she had no acquaintance of Mrs. Autrey nor any idea what had become of Mr. Watson. When she'd tried to inquire about him from one of the library's founders—and she nodded toward the door through which Aunt Sophia had made her getaway—she was told that as far as his whole clan was concerned, Elijah D. was dead. "He's what the old folks used to call a shadow cousin. They just don't talk about him, kept him clean out of the census. When his name comes up, you never heard a subject changed so fast!"

Unaware that we were speaking of my father, yet sensing an unhealthy curiosity, she remarked tactfully that Mr. E. D. Watson was not the only shadow cousin in this county, not by a long shot, mostly because of Edgefield's long tradition of violence. There had been so many killings here, right to the present day, that no man in this district went unarmed. Not long ago, a mad dog was wandering Augusta's streets, and all the men ran around trying to find a gun. At last someone thought to poke his head into a saloon and holler, "Any man here from Edgefield?" I smiled politely, but Miss Mims assured me it was not a joke.

If anything, the violence had worsened after 1877, when the new President, Mr. Hayes, withdrew the Union troops, leaving the "darkies," as she called them, to the mercies of white vigilantes. She brought me a newspaper account by a local black attorney. "Colored men are daily being hung, shot, and otherwise murdered and ill-treated because of their complexion and politics. While I write, a colored woman comes and tells me her husband was killed last night in her presence and her children burned to death in the house. Such things are common occurrences." In the same period, it came out that only half of the 285 black convicts in this county contracted out for labor on the Greenville-Augusta Railroad had survived the job.

I caught Miss Mims observing me to see how much I knew. Those Herlongs had told Mama that not long before they left, Lige Watson had found work as a state prison guard. Had he also been a road gang guard during the building of that railroad? An embittered Confederate veteran who had lost his land and reputation and was prone to drunken violence was just the man to oversee black convicts.

"E. D. Watson," I said tersely. "Any record of illegitimate children?"

She located a handwritten note, dated 1889, in what looked like Colonel Robert's hand. "E. D. Watson: Son Jacob, Mulatto. Born Augusta 1854. Lynched in southeast Georgia ca. 1882."

*

Aching with peculiar feelings, I went outside into Court House Square and gazed about me in the cold spring light. The town seemed empty, with not one soul to be seen. Where the famous homicides had taken place, the name A. A. Clisby could be made out on the faded sign over the door. I tried to imagine my red, sweating father, pistol in hand, reeling across these dusty cobbles on a stifling August afternoon. How many times since his family had deserted him had he been haled up those courthouse steps in full view of his neighbors, to be shoved into the cells by shouting bailiffs?

Before riding all the way out to the Ridge, I made inquiries about him at the tavern.

Elijah D.? You mean ol' Ring-Eye? Pretty bad drinker? Lived with the Widder Autrey, one we called Ol' Scrap? Well, that feller lost his work gang job a few years back. He was usin up too many niggers building track beds for the Greenville railroad. Went through chain gang hands like goobers, worked 'em straight to death, ol' Ring-Eye did. They told him, Ring-Eye, dammit all, maybe them monkeys come down out of the trees, but they don't grow on trees, goddamnit, and good green money ain't the same as leaves! And he had him a feud with the Booth boys before that, a real bad fracas right there by the courthouse, three, four men was laying dead by the time them fellers finished. Nosir, ol' Ring-Eye could not stay out of trouble, he was givin his family a bad name. So finally them Watsons come to fetch him, hauled him over to Ridge Spring—don't know Ridge Spring? That's the new railroad crossin. Reckon it's still "the Ridge" to the old-timers. Got Ring-Eye out there at the boneyard tendin their Watson dead, cause he sure ain't welcome around any that's alive. Ol' Ring-Eye! Yessiree! Now there's a feller could tell you a war story or two, and never bother his head one bit about the truth of it.

That's where I caught up with him, digging a new grave in our Rock Wall cemetery at Ridge Spring. I watched him wheezing in his pit not forty feet away, resting after every spade of dirt. Seeing a horseman on the highroad, he doffed his soiled slouch hat. "That you, Will? You looking for me, Will? Yessir, you just name it, Will, Lige Watson is your man and proud to help."

Realizing the rider was not Coulter, he cursed and turned away. But after a few more aimless pokes at the cold earth, he leaned the spade into the corner of the grave, put his hands on the brown grass behind him, and kicked himself up and back a little so that he was seated on the edge. All set to engage in civilized palaver with a passerby, he mopped his brow. "Yessir, it sure is hot enough," he offered.

For the moment, I ignored him, let him sweat a little. With the Watson archive still fresh in my head, I inspected the walled cemetery with new interest, recalling all the family lore about the fabled Michael's widow, Martha, who had felt obliged to wed one Jacob Odom, a churlish man of muddy origins and low degree who had lived back down this road. Annoyed by the widow's reduced expectations, Odom had confirmed the family's poor opinion of him by making poor Martha pay room and board for her four small children.

On Saturday, May 21, 1791, General George Washington had honored the hero's widow and her children by lodging with them overnight on his journey from Augusta to Columbia. On this occasion, "the odious Odom," as Aunt Sophia called him, attempted to charge the first president of the United States for bed and board. Fittingly, it was young Polly Watson (rather than some malodorous Odom offspring), who was taken upon the presidential knee and presented with an enamel snuffbox containing a new twenty-dollar gold piece. That coin was in the proud possession of Aunt Polly's daughter over in Greenville at this very moment.

When Martha died in 1817, her remains, contaminated by Odom's name, were forbidden interment in this cemetery. One of her two Odom children was subsequently installed there surreptitiously, and Aunt Polly—the keeper of the presidential gold piece—had raised an immemorial rumpus. *An Odom has snuck himself inside the Rock Wall, and I want him out!* Exhumed forthwith, the half-decayed half brother passed dusty days right here beside the highroad before the disgruntled Odoms would collect him.

"Looking for somebody?" bawled Ring-Eye Lige. For I had dismounted and climbed the wall to inspect the headstones. "Private property, Mister," he hollered next. "Watson property, dammit!"

Our Watson stones were of white marble set on brick foundations. Captain Michael's son Elijah Julian (the Old Squire)—who as a boy had met President Washington right down this road—was there, as well as Elijah Junior (the Young Squire) and his brother Artemas, who shared an obelisk with my grandmother Mary Lucretia ("Come unto me all ye weary and heavy-laden and I will give you rest"), and also the Old Squire's youngest daughter, Ann, late wife of Robert Myers of Columbia, dead at age twenty-two. Scraping at black lichen with an oak twig, I traced part of Ann Watson Myers's inscription.

A MYSTERIOUS PROVIDENCE VERY SUDDENLY REMOVED
THIS WIFE AND MOTHER OF THREE SMALL CHILDREN FROM THE
RESPONSIBILITY OF TIME TO THE AWARDS OF ETERNITY.

Of course. Robert Myers's brother had married Laura Watson. These "three small children"—now older than myself—included the nephews in William Myers's will who were supposed to inherit his plantation but would only do so over Sam Tolen's dead body.

*

Wary, my father had clambered to his feet, gripping his shovel. Behind him, in the corner of the wall, brown leaves swirled in the wind eddies like small winter birds.

Awaiting him, I let the revolver slide into my hand. I hoped he would make my mission easier, permit me to get it over faster, by attempting to drive me violently out of the cemetery. He was considering this as he crept forward, but something about me gave him pause. When I turned to face him, he retreated a little toward his fresh grave. "Looks snug enough to curl right up in, don't it?" he called cheerily in a hoarse whiskey voice. "Got half a mind to lay down in there myself."

"Good idea," I said.

My father laughed too loudly and too long. I winced, remembering how quickly his drunkard's conviviality could turn mean. Hearing my voice, he squinted in suspicion, trying to peer at the man behind the beard.

Lige Watson had changed, too, not for the better. He was glaze-eyed, shiny-skinned, unshaven, with a red pulpy nose and greasy gray hair with yellowed hanks down to his shoulders. When he saw the revolver in my hand, his eyes narrowed and his nostrils dilated in a kind of snarl and his hand groped the air behind him for the spade. The scar circling that half-popped eye of his turned livid.

Ring-Eye straightened kind of slow while he figured out what he was going to do next. "Old soldier," he blustered, pointing at the scar. "And a pauper, like you." He pulled the empty pockets from his britches.

A moment later, his eyes widened and he forced a dreadful smile, spreading his bony arms for an embrace. "Edgar," he gargled. And he shook his hoary head in awe of that Mysterious Providence which had returned the long lost prodigal to the pining father. Then he abandoned this course, too, crouching a little, hefting the shovel, undecided whether to charge now or work his way closer first. I made an impatient sideways gesture with the revolver, and he tossed the shovel down.

"So you've come to kill your father in cold blood." Sneering, he lifted his filthy coat, tugged at his empty pockets. The sneer was for his rags as well as mine. He hiked his pants, exposing begrimed white shins and broken boots—he had no stockings—to show me how paltry the murder would be, how empty my revenge, how little it would signify to either of us. He dropped his pant legs and stood straight. "Well, from the looks of it, you never come to much. You're no damn better off than I am."

Ring-Eye's tone was sardonic but his wheeze was rapid. His old pants snapped in the wind, his eyes were darting. He could not fathom why I remained silent. "Your mother and sister," he pled next. "They're getting by all right?"

I waved the revolver toward the open grave. "Lie down in there," I said.

He took a deep breath and composed himself a moment, looking around the little cemetery at the stones of buried kin. "Might be the only way I'll get into this place." His grin was brief, more like a wince, but it was genuine enough. "Still looking for revenge, boy? After twenty years?" Frowning, he brushed red dirt off his soiled knees, then lowered himself with a desultory groan into the grave. "Of course you are." He spat forcefully in my direction. "You ever read all those Greek books? Retribution? Was it Plato who said that life was terrible but it wasn't serious? Your grandfather could quote such things, they say. I never knew him. Never knew much of anything, when you get right down to it."

When I didn't answer, he just shrugged. He lay down in the pit and folded mottled hands upon his chest. "Send your sainted mother my respects." He sighed, closing his eyes. "Shoot straight if you are man enough," he growled, mustering up some last-minute contempt. Though he would not beg, he was clenching his eyes tight, for he was not a steadfast man. A moment later, he was choking on his terror. "You cold-eyed son of a cold-hearted bitch!" he yelled, to keep his nerve up. "Finish it!"

Standing there over the grave, I knew I had come all this long way for nothing. I no longer cared whether Ring-Eye Lige Watson lived or died, so I would do well to forsake my vow of twenty years in the hope of returning to Clouds Creek in the future.

His eyes were still clenched as I moved away. From the damp hole his voice rose in despair. "Shoot, then, damn you. *Shoot!*"

His punishment today would be not death but the emptiness of life. When he dared open his eyes, in two minutes or ten, all he would see was the hard rim of the grave, framing the high swift clouds out of the north and the bare branches of the graveyard trees, the dark wind-borne autumn birds which left no trace of their passage down the sky.

*

From the cemetery I rode over to the Artemas Plantation. The old house was gone, sunk away in punky rot, grown over in vines of creeper and dark ivy. In the mourning grove of black walnut and oak, the ancient sheds leaned away into the weeds. My fields, descending to Clouds Creek, had been hacked to ragged triangles by transient sharecroppers, gullied and eroded down to raw red iron clay.

I rode on eastward toward the Ridge, now called Ridge Spring, where I dismounted near Colonel Robert's house. I did not know what I hoped for after twenty years—recognition, I suppose. Hearing the dogs, he came outside before I reached the steps. The silence in the house behind made me wonder if Aunt Lucy had passed away. He drove the dogs off me.

Robert Briggs Watson looked very much the same, though grayer, more granitic. Unlike my father, he knew me at once despite my heavy beard and begrimed appearance, which told him everything our clan might care to know about how Ring-Eye's son had fared in the great world. His expression was neither cold nor warm. He did not speak because he had not seen me. Edgar Watson, like his father, was a shadow cousin. In a moment he would return inside and close that door.

"I named my first son after you," I blurted. Awkwardly, I offered my hand. He pretended not to see it, gazing away over the road. Looking past me was his warning that I was still an outcast and a fugitive. I understood that if I left at once and kept on going, he would not betray me, even to this household.

I rode away bruised by his disappointment. But he had kindled one small flame of hope. Had I imagined it? Before he turned and went into the house, without once meeting my gaze, Robert Watson had spoken two brief words. "Not yet," he said.

*

On the way west toward Edgefield Court House, I rode into the old carriage-way at Deepwood, seeking some sort of empty absolution in paying this useless homage to Selden Tilghman. The old trees seemed larger, while the black ruin shrouded in thick binding vine seemed smaller, drawn in on itself. I sat my horse awhile, not daring to dismount, in dread of spirits. Since the Owl-Man's death, I had dreamt of Deepwood many many times, a terrible dream involving a hidden body which in the end would surely be discovered. The grave, too shallow, was quaking underfoot, as if the cadaver, bloated and rising, was on the point of bursting through the grass. Unable to flee it, I would wake up howling.

Selden Tilghman, who died violently, had detested the legendary violence in his family, Mama had told us. Attributing their uproar to plain ignorance, her cousin reverted to the ancestral Tilghman in order to separate himself, he said, from "those among my kinsmen who have grown so contemptuous of learning that they no longer know the correct spelling of their own name."

Cousin Selden would not have been surprised that in this Great Depression year his cousin Ben Tillman and his rabble-rousers would found their own Populist Party, which jeered at the other parties and the press for their shameful subservience to the industrialists and the bought-and-paid-for politicians they put in office. Mostly redneck farmers and farm laborers, the Populists joined with factory workers and solicited black votes to go after the capitalists who hogged all the profits and permitted the poor to starve in the name of progress. Pitchfork Ben would go on to win election to the U.S. Senate, taking his safe seat away from Calbraith Butler. Very soon, Ben Tillman would revert to the know-nothing nigger baiting of his snag-toothed rednecks, who had only a passing acquaintance with the language—*Maht not know nuthin, but Ah know whut Ah know!* By that time, Pitchfork Ben had lost his black supporters. "The Negro has been infected with the virus of equality," Old Ben complained.

*

I rode hard toward the west, reaching Hamburg on the Savannah River after dark. In this place, in 1819, a slave rebellion led by Coot or Coco had filled the entire Piedmont region with night fear. Since I'd passed through here twenty years before, this once Radical town had been burned half off the map, and what was left had been given a new name, North Augusta—a sad and sorry place where I had trouble hunting up something to eat.

An old hostler whose bad cold grub I shared confirmed the story that this former nest of Republicans and their smart niggers was the place where Selden Tilghman had been taken to be tarred and feathered, no doubt as a lesson to the inhabitants. "Whipped that dang traitor into strips, he was just a-*beggin* them to kill him. Looked horrible when they got done with him."

Redemption arrived on Independence Day of 1876, when the Edgefield Sabre Club in their red shirts had shot down those black militiamen out in this street. The old man had seen that with his own eyes, too. When I asked if a big rufous man with a staring red ring around his eye had taken part, the man gave me a queer look and said, "You know something? He *did*! Took part in the tar and feathers, too."

Next morning I crossed on the Savannah River ferry and headed south to Waycross, over east of the Okefenokee. There I went hunting for Lem Collins, being curious to hear my erstwhile friend explain why he had shifted the blame for the John Hayes killing onto Edgar Watson, and obtain his opinion on my proposal that he notify the Columbia County Sheriff that Watson was innocent and always had been. I could not find him because he had changed his name, though I never learned that until I reached Fort White.

In Waycross, I hunted up a man named Smith who had kindly befriended me on my first journey south back in 1870. We went to a tavern for some talk. He kept cocking his head to look at me more carefully, and finally he told me that a man of my same name had got himself lynched here in this district just a few years back. "Reason I think of it," he said, "he looked somethin like you—same kind of colorin." He grew red in the face. "Jacob Watson," he said, as I got my breath. "Ever hear of him?"

"Never did," I said, maybe a second too slow.

"Well, you never know," he muttered, strangely disturbed. "Called himself a nigger, he was proud about it—*nigger to the bone*, he said. And him just as white as you or me, to look at. Crazy man. But he sure showed some guts, there at the last of it. Nobody ain't never forgot that feller, not around here."

Eager to relate the whole grim story, Smith was restrained only by my show of indifference. He invited me home for the night, to wash my feet and meet the daughters. There were four if I counted correctly, and every one a head taller than the guest—huge strong young females twice my weight who ate like horses and drank me under the table. Once their daddy had turned in with a loud snoring, those giant girls came down there after me, they actually tore the nice clean duds their dad had lent me so mine could get a wash. I never saw such love-starved critters in my life. One lugged me over to her corn-shuck mattress to finish up the job, and I do believe all the others had their way with me before the dawn. I did my best but, being drunk, I never got the hang of 'em some way, they just weren't made right.

I was glad to make my getaway next morning, clawed and gnawed up pretty good but in one piece. One of those strapping daughters, Little Hannah, would loom large in my life again years later, by which time—with no sisters around to steal her thunder—she had become known as Big Hannah instead. By then we couldn't quite recall just what had taken place under that table, but Big Hannah blushed. "You had you a whole heap of womanhood, all right," she said, "and done pretty good, too."

*

Crossing over into Florida, I headed south along the river road on the west bank of the Suwannee. All that bare cypress, all that Spanish moss hanging everywhere like gray dead hair, and doleful vultures hunched on the black snags. *All the world is sad and dreary, everywhere I roam*—that old song really got the feel of that swamp forest in dark weather, reminding me less of the old folks at home than of black Joseph, dead among the roots in the Clouds Creek swamp. I sorely missed dear Mandy and the children, and worried how Baby Lucius might be getting on.

Cypress Creek, White Springs. The next day, I knew the country and waited till night to ride down past Lake City. Though no one at Fort White would expect me, I stayed close to the woods, taking no chances. On the books I was a dead man, drowned in the muddy Arkansas, and I meant to keep it that way, because being dead was the best way I knew of to stay out of trouble.

In those long days in the saddle, I changed my name for good to E. Jack Watson. For a fugitive, new initials made good sense, and anyway, my great-grandfather had been Elijah Julian. As "the ramrod of the family," the Old Squire might be just the man to change my luck.

*

Determined to get things straight with Billy Collins, I went to his house first. This was December 1892. Little Julian Edgar, close to my Eddie's age, was already a sweet-faced young feller, and we went hand-in-hand to find his mama, who had an infant toiling at the breast. A second boy was already up and toddling. His name is Willie, little Julian whispered, and that one at the teat is Baby May.

With the baby fussing, Minnie did not notice our delegation in the cookhouse door.

"Company for supper, Min," I whispered.

She gasped, backing away. She was deathly afraid for her dear Billy, and her eyes implored me even as she babbled how happy she was to see her long-lost brother. I promised her if she stayed out of the way while I finished up my business, everything would probably be all right. Not knowing what "probably" might mean, she started crying.

When Billy came, I was sitting on his porch, the exact same place I sat five years before. He stopped short at the gate. Seeing little Julian on my knee, he mustered up some courage, came ahead. "Well, Edgar," he started, kind of gruff, "this sure is a surprise."

Minnie came rushing out to greet her husband. She told me how thrilled she was that I had made such good friends with Julian Edgar, and even claimed the child was named for me, which was no less a lie than it had been when she first told it right after he was born. I waved her back inside, intent on Billy. When he sat down, I passed him his child, which needed changing, and questioned him about local attitudes toward Edgar Watson. I wanted to know if it was safe to bring my family home, and I wanted an honest answer. Billy asked for a little time to think that over.

A pretty wench with shadow in her face brought a pail of milk, waved cheerily, and went away again. Who's that? I said. Depends, Billy said. She is called Jane Straughter, Minnie giggled. Might be a Robart, Billy said. Her daddy might be your old friend J.C. I thought about Jane Straughter all that evening. She had got under my skin some way, she made me restless, and one day I meant to have her—kind of a life promise, like Clouds Creek.

At supper I told most of my news, how a son Lucius had been born in Arkansas, how I had paid a call on Ring-Eye Lige.

Minnie said, "O Lordy, Edgar, you didn't—" She could not speak it, and I had no intention of explaining. Minnie would never face the truth—that if I shot her father and nailed him into his box, ending her nightmares that Ring-Eye Lige might track her down in Florida, she would be overjoyed, yet flail herself for her inability to grieve. She was condemned by her badly broken nature to find nothing but torment in every circumstance while seeking in all directions for forgiveness.

*

Having stolen Cousin Laura's poor old heart, Sam Tolen was hot after her money and had already renamed our place Tolen Plantation. Sam was so messy that he took up all the air in the old cabin, and since more room was needed for this happy household, Great-Aunt Tab had gone ahead with the construction of the two-story plantation house that William Myers had been planning when he died.

Meanwhile, our dear mother, Minnie said, had been made to feel unwelcome under the Tolen roof and was anxious to come live here in this little house, help take care of her grandchildren. "But unless she brings Aunt Cindy, she'll be no help at all," Minnie complained. "Of course we'll be sure to give her your respects," she added nervously, as if I were just leaving.

I wasn't figuring on going anyplace, I said. I wanted to bring my family home and settle down here. I turned to Billy, all set to receive his honest opinion.

Billy frowned deeply, weighing his words. "You asked for an honest answer," he reminded me, with a glance at his pale wife. "So to be honest—to be *real* honest, I mean—I wouldn't honestly come home as yet if I was you." He blurted out his speech all in a breath. This community was still looking for someone to pay for the killing of John Hayes. I was sure to be arrested, and even if I escaped conviction, I was a wanted man in Arkansas, where I would be returned in chains.

Billy and Minnie had made it plain without quite meaning to that the Collins clan, not to mention the Watson women at the plantation—the whole damned bunch, in short—would be greatly relieved if Edgar Watson would make himself scarce for a few more years if not the remainder of his life.

"What makes you think that I'm wanted in Arkansas?"

Billy was ready. "Sheriff's office in Lake City was notified by telegraph to be on the lookout for an E. A. Watson."

"That was the first news we had that you might be alive!" cried my pale sister as Little May suckled, watching me with round shining eyes over her mother's tit.

Minnie was pleasured in her nursing in a way that could not be concealed by that innocent air of milky sweet self-satisfaction peculiar to the young mother, who imagines herself and her yowling, stinky bundle on a golden cloud at the heart of all Creation. But being able to stand back a bit and consider my sister after these years away, I had to acknowledge that other men might admire this dim scared creature more than I did. Minnie was pretty, even beautiful, I suppose, with her alabaster skin and full red lips, but her flesh looked spiritless, with no more spring in it than a lump of suet.

"Also," Billy was pleading, "Will Cox is taking good care of your cabin, so you won't have to worry about that."

"You have any safe place I can sleep?" Sprawled in the old family rocker while they scurried to find bedding, I felt saddle sore and weary and begrimed by life, and mortally homesick for a home I had never had except across these woods in that old Robart cabin with my Charlie. Here I was in my mid-thirties, a damned drifter. I couldn't go home to Clouds Creek and I couldn't go home to Fort White, and the Indian Territories were dangerous, too. I would have to start all over someplace else.

Not knowing that my grim expression had nothing to do with them, these kin of mine were sick with dread, looking away like they'd been whipped across the face. I sat quiet, thinking my life over. Life was great and life was terrible and life could not be one without the other—that was all I knew, which is not to say that I understood it.

Leaned way forward, arms upon his knees, Billy was too eager to tell me about the Smallwood and McKinney families which had moved south to Fort Ogden and Arcadia. "Man could do a heck of a lot worse than a fresh start down in that new country, that's what they wrote back to their kinfolks." He frowned to show how much real thought he'd put into this matter. "Yessir, Ed, a *hell* of a lot worse!" That was the first time I ever heard a Collins swear in the presence of a woman. I winced and shifted as if mortally offended, to see if Minnie would squeal "*Bill*-lee!" which she did.

I said, "I will head on south, send for my family when I find a place." Nin rushed to fetch me Mandy's address—c/o Bell, Broken Bow, Indian Territory. She was so relieved I would be gone by daybreak that she promised faithfully that the family would send to Arkansas for my wife and children and take good care of them until they could rejoin me. Those Collinses were overjoyed to see me go.

I told them to keep their eye out for a black man named Frank Reese, find him some work. "Don't forget, you never saw hide nor hair of me," I reminded Billy, who came outside as I swung up into the saddle. The moon was going down behind the open pinelands, waking the first crows and bobwhite quail. "So far as you have ever heard, Watson is dead, all right?"

"All right by me." Billy Collins didn't crack too many jokes, but I gave him the benefit of the doubt and laughed a little. He laughed, too, but his heart wasn't in it.

Arcadia

I forded the Santa Fe below Fort White and headed south across the Alachua Prairie where the early Indians and Spaniards ran their cattle. To the east, early next morning, strange dashes of red color went drifting through the blowing tops of prairie sedges where the sun touched the crowns of cranes, which I had last seen in the Oklahoma Territory. As they moved away over the dew-sparkled savanna, their strange wild ancient horn and rattle drifted back on the fresh wind. That blood-red glint of life in the brown grasslands, that long calling—why should such fleeting moments pierce the heart? And yet they do. That was what Charlie Collins made me see. They do.

Wolf, bear, and panther sign was everywhere in this wild country—I heard a panther scream more nights than not. Plenty of game and wild boar, too, and a lot of scrub cattle on the wandering dim trails through the palmetto. I tended south and east along the Yeehaw Marshes—Muskogee for red wolf, some said, while others claimed it came from the *yee* and *haw* of wagon harness. Where a trail turned off southwest toward the Peace River,

I stayed overnight with Captain Billy Smith, a cousin of those big man-eating Smiths in the Okefenokee. Captain Billy was planting some wild oranges for his first citrus grove, said he had high hopes that citrus would do well in the Peace River country. He invited me to throw in with him, and I thanked him but said no, I aimed to clear off a piece of the back country, get established on my own. Next morning I rode down along the river, and on into Arcadia that afternoon, dead broke and dirty.

As far away as the Arkansas prison, the word was out that a resolute man who was easy with a horse and gun and kept his mouth shut could make good money a lot faster in De Soto County, Florida, than anywhere west of the Mississippi. Unlike most prison rumors, this one turned out to be true. For a few years in the early nineties, the range wars around Arcadia beat anything the Wild West had to offer. The ranchers were advertising for gunslingers as far off as St. Louis, and every outfit had its own gang of hard riders. With so many rough men in the saloons, a man could get his fill of fighting any time he wanted, and be lulled to sleep at night by the pop of gunfire. A lot of these brawls might start with fists, but every man was quick to use a weapon before the other feller beat him to it. Fifty bloody fights a day were not uncommon; four men were killed in one shoot-out alone. The year before, a new brick jail had to be built to hold the overflow, and as it turned out, that new jail saved my life.

A rancher with the wherewithal could hire new riders every day at the nearest whorehouse or saloon, but Arcadia House was where you met all the best people, including the famous Bone Mizell, who liked to chew on a steer's ear to put his brand on him. One time, folks said, ol' Bone was so darn drunk they figured he was dead so they laid him in his grave, got set to bury him. When the first clod hit him in the chest, Bone sat straight up and looked around, yelled, "Resurrection Day! And guess who is first man up!"

At Arcadia House, any hard stranger leaned back on the bar and waited like a whore to be looked over. I wasn't through my second whiskey when a big man, Durrance, bought the third. Will Durrance spoke of the hard feelings over the rangeland on Myakka Prairie, and the cattle rustling all across the county—not just a steer or two shot by some mangy cracker in the piney woods but whole damn herds, up to three hundred head. Most of that range was unfenced, choked with dry palmetto thicket. A steer could wander halfway across Florida, get lost for two years before it wandered out again, and not be missed. Plenty of calves were dropped in the deep scrub and went unbranded, so naturally, you burned on your own brand as fast as you could get a rope on 'em and drag 'em to your fire, figuring another man would do the same. Local hospitality for any stranger on your territory was to hang him from the nearest live oak, go your way with a free mind. "Better safe than sorry"—that was the motto. A lone rider who wanted to turn up some-place alive avoided the woods roads and picked his own route across cattle country, telling no one.

Durrance warned about a feller named Quinn Bass, the bad news in a big cattle clan around Kissimmee. This Quinn liked to play with gun or knife "with any man at any time on any terms and on any provocation." The Sher-iff himself wouldn't mess with Quinn if there was a choice about it, because even for lawmen, a showdown with a Bass was the worst kind of trouble you could ask for, and no local juryman nor judge would go up against them. Why, only this week, Bass and a partner had been acquitted in the killing of a nigger because the white man set to testify he'd seen the killing had been wiped out, too. The whole county knew the ones involved, something to do with a fight over counterfeit money. Nobody believed Bass's story, but no ju-ryman would vote to convict him, either, not over a nigger. ("While every-body was satisfied that they killed the Negro, the evidence was not sufficient to convict them"—those were the words of the jury foreman, quoted in the paper.) So Bass and his partner had been charged instead with the murder of the white man, with the trial coming up next week, and since he was a local feller, they had let him out on bail.

I was here to put a stake together for a new start in life. I had made a promise to myself to avoid trouble. But in Arcadia, I could not say that out loud, not if I wanted a good job as a rider.

"Well, now, Jack," this Durrance said. "I reckon you know how to ride."

"Well, now, Will, I rode all the way from Arkansas by way of Carolina and didn't break my ass in two, not so's you'd notice, so I reckon I'll make it the ten miles out to Myakka Prairie." Durrance laughed and paid my supper and a bed and breakfast and the first bath since I swam the Arkansas, and threw in an advance on a week's pay.

*

Next morning I bought me a shave and a new denim shirt and rode out to the ranch. Will Durrance lived with four rangy hounds in a cleared-off woodlot fenced with barbed wire, in a two-story house with peculiar win-dows high up on the outside wall, so high that no riders could shoot through them at night even from horseback. He set out a tobacco can, gave me and two other hands repeating rifles, said, All right, boys, let's see how good you shoot these Winchesters. The other two shot all right but they had to aim each shot. Fine, said Durrance, and they grinned, sliding their new repeaters into their saddle scabbards. A new Winnie was worth about two months' pay. Come my turn, I danced that can across the cow pen, about as fast as I could pull the trigger, until Durrance hollered, Don't go wastin them good bullets!

His cow hunters, as they call 'em here in Florida, looked me over sideways, rolling smokes. They were two backwoods brothers by the name of Granger, bony men with thick black brows grown right across the forehead in one line, then curving down the sides. Looked like raccoons. Durrance must have signed them on to keep them from shooting his stray beefs to feed their kin. I knew this kind, just getting by in life, losing no sleep. Looked worried that this stranger might bring trouble. This man Jack Watson out of Oklahoma was no sodbuster, the way he said, not the way he handled that repeater. This feller had gunslinger written all over him.

"They turned Bass loose," one Granger said. "Made his acquaintance yet?"

"Nope." I swung onto my horse. "But I look forward to it."

The Granger boys looked skeptical and sour. Will Durrance let us ride away with his new rifles, but from the look of those two backwoods brothers, he could not have been too confident they would be back.

*

One night I was at a bar with Tommy Granger, who was leaning with his back against the rail when a man banged through the door and scanned the place. What I saw in the bar mirror was a squat and squint-eyed runt with bushy whiskers and a big lumpy tobacco chaw which made his mug look too big for his body. Granger turned around too quickly, not wanting to be noticed—a bad mistake with a mean dog with a nose for fear. When Bass saw him turning, Tommy stopped short—mistake number two—then nudged his drinking partner with his elbow. "Bass!" he whispered. That was number three.

Though I hadn't turned, Bass had seen me in the mirror. He strutted up to us, to get a bead on any stranger. His eyes sought mine in the bar mirror, and he took his time sizing me up, in a nodding curled-lip style I didn't care for. "You boys signed on with anybody yet? That fuckin Durrance?" He spat between our boots. "Any sorry sonofabitch would take orders from that shitty bastard ain't no kind of a man at all."

I didn't even blink, and this enraged him. "You some kind of a dummy, Mister?" He slapped my upper arm with the back of his hand. "I'm talking to you," he said. "What's your damned name?"

Not wanting to toss him any bone to gnaw on, I remained silent. He took this as an insult and he was right. He had half a mind to put me out of my misery right here and now, he growled, starting to pant a little, because I sure looked like some sorry skunk on the run from someplace else, so he would be doing somebody a favor.

Arcadia was no different from Edgefield or Fort White or anywhere else on the American frontiers. Not to defend your honor was your finish. A sudden show of his dirt-colored teeth was sign that Bass had me figured for a coward, a man willing to back down from mortal insults. However, he'd had a good look at my eyes and saw that they were steady. Maybe this stranger was unacquainted with his reputation. Maybe this stranger did not fear him after all.

Bass was still panting for some reason. "Let's have some fun," he said. Tommy grinned to be obliging, and Bass hoisted a tobacco-stained forefinger under his nose. "Yank this lever, friend," he said in a thick voice, shifting his chaw to the other cheek. "Just for the fun of it."

Granger had a stiff grin pasted on his face that might have looked more natural if he were dead. He seemed to know—and he turned out to be right—that when he yanked that finger like a lever, Quinn would open that brown mouth—here comes the joke—and let fly a jawful of spit and tobacco juice onto Tommy's face.

Granger glanced at me with an aggrieved expression—a backwoods ruse, because his long frame was already uncoiling. Bass was drunk enough to follow Tommy's eyes, and Tommy's fist cracked him hard in the black bush around his mouth and knocked him sprawling.

If Tommy Granger had meant business, he had plenty of time to put Bass out of commission by kicking him fair and square in the balls or head. But this was Quinn Bass, and Granger knew he had gone too far unless he aimed to kill him. When Bass raised himself onto his elbows, his knife was already in his hand, upright. He looked relaxed. He even smiled a little. Taking his time, he shook his head to clear it. Then he rolled onto his feet, and he was not smiling anymore.

Granger threw me a whipped look as he backed onto his stool. He never even wiped the slime off of his face. "I sure ain't lookin for no trouble, Quinn. You and me always been friendly, ain't that right, Quinn? Hell's fire, Quinn, you wouldn't want no man for a friend who let another feller spit his chaw into his face." He turned to me because he could not look at that knife a moment longer. "Ain't that right, Jack?" This cracker aimed to drag me into this, he was counting on ol' Jack to get him out.

"Let's go, Peckerhead," Quinn rasped, holding the knife blade high. He had backed off enough to give them fighting room.

Granger took his Bowie out and stared at it as if astonished to find such a dangerous weapon on his own person. His nerves were going. When Bass shot a look across at me, Tommy kicked off from the bar, launching himself with an awful squawk like a dying goose. In a moment, they were down rolling around, holding each other's wrists. Granger was bigger, wiry and strong, and in a minute he had Bass's arm twisted up behind his back. Dropping his knife because he had no choice, Quinn yelled, "Okay, you win," and growled at Tommy to let go. Well, that's what that fool did. "Okay by me! Let's quit!" he hollered with a kind of sob, and flung his knife away.

Quinn Bass grabbed up his own knife and sprang astride him, holding the weapon to his throat. He poked Granger with small stabs through his blue shirt, drawing red blots. Because Granger had struck him first, in front of witnesses, the Sheriff would have to call this self-defense. Quinn Bass knew he could take this life for free.

Tommy's arms were stretched wide on the floor. He was coughing pitifully, too scared to talk. "Which ear can you spare?" Bass panted at him, very excited. Tommy's eyes were darting, trying to find me, as Bass awaited the last panicky thrash which would trigger his need to slip the knife in deep. "Which nostril you want slit, you stupid fucker?"

I toed Quinn in the back. Bass twisted around quick as a snake.

"That your fuckin boot?"

"Nosir, it's not. I never saw that boot before in all my life."

Such insolence bore out his worst suspicions. He jumped up and came for me, knife blade out front, held flat and low, as if his dearest aim in life was to cut my heart out. He was only stopped by the sight of my revolver, aimed at point-blank range. One more step and I would have shot him dead. He knew that, too. Being Quinn Bass, he would feel obliged to bait me again, test me again, and sooner or later he would force a fight, unless he became confused and killed me first.

Bass had forgotten about Granger, who had slipped away. "Stranger, this ain't over yet," he promised, as I tipped my hat and backed toward the door. "You and me is going to settle this once and for all."

*

Hearing Granger's report, Durrance exclaimed that I should have shot Bass down in self-defense. After Granger left, I said, "What's in that for me? Besides a murder charge in the dead man's own hometown?" He thought that over. Then he made me a financial proposition and I accepted it, though not without regret.

For all my troubles and my time in prison—where I had been well-tutored in the lethal arts—I had never thought I might become a hired gun. But capital would be needed in south Florida, and the time had come to turn my life around. I could even argue I was doing a good deed. But no matter how often I told myself that Quinn Bass was the worst kind of news, I had no right to take his life on that account. For a Watson of Clouds Creek, it was dishonor. I had to accept that, and I did, and I do today. Will Durrance withdrew his offer after Bass was convicted of first-degree murder and sent away for life. The county was scared of Bass but also tired of him. This was late November, 1893. A month later, Bass escaped with another killer named Jim North, causing an uproar in the county over all the money thrown away on that new jail. The Sheriff, posting his reward notices—*Two Thousand*

Dollars in Gold Coin!—refused to talk about it, and Durrance came to me, nerves shot, to renew his offer. All right, I said. You double the payment, with half in advance, and I will risk life and limb so you can get some sleep. He yelped, Hell, no, I ain't payin in advance. Suppose somethin goes wrong? It don't make sense, some Oklahoma outlaw carryin my money. It ain't that I don't trust you, Jack, but you already got my Winchester, and anyways, you'll be collectin the reward.

All right, I said, I am a man of trusting nature, so I will trust you for my payment, but you better have it ready the same day I earn it, because I will be heading out real quick for other parts. I held his eye. I sure would hate to have to shoot you, Will, but you know I'll do it, and you won't get your Winchester back, either.

This was mostly guff but Durrance thought I meant it. He reckoned I was cynical as well as greedy, and perhaps I was, because my heart had hardened. I wanted Durrance's bounty and the Sheriff's reward, too. I had lost too many precious years and had no prospects. To seize my life and take it back, I was desperate enough to commit a desperate act. If I had to, I would kill Quinn Bass as a business proposition.

That is how E. A. Watson became E. J. or "Jack" Watson, fugitive and frontier desperado. Edgar Watson of Clouds Creek would never make his peace with being a bounty hunter, but Jack Watson, fugitive from the Arkansas federal prison, was another story.

*

A certain scarlet lady had taken some coy pains to scrape acquaintance with Jack Watson at the cathouse. She confided that Bass was hiding out in the vicinity and had sent word that Durrance and Watson better watch their backs. Though this news came as a relief (I could now act in self-defense and lose no sleep over my honor), it was also a trap. She soon confessed what I already knew, that she was Quinn's favorite and his spy. However, he was very jealous, and had made the mistake of knocking her around at the hideout cabin where she met him three times weekly. Quinn's plan was to lure Jack Watson there and kill him.

One night at the whorehouse, having agreed that her Quinnie was an ornery low hog, also a menace to polite society, we decided that it was our civic duty to put a stop to him and collect the reward. Next our conversation turned to a cache of money she had come across one afternoon while idly ransacking his hideout at Coon Prairie, across a creek off the old Pine Level road, some four miles west of town. Since her Quinnie intended to murder me, it seemed only just that I share in this money as well.

Once I had closed my deal with Durrance, my whorehouse associate got word to Quinnie that everything was working out just as he'd planned. Mr. Jack Watson at the Durrance Ranch had been happy to accept an invitation to enjoy her favors on a complimentary basis at her sylvan retreat out at Coon Prairie, where he planned to call on her tomorrow evening. All Quinnie had to do was shoot when Jack walked through the door. What Jack would do instead, of course, was bring a posse. Hearing hooves and shouts, Quinn would light out the back window, heading for an old overgrown corncrib in the holler where he tethered his horse in case something went wrong. That was where Jack Watson would be waiting.

This was the rough plan, which had two things wrong with it. First, this woman might truly love Quinn Bass or be scared to cross him, and I might walk right into my own trap. Second, it would be unwise for any stranger to claim any reward for killing any member of the Bass clan, even this one. What I did was notify the Sheriff that the fugitive Q. Bass (who had made such a laughing stock of his new jail) could be found at his secret hideout on such and such an evening, and that under my guidance, a posse could sneak up and take him. I had two conditions. I wanted to be deputized, tin badge and all, and I wanted the reward if the fugitive was taken, dead or alive.

The Sheriff didn't care much for my proposition, but as he was still smarting over those escapes, he decided to accept. He could not go himself, he said, because he was tracking a fresh lead on the other fugitive, Jim North, so he assigned Bass to his deputy instead. The Deputy knew as well as I did that the Sheriff was ducking this tough case because Quinn's large clan voted.

Near Coon Prairie I told the Deputy I would scout the place to make sure Quinn had arrived. The posse was to come ahead at the first shot or in fifteen minutes, whichever came first. I circled the cabin and located Quinn's horse in the place my confederate had described, out of sight of the cabin in a hollow down behind the corncrib. I crept near on foot from the downwind side, but not too near, in case Quinn was waiting there in hiding. The tethered horse lifted its head once, then resumed grazing, yanking loudly at the grass. It did not whinny until it heard the posse's horses.

Quinn Bass heard that whinny, too, and jumped out the window before he was surrounded. I ran forward and ducked behind that corncrib. When he ran past, I said, "Hands up!" and when he spun, going for his gun, I had no choice but to shoot in self-defense.

Quinn was a tough customer and took some killing. He had grabbed onto a sapling to keep from falling. His gun had dropped out of his hand, so I held my fire. Swaying, still upright on his knees, he stared past me with his grizzled jaw dropped open. "Well, shit," he said—famous last words, and about as sensible as any. He coughed up blood and fell.

I ran forward, grabbed and fired his gun once, then dropped it beside his hand. Returning to my place, I squatted down and replaced the spent cartridge in my own weapon as the dismounted posse came running toward the shooting. I yelled, "Watch it, boys!" and fired a round to panic them. Sure enough, they sprawled out on their bellies and blazed away at the sagged body. When they finally quit, Seph Granger, slapping his new Winnie, gave me a broad wink. Ol' Seph was proud to be in on a real posse and proud he had done the Grangers proud by helping to blow a deep-dyed criminal to kingdom come. Seph was just plain proud all over, like a happy dog.

Inspecting the dead man's weapon, the lawmen established that the fugitive had fired at Deputy Jack Watson, who returned his fire before the posse finished him. I saw no reason to dispute that, but the Deputy Sheriff, viewing the body, scratched his neck, unhappy. "Never heard me holler not to shoot? Hell, Quinn's a *local* man!" He contemplated the corncrib and the tethered horse. "Looks like you knew right where to find him, Watson. Let's see your gun."

Well sir, I told him (while he checked to see how often I had fired), this heinous outlaw lying here had sent word that he aimed to kill me, so when I told the fugitive to put his hands up and he drew down on me and fired, I felt obliged to return his fire in self-defense. Same as the rest of you, I added quickly, as the posse nodded. It was me or him.

The Deputy handed my revolver back with that cold look of hard and stupid skepticism which is always very popular among law officers.

By the time the posse went back to the cabin, there was no sign of my associate, who had hid her own nag well off from the cabin. The men threw Quinn across his saddle and galloped his bloody carcass back to town. I hung back pretending I had dropped something. As soon as those hooves died away, I hunted up Quinn's cache, which in broad daylight looked more like a packet of dried frog skins than real money. That was because this stuff was counterfeit—I should have known. On the other hand, it seemed quite suitable for the Everglades frontier, where folks had more experience with frogs than frogbacks. They'd be glad to accept a fake ten-dollar bill, having never laid eyes on a real one. Meanwhile I would hold my sweetheart's half just for safekeeping. I hid the money in a sack and shoved that into my saddlebag, and my bad conscience with it, and rode away with a light heart and eight hundred green bills of ten dollars each, not counting Will's bounty fee and the reward.

*

Quinn Bass was not the first man killed from ambush in that county—in fact, he had bushwhacked one or two himself. The practice is useful on the frontier and always has been. Men who never took a life and don't know what they're talking about are the ones who call it cowardice or back-shooting. I don't think the victim would agree. If anyone thought to ask him his opinion, the dead man might call it the Lord's mercy and also a chance to die with dignity, which very few men get, in bed or out. He rarely sees who struck him down or knows what hit him, and never suffers pain or fear, which can be a great comfort to his family. And if no one knows who did the deed, then the family won't have to crank up their old honor and go out killing in return, eye for an eye. Compared with mayhem of the common kind, bushwhacking is clean and it is merciful, a very safe, efficient way of taking care of business, which is why it is so often chosen by professionals.

As for the bushwhacker himself—assuming he's not one of that warped kind who gets a kick out of it, but just an ordinary kind of feller trying to get by—he can thank his Maker that he never had to face the terror and reproach in that last doomed stare. I talked to some killers while in the Arkansas prison and they all said the same—if it has to be done, then do it quick and merciful and from behind, and never let 'em see you. First, it's a lot harder to shoot straight when that wild-eyed feller in your gun sights not only sees you but knows who you are. This is distressing to both parties, and might earn you a dead man's curse, and it can be dangerous if he jumps aside and draws his weapon. Jack Watson faced Bass out of some false idea about self-defense and honor, but Bass was killed in cold blood just the same.

Quinn's partner Jim North would remain at large for two more years before he was bushwhacked by a friend for the reward. When his friend's turn came, he was bushwhacked, too, over near Fort Thompson. June 6, 1898— I remember the date because my daughter Carrie would be married down the river at Fort Myers a month later.

To make a long story short, I did what I was paid for. I'm not proud of it, but I'm not ashamed. Many a successful man of business revered in his community got his start in a way he would not care to talk about today. Arcadia needed Quinn Bass killed and I needed the money, so everybody was better off, even Quinnie, who needed killing worse than anyone I ever met except Maybelle Starr.

*

Back in Arcadia, I rode around the block and came up to the jail from the far side, arriving at the same time as the posse. Quinn's body had drawn an excited crowd from the saloons. A lot of Bass men prowled that crowd shooting guns into the air, wanting to know who had led the lawmen to Quinn's hideout. And pretty soon a voice sang out, "Better ask that gunslinger who rides for Durrance! Ask Jack Watson!"

The Sheriff arrived dusty and sweating, in bad temper. His mouth was tight as a sprung trap. He shouted, "Hell, there's enough men out there to steal my jail!" The Sheriff wasn't happy Quinn was dead, nor was he sorry. Bass had made a hard job that much harder. "But them boys in that crowd out there are Bass clan first and Bass clan foremost. Maybe you done this town a favor, but that don't mean that they won't take and string you up. And there's others out there that is good and drunk, just rarin to string up some damn stranger, not for the justice of it but for the hell of it, to pass the time of day." He wouldn't advise me to loiter in Arcadia, the Sheriff said.

When I said I was only awaiting my just reward, he asked me coldly how it felt to be a bounty hunter. "I served as your deputy," I reminded him, my thumb pushing out my badge.

"That badge don't mean nothin to them men out there. They're callin you a bounty hunter, and I agree." He wrenched my star right off my shirt, leaving a tear. He said that if I aimed to risk my neck by hanging around until the bank opened tomorrow, that was my own goddamned responsibility.

All right, I said, lock me up for my own protection. He refused. I went into an empty cell and slammed the door and told him from behind the bars to do his duty and bring me my supper. "Come out of there!" He threw the cell door wide. "I ain't gettin my new jail burned down, not for no gunslinger!"

I lay back, put my hands behind my head. "You'd turn your own deputy over to that mob? That's cold-blooded murder."

"How can I turn you over if you ain't in custody, you stupid shit? You got no business in that cell! You are *trespissin* in my new jail, layin in there like that!" He became still more outraged when I grinned.

"Nosir, I ain't so sure about no damned reward. I believe you knew where Quinn tethered his horse. My deputy reckons you foxed them men into shootin Bass down after he was dead so it wouldn't look like you was layin for him. Anyways," he said, frowning at the floor, "we ain't talkin here about innocence or law, we're talkin about savin your damn life. If it's worth savin. Who are you, Mister? I heard you was pretty handy with a gun." The lawman shook his head, disgusted, looking out the window at the crowd. "And a fast talker, too." He turned to look at me. "You on the dodge?" He didn't expect an answer, and he didn't get one. "Know something, Watson? If the dead man was anybody but Quinn Bass, I'd hold you for a grand jury hearing, get an indictment. I might do that anyway." He was fuming again. "We think you tricked Quinn into an ambush. Cold-blooded murder."

"Your own deputy murdered the fugitive who escaped from your new jail, that what you'll testify? Murdered that murderer with the help of the Sheriff's posse—that what you want the grand jury to hear? When you have no proof that Jack Watson even fired?" I let that sink in. "Sheriff, no one has to know who tipped you off about Quinn Bass. You hand over that reward this evening and I'll be long gone before daybreak. Tomorrow the word gets out that your special posse surrounded the escaped killer in his lair and had to shoot him when he fired at your men. You get the credit and the votes."

Brooding about the nature of justice and injustice, the Sheriff grunted real low in his chest, like a prime hog. "If that mob was to take and hang you," he said finally, "you might not have much use for that reward."

"Where I come from in Carolina, there's an old headstone that reads, 'Hanged by Mistake.' Want that on your record, too?"

*

When Durrance showed up, the Sheriff pushed him right into my cell. He locked the door with a hard slam and went out again. "Jack, I come quick as I could," pled Durrance, not happy to be cooped up with me at such close quarters. He cocked his head toward the noise outside, where the Sheriff was trying to parley with the crowd. "Hell, Jack, them people aim to *lynch* you, that's the way they was yellin when I come in."

"You probably hoped they'd have me hung by the time you got here, Will," I said. "But here I am, so you better pay me while I'm still alive."

Will Durrance reached into his coat, his brow all beetled up with honest worry over good money laying loose in a lynched man's pocket. "Jack, it ain't like you killed Bass for Will Durrance. You done it cause he threatened you, now ain't that right? Ain't he just a fugitive killed by the posse? That ain't nothin in the world to do with me!"

"You offered me blood money, Will. Want me to tell that to the Bass boys?" I nodded toward the window. His fingers had emerged empty from his pockets, but now they went back in. He forked over a bag of twenty-dollar gold pieces.

The Sheriff came back and unlocked the cell and waved me after Durrance, spelling out my choices. If I insisted on staying in the cell, he would try to save his jail but he wouldn't die for it. If the jail and I survived the night, he would hold me on suspicion of first-degree murder and see to it that I was indicted. And if by some miscarriage of justice I was acquitted, he would turn me over to the mob. That was one choice.

The other choice was, I walked out of here right now.

"Them boys are lookin for some fun, but they ain't lookin to get shot, not for Quinn Bass." He jerked his chin toward Durrance. "He told me the Grangers have your horse out there. Told 'em to empty their six-guns in the air when you walk through the door. Scatter the crowd, to give you a head start."

He handed me the Winchester and still I waited. Scowling, he handed over the reward.

"Good luck," said Durrance, who was almost cheerful. He was confident I would be killed, after which his gold could be removed from my remains. I believe this was the Sheriff's plan, as well. "I'm givin you a better chance than you give Quinn," he said.

Seeing us in the jailhouse door, the Grangers fired off all chambers of two six-guns each, scattering the mob. A few guns answered but we drew no fire. I poked Durrance in the back with the revolver and trotted him over to the horses. "Good luck," he said again. "You're the one needs it," I yelled. "You're riding up behind." I hauled Will aboard the horse, with the Grangers shooting as fast as they could reload.

From the safety of the darkness, the crowd groaned, milling stupidly like cows at the pasture gate. Durrance was bellowing, Don't shoot, boys! It's me! Right then, some silly bastard opened fire, and a bullet sang close past my ear.

I rode that man all the way to the Peace River, where he half fell off, sore-assed and stiff. No one had followed. The night was dark, with no curve of the moon, and the river flowed past in the direction I was headed, south and west.

Having coughed up the money, Will Durrance was bellyaching about my rifle. Said he was scared of bears and panthers, and scared of the dark, too, and anyway, that Winchester was not part of the deal. This was true, and anyway, I had been lucky for a change, and did not want to risk that luck by being greedy. I emptied out the breech and tossed the rifle. He didn't thank me. He was looking back over his shoulder toward the woods.

*

I rode to the Calusa Hatchee River, crossed on the cattle barge from Alva, and went on down the south bank to Fort Myers, where I boarded my lame horse in the livery stable. Next day I sailed out on the schooner *Falcon*, which rolled and pitched all the way south past Key Marco and Cape Romaine to the Ten Thousand Islands. My first sight of the open Gulf dismayed me, that vast and unforgiving plain of ocean emptiness, the frail craft and its tossed, clinging sinners under the eye of Heaven—was this Judgment Day? However, I struck up acquaintance with the captain, W. D. Collier of Marco, and when the nausea let up a little, Cap'n Bill straightened me out some with a cup of whiskey. He answered a few fundamentals about coastal piloting and navigation, even gave me the helm so I could feel the sea myself, and the great might of it.

Soon the few poor shacks perched on the outer islands disappeared.

Seeing so much wild, virgin coast awaiting man's domination, I felt better and better. I was still on the run, still headed south, farther and farther from my family, but for the first time in my life, I had the capital to establish my own place. I would find good soil, lay out a farm, get a cabin and a first crop under way, and bring in pigs and chickens, then send for Mandy and the children—that was all the plan I needed for the next few years. After that— well, this Everglades frontier was still a wilderness. I had a name to make, and I had energy and great ambition. If the great Everglades to eastward could be tamed and harnessed, I was just the man to do it. It was up to me.

Chapter 4

Ten Thousand Islands

Early in 1894, the *Falcon* set me on the dock at Everglade, a trading post on a tidal creek called Storter River. George Storter Junior ran the trading post, and his brother Bembery ran its trading schooner. Captain Bembery, who became my good friend, shipped local cargoes such as sugarcane and syrup, charcoal and farm produce, furs and alligator hides, bringing back trade goods for the Indians and supplies for the three small settlements—Everglade, Half Mile Creek, and Chokoloskee Island—that perched along the eastern shore of Chokoloskee Bay.

Three miles inland from the Gulf, between the barrier islands and the mainland, the Bay was a broad shallow flat almost nine miles long and up to two miles wide. At low tide, it was so shallow that herons walked like Jesus on the pewter water a half mile from shore, and all the rest of it looked like the end of nowhere—mudbanks and islets gathered into walls of dark and shining mangrove jungle, with strange stilt roots growing in salt water and leaves which stayed that leathery hard green all year around. For a man from the North, used to the hardwood seasons and their colors, this tide-flooded and inhospitable tangle was going to take a lot of getting used to. On this southwest coast, called the Ten Thousand Islands, there were nothing but lonesome bays and estuaries where the sawgrass rivers and alligator sloughs snaked through the mangroves. Tobacco-colored from the tannin, turned brackish by the tides, they continued westward to the Gulf as tidal rivers swollen with rain and mud, carving broad channels through the barrier islands.

That professor at the World's Fair in Chicago who claimed there was no more American frontier had never heard about the Everglades. No roads, not even a rough track, in all this southern part of Florida, only faint Indian water trails across the seas of grass to the far hammocks. The trail closed behind after the dugout passed, and all was as empty and silent as it was when this limestone peninsula first arose out of the sea.

*

The C. G. McKinney and Ted Smallwood families from Columbia County had located on Chokoloskee Island, a high Indian mound of 150 acres at the south end of the Bay, where both men would establish trading posts. C.G. also had a farm and a sawmill, pulled teeth, and delivered babies—he learned how from a book—and caught male redbirds and sold them at the Key West market for fifty cents to a dollar and a quarter. Both were smart self-educated men, among the very few on that wild coast who knew how to read, and their friendship would stand me in good stead from start to finish. As it turned out, Ted Smallwood had read around in the Greek literature, and so had an old French plume hunter down the coast named Jean Chevelier, who had "scraped acquaintance with every field of knowledge except the society of humans," as Mr. McKinney put it.

I took some rough work cutting sugarcane for Storters, who had a cane farm down at Half Way Creek—halfway between Everglade and Chokoloskee. Cutting cane was mean hard labor done mostly by drifters, drunks, and niggers, but I never was a man afraid of sweat, and any old job suited me fine while I figured out how a man might work this country. I saw straight off that these palmetto shack communities, backed up against dense mangrove that a damn cottonmouth couldn't sneak through, were no place for a wanted man who had no boat. I did not know when someone from up North might come here hunting me, I only knew he would show up sooner or later.

Old Man William Brown at Half Way Creek, he liked the way I went about my business, saw some future for me. William Brown accepted some Arcadia cash as down payment on an old and worn-out schooner, the *Veatlis*. Having had no experience of homemade bills, he reckoned he'd got the better of this inlander, so both parties were happy and we made fast friends. Young Henry Thompson of Chokoloskee signed on to teach me the sea rudiments, and as soon as we got some stores aboard, we headed south into the Islands, cutting buttonwood for charcoal to sell down at Key West and shooting a few plume birds where we found them. It was Thompson who showed me the high ground on the great bend of Chatham River which became my home.

In all of the Ten Thousand Islands, Chatham Bend was the largest mound after Chokoloskee, forty acres of rich black soil all going back to jungle because the squatter on there with his wife and daughter would not farm it. Like more than one Island inhabitant, Will Raymond Esq. was a fugitive and killer, glowering from Wanted posters all the way from Tampa to Key West. He liked the Bend because it was surrounded by a million miles of mangrove, giving the lawmen no way to come at him except off the river. There was a loose palmetto shack on there, and smoke. We drifted off the shore, keeping our distance. When I hailed, no answer came back, only the soft mullet slap and whisper of the current, and a scratchy wisp of birdsong from the clearing.

The boy slid in under the bank, put me ashore. He had heard about this mangy bastard and was scared to death, so I told him to row the skiff out beyond gunshot range, but to stay in plain sight as a warning to Will Raymond that there was a witness. Once he was safe, I hallooed once or twice before sticking my head over the bank to have a look. Nothing moving, nothing in sight. I rose up slow, keeping my hands well out to the sides, and nervously wasted my best smile on a raggedy young girl who retreated back inside the rotted shack.

All this while, Will Raymond had me covered. I could feel the iron of his weapon and its hungry muzzle, and my heart felt naked and my chest flimsy and pale beneath my shirt, but I was up there in one piece with my revolver up my sleeve, smiling hard and looking all around to enjoy the view.

Hearing a hard and sudden cough, like a choked dog, I turned to confront an ugly galoot in a broken hat, hefting a rifle, who had stepped out from behind a tree. Unshaven, barefoot, in soiled rags, red puffy eyes like sores, and a thin split for a mouth, he stunk like a dead animal on that river wind. Even after I presented my respects, his coon rifle remained trained on my stomach, his finger twitching on the trigger. Will Raymond looked rotted out by drink but also steady as a stump—a very unsettling combination in a dangerous man.

The muzzle of a shooting iron at point-blank range looks like a black hole straight into hell, but I did my best to keep on smiling. Mr. Raymond, said I, I am here today with an interesting business proposition. Yessir, I said, you are looking at a man ready and willing to pay hard cash for the quitclaim to a likely farm on the high ground—this place, for instance. Two hundred dollars, for instance. According to Henry, this was a fair offer for squatter's rights in this cash-poor economy, assuming that nobody looked too hard at that cash money.

Will Raymond wore a wild unlimbered look, and his manners were not good. He never so much as introduced me to his females, who kept popping their heads out of their hole like prairie dogs back in Oklahoma. In fact he made no response at all to my fine words except to cough and spit in my direction whatever he dredged up from his racked lungs. However, that mention of cold cash had set him thinking, because his squint narrowed. While estimating how much money he might take from my dead body, he was considering that boy out in the boat, who was doing his best to hold that skiff against the current. Will Raymond had reached a place in life where he had very damned little left to lose.

He coughed again, that same hard bark. "If you are lookin for a farm at the ass end of hell, seventy mile by sea from the nearest market, and have a likin for the company of man-eatin miskeeters and nine-foot rattlers and river sharks and panthers and crocky-diles and every kind of creepin varmint ever thunk up by the Lord to bedevil His sinners—well then, this sure is your kind of place."

"My kind of place is right, sir!" I sing out cheerily.

"Nosir, it sure ain't, cause I am on here first. And next time, sir, you go to trespissin without my say-so, sir, I will blow your fuckin head off. Any questions?"

"Not a one," say I in the same carefree tone, and I signal for my boat. While waiting, I venture to look around a little more, thinking how much my Mandy might like these two huge red-blossomed poincianas. "Yessir, a fine day on the river. Makes a man feel good to be alive."

"You got maybe ten more seconds to feel alive in, Mister. After that you ain't goin to feel nothin."

Under my coat, the .38 lay along my forearm, set to drop into my hand. To drill this polecat in his tracks would have been a mercy to everyone concerned, especially his poor drag-ass females. But what I needed more than anything right now was a reputation as an upright citizen, so I put aside my motto of "good riddance of bad rubbish" in favor of "every dog must have its day." This dog had had his day at Chatham Bend and mine would come next or my name wasn't Jack Watson, which it wasn't.

Will Raymond observed our skiff all the way down around the Bend. The man stood there as black and still as a cypress snag out in the swamp, his old Confederate long rifle on his shoulder like the scythe of Death. Passing through the delta, looking back, I noted with approval that the river mouth, all broken up by mangrove islets and oyster bars, would pass unseen by any boat, even from a quarter mile offshore.

*

That same week, on the way south to Key West with a cordwood cargo, I had my first look at Lost Man's River, said to be the wild heart of this whole wilderness. Beyond Lost Man's lay Harney River, where that old Indian-fighter Colonel William Harney found his way out to the west coast after hanging Chief Chekaika in the Glades. In Shark River, farther still, lay a jungle of huge mangroves which rose to eighty and a hundred feet in unbroken walls, "the highest in the world," claimed Henry Thompson. From there the mangrove coast curved south toward Cape Sable and the long white beach where Ponce de León came ashore and all those Spaniards in their armor went clanking many miles inland in the wet and heavy heat to conquer the salt flats and marl scrub and brown brackish reach of a dead bay.

From Cape Sable our course led offshore along the western edge of vast pale banks of sand and coral marl, with the turquoise channels and emerald keys of Florida Bay on the port side and the thousand-mile blue reach of the Gulf of Mexico out there to starboard. Henry would point when he heard the puff of tarpon, and sure enough, one of these mighty silver fishes would leap clear of the surface like the black-winged manta rays farther offshore, crashing down in explosions of white water.

In late afternoon the spars of an armada of great ships rose slowly from the sunny mists in the southern distance—Cayo Hueso, or Bone Key, announced Henry Thompson, who turned out to be an authority on Key West, having been born here. Early in the nineteenth century, Cayo Hueso had been built up as a naval base, mostly to suppress piracy on the high seas, but now most Key West pirates lived onshore, preying on the unsuspecting as shipwreckers, ship's chandlers, and lawyers.

On a southwest wind, the *Veatlis* passed the Northwest Light and tacked into the rough water of the channel. Who would have imagined such a roadstead as the Key West Bight, so far away at the end of this long archipelago of desert keys, or so many masts, so many small craft, so much shout and bustle of triumphant commerce? New York merchantmen and Havana schooners mixed with small schooners from the Cayman Islands, fetching live green turtle to the water pens near Schooner Wharf for delivery to the turtle-canning factory down the shore. My jaw must have dropped comically at the spectacle, for my glum guide uttered a hiccuping grunt that I took to be a rare spasm of mirth.

Tacking and luffing, servicing the ships, were whole flotillas of "smackee" sloops with baggy Bahamian mainsails, dropping their canvas as they slipped alongside—reef fishermen, mostly, with live fish in wells, hawking their snappers to the Key West Market and their king mackerel to Havana schooners. Sponges, dried in open yards ashore, were shipped to New York on the Mallory Line, which supplied and victualed this island city. America was nearing "the end of the Gilded Age," the papers said, and entering the Great Depression, but no foreigner would have known that at Key West.

Our cargo was unloaded into a horse-drawn cart backed down into the shallows, and we went ashore. Key West was a port city, with eighteen thousand immigrants and refugees of every color—eighteen times as many human beings as inhabited the whole west coast, all the way north two hundred miles to Tampa Bay. The island is seven miles by three, and the town itself, adjoining the old fort, is built on natural limestone rock. The white shell streets were potholed, narrow, with makeshift sidewalks and stagnant rain puddles and small listless mosquitos. Coco palms bent over the small roofs of green-shuttered white houses, with their shady yards of paradise-colored flowers and tropical trees—sweet-flowered citrus trees, banyans, date palms, almonds and acacias, tamarind and sapodilla, Henry said.

While in Key West, I paid a call on the Monroe County Sheriff, Richard Knight, in regard to a certain notorious fugitive depicted on the Wanted notice in the post office. The murderer Will Raymond, I advised him, could be found right up the coast, in Chatham River. The Sheriff knew this very well and was sorry to be reminded of it. He sighed as he bit off his cigar. My report would oblige him to send out a posse when, like most lazy lawmen, enjoying the modest graft of elected office, he much preferred to put off such thorny matters.

Taking the chair he had not offered, I said I sure hated to cause trouble for Mr. Raymond, but as a law-abiding citizen, I knew my duty. Looking up for the first time, Knight said, sardonic, "That mean you won't be needing the reward?" Sheriff Knight and I understood each other right from the first, and our understanding was this: we did not like each other. We did not even honor and respect each other as fellow citizens of our great new nation.

A few days later, the Sheriff's posse laid off the river mouth until three in the morning, then drifted upriver with the tide as I advised them. They had four men ashore by the time Will Raymond opened fire, and he never got off a second round. Raymond's executioners offered their respects to his loved ones and gave them a nice boat ride to Key West, where Sheriff Richard Knight accepted all the credit. You'd think that might have won me his affection or at least a benign tolerance. It did not.

On my next visit, I went to Knight's office to offer my congratulations. He winced and slid open a drawer and forked over $250 in hard cash without a word. I never kept a penny of that money but went straight over to Peg's boardinghouse on White Street and offered it to the dead man's widow as a consolation in her time of bereavement. By now, she was looking a lot better, or at least a good deal cleaner. Kind of perky, she said, "Stranger, this sure is my lucky day and you sure are my savior, bless your heart!" She offered corn spirits and a simple repast, then took me straight to bed, out of pure gratitude and the milk of human kindness.

Buttoning up, I happened to mention Mr. Raymond's quitclaim, and she implored me to take it over with her compliments, declaring her sincere and fervent hope that she would never see that hellish river again. Altogether, a very touching story with a happy ending. I strode away to the docks with a lilting heart, confident at last that my path had made a turning in the right direction.

*

On that first voyage to Key West, I encountered Captain Penny, an enormous, fine, ferocious-looking fellow, famous in his day as a slave runner who would cheerfully dump an entire cargo into the sea rather than risk capture by a federal vessel. We exchanged but a few words before he recognized me as a man who intended to get ahead in life, and entrusted me with the information that the slave commerce which had made our country great was by no means dead. These days, however, the slaves sold themselves (as Tap Watson had done after my grandfather freed him). Chinese coolies and other illegal immigrants would pay enterprising captains to set them ashore in Florida, where most wound up as indentured labor for the new railroad companies and their drainage schemes, large-scale development enterprises and resort hotels designed to bring Florida's virgin coasts into the modern world. It made his red blood tingle and his pockets jingle, quoth this jolly patriot, to furnish "Chinks" for Florida's exciting future.

Imagining I shared his turn of mind, Captain Penny suggested that we stay in touch and "do some business." However, I very soon realized that a man like Penny was only a small cog (a very large small cog) in the great engine of our nation's progress. The very next day, at the house of the cigar tycoon Teodoro Perez, at Duval and Catherine Streets, I was introduced to Napoleon Broward, who was already preparing for the dashing role in Cuban liberation which would get him elected governor of Florida a few years later. With Mr. Broward was the Cuban revolutionary José Martí, a pale small man, very thin and tense, with much more hair in his long sad mustachios than on his pate. José Martí's support in the fight for Cuban independence came mostly from these rich cigar manufacturers in Key West and Tampa.

Napoleon Broward was a bold sanguinary man of direct action, in the mold of Gould and Astor, Frick and Carnegie—in short, a man who could be counted on not to be squeamish about how the nation's progress was achieved, and never lost sight of his private interests, whether in politics or in industry and business. To the sweet chortling of redbirds, which our cultivated Spanish host kept in small wicker cages like crimson canaries, Broward spoke admiringly of Hamilton Disston, who had pioneered the shipping canal connecting Lake Okeechobee to the Calusa Hatchee River and the Gulf, and I mentioned some of my own ideas about the drainage of the Everglades for agriculture and also long-range prospects for the magnificent Ten Thousand Islands—here Broward raised his brows. "Not so fast there, Mr. Watson," Broward said. Forgetting that Señor Perez, our host, was not the butler, he raised his forefinger and ordered him to fetch Mr. Watson and himself another round of brandy and cigars.

By the time we met again in the year following, I had studied all the Everglades reports, even the visionary schemes of Buckingham Smith, who had written a drainage recommendation way back in the days of the Seminole Wars. I described General Harney's grand proposals for the drainage of southwest Florida and furnished Broward the details of that 1850 Act of Congress which had patented this entire swamp-and-overflowed wilderness to the state of Florida. As early as the 1860s, a Colonel Thompson of the Army Engineers had estimated that if Lake Okeechobee's water level could be lowered by six feet, nine inches—the approximate fall from the lake to the Atlantic—the wetlands from the Kissimmee River south through Dade County could be settled and cultivated without fear of annual overflow and flood.

"By God, Watson, you intrigue me!" Flushed and fulsome, Nap Broward swore that E. J. Watson would be summoned to the state capital to help set Glades development in motion just as soon as he was elected governor. "You're an up-and-coming feller, Ed," Broward said warmly, taking my hand as we parted. "If I am elected, you can write your own damn ticket." By God, I thought, it's happening at last. I am on my way!

*

Taking a Key West nigger called Sip Linsey as well as a few chickens and a mule, I went straight home to Chatham Bend and got to work. With some half-hearted help from Sip and Henry, I had that high ground in production in a hurry, having no real forest to contend with. The Indians who had a village here before the Seminole Wars had kept the jungle down, and since then, the old plume hunter Jean Chevelier, then a halfbreed Indian, Robert Harden—the last occupant before the late Will Raymond—had burned it over every year to discourage a surging jungle scrub of pigeon plum and stopper berry, gumbo-limbo, mastic, ash, Jamaica dogwood. What settlers wanted all around the shack was a dead bare ground which provided no cover for snakes and varmints, not to mention the no-see-ums and mosquitos—the most pernicious of God's creatures in the Glades in regard to bloodletting, discomfort, and disease. In this burdensome humidity and heat, the early Spaniards had worn armor, and these whining demons might have been one reason why.

Clearing off the second growth was hot and wearisome, and turning over the black soil, packed hard with heavy shell, was worse. That shell ground had to be chipped out with a pickax, though once it was reduced to soil, it was black and fertile. I started out with tomatoes and peppers, then peas, beets, radishes, and turnips. Came up fine, but in this climate, that produce looked old and limp, half-spoiled, by the time we got it to Key West. Truck farming would never make my fortune in the Islands. We grew our kitchen vegetables, of course, and planted fruit trees—bananas, mangoes, guavas, papayas, a variety of citrus. (In the early days, the only fruits we had were small wild grapes and the small fragrant key limes.)

With the rains in spring and fall, the river became a broad and burly flood, sandy brown and heavy with Glades silt, without light or sparkle, which left pale crusts on the marl wastes behind the mangrove fringes of the larger islands. Because the river was brackish from the tides moving upstream, what we drank was the dead water from a rain barrel, and very glad to have that, too, in this salt country.

Chatham Bend was the first good ground I ever worked on my own behalf, not leasing or sharecropping for someone else. That first year I built a palmetto log house with palm thatch roof—two big rooms and an outside kitchen. Next came a big shed, then a small dock, then a pasture with fence posts cut from the reddish gumbo-limbo, which will take root when stuck into the ground. By the end of the year, a milk cow and five hogs were lodged in the old Raymond shack to keep Sip company. I had more livestock on the Bend than any settler south of Chokoloskee. All that was missing was Mandy and the children (though I knew already that Mandy might not care for such unrelenting isolation and uncanny silence).

The following year we cleared more ground and grew a crop of sugarcane on about ten acres, with another acre set aside for kitchen produce. The Storters and my friend Will Wiggins were already growing cane at Half Way Creek, and also Mr. D. D. House upriver at House Hammock, so I had good neighbors who would give me cuttings. Will Wiggins also lent an experienced field hand called Nig Wiggins, who helped me get my plantation started in the right direction. Cane is known as a cast-iron crop that can survive flood as well as fire, even brief freezing. Furthermore, it would not spoil in shipping like fresh produce. However, the Bend was eighty miles by sea from the nearest market, and I had learned that cane stalks were too bulky to ship economically to a distant market. I increased crop acreage, brought a crew in for the harvest, and went straight over to the manufacture of cane syrup—the first farmer in that region to try it. By now, I had replaced the small *Veatlis* with a sixty-eight-foot schooner called the *Gladiator.*

The cane harvest extended till late winter, early spring, when I got rid of all my crew except Nigger Sip and Henry Thompson and my new housekeeper, Henrietta Daniels, known as Netta, who was Henry's mother. She brought along Henry's older brother Joe and Baby Jenny, very glad to have a roof over her head. But she was terrified of the wild people, and hid back in the house at the first glimpse of a dugout on the river—very strange, since her Daniels clan had some Injun in 'em, like many on this coast.

Joe and Henry's father had been a Key West seaman, Robert Thompson. Since his death ten years before, poor Netta had led an errant life, working as a tobacco stripper in the Key West cigar factories and marrying often. Her most recent consort, Mr. Williams, had died earlier this year, but not before presenting her with little Jenny. Despite all her trials, she remained a fervent Catholic, never danced nor swore nor slept in the same bed with a man who had been drinking, as I discovered on the night of her arrival.

Netta Daniels was a few years older than myself, small and wistful in her face, with hazel-green eyes and light brown hair and small cupped ears that made her look crestfallen, but she was still a pretty woman and a willing one. She would clean a little but not much, cook, can preserves, and feed the chickens, and do her bounden duty by her lord and master, namely me. "Listen," I told her the day after she arrived, "it's not seemly for a lady to sleep in the same room with her own sons. That kind of behavior will not be tolerated on the Bend." After that, she bunked with me, at least when I was sober, which is pretty much the way I'd planned it in the first place.

Henry mostly ran the boat and helped the nigger slop the hogs and fetch them water and do a few odd jobs when we could find him. Young Joe, who disapproved of me, was soon replaced by Netta's half brother Stephen—Mr. S. S. Jenkins, as he introduced himself—better known as Tant. Tant made good whiskey from raw sugar and chicken feed (a half sack of corn and a half sack of sugar to each fifty-five-gallon charred oak barrel—that was his recipe). Ferment worked quickly in this climate, and the buck was ready to distill in about ten days, but Tant was tasting it for flavor every minute. "I got her right this time, Mister Ed!" he'd holler, to keep up my hopes. By the time he got that shine distilled, he had drunk most of it and had to start all over. Although still a young man, Mr. S. S. Jenkins was twitching like the dickens, and every time he tried to quit, he'd have to fold his arms around his chest just to stay put in his chair. Sometimes all I got out of the deal were the colorful feed sacks which Netta used to make us nice checkered shirts.

Tant fished and hunted our wild food, harvesting wild duck or "squawks" in the creeks and sloughs, and sometimes a few of those black pigeons which hurtled up and down the river in the early morning. He was a tall and lanky feller with a small head and a comical tuft for a mustache, and he made me laugh right from the start, which deflected attention from his natural traits of bone laziness and alcohol addiction. Tant Jenkins realized long before I did that I would tolerate his flaws of character only so long as he kept me amused. One day at Chokoloskee, knowing I was watching, this fool snuck up on Adolphus Santini's cow pen, causing a regular stampede by poking his head over the fence and ducking down again, over and over, until those critters went crazy with suspense, galumphing around colliding with one another. I got laughing so hard I could hardly find my breath, even when Dolphus ran out hollering.

Tant sauntered over, frowning. "Hellsfire, Mr. Watson, what are you laughing at? This here is *serious*. Why, it's just like you told me, them crazy critters *like* bein drove crazy. If the moon was to come out, they'd jump right over it, ain't that what you was sayin?"

Old Man Dolphus folded his big arms upon his chest like an old blue heron folding its big wings. He was glaring but he never said one word.

Another day we were out shooting curlews for our supper, back over toward what is now called Watson Prairie. A big ol' gator maybe twelve foot long was crossing some dry palmetto ground between two sloughs, and ol' Tant, being drunk as usual, says, Looky here, boys, I aim to show what I can do. Damned if he don't run across the clearing and climb onto that reptile kind of piggyback. Threw an armlock around the jaw, crossed his ankles under the belly, all the while whooping like an Injun. That big gator was so scared it tried to get away, hauling Tant through the palmettos, you never heard such a racket in your life. Another time a young buck jumped the creek and Tant reckoned he should try that, too. He ran and leaped and splashed down in the middle. "That's the first time and the last time I will ever take a bath," he said. "Don't see no sense to it."

Tant never considered female companionship except when drunk. One evening he crawled up to his half sister on his hands and knees, said, Netta, I aim to go get me a *bride*. All you got to do is give me a good recommendation, Netta, and I'll sure try to live up to it. Netta just smiled. She loved Tant the way he was, she never tried to change him as most half sisters would have done, and never tried to find him a wife, either, knowing that was hopeless. Like many a lovable, whimsical feller, Tant Jenkins was a very lonesome man.

*

In the breeding season, in late winter and early spring, we hunted the egret rookeries, stripping the white plumes. These were traded to Lewis and Guy Bradley of Flamingo, who knew this coast from their first plume-hunting expedition with the Frenchman Jean Chevelier back in the eighties. In October, when the long chill nights would knock down the mosquitos, Tant baited a few traps, using salt mullet, and set a trap line along the creeks for otter, coon, and possum, which humped along the shoreline at low tide. The rest of the year, he journeyed deep into the Glades, as far from honest toil as he could go—that was the Injun in him. In a few days, he would be back with turkey and deer from the hammocks and pine islands. The venison hams and turkey breasts were salted overnight, then smoked for a few days on palmetto platforms over cypress coals. That smoked meat would keep a good long while, until it was soaked to remove the salt, then cooked and eaten. The deer hides were stretched on frames, salted and dried, then sold for credit at the trading posts, along with his gator flats and coon and otter pelts. Occasionally Tant lugged in big pinewoods gophers or swamp rabbits or possum; roasted possum tasted almost like young pig if you tasted hard enough, and the firm white tail meat of a young gator was good, too. Tant ate the big rattlesnakes he skinned out for sale to tourists—"fit for a king," he'd say—but he had that snake meat mostly to himself.

Netta was always disappointed when he did not bring fresh greens. She doted on wild butter beans from the hammock edges and dug out prickly pears for pie, and occasionally Tant brought palm hearts from the inland hammocks, also coontie, which sold well at the market as "Florida arrowroot," a fancy starch for cakes and puddings. Tant detested the insect swatting and hard grubbing in the windless woods that went into every barrel of coontie at seven cents a pound, and always let others take care of the washing and grinding of the pulp, the soaking, fermenting, and drying. In short, he despised all common labor—"can't stand the feel of sweat on me and never could." So Netta mostly baked her dough using salt and boiling water, and her bread came out like a loaf of hardtack cracker. Even that was better than Mr. McKinney's gray store bread, which C.G. himself reviled as "wasp nest."

Cash being scarce on the frontier, the greenbacks minted at Arcadia were welcome, but most trade was still done by barter. I'd swap cane syrup for big oranges, two for a penny, or salt-water oysters, sixty cents a barrel. At Key West or Tampa Bay, such treats as coffee beans and olive oil and chocolate were available, along with the sacks of onions and potatoes from the North.

We always ate well on the Bend, better and more than I had ever eaten in my life. In South Carolina and out west in the Nations, there had rarely if ever been enough. Crossing the hinterlands from Arkansas to Carolina, then south through Georgia to Columbia County, I was glad of the shelter in many a dirt-floor shack, but where the people weren't half starved, I gagged down grub that would tumble the guts of an old turkey buzzard—sow belly and grits slimy with lard, old corn bread dead as attic dust, half-rotten potatoes boiled down to a smelly gruel. Where these frontier folk weren't too drunk and shiftless to step outside and trap or shoot wild game, it was gulped down shiny purple raw or fried to a hard chip, and very few took the trouble to catch fish, though they were plentiful in every branch and pond. All over the back country of America, wild things were plentiful, yet good food was as scarce as a good cook.

*

In April of 1895, a baby daughter—Minnie Lucretia, after my sister—was delivered to Netta by Old Man Robert Harden. Having wanted a son, I was ready to call her Ninny and be done with it, but her mother would not hear of such a joke. For a small and gentle person, Netta Daniels had great courage when she needed it. One day that Key West mule of mine refused to pull no matter how I beat it, until finally I lost my temper and grabbed up a length of two-by-four, thinking to wallop it between the ears to knock some sense into its head. Netta called out, "Mr. Watson! Mr. Watson! That's enough!" She stopped me, all right, and I felt pretty sheepish, too. "I'm a damned fool, Netta"—that is what I told her, and she said all men were damned fools but it was nice to meet a man who knew that.

Netta's mother had made Catholics out of her children, and Netta's sister had married Tino Santini, a Corsican from a hard Catholic family with no tolerance for common-law marriage nor for bastards. Their gossip would lead to a bad scrape with Tino's brother at the produce auction house down at Key West. I was drunk, or so they tell me, and Adolphus was, too, and he wound up in the hospital with a sore throat. I meant to leave him a thin scar as a reminder to be more civil to Ed Watson, but unfortunately the knife nicked his jugular and his Corsican blood spurted out between his fingers all over eight bushels of asparagus, making me look like a bloodthirsty villain. His hints about my past were what had started it—"he cast asparagus on a man's honor," as Tant said—but even so, I had to fork over what was left of my handmade money to settle this matter out of court.

Sheriff Knight wanted to hold me in the Key West jail while he looked into Santini's story that E. Jack Watson was a desperado, wanted by the law somewhere out West. With his bald eye and sour nature, Knight had followed my career since the Will Raymond episode, and now he sent away on his new telegraph to find out what he could about E. Jack Watson. I paid my bail with my last bona fide cash and left Key West before word came that Jack Watson was an escaped felon from Arkansas. I did not return to Cayo Hueso for a year.

As I might have anticipated, Dolphus Santini learned about that phony money. He grew suspicious and had it checked at the Key West bank. Not only did he unfairly accuse me of being a counterfeiter, but he wrote to the Governor with the complaint that his assailant had never been brought before the bar of justice for attempted murder. According to my legal counsel, who also served as part-time U.S. Attorney, the Governor's office sent a query to Sheriff Knight, who was obliged to call me in for questioning. When Dolphus heard that I knew about his letter, he lost his zeal for justice, sold his Chokoloskee house, and sailed away to the east coast at Lemon City.

Being too busy to come hunting me, Sheriff Knight delegated a young deputy who planned to run for Knight's job in the next election—the ideal man to be sent up that wild river to arrest Desperado Watson single-handed. This feller had more guts than brains and he sure tried, but I got the drop on him and took his guns away and put him straight to work out in the cane. After two hard weeks I told him, Clarence, let that be your lesson, and put him back into his boat and waved good-bye. Clarence Till thought the world of me because I spared his life, and he waved back with a big grin on his face. Though still disgusted with the Sheriff for never sending to inquire what became of him, he returned to Key West singing my praises as the only man of progress on this coast. In later years, he looked the other way even when I cut up rough while in that city.

*

According to a comic card sent by Sam Tolen, the Santini episode made headline news in the Lake City paper, the culprit Watson being locally well-known as a dangerous drunk and an alleged accomplice in the killing of John Hayes. Yet Mandy, who had now returned to Columbia County with the children, made no mention of that story in a gentle letter, but simply inquired if she and the children might not come join me. Despite all her poverty and suffering, including five long years with no word from her wandering husband, this excellent woman had forgiven me entirely. Mandy had always known the dark side of my nature—she would not pretend—but for some reason, she loved me anyhow and I was grateful.

I don't suppose that I missed Rob, but I did miss my pretty Carrie and young Eddie, and was curious to see how Lucius had turned out. "He favors me a little, more's the pity!" Mandy had written. I chuckled, imagining her shy smile as she wrote that, but a moment later, that memory was rudely ousted by a vision of Mandy's girlish rump, which always brought to mind a hot pink muffin. I laughed out loud, that's how happy the prospect of my family made me.

Hearing that laugh, Netta smelled trouble. "A penny for your thoughts, Jack Watson." I told Netta I was sorry but she would have to make room for my lawful wedded wife and legal children—in short, she should clear out as soon as possible, down to the last hairpin, and take her Jenny and our sweet Little Min right along with her. She stood right up to me—Mr. Desperado Watson! *Huh!*—the only time I ever saw this woman spitting mad. She called me a liar for telling her that common-law marriage was no different than Catholic, and said she had been worried sick about the safety of her children ever since that horrible Santini business. Now that she knew I was already wed, which made me some kind of a dirty Mormon, she was only too happy to leave forever and never darken my door again.

I was sad, for I loved Netta, too, but my past life had overtaken us and that was that. I left the Bend that afternoon so as not to have to listen to her bitter weeping. At Caxambas I notified her brother Jim that in a day or two, somebody should go fetch Netta at the Bend. Then I went on to Fort Myers to talk business with Dr. T. E. Langford and a Mr. Jim Cole, who wished to invest in my cane syrup operation.

The Santini story had arrived ahead of me, so I was surprised that these upright citizens not only wanted to do business but were ready to fork over some cold cash. As businessmen, they were less interested in Santini than in what Captain Bill Collier had told them about how fast that feller Watson got his sugarcane plantation up and running. Captain Bill informed 'em that Ed Watson was a newfangled kind of feller with enough brains and ambition to develop the whole Ten Thousand Islands.

Only thing, Bill Collier added, Ed has a temper, and never lets too much stand in his way. This was his wry joke, meant as fair warning. Jim Cole just grinned. For a good businessman, said he, there were far worse recommendations. A nose for opportunity and the nerve to see it through outweighed all other business virtues or the lack of them.

*

Though not a native of Lee County, Jim Cole was a big man in cattle and shipping and one of the first county commissioners, and he was engaged in various enterprises with the Hendrys, who owned most of the town. Because he had political ambitions, Cole was civic-minded, using his cattle boat to bring royal palms from Lost Man's Beach for planting along Riverside Avenue. A few years later, he paved over the white seashell streets for his new auto. I associate concrete with Cole—he loved that stuff.

Jim Cole aimed to drag Fort Myers into the twentieth century whether folks liked it or not. He was a big-bellied friendly feller, loud and jokey, and plenty of folks got on with him just fine. I never liked him much myself, maybe because, for his own reasons, he was always putting me into his debt. I did not feel grateful, only resentful, and I guess he knew that, but as a politician, he could not accept it, he was out to win me over to his side or know the reason why. Hearing about the Santini case, he sent a wire to the Key West Sheriff: *Friend Watson comes out of the Wild West, he's one of that freewheeling breed that made this country great.* Knight wired back, *Freewheeling? Freebooting is more like it. Don't tell a lawman not to do his job.* Jim Cole thought this was pretty funny, and looked a little rattled when I did not smile.

Jim Cole, being a politician, bent over backwards for me because he didn't understand why I didn't like him. He lined up the local business interests to capitalize my syrup operation and advance me credit, and Doc Langford nodded and went right along. When it came to business, the Langford family would do what Jim Cole told them.

I was elated. A man who has the businessmen behind him, that man will be forgiven damn near anything, because real businessmen are like good mothers, they will stop at nothing to advance their investment. Before anything occurred to change their mind, I placed an order with Bill Collier for a cargo of Dade pine, hired three carpenters, and ran them south to build a big wood house and a dock, a boat shed and a barn for workers, with down payment in advance and the balance billed to the Watson Syrup Company, Chatham River, c/o Chokoloskee, Florida, U.S.A.

*

The great day came when I sailed north with Henry Thompson to meet my family at the new railroad terminus at Punta Gorda. For the first time since he was one month old, I gazed upon Lucius Hampton Watson, a fair-haired, handsome, quiet boy with a friendly smile. Pretty Carrie skipped and ran to jump and hug me—*Papa! Papa!*—while Eddie, due to the seriousness of the occasion, frowned at his sister and furrowed his brow before stepping up and shaking hands in a stern, manly fashion. "Good day, Father," said Master Edward Watson. "I am very glad to see you once again." Then my Mandy, bless her heart, curtsied minutely and took both my hands, bending her forehead to my chest to hide her tears. Only Son Born—I might have known—stood to one side, spoiling for a showdown. I was struck afresh by Rob's resemblance to his mother, the pallid, almost pretty face with the vivid red spots on the cheeks and the long black locks of a sissy poet hanging in his eyes.

When he learned that a boy younger than himself was the ship's captain, Rob wasted no time picking a fight with Henry Thompson, and a moment later, they were rassling around down on the ground. I did not intervene, only watched calmly as Henry pinned him and twisted Rob's arm up behind his back. Having lost the fight—and defying his stepmother, who sought to hush him for his own good—Rob became rude and disrespectful. I took him by the arm and shook him, fighting down an urge to beat him, hurl him from me.

I led my poor exhausted troupe to a dinner at the Hotel Punta Gorda, an immense pile of masonry with corner turrets and big central tower, thrown together too quickly a few years before when this Gulf fishing camp became the southern terminus of the west coast railroad. The hotel contained over five hundred rooms, more than enough to bed every human being on this empty coast. As Eddie rolled his eyes for my benefit, Carrie ran wild down the corridors with Lucius right behind her, although both were near tears with fatigue from their long journey.

At supper, my overexcited daughter exclaimed for the whole dining room to hear, This big dinner we are going to eat, I bet they wouldn't never dare to serve us beets! Then the waiter arrived, and he says, Folks, if there's one item on our menu you just better try, that's our fresh beets. And Carrie squints at him, then growls, Well, Mister Waiter, if I was you, I'd just *retire* them old beets! If it looks like a beet or tastes like a beet, let alone *stinks* like a beet, don't you dare bring it to this Watson table! The boys seized this excuse to whoop, we were all laughing, even Rob and even poor dear Mandy, although she had flushed, upset by Carrie's wild deportment, not to mention her un-couth speech and frontier grammar. Henry Thompson smiled, too, he who never *ever* laughed if he could help it. His smile was as thin as a hairline crack in glass.

*

Sailing south next day, we stopped off at Panther Key to let these inlanders hear some of the old sea stories told by a fabled ex-pirate and world cham-pion liar called Juan Gomez. Panther Key was named for the panthers he claimed would swim out from Fakahatchee to eat up his goats.

Next morning we trolled fish lines south with good fishing all the way, and everyone but Rob was in high spirits as the schooner came in off the Gulf and entered Chatham River. Having contracted from Old Gomez the ambi-tion to be pirates, the boys shouted in excitement as the schooner negotiated the hidden entrance where the narrow channel parted the shallow oyster flats and mangrove clumps. Upriver, as we neared the Bend, I pointed out the inland trees that were rising over the mangrove walls along the river, the light green tops of the big gumbo-limbos that favored old Indian mounds and were always sign of high ground and good soil.

"Gumber-limber," Lucius said, enjoying those funny words.

I hoped that Eddie would not shake his head again in that superior way, but I'm afraid he did. As for Rob, he was learning seamanship, asking no questions but fiercely intent on every move Henry Thompson made.

Once they realized the new house was ours, the children could not stop hollering, they were so excited. They scarcely heard my history of this mound nor glanced at my thirty-acre cane field. Mandy gasped, "Oh, Edgar—oh, at last!" She dabbed her eyes and sniffled as she smiled, she could not speak.

I boasted that both outside and inside walls were painted white—real oil paint, too, not some old limestone whitewash. The Watson Place was al-ready renowned as the only painted house on all that coast between Fort Myers and Key West, with shingled roof and polished hardwood floors and a parlor in front with a fine river view. There were two full bedrooms on the west side, also a sewing room which Mandy could use for her schoolroom. A separate dining room and a good big kitchen with a good big wood stove were in the wing on the north side. Mounting from the hall was a full stair with a polished mahogany rail—the only stair so grand on all this coast. "Can you really afford this, Mr. Watson?" Mandy said fearfully, running her hand down the rail. "No, I cannot, my dear sweet wife"—and I hugged her happily—"but I am on my way at last and you need not be afraid for us ever again."

On the second story, two full bedrooms faced the river, and behind were five small children's rooms, with a big linen closet off the stairwell. All the rooms had double beds, and the bigger rooms two doubles each. Planter Watson's house at Chatham Bend, proclaimed Planter Watson, was the biggest and the best-built house in all the Islands.

Before mesh screens became available, we tacked a sheer cotton fabric over the windows. Palmetto frond brooms stood at the entrance to sweep mosquitos off people coming through the door. The cow was swept, too, as she entered her shed, and a gunnysack door covered that entrance, for otherwise even this dull uncomplaining creature would gradually weaken and die from loss of blood. Mosquitos were at their worst from June through September, when kerosene smudge pots and wick lamps filled the house with filthy smoke all around the clock.

*

On Chatham Bend, we watched out for snakes—rattlers and coral snakes, especially—and occasionally we found a track of bear or panther. These creatures were not dangerous unless cornered in a pen or chicken house. The children reserved their most delicious fear for a creature the size of my middle finger—the vinageron or whip scorpion, which Sip Linsey called a scruncher due to the noise it made, trod underfoot. Though the vinageron was harmless, Sip would tell them in hushed tones, *Mine he doan hit you a lick o' dat tail, you sho nuff a goner!* (Rob was forever imitating Sip to amuse Lucius, who despite the ten years' difference in their age was the only one Rob cared for much among the children. Rob was already seventeen—I could scarcely believe it. I still heard his mother's voice in him and glimpsed her smile, as if time had stopped that day she died, or perhaps gone on without me.)

Of the three boys, Lucius was most interested in the wild creatures. He trailed Tant everywhere, he could never learn enough. Because of his love of wilderness and fishing, Lucius alone among my children seemed altogether content at Chatham Bend. Excited that we lived mostly off the land, he gathered fiddler crabs for bait and handlined sheepshead, mangrove snapper, snook, and grouper from the dock. Sometimes Tant or Sip, using the tides, would row the kids downriver to gather oysters and dip-net blue crabs or trap diamondback terrapin in the bays. In the sea-turtle nesting season, on the outer beaches, they followed the broad tracks leading mysteriously out of the Gulf to a place above the tide line where buried clutches of the warm white leathery eggs might be gathered. On trips north and south along the coast, tin lures were trolled for kingfish, pompano, and Spanish mackerel.

With Mandy in the house, we could always count on good fresh bread and even cake or cookies. She also tinned vegetables and made preserves, using wild fruit. We all agreed that there never was so much good food anywhere on earth.

My only worry was the children's love of playing at the water's edge and paddling in the shallows. Sharks came upriver with the tide, Henry Thompson told me, and there were also immense alligators, fifteen foot and better, which came downriver from the Glades in the summer rains. Drawn to commotion, these grim brutes would be on the lookout for unwary kids and dogs.

When the fresh flow weakened in the winter dry season, these gators returned upriver to the Glades, forming congregations at the heads of rivers. During March and April, they hibernated in deep holes in the hammocks, emerging again during the rains in May. According to Tant, the female built a mound nest four or five feet across, where she laid up to fifty leathery long eggs larger than hen's eggs, then covered them with mud. She guarded the nest faithfully, and when the young ones started grunting in the eggs after ten weeks or so, she uncovered them as they hatched and carried them in her delicate great jaws down to the water. Tant showed the children how to find big nests, and when to listen for bull gators roaring.

A gigantic alligator, strangely colored, would haul out on the far bank, where it sometimes lay all day like a dead tree. Often its long jaws were open, and the glint of white teeth could be seen across that wide bend in the river. Because of the children, always playing around the water's edge, I became uneasy when that thing was missing, knowing it might be sliding along like an underwater shadow off this bank.

Mandy observed this creature, too, and kept an eye on the children and her cats while reading in her chair beneath the trees. These days she was feeling poorly, and spent long hours in the thin shade of the poincianas. One afternoon over lemonade and cookies, she discussed wilderness and wild things with the children, quoting some opinions of the poets. A certain New Englander, Miss Dickinson, had concluded (God knows how) that the true nature of Nature was malevolent, whereas the famous Mr. Whitman from New York found undomesticated Nature merely detestable. What did such sheltered people know of Nature, I demanded, pointing at that huge motionless thing across the river. It was simply *there*, oblivious, indifferent, and that indifference was more terrible than their literary notion of malevolence could ever be. Only an egotistical pontificator could regard such an engine of danger without awe, or dare to dismiss it as detestable—unless, of course, this poet was privy to some heavenly information that the Creator detested His own Creation.

In his own odd comment on this matter, Lucius led the family down the riverbank to show us a nest of white-eyed vireos he had been observing. The tiny male had lost its mate after the eggs had hatched, and in its blind urge to reproduce had started over with a second courtship, singing to attract a second female. Together this pair were building a new nest on top of the old one—that is, right on top of the live young, which still struggled weakly to push their hungry bills up through the twigs. We cried out in horror as Lucius explained what was taking place. The children, of course, longed to rescue the innocent victims, although this meant that the second clutch would be destroyed. Lucius forbade this. "They are not innocent," his mother agreed in an odd tone.

I felt odd, too, perhaps we all did. One moment a man swimming in clear salt water celebrates his sparkling life and the next he is seized and dragged down by a shark and never seen again. Is that fate or is that "God"? Are they the same? If it is God, and God gives life, then takes it away again for His own purposes, then why—if man is created in God's image—why is man not free to do the same? These are the sorts of questions I asked Mandy. But she knew I did not believe in God and knew it was useless to discuss it, and anyway, she was troubled by that question.

The Crocodile

Eighteen ninety-eight was a real dry year out in the Glades, and the gators were piled up in the few holes that still had water in them. Taking a skiff load of coarse salt in 160-pound sacks, ammunition, bread and coffee, we set up camp on the long piney ridge near the Big Cypress. Tant and Henry were with me, also Lucius, who came along to help. Working our way east into the Glades, we killed gators for three weeks, shot and clubbed and axed until those ponds turned smoky red, then stayed up late stripping the soft flats off the bellies and rolling them up in the coarse salt by firelight. It was exciting for a while, because stacking flats at such a rate was like heaping up cash money. Exhausted—having drunk up so much coffee we could scarcely sleep—we lay flat out watching the stars fade away in the dawn sky. All around hung that purple smell of the heaped carcasses around our camp. It soon turned to a stink of putrefaction, as if the Everglades had rolled over and died.

Lucius became more thoughtful and subdued as the days passed. He no longer nagged me to let him shoot the rifle, and tended to lag a bit behind. One day we came across a big boar gator, fourteen, fifteen feet, lying like a rotted log in a little slough under a willow head. Having scared off other gators, it did its best to scare me, too, coming slowly up out of the water, huge head waving back and forth, to run this damned two-legged thing out of its territory. I didn't waste ammunition but jumped around behind and fetched it two good ax blows to the nape. The scaly brute thrashed back into the pool and kept on thrashing, and pondweed stuck to the bloody wounds as it rolled and shuddered and finally lay still.

I got my breath and mopped my brow in the steaming heat. Lucius stayed behind me. "These big ol' dinosaurs sure take a lot of killing, don't they, boy?" I was set to move onward, but the boy protested. I explained that the belly flat on a gator of this size was too horny and scarred to be worth stripping. He gazed at me politely in that open way he had inherited from his mama, then knelt and touched the head of the dead gator. Leaving his hand there, he said in a small voice, "Well, then, why kill it, Papa?" That turned me right around. "Why kill it?" I demanded. "Well, son, I mean it's dangerous. That's one big gator less to come downriver, take a dog or child."

This sounded like bluster to my son because that is what it was. "Papa? Are we going to stay here till we kill 'em *all*?" I shook my head. We went back to camp without a word. I told the others we were heading home and they looked relieved. We all knew we had killed enough, but it took a nine-year-old to put a stop to it. Sure enough, when we loaded the boats, the flats stacked right up to the gunwales. Any more would have been left to rot.

At Everglade, we laid the flats along the dock to be checked and measured by George Storter. We were tangle-haired and bearded, sun-cracked, filthy, clothes caked stiff and dark with reptile blood. Folks moved away when we went into the store. Lucius asked me if they smelled the death on us. As far as I know, that boy of mine never went on a gator hunt again.

Chevelier

To provide poor Mandy a distraction from our rough, mosquito-ridden life, I rowed her upriver one fine Sunday for some cultured conversation with Jean Chevelier—"Shoveleer," as the local people knew him—that ancient ornithologist and plume hunter turned archaeologist who was living out his bitter life on Possum Key. His only friend was Robert Harden, who had built his last home for him, whose family took good care of him, and who was regularly denounced by this bad old man.

One day years before, back in the rivers, I shot the Frenchman's straw hat off his head—a warning to stay away from Watson's plume bird territory. Not long thereafter, Chevelier and two henchmen made a botched attempt at a citizen's arrest and he had been maligning me ever since. Seeing Watson's boat, the old man went ricketing into his hut to fetch his shotgun, fearing I had come to steal his secret treasure, which he valued far more than his life. Visitors were never welcomed by the Frenchman. Not until he was reassured by Mandy's gentle bearing did the old man lay down his fowling piece and resign himself to a neighborly visit.

The Frenchman had never changed, he had merely shrunk. He was humpbacked and skinny-legged, sniffing crossly, picking his way about like a wet raccoon, and those hooded eyes of his were a raccoon's eyes, bright black and burning. Formerly a gentleman, he had now lost all his graces, a snappish little know-it-all who would bark out his last orders to the firing squad lined up to shoot him. Introduced to my wife, he neither greeted her nor welcomed her to Possum Key. Instead, he thrust under her nose the queer black blisters on his withered forearm, jeering in triumph when I could not say what caused them.

"Man-chi-neel!" he cried. In the spirit of scientific inquiry, he claimed, he had taken shelter from the rain beneath a manchineel, or poison tree. He warned her sternly to avoid any smooth-barked reddish tree seen in the back country. To tease him, I claimed I had recently seen such trees on Gopher Key—was it Gopher where he got those blisters? Very rattled, he cried Ampo-*seeble!* then tried to pretend he knew nothing of *Go-phaire,* even though the whole coast knew he had dug up that entire mound in a frantic late-life hunt for Calusa treasure. Gopher Key was little known, being off the main channels and barely accessible by a small hidden creek that led in from the inland bays. There was also an old Calusa waterway known as Sim's Creek, which flowed west through the forest to the Gulf. A narrow canal around the key was steep-sided, as if dug by implements, and it had a hard bottom of white shell—very peculiar in a region of dark mud-bottomed creeks and swampy mangrove. To the Frenchman, it was certain evidence that this so-called creek was actually a moat dug by the Calusa, and that its white-shell lining had ceremonial significance. In this old man's feverish imaginings, the mound's sudden elevation way back in a hidden jungle identified it as a burial mound, which might contain ancient artifacts superior to those which Bill Collier had stumbled on the year before, digging his new tomato patch on Marco Island.

I was eager to pick up anything I could about natural aspects of southwest Florida that might be of use in developing this coast. Gopher Key with its white canal, I thought, might serve as an excursion spot for visitors. As for Mandy, she was very entertained by the prickly scientific stance of this old Frenchman, and could scarcely wait to report back to Lucius that the delicious table bird we called the curlew was actually the white ibis, that the "ironhead" was the large wood ibis (not a true ibis, in Chevelier's view, but a New World stork), and that the "shit-quick" was the reed heron or bittern.

"*Sheeta-queek!*" he had yelled at Mandy, who shifted in her seat. "*All* birts *sheeta-queek,* for fly away queek, *voo com-prawn, Madame?*"

The Frenchman and Mandy spoke animatedly of Poe, agreeing that he was more esteemed in France than in this country. Poe had died heartbroken at age forty, but not before he had been discovered and translated by the great Baudelaire, *ness pa, Madame?* But what Chevelier was most anxious to discuss was the inferiority of the U.S.A. when compared, say, to *La Belle Frawnce,* a paradise to which he would return before his death. He declared that France had conquered Florida back in the 1590s, as proven by such geographic names as Cape Sable and Cape Romaine, and that *La Belle Frawnce* was the rightful ruler of the New World. To prove this, he scurried inside and dug up his old books by a smart pair of Frenchies, de Crèvecoeur and de Tocqueville, who knew a great deal more about Americans, he said, than Americans could ever hope to learn. He even read aloud from old de Crève-coeur, as Mandy translated his outlandish tongue: *What, then, is the American, this new man? He is neither a European nor the descendant of a European; hence that strange mixture of blood you will find in no other country. . . . Here individuals of all nations are melted into a new race of men!*

As for de Tocqueville, who had visited this country in the 1830s, he had been astonished on the one hand by the callous indifference with which most Americans regarded slavery, and on the other by a strange apathy and acceptance of their lot which not only inured blacks to their wretched servitude but encouraged them to imitate their oppressors rather than hate them. In my own experience with cane crews, this was true of every color, not just blacks, but Chevelier dismissed my objection by flicking his fingers at me in a brusque gesture, as if brushing crumbs off of his knee. On the other hand, the *redda-skeen, les peaux rouges—*

Here dear Mandy remarked that Europeans seemed to cherish a romantic view of Indian peoples, perhaps to make up for their harsh opinions of the blacks. And she reminded him that Indian forces in the Seminole Wars had often been led by black warriors. To avoid capture and the bitter return to slavery, blacks sometimes led and often reinforced Seminole resistance, as was recognized by the embattled U.S. Army if not by most historians: "This is a Negro and not an Indian war," a general in the First Seminole War had assured the Congress.

Mandy must have been right, because Chevelier instantly returned the subject to de Crèvecoeur's "new race of men," citing "the half-a-breed family of that fockink Robert Harden," who represented what the Frenchman called "the new American." The Hardens embodied the tough, enduring qualities of all three races, which would one day be seen as the true character of *thees ray-poo-bleek*. De Tocqueville had said that escaping slaves who in the early days had turned up among Indian tribes throughout the South had to be men of exceptional courage and fortitude to risk a hostile wilderness and a wild people; and that those who survived were much admired by the Indians and valued for their knowledge of the greedy white man who exploited and killed blacks and reds alike. Being seen as heroes, they were often married into the head families, producing a mixed-blood progeny of fine physical specimens of high moral intelligence.

Hoping he would find no way to claim this brute for France, I asked Chevelier his opinion of that huge greenish gator which had made itself at home in Chatham River. After a few snippy questions designed to display my ignorance to my wife, the Frenchman sneered that my "alligator" was no gator but the salt-water *cro-co-deel*, rare in south Florida though not uncommon on the shallow shores of Florida Bay east of Cape Sable. Had I been educated, he declared, I would surely have noticed its gray-greenish color and a pointed snout that was quite unlike the shovel snout of the brownish, blackish gator, and that even when its mouth was closed, its teeth showed along the entire length of its lower jaw. What was more—just as I feared— the first naturalist to describe this beast had been a Frenchman, one Constantine Samuel Schmaltz Rafinesque, although the crocodile, like so many new species in *thees fockink ray-poo-bleek* (here Mandy batted her eyes prettily and smiled, as a signal to me that her honor would survive even if I did not rise and shoot this foulmouthed villain), had been falsely claimed by a colonial *Frawn-say*, the rascally Jean-Jacques Audubon, who wrote contemptuously of Rafinesque after cheating him of his discovery. *Audu-bone! For Christ swit sek!* Chevelier's hatred of "fockink Audu-bone" was only exceeded by his hatred of God, which he now launched forth upon.

To spare poor frail Mandy any more of his vile heresies, I referred again to that white-shell canal at Gopher Key. The old man stiffened on his bench. Even if there was such a canal, he said, as a gleam of pure duplicity crossed his eye, all it would prove was the existence of a huge clam bed offshore. Though the Islanders gathered a few conchs and clams, no one had discovered the vast mollusk bed which would be required for all the Indian-mound construction on this coast. Most likely that clam bed lay close by, perhaps on that broad and shallow bank off that empty stretch of coast north of Chatham River.

If he were a younger man, Chevelier assured me, he would stake out that clam bed for a canning industry, because the plume birds and alligators were doomed to disappear like all the rest of south Florida's wildlife. Nature cried out—and saying this, he actually cried out himself, a sharp yelp like a fox— for vengeance against Lum, whose wasteful rapine could only end in famine and destruction—

Who is Lum? I interrupted, annoyed because my wife seemed taken in by this old fraud. Mandy spelled it for me—*L-h-o-m-m-e*—and Chevelier pointed his old finger at my eyes. *"L'homme!"* he hollered. *"Voo, Msieu! Voo zett l'homme!"* I shut him up by mentioning what I'd been told by Nap Broward at Key West, that it was my destiny to develop this Lost Man's coast. *Lemper Roo-er!* this old man scoffed rudely. *Lemper Roo-er Wat-son!* Mandy laughed, which annoyed me further. Later she would use "Emperor Watson" as a nickname just to tease me, also "Lum" and "Lem" and sometimes just plain "Mister," short for "Mr. Watson." All these names were slightly disrespectful, but I enjoyed the whimsy of them because she truly loved me.

Before leaving, Mandy asked Chevelier his opinion of something said by our Chokoloskee friend Ted Smallwood, who had observed that the Ten Thousand Islands, with their myriad shifting channels, put him in mind of the Labyrinth in Greek mythology. Doubtless recalling the episode of the shot-off hat, the Frenchman retorted that if the Islands were indeed the Labyrinth, her own husband must surely be the *Mee-no-tore.* He glared at Mandy when she tried to make a joke of that, noting that the Minotaur could be gentle, too. "No fockink *choke!*" he snapped, still giving me that evil eye of his, mouth twisting cruelly. (Elderly indigestion, Mandy would tell me. I was not so sure.) I stood up abruptly, saying we must go.

Mandy thanked Mr. Chevelier for his kind hospitality, though that old wretch hadn't offered us so much as a cup of rainwater. The Frenchman liked her, that was clear, but he and I parted without shaking hands, as disgruntled and wary as ever. *Bun shawnce, share Madame, bella fortuna!* he called across the water, lifting his hat and making a small bow. Mandy said the old man was wishing her good fortune in two languages, perhaps he had sensed her illness, but I assured her he was only commiserating with her for being married to a minotaur like me.

All the way home from Possum Key, descending Chatham River, Mandy's eyes shone with excitement, but even before we reached the Bend, her mood was changing, and at the dock she seemed almost too tired to leave the boat. Watching the silver mullet flipping upward toward the moon, only to fall back helplessly into black water, she even wept a little. She could not explain her sudden dread and said it was not serious, but I believe she had some premonition of her death.

That year my dear wife seemed to waste away, perishing from the inside out, like a hollow tree. When she grew weaker, I took her to Fort Myers and put her in the care of Dr. Langford, who had a big house near the river between Bay and First Streets. Carrie went along to tend her, and the younger boys followed in late summer and stayed for the school year. Of all my children, ironically enough, the only one left at Chatham Bend was Rob.

*

One gray day, disturbed by a kind of hollowness in the air back in the mangroves, I went ashore at Possum Key to see how that old *Frawn-say* was getting on. At the door I smelled a dead mouse smell, which I thought at first might be his wild bird egg collection, knocked off the shelves by some foraging varmint and scattered on the floor. Then I saw him in the shadows, stiff as a poisoned rat in his mildewed blanket—long white whiskers, little paws up in the air, long yellow teeth in the dry mouth stretched toward the nose bone as if seeking water. Seeking was the story of the Frenchman's life, and judging from his famished face, he never found whatever he was after and probably never knew just what it was. All that was left him at his lonely end was his dream of *La Belle Frawnce*, lost long ago.

I hunted up his shovel and dug a grave in the soft soil of his overgrown garden. Putting rags over my hands against the odor, I lifted the light bundle in the blanket and carried it out like an offering into the light. Kneeling slowly, I lowered him into the earth, remaining there on my knees a moment, out of respect. I could think of no prayer that might help such a fierce God-hater, in the hereafter or anywhere else. "Jean Chevelier." I recited his name quietly, in witness. What else was there to say? I had delivered him to God in case God wanted him, and those two could thrash out which was the worse fraud now that he was dead.

In the clear stillness, the only sound was the harsh tearing squawk of a great blue heron from across the water. Chevelier had loved birds better than people. Here was his grim crier. And raising my head, I saw the staring eyes of a young owl. It had been there throughout our little ceremony, and did not fly off into the shadows even when I rose to shovel the black dirt back in the pit.

I had a look around the cabin for Chevelier's dug-up treasures before some thieving fisherman or plume hunter stripped the place clean, and was able to walk out of there with a clear conscience, having been tempted by nothing in the place. Outside, I was confronted by two of the young Hardens who brought food and cleaned house for the Frenchman. They had been coming every day for the past week. They were startled to see me, knowing how much the old man had feared and disliked me. When I told them that Chevelier was dead, the girl glanced at her brother, getting scared. Lee and Libby were fine young people, and their daddy Robert Harden was my friend, so I can't be sure who started the new rumors, but I knew right then that no matter what I said, Ed Watson would be connected to the Frenchman's death sooner or later.

*

In his instinctive guess about the lost Calusa clam bed, the Frenchman had distracted me from whatever he was up to back on Gopher Key. Even so, his instinct was correct. One day at dead low water, I anchored off Pavilion Key and eased myself barefoot over the side, a little gingerly because of stingrays. Sure enough, my toes located the numerous hard shapes of upright clam valves just beneath the sand, in what proved to be (when I got it all mapped out) a clam bed close to a mile wide, extending almost six miles north from Pavilion Key. I was pretty excited, because a clam industry right close to home where I could keep an eye on things might finance all of my great plans. I would get things started as soon as the cane harvest was finished, in late winter.

At this time, young Bill House and the House nigger, Henry Short, were working upriver from the Bend on Old Man D. D. House's small plantation at House Hammock. For a year or two, in their spare time, those boys had collected bird plumes and rare bird eggs for the Frenchman, and perhaps he had mentioned his clam theory to decoy them away from Gopher Key, because the next time I stopped by at House Hammock, I found Bill constructing a crude dredge. Clams? I said. He kind of grinned, a little sheepish, then led me away from that whole subject.

I gave Bill House no sign of my own interest. I went straight to Marco the next day and confided my discovery of that huge clam bed to Bill Collier, inviting him to join me as a partner. This man had always been successful in his enterprises and could make up what I lacked in experience as well as capital. To my surprise, Captain Bill seemed skeptical of the whole proposition, even when I mentioned my clam-dredge idea.

Because young House was a slow mover, I was not discouraged. I would find a partner or at least a backer among my business acquaintances in Fort Myers.

*

My friend Nap Broward was making his name by smuggling contraband arms to the Cuban rebels, and was urging me to use the *Gladiator* to help with his night runs. Broward was anxious to avenge José Martí, who had been goaded into returning to Cuba by Cubans who claimed he was doing too much talking and not enough fighting; they got that poor frail feller killed the first time he went out to prove them wrong. But I had known Martí only slightly, and on my next visit to Fort Myers, Mandy implored me to avoid such a reckless venture, reminding me that our family was reunited after years of hard separation, and that we should make the most of this precious time. Already very sick and weak, she gazed into my eyes in an odd way, for

Mandy knew she would not live much longer. She had never asked much of me and so I nodded.

To lighten our spirits, she showed me a Copley print called *Watson and the Shark*, which portrayed a man overboard being attacked by a huge shark in Havana Harbor. She teased me, saying, "You had better stay away from *that* place, Mr. Watson!" The doomed Watson was a soft, pale, naked fellow, wallowing helplessly in the shark's jaws and rolling his eyes to the high heavens, and the sole longboat crewman who was trying to toss a line to Watson was a black man. "Well"—I laughed—"if that is E. J. Watson, it's a damned poor likeness."

1898

In July of 1898, our Carrie would marry Dr. Langford's son, a handsome young fellow who lived in his father's household and had plenty of opportunities to pull the wool over the eyes of my young daughter. Carrie imagined she was in love with him, of course, and the Langfords loved Carrie—everybody did—but I believe their main idea was to settle Walter down. Because his father was my business partner or at least a backer, and because his family had been so hospitable to my own, I felt obliged to go along with the arrangement.

Young Langford had worked as a cow hunter in the Big Cypress, real hell and high water. Every Saturday, he rode into town, drank up his pay at the saloon, and rode out again, half dead, rounding up scrub cattle the rest of the week to pay for the next weekend of debauchery. But after one cowboy was shot and killed in a senseless accident in which he played a part—this was before he met Miss Carrie Watson—Walter decided he was through with those wild Saturdays and would now make something of himself. He still had his bad drinking bouts from time to time, but instead of shooting up the town, he would go down to the Hill House, turn his gun in, rent a room, and pay the colored man to bring him moonshine. The nigger would keep him locked up with his jug until he had drunk himself stone stiff and blind and worn that craving for hard liquor out of his system. Then he would totter home, gagging at the mere whiff of alcohol for the next six months.

I had known Walter for some years and liked him well enough, but I was not delighted by this match, which had been brokered by the Langfords' friend Jim Cole. In fact, I had misgivings from the start, not only about my little Carrie but about what I used to think of as my honor. And so I had a formal meeting with the would-be bridegroom in which I laid out a father's thoughts on honeymoon etiquette.

At Hendry House, we sat down over a brandy. Unfortunately we had two or three before I warned Walt more or less abruptly against getting drunk and taking my daughter by force—against taking her at all, in fact, until she was good and ready. My beloved little daughter, I reminded him, was scarcely thirteen, and I was already being condemned by this society for delivering my daughter to his mercies at this tender age.

Walt Langford took my good counsel as an insult to his honor as a gentleman, which had never been questioned, he informed me, until now. Though he struggled to contain his anger, he finally burst out, *Well now, Mr. Watson, sir, if she is too young, then why do you permit this marriage in the first place?* But we both knew why I was permitting it, and we both knew better than to speak about it, since it was unspeakable. Nevertheless, he felt humiliated, and being drunk—he was red in the face with brandy and embarrassment—he much resented the insinuation that he drank so much that he might ravish a young lady as if he had no more control over his lower instincts than one of those black animals who were conjured up by Pitchfork Ben before election.

The young man's anger in a public place triggered my own. "I am not *insinuating*, sir!" I interrupted. "I am stating a well-known fact about men's lust, a fact as plain as that red nose on your face!" To which he retorted that I had no right—*with all due respect, sir*—to instruct another man about how to comport himself with his own bride, especially when her father had approved the marriage for financial reasons. I was making the bridegroom pay, he said, for my own shame.

That was the first time and the last that Walter Langford ever dared to speak to me in such a way. I let the silence fall. He had sobered quick and had started to apologize, but I raised my hand to cut him off while I got my own outrage under control. Finally I said that I had spoken as I had because I knew about his years of drunkenness and fallen women. True, I had let my daughter go in consideration of my business circumstances. And I had no right, just as he said, to meddle.

I had my eyes down, gazing at my hands, and Walt awaited me, uneasy. He did not know what to make of such a speech or whether it was an apology or not. When I raised my eyes and looked at his, he shifted in his seat.

"But right or no right, boy, let me say this. You will answer to me and you will pay dearly if you fail to protect Miss Carrie Watson from all that is unseemly in yourself."

Walter was licked. He would never stand up to me again, although he would work against me, using Carrie. In a hushed voice, he said that he loved Carrie very much, and that he promised to be gentle, which indeed he was—gentle to a fault? Their first child would not be born until years later.

*

For all cautionary spite of bad-breathed old Aunt Etta, the Langfords were glad to get our lively Carrie, despite her father's shrouded reputation. Once my frontier family had been fitted with town clothes, we became quite fashionable by Fort Myers standards, thanks to Mandy's education and good manners, and were even included in Langford dinner parties and soirees. Eventually we were introduced to "America's Electrical Wizard," Mr. Edison, who had built his huge Seminole Lodge on Jake Summerlin's old place on the river and would later invite his friend Henry Ford to share the property. Though I never had that privilege, my daughter would meet the great automaker when he visited the Edisons, who also expected a visit any year now from their friend Sam Clemens. "*Mark Twain,* dear!" Aunt Etta gushed to Mandy, who had probably read more of that man's books than every Langford in the state of Florida piled up together. It was poor Mandy's fondest wish that she would live long enough to behold Twain in Fort Myers, "if only from afar," said this dear modest woman.

Because I could speak knowledgeably of the Tillman family in South Carolina, and especially that Populist radical Pitchfork Ben, the Langfords and Jim Cole introduced me into a meeting of their business club, to which I held forth over coffee and cigars. Back in '93, Tom Edison's General Electric Company had failed in the Great Depression, which propelled Ben Tillman into the U.S. Senate in place of Calbraith Butler. Tillman pointed out that Mr. Edison had been bailed out by the bankers, leaving the starving poor to their Great Redeemer, and like all capitalists had been inconvenienced not at all in his comfortable way of life. That an American industry led by Tom Edison could be brought down by unpatriotic agitators and syndicalists had greatly alarmed our new cattle capitalists, who denounced Ben Tillman as the Devil Incarnate, and welcomed anything I had to say.

I enjoyed being included by our civic leaders in excited discussions on the historic events taking place at the approach of the new century, especially when all these men might be very useful in my future plans. (Carrie proudly reported that I was considered "eloquent, humorous, and lively.") I always spoke as a stern supporter of the capitalist system, since I meant to become a capitalist myself, but privately I had to agree with Pitchfork Ben that the Populists were the only political party in America that was not for hire by the banks and corporations, or not yet, at least.

*

In the winter of 1898, we accused the Spaniards of sinking the battleship *Maine* in Havana Harbor. (Nap Broward told me our Government knew she had exploded without Spanish assistance, but nobody wished to hear anything so unpatriotic, and anyway, it was the excuse needed to begin a war with Spain.) Admiral Dewey steamed halfway around the world to destroy the rickety Spanish armada in Manila Bay, and the whole thing was over in four months—that "splendid little war" as it was called by our splendid little Secretary of State, who like most of the world's well-fed statesmen had never in his life seen red blood spilled nor heard a terrified man scream out in agony.

Theodore Roosevelt, the thick-spectacled Yankee in charge of our Cuba expedition, was calling Americans a "masterful" people whose bounden right and duty was to bring our superior civilization to the darker breeds. Our nation's new imperialistic arrogance, as Mandy called it, distressed my poor sick wife so much that I dared not confess what good sense it made to me. After all, as the newspapers reminded us, the European nations were seizing enormous territories in Africa and Asia, and the U.S.A. had better grab while the grabbing was good. As it turned out, what our nation was grabbing was a big fistful of thorns, but better that than missing out entirely, said the public.

In early June, a month before Carrie's wedding, the U.S. troops—66,000 restless men, including black conscripts and the pudgy T. Roosevelt's Rough Riders—disembarked at Tampa. Already the nigger soldiers were offending the good citizens, complained the Tampa *Tribune*, in an editorial I read out loud to amuse my wife.

"A number of disturbances resulted, the most serious when black troops objected to white soldiers from Ohio target-shooting at a black youngster. A riot ensued, injuring twenty-seven persons. . . . It is indeed very humiliating to the American citizens and especially to the people of Tampa . . . to be compelled to submit to the insults and mendacity perpetrated by the colored troops."

"Stop. Please, Mr. Watson." Pins in her mouth, Mandy was basting Carrie's wedding dress. The editorial had upset her so that she pricked her finger, and there was a round red dot on the cream satin. She had not noticed the red dot, and for some perverse reason I did not tell her, although even I knew that cold water should be applied at once to remove the stain. "I don't know which I detest more, those Ohio soldiers shooting at that child or that cruel, hypocritical editorial. Or my own dear husband finding it amusing—"

"No, no, I was smiling at what follows." I regretted having been amused in Mandy's presence, and detested the craven lying I resorted to in my secret need of this dying woman's good opinion. Hastily I read on about the hordes of soldiers rampaging through the streets and bars and brothels, all the drinking and wreckage and shooting at the ceiling. It seems that one poor prostitute had been punctured in the buttocks while plying her trade upstairs. "First casualty of our Splendid Little War," I commented, frowning hard to hide my chuckle in a fit of coughing.

"That can't have been funny for that poor young woman, Edgar Watson!" Mandy cried out, with more vigor than she'd shown in months. "What's the matter with white people anyway! Maybe all of them should be taken out and shot in their white buttocks, give 'em something to think about besides their own darn meanness!" But despite herself, she smiled a little, and again I felt ashamed, for the mere mention of whores' buttocks had reminded me how long it had been since I made love to Mandy, due to the painful ravaging of her body by her cancer.

Sucking her pricked finger, she had taken up the newspaper to read that story and make sure I wasn't joking. She detested everything she read about this war. "How can something so completely idiotic be so very evil at the same time?"

*

By the time I returned to Fort Myers some months later, all sorts of new stories had sprung up, some of which my daughter had passed along to Mandy. I went to Carrie, demanding to know what was being said, and she dismissed it as mere ladies' gossip overheard at Miss Flossie's Notions Store.

It seems that Mr. Edgar Watson, well-educated and well-mannered, had come from a wealthy Carolina clan. Unfortunately he was the black sheep of his family, getting in so much trouble that he had to flee. Eventually he opened a saloon and gambling joint someplace on the Georgia frontier. There were women, too, one lady whispered, so Belle Starr joined forces with him. Her method was, when a gambler won, she would have him followed, killed, and robbed (and she could take care of this end of the business if no henchman was handy). "Oh, Edgar and Belle were bad as bad could be!" my Carrie mimicked, smiling to show me how silly all this was. Finally this dangerous pair had been run clean out of Georgia, so they went to New Orleans for a while, then somewhere out West. Next, Belle disappeared and Mr. Watson moved to Florida and married a nice girl from a nice family in Deland who never knew a thing about his past. They moved down to the Islands and built a great big mansion on Chatham River.

"There's more, Papa." Carrie sighed. "The Langfords—" She stopped there, unable to continue. I returned to Mandy, who told me the rest of it in straight-faced innocence, trying bravely to make light of it, even amuse me.

It seems that Desperado Watson had a telescope in a lookout high under the eaves, from where he kept close watch on Chatham River. He spent most of his day scanning the Gulf, in case men came after him (or "his past caught up with him," as the case may be). One day he shifted the channel marker at Shark River—it was just an old post stuck into a sandbar—and on a night of storm, he shone a light to attract a Spanish ship which was on her way north to Punta Rassa to pick up a cargo of cattle for South America. Since she could not continue up the coast and round the shoals of Cape Romaine in these high winds, she entered the river mouth, missed the channel, and went hard aground, just as he'd planned. Watson rowed over ever so courteous and worked hard to get her off, and afterwards they invited him aboard to drink some rum. As soon as the Spaniards were drunk, he killed them all and took the gold they'd brought to buy the cattle. He took all the valuables, then towed the ship out to deep water and chopped a hole in her and sank her, having locked the cabin so that no telltale bodies would float to the surface.

"Telltale bodies," I repeated, nodding. "Looks like Mr. Desperado Watson knew his work."

"Mr. Desperado's Island neighbors revealed that story to somebody's lawyer's sister," Mandy assured me. We were both nodding now. "However, everyone agrees that Mr. Desperado has always been very kind to his beloved wife and children." Here she batted her eyes primly, trying not to laugh. "Also, it turns out that Belle Starr was not killed after all, her death was a trick Belle and Edgar played to get her out of trouble. Belle even came East and helped him nurse his poor sick wife while she was down there wasting away in those awful Islands." She looked up. "Perhaps they confused Maybelle with that Netta woman you had living there before I came." This teasing was as close to a reproach about Netta Daniels as Mandy would ever come, but mild as it was, it changed her mood.

Mandy chose this day almost a decade after the death to take a deep breath and ask me quietly if I had been Belle's slayer. "I answered that way back in Oklahoma," I said shortly. "I know you did," she said, gaze unrelenting. When I remained silent, she nodded carefully, closing her eyes as if satisfied, which she was not.

Mandy had never asked why I had changed my name to E. J. Watson, but one evening—we were still at Chatham Bend—she inquired politely what that J might stand for. "Jesus," I snapped at her too sharply, and went right on with what I was doing at the table, which was molding bullets. A moment later, I looked up, defiant.

She was awaiting me, as I knew she would be—a born poker player, watching me over her cards. Eyebrows raised in that way she had, her pale brow as cool and clear as porcelain even in this heat, she held my gaze. Her fixed expression made me feel she was looking into me, looking straight through my black pupils at Jack Watson. Clear-eyed, unblinking, she gave nothing away, for my wife was an unmuddied soul who could outstare Jack Watson without even trying. Right then I knew with the greatest relief that whatever this good woman had perceived in her husband's face, she would always love him.

Arranging a bank loan on good terms, I bought her a little house on First Street, opposite Franklin's Hardware. "It's small," I told her, "but I reckon it will hold most of your cats." She smiled in a soft burst of joy, so happy was she at the prospect of living independently under her own roof while she was dying.

*

Not very long before the wedding, a book entitled *Hell on the Border* was brought to the Thursday Reading Club in town. Among its tales of the Wild West was the author's version of the life and death of Mrs. Maybelle Shirley Starr, in which a man named Watson was identified as her slayer. It was soon confirmed by Sheriff Tippins (who had learned of it from the Sheriff at Key West) that the said assassin was none other than Mr. E. J. Watson of Chatham Bend, an escaped felon from Arkansas State Prison. The word spread quickly.

As everyone knows, Americans love a desperado, especially a well-dressed rascal of suave and courtly manner. Having already made a dangerous reputation at Key West and Tampa, Mr. E. J. Watson couldn't walk the street without folks pointing. Overnight, I became the most celebrated citizen in town after Tom Edison—or the most notorious, as Jim Cole liked to say, trying to bend things in the Langfords' favor in our transactions over the terms of Carrie's marriage. Cole also persuaded the Langford family, and eventually my own, that a fugitive from justice and accused murderer should not be permitted to show his shifty face at a formal wedding. (Cole also saw to it, I suspect, that I was no longer welcome in the business circle.) Though Mandy and Carrie assured everyone I was not Belle's killer, the social pressures proved too much, and in the end, Mandy had to suggest on behalf of Carrie and the Langfords that I stay away from my beloved daughter's wedding. Asked her own opinion, she looked me in the eye and said she would stand by me whatever I might decide. "It is up to you," she said.

I said nothing. I was very bitter. I longed to invade the wedding drunk and outrage them all. But in the end I did not want to do that, and to make sure I didn't, I left the house and went down to the docks and prepared to sail.

Rob came aboard the *Gladiator* at the last minute and called good-bye to Carrie from the masthead. She was thrashing both arms back and forth holding two white hankies, trying to bring me back to say good-bye, and perhaps Rob responded when I didn't, pretending he thought her frantic waving was for him. I suppose he meant well, but it seemed pathetic any way you look at it. I never asked him why he joined me and I never thanked him. On that voyage south, father and son never exchanged one word.

*

Down in the Islands, folks felt left behind by great events—"We are coughing up the dust of progress, none the wiser," C. G. McKinney said. The only memorial to the great victory over Spain was the mahogany tree that was planted by the Storter family over on the east side of the trading post in Everglade. That tree will be there a lot longer than all the flags and bombast and parades.

The Philippine Islands had joined Cuba in declaring independence, but after we freed them from the Spanish yoke, there was loud talk of annexing all those islands for their own damned good, and Puerto Rico, too, while we were at it. (Drive some sense into them Filly-pino heads, said Tant Jenkins wisely, make them little fellers see things *our* way.) Uncle Sam's blood was up, all right, now that we had realized how far ahead of us those Europeans were in bringing Christ and capitalism to benighted lands all around the globe. But our cane planters felt threatened by the acquisition of these backward places, suspecting that what attracted the U.S. was the rich sugarcane industry in all three countries.

"Progressive" versus "Populist"—that was the great struggle of our nation as the old century was drawing toward its close. I actually preferred Ben Tillman's populism to the so-called Progressive platform of T. Roosevelt, who was making up for his weak eyes and sickly childhood with his noisy trumpeting and brandishing of flags and guns. Aside from Tillman (who would protest that fooling with these Filipinos was bound to inject the inferior blood of a "debased and ignorant" people into "the body politic" of the U.S.A.), the one notable American who denounced our glorious bullying of small brown countries was Mandy's revered author, Mr. Clemens. As a turncoat Southerner who had dared to blame the War of Northern Aggression on the South, he now declared that our nation's bold new spirit of industrialism and imperialism was based on nothing more nor less than racism and greed. When talking at our business circle, I had strongly disapproved of his radical tendencies, but privately I had to own that he was sharp-witted and comical, and that even his thorny political views were pretty close to my own ideas of what was true.

The Spanish War was a great boon to our Lee County businessmen, in particular those patriotic cattlemen whose cow hunters were out beating the scrub for every head of beef they could lay a rope on. These scrags were herded over to Jake Summerlin's corrals at Punta Rassa and shipped off to the U.S. troops in Cuba—a real hog-killing, or what business people like to call "a tidy profit."

Naturally I felt patriotic, too, since in its small way the cane syrup industry was also prospering. Mostly I traded at Tampa Bay, which was now dredged out for coastal shipping and accessible by railroad, and mostly I stayed at the Tampa Bay Hotel on the Hillsborough River, with its curlique arches and fancy minarets that made it look like a five-hundred-room whorehouse up in Heaven. I wanted to take Mandy there to see the sights and attend a concert and do some fancy shopping, but by the time I finally got around to it, she was too weak to enjoy herself, and I brought her home.

*

By 1900 Tampa Bay had its first automobiles and hard-paved streets where horse hooves skittered on the fresh manure. The Tampa Electric Company had more business than it could handle, and the cigar industry was booming, with over two hundred factories out at Ybor City. Having had a little trouble at Fort Myers, I was now conscripting field hands in the Scrub, a makeshift settlement east of Ybor City where the blacks huddled in their shacks in the scrub palmetto.

I never cared much for the cockpits, though cockfighting was very popular in Spanish Tampa. Instead I visited the Misses Metz, the young kindergarten teachers at the school. The sisters became my close companions, not only at Tampa Bay but later at Key West, where these jolly girls opened a nice lodging house over on White Street. Their dauntless willingness to accept my rough side with my smooth lightened many an hour not otherwise engaged in business dealings, which were mostly held in the saloons.

One afternoon, forsaking the saloon to go trade for supplies at Knight & Wall Hardware, I became unduly irritated by the clerk, who kept me waiting while he preened over some damn foolishness he had learned at dancing school. To command his attention, I drew my revolver and fired into the floor beside his shoe. "If you prance as fancy as you talk," said I, "let's see you prove it." Someone ran out when the shooting started, the deputies arrived, and I went off to jail. One deputy said, "I'm sorry, Ed, but nobody saw no fun in it exceptin you." Of course, Tampa was becoming a large port where few folks knew me, and when I grew unruly, nobody at home heard much about it. However, my luck was changing, because this news reached Fort Myers before I did.

*

With my wife an invalid in Fort Myers and no woman to run the household at the Bend, I installed Tant Jenkins's baby sister as my housekeeper. Josie Jenkins was spirited and pretty, with very wide-awake round dark brown eyes. "Our daddy Mr. Jenkins loved his Seleta," Tant had told me. "When she left him, he got over her, I reckon, but he had to kill himself to do it." I had a long laugh over that one, and glad to get it, too, because I hardly got enough work out of Tant to pay his feed.

Though Tant was still with me, Henry Thompson had left the Bend before the century's turn, joining his mother at George Roe's boardinghouse in Caxambas, where Netta had taken up her duties as Mrs. Roe. That year young Gertrude Hamilton came up from Lost Man's to go into the school, and pretty quick she and Henry had to marry. Gert's granddad was Jim Daniels, Netta's brother, so those two youngsters were close kin to start off with, though not as close as some folks in these parts.

The Watson Syrup Company

Although still short of capital, my syrup trade was growing fast and had great prospects, with buyers lined up for every drop I could produce, and meanwhile I learned more and more about the business. Sugarcane is a giant grass and a perennial, yielding four or five crops before new cuttings must be planted. I double-cropped with cowpeas to restore the soil and would rest each section every few years, leaving it fallow.

In south Florida, the cane begins to ripen with the first drop in temperature, in September. In October, an experienced hand goes out with a firepot to burn it, for I had learned that good strong stalks lose little sugar to fast-moving flames. It all depends on how well you gauge the wind. Without the long leaves and tops, which clog the mill, the stalks become much lighter and more easily handled. Also, the burning clears the field of snakes and scorpions, and chases out strayed hogs as well as game, so a good gun ranging down along the field edge could generally bring down more than enough to feed our crew.

Dry cane ignites all in a rush with a heavy roaring as in storm, and the fire produces a black smoke so thick and oily that it takes on a kind of a muscled look as it rolls skyward, leaving the earth in deep sepia shadow and strange light. When the field was dry, I would organize the burn on the day before harvest, in late morning. Burning too early harms the plant and causes the cane to grow back with thinner stalks, until finally it leans and sprawls before it can be reaped, especially where cane rats (which throw big litters six times in a year) gnaw the stalks. Yet this plant is hardy and keeps right on growing, causing a problem where stalks tangled by the wind form a thick green matting on the ground.

The cutters use the cane knife, like a big machete. Because the long blades are honed to a singing edge as sharp as sawgrass, trying to clear the tangle can be dangerous. Bloody accidents are pretty common, especially among bad drinkers, but also among the older men, green hands, and the exhausted. They go bleary. The veterans rig themselves crude shin guards or hide leggings, having hacked a shin or sliced off toes at one time or another, often those belonging to the man beside them. When a tired cutter stoops carelessly to grab a stalk for chopping, a sweat-filled eye or even an eardrum can be pierced by the hard tip of the cane. In this humid climate, there is heat collapse, and sprained backs are common. Every little while, one sees even the strongest straighten in a slow half turn, arched like a bow, the heel of one hand pressed into his lower back to ease his muscles.

A steam engine ran the mill which pressed the stalks. I rigged a frame for a big kettle over a buttonwood fire for boiling the syrup, which smelled so good that the Hardens claimed it made their mouths water three miles away, off the river mouth at Mormon Key. My kettle, 250 gallons, was twice the size of any kettle on this coast. Once the syrup works got under way, our plantation produced 10,000 gallons every year, at least three times what was produced by Storters, who had to haul lighter-loads of stalks from Half Way Creek to their mill at Everglade. We packed the syrup in one-gallon tins and saved the skimmings to make moonshine, sold off that white lightning by the quart jar along with the fine product of the Watson Syrup Company.

Cane harvest began in October, when I fetched a crew of cutters to the Bend. I promised free transportation, a dry bunk, and three square meals a day. Most of the crew were derelicts and drifters from the shantytowns and saloon alleys of Tampa and Key West, and later some of this riffraff bitched that they had been kidnapped while drunk. I'd take out a coiled whip and rap it on my palm, or maybe inspect my revolver. I'd say, Well, boys, you might as well work now that you're here, otherwise you might be shot as an example. That made the complainers back down fast and work a little harder, because we were way out there beyond the law where the boss was not responsible to anybody, and they were not confident that this man Ed Watson was joking. In scarcely a fortnight that bunch would be broken the same way wild horses are broken, and would instantly obey my every order. Instilling fear got the work done faster, but I had some bad luck and made some mistakes which would cause me serious trouble later on.

My new mill turned real fast with its ten-horsepower motor. All the hands wore baggy clothes on account of the damned bugs, and one young nigger's shirt was an old hand-me-down, a lot too big for him. It caught a loose cuff, then his hand and forearm before Sip Linsey jammed a log into the flywheel, stalled her out. I heard him scream and came running from the fields, but he had already passed out from shock and loss of blood. Poor Josie wept at the sight of so much blood and entreated me to run him to Key West, but one look told me he wouldn't make it to the boat, let alone Key West. His arm was ripped right off the shoulder, with nowhere to tie a tourniquet and slow the bleeding. All we could do was lay him in the shade and slip a folded gunnysack under his head. He came around just once and asked weakly for water, and while he sipped at it, he watched our faces. Scared and sleepy, he asked if he was dying. No, I said, you will be fine tomorrow. He closed his eyes, which were suddenly full of tears. He was still hemorrhaging and soon slipped away.

Next, a big cutter, Little Joe, nearly sliced his foot off when his blade glanced off a clump. He was working tired. That foot was sewed back on some way by Robert Harden, but not before the man half-bled to death. He recovered all right but would not come back to Chatham Bend. He forsook his pay. Robert got stubborn about it, too, said he would not bring him back against his will. There weren't too many who stood up to me around the Islands, but that time Robert did it, and we stayed pretty good friends. I had a sugar plantation to establish and needed no enemies among my nearest neighbors, especially an enemy who had three sons who all knew how to shoot.

Like Old Man James Hamilton on Lost Man's Beach and many others on our coast, Robert Harden had outrun a past he never talked about. Those two old men were kin by marriage, though they didn't talk about that, either, due to real or imagined differences in their blood. The Hardens were American, Choctaw, Seminole, and Portugee, to hear them tell it. If something else was in that mix, that was their own business, and anyway, they had plenty of company around these parts. Those Hardens stood by me, and I could count on 'em. I don't know if they were "new Americans" or not, but as the Frenchman found out years before me, they were the best friends a man could want down in the Lost Man's country.

The Tuckers

My Island neighbors, Robert Harden warned me, were already leery of "Desperado Watson," and of course this was partly my own fault. In my early years, planning a great future for this coast, I had not discouraged dangerous stories that might scare settlers off the few pieces of high ground down in the Lost Man's country. But now these stories were coming back to haunt me, and everything that happened seemed to make them worse.

First of all there was bad trouble with my foreman, a likable young feller from Key West named Wally Tucker, who had come here with his wife the year before. I owed Tucker his year's pay, but as I had warned him when he came, I never paid off help until the end of harvest, so my riffraff would not quit me at a crucial time. If I paid the Tuckers, I had no excuse not to pay the others, and until the new syrup had been sold, I could not afford that.

Tucker protested angrily that I'd said the same damned thing six months before. He only backed off a little when his wife cautioned him. The matter was still unsettled when my hogs, which ranged free in the daytime, snuffled a corpse out of a shallow grave out behind the cane fields. Tucker and his pretty Bet were the ones who came across it. Though the dead man had no face left, they claimed to recognize him.

That damned Rob never said a word about this until they left—that was the first mistake. I told him this must be the man who got his arm chewed in the mill. More and more upset, he told me that this could not be that same man because he himself had helped Wally Tucker carry the body from the house, wrapped in a sheet, and let it go into the river. After another pause, he added that when he went out there to see for himself, he had found a second body near the first one. The field hand the Tuckers had recognized was Ted and the second man was Ted's work partner, Zachariah.

When Little Joe was hurt the year before, this black Ted had stirred up trouble, claiming the work was much too dangerous for such long hours and poor pay, and threatening to quit or start a strike. Spouting that union syndicate talk that was causing so much labor trouble on the east coast rail-road, he had infected all the rest with discontent.

My syrup enterprise, which was to be the foundation of west coast development, would suffer a setback it would not survive if this man was allowed to start a strike here. I called him in and promised him more pay, and when he told me he was fighting for the workers of the world, not just himself, I cursed him for a fool communist and threatened him. Ted backed down, but he had spirit, and I knew he would be back. Sure enough, when that man bled to death a few months after Little Joe was hurt, Ted came to see me and demanded improved pay and better work conditions, starting next day.

*

"Bet was out calling the hogs," Rob was telling me as I tried to focus. I growled, "Out screwing in the woods, more likely," and drove him from the room, pouring myself a coffee mug of whiskey. It seemed inconceivable that my whole enterprise might fail because hogs had sniffed out the graves and these damn Tuckers had stumbled on their mess.

Wally Tucker had known Ted was a troublemaker, trying to blackmail Watson Syrup at harvest time, but seeing the body, he decided that life might be dangerous around here because he and his pregnant Bet knew my dark secret. Telling Rob they feared for their lives, they went off in their little sloop, leaving me with no foreman for the harvest. Tant was over at

Caxambas, having his last binge before work started. I ordered Rob to forget
the whole damn business and not mention it to Tant when he got back.

Due to bad winds, the Tuckers ran short of food and water and got no farther south than Wood Key, where Robert Harden and his family were now
living. Robert encouraged them to settle on that coast, at least until he could
deliver her baby. The Hardens helped them plant a vegetable patch back of
Lost Man's Beach and build a shack across the channel on Lost Man's Key
which would catch the onshore breeze. When I found this out, I bought the
quitclaim to Lost Man's Key from Winky Atwell up in Rodgers River and sent
a letter back with Winky, ordering those Tuckers off my property. Tucker
sent back a sassy note, claiming he had squatter's rights until I paid him his
full wage or hell froze over, whichever should come first. That note enraged
me all over again, because Tucker had already told Hardens that E. J. Watson
was killing off his nigger help on payday. Said he aimed to notify the Key
West Sheriff as soon as his small crop was in and his Bet felt strong enough
to make the journey.

Tucker had no proof anymore because I had slipped those remains into
the river. I would say he had told that story out of spite after a salary dispute.
However, I could not afford more rumors just when my larger plans were
getting under way. Having befriended the surveyor Mr. Shands, I had made
progress in establishing legal ownership of Chatham Bend and also a
smaller tract across the river, and I also had claims to other pieces of high
ground, to ensure control of the development that was bound to come to the
Lost Man's region with the large-scale drainage and development of the
Glades. Most exciting of all, my plans had been promised full support by my
friend Nap Broward, whose election as governor now seemed assured. But
Broward had warned me that before I could work with his administration, I
had to restore my name as a good citizen, to go with my fine reputation as
planter and businessman. This I could never hope to do while Tucker was
threatening me with his bad stories.

Whenever someone threatened to tell tales on me, get me in trouble, a
taste of iron came into my mouth and my hand hardened, in a rage or perhaps fear from the oldest corner of my brain. My chest would bind tight and
unless something gave way my heart and mind together would explode. In
panic, I knew that something terrible was on its way that I could not stop but
only watch it come.

It. I've tried over and over to find words for this It. I don't know how. It is
just *there*, it is always there behind my brain, ringing and intense. Like
death in life. The one hope was to seize it quick, meet its force and twist that
force back upon itself, before it unraveled beyond reach. By the time that
wild unraveling is under way, I am already caught up in it, like a coyote I

saw in an Arkansas tornado, a pale dog spinning skyward, turning white against black clouds, then black against white, then lost into that apocalyptic funnel.

Afterwards that chaos gives way to a dead stillness, a glassy clarity and a cold ecstasy that shivers every nerve and muscle. With this came a precise *knowing* that what this self was about to do was the universal will.

Moonlight on its whiskers, muscles gathered in a coiling crouch, the wild cat leaps. The leap is the It, and It is the cat and It is I. In this moment I am the instrument of light and dark and death and life, for I am everything. It is like loving at the lost wild end of it, but many times more powerful, and dark.

*

Having read Tucker's note, I tossed it away and sat down hard in my corner chair, to calm my heart. When that didn't work, I yanked open my jug and sat at my long empty table while I drank it, as Josie and her new baby watched through the back door.

Through the window—he did not dare come inside—that damned Rob was pestering me with questions. He was full of dread and would not let go. Son Born, I said wearily. Son Born, I repeated. Son Born, dammit, this fucking Tucker is out to spoil all our great hopes. We have to do something.

Rob cried desperately, Wally Tucker might be pigheaded but he is sincere. He thinks you owe him a year's pay. And now Atwells have sold that key right out from under him, and poor Bet having her baby any day now.

Son Born had some spirit, yes he did, but he was too high-strung and oversensitive to be much use. When I think of Rob, I think of that day three years before when he brooded for a week over some damned thing I'd said, then took my revolver and kneeled in front of Pup, my bluetick hound. I was dozing after the midday feed when I heard Rob's voice drift through the sunlight in the window. *Pup?* it said. *Want to play Russian roulette?* I didn't even know what the hell that was, but through the window I could hear Pup thump his tail. Rob removed the cartridges, all but one, spun the chamber a few times, put the muzzle to Pup's head. Wasn't much of a roulette game. He killed that dog dead first time he pulled the trigger. The noise shocked him so, and the blood and the dead dog, that he hurled the gun against the tree and lit out around the house. He was shocked by the result, I don't know why. How many times did that fool aim to try it?

When I heard that *bang,* then screams and crying, I thought at first that one of the children had been killed. When I ran out, that crazy boy was running round and round the house, screeching each time he passed that poor hound's body. I went back and put on my boots and came outside again. He was still running. Wanted to run right off the map. I intercepted him at the house corner and hoisted him, kicking and screeching, off the ground. I laid him down—I *held* him down—and shook him, stopping those hysterics by main force. Finally, having made him understand just what he'd done, I beat him. I beat hell out of him. That made the other children cry, but to this day I believe that is what he wanted of me. That's why he played that fool game in the first place, to get my attention. Son Born, I said, you're going about your life all the wrong way. And he screeched, Papa, don't call me that name ever again or I will kill you!

Well, that's what he was doing now, through that same window, fighting for Papa's attention while plaguing him with his upset and loss. I had to shout before he would be still. I told him, "Never mind, boy, I'll take care of this. Stay out of my way, that's all. Stay here with Josie and the baby, keep your mouth shut, and don't go acting crazy, understand?"

"I'm your *son*, Papa! Why won't you listen? Someone *killed* those field hands!"

Son Born never did know what he felt, didn't even know where to begin. He was half furious, half close to tears. Most of all, he wanted my approval, wanted to stand by me, when the one he should have stood by, as I realized much too late, was the one who saw that his father had gone crazy and was trying to stop a crazy man from doing more harm.

*

Sometimes when I drink, like any man, I am full of piss and vinegar. Pick a fight or horse around or wrestle, shoot out the lights or smash up something out of the energy of life, just for the fun of it—just for the *fun* of it—if only to hear the other sinners howl. The glee of breaking, that's all it is, the glee of breakage. Not glee so much as a well-being that can only be expressed in senseless wild destruction—joy and destruction all at once, a whirling and spinning clean out of my sin-burdened self into that nothingness which poor Mandy glimpsed that evening in those mullet, the yearning leap and fall back to oblivion.

I have always done my best to pay for all the damage, but as a moonshine drinker, I was losing my grip. Since those two corpses had been found, I had been gutted by black-hearted moods or an inchoate rage or by dead apathy. Or by dangerous brawling in the bars—the same signs I recalled from those bad spells of hard drinking and disruption long ago. For the first time in years, Selden Tilghman had returned in nightmare, and the Owl-Man, and also black Joseph, dead out in the swamp. What Joseph might signify, if anything at all, I never knew.

In this crisis, with everything at stake, I was too sick with weeks of heavy drinking to think clearly. Son Born silhouetted in the window, always pleading. I refused to answer. Where was Lucius when I needed him? Yet I did not want Lucius to see this. The farther away he was from what was happening the better. Right now I had to drink to knock my heart down. I sat up, waving Son Born from my sight.

I was afraid. I was sick afraid of losing everything I'd worked so hard for just because some bastard agitator had turned up like a withering disease on this small plantation, just because my horny foreman went out screwing his young wife in the woods instead of tending to his business. And the hog? Which one? That young black sow the Tucker girl had raised up to do tricks. Betsy. Named for that girl. And turned around and gobbled up her litter. I should have slit her bristled throat right then.

*

Over there on the east coast, Henry Flagler was dealing with dago Italians and union syndicates and I don't know what, mixing their dirty immigrant tricks and communist ideas with Ben Tillman's homegrown rantings. But Flagler had hard foremen to take care of troublemakers—move in quick, let the fur fly, before the trouble spread, the same way the owners were doing in the mines out West. Flagler's wish was law on his new rail line as well as in his kingdom at Palm Beach, up to and including capital punishment, and all the other big new businesses around the country were the same. The great capitalists building America let nobody and nothing stand in the way of progress, especially their own—that's what made them great. "Hardest fight I ever fought," Flagler boasted to the papers, except that Flagler didn't have to fight, he was spared all the rough stuff, and the blood and guilt. Employers are proud to sacrifice the workers' lives for business principles as long as their underlings do the dirty work and spare their consciences. Never have to bloody their soft hands or even know about it, not if the foremen really know their job. *Go on out and play some golf, Boss, get some fresh air.*

"You boys want progress American style or dirty European communism?" they asked the strikers. Never even waited for an answer, because no reporters had showed up and no law either, so they sailed right in. Flagler's men went after those crews with clubs and pistols, broke some arms, bloodied some heads. The ones who never got up again served as examples to the others. Just happened to be the troublemakers they were after.

We could have gone after Ted and Zachariah that same way, whipped a few others as they ran, and the little strike at Watson Syrup would have been over. But Foreman Tucker wasn't up to that, not for a boss who owed him a year's pay. Tant did not want the responsibility for strike-busting or anything else, that's who Tant is. Rob would have jumped right in if I had asked him to, but he would have been useless, trying to reason with them when he was really on their side.

I knew what had to be done and done real quick, but I didn't have the man to do it. It was up to me.

Those two bad apples had to be removed from the barred because that one called Ted had heard about those unions and carried that infection with him, and the other one, Zachariah, was a crew leader and went along with it, helping Ted persuade the rest to go on strike the first day of the harvest unless Watson Syrup met all their demands. They would not listen to reason and I could not scare them—they were both tough niggers. I wasn't a Flagler or a Carnegie but only a small planter in a frontier wilderness where a man had to make his own law or go under.

One Sunday, having steadied my nerves with a good jolt from the jug, I called those two out of the bunk room, marched 'em to the boat, yelling out so the rest could hear how I was running these sonsofbitches north to Everglade, from where they would have to work their own way home. Those boys only snickered, waving good-bye to their friends, they were sure I was just bluffing about Everglade, and they were right.

I had a shovel on the boat. Down around the Bend, I tossed 'em the shovel and ordered 'em ashore. Marched 'em straight across the forest on the far side of the fields. Knowing something was coming, they tried to tell me, stumbling along, that having thought things over, they would now work hard and make no further trouble. They were too scared to run, and anyway I knew better than to shoot them since the sound would carry. I told them to dig their graves.

They were both strong workers, good smart boys, probably the best cutters on that crew, and I didn't like this any better than they did. I stood them in their graves, took a deep breath, and brained Ted first with the revolver butt. Zachariah saw him drop and cried out, "Dere Lawd God!" but I told him to be quiet and stand still if he knew what was good for him. He asked if he could pray and I said yes, and as soon as he bent his head, I dropped him, too. I covered 'em up as best I could, shouldered the shovel, and went back to the boat the way I came. That afternoon, I kept on going north to Everglade to make sure I was seen where I said I was going, and I spent the evening with Bembery Storter over a jug of shine. I felt relieved that the Watson strike was over, but also sorry. Listening to ol' Bembery singing "Amazing Grace" in his own funny idea of a darkie accent, I swore I would never take a life again.

I sailed at daybreak, and was back out in my fields by afternoon. *Once I was lost, and now I am found . . .* I was still singing that old hymn, full of strange grief. Next thing I knew, the Tuckers found those bodies.

I don't excuse what I did. There is a difference between right and wrong, always was and always will be, but each man's wrong and right is somewhat different. Just depends, as the old fellers say. Everything depends. But what I did was wrong by my own lights, and I hated the doing of it, I felt sick. Even so, I don't regret it because progress was at stake, which is something much, much more important than my conscience. Or even two brown lives, if we are honest.

On the Everglades frontier as the new century came in, rough methods were sometimes necessary in the name of progress. Any man standing in the way of progress in America was going to be knocked flat, and some were not so likely to get up. *Can't scramble eggs without breaking one or two*—that's a pretty good motto.

*

Too much had already gone wrong, and too much was at stake, after too many hard years of loss and failure. Enraged that Tucker was forcing me into this corner, I got drunk. When I read his note again, I roared like a baited bear. Soon after that, I fell down on the bed face first, I could not even roll over. In my dream, my blood was boiling. I was in hell.

In late afternoon, a murderous hot shaft of sun through the west window burned my temple. My eyes opened to see a man silhouetted in the window frame. He was burning me. No, it was Rob, still watching me, not knowing what to do. Lying weak and motionless, with a great headache, I heard that shrill ringing, felt it grow like a tornado, all around me. Then Edgar was gone, as in one of those flying dreams he suffered as a child, falling and falling till the moment he awakened, whimpering in terror.

That night I blamed Rob for all my troubles, who knows why. Perhaps—though he could not admit it to himself—he hated me for hating him, and had taken the side of those Tucker people. For all I knew, he'd put them up to leaving, and had not awakened me in time to stop them.

It was my life or the life of Wally Tucker.

Inert as any dead man, watching Son Born's silhouette through lidded eyes, I said, "I'm going." I never told him that he must go with me or suggested it or urged it. Never. His voice said, "Please, Papa. I am going with you."

*

Josie Jenkins was afraid who was ordinarily afraid of almost nothing. With her cat instincts, she understood something. She knew me. Clutching our Baby Pearl, she said, Where are you going, Jack? It's late. I told her what I had told my son, to shut up and get the hell out of my way. She retreated and ran outside when I raised my arm, but she screeched back at me. *Why would you take him with you? Why are you doing that?*

"He is not taking me," Rob told her, "but I must go." He was still in hopes that he might stop me. She ran forward and hugged him. "Honey, you stay out of it," she whispered.

I was halfway to the dock when I heard his steps.

I am going, Rob had told her—a sane answer. *Row the damn boat, then, and shut up*—there was another. One sane answer at a time.

*

There was no wind. Until near midnight, under a full moon, the skiff creaked along inside the Islands. We rested a few hours at Onion Key. He pled with me for the last time, he wept and begged me. *Look at me, Papa. Please, Papa. Answer me.* I was coating those noisy oarlocks with a heavy oil and did not answer, only waved him aboard and took the helm and drifted Lost Man's River with the tide, out across the morning mists on First Lost Man's Bay. Soon I dropped the sail and took the oars, but this time I faced forward, using small and silent strokes as the skiff drew near the dark mass in the river mouth that was Lost Man's Key.

In the Home Cove on the east side of the key, I drew the boat softly up onto the sand. I whispered over my shoulder, *Stay with the boat. The less you hear and see and know the better. If I'm not back in an hour, don't come looking for me. Get out of here quick, you understand? Get the hell home. You never knew anything about this.*

But when I headed through the woods toward the Gulf shore, he followed me. He was clumsy with distress, making too much noise. I turned and scowled, pointing back toward the skiff. He shook his head. He was trembling so hard he could scarcely walk.

Soon the sea grape opened out on the Gulf shore. On the dawn horizon was a shadow squall full of dark rain, but the sunrise from the Glades, touching Lost Man's Key, turned the leaves over Tucker's head as bright as metal.

Wally Tucker in a worn gray shirt was perched on a driftwood tree down by the water. He was mending his britches, rifle leaning on the wood beside him. Every little while he'd lift his head to look and listen, then spit his wad before bending to his needle. Expecting Watson to come south along the coast, he was keeping an eye out in the wrong direction. His wife was in the shack, which was a mercy. There are things no pregnant girl should have to look at.

He sensed something, he whirled, stared down my barrels. Startled, I held my fire while he asked Rob to take care of his poor Bet. This did not fool me. I pulled the trigger as he lunged for his rifle, and he spun and crumpled like a bird and hardly quivered.

"Oh Papa, *NO!*"

Rob's screech shattered the echo of the shot. He was unable to take in what had just happened. A man is quick, eyes bright, mouth shining, and the next moment he is extinguished, twitching the last of his lost life away in his own mess. There is no being anymore, only the soiled carcass, eyes wide, mouth wide, shivering and jerking as death takes it. A life is gone like the sun flash of a minnow in the current.

In a white shift, Bet Tucker flew across the sand. I had forgotten her. She did not fly to her husband's side but down the shore toward the point. That meant their skiff was hidden in the mangroves in case Watson came, and I cursed my carelessness in not having noticed that their little boat was missing. Even now, I could have brought her down, but in my condition, I could not be sure of a clean kill at that range. She'd be kicking and bleeding on the sand, or even screaming.

That is why I tossed Rob the revolver. I told him gently to go finish it because I could not catch her. He dropped the weapon in the sand but picked it up again. Clutching it, he backed away, still staring at Wally, still telling me that this was crazy, still weeping that I must be crazy, too. He was pasty, going green, trying not to vomit. He was stuttering aloud that he could not do it. I told him quietly that if Bet got away, he was going to hang right alongside his crazy daddy. "Just *do* it," I told him, "quick and merciful. Temple or the base of the skull. Don't meet her eye. Don't say one word."

Rob moaned like a doomed soul and ran off after her, casting me one last wild-eyed look over his shoulder. That boy was not cut out to take a life. But the gun went off as I approached, and in the echo of the shot, there came loud ringing silence. I saw his legs on the white sand between low bushes, and I thought, He's killed himself. I was mistaken. He had done what he had to do and done it quick.

Perhaps at the sight of blood and bone and brain on his own trousers, Rob had fainted. He lay curled like a child beside the dead girl, like the mythic brother of this mythic sister in her virginal white shift, swollen with child, and the blood pooling in the sun in a crimson halo all around her head.

She was not decent. I stepped forward and tugged the shift down, then stood Rob on his feet. When he fell again, I let him go and hoisted her warm heavy body, carrying it to the water's edge, setting it down. *I'm sorry,* I told her, and I meant it. I went to her husband and grasped him by the ankles, hauled him to the water, laid him beside her. We could not stay there long enough to bury them, since the Hamiltons on Lost Man's Beach might have heard the shots. When I moved the bodies into the slow current, both sank slowly to the bottom, where sharks following the blood trail upriver would nose toward them on the first incoming tide.

Rob had come around by the time I reached him. He was a gray color, still trembling. He whimpered when he saw dark sand where she had lain. I helped him up and with my fingertips brushed the human bits off him as gently I could. He stared at my hand in astonishment, then turned away and would not look at me again, but trudged behind me through the trees toward our boat like a kind of half-wit.

I no longer blamed Rob, nor the Tuckers, either. Gone was that rage which had choked me all these years. In its place there rose a love for my firstborn, locked in my bitter heart, set free too late.

Oh Papa, NO! Those were to be the final words that my poor Charlie's child would ever speak to me. I would never be forgiven. Rob was lost forever.

The tide was against us, and the humid air was much too light for our small flapping sail. I rowed my son all the way up Lost Man's River. Trying to drive the dark out of my lungs, I took huge breaths and hurled my shoulders back into each stroke, until my hands were blistered and my arms were burning. Even so, the journey home through the back bays took all day. At Possum Key, the Frenchman's cistern had been fouled by a creature fallen in; there was no water. With the heat and the exhaustion, I was almost blind, and a great blackness settled on me that I could not name. All I could think of, all I could look forward to, was my faithful jug.

Rob seemed to doze in a kind of dull stupor. Two or three times during that long journey, I saw his eyes slide toward the revolver butt protruding from my jacket, which lay beside him in the stern. I believe he considered seizing it, or slipping it beneath his shirt, though whether to destroy his father or himself I did not know. It seemed to me that day that I did not much care. Perhaps it was only my exhaustion, but my thought was that it might be a great mercy.

Except that I had hesitated one moment too long, when he turned and saw us and pled before he died, I did not regret the death of Wally Tucker. As for his wife, I would mostly regret that I had permitted my unlucky son to follow me, and to act against every instinct in his being, and crush his soul with a burden that was mine. I believe now that the murder of his spirit was the most grievous sin that Jack Watson had ever committed.

*

Whether or not sharks took those bodies, the evidence of murder was all over that key, and people were certain to suspect Ed Watson. I had behaved crazily as Rob had said, and this business would end badly, but not so badly as it would have done had the Tuckers lived to tell their story at Key West. No, there had been no choice about it, as I intended to explain to Rob when he felt better—when he realized not only that his father loved him but that I was asking his forgiveness.

At the Bend, poor Rob could scarcely drag himself out of the boat, or so I thought. That night he slipped the schooner's lines and drifted her down-river. I did not discover he was gone till daybreak. I jumped into the sailing skiff and took off after him, so outraged—that he had left without forgiving me?—that I forgot my hat and took along no water. I was off Cape Sable by the time a coasting vessel picked me up and took my skiff in tow. I was sun-parched, raving. I don't remember what I yelled, I only know I scared hell out of that crew. Those men were very glad to put me back into my skiff and let me row myself ashore there at Key West.

With the help of his Collins uncle at Key West, my son had shipped out a few hours earlier on a New York freighter, but not before selling my schooner cheap to this same kinsman, who was all set to resell her when I got there. I knocked Lee Collins down into the mud in front of the new bank on Duval Street, where he had thought it might be safe to meet me, and I threatened to blow his brains out there and then. *Any man lowdown enough to encourage a son to rob his own father like some common criminal—!* I stopped. From the look he gave me as he picked himself up, I knew Rob must have told him something. I backed off a little. All right, I said, how much do I have to pay for my stolen schooner? Two thousand dollars, said Collins, pulling out a bill of sale as proof. He said he had given that sum to Rob to give him a good start, and he offered to tear up this bill of sale if I reimbursed him. I took that paper and tore it up myself, then tossed two hundred dollars on the ground. "You deserve to be jailed for brokering stolen ships," I shouted. "If you weren't Charlie's brother, I would get the law on you!" And he called back, "I would not go anywhere near the law if I were you."

We stood a moment. Then I said, "He'll be all right." This came out suddenly and took us by surprise. Lee Collins considered me. "How would you know?" he said, and walked away.

By now Winky Atwell had spread the tale of my dispute with Tuckers, as I learned from my old friend Dick Sawyer when I stopped by Eddie's Bar for a stiff drink. I decided to pay a call on Winky, who was now residing at Key West, but Dick advised me to set sail before the Sheriff sent his deputy around to ask some questions.

"About what?" I demanded loudly so that everyone could hear that Ed Watson hadn't one damn thing to hide. Dick Sawyer backed up just a little, saying, "Ed, I'll be goddamned if I know, now that I think about it."

The only trouble was, I could not leave town. I was shaking with a heavy fever and delirium, and scarcely had the strength to reach my boat. That night I lost all track of where I was, thrashing in the bunk with those hoary Deepwood nightmares, carrying me back over and over to those childhood horrors.

It was probably typhoid. Nights and days later, learning that the *Gladiator* was still in port, Dick Sawyer became worried and ventured aboard. Later he told me he thought I was a goner, he just could not rouse me. He fetched Dr.

Feroni, who brought me back to life, though for two more days I lay motionless in what I would have thought was a state of death. He said, *Mr. Watson, you're a very lucky man!*

Hearing that, I opened my eyes wide, which startled him. He dropped my wrist at once, jumped to his feet. In a thick voice, I thanked him, he had saved my life. Trying to joke, he blurted nervously, "Well, I don't know if that was a good thing or not!" When I failed to smile, he backed out of the cabin with Sawyer right behind him, never left a bill.

I called after him that he would be paid on my next visit if he forgot all about this business in the meantime. I refused to admit how helpless I had been, even to Dick Sawyer. I was warning Sawyer, who talked too much, that he better forget about it, too. I don't like feeling beholden, not to anybody, that's the way I am, and I especially dislike any damned story about how Jack Watson was so ill he could not defend himself.

That afternoon at Eddie's Bar, Dick was already boasting how he saved my life. "*I don't know if what we done was a good thing or not,* that's what I told Doc Feroni! You should have seen ol' Desperado's face!" Dick had not seen me come in and did not know I was there behind him until the bar fell quiet. When he got up his nerve to turn around, I told him, "You're a liar, Dick. You always were. So you buy me a drink."

In a little while, Deputy Till showed up. I followed him outside. "Better keep on going, Mr. Watson," Clarence warned me. "Better sail tonight."

*

The day after I left Key West, Earl Harden showed up there from Lost Man's, claiming he and his brothers and Henry Short had found the Tuckers' bodies at Lost Man's Key. Did that mean I could no longer trust the Hardens? The Hamiltons had heard two shots but had not seen our skiff because I had hidden it in the Home Cove; that was about the only thing that I did right. Earl did his best to hang it all on Watson, though he had no real evidence, only his fear. With Rob gone, Lee Collins's account was also useless and Winky Atwell knew better than to testify. However, Deputy Clarence Till sent word that I should stay out of Key West, that the Sheriff would do his best to make a case, if only to get me extradited back to Arkansas. Since I might be liable to arrest as far away as Tampa, I decided to head north for a year or two—a serious setback to my schedule for expanding my plantation to the south bank of the river, not to speak of my plans for the future of this coast.

My friend Will Cox, who leased my old cabin at Fort White, had written some time before to say that folks had mostly forgotten Ed Watson in Columbia County. Will had grown up in Lake City with the new Sheriff, a man named Purvis, who was willing to let bygones be bygones if Will's friend should decide to come back there and try his chances.

*

Tant Jenkins had disappeared for good, leaving no word, but Josie said he had been fond of those young Tuckers and did not care to work for me any longer. With misgivings, I left the Bend in charge of a new hand named Green Waller. He was a drinker but he knew his hogs and could be depended on to stay, being wanted on three counts of hog theft in Lee County. As for companionship, those pink-assed sows would probably see him through.

Henry Thompson was at Lost Man's with the Hamiltons, and I got word to him that he could use my schooner if he helped the Bend when needed and brought my hog man Mr. Waller his supplies. Finally I arranged with my friend Bembery to scrape up some field hands for this fall's harvest next time he was in Fort Myers, then pick up my syrup in late winter for marketing to my wholesalers at Tampa Bay.

Right after I left, Sheriff Knight himself showed up at Chatham Bend, where a Mary Josephine Jenkins would inform him that Mr. E. J. Watson was no longer in residence at this address, having departed on a business trip to parts unknown.

*

I stopped over at Fort Myers to pick up my horse and bid good-bye to Mandy and the children. Mandy had moved to the ground floor because she could no longer make it up the stairs, and though it was midday, I found her in bed. Entering the silent room with its strong cat smell and its shuttered heat and shadows, I knew at once that this was the last time in this life I would set eyes on her. Already death inhabited her eyes and skin—a blow to the heart, to see my dear old friend in this failed condition. Mandy looked up with that bent shy smile which had first drawn me to her years ago and which she had passed along to our son Lucius.

How impossible it seemed that the creature who lay here helpless was the former Miss Jane S. Dyal from Deland, already on her deathbed in her thirties. I fought off an image of long years before, our Fort White cabin in early afternoon, the hot moss mattress, and this shy creature, all soft and strong astride me, eyes lightly closed and sweet mouth parted, releasing my hands and curving backwards, spreading her arms gracefully as if to embrace the firmament above, as if our ascent depended on that joyous arching. The remembrance of those firm thighs, even at this moment, caused a disgraceful swelling in my britches, although I knew how they must look now, blue-gray and shrunken under these covers.

To hide my shame from Mandy's sight, I buried my face into her neck and hugged her tight—too tight, because I hurt her, and she made a sound. How thin she was, with her watery bewildered eyes and lank dead hair! Smelling the death in her, I must have flinched, because when I drew back, she nodded just a little in humiliation.

I sat on the bedside and took her hands in mine, the tiny bones. "Well, Mrs. Watson. And why are you lying about in bed on this fine day?" I rose again, drew back the curtain, thinking the sun might comfort her, but of course it was the husband, not the wife, who needed light and comforting. "Oh, I'm so happy you have come!" she sighed. Relieved by each other's company, needing no words, we sat there a good while in the midday quiet, never mind that Death sat there beside us. Quite suddenly, as foolish as a boy, I gasped out that I loved her very dearly and I always would. "*Very* dearly, Mister?" she said, teasing. I assumed she had heard about the other women in the Islands, and those other children, but more likely she was thinking about Charlie Collins.

To Charlie, I would have simply said, I love you.

"Edgar? I am failing fast. You knew that."

"Yes."

"Oh, good! I am so weary of this pussyfooting!" She squeezed my hand. "Poor Dr. Langford clings to that cheery tone and bedside manner to cover his distress, and Dr. Winkler puts his finger to his lips to hush me when I try to talk to him. Tells me to rest, be a good little invalid. Isn't it astonishing? Even the children—they're so brave and tactful I could smack them!"

Smiling at the idea, she blew her nose. "I want to tell them, 'Be with me now. I'm lonely.' " She looked up. "Is death so dreadful, Edgar?"

"Good Lord, dearest! How would I know!" I tried to laugh a little, for her question had embarrassed her. She feared she had hurt my feelings. Yet there was something she had left unsaid, and I was not so sure I wished to hear it. Taking her hands again, I promised I would look after our children, make sure that they got on all right in life.

Oh Papa, no!

Just as those words erupted in my brain, Mandy peered at me in a queer way, saying, "I beg of you, dearest, don't turn your back on Rob. For her sake, and your own. He's your firstborn."

I grunted. "You've told Lucius, I imagine."

"I didn't need to. Carrie and Eddie know though they pretend not to. They don't want to deal with it. Not that Lucius speaks of it, although I wish he would." She seemed wistful. "He loves you so much. Perhaps you can comfort him a little. He'll be right home after school."

I was passing through town quickly, I explained. I had to go.

"My goodness! You're in such a rush that you can't wait even an hour for your youngest son?" She stared at me, intent, then closed her eyes, turning her head away. "Oh, Edgar," she murmured, the tears coming. "I'm not sure I can bear more."

"More?" I said.

It all came out. The murder of Mr. Chevelier, the killing of the cane cutters on payday—

"Is that what people say?"

She nodded, wiping her eyes. "Lucius is being teased at school. He won't believe this nonsense, goodness knows." In a different voice, she said, "Rumor has it that when Mr. Watson goes to Colored Town, the darkies run away. They hide from him, that's how scared they are that he might kidnap them as field hands." She hesitated, her hand kneading the coverlet. "And then kill them," she finished. She shook her head, as if talking to herself.

Overcome by what could never be undone, I sank onto my knees beside the bed. Because she was dying, I longed to confess all and clear my heart. I could not do it. I leaned and kissed her, astonished by my own impulse to weep—a man whose eyes had been bone-dry for years. I ached with need of solace for so many losses, I almost whined. *I could have been the best farmer in south Florida. I had great plans. But now I have done myself great harm*—disgusting! A disgusting, low, self-pitying speech to a dying woman who knew very well that for all the harm I might have done myself, I had done more to others. True, there were reasons, or at least excuses, but none of these would avail me much on Judgment Day.

I pulled myself together and sat up straight. Gruffly I said, "I don't believe the Good Lord will forgive me. What do you think, Mandy?" She did not recognize that reference to our Oklahoma days and that huge and bloody hellion, Old Tom Starr—either that or she was simply not amused. I stood up, pressed her hand in parting, crossed the room.

She did not detain me. She remained silent even when I faltered, turning in the door. She had not forgotten my old story. Now she finished it. "No, poor dear Edgar," her voice came quietly, "I don't believe He will."

Her cool tone stunned me. I felt betrayed and longed for comforting, if only one loving smile which, after all these years of deference, she now denied me. I had defended myself with the tin armor of irony, and she had pierced me with hard simple truth.

Weakly I came back to the bedside. She saw that my agony was real, but she was resolute. "Before I die, I want the truth," she whispered.

"You never believed me?" I went short of breath and my heart pounded. "You even testified in court—!" Her gaze stopped me.

"The truth, Edgar. It's late."

So long ago, twelve years, and yet . . . one escapes nothing. Perhaps, in the end, that is all one learns of life.

My silence was all the answer Mandy needed. "May God forgive you," she whispered. "May God rest her soul."

"Do *you* forgive me? That's all I care about."

She squeezed my hand a final time, pushed it away. I seized the gray fingers, pressed them to my lips, and our gaze held, but her big eyes did not soften, nor did she speak. I went away bereft and unforgiven, and suffocating for want of any way to cry out the love I had not found words for while she searched my face.

I crossed the Calusa Hatchee on the Alva ferry, in river wind under a hard blue sky. In the old horse coach through the piney woods to Punta Gorda, from where the railroad would carry me northward to Fort White, the sun glinting down through the sharp needles was liquefied by the hot tears that had been so long in coming. Who was I grieving for, Mandy or Edgar? I had to laugh a little then, astonished that Jack Watson, with his fury and cold nerve, could come apart and weep like a young boy.

In April, when my dear wife died, I knew I had loved her as much as my darling Charlie and perhaps more deeply, though I don't suppose that love, if truly felt, can ever be compared in such a way.

Sometimes I think we do not know whom we loved most until after they are gone. Looking back down our long road in life, these are the peaks which still rise higher than the rest, like the far blue Appalachian peaks on that boyhood day when Private Lige Watson of the First Edgefield Volunteers lifted me so high into the sun above the courthouse terrace. The light (so Mama always said) was like an angel's halo in my hair.

Chapter 5

Crazy Watson Eyes

Even before Cousin Laura died, my mother had started scrapping with Aunt Tabitha, and finally she quit that lady's roof and went to live with Minnie and her Billy. In 1901, when I returned from the Ten Thousand Islands, I went straight over to pay my respects as a good son should.

"Well, Mother, I'm home."

"I don't recall that I laid eyes on you the last time you were here. How long ago was that, do you suppose? Six years?"

"Seven, mother."

"Well, that's long enough, wouldn't you say?"

Skillfully she dispensed with her incivilities just as I was ready to snipe back, that's how perverse this little woman was. She did not ask after Mandy's health, far less inquire about the children, nor did she make the least effort to embrace me. Going unhugged by her twiggy old arms and unpecked by that dry scar of a mouth, I felt oddly incomplete, I must admit. As for Aunt Cindy, fixing supper at the stove, she never looked at me. For the first time in my life, that bony black woman did not come forward to hug me, nor take notice of me, not even enough to sniff or turn her back. She ignored me throughout the few minutes that I stayed. What Aunt Cindy had heard and what she suspected I did not know, and I did not inquire, knowing my account of it would do no good.

Mama settled down and made some tea while relating in detail how Cousin Laura had died in '94 when Aunt Tabitha's new manor house was scarcely finished. "Laura bored herself to death, that's all," said Laura's life-long loyal friend, "and darn near took the rest of us off with her."

The widower, on the other hand, had fattened up like a prime hog with his good fortune. The former Ichetucknee or Myers Plantation was now known as the Tolen Plantation, and the homesteads all around were called the Tolen Settlement. There was even a post office called Tolen, Florida, at the turpentine works down by the railroad crossing. All that was missing was the Holy Tolen Church. Meanwhile, Sam had married off his brother Mike to a Myers niece, then moved him into William Myers's big log cabin to strengthen the Tolen death grip on this property. What's more, the Russ clan—Sam's step-brother John Russ and his four mink-jawed sons—were infesting another Myers cabin on Herlong Lane.

Mama showed me without comment an obituary clipped from the newspaper in Columbia, South Carolina, dated June 19 of 1895, relating how Captain Elijah D. Watson, aged sixty-one, had succumbed to Bright's disease, perishing peacefully in his sleep at a rooming house in that city. She read aloud from the obituary:

> Before the War, he was a well-to-do farmer in Edgefield County. . . . A gallant soldier during the War between the States, he distinguished himself on many battlefields for acts of great bravery and daring . . .

"You must feel very proud of such a father, dear." Mama did not have to explain that the rank of captain, like the deeds of heroism, was an obituary courtesy to a private who returned from war with a secure reputation for dereliction of duty, drunkenness, and insubordination.

When I told her I'd seen him back in '93, she did not inquire about his appearance. Instead she produced a yellowed daguerreotype, pressing it down on the table with a kind of grim finality, like a poker winner laying down his final card. Her hands were shaky now, with pronounced liver marks.

Wild-haired Lige in Confederate uniform had a cocked cap and jaunty style and looked nothing at all like the handsome soldier I wished to remember from the courthouse terrace. Even without his ring eye, he looked bug-eyed, truculent, kind of half crazy—Crazy Watson Eyes, Mama used to call them. "I never knew you'd treasured his picture all these years." I set it down.

"Cindy saved it. For you children. Wasn't that sweet?" She curtsied minutely and I made a small bow as we sweet-smiled each other, not entirely without amusement and affection. "Oh Lord, Edgar!" She was cross again. "And how long are you to be here *this* time?"

Aunt Cindy rapped the iron stove with her wood spoon, then turned and left. According to her mistress, she had finally accepted the hard truth that her man would never again be seen on earth and she prayed for a reunion of some kind in Heaven's mansions. Deprived of her own family, Aunt Cindy had given herself to ours, devoting her long narrow days to tending Mama's every whim (unabashed, Mama used this phrase herself) and running the Collins household for her Miss Minnie. Minnie had become a blight upon her family with her "American nervousness," as the quacks now called it, her "neurasthenia" (which included hysteria and insomnia, dyspepsia and hypochondria—any ailment resistant to known cure which had an -*ia* at the end of it, said Mama). Mercifully, one symptom of her malady was a horror of being seen in human company, even at home.

As for Lulalie, everyone feared the worst. Such a warm busty young girl, did I recall her? She frowned and switched the subject, not because I hesitated, but because she did not wish to dwell on warm brown bosoms under the bald eye of Lige, the famous lover of brown bosoms in the photograph. (Guessing at her mind's quick turns, I saw a light mulatta woman in Augusta, elderly now but never older in Mama's mind than the young house wench who became Jacob Watson's mother.) Mama proffered the daguerreotype and an enigmatic smile. "I'm sure you'll want this picture as a keepsake." I shook my head, keeping my arms folded. I wished to hear no more about my father, nor could I bear my mother's company a moment longer. I rose to go.

Mama took my arm as she accompanied me outside, and her face actually softened as she related what Private Watson had confided on his return from war. Sleepless and restless for long nights, he had finally broken down and wept, confessing his terrible fear of being bayoneted, his nightmare horror of the battlefield at dark, when the musket fire died to the last solitary shots even as the dreadful cries of those left on the battlefield, the thousands of thirsty, maimed, and dying on both sides, rose in a wild moan like wind from the blood-damp night earth of Virginia, until the no-man's-land writhed under the moon like one huge tormented creature, all the way across the wasteland to the Union lines.

In the dawn of one dreaded day of battle, he had broken out in a soaking sweat, then come apart, shaken violently by his own unraveling like a muskrat shaken by a dog. Then his gut let go and he soiled his only clothes without any means or hope of restoration. He began crying and could not hide even that and so he fled.

It was William Coulter who came after him, who pulled him down behind a wall and slapped him hard, who ordered him to return into the lines or he would shoot him then and there where he lay stinking. And after the War, in their Regulator years, that man with the hard, black crow-wing hair had used his knowledge of Lige Watson's terror and humiliation to manipulate him and ensure his loyalty in those night activities of which "Captain Watson" had been secretly ashamed. (This was untrue, of course.) My mother's eyes pled with me to relent, to forgive my father, to forgive his wife, to forgive Minnie, to forgive myself. She said, "There is still time." I shook my head. "No, Mama," I said.

*

For a time I lived with my friend Will Cox, who sharecropped a piece of Tolen land and was living in my old cabin near the junction where Herlong Lane came into Tolen Road, near Tolen Post Office and Herlong Station. I was building a house on former Collins land on a hill overlooking the Bellamy Road. Though not much of a hill, it was the highest for many miles around, and the site of a seventeenth-century Spanish mission destroyed by the British when they came to north Florida from Charleston at the start of the eighteenth century and killed every Spaniard and Indian they could lay their hands on. When the wind shuffled the leaves of the ancient red oak on that hilltop, I heard a whisper of its old sad history.

I planted pecans right down to the road, also a fig tree. Built a work shed, horse and cow stalls, sugar mill, syrup shed, corncrib, beehives, chicken coop, and muscadine arbor. William Kinard dug me a well, and my new friend and devoted admirer John Porter got me started with some hardware. (I suppose John liked me well enough, but mainly he was anxious to be known as the confidant and inseparable friend of "the Man Who Killed Belle Starr," a local rumor I neither confirmed nor denied.)

John Russ was a fair carpenter, and together we got my house done in a hurry, using heart pine lath and heavy tongue-and-groove pine siding. My roof of cedar shakes clear of the smallest knothole was the talk of the southern county, because times were changing and men already begrudged the time and craft required to make them. Folks were going over to tin roofs, which turn a house into an oven in the summer. The tin starts popping toward midday, and in late afternoon, as the house starts to cool off, she pops some more.

Inside, I dispensed with a parlor in favor of three good bedrooms and a larger dining room with a kind of window counter through which food could be passed when it came in from the kitchen—my own innovation, built originally for the house at Chatham Bend. The new house had no second story, only a garret with end windows to vent the summer heat. With the lumber saved, I built a broad airy veranda with split-cane rockers where social occasions, such as they were, mostly took place. The porch had a hand-carved railing which became famous in our district, and the whole house was set up on brick pilings to let cool breeze under the floor and shade the hogs and chickens. As for the windows, they were high on the outside walls so that even a man on horseback could not shoot someone inside—a trick learned in Arcadia that I never troubled to explain here in Fort White.

*

Black Frank Reese from Arkansas had turned up at Will Cox's place while I was in the Islands, and I gave him some rough work moving materials. Frank had found that faithless woman he had sworn to kill, but by the time he got there she had grown so fat and ugly that he belted her hard across the head and let it go at that. From this I knew he had matured somewhat since I last saw him.

Will Cox, who had been sharecropping for Tolen, could take no more of Sam's abuse and came over to farm with me instead. Sam still owed me for those hogs he'd all but stolen when I went off to Oklahoma, but I had to threaten him with arson before he produced a few razor-backed runts, thin and uncared for. "Ain't goin to thank me, Ed?" With a rough boot, he drove them off the tailgate of his wagon into my new pen.

"The hogs I gave you were fine animals," I reminded him, "not like these."

Fat Sammy laughed. "Fine animals and fine eatin." He winked. "Get fine money for 'em, too." I mentioned that better men than Tolen had been hung for hog theft back in the old century. "Is that a fact?" he said. "Yessir," I said, "that is a fact, and here's another: a dispute over a pair of hogs caused that feud between the Hatfields and McCoys. More than twenty came up dead before the smoke cleared."

"You threatenin me, Ed? I'd go easy on that kind of talk if I was you. Folks around here ain't forgotten who you are, and ain't all of 'em has forgiven, neither."

I looked him over, saying nothing. In Arkansas, I had been sentenced to fifteen years at hard labor for boarding stolen horses. Almost anywhere in the back country, a man would pay more dearly for stealing a horse than for exterminating this fat varmint. Of course, I had sworn I would ease off on my drinking, put my gun away for good—I meant it, too. But Sam Tolen didn't need to know that.

*

Carrie sent word from Fort Myers that her mother had passed away only a few months after my visit. When I wrote back to commiserate, I told her to send Eddie north to help on the new farm. As for Lucius, he had moved in with his sister while he finished school. Unlike Eddie, he had not been born here and had no interest in Fort White at all. All that young feller cared about was Chatham and the Islands, which were his first real home.

Eddie was not handy out of doors. A nigger named Doc Straughter, who usually showed up, taught that young feller how to do the yard chores, tend the animals. Doc was stepbrother to that girl Jane Straughter, who was so light-skinned that at any distance she would be taken for a white, and so desirable that half the men in the south county, black, white, or polka dots, were sniffing around her like wild tomcats, even that dignified widower Mr. Watson. Jane helped out some in the house, where I could keep an eye on her, so to speak.

Jane was just over twenty, child-like and graceful but very smart and grown-up for a nigger, which of course she wasn't, having been got upon Fannie Straughter—very light-colored, too—by my friend Calhoun Robarts. That family never did deny her, in fact welcomed her into their homes and paid her visits and hugged and talked to her like one of their own. Being close kin to Robartses, the Collinses regarded her as "family," too. All the same, she knew her place and worked as a house nigger.

I told Frank Reese to keep his hands off Jane, told him they looked like chocolate and vanilla. Made a joke of it, the way we used to. But this time my old partner was rankled. He dared to say, "I thought you told me how just one black drop made a man a nigger. That go for females, too?" And I said, "Oh she's got that drop in her, no doubt about it. But she is a Robarts all the same, so if a nigger with as many drops as Black Frank Reese was to go fooling with her, he might be hunting up more trouble than he'd care to handle."

Since we rode out of Arkansas, our teasing had been rough for want of a better way to deal with our strange partnership. But this day Frank disliked my tone and did not hide it, knowing that when it came to Jane, only one of us could tease and that was me. Sucking his lips as if tasting this hard truth, he gave me that flat look of his, the kind of look that a tough nigger might get away with in the Territories but would get himself hung for anywhere east of the Mississippi, as Jacob Watson learned in Georgia.

"You're not a home nigger around here," I reminded him. He looked away. With Jim Crow law spreading like wildfire across America, any black man could become fair game for whites out to raise hell, and a story in the papers here had only made things worse. Some lunatic black man in New Orleans, resisting capture, had gunned down a whole covey of police before they finished him. Niggers, I explained to Frank, were set afire and strung up like burnt hams just for looking like they *might* be looking at a white woman, and Jane Straughter would pass for a white woman around here, at least for purposes of justice. Nosir, boy, our local men would not hesitate to use the torch and rope on a black from other parts who dared to snoop around that little Robarts girl, dared lust after young Miss Jane the same way they did.

"Burnt hams." Reese drove his pitchfork hard into the earth. "Justice," he said.

*

In the next year, while I finished the Fort White house and got my crops in, I was glad to have the income from the Bend. The new farm was up and running, but I had a mortgage to pay off and I still owed John Russ for some carpentry. All the while I had to worry that Green Waller and his makeshift crew might make a mess of my cane harvest just when I counted on that syrup to pay my debts.

Toward the end of 1902, I decided it was safe to pay a quick visit to the Bend. On the way through Fort Myers, I would talk to Carrie's husband about his proposed citrus farm out at Deep Lake and continue discussions with the Lee County surveyor about establishing a bona fide claim on Chatham River, because all my quitclaim amounted to by law was squatter's rights. Finally, it was high time I got moving on Bill House's idea for a clam-dredging operation before some feller like Bill House beat me to it.

Leaving the Collinses to oversee young Eddie, I took John Russ and two of his four sons to the southwest coast. In exchange for repairs and additions at the Bend, I would use this winter's syrup sale to pay off every last cent that I owed him, I told Russ, who went along with this mostly because I also took Miss Jane, to keep her out of trouble while I was away.

Though he knew better than to say so, Frank Reese had not taken kindly to my news. He put on a kind of humble show, as was expected from the blacks when they received orders that upset them. They had to act "natural," which meant not merely compliant but eager and cheerful. They had to grin like minstrels till that smile slipped off like sweet butter off a cob of corn. Frank tugged his cap and ducked and writhed, to rub my nose in that hideous false smile, and when I yelled at him—"Stop that, goddamnit!"—he straightened slowly, throwing his shoulders back, not defiant, no, not quite, his dark face closing like a fist.

*

In 1901, the state of Florida had passed a plume bird law against killing egrets, and it was true that the white egrets, at least, were almost gone. With plume birds and gators mostly killed out, and fishing and hunting generally so poor, ricking charcoal and digging clams were almost the last ways for a poor man to make a living. Word had spread about those shallow water clam flats which ran from Cape Romano and Fakahatchee Pass all the way south to Lost Man's River and up to a mile and a half offshore in certain places. Men waded out in canvas shoes in waist-deep water and raked 'em up with a two-prong rake until they filled the small skiff riding alongside. Some clammers dug thirty bushel on a tide, that's how thick they were. On wind-less days, the mosquitos got so bad that men had to go ashore and slather on black mangrove mud for some protection. In the evening they'd go back to the key and unload their clams into the clam boat for the factory, then go wash off and fix their supper after building a smudge fire to fight the bugs. By the time I came back from north Florida, the shantytown on Pavilion Key—mostly tents and canvas lean-tos—had close to fifty men, and the women and children included my former housekeepers and my daughters, Minnie and little Pearl. They even had their own post office and boarding-house run by George Roe, Netta Daniels's latest husband, a Yankee who quit medical school in Chicago because the sight of blood made him sick but oth-erwise not a bad feller at all.

On the way south on the *Falcon*, I was eager to discuss my clam dredge op-eration with Bill Collier, who knew me for a good businessman who paid his bills—that's all he cared about. My reputation never bothered him a bit. Cap'n Bill was a steadfast man who had tended to business ever since a boy, and today, he controlled almost all of Marco Island. Besides the cargo and passenger trade on this fine schooner—lately converted to an auxiliary ves-sel with a two-cylinder engine, the first motor vessel on this coast—he owned the Marco Hotel and general store, a good farm and copra plantation, and the local boatyard and shipbuilding company.

Knowing how keen this feller was for smart investment opportunities, I asked him if he had reconsidered going partners with me in that clam-dredging operation I'd mentioned once before. Already some Yankees had set up a clam-canning factory in Caxambas, so there seemed to be quite a call for clams. A mechanical dredge could make us both a lot of money.

Thinking this over, Cap'n Bill squinted out over the sea for a long long time. When he finally spoke, he was matter-of-fact, describing in more detail than I needed the dredge he was having built there in Caxambas—hundred-and-ten-foot barge, thirty-foot beam, with a clam well forty feet in length amidships. Lowered an eight-hundred-pound anchor, then drifted back on a twelve-hundred-foot cable, then winched herself forward while the dredge dumped its clams onto a conveyor belt under the hull. "Bill?" I said. With nine in crew counting cook and engineer, she could work day and night, Bill continued in that same flat voice. Feed the men mostly on cooked clams and canned corned beef. Very small overhead. The dredge could work in deeper water than the men with rakes, and the flat was so big that he figured she could harvest up to five hundred bushels every day eight months a year for maybe twenty years before the clams gave out. He told me that my friend Jim Daniels, Netta's brother, had signed on as her skipper, and my friend Dick Sawyer would be mate. The dredge would be ready to go early next year.

The *Falcon* was running south before a stiff northerly wind. "Is that a fact," I said, holding my voice down.

He looked at me half sideways and coughed into his fist. "Go slow now, Ed." He lit a cigar and blew out smoke before he said, "That dredge idea weren't yours back in the first place."

"Watson is where you got it all the same."

"Bill House," he said mildly, "gets a lot of good ideas, but other people always make the money. Bill House don't know how to move ahead instead of talk about it, and he don't write it down and date it, show he had it first. That's because he always worked hard for his daddy, never got no education—he can't read nor write." Bill Collier shrugged his shoulders. "If a man don't make the most of his idea, another man will step in there and make it for him."

For once, I only grunted and shut up. Cap'n Bill had me licked coming and going. Anyway, it was hard to stay angry with this man, who was always soft-spoken and straightforward. He took care of his own interests better than any man I ever came across, and that was because he never drank much and knew when to let others do the talking. He also took the excellent advice he dispensed to strangers in this region, most of whom had to travel on his boat. When you're dealing with these Islanders, he told 'em, state your name, your business, and your destination, and don't ask no questions, cause you might get an answer you won't care for.

*

Unfortunately for all and sundry, Jane Straughter was no less desirable in south Florida than she had been in Fort White, and there were long nights, I will confess, when my mind was a low and stagnant swamp aswarm with fevered images of a pale golden shape which would open up in the bed of E. J. Watson like a sun-warmed split peach glistening with nectar.

Miss Jane and I got along fine, I let her tease me and I made her laugh. Since my first wife had been kin to her natural father, I told her we were "kissin cousins" and maybe she should call me Cousin Edgar. This made her nervous, and after that, she shied off and hid when I was drinking. I believe this was due mostly to John Russ, who was filling her pretty seashell ear with his bad stories. As a Tolen stepbrother, John disliked me on general principles, and away from his worn-out old wife, this gawky man was coveting my cook, he couldn't take his rheumy eyes off her.

Not that Mr. Watson was much better, and we weren't alone. Two of the young Hardens, Earl and Lee, were newly wed, but even so, that young Jane made 'em itch. (Earl had tried hard to get me into trouble in that Tucker business, so he never showed up at the Bend unaccompanied by his brother.) Henry Thompson came, too. Never missed a chance for a long gloomy look, forgetting he was hitched up to Gert Hamilton. As for Bill House, he got hot and bothered every time he happened by, and so did Henry Short, who was always with him. All these fellers believed I killed those Tuckers, but they never turned in their neighbor the way Earl did.

This Henry Short was young Bill's shadow, a tall strong good-looking redbone boy, as we used to call 'em back in Oklahoma. White man's coloring, thin features, with high Injun cheekbones. Knew his place, always courteous and quiet. Hard to tell what he was thinking or even if he thought at all, but watching him, I could see he didn't miss much. Henry Short was no darker in his skin than Henry Thompson, but we called him "Black Henry" when Thompson was around, to avoid confusion. You sure wouldn't confuse 'em if you watched 'em work. Black Henry Short was handy with a gun or gill net or any farm or fishing implement he put his hand to. He was a steady and painstaking man, honest as wood and as good a worker as I ever saw, which nobody ever said about Henry Thompson. This brown boy was a very uncommon nigger, one of the most able men on the whole coast.

There's men will tell you that niggers don't fall in love, not the way we do. Well, I believe that Henry Short fell in love with our Jane Straughter—it was all that white in both of them, most folks would say. The rest of us might want to hump and rut her half to death in grand old-fashioned drunken Southern style, but Henry *loved* her. Jane saw the difference right away, and very soon, she loved him dearly, too. She couldn't hide it any more than he could. So John Russ started abusing him, nigger this and nigger that, until I told him to save that kind of white-trash talk for his half brothers. I knew just how John felt, of course, because I was jealous, too, and finally I had to tell Black Henry to stay away from Chatham Bend because I didn't trust him not to run off with my cook.

Not smiling when a white man cracked a joke was as close to insolence as a nigger dared to come, but I don't believe Short was insolent so much as shocked. He never squinted doubtfully the way Reese did, never hesitated to obey, never even asked permission to tell my cook good-bye. He murmured, Yessir, touched his hat and turned away. Even when Jane ran out and waved, he never looked back. But being in love, he had eyes in the back of his head and knew right where she was, because he lifted his straw hat, held that arm high in a lost and desperate wave, then kept on walking down toward the dock. Only the stiff set of his shoulders told me how upset he was. Like Frank

Reese, this feller knew that Mr. Watson wanted Miss Jane for himself, and like Frank Reese, he was a nigger to be reckoned with. The difference was that Short had learned an iron self-control. He was not a man to show his hand or make stupid mistakes.

*

John Russ was plotting day and night to get that poor young Jane into his bed. As I later learned, he was letting on how Good Man Russ would protect her from the Killer Watson. When he was drinking, this stupid sonofabitch would drop hammer-like hints about my deadly past right at the table, then laugh in that noisy squawk of his while the rest studied their turnips for fear of what the Killer might decide to do. Restraining my temper, I warned him as patiently as I knew how that if E. J. Watson were the dreadful criminal that Mr. John Russ claimed he was, it might not be wise to blacken the man's name right there at his table, he'd better stick to doing it behind his back. But John was so crazy with the rut that he just hee-hawed louder, out of his loose-cocked donkey lust and twitching nerves.

John's two boys, who might have tattled to their mother, had gone off on the schooner to Key West, so this rawboned Russ was living in some Damn-Fool Paradise. Being plagued by Jane myself, I couldn't blame him all that much. What I held against that fool were his dirty tactics—not that they did him the least bit of good. When it came to women, as Tant Jenkins used to say, John Russ could not pour piss out of a boot with the instructions written right there on the heel.

Miss Jane stayed leery of me, thanks to John's calumnies, and she was still sulky over Henry Short, who had told her in all earnestness that he wished to marry her. She hadn't minded when I'd warned off Black Frank Reese, but now she came and tried to plead with me, eyes full of tears. When I shook my head she ran away around the house.

*

What happened not long after that, Mr. John Russ choked to death. He was eating his supper with me and my noted hog authority, Mr. Green Waller, and he ate too fast, got a sweet potato in his lung or some damned place. He turned a darkening gray-blue, seemed to be choking, then fell down heart-struck before anyone thought to whack him on the back. One minute he was packing in the grub like Judas Priest at the Last Supper, and the next he gave an almighty cough and went down like a stockyard beef, that's how fast Death took him. Before we could lift a hand to help, that blue-gray mask was staring up at us, mouth oozing sweet potato like the hind end of a turkey packed with stuffing.

Green Waller, looking unwell himself, sidled bandy-legged for the door, keeping a walleye on Ed Watson while his hand groped for the way out. "Dammit, Green," I shouted, "give us a hand with these remains!"

Jane had run in from the kitchen. Seeing John, she raised her hand up to her mouth, then burst into tears of fear. Before she could stop herself, she whispered, "Poisoned!" And hearing that, my hog man hollered, "Beggin yer pardon, Mr. Watson, but anyone who says Green Waller poisoned him is a damn liar!"

Jane Straughter had been spoiled by the Robarts family, for she dared inquire for everyone to hear, How come you don't run him to the hospital? There was a challenge in her tone I didn't care for. Well, first of all, there's no hope for him, I told her, as you would know yourself if you weren't too scared to look. Second, I said, growing angry, whether I take him or I don't is not your nigger business, Missy, which if I were you, I would mind more carefully in the future. Even then, she was upset enough to toss her hand up in exasperation as she turned away. She had not forgiven me for sending Short away, that much was clear.

I laid my hand on my heart and swore that E. J. Watson had not poisoned John J. Russ. He had perished of a heart attack, and that was that. I was outraged by their insinuations, but defending myself too fast that way when nobody had accused me—that upset me even more. "Good thing he never sniffed his way into your bed," I snarled at Jane. "He might have had his heart attack on top of you."

Upset and offended, she offered his cadaver a look more fond than any she had bestowed on him in life. "Might have died happy, at least!" said this saucy wench, to spite me. Jane had no doubt that E. J. Watson had poisoned that fool carpenter, and probably Green Waller agreed, having heard my fierce disputes with Russ over the amount of back pay he had coming—disputes mostly fired up by drink and old bull horniness over the girl.

I told Jane Straughter that she better mind what she told people at Fort White. "Or else you'll kill me?" The girl's words came out in a squeak of terror, she looked paler than anybody there. But a girl who tries to make you jealous of a blue-faced corpse is not too worried you are going to kill your friend J. C. Robarts's daughter. In later years she would let on at Fort White how Mr. Russ might have been poisoned in the Islands, but she did not mention those suspicions until after my troubles with the Tolens, by which time it didn't matter very much. Anyway, I knew what John Russ's people would conclude, and most of the neighbors, too, no matter who said what.

Mercifully, John Russ's boys did not show up for another day or two, by which time their daddy was safe underground. With no family present, we didn't take time to make a box, and by the time we laid him in, enough river water seeped into that grave to almost float him. As Green Waller opined, resting on his spade, Them boys seen their dad in better days, they don't need to see this thing that's layin in the mud and water without no box to it. Still sweating out his considerable drink of the night previous, the hog man himself was a very poor color. They didn't call that feller Green for nothing.

The burial done, we trooped back to the house to toast the dead man's journey with a cup of moonshine. I sat quiet in my usual place in the room corner, in the green velveteen armchair from Black Betsy's whorehouse near Flamingo. Green Waller sidled up, kind of confidential. "Please, Mr. Watson," Waller begged. "I never did believe them things John told about you. I never even *listened* to them dretful stories!"

Green sprang backwards, scaring everybody, when his boss leapt up and punched that wall. All this misfortune, just when I had a chance to recover my life! I took a deep breath and sat down again, not trying to explain, and devoted myself to getting drunk, in ugly humor. As the evening wore on, it became clear to me that after so many years of trials and tribulations, even God must acknowledge that Edgar Watson deserved a little something— young Jane, for instance. But Jane saw my mood and guessed my line of thought, and when I went looking, I could find neither hide nor hair of her, just when I was most in need of both.

In the end, I went crashing and cursing to my bed and there she was, in the last place I would have thought to find her. She whispered, Please now, Mist' Watson, don't go hurtin me. What she meant was, *Don't go killing me.* She was terrified.

Sighing, I took her in my arms, feeling that old sweet shiver of relief waft over my skin like holy balm—like frankincense and myrrh, for all I know. Her breath was fresh, she was light and quick, she had no clumsiness in her. I ran my fingertips over her neck and pretty shoulders, over that silken rump of hers that until this night had shifted so elusively under thin cottons.

I muttered, Jane, honey, why would I ever hurt you? She whispered that this was her first time, which made me grin in disbelief. I was mistaken. She was a virgin, the dear little thing, though not for long.

That mulatta girl slept in my bed the rest of the time that we were in the Islands, and I like to believe that after the first time or two, she was neither unwilling nor unduly horrified that a large male creature was easing his passion on her person, stirring his strong pine house with rhythmic creakings. I never wished to take advantage of a young girl's fear, but life is hard and life doesn't relent, and a man would do well to take such solace as life puts in his way.

*

Sometimes, bound homeward from Key West, I stopped at Lost Man's Beach to take some supper with the Hamiltons and Henry Thompson. Other times I would put in at Wood Key for a good fish dinner. On that narrow little island, the Hardens had nice cabins painted white, with coconut trees and bougainvillea and periwinkle flowers all around a white sand yard, which they raked clean to discourage serpents and mosquitos. And they had their own fish house, built at the end of a long dock on that shallow shore. Dried and salted mullet for the Cuba trade during the running season, late autumn and early winter, then went offshore in summer for mackerel and kingfish, sent eight or ten barrels of good fish to Key West maybe twice a week. These days motor boats were permitting a new trade in fresh fish, with run boats bringing three-hundred-pound ice chunks to fish houses up and down the coast and taking fish away.

The youngest Harden daughter, Abbie, came to my place to help out. This girl was light-skinned and had nice manners, having been trained at the Convent of Mary Immaculate in Key West. Abbie would arrange the parties, sometimes for as many as fifteen guests. Her folks and most of the other settlers were invited, and of course I'd attend the Harden parties, too. The three Harden boys played musical instruments, and sometimes I'd yell for "Streets of Laredo," my old Oklahoma favorite, which made everybody gloomy except me.

Hardens always expected I would bust out wild, shoot out the lamps, tear up the party, due to wild stories which came back from Key West. I never did. Except in public places, I never drank too much. There were always strangers in the Islands, fugitives and drifters, and I never knew when some unknown avenger out of the past might come for me. Outside, I stayed back from the firelight, and inside, I kept my back into the corner. I took that chance of being sociable but kept my eye open.

The Hardens had been wronged, they claimed, by the 1880 census, in which Robert was marked down as a mulatto—one reason they had moved away to the Ten Thousand Islands. They blamed this listing on the malice of the Bay people, who still resented him for running off with John Weeks's daughter. In 1902, harried by his family, Robert traveled to Fort Myers and signed an affidavit claiming his mother was a full-blood Choctaw and his father a half-Portagee slave owner, which accounted for the tight curl in his black hair. His wife Maisie put him up to that because Old Man Robert didn't give a damn. He was mostly Injun in his own estimation, and had settled at Lost Man's River, as he put it, "to get away from all them other colors." When nobody paid that deposition much attention, the family felt more cut off than ever, and lately they had started quarreling amongst themselves. His sons Webster and Earl hardly spoke to each other anymore because Earl was ashamed of Webster's darker color and reluctant to admit to his white friends on the Bay that they were full brothers.

The way I looked at it, the Everglades was a frontier like Oklahoma, with plenty of fugitives and halfbreeds in the mix. If the Hardens wanted to be white, they had as much claim to that distinction as the next bunch. I needed their friendship in the same way they needed mine, and the way things were going, I was very glad I had them there to back me up.

An old Bahama conch named Gilbert Johnson was the Hardens' only neighbor on Wood Key. Every time Gilbert got drunk, he would revert to the King's English and rue the day he had ever got mixed up with this "mongrel" bunch. He'd expressed this opinion to Robert every day since his daughters married Earl and Lee instead of staying home to tend their poor old daddy. Here at the bitter end of life, in his decrepitude, he was condemned to live amongst his in-laws, and he made the best of his bad situation by telling them his poor opinion of them to his heart's content.

Like Robert Harden, Old Man Gilbert had married a halfbreed Seminole, and he liked to spend his leisure hours—all day, on most days—on his enemy's veranda expounding on the deficiencies of Indians as human beings, as exemplified by various members of both their families. When his wife Maisie wasn't listening, Robert thought that most of Gilbert's guff was pretty funny, and Gilbert did, too. He meant no harm by it, he just enjoyed ranting and raving.

In other days, sitting on his porch watching the sun go down behind the Gulf horizon, Robert had enjoyed long talks with Jean Chevelier. Struggling to recall the precise words, he would pass along his understanding of the Frenchman's idea about the Original Race of Man, which had separated into different shades of black and yellow, red and white, and maybe even blue, for all they knew. Chevelier's point had always been that human beings were essentially big itchy monkeys, unnaturally cruel and violent in their behavior. They were screwing their wits out and spreading their malignancies across the globe, killing off the other creatures as they went. But human races with their differences in skin color were bound to disappear with interbreeding, he had claimed, with man returning to the primordial mud-colored dimwit who started all the trouble in the first place. In Chevelier's view, this fundamental mix was already emerging in the Americas—what the Frenchman called "the true Americans."

To tease Old Man Robert, I would say, "I suppose you're talking about true Americans like Charlie Dixie," referring to a thieving feller who, as far as we could tell, had almost all of the most sorry traits of the red, black, and white races. Robert, unruffled, would sniff and say, "Charlie ain't nobody, he don't count." By that he meant that Charlie might as well be dead, having been banished by the Mikasuki for trafficking with whites. In Indian terms, he no longer existed in this world, even though, to the unknowing eye, he still appeared to be running around loose. Charlie Dixie never fled his fate but accepted his death sentence without complaint. In that one way, he was Indian to the bone. He passed his time getting by as best he could while waiting for his people to put him to death, which one day they did.

The feller Robert mostly talked about was Henry Short, who in Indian way had been adopted by the Hardens. When Henry had his hat on, he would pass anywhere outside the Islands for a white man. In fact, he was lighter than many so-called whites at Chokoloskee, who would have lynched him if he'd ever dared to point that out. Though Henry himself never denied his ancestry, his color would change according to the beholder, according to how you turned him to the light. Robert would say, "Them House boys claim that Henry has some tar in him, but I believe he is pure white and Injun, the same as me."

There was a half-secret story around Henry. According to Old Man D. D. House, who raised him up, he had a white mother and a mulatto father who was lynched. Old Man Dan knew what he was talking about, too, because he'd seen the battered corpse himself, strung from an oak limb back in Redemption days. "Course you'd never know *what* color he was, not after them Georgia boys got done with him." D. D. House was a very hard old man. He said he'd been a witness to the lynching, and he sure had the details, but I couldn't make out if this was his own truth or a dark myth known to all Americans after the early nineties, when reports of lynching came from everywhere across the country.

*

One day I was sitting on the Hardens' porch there at Wood Key when two passengers came in on the mail boat. Young Dan House was captain and Gene Gandees Junior was crew. Dan House hollered that these strangers had some business with "Mr." Henry Short—Dan winked when he said the "Mr."—and he wanted to know where they could find him. Henry was back upriver at House Hammock, and Dan knew that, but being a local boy, he would not reveal a man's whereabouts to strangers, and as for Lee Harden, he told the strangers he had never heard of no such Henry.

I shifted in my seat a little, freed my weapon. These men might be hunting me, not Henry Short. Seeing Ed Watson sitting there in the shadows of the porch, the Gandees boy was nervous as they came ashore. The passengers stood in the noon sun, hats in their hands, and nobody invited 'em to have a seat, not even Sadie, who was right behind the screen with Lee's gun loaded. Young Gandees had eased up onto the porch, to separate himself in case of trouble, and once he was safe out of the line of fire, he told the strangers, "These folks are friendly with the man you're after. Might as well tell 'em what you come for."

The two glanced at each other, nodded, took a breath. The older one, not yet twenty, said, "Why not? There is nothing to be ashamed of." By that I knew he was ashamed, and ashamed of being ashamed while he was at it.

Then the other one spoke out, more resolute. Not long after Henry had been sent away, he said, Henry's grandfather had married off Henry's mother to a cattleman named Graham who was moving his herds south to Kissimmee. The young woman welcomed this as a new life, but she needed to know about her firstborn little boy because when she'd last seen him as a four-year-old, he had been frail and nervous, and she was worrying herself to death, wondering if he was all right. These two young fellers had come south on her behalf to find out what had become of him and how he was getting on.

We looked at one another, puzzled. "We didn't catch your names," I said.

"Graham," the older said, looking around at every face, one at a time. The other nodded. "Henry's mother is our mother, too." Their hard truth, laid out as bare as that, made my temples tingle, because these two were white boys as fair-skinned as myself. "Our dad don't know we're here," the younger explained.

"I'll bet he don't!" blustered that fool Earl, banging his chair down.

Sadie Harden leaned the gun inside the door and came outside. "Don't matter who you are," she said, with a cross look at her men. "You fellers come on up here on the porch out of that sun." And they came up the step into the shade to enjoy a cool lime squash. They had stopped all along the coast without locating Henry, and now they had to go back to Arcadia.

"Henry is gettin along just fine," Old Man Robert told them, clearing his throat. "He has grown up to be a big strong feller and a fine man, too. You can be proud of him." And Lee chimed in that Henry had always lived with Houses, and that family had been good to him, as far as he'd ever heard.

"He's been treated all right, then?"

"For a nigger," I said. "Right, Earl?"

Earl had niggers on the brain, and I liked to tease him. If he hadn't been so scared of me, I honestly believe Earl Harden would have waylaid me and shot me, so I made damn sure that he stayed scared and never came around behind me. Earl was jolly as could be most of the time, he worked at it, but you couldn't joke him on a racial subject. He was a white man by his skin, the same as Lee, but he had that shadow.

Two Harden sisters had that same shadow in their color, a kind of thickened look behind the white, and another one was coffee-and-cream, though no man on the coast noticed her color. Libby Harden was clear-skinned and small-featured, she was rounded and sweet-smelling, she was a blessed gift to man on Earth that a grateful soul such as myself was aching to take home and unwrap.

Sadie said, "Henry is welcome at our Harden table whenever he comes through, he is our friend."

They looked at me. I said, "Henry Short is a good worker and he knows his place." And the older boy asked, "What place might that be, Mr. Watson?" They got up to go. The mail boat crew had whispered warnings when they first glimpsed me on the porch, and these young Graham fellers wanted no trouble, not because they were afraid, I saw, but because all that concerned them was their half brother. They said they would be back another year, and they left a letter for him.

Next time Henry showed up at Wood Key, he read that letter over and over, Lee Harden told me. Then he refolded it very carefully—as if it had a gold piece wrapped in it, Sadie said—and put it away in his breast pocket. He never spoke of it, and they knew better than to ask him. "I reckon his kinfolks are Henry's only secret," Sadie said.

"Henry is *their* secret," I said. "He's keeping their secret for them, out of gratitude that they never forgot him."

"Gratitude!" scoffed Earl Harden grimly. Nobody knew what the hell he meant, least of all Earl.

*

Word was out at Chokoloskee Bay that Watson had come back to the Islands. I had to leave before somebody came looking—whether the Sheriff or some local posse didn't matter.

The Russ boys had left for Fort White ahead of me. Never spoke, not even a good-bye, except to demand their father's pay. I couldn't oblige 'em yet, I said, because I didn't have it, not until I'd sold my syrup at Tampa Bay. Those boys rolled their eyes and scowled, very angry and suspicious, but said nothing.

Before returning to Fort White, I had written Izma Virginia Russ a letter recounting the misfortune of her husband, and offering to help her boys get off to a good start in southwest Florida. I was a good talker, but the written word came hard, since I had barely learned to write and had no spelling.

Dear Maddam I am very sorey to inform you that Mr. John Russ is ded. I can ashore you I will do all I can. If the boys will try they will get along all right. I think Mr. Russ dide of hart failer. You have my simpaty and if

there is anything I can do for you let me know. With much respect to you
and the boys.

Edgar J. Watson

I guess I kind of hoped she might come join us. Izma was a female of my
own age, dun-haired and dull of eye, due to a resigned spirit or a stupid one.
However, a woman was needed in my house, and I was willing to overlook
her defects if she overlooked my financial debt to her late husband and took
good care of me. But Izma had never answered my kind letter, which told me
what kind of reception to expect, back home.

I made a fair profit on my syrup sale at Tampa and continued northward
to Fort White, where I went at once to offer my condolences to the Widow
Russ. With those sad silky dark hairs above her mouth and sharp short lines
beneath, her lips looked sewn up tight as a bat's bottom. When I doffed my
hat and made a little bow, she closed her door down to a crack, leaving me
out there in the rain. Through that slot I was informed in no uncertain terms
that Izma and her boys, and the Tolens, too, had all concluded that Edgar
Watson had murdered Mr. Russ because he had demanded his rightful earnings, which aforesaid Watson had never intended to pay.

I handed her the full amount in a brand-new store-bought envelope with
posies on it—"to the last penny," I declared. But I could have worn a big
black cowl and carried a scythe across my shoulder for all the thanks that
homely woman gave me. I grabbed her cold and bony hand and pressed it,
and spoke out plainly from the heart. "Mrs. Russ, ma'am, Izma dear, your
late husband died untimely of a heart attack and that is God's truth, as I
wrote you."

Izma said, "What would a man like you know about God?" She closed the
door. That twisted, unforgiving face told me how useless it would be to go
among the neighbors saying Edgar Watson had not killed John Russ.

*

Great-Aunt Tabitha had sent a summons. I rode over to the plantation
house. Very frail after her long life, the old lady spent most of what was left
of it rotting away under the covers. She was now ninety, and in her white
hair and threadbare nightgown, she looked as dry and crumbly and poor as
a bit of old bread left out for the jaybirds. The window was tight closed and
there was no scent of cigars, which told me her son-in-law's visits were in-
frequent. It was Calvin Banks's crippled-up old Celia who now hobbled over
to look after her. However, Aunt Tab was still sharp-eyed and nosy, demanding to know without preamble if I had murdered what's-his-name, her son-
in-law's stepbrother.

"No ma'am, I did not."

"Nephew, there's been bad rumors aplenty, all the way back to Edgefield County." She peered at me as if some vile wart had grown out on my nose since she'd last seen me. "What in the dickens is the matter with you, Edgar?" That's what the old package had always said—*What in the dickens*—perhaps because Dickens was the one author she would read.

"Is something the matter, Aunt?"

"A great deal is the matter. All those bad rumors. Nothing but trouble around here since you darn people came." She pointed her bony finger. "I revised my will, you know! Cut you clean out of it!"

"Yes ma'am. I've heard."

"Your mother and sister are complaining, are they?" She spoke with satisfaction. My courteous manner had mollified her but not much. "That's because I left my piano and some silver to your Mandy, who would have appreciated such fine things. Unlike your sister, she came regularly to call in the year she lived here with the children." She cocked her head. "I don't suppose that you killed Mandy, did you?"

"No ma'am. Please don't say such things."

"Well, you never deserved a person of such quality, I know that much. Of course she failed me in the end, like all the rest of you. Never acknowledged I'd left her my piano, far less thanked me. She might have been dying by that time, of course, for all anyone told me." The old woman frowned, losing her thread. "Precious little thanks from *any* of you Watsons, the more I think about it, least of all that wicked little Ellen Addison, pretending to be such a friend to my poor Laura."

Suddenly incensed by my intrusion, she drew the covers to her chin.

"What is it this time, Edgar? What do you want here?"

"You sent for me, Aunt Tabitha."

"Of course I did! I wanted to tell you that you should be horsewhipped!"

"My mother plays the piano, Aunt. I'm sure Mandy would have wanted her to have it."

"Too old! Too *spoiled*!" She waved the very idea out of her sight. "That Addison girl was rotten spoiled right from the start! Orphaned at ten, married at twenty, lived through the War and Reconstruction, and never even learned to boil an egg!" She masticated a little while, building up spit. "I cut her right out of my will, and her fool Minnie right along with her. I cannot imagine what Laura saw in those two females."

I held my tongue. From the window here in the south bedroom, I could see all the way down the long drive to Herlong Lane.

Spent, my great-aunt vented a deep sigh. "I suppose Laura was foolish, too—that might explain it." A tear came to her eye. "And this old fool who banished both of us to these dark woods for life— !" She raised her fingers to her collarbones, the gesture wafting sad old smells from beneath the covers.

"It's hard to put your finger on the fool. Haven't you discovered that in life, you of all people, Edgar, who had such energy and promise? Aren't *you* a fool, an accursed fool, to ruin every chance that comes your way?"

Her eyes rose to meet mine, beseeching me. "Tom Getzen told me after you left for Oklahoma that you might have become the leading farmer in this county. Did you set fire to his barn? Oh, never mind that now." She shook her head. "Look at your mother. *Still* rotten spoiled, after so much hardship in her life. As for your sister—well, let's not be unkind. The only one in that whole household who is not a fool is Minnie's daughter. What did they name her? Maria Antoinett? Where did these up-country Methodists hear tell of a French queen? Got the name wrong and the spelling, too."

"May." I nodded. "A lovely young girl."

"She is nothing of the sort! She has had no upbringing, she has no manners, she is wayward and hard and discontented. I left that child three hundred dollars in my will, but from what Mr. Tolen tells me lately, I have a good mind to take it back. She hasn't been to see me in two years!"

"What else has Mr. Tolen told you, Aunt?" I paused. "That I killed John Russ?"

"It's not your business what he told me." Again she cocked her head, fierce as a wren. "What in the dickens is the matter with you, Edgar? We had such hopes for you! Do you really suppose I would have let these Tolens into our family if you had fulfilled that early promise?"

"Yet you let Cousin Laura marry him."

"I had no choice. She was always jumping on him, she was shameless. Silly fool got herself pregnant first time out. We have only the Merciful Lord to thank that she miscarried." Aunt Tab was weeping. "Oh, Nephew," she entreated suddenly, "this vulgarian is selling *everything*! Why did you choose that Russ fellow instead?"

She had spat up the unspeakable, this kinswoman of knife mouth and burning eye. I crossed the room and closed the door, came back. She held my gaze, eyes glittering with retribution. She had meant precisely what her words had said. But now, with a jerk as stiff as a last death throe, she snapped her head away, closing her eyes to banish me and waving her own thought from her brain like some evil fume released by the family dog.

For the moment I went along with this, though I was eager. Taking her wrist, I whispered gently, "Tell your son-in-law I will call again on Sunday."

Eyes tight closed, she was still shaking her head. "Please, Edgar. I didn't mean that, not the way you're taking it. I was upset." She wept and trembled, very agitated. "I shall warn him—" But she stopped struggling and opened up her eyes and we regarded each other in silence. We both knew just what she had said and knew she meant it.

Aunt Tabitha turned her head aside as if all this unpleasantness would vanish in her sleep. Her face had softened. To her yellowed pillows, she murmured sadly, "Oh, how I longed to write back to Clouds Creek, to tell those stingy Watsons how young Edgar had made good, to tell them . . ."

"Aunt Tab? Why not write and tell them Cousin Edgar has two farms and a fine syrup business? Tell Colonel Robert—"

"And tomorrow?" She had tired of me and tired of her life. "What will you have tomorrow, Edgar? Go away." And as I unlocked her door, she said, "If you harm him, I shall testify against you."

Returning along the white tracks through the woods, I thought everything through. Before faltering, Aunt Tabitha had approved our right to remove Sam Tolen from our lives before he brought utter ruin to our property. That would be easier said than done, because Tolen had a large clan behind him, brothers and stepbrothers who would swarm out like red ants to defend him. He would not be ousted easily from an anthill as large and bountiful as this plantation, at least not lawfully, and probably not alive. In that event, Edgar Watson would be the first to be suspected and might well get himself hung, not because his neighbors cared about Sam Tolen but because nobody, including E. J. Watson, should get away with murder in this community more than once or twice.

*

On Sunday when I came back to see Tolen, I rode right up to the front door with its fake Georgian columns. I did not dismount. Aunt Tab had heard my horse or had been spying from the window, likely both. She called, "Sam!" sharply from upstairs. Eventually, taking his sweet time, the Lord of the Manor appeared in the front door, then waddled out onto his broad veranda. He was wearing his black frock coat from church in this thick midday heat, by which I knew he carried a weapon and more likely two, but he stripped off his Sunday collar in his visitor's presence in a typical gesture of cracker disrespect.

Sam had lost some of his lard, and a lot of his jolly manner along with it. He didn't smell good even at ten paces. After years of sloth and rotgut liquor, he looked like some squat nocturnal varmint poked out with a stick into the sun. His dirty hair was not trimmed neat in side whiskers or beard, it was just head growth in a thin black frizzle. The mean red eyeshine glinted through the fur, and the soiled pate shone through his crown like a dog's belly.

"Well, Sam, you haven't changed a bit."

"Not so's you'd notice. Only thing is, I'm richer." With that hoggish leer, he tossed his head back toward the house. Sam enjoyed teasing me so much that he clean forgot how upset he was over Ed Watson's alleged murder of his stepbrother. Sam wouldn't care too much whether I'd done it or I hadn't if it gave him an advantage either way.

Mike Tolen, in the door behind him, was thickset like Sam but his small paunch was hard. He looked sober as Sunday, all scrubbed up, while his brother looked like late Saturday night. From the day he was born until the day he died, Sam Tolen looked soiled inside and out.

I nodded at Mike but did not let him distract me, though I kept him in the corner of my eye. What I had to say was between me and his older brother, I told him, still looking at Sam, and this was true. I never had one thing against Mike. Everybody but my friend John Porter, who lost out to Mike when they ran for the County Commission, had a good opinion of this younger Tolen, who could not be blamed for the name Tolen but only for blind loyalty to his rodent family.

On account of John Russ, Mike ignored what I had said, though acting impolite and cold came hard to him. To gauge him, I skittered my horse out to the side, watching Mike's boots. From where he placed 'em when he shifted with me, I knew he was armed, too. They'd been expecting me. I caught Aunt Tab ducking back behind the curtain in the upper window and gave her a little yoo-hoo kind of wave.

From his big grin when I did that, a stranger might have thought Sam was glad to see me, and as a matter of fact, I do believe he was. Because I had let him hang around when we were younger, this fat feller still looked up to me, he even liked me. But being afraid, he might pull that gun at the first chance, especially with his brother there behind him. That old Watson skulking up there behind her blowing curtain was the only thing that might deter him—not that I had confidence in her support.

In this standoff, we looked each other over. I had no doubt about the outcome. Sam could not shoot a nickel's worth, not even with a rifle, and very few farmers besides E. J. Watson could hit anything at all with a revolver. I doubt if either of these two knew how to draw. They'd be dead before they dragged those guns out of their linty pockets, and Aunt Tab would testify that they drew first.

That's what was going through my mind while Sam was grinning. I wiped that damned smile off his face real quick. "Nope, you haven't changed a bit," I said. "You still stink like a skunk, because you are one. And you have been telling lies about me, as usual."

"Lies?" he growled. His half glance alerted his brother to get ready. "You told Izma and that old lady upstairs that you never killed John Russ. If that ain't a lie, me'n Mike here never heard one, ain't that right, Mike?"

Mike Tolen grunted but said nothing. Not being a gunman, poor Mike was uneasy, knowing Sam's drunken nerve was fraying. Sam started blustering. "When all you was doin was shootin your nigger help on payday— hell, nobody never paid no mind to that. But when my stepbrother goes south with you owin him money, and he don't come back—" Sam shrugged his shoulders. "Come on now, Ed," he complained, "how can you blame folks?"

"I don't blame folks," I told him. "I blame you."

Will Cox's oldest boy rode up alongside while we were talking, a big husky young feller, long-legged on a mule. Smelling trouble, he let out a kind of eager snicker. I nodded to Leslie without turning my head. My old cabin, which the Cox family was still using, was not far away on Tolen Road. Will Cox did not like the Tolens, and his wife Cornelia liked them even less, because Sam's brother Jim had wronged her sister before hightailing it back to Georgia with his daddy. No son of theirs would ever jump in on the Tolen side against Ed Watson, and anyway, Les was probably unarmed.

"I am notifying you right here and now—and your brother Mike and this Cox boy here are witnesses—I am notifying Sam Frank Tolen that E. J. Watson did not kill John Russ. So the next time you accuse me, you will be calling me a liar. You can try that now"—here I shifted in the saddle, getting set—"or you can say it behind my back. Either way, boy, I intend to shoot you."

Hearing that kind of dangerous talk, the Cox boy grinned a hungry grin that drew his ears back. He looked like some kind of sleek water animal. Though I hid my mirth by hard coughing in my neckerchief, I was grinning, too. It did my heart good, it was just plain fun to talk in that Wild West way to Sam Frank Tolen.

Sam would never have a better chance to repay me for that long ago day when I faced down Woodson Tolen in the field. He had two against one, and though Mike was not so willing, he was ready. Also, it would gall Sam something fierce to back down in front of his brother and the Cox boy. But Sam had seen me shoot too many times. His green eyes flickered. "You aim to back-shoot me?" he sneered finally, then belched, contemptuous. Leslie laughed aimlessly out of sheer eagerness. Mike did not laugh. He did not know what I would do, and for one burning moment, I did not know either.

For that insult, I told Sam, I would challenge him to shoot it out on the field of honor except for the fact that Tolens were poor whites without honor and much too trashy to call out in a duel. Anyway, the duel would not be even, not unless I left my gun at home.

Both Tolens sneered at this. When Aunt Tabitha called out, they returned inside. I went away as frustrated as I had come.

*

Leslie Cox came to the plantation house that day because he was the star pitcher on Sam's baseball team, which played on a diamond on a piece of pasture east of the Fort White Road. Like the plantation and the post office and the mud ruts that ran north and south along the railroad track, the baseball team was named for Sam—the Tolen Team—though Sam could hardly throw a ball, let alone catch one. The team was mostly young Kinards and Burdetts, who lived near the ballpark and never thought about much else, but Les Cox was the star and Fat Sam spoiled him, so he often hung around Sam's fancy house. San ran the baseball club and owned the diamond, and Leslie wanted to pitch in the worst way. Besides being the star, he also enjoyed using his fastball to scare and humiliate opposing batters. Les Cox was a big strong boy who took what he wanted, whether it belonged to him or not.

At fifteen, Les had chin stubble and a heavy voice and was solid and hard-muscled as a man. He was handsome, too, so women said, though I mistrusted those ears, which were too small and too tight to his head. On his left cheekbone was a pale crescent scar, courtesy of a cranky mule which had fetched him a hind kick that blacked him out for close to forty hours, scared his poor folks half to death. Broke the cheekbone, nearly blinded that one eye. Might have shifted his brain, too, to judge from some of his behavior later on.

One day another boy cut himself in the schoolyard and was screaming at the blood. Leslie ran over not to help but to holler at him to shut his mouth up or he would beat him. He did it, too. A dog will attack another dog that's hurt and yelping, but among our human kind, it's not so common. Even his own people were troubled at the time. Leslie was the oldest son, but he had remained childish in some ways. Wore a toy pistol up till age fourteen, and never learned to handle himself when things went wrong.

Lately my niece May Collins had imagined that she was in love with Leslie Cox, she saw the trouble he got into at the school as quite romantic. He was often a truant, and was always picking fights, pushing the smaller boys and grabbing things that did not belong to him, even their food. He was quick to anger and quicker to attack any boy who dared protest. In fact, none of the children liked him except May and her young girlfriends. He wasn't stupid, he was utterly indifferent, and when he was sent back to repeat his grade, he gave up on his education, contemptuous of teachers and pupils alike.

I never had much doubt about who Leslie was. He was a back-country boy who would grow hard and vicious. All the same, I admired how he stood up for his daddy against Sam Tolen even when he was star pitcher on Sam's team.

Because I was friendly with his daddy, Les liked to boast how he was friends with "Desperado Watson." He had made me his hero in some way, and with his education at an end, he started showing up over at my place, asking questions about the Wild West and Belle Starr. Les had studied up on the Belle Starr story, and he informed me that it was my small footprints which got me into trouble in Oklahoma, having learned from a dime novel that Jesse James had small feet, too, and Jesse was Belle's jealous boyfriend and had killed her. Also, Belle was shot in the back, and everyone knew that a man like E. J. Watson would never shoot anybody in the back. "No matter what, my daddy says, Ed Watson would look a man straight in the eye!"

I spat on the ground and looked Les straight in the eye just to oblige him.

Les asked if I'd known Jesse James, and I said I sure had. I told him Ol' Jess was mostly talk, it was Frank James I could always count on in hard situations. "Hard situations?" Leslie whispered, those green wildwood eyes of his just smoldering. He nodded eagerly when I gave him a hard squint, smiling an ironic little smile and shaking my head—the frontier code. He went off practicing his own squint and also that frontier code of stoic silence. For a while there, his daddy told me, they could hardly get their oldest boy to speak a word.

Sam purely hated it that his young baseball star admired Edgar Watson. Though Sam heeded my warning and shut up about John Russ, he fed Leslie all those Carolina tales he had got from Herlongs, not knowing that this would only make this boy admire me, and Leslie, who liked nothing better than stirring up some trouble, passed Sam's stories right along to me. Naturally, he would run right back to Sam with my response, and so I boasted some. To sting Sam up a little, I told Les how I ran that yeller-bellied Woodson Tolen right out of the field back when I was Leslie's age. While I was at it, I confided how I had dealt with the Queen of the Outlaws and her gang of halfbreed Injuns, and how I took care of a bad actor named Quinn Bass—in short, what you might call the varnished truth.

Sure enough, one Saturday afternoon after the baseball game, Les drank whiskey with Sam Tolen and told him all about Desperado Watson's scrapes, even mentioned how I'd wanted "to sting Sam up." Sam Tolen bollered, "I'll show you somethin about 'stingin up'!" That same evening Sam rode him over to the sawmill at Columbia City to sting up two nigger brothers who had failed to show Sam due respect. Sam had been brooding about those sassy niggers every time he drank, aimed to teach those two a lesson with some bird shot.

The lesson Sam Tolen taught them was the following: he blasted 'em clean off their mule after halting them on the road, waving his shotgun. Being dead drunk, he had his loads mixed up, used buckshot instead of bird shot, and because his aim was poor, he shot 'em around the head instead of the legs—made a real mess of that stinging part, Les said. Sam's nerves gave way, what with all the blood and screeching, so he yelled at Les to jump down off his mule and finish those boys off before their nigger racket brought the whole countryside down on top of them.

"I ain't never took a life! Made me feel funny!" Les was very overexcited, even scared, but also just as thrilled as he could be. "Reason I'm tellin you, Mister Ed, you had some experience, but don't go tellin nobody I told!" He laughed loudly just to ease his nerves. "Thing of it is, Mister Sam is claimin how he was dead set against killin 'em, all he aimed to do was sting 'em up a little. Says what that Cox boy done of his own accord were not his idea at all, it were all Les Cox's doin."

Les and Sam would never be arrested for a thing like that because Will Cox's old friend Purvis was Columbia County Sheriff and had known Les ever since he was a boy. However, with both of them shooting off their mouths, there was too much talk. Leslie's account fit what I had heard, so I didn't doubt that it was mostly true. What troubled me about it was the way he told it—the way he tasted every word, licked at it, even. And that bad grin, in this sullen boy who hardly grinned from one week to the next. He had come over to my house not because he was upset by senseless killings but to brag about them to his hero E. J. Watson.

"So you didn't mind—?"

"Hell, no," he squawked, loud and derisive. "That don't bother me none!" He actually gave me that stupid frontier squint, then grinned and winked. Will's boy had gone wrong, all right, worse than I feared.

The Columbia City shooting was in early winter. Knowing Sam, he would be scared by what he'd done once he was sober, and more scared still by all of Leslie's talk. Those amateur killers avoided each other until baseball came around again in early spring. Leslie pitched for the Tolen Team that year but they never saw him anymore at the plantation, where Sam blamed the whole business on Watson's bad influence.

*

One day Sam sent word through Coxes that if Watson would meet him in a public place, namely the J. R. Terry Grocery in Fort White, we could talk things over and patch up our differences. However, I was suspicious of the invitation because I happened to be scrapping with the Terrys.

My mother was Episcopalian, and Minnie, too, and Minnie's three children had been baptized in St. James Episcopal, Lake City, but there was no Episcopal church around Fort White. The Collins family were Methodists, but Billy got cranky in the last years of his life and went over to the Baptist persuasion, so the family got the habit of Elim Baptist, which was over east of the Fort White Road and had Captain Tom Getzen for the deacon.

However, there was trouble with the Terrys because their mean dogs were scaring the three Collins kids on their way down the Bellamy Road to the Elim Church. My sister spoke to me about it—only time she spoke to me all that whole year. I went over there and warned those Terrys but they paid no attention, never chained their dogs even on Sundays. So the following Sunday, I took my gun along, and I shot those dogs dead as fast as they ran up. Terrys never forgave that, never forgot it, and I don't suppose they ever will. From that day on, I had to watch my back every time I went over to Fort White. Even gave up my Saturday midday meal at the Sparkman Hotel, where I'd always enjoyed the lively conversation, mostly because I was doing all the talking.

When I was invited to meet Sam at the Terry store, I sent my son Eddie over there to reconnoiter. Just you duck around the back, I told him, peek in the window, see what's going on. It was just a frame one-story building and still is. So Eddie snuck around the back and peered in through the spiderwebs and shadows. He could just make out a big old iron safe and the tools and harness hanging from the walls and the potbellied stove. What he didn't see at first—it gave him a bad start—was the shape of a heavy man sitting on a nail keg with his back to him.

Eddie rode home and told me what he'd seen. This man had a shotgun across his lap, facing the door, and Eddie said it looked like Samuel Tolen. I decided that man with the shotgun wasn't sitting on that nail keg just for the hell of it. Mike Tolen or some damn Terry might be elsewhere in that room, which had dark corners—the last place I would ever go to patch up differences.

By now, I trusted nobody around Fort White. I jumped at shadows every time I rode along those roads. I decided I would be safer in the Islands.

*

While I was absent in Fort White, Bembery Storter had found a carpenter named Fred Dyer who would make improvements and repairs while overseeing the sugarcane operation at the Bend. He built a small one-story cabin not far downriver from the boat sheds for his wife Sybil and their little Lucy, then set to work on a big underground cistern back of the kitchen. He also built a screened porch across the front, where in the spring our folks could look out through the red poinciana blossoms to the river without being carried off by the mosquitos. Those darned mosquitos were God's Malediction, sighed Mis Sybil. Lucy's little nostrils were black with smudge from the kerosene rags burned in the smudge pots, and Mis Sybil had to rig netting to her hat and wrap old newsprint around her legs every time she went outdoors or to the privy. In wet weather, the ink came off the paper and turned her legs a dark bruised blue—Mis Sybil hated that, too. At night nobody walked around due to poisonous snakes that came up on the high ground in time of flood, so everyone used chamber pots—chambers, Lucy called them. Day in, day out, in the wet season, that poor child was shut up indoors, which in dark rainy months was damp and stifling, with air so heavy that the lungs became exhausted hauling it in. A clear day with wind was what Mis Sybil called "the Mosquito Sabbath," when these demons rested—the only days when she could romp along the river with her little girl. So her husband built a screened porch on both houses—the only screens in the Islands back at that time.

Fred Dyer was handy and did most of his work, but found too many excuses to go off on the *Gladiator.* He was gone a lot, he drank a lot, and there were women. I learned all this from Henry Thompson, who was prone to gossip when he talked at all, not wanting anyone to get away with anything. Sometimes Fred didn't show up on the dock for the trip back, and his little family might not know his whereabouts for the next fortnight. Even after my return, he went off with Henry every chance he got, claiming we needed various stores and supplies, and I let him go and didn't say much because he was smart and kept the syrup operation right on schedule, and because it suited me to have him elsewhere. Mis Sybil seemed to welcome this, as well.

Often we sat on Fred's screened porch on those long river evenings. I missed dear Mandy, I was lonely, and Sybil Dyer cheered me up, she was delightful. She was more educated than her husband, bright, lively, and pretty, and would pass for a lady by back-country standards. Mis Sybil asked about my childhood and I found myself confiding in her, recalling those dark days in Carolina and the loss of the Artemas Plantation. Yes, she crept into my soul in a way that Netta and Josie—though good country women—never had, and in a way that Jane Straughter never could.

At Christmas I brought the child a beautiful big dollie from Key West. I brought Mis Sybil presents, too, but as a married woman, she could not accept them, she said—this may have been our first little flirtation. However, I heaped toys on Lucy, and after a while I persuaded Lucy's mother that my gifts to her were not presents at all but were practical things for use in the household—the sewing machine, for example, with which she would soon be making all our clothes and sewing mosquito bars for every bed.

Lucius came to Chatham for the holidays, and I embarrassed him one evening, maybe more. Exasperated by the general torpor of the table conversation, I made a drunken public declaration that Mis Sybil was the only soul worth talking to on the whole place. I needed her too much, I guess. When I looked back on the women I had loved, I realized it was probably not so, but at the time it seemed to me that I was in love with little Mrs. Dyer.

Trying to mend my civic reputation, I did not want scandal any more than she did. Yet I couldn't trust myself when drinking, which meant she couldn't trust me either. Fearing what might happen if I drank while Dyer was absent, I bought her a small silver revolver for her own protection. After teaching her how to target-shoot, standing close behind her and supporting her arm while she aimed, I urged her to carry the weapon in her apron pocket whenever her husband was away, and to bar her door to Mr. E. J. Watson even if he yelled that her cabin was on fire. She laughed in protest at such an idea, but I was serious. I also commanded her to shoot right through the door if I made any attempt to break it down.

Mis Sybil was horrified. She cried out, Oh pshaw, Mr. Watson, you are pulling my leg! Anyway, I couldn't even shoot a snake! And I said, Well, ma'am, you had better learn, and the sooner the better.

*

At the end of the cane harvest in late winter of 1904, I had to return to the new farm in Fort White for the spring planting. I was already at the dock when Mis Sybil told me simply that she was with child. There was nothing to be done about it, and she said nothing more. Well, I said, and what does your husband think about it? And she said, He doesn't care to think about it. Nor do his arithmetic either, I laughed, to cheer her up.

She shook her head, picking at her dress. "I've discovered one thing that I don't love about you, Mr. Watson. You are kind and generous, but you also have a cynical and brutal streak."

"Yes, ma'am. I fear that a hard life has turned me hard." I looked down at my boots in honest shame. "I truly regret it, and I hope you will forgive me." But of course she knew about my childhood, and besides, she needed my affection at this painful time and embraced me fervently. "It is you who should forgive the world, my dear, dear Mr. Watson," she murmured gently, as I did my best to look brave and demure.

On the way north I passed through Tampa Bay, where a raucous crowd of businessmen and boosters were staging a mock piratical invasion of the town, calling themselves Ye Mystic Crewe of Gasparilla. This Gasparilla the Pirate nonsense was cooked up by Juan Gomez, that lying old Cuban out at Panther Key who had thrown himself overboard and drowned in his own cast net a few years before at the age of 123. Claimed that Napoleon had patted him on the head before he sailed as cabin boy with a buccaneer named José Gaspar or some such. Not a word of truth in it, nor in Juan, either, though I was fond of that old rascal in small doses. Anyway, this painted scow, crewed by soft and pasty merchants in queer pirate outfits, went tooting up the Hillsborough River, wood cannons, wood cutlasses, skull and crossbones, eye patches, and all. It was a pageant for the tourists, and I hope the poor fools loved it, because they plan to call it Gasparilla Day and perpetrate it on the public every year.

My friends the young Metz sisters, schoolteachers at Tampa, who disapproved of my sardonic attitudes toward black citizens, escorted me one afternoon to the grave of William Ashley, Tampa's first city clerk, who had written a strange epitaph before having himself buried with his former slave and lifelong mistress, Nancy.

IN DEATH THEY ARE NOT SEPARATED. STRANGER CONSIDER
AND BE WISER. IN THE GRAVE ALL HUMAN DISTINCTION OF RACE
OR CASTE MINGLE TOGETHER IN THE COMMON DUST.

I made a joke about common dust but my heart wasn't in it. In fact, it troubled me a little, bringing to mind those Graham boys and their half brother Henry Short. From there, my mind turned unwillingly to Sybil Dyer, standing alone on the dock at Chatham Bend.

Chapter 6

1905–1907

William Parker Bethea, a Baptist minister who claimed descent from an old French Huguenot family in the Tidewater, had lived down south of the Santa Fe River before moving up our way with his second wife late in 1904. He sharecropped a piece of the plantation, right across the Fort White Road from Joe Burdett, and his family grew close to the Burdetts and Porters. His widowed daughter from his first marriage came to visit, and John Porter, a born snoop, suggested to both parties that Mrs. Lola McNair and Mr. E. J. Watson might take kindly to each other. Having nothing in the world against sweet widows, I fluffed up my whiskers, borrowed the Collins family's nice red trap with bright gold spokes in which Billy had once courted his Miss Minnie, and sparkled over there on a nice Sunday to pay my respects.

The Reverend in black preaching suit, white socks, and high black shoes was sitting in a rocker on his front porch. "Good day, sir," said I. "E. J. Watson is my name. I am a friend of John L. Porter, come a-calling." When I lifted my hat and introduced myself, he rose from his chair as if preparing to defend his hearth and home. Like so many of the preaching persuasion, he looked like a more steadfast man than he turned out to be.

"Yessir," he said in a stiff voice. "We know who you are."

Hearing those cold words, I almost left without another word. Because of John Russ's idiotic death, I remained suspect in my home community. But even as he spoke, Preacher Bethea was hastening out into the sunlight for a better look at my red trap with its fringed canopy, and after an uneasy kind of pause while he scratched his neck, this man of God stuck out his knobby hand. I gave it a good honest shake and he waved me up onto the porch, saying, "Make yourself to home here, Mr. Watson."

Watching me was a young girl in a white frock who stood behind his rocker like a servant. She had wide brown eyes in a calm and kindly face and long soft taffy-colored hair down past her shoulders. This was not Lola but her younger sister Catherine Edna, who was of that age—about sixteen— when a female creature can be handsome and pretty both. Showing nice manners for that part of the country, she curtsied to her father's guest and skipped away ever so winsome to fetch her sister.

What Preacher Bethea was up to in that moment only his Lord knew, but my guess would be, he was tussling with the Devil. And ol' Beezle-bub whipped God's messenger well and quick, because even before I flapped my coattails up and sat my arse down in his rocker, I knew this man would never give me trouble. As farmer and preacher, he was well-acquainted with my neighbors, including his landlord, the loud and loose-mouthed Tolen, and surely he'd heard rumors about E. J. Watson. Yet never once, on this day or later, did Bethea seek to assure himself that this stranger of ill repute would bring no harm to his dear daughter.

By the time I left, I had concluded that the Preacher's plan was to sweep out the leftover girls from his first marriage, make room for the second batch coming along. He had two new kids and a third one in the oven, and probably he dreaded the burden of the Widow Lola and her children somewhat more than permitting the younger sister to fall into the grasp of a known criminal.

By now Catherine Edna had returned, busting out onto the porch all in a flurry. When she smoothed her skirt to sit down on the steps, I could not help but take note of the apple bosom swelling in her frock. However, that was my own need, there was no guile in her. If she noticed all my noticing, she gave no sign, just sat there beaming up into my face like a fresh fruit pie. By the time Lola and her little girl had joined us on the porch, it was already too late. I had my wicked sights set on Catherine Edna.

"We expected you Sat'day," the Preacher said, a little sour. "Lola's just fixin to leave."

The Widow Lola had the same calm, kindly manner as her sister, but also the sad quiet in her face of a young woman who already lives mostly in the past and expects very little from the future. Her hair was up in a big roll on her head, the way all married women wore it, and childbearing had thickened her a little through the midriff. She was handsome, yes, but no longer apple fresh like her young sister. All in a moment, Catherine Edna, whom I would call Kate, had twisted my loins harder than any female since poor

Charlie Collins, who had moldered in the Bethel graveyard many a long year by the time this randy man of God, panting and croaking, had clambered aboard his wife and fired up her womb, setting this sprightly Kate on the path to Glory.

Lola McNair, very pleasant, not flirtatious, did not stay long. She was taking the afternoon train to Lake City, and the Reverend went off to hitch up his buggy to drive her and her children to the Junction. When she rose to go, she took my hand, smiling a little, having sensed what was already taking place. "So-o"—she drawled that small word slowly—"Mr. Watson." I bowed minutely, we exchanged a smile. Releasing my hand, she said how much she'd enjoyed meeting me, adding, "Next time, y'all come calling just a little sooner."

Miss Lola was not teasing me, only herself, having lost a suitor even before she had laid eyes on him—even before she knew whether she might want him. And she did not mind that I had seen her bittersweet glimmer of regret—all of that went back and forth between us with not one word spoken. That woman and I were friends from the first moment, as if we had been lovers in some other life. I loved her and her sister both, being full to overflowing with a grand bold feeling. But Miss Lola was protective of her sister, and her eyes were troubled. Unlike her father, she did not pretend she had not heard the rumors—that shadow went back and forth between us, too.

By reputation, I was two men in this district, the jovial, hard-working brother-in-law of Billy Collins and the cold-blooded desperado—the Man Who Killed Belle Starr. While the Preacher might claim he knew only of the first, he stood ready to practice his divine Christian forgiveness on the second or know the reason why. This man Watson was not straddling a dusty mule, like all the rest of the young bucks around this section. He was a planter and a gentleman of property with a second plantation on the southwest coast, a man with manners who came calling in a fine two-horse trap, bright red with a gold trim, the only one like it on this side of Lake City. Once the Preacher had seen that side of E. J. Watson, the rest went right out of his mind. His wish was to make a good marriage for his daughter, just as I had done for my daughter in Fort Myers, never mind that I had been invited not to attend the wedding. No, it wasn't for me to disapprove of this hungry man of God, but I do know this: I would not have let Carrie anywhere near a suitor with Watson's reputation, no matter how rich that rufous rascal seemed to be.

Although Bethea didn't know it yet, I wasn't rich—I had borrowed that red trap—but I was an old rascal, no doubt about that. From the first day I met his daughter, all I could think about was snuffling up under that sweet dimity like some bad old bear, just crawling up into that honeycomb, nose twitching, and never come up for air till early spring. Think that's disgusting? By God, I do, too! But that's the way male animals are made. God put those strange delights there to entrap us, and anybody who disapproves can take it up with Him.

In their capacity of knowing the Lord's mind, churchly folks will tell you how the Lord would purely hate to hear such dirty talk. My idea is, He wouldn't mind it half so much as churchgoers would have us think. Because even according to their own two-faced creed, man is God's handiwork, created in His image, anger, lust, shit, piss, beauty, brains, and all. Without that magnificent Almighty lust of God's Creation that we mere mortals dare to call a sin, there wouldn't *be* any mere mortals, and God's grand plan for the human race (if He has got one, which seemed to me more doubtful than God himself) would turn to dust, and dust unto dust, forever and Amen. All those other creatures would step up and take over, realizing that mankind is so weak and foolish they can hardly breed. No, no, no, it must be hogs who will Inherit the Earth, because as long as there's plenty, they love to eat any old thing God sets in front of them, and they're ever so grateful for God's green earth even in the rain and mud, and they just plain adore to fuck and frolic and generally fulfill God's Holy Plan. And hogs might be created in God's image, too, for all we know.

So only church folks would think God's poor old Edgar J. should be cast into Damnation for longing so to become One with His Divine Creation, namely Miss Kate Edna. In God's eyes, the dirty-minded one might be this preacher who whistled the girl's sharp-eyed stepmother onto the porch while he took her big sister to the railroad, to protect his investment and make sure that rich Watson feller didn't get something for nothing.

Soon we were joined out on the porch by young Clarence, who claimed he was the first fellow in these parts to work a camera. He wanted to show a photo he had taken single-handed of this very porch on which we sat. When the ladies went inside, I encouraged Clarence to tell me something about his family background, from which I hoped I might deduce Kate Edna's expectations. The obliging youth reared back and gave me in one blurt the background information on the Bethea tribe as best he understood it, which—to judge from his very first sentence—was not well at all.

"Columbus thought the world was round, but the Queen told him it was square, so he ended up at the Little Peedee River. And the first Betheas, they come there, too, but they was Frenchmen, French Hoogen-knots, y'know, and they was signers of South Carolina's Secession where we split off from the damn-Yankee Union. But life got too crowded in the Tidewater, so our bunch spread out.

"One day my Granddaddy W. P. Bethea Senior got it in his head he was comin to Florida, so he hitched up his ox team and he come ahead, driving his stock, y'know. Come south in a covered wagon by the old Cherokee Trail to Cow Ford, where it's Jacksonville today. But the St. John's River was too high, stock couldn't swim it, so he headed 'em off west to Little Bird, crossed over at a tradin post that had a moonshine still and a 'brush arbor' with no roof onto it where them pioneer Baptists went to worship before wood churches was put up—probably how they got that name First Florida Baptists.

"Now Granddaddy Bethea went west and south and homesteaded down yonder past Fort White on the Santa Fee River, which flows on over west to the Suwannee. My daddy, W. P. Junior, was ordained a minister by age twenty-one, had thirteen children by Miss Josephine Sweat, who died of it all back at the century's turn. Seven head of us was still under his roof when he got hitched again. Oldest still at home amongst us is Kate Edna, who was borned down yonder back in 'eighty-nine. Bill P. the Third showed up only last year.

"Daddy don't hardly make a livin preachin, he got to raise his cows and chickens, got to sharecrop, too. Corn, peanuts, peas, okra, tomatoes, hot peppers, common greens, and velvet beans for our cow fodder. Mama Jessie got her a crank churn, she turns out three, four gallons of good cream every other day. Daddy goes up to town on Saturdays, peddles eggs and butter—"

Clarence's voice was dying down at last. Pretending he'd heard something in urgent need of his attention, he frowned and ran off behind the house, as his stepmother screeched after him to mind his manners. But of course the poor boy had lost interest in our talk because he saw that I had, too, having heard more than I would ever care to know about this family.

The womenfolk came outside again, bearing lemonade. Sitting there in the old man's rocker, I noticed how Kate Edna and her chaperone got in each other's way. With Lola married, this young girl had been taking good care of her widowed daddy, and even when Mis Jessie had shown up, it was hard for the girl to turn her papa over to a stranger. It was plain that she felt unwelcome in this house and was set to flee the coop, though not with me.

During my visit, a boy rode up on a mule, nice-looking young feller with black hair cut in a bowl. This was Herkie Burdett, son of Josiah Burdett from across the Fort White Road. Herkie played a pretty good third base, I'd heard, for the Tolen Team. When Kate Edna came out, Herkie went rose red in the face and tripped over his boots, couldn't make things work at all. Kate Edna blushed at his hello, but whether that girl blushed out of young love or pained embarrassment for her tangle-footed beau, she was too kind and discreet to let me see.

Right in front of me, Mis Jessie reprimanded Kate as if Herkie wasn't there, saying Herkimer must go home at once and stay away from here. Seeing Kate's cheer die in her face, I knew it was high time I left, so that this girl would not blame the guest for being the cause of Herkimer's dismissal.

*

As it turned out, Leslie Cox had his eye on Catherine Edna, too. One day he let drop something smart and sly to give the impression that he knew her somewhat better than a modest and honorable frontier character such as himself would choose to reveal. Without really acknowledging that he had noticed her, he managed to hint that the Bethea girl had been trailing around after him at school, panting for the smallest crumb of his attention. With her tearstained face poking around every tree and corner, it had got to the point where this poor scholar was plagued and distracted from his studies and finally abandoned his education altogether.

Besides being ridiculous, and a plain lie, his conceit was annoying and it stung, reminding me that I was close to fifty while this girl was not yet sixteen. And maybe she did love Leslie, just a little, because if she didn't, she was the only adolescent female with good sense for miles around.

My niece May Collins, her best friend Eva Kinard, and that whole flock of linsey-woolsey damsels at the Centerville School, were all a-flutter over the handsome pitcher on the baseball team. They blushed and gushed over their hero's husky voice, so low and easy and confiding, and that romantic cheekbone scar obviously suffered in a duel—these addled girls knew a lot more about dueling scars than about mule hooves. What May went all to pieces over were those dangerous black brows, which contrasted, said she, with his sensitive mouth and soft brown hair. According to May (who had a poetical nature, like her grandmother), the Cox boy's hair turned "gold and light-filled in the summer." She loved the graceful way he moved and ran and threw, doubtless imagining how all that rampant youth would feel in her loving arms. So it was not Kate Edna but May Collins who tagged after the star pitcher every chance she got, at least when her daddy wasn't looking.

"That young man's scar is the mortal imperfection that makes immortal the beauty of his face," pronounced Granny Ellen—that's what Minnie's children called my mother. Granny Ellen got her fanciest ideas from her old book of English poems, brought south from Edgefield. "*Beauty is truth, truth beauty,*"—*that is all ye know on earth, and all ye need to know*—I recalled that one from earliest childhood. But Les Cox's "beauty" was no kind of truth that any woman of right mind would wish to know, on earth or elsewhere. Later on, when his bad character began to twist his face, the ladies would assure one another that his horrid scar must be the mark of Cain.

I told Les sharply to watch his tongue when referring to young ladies, in particular Miss Kate Edna Bethea. He cocked his head with a knowing grin and tried his frontier drawl. "Never reckoned Desperado Watson would bother his head none about them young fillies." I suppose he meant that no true gunman from the West would get so hot and bothered over a woman, let alone a girl, but in my experience, desperados—like most men of perilous and uncertain occupation—rarely got hot and bothered about much else. However, I did not impart that information to Les Cox, not wishing to spoil a young person's illusions.

In the end the Preacher was forced to acknowledge my poor reputation, and it never changed his plans even a little. As a last-minute precaution, when the day drew near, he found some weak excuse not to perform our wedding, and once his Kate Edna was safely off his hands, he assured people that he had strongly disapproved this match right from the start. Kate Edna was hurt, having done what she thought he wanted, but by now she was learning who her father was. She said, "You see, if Daddy disapproves of us, he won't feel obliged to provide a dowry"—the one bitter remark I ever heard this loyal daughter make. She was shocked when it turned out she was right.

*

On May 20, 1904, we were married in a civil ceremony at Lake City's City Hall by County Judge W. M. Ives, with whom I would have less amicable dealings later on. (Granny Ellen was disgruntled that the groom's mother had not been invited to our nuptials.) As a wedding present, sweet Kate gave me a white shaving mug in floral porcelain with gold trim, the first elegant object I had ever owned, and a beautiful token of our wealthy future.

The wedding was celebrated on a two-day honeymoon at the Hotel Blanche, where Kate tasted her very first champagne and oysters. For a girl who had grown up around farm animals, she set out on her erotic life distinctly nervous—not jumpy so much as inert and damp, like suet, breaking out in sudden little sweats. But I stroked her back and rump real slow and gentle, murmured her down and murmured her down, same way you might calm a foal. Pretty soon, with more champagne, she got taken by surprise by her own free nature. She opened up wide and hung on tight and commenced to pant and moan, turning a lovely sweet pink in the face, which got me going, too. In the midst of it, I had a revelation that God's Creation might be nothing more nor less than the simultaneous joy and energy of animal ecstasies, all exploding into the universe at once.

After a high time or two, it was the bridegroom E. J. Watson who was acting kind of shy or at least retiring—the first time it ever bothered me that I was getting on toward fifty. HERE LIES BILL WILLIAMS: HE DONE HIS DAMNDEST—

that's a tombstone epitaph somewhere in West Texas. I gave it hell, but after a while I was less hard than hard put to keep up with her. Even so, we raised such a jolly rumpus in our big and squeaky bed that poor Kate felt too giggly and peculiar to dress in front of me next morning or appear at breakfast.

*

Granny Ellen was distracted by a letter recently arrived from Colonel R. B. Watson at Clouds Creek, who inquired after her son Edgar, wondering what had become of him, how he was faring. Had he made his mark, as the Colonel hoped? Colonel Robert's interest moved me more than I cared to show her, so I feigned indifference. In his letter, Colonel Robert—apparently the only Watson to visit his shadow cousin—regretfully described the last days of Ring-Eye Lige, "all purple bony knees and puffy belly, all eaten up with big sores on his legs that would not heal, wheezing and moaning and crying, and he smelled just terrible." In the last two weeks before he died, that wretched sinner howled for light all day as well as the night through, that's how scared he was of the coming darkness and the vengeful spirits. In his last coma he had raved and muttered about those terrible nights after a battle, and the wails of agony and woe among the dying. A name he had mentioned repeatedly was Selden Tilghman, and Colonel Robert asked if Cousin Ellen could explain this. "You might ask your son. It's very curious."

Mama looked hard into my face. Startled to hear Cousin Selden's name, I only shook my head. Mama shrugged, too. "I'm not surprised he was scared to meet his Maker, after such a life. And of course he always hated Cousin Selden." She scrutinized me but dared go no further.

*

Fred Dyer had heard the rumors about the Tuckers, his wife told me when I returned to Chatham in the autumn. Fred came reeling to the dock and with the drunkard's ferocious belligerence informed me that he wanted to be paid off right now since he aimed to leave. I looked him over up and down and crossways until he started glancing back over his shoulder for his wife's support, and then I said that this plantation had always required a year's notice from a foreman. If he left before the harvest, he would have to forfeit a year's pay. Nothing came out of that flushed face, but when he sobered up, he had changed his mind.

At Christmas, Mis Sybil was near term and her husband was off at Tampa on a bender. That poor young wife delivered her baby with only the help of our Injun woman, who told her to get out of bed and squat. That squaw ignored the boiling water and hot towels I fetched to her cabin door, just hacked and coughed and spat and closed the door again. Having broken in her own tough old vagina, she could not imagine what the fuss was all about. Giving birth, for her, was more like yawning. In sign language she indicated that when that weepy white woman got her breath back, she could go on down to the river and wash off.

Hurt by her husband's absence—and confused that I had remarried—Sybil tried to be happy for me, and was grateful for my tenderness. She was still determined to name her son Watson Dyer. She never reproved me for forcing her door, saying I had warned her, and had even given her that pistol to protect herself. It was not my fault she could not bring herself to pull the trigger.

When Fred got home, red-blotched and shaky, he was so ashamed of abandoning his family not only at Christmas but for "Wattie's" birth that he put up no fight over that name. I went to Key West on business, bought late Christmas presents, including ten yards of fine silk for the new mother. By the time I got back to the Bend, the Dyer family was gone. Green Waller said they had departed on the mail boat, leaving only a scrawled note saying where to send the five hundred dollars that Dyer claimed was due him in back salary. I was cross about buying all those Christmas presents I could not afford, but I was also a lot easier in mind. Considering the suspicious husband and the baby—and Mis Sybil saying dangerous things like *I think I have fallen in love with you, Mr. Watson*—it seemed like things had worked out for the best. I certainly felt no obligation to send money.

Young Lucius had been living at the Bend, going to school in Everglade when we could spare him. He told me Mis Sybil had wanted her husband to wait till he was paid. Dyer was adamant, however, telling his wife that he was going and that if she did not come with him, she would never see hide nor hair of him again. By now he had persuaded himself that I would send his salary after the harvest. "Mis Sybil knew better," Lucius said in a wry tone that seemed too skeptical of my business practices for a man's own son. Finally Sybil had agreed to go, saying good-bye to everyone, in tears.

Little Lucy, who adored Lucius as much as her mother adored me, left "Chatham" in a flood of grief. I believe Lucius stayed in touch with the mother and daughter, but I did my best to forget them all. Baby Wattie was still blind when he left the Bend, so he never laid eyes on his natural father. For everyone's sake, I never claimed or recognized Watson Dyer as my son.

As for my daughters by the Daniels women, I stopped off to visit Netta's Minnie and Josie's little Pearl every chance I had, which was never enough for the two little girls. Minnie said, "Daddy, how come you go away and don't come back?" Already eleven, she was a shy and pretty child with dark brown hair and eyes that were near black, and I was happy she had forgiven me for that mistake two years before when I got drunk and took her away with me because I felt so lonesome. Because she never stopped crying for her mama, she stayed only one night at the Bend before I brought her back.

*

Not long after my marriage, Great-Aunt Tabitha had summoned me to her stale bedside. She got my wrist in a bony grip, then whispered with weak sulfurous breath that she wanted her Watson silver to stay in the family. That silver was to go to my new bride. Aunt Tab was frail, with the smell of decay already rising from her yellowed linen, and maybe her son-in-law hurried her along before she could get that last wish down on paper, because on a soft hazy day of spring, she gave up the ghost. Her mortal coil had been boxed and trundled up the highroad to Lake City, where she was laid in next to Cousin Laura, under that high and haughty stone she had ordered right after her daughter's death, more than ten years in advance of this great occasion. WE HAVE PARTED—whom could she have meant? Her Laura, I suppose. She did not sound sorry.

Her loving son-in-law, Mr. S. Tolen, did not attend the funeral, being snot-flying drunk in premature celebration.

Paying a call on the bereaved, I mentioned the Watson silver that kind Aunt Tab had left to my new bride. Sam just shook his head and chuckled, saying, "I wouldn't hardly know nothin about that. Wouldn't hardly know what bride you're speakin of. The one your old aunt was thinkin about must been the one who died a few years back, cause there ain't a word about that silver, in her last will."

He looked around at his big house, thumbs tucked up into his armpits, as if to say, *I reckon I got it all now, ain't I, Ed?*

"That silver came down in our family," I informed him, speaking each word carefully to make sure he heard. "That silver belongs in our family, like this property. That's a warning, Sammy."

"That a warning? Or is that a threat? Cause a feud won't do you Watsons any good. Even if you was crazy enough to shoot me, my brothers are in line for the whole thing. I know that better'n anybody, cause I done the papers. And after Tolens come them Myers nephews, which is only half Watsons on the mother's side. So you people are way back in the line, suckin hind tit."

In 1903, the two Myers nephews and their sister, contesting the flouting of their uncle's will, had acquired by tax deed nearly half of the mismanaged plantation and had filed a suit to lay claim to the rest. That suit was opposed by the last will and testament of Tabitha Watson, who had disregarded William Myers's wish, bequeathing everything directly to Sam Tolen. Since her reasons were incomprehensible, our family assumed she had been starved, terrorized, and otherwise coerced.

A man lacking shame can go far in life, especially one who can get by without friends. Tolen was all ready for those nephews, he'd had a lawyer on the case for years, but as a precaution, he had sold much of the land and invested the proceeds. Even if he lost the case, he had most of the loot salted away through common robbery. This great plantation that could have been the pride of northern Florida under sound management was being chewed apart by rats right before my eyes, and my hopes with it. Suffocating, I walked out to my horse without a word.

Deep Lake Plantation

In May, our small pink-haired Ruth Ellen was born in my new house at Fort White, and as soon as Kate was on her feet again, we made our preparations to head south. We were happy to escape the evil gossip at Fort White, not to speak of the festering family feud which Kate felt was a danger not only to me but to our firstborn child. One night not long before we left, driving my son Eddie and my nephew Julian Collins along Herlong Lane, I halted the buggy on a sudden premonition, listening and peering, that's how sure I was that a bushwhacker crouched behind one of the surrounding forest trees. Perhaps I was mistaken or perhaps he slipped away, but after that I kept a sharp lookout wherever I went, so as not to be murdered by a Russ or Tolen.

We traveled on the new railroad to Fort Myers, to introduce the baby to my older children. Walt and Carrie had recently lost their infant boy and they were melancholy, but Carrie walked Kate right over to Miss Flossie's and decked out her young stepmother in an egret bonnet in the latest fashion. From there, these two lovely young ladies ankled over to the photo parlor, where Kate had her portrait taken with Ruth Ellen. I carry that picture in my billfold, show it to anyone who wants a look and some who don't.

Though both girls worked hard to be charitable and understand each other, Kate and Carrie had no more in common than chocolate and grapefruit. I hoped to be a bond between them—quite the contrary. My wife, who was four years younger than her stepdaughter, was calm and rather quiet ("bland," Carrie might say), while my daughter was headstrong and rambunctious ("a little wild," said Kate), though she mainly stifled that obstreperous side for her young banker's sake.

One day Jim Cole came around, became uneasy when he saw me, which caused him to talk much too loudly about Henry Ford's prospective visit to "Tom" Edison. Eventually he got around to the great prospects for Walt's citrus plantation at Deep Lake, in a way which told me that Big Jim Cole had cut himself a large slice of that pie and also that Deep Lake must be in trouble. These partners knew all about my extensive plantation experience, and also that Watson Syrup Company was the most promising business on the southwest coast. Though Cole tried to be casual, my son-in-law made no bones about the fact that he needed some advice. As the first President of the First National Bank, Walt was twice the weight and half the fun of the hard-drinking cowboy I first met ten years before.

From Fort Myers to Deep Lake was a long, slow forty miles over poor trail through the Big Cypress. I rode out there with my son-in-law, spent a few days. The forest floor was crisscrossed by bear and panther tracks, all kinds of game, and a hundred turkeys came to that clearing early every evening. The soil was dark and soft, just beautiful, and all the young trees were doing well, yet that golden fruit lay rotting on the ground. Deep Lake was the plantation a man dreams about, but it was way out there in a vast and trackless country of rough thorny limestone thicket, with no road or river to bring in labor and supplies, and no way to get the citrus out without fatal spoilage.

My son-in-law took the expansive view of all bankers and businessmen, pasting on big friendly grins to paper over all the lies they have to tell. Being new at the game and anxious to look the part, Walt lit up a cigar and hooked his thumbs into his armpits, rocked back on his heels and smiled unmercifully for no sane reason before letting me know with a big wink that when Lee County got around to putting in its western section of the proposed Tampa-Miami road across the Glades, which would pass Deep Lake only a few miles to the south, their marketing problems would be over for good.

Well, there had been talk of a cross-Florida road long before Nap Broward became Governor, and not one cypress tree or saw palmetto had bit the dust so far. Deep Lake's beautiful crop might lie rotting in this grove for years. He'd be a hell of a lot better off, I told him, to persuade his railroad partner Mr. Roach to lay a narrow-gauge rail spur line south twelve miles to the salt water at Everglade, get that citrus out on the coastal shipping.

Walt stared at me. He'd never thought of that. "As for field labor," I continued, "your friend Sheriff Tippins would be glad to rent you big buck niggers cheap, right off the chain gang. Hell, he could set up a road-gang camp out here, kill two birds with one stone." By the time we got back to Fort Myers, young Banker Langford was so excited by my ideas about citrus railroads and sound labor management that he promised to ask Mr. Roach about my participation in the venture.

Hearing her Walter talk with such enthusiasm, Carrie perked up right away, she was delighted. "Daddy, your dreams are coming true!" she said. And Kate was smiling, too, of course, trying to feel part of the celebration but not yet clear why my own family had not sought and welcomed my participation before now.

*

Strolling around the growing town, I was astonished by the changes in Fort Myers in the past decade. The oil and gas lamps and horse-drawn carriages of the nineties were all but gone, replaced by electric light and gasoline engine, automobiles and the new railroad with its bridge across the river, which now connected our frontier cattle town to the outside world. The telephone and radio, the camera and the typewriter, were becoming commonplace, and the new diesel engine was on the way.

One day soon, Jim Cole predicted, the winter visitors would come here on an aeroplane, which had had its first flight in North Carolina just three years before. For two thousand years, there had been no improvement on the horse as the speediest mode of human travel, and now, in a few decades—and just in time for our new century—petroleum had fueled an industrial age which inspired marvels of new engineering. America had led the world into the twentieth century with what the newspapers were calling "a veritable explosion of invention," with two of its greatest pioneers, Mr. Edison and Mr. Ford, exchanging ideas right here in our little frontier town.

How painful and humiliating, then, that at Chatham Bend we were still mired in the living conditions that folks had suffered at Edgefield a half century ago, during the War, and for many dark centuries before that. It was enough to drive a man of worth half mad, to be excluded and left so far behind in this rush of progress. My head ached with frustration and throttled rage every time I thought about it.

All E. J. Watson had contributed were a few modest improvements, including a new strain of sugarcane that produced what Tampa wholesalers were calling "about the best darned syrup ever made." The citrus railway, the pass-through window for the modern dining room, mesh window screens primed with cylinder oil from the boat motor to keep out no-see-ums as well as mosquitos, an improved hand pump which raised three hundred gallons to a roof tank, from where gravity feed delivered it to a kitchen tap and sink. All these made wilderness life so much more tolerable that my Kate declared that E. J. Watson compared with Messrs. Ford and Edison as a man of genius. But how could such puny innovations be compared with electricity and the combustion engine, which would change the world?

The one new "gadget" that consoled me just a little was the first motor launch ever to ply the waters of this coast south of Fort Myers—a twenty-eight-footer with nine-foot beam, painted white with a red trim at the waterline, a large cargo space aft, and a framed canopy of black canvas forward, forming a cabin. I named her *Brave*, to remind myself to keep my courage up until I made my mark once and for all.

*

My young nephew Julian Collins had married a Miss Laura Hawkins on the first of April. (Why a humorless fellow like my nephew had chosen April Fool's Day to get married, no one seemed to know, Julian least of all.) I never understood what that girl saw in him, for that nephew of mine was ingrown as a toenail. There was no fun in Julian whatsoever, whereas Laura was fun-loving and lively and pretty, with big soft eyes that could drive a man of sensibility and taste, such as myself, to groan aloud with heartache and romantic longing. To Kate's delight—for she and the Hawkins girl were bosom friends—the newlyweds would join us in the Islands in the summer, planning to stay on for a year. We went in two boats to meet them at Everglade, where they arrived on Bembery Storter's *Bertie Lee*, but returning south to Chatham Bend, the *Brave* encountered heavy weather off Rabbit Key. The women begged me to head in to Chokoloskee, but I didn't, being anxious to get home. I had Kate and our baby aboard, along with Laura Collins and Jane Straughter, whom the Collinses had brought along as cook. At seventeen, Lucius was already handy with gasoline engines, and he had his cousin Julian with him in his motor skiff, toiling behind. In a squall, he took a following sea that drowned out the wiring on his little motor, and Kate and Laura got a terrible fright when they looked back and saw that small craft wallowing.

I swung the *Brave* around in a wide circle. Coming up astern, with both boats jumping all over the place in the rough chop, I heaved the boys a line as I went by, took them in tow. With Julian steering, trying to hold her in my wake, Lucius returned to tinkering with his motor. But the wind was gaining all the time, with both boats taking a godawful pounding, and damn if that tow line didn't part southwest of Pavilion Key, the very last good line I had aboard. There was such a surge that Lucius's boat would drop clean out of sight, as if the sea was swallowing her, spitting her up again. There was nothing to do but get the women safe into Chatham River and pray that my son got that motor started, because night was falling and the weather worsening each minute.

Laura Collins spread her wings for balance, pitching forward to the helm, and yelped at me like a gull across the wind. Only a cold-hearted rogue or a dastardly coward, she cried, would abandon those young men to their fate. I told her that if we turned back, nobody would make it. The new bride went down onto her knees and prayed and begged me. *Turn back! Turn back! For pity's sake, sir, won't you please turn back? I beseech you!* She wailed that if Julian had to drown, her most fervent wish was to drown with him. I bawled at her across the wind, Maybe the other passengers don't feel that way. When she threatened to hurl herself overboard, I seized her arm. *No,* miss, I told her, you better not, because if Lucius pulls his cousin through this, you will feel kind of lonely and foolish up in Heaven. I was finally obliged to make Kate hold her in order to pilot the narrow channel into Chatham River.

By this time, Kate was also weeping because Ruth Ellen, losing her grip on her dear Jane Straughter's frock, had been tossed around like a beanbag and had barely escaped flying over the port side. Losing my head in all the shrieking, I roared at Jane, I sure hope you can swim, cause if that child goes overboard, you're going after her. That threat terrified poor Kate, who was already a bad puce color with seasickness. Her eyes were rolling like the eyes of the doomed Watson in the maw of the great shark, pleading for succor to God Almighty in the stormy heavens. Her only wish, she confessed later, was to set foot on dry land before we died.

Inland people dread unruly winds and huge, wild waves—the shapelessness and chaos and the death of color, when sea and sky and wind all rush together. Once in sight of shore, they feel much safer, not realizing that where sea meets land lies the greatest danger. When Kate made out low mangrove shadows in the spume and mist, she thanked the Lord. But with that onshore wind, at dusk, in such poor light, the *Brave* could strike an oyster bar and go aground, get pounded to pieces, since I had no men to help me heave her off.

With good timing and some luck, I rode her on a cresting sea that carried us all the way through into the estuary. In this delta broken by small clumps of mangroves, there was no good place to put passengers ashore. I wanted to head back out to search for Lucius, but if I failed to return, they would probably die here, unable to swim upriver or travel miles through the dense river jungle. Having been here before, Jane Straughter understood what I was trying to explain, but having been shouted at, she was impassive, arms around Ruth Ellen. Her cool eyes mocked me. *You sure you're not forsaking them to save yourself?* I scanned the waters visible over the stern before the Gulf mists closed behind. We went upriver.

Hearing the motor, Green Waller and Sip came down to the dock and took the lines. Old Green moved as stiff and careful as a drinking preacher, but he had picked up fancy manners somewhere on his road and was raring to try 'em out on all the ladies. Howdee do, ladies, he said. I cut off this fool's palaver in a hurry. "Lucius's boat is adrift out toward Pavilion Key. Light a bonfire! Give 'em a beacon!" I gave that order to calm Laura, because the Bend is a good three miles inland, and in such thick weather, no boat offshore would ever see a glow over that jungle, not even if Green set the damn house afire. Green knew this much and at once started to say so, being insensitive except when in the company of hogs. I stopped him with a look, and he jumped to it.

I never slept that night. I ranged up and down the riverbank like a trapped panther, worried sick that leaving that boat behind had been a fatal error. Toward midnight I sagged down on the porch steps and drank off some of our white lightning. Laura sat up, too, though she stayed out of sight behind me and refused to speak. During that long night, the storm died, and at first light, when I went down to the dock, she followed. I waved her away when she tried to come aboard, because a woman and her grief would only be in the way if I found a body.

I went offshore as far as Pavilion, searching that gray and sullen sea for a sign of life, all the while knowing that drowned men usually sink for a few days before they rise again. I went ashore there, asking in vain if anyone had seen a sign of them. My daughter Minnie escorted me around, holding my hand.

Unless they had got ashore someplace, those boys were lost. At noon, with my fuel almost spent, I headed back into the river, leaden-hearted. The day was dark, and the roiled water pouring down out of the Glades moved between the banks as strong as molten metal. Dark cormorants swam down the raining river, faster than the curling eddies, faster than the turning limbs and leafy branches.

Kate and Laura stood on the bank before the house, clutching their bonnets. The onshore wind flew their red hat ribbons toward the east. From the distance between them, it was plain that Kate could find nothing more to say to comfort her dear friend. Seeing the *Brave* coming upriver with only the lone man at the helm, Laura turned and ran into the house, her cries high and faint as the mewing of a gull, banking downwind.

"She's beside herself," Kate warned as I tied up. "She doesn't know what she is saying." Laura ran outside again to scream at me, "Why aren't you searching? How dare you look so calm!" When I only nodded, calling to Sip Linsey to refuel the boat, she burst into tears, too exhausted to protest further. Kate led her back into the house.

*

Lucius brought Julian back that afternoon. Sometime after midnight they had drifted in behind a mangrove islet, which hid them from both the Chatham delta and the Gulf. At daybreak, they heard the *Brave*'s motor, but its loud *pop-pop-pop* drowned out their yells. All this while Lucius was tinkering—it was water in the carburetor—and toward noon he got the motor kicking over and they came on in. Hearing the boat, I yelled toward the house, but Laura dared not come out to look until she heard Kate's peal of joy as two figures standing side by side came into view.

I shook Lucius's hand as he came ashore. "What kept you fellers?" I said jovially. My son gave me that bent smile he got from Mandy, as if to say, Don't joke about it, Papa. Though he loved me dearly, Lucius knew me somewhat better than I might have wanted.

Julian gazed blankly over Laura's sobbing shoulder. Stroking her, he would not meet my eye. His wet dark hair was slicked close to his head so that his ears stuck out. Like all those Collins men, he looked slight and boyish despite his thin black beard, and he still shook because he was still frightened through and through. On a day warm and humid with Gulf haze, Julian's teeth chattered. Coddled by his wife, he spent three days in bed complaining of the ague, and he never forgave me. But being afraid some way—afraid of his own timidity, heretofore untested, would be my guess—he never spoke about his adventure, or not at least to his callous Uncle Edgar.

It was his young wife who was to suffer most from his adventure. She would lose her baby. Unlike her husband, Laura would forgive me.

*

Green Waller had told us that Henry Short had left yesterday morning bound for Key West in the *Gladiator* with a cargo of hogs, eggs, syrup, and general produce. The storm had built all day in the southwest, and when it broke, he must have been somewhere off southwest of Cape Sable, managing that boat alone in violent weather. Henry Thompson, who was supposed to be her captain, had hired Short from Old Man D. D. House, who had his cane patch at House Hammock, a few miles upriver, but he had no business entrusting my ship and cargo to Short without permission. Henry Short was strong and conscientious, but a schooner, even a small one, needed more sea experience than Henry had for an eighty-mile voyage south over those banks west of the Keys.

When she heard me say this to Green Waller, Jane Straughter's eyes opened up wide and filled with tears, as if it were Old Man Watson's fault that Henry Short was all alone out there in that bad storm—as if this danger had befallen him because I had driven him away from her out of my jealousy rather than let them jump onto each other the way they wanted.

*

Two days later, Henry turned up at the Bend without the *Gladiator*, which lay sunk on the banks west of Florida Bay. Short had been out of sight of land, rowing northeast toward Cape Sable, when my friend Gene Roberts, bound for Chokoloskee, spotted that lonely skiff on the horizon.

It was Gene who related the whole story, while Short stood off to the side like a wooden Indian. "Her spars are sticking up, so you can spot her maybe two miles off across the shoals. But if it was me, Ed," Roberts said, "I'd get down there quick before some Key West pirate comes across her."

While Gene was speaking, I watched Short, who nodded fervently that all of this was true. The squall had come up fast, he whispered finally, and he tried to run before the wind. By the time he came about, to head up into it, the schooner, responding sluggishly due to her heavy cargo, remained broadside one minute too long, and the seas she took over her starboard beam had swamped her. "Jus' lacked the knowledge, Mist' Watson," Henry whispered. Frightened though he was, he made no excuses but took responsibility, holding his straw hat to his chest, toeing the ground.

Gene chuckled, trying to ease things for Henry. "He wouldn't never of signed on to sail your schooner, Ed, not if he knowed you was on your way home to Chatham Bend." Kate took my arm to keep me calm, but the fury was already dying down. In fact, I had to give Short credit for coming back at all, because ever since that Tucker business, when Henry and the Harden boys found those two bodies, this nigger had been scared to death of Mr. Watson.

My friend Gene Roberts was the famous man who licked the cane rat problem at Flamingo, where almost the entire crop of cane was devoted to the manufacture of deluxe cane liquor. Gene sailed to Key West and put up a sign—ten cents apiece for every cat delivered to the dock. Took home a cargo of four hundred cats—"worst voyage I ever made," Gene said. But those cats fought those cane rats to a standstill, then disappeared into the Glades, where the bobcats and the panthers probably ate 'em.

That summer of 1905, our friend Guy Bradley of Flamingo, the Florida game warden around Cape Sable, was murdered by a sponger and plume hunter named Walter Smith. I knew Smith as a hard man and a mean sonofabitch, having crossed paths with him around Key West. By the time I heard the details from Gene Roberts, the story that E. J. Watson was the killer was already spreading, even though Guy was my friend, and even though I was in Tampa on the day he died. Simply because I had been absent from the Bend, some folks concluded I had murdered Bradley because he'd threatened to arrest me for plume hunting next time he saw me. This was pure nonsense. Guy had never threatened to arrest me or even mentioned such a thing, and anyway, with so few birds left to hunt, I had not shot an egret in three years.

Dick Sawyer had been aboard Smith's boat when Smith murdered Bradley, and he told me a year later at Key West that once the grand jury refused to indict him, Smith started boasting to his cronies about the public service he had done by wiping out that warden, said he was "proud about it." I went over and banged on his door, and a woman's voice yelled that Captain Smith was not in port. I left my name, telling her to let him know I wanted a word with him next time I came to town. At that, she opened the door a crack to have a look at Desperado Watson, grinning in a way which told me that she might not mind if I was to shoot that skunk once and for all.

Gene Roberts was the man who found Guy Bradley's body and the first to inform me that the real killer, Walter Smith, and his sons Tom and Danny, had later started the rumor that Bradley's murderer was probably E. J. Watson. Before Gene left, I sat him down with Lucius, made him tell my son the whole true story so that Lucius would know that his papa was innocent. Lucius protested, denying that he needed the true story, having never believed the false one in the first place. And I said, Well, I know that, son, and I appreciate your attitude, but you'd better listen to Gene Roberts all the same. Gene said, Let me think a minute, so I get this right. We sat on the dock, leaning back against the pilings in the river sunlight. Then he started talking.

*

Guy Bradley had a quarter mile of shore west of Flamingo, and us Robertses was the next section west, toward Sawfish Hole, and we was huntin partners. Still had fair numbers of plume birds around Cape Sable, but every place else, them birds was already slaughtered out, they was almost gone. Guy weren't but a boy back in the eighties when he was plume huntin with Old Chevelier on the *Bonton*, but now he had him a new family to feed. Before the rest of us, he seen that there was no future for the plume birds, nor plume hunters, neither. Used to tell my dad how them egrets was bound to disappear, same way as the wild flamingos that give our good ol' Filly-mingo settlement that name. Used to see them gorgeous birds back there in the savanna pools, and as recently as 1902, there were still close to a hundred on the Cape flats. But flamingos never stood a chance against the plumers. They are gone now, and I don't reckon they'll be back.

Guy and Lew Bradley was the first plume hunters to shoot egrets out of Cuthbert Lake. The reddish and blues and blue-and-whites, they wasn't worth much, but the plumes of the white egrets brought thirty-two dollars an ounce, more than pure gold, and the pink spoonbills brung good money, too.

In 1903, Guy guided some them Audi-bone officials from New York to see all the shot-up rookeries. Mr. Job and Mr. Bent and Mr. Chapman, Mr. Frank Chapman—it was them three men who give Guy the idea to be the warden. They got him hired for that job by Monroe County, said Guy was just the man to protect the birds. Course the County never aimed to pay no goddamned warden, it was Audi-bones up in New York that paid his salary. Guy took the job kind of reluctant, cause as he told us more'n once, "Sooner or later, some riled-up sonofabitch is goin to take and shoot me." He told that to Mr. Chapman, too. But Guy wanted the job anyway, he was that kind.

Ol' Guy was about thirty-two, I reckon, hardenin into a stubborn streak which come down from his daddy. Edwin Bradley in his younger days had walked the U.S. Mail down the east coast all the way from Palm Beach to Miami. Later he worked as manager at Flamingo for the Model Land Company and Henry M. Flagler, King of Palm Beach, who had been given most of southeast Florida by the U.S. Government as a payoff for building the new east coast railroad.

Guy figured if he was goin to warden, he would give it hell, same as he done when he shot the shit out of the birds. Never had no uniform or nothin, just stuck a badge on his ol' mattress-tickin shirt and hitched his galluses and went right to it, making life miserable for all his neighbors. I don't hold with what was done to Guy, but I weren't surprised when some of his old partners turned against him, took to wingin bullets past his ear to warn him off. Bein Guy, he never cared if you was friend or stranger; if he'd of caught his brother Lew, he'd of run him in.

Course these arrests never come to nothin, cause he couldn't *prove* nothin, not in Monroe County. Judge at Key West would be plain crazy to jail a man for doin what our people always done—what it was our God-given damn *right* to do, ain't that a fact? Who was here first, our local hunters or them Audi-bones from New York City? Judge figured the plumers had punishment enough, what with all that time lost sailin seventy miles down to Key West and back for nothin, missin day after day in the best part of the season, knowin that while the warden was gone, their neighbors had went right back into the rookeries and finished off what few white birds was left.

Spring of 19-ought-4, them birds was farther in between than ever, and prospects was lookin very very poor. Before the next breedin season come around, Cap'n Walt Smith, a sponge fisherman and wreck salvager out of Key West who kept a plume bird huntin camp at Flamingo—this Walt Smith applied to take Guy's job away from him. Smith spread the word that if his fellow citizens would vote for him instead, persecution would stop and honest men could go out and break that law to their hearts' content.

You couldn't blame Smith in a way, because before Guy got to be the warden, them two men was partners at Bird Key when the nigger geese was nestin. They'd salt down the young 'uns, sell a bushel in Key West for a few dollars. But a dollar was a dollar then, a man could get by on one hundred a year for them few needs he couldn't take care of by himself, so Smith was countin on it. Anyways, them two fellers had always been in the same line of work, and not only that but Guy's mother and Smith's wife was best of friends from way back in their early years, up the east coast. Yep, Guy had known him most all of his life, they had shot birds side by side, and when the warden knows all the plumer's ways and what he's mostly likely to do in ever' weather, well, that makes it hard. Because what we called "white birds" was gettin so scairdy that a shot a mile away would rise 'em up out of their rookery. It was hard enough to get in close without keepin an eye over your shoulder for some damn warden lookin to arrest you.

All the same, after Guy got to be warden, he told the Smiths to stay out of them rookeries or he'd take 'em to court and do his best to get 'em jailed. And Old Man Smith said, Lookit here, goddamnit, Guy, I been shootin out here for many years and you right next to me, so don't you go to messin with me, cause them birds is my livin and I aim to keep it that way. Well, Guy just went ahead the same as always, and before the year was out, he arrested Smith's boy twice for plume bird violations. Tom was sixteen. Smith had a fit. He said, You pester my boy again, I aim to kill you.

Thing was, our Flamingo folks always liked Guy Bradley, leastways before he went to wardenin, and even them few that didn't care for him too much, called him too upstandin, they liked him a lot better than they liked Walt Smith. At least they had respect for Guy, and nobody respected Smith at all. Loaded his sponges up with sand to cheat a few extra pennies in the market, claimed he was a Confederate hero, a damn sharpshooter—that's where that "Captain" come from. Captain Sniper! He could shoot, I won't deny that, but he was a mean skunk and his sons took after him. His boys and crew was about the only ones as voted for him.

When he lost out on takin Bradley's job, Smith come to see this as a feud, insult and injury. To his way of thinkin, Guy had robbed him of what was rightfully his, and he hollered to anybody who would listen that he had swallered all he meant to take. Said no man could shit upon Smith family honor and live to tell about it. That was the first us Filly-mingo folks had ever heard about Smith family honor. As my dad said, a feller'd have to hunt long and hard to come up with enough of *that* to shit upon!

No, the Smiths were not so famous for their honor, but they were pretty well-known for revenge. They wasn't boys you would want to turn your back on.

One daybreak not long after that election, eighth day of July, the Smith bunch come in and shot up Bird Key just like they promised, not two miles out in Florida Bay from Bradley's house. Guy was woke up by all the shootin, and when he looked out and seen the old blue *Cleveland* over there, he sighed and told his young wife Fronie, Them Smiths is out there killin cormorants—Audi-bone lingo for plain ol' nigger geese—and I'm goin over there and put a stop to it. But Guy must of knowed that nobody would shoot so close in to Flamingo that wasn't lookin to bring the warden runnin. It was kind of funny how much pains he took to say good-bye, that's what Fronie told us the next day. Picked up his two little fellers and hugged 'em hard although he weren't goin but only that short distance and be back for supper. Later she figured he had a feelin what was comin down on him but was too stubborn to mention it or head the other way.

Always puzzled us when Fronie Bradley said she knew better than to try and stop him, cause that young woman could back up her opinions with her fists. Boxinest damned thing I ever seen, she'd put the gloves on with anybody, man nor woman. Yessir, Mrs. Bradley loved to *box*! Me, I could never hit a woman, fraid I'd hurt her, but one feller held the opinion that this darn female should be taken down a peg before all women got that habit, so he took her on. Hell, I was there, I seen it. She knocked him down as fast as he got up. Finally he dusted himself off, said, Thanks for the boxin lesson, ma'am, but I reckon I have had about enough. So Fronie said, Hold on, Mister, I ain't done boxin. Darned if she don't knock him flat again!

Like I was sayin, Lew Bradley was around there someplace, but Guy never asked his brother to go with him. Just set sail in his little sloop, out across the bay. No question he knowed who that blue schooner belonged to. But Guy never did like askin nobody for help—sin of pride, I reckon.

That morning of July 8, it was a norther, wind backing around from southeast to northwest, and a heavy sky over the Cape. Long strings of them curlews, white as bones, crossin that pewter sky inland toward the Glades. Offshore, the sky was turnin into silver, and the bright green of the mangrove clumps was turnin black. I seen a kind of transparent line on the south horizon, a real peculiar light, made them little keys look suspended in the air. I didn't like the look of it, and I don't imagine Guy liked it much, neither.

According to what Dick Sawyer and the other crewman said in court, Tom Smith and his brother Dan was still out huntin, over on the key. When Guy's skiff come up alongside, Old Man Walt fired a shot and they come in. Never bothered to hide their birds, brought 'em right in under the warden's nose, made sure he saw 'em. Guy told 'em to stop but they paid no mind, went aboard and down into the cabin, as if to say, Well now, ye Audi-bone sonofabitch, what you aim to do about it? So Guy told Walt Smith that his older boy was under arrest, and Smith said, You want Tom, you better come and get him. Walt Smith had his Winchester on his arm, never tried to hide it. Claimed he expected him to back down, but I believe he knew the man too well for that.

Dick Sawyer didn't want no part of it, so him and the other crewman, Ethridge, stayed below, but both of 'em heard Bradley's answer. He said, Put down that rifle, then, and I will come aboard. He had hardly spoke when there come two quick shots.

That evenin, we seen Smith's boat come into Flamingo. He picked up his family and took off again. When Guy never showed up, Fronie got worried and come over to see me. She said, Gene, my man ain't home, so I'd sure appreciate you have a look around first thing in the mornin. At daybreak I started across. Not a sign of nothin at Bird Key, but lookin back toward the coast, I seen Guy's little sailing sloop drifted up on shore. I found the poor feller slumped over forward, shot through the neck.

Old Man Smith had went straight back to Key West, and first thing he done was spread the word that the warden was dead. Someone said, Ed Watson kill him? And Smith said, Sure looks like it. When it turned out Watson was away up north, he changed his story, admitted he might of done the job himself out of self-defense. Said Guy fired first, malice aforesight or some such, and he showed two bullets he had dug out of his mast to prove it. Guy Bradley not being the kind to miss a man at point-blank range, folks had to suspect that Smith had took and shot them holes himself, but Dick Sawyer and the other feller had cleared out of Key West. Didn't care to testify for nor against, just didn't want no trouble.

I went to Key West and told the court that all six cartridges was still in Guy's revolver when I found him. Smith's bullet had gone in his neck and down his spine because it was fired from above, and he must of took a very long time dying. And my daddy Steve L. Roberts, who built Guy's coffin and helped us bury him in the white-shell ridge back of Guy's beach, he told that jury what Smith told him only two months before, that next time Bradley tried arresting any Smiths, he aimed to kill him. That was a message he meant Guy to receive, and Guy received it. Guy Bradley knew about that threat when he sailed out there.

Well, them young Smiths stepped up to that witness stand and swore on their Smith family honor that Guy Bradley weren't nothin but a deep-dyed plumer hidin behind all that Audubonin, that he was still partners with his brother Lew and all us Roberts boys, who was not only Mainlanders but the most bloodthirstiest butchers of them pore li'l egrets in all south Florida. And they swore that Bradley had been harassing God-fearing Key Westers cause they give his Mainlander partners too much competition. He also swore that Bradley had pulled his revolver, which obliged his daddy to fire in self-defense. Maybe Guy's revolver dropped overboard or somethin. Well, I seen it next day, dropped in the bilges. He never fired.

The grand jury was dead set against putting a Key West man on trial, especially a former officer of the Confederate Army. They refused to indict a well-knowed poacher who admitted to common murder of a lawman, and they opened up the jailhouse door and sent him home. Yessir, old Walt come clear in court, and he hardly took his first breath of fresh air out in the street when he started boastin how he'd kept his word, Smith family honor. Told all about how he'd stood up to that sonofabitchin warden and killed him deader'n a doornail with one bullet.

Not knowin what else we could do, us Flamingo folks burned down Smith's shack, but it weren't much more than a henhouse to start off with. Burned Cap'n Sniper right out of our settlement, and his family honor along with him, but none of that done too much good for the Widow Fronie and her two fatherless boys.

Course them Audi-bones made Guy a hero, got the case all writ up in the New York newspapers, but they didn't do nothin at all to help the widow. Later them bird lovers come back—I hobnobbed some with Frank Chapman and A. C. Bent. Guy's brother Lew and my brother Melch took them men to Cuthbert Lake, and Mr. Chapman told me on his way back that Cuthbert Lake was the best of the big rookeries left in the whole darn country of America. Good thing you boys never come acrost it earlier, he said, and give us a big wink.

*

Gene Roberts told Lucius that thanks to Walter Smith, a lot of people still believed Guy's killer was Ed Watson. "So when people talk about your daddy, you has to remember there's been many killins blamed on E. J. Watson that he never done. Compared to some of the low skunks I seen around the Glades, your dad here is a fine upstandin feller—kept his eye on progress and the Devil take the hindmost. I myself have heard Nap Broward say that E. J. Watson was that old breed of frontier American that made this country great." I believe Lucius felt much better, hearing these things.

Maybe four years later, around 19 and 09, the same breed of skunks would waylay another warden named MacLeod at Charlotte Harbor. Found his sunk skiff, found his hat, which had two ax marks through it. They never came up with the body, and nobody was ever brought to court. I believe that one was blamed on Watson, too, but Lucius knew I was at the Bend all through that period. He never doubted. Lucius is the only son I can count on to love his Papa no matter what, and I love him back as well as I know how, which is probably not as well as other fathers. On the other hand, I am the best he's got.

*

With Lucius and Henry Short, I went south to Wood Key to pick up the three Harden boys and their three guns. I don't think Short wanted to come, but he thought he owed me. At Lost Man's Beach we anchored the *Brave* in the cove at the north end, taking Thompson's little eight-ton schooner for our salvage expedition—never asked permission, we just took her. As we hauled anchor, Frank Hamilton and his bunch came out onto the beach. They did not call or offer to come with us. Then Thompson came out—he was hanging back. If he wanted to stay home from now on, I yelled across the water, that was fine by me.

We kept on going that late afternoon, down toward Cape Sable. Lay to that night on the open Gulf with the sea silver calm under the stars and came in off Sandy Key at first light next morning. We had no trouble locating her masts stuck up in a thin line out of the sea. Sure enough, there was a blue sponge boat tied to her spars that I recognized as the old *Cleveland,* Captain Walter Smith.

The Smith crew was still asleep below. We reckoned they had sent back to Key West to get some help. We stood off a little ways, eased down the hook. In a while, a man came up on deck to piss. Seeing us, he made a move toward the hatch to wake the others, but Lee Harden waved him back at rifle point.

Sponging started in Key West over fifty years ago, and at one time that port controlled nine-tenths of the U.S. trade. Even a decade ago, when I first went there, there were three hundred boats unloading sponges at the foot of Elizabeth Street and spreading 'em out to dry. But now the sponges were getting fished out like everything else, and by 1904 there was new competition from the Greeks at Tarpon Springs—unfair competition, the Key Westers decided, because those damned immigrants used diving helmets. Cap'n Walt got the spongers fired up, and they went up the coast and slashed their air hoses and burned their boats.

In short, these Smiths had earned a reputation, being too quick to shoot when anything got in their way. If it came down to a fight, I was glad that it was Smiths, first because these skunks deserved some shooting, and second because the Harden boys were the right men for the job. The Hardens had been good friends with Bradleys when they lived at Flamingo for a year at the turn of the century, and wouldn't need much provocation to straighten out Walt Smith once and for all.

Henry Short had his ancient Winchester along, and Henry shot better than the Hardens—better'n any man along the coast, I'd heard, excepting me. All the same, I ordered him not to show his weapon if it came to any showdown with Key Westers. "Next time these skunks caught you alone," I said, "they'd lynch you just on general principles." Henry nodded. He knew what I meant by "general principles," but maybe he wondered why I didn't apply them to Webster Harden, who was much darker than he was—not that skin color meant much. What with Injuns and niggers, half the so-called whites along this coast were darker than this brown boy I had here. And Henry Short was a painstaking man, honest as wood and as good a worker as I ever saw, which nobody ever said about Henry Thompson. Short felt obliged to stay with Houses, who had raised him up, otherwise I would have hired him myself, made him my foreman.

Pretty soon there were three spongers up on deck—Cap'n Walt, small, mean, and quick, and his offspring Tom and that scraggy feller the Hardens called Coot Ethridge. Those three had been aboard this scow when Guy was murdered but had declined to tell the truth in court. And I said, "You know who I am. Cast off your lines."

Smith crossed over to the rail and took a piss in our direction, to relieve his feelings. In that silver early morning calm, in that dead silence, in that red sun rising from the fiery shimmer of Florida Bay off to the eastward, that tinkle of his worn-out bladder would have woke a crocodile a half mile off. While he pissed at us, his glasses glinted, and his brain buzzed like a rattler as he figured out what he was going to do next. Finished, he shook the last bitter drops in our direction, hawked, spat, and farted. If he could have mustered up a shit, he might have done that, too. Taking his time, he straightened up and stuffed his mean old prick back in his pants, all the while squinting toward the southward, as if confident that help was on the way.

Seeing him being so obnoxious, his crew got nervous, and Coot Ethridge's voice broke as he called over, "Mr. Watson, we don't want no trouble, so there ain't no call to keep pointin them guns." Hearing that, Smith whipped around, quick as a moccasin, so quick that he damn near got himself shot. "This vessel was abandoned and we found her first. We are aboard of her right now. That's the law of salvage. Law's the law."

My temper came up just as quick as his. "And Bradley? Law was the law, you sonofabitch, you would be hung. Anyway, you're not aboard my schooner, and you're not going aboard her, either, cause she's on the bottom. There's five witnesses to that standing right here. So you cast off real quick, the way I told you, cause I don't aim to explain it all again." When I raised my shotgun, there was a big moan and scuffle as Smith's crew dove for cover.

The three Hardens had raised their rifles, too, and Lee Harden interrupted Cap'n Walt's thoughts before he could speak again. "You're fixin to tell us it's your word against ours, now ain't that right? Only thing is, your word ain't worth a shit no more on this whole coast, nor your ass neither if you don't get movin."

Old Smith did not like hearing such hard words, never mind looking down so many gun barrels, but he reckoned this was not the time to say so. He gave Lee a wink to let him know that accounts would be settled later. "We got witnesses, too," he snarled. "And more men"—he tossed his jaw toward the south—"will be showin up here any time now." But the Smith boy and Coot were hustling to cast off their lines.

In the still air, Smith's ketch, adrift, moved hardly at all on the weak current. They did not hoist her sails, they were just drifting, still in gun range.

Finally Smith called across the water, "You'll need hands to raise her, Watson, let alone careen her. We can split the salvage."

"The cargo is spoiled and the boat is mine. No salvage. I'll pay one day's wage."

That's how we settled it. Fished up her anchor line, rigged a block and tackle amidships and a second line astern, and raised her inch by inch between the boats, like a drowned whale. Took till noon before her gunwales finally surfaced, that's how slow and hard that winching was. Then all hands bailed till her deck came up a foot out of the water, and she wallowed.

A sail rose on the horizon after midday, drew near in early afternoon. I sat back in the stern where I could cover all three boats, and kept that gun stuck up where all could see it. I am pretty well-known at Key West, and there wasn't a man on that other boat who wanted trouble.

By now a little breeze was picking up. At high tide, we towed the *Gladiator* eastward, ran her aground on a steep sandbar. We careened her six hours later when the tide was out, long about midnight, emptied the cargo out, set things to rights. Her cargo was a total loss, a mess of rotted eggs and slimy vegetables, waterlogged chickens, a drowned milk cow and swollen hogs, but the hull came out of it undamaged.

The Smith crew refused to help us clean her out. "Where's our money?" Walt Smith said, yanking his shirt on. The sea salt crusted on his glasses made this old wharf rat look even more mean and bitter than he was.

"You'll have to wait. Next cargo to Key West."

"Don't go drinkin it all up before we get what's owed us."

Six hours after that, the tide floated her again. She was riding as high as a white gull when the sun came up like a fireball over the keys.

*

Lucius took the *Gladiator* north from Lost Man's. I told Henry Short to come with me on the *Brave*, I would take him home to House Hammock through the inland bays. Lee Harden said, "You come see us, Henry," which was Lee's way of warning me to be good to Henry Short, in case I was upset over that cargo. Henry was well-liked by the Hardens, all but Earl, who groaned and rolled his eyes.

Henry shook hands with Lee and Webster and got into my boat without a word. At a sign from me, he took the helm, heading her upriver and inland across First Lost Man's Bay. We passed the place where Henry and the Hardens had come across the Tuckers but he did not look over there at all. Where the bay narrowed, he stared around him at the mangrove walls as if seeing the darkness in them for the first time. And he watched me sip my flask, more and more uneasy. He said, "I'm sorry for all the trouble, Mr.

Watson." He meant that, too. But knowing how the old *Gladiator* yawed when she was overloaded, I didn't feel right about blaming him. The man responsible was Henry Thompson, who stacked up two cargoes, then hired an inexperienced hand to take her south despite the signs of storm. I said, "Well, I know you are, Henry, but you did your best, so never mind about it." And he said, "Nosir."

After a time he gave a little cough, but not until I looked his way did he come out with it. "Sir? How is Miss Jane gettin on?" And I growled, "*Miss* Jane? The mulatta gal?" And he said, "Yessir." And he paused. "The mulatta gal."

That was a pause I didn't care for. I took a draw on my cigar, breathed the smoke back in his face. I said, "Jane aims to get married off to a coal-black nigger by the name of Reese." Not counting Jane Straughter herself, that was the first and only time I ever saw blood rise to a nigger's cheeks, which goes to show how light this feller was. "Something wrong, Henry?" I said.

After another of those pauses, he said, "Nosir. Nothing wrong with it. Please give Miss Jane the respects of Henry Short."

"Give *Miss* Jane the respects of Henry Short."

"Yessir," he said slowly, scared but stubborn. "Miss Jane Straughter."

"Give *Miss* Jane the respects of *Mister* Henry Short?"

"Nosir."

"Mind that kind of fancy manners don't get you in trouble, Henry."

We went inland up Lost Man's River and north through Alligator Bay. Henry flinched when I swung my gun up kind of sudden to shoot a white ibis passing overhead. I took the helm. He went to the stern and plucked our supper as we went along, and I still recall how those white feathers danced and disappeared in the pale wake as the boat passed through those narrow channels. It was a dark evening, overcast, no moon to travel by and dead low water. Twice the *Brave* went hard aground before I quit and ran ashore at Possum Key.

The jungle crawled over Chevelier's grave, and the door had blown off the old cabin. "We'll lay over here tonight," I said. Henry built a fire and cooked some of his stale grits with the ibis. I sat there in the fire smoke to spite mosquitos, brooding over my cargo and wondering where the capital to put the Bend back into shape was going to come from. Every time I recalled how Bill Collier had stolen the clam dredge idea that I had stolen from Bill House, I grunted in resentment, that's how worked up I was, even though I knew this was ridiculous.

Henry was more and more uneasy, watching me polish off that flask. Niggers smell trouble on the way quicker than we do. He was afraid I might get drunk and take his life.

"Fine-eatin bird. Call this 'Chokoloskee chicken.'"

"Well, I *know* that, Henry."

He served me my tin plate, then squatted down to eat out of the pot. He stayed behind me and on my right side, where I'd have to swing against the grain to get a shot off.

"What's this 'Pentecostal'?" I demanded suddenly. Everyone on Chokoloskee Bay was talking about this new religion out of California that was signing up all our local Baptists, this one included. Politely and carefully Henry explained about Acts 2:4, the Day of the Pentecost, fifty days after Passover—

"You some kind of a Jew, Henry?"

"—after Jesus went to Heaven, and a mighty wind or Fire from Heaven rushed into Jerusalem, and the apostles filled up with the Holy Spirit and went around jabberin in funny languages—sign of the End of the World, same as Revelation—"

"Let's hear some of their jabber."

"Got to be in the Spirit, Mist' Edguh. Got to speak in tongues."

" 'Got to speak in tongues.' " I nodded wisely. "Helps to be drunk, too, I reckon." I drank some more, feeling mean and yet exhilarated. "Might get to be Jesus for a minute, or the Holy Ghost, what's your opinion, Henry?"

Henry's face had less expression than a conch. He scratched the black ground with a small stick from the fire.

One time out there in the Nations—out of gun range, down the river narrows—I saw a panther come off a rock ledge, take a bay foal. That foal was a lot bigger'n the cat was, and the mare was right there, big horse teeth bared, right alongside. These were half-wild Injun ponies, knew how to kick and bite. They could have run that cat back up that rock with no damn trouble. But that little horse just nickered once, and the mare whinnied, made a little feint, and it was over. Never even laid her ears back, the way horses do when they fight with other horses. That mare and her foal, too, they just gave up, like offering the young one to that panther was in their nature. The mare went back to grazing before her foal was dead, not thirty yards from where that cat crouched, feeding.

Why I recall that—Henry Short was armed, and a dead shot. He had plenty of opportunity to get the drop on me, but he would never do it, never in this world, not even if he thought he could cover it up and get away with it. And that's because it wasn't in his nature.

Your common black man knows much better than to raise his hand against a white man, or his voice, either. In Henry's place, ol' Frank Reese might have drilled me just for baiting him, then covered it up some way, taken his chances, because a man's color never counted for much out in the Territory.

"Henry? Ever hear about a crazy nigger they called Robert Charles?" At the turn of the century, this Robert Charles had shot up a whole posse of New Orleans police and killed some, too, before they tore apart his hideout in a hail of bullets. All over the South, the white men talked about Robert Charles, trying to figure where that crazy nigger learned to shoot.

Henry was guarded. "I guess I heard sump'n about it, Mist' Edguh. That boy must been dead crazy, like you say."

"Oh, he's dead, all right." I took another swig.

This brown boy I had here was very complicated—not humble or subservient, not exactly, he kept his dignity to go with his good manners. It was more like he was doing penance and would bow his neck for any punishment that came his way—his own penance, not for the white man's sake. Not so much ashamed, I'm trying to say, as forever damned by those few drops of black blood he had in him. Having been raised by white people since a small child, in a community where other blacks were rarely seen from one year to the next, the nigger in him was a man he scarcely knew, for whom the white man in him took responsibility. In Henry Short, the brother's keeper and the brother were the same, kind of like me and Jack Watson. Judgment Day would come, sooner or later, or maybe in his case it was here already. For some damned reason, this man figured he deserved his cross, and he aimed to tote it.

*

Henry's mulatto daddy, said Old Man D. D. House, was one of those smart niggers the journals used to condemn as "the New Negro." Not having been born a slave, this New Negro hunted white women to ravage, just as young white men would tomcat around after the darkie girls. But according to House, whom nobody could call a sentimental man, Henry's daddy loved his white girl truly, and she loved him, too. Between the races, true love was a lynching offense if ever there was one, and that's how the neighbors handled it. Mr. House said he could not remember the man's name.

The day I heard about it, I had gone to House Hammock to try to hire Henry Short away. The old man said, I reckon I'm dead set agin that, Mr. Watson. But he offered me a cup of his good shine to speed me on my way, and we got to talking, and it came out that he had witnessed that man's death. He described the hungry faces in the crowd, good Christian folks who might pass for Christians anywhere. Set up a platform, scrawled JUSTICE in black charcoal on the planks in front in case anyone wondered what this event was all about. Had a barbecue picnic, sweet corn and spareribs, a regular holiday excursion.

Old Man House believed that Henry's daddy could have flat denied his blood. Being so light, blue eyes and brown hair, he probably would have got away with it, because the girl's father had a lot of influence, and some folks resisted the idea of lynching a handsome young cavalryman in the first place. But this man would not deny that he had served as a buffalo soldier, nor would he humiliate his regiment or himself by crawling to a mob of whites, not even to save himself, not even to spare Henry's young mother her lifelong shame. Instead, he declared that he might not be full-blooded but he had spilled some red blood for his country, and some Injun blood, too. He was an American soldier and a full citizen with constitutional rights—that was his statement.

So they said, Boy, your rights just ain't the point here. Are you a nigger that has nigger blood or ain't you? And that soldier paused, realizing they would have their fun no matter what. He took a deep breath and he said, I may look like you red-faced sonsofbitches but I'm proud to say I am nigger to the bone. He bellowed that right at the crowd, *Nigger to the bone!*

To punish him, they ripped his pants down to castrate him. They had a special hatred for this man with skin like theirs, and being drunk, they made a bloody mess of it. When finally a moan was wrung from his clenched mouth, they laughed to beat hell, Old Man House remembered. Their lank-haired women stood around barefoot and grim, arms folded on their chests or nursing young.

With such a fine turnout for the barbecue, folks got into a festive spirit and prolonged it, lowering the rope so that his bare feet touched the ground. They gave him enough slack to gasp up a breath so he could scream or beg to them, and when he didn't do that, they yanked him up again until his face turned blue. His eyes bugged out and his mouth opened and closed just like a fish until finally it fell open for good, skewed kind of sideways. Being so ornery, he would not come back to life, making no response whatever to poked sticks or torches. Disgusted, they let the crowd do what they wanted with him. Folks came and stood there next to him, got their pictures taken for half a dollar. Dad with a buttered corn cob in one hand, Mom and kiddies, only two bits each. Finished up by hacking off nice souvenirs, and finally target practice. Man and boy, they whacked him with so many rounds that the body turned and turned in that summer heat. That was the sport of it by the end—*keep that nigger turnin!*

In Tennessee, on my ride from Arkansas to Carolina, I had witnessed something like it, and I don't care if I never see another—it wore out my spirit. It brought back the Owl-Man, gut-shot, and dying, in his cold gutted house. Mr. D. D. House felt disgusted that same way—about the only thing that old man and I ever agreed on. What I forgot to ask him was, Did Henry know this story? Old Man House being so hard, he probably did.

"Henry, come over here. Sit down." I pointed at the ground beside me, grinning to ease his mind. "Ol' Massuh ain' gwine whup you, boy." I enjoyed talking black to Henry, who talked white, having no nigras at Chokoloskee to teach him his own language. The only other colored man within twenty miles of Houses (not counting Nig Wiggins at Will Wiggins's cane farm out at Half Way Creek) was George Storter's man at Everglade. Good fisherman, pretty good worker, too, played a fine banjo. But that one was a stowaway from the Cayman Islands, he was blacker'n my hat, and maybe Short looked down on him, for all I know. Not that they ran across each other much. It's like my kind Kate always says, "These poor darkies in the Islands must get kind of lonesome."

Hearing Henry's voice, there was no way to tell what kind of man he was, and seeing him, you could hardly tell it either. Henry Short looked a lot more Injun than nigra and a lot more white than Injun, come to think about it. But when I asked him what he was, as I did presently, he whispered, "Nigger. Nigger to the bone." There was no mistaking the slow pause which followed that first *nigger.*

Nigger to the bone—that's what Henry thought I wished to hear. But I had heard those words before, and so it nagged me. I turned to look at him. Trying to pin down what this feller was thinking was like trying to nail an oyster to the floor.

We sat there hunkered in the fire smoke, slapping mosquitos. *Hoo-hoo, hoo-hoo* went a hooter in a tree behind us. *Hoo-hoo, hoo-aw.*

"Nigger to the bone," I mused. Before it struck me that I might not want the answer, I blurted out a question. "I suppose your daddy's name was Short. *Mister* Short, maybe?"

"Nosuh, Mist' Watson. I didn't rightly have no name. Dey called me Sho't jus fo' de fun, cause I so puny." But he could not hide his alarm, and so I knew.

"Your unrightful name, then? Anything like my name, Henry?"

"Yassuh." He said quickly, "Called him Jack or somethin."

"Jack or something." I emptied my pint and threw the bottle high over the night water. It made a small splash at the far edge of the firelight. "I can't pay your wages for a while," I snarled. I couldn't look at him.

*

Minutes passed. We watched the flask. It had gone under for a moment, but then the neck popped up like the small head of a terrapin up in the salt creeks, or the tip of a floating mangrove seed that has not taken hold.

"Tell you what." I picked up his Winchester, which looked like the first model ever made. "Let's shoot for your wages. Double or nothing." Despite all that Chokoloskee talk about Henry's marksmanship, niggers generally shoot poorly, not being mechanical of mind. I figured he might shoot better than the local men but nowhere near as well as E. J. Watson.

"Ah sunk yo' boat. Ain' got no wages comin, nosuh, Mist' Edguh." He was scared now. Trying to speak like an ignorant field hand was the sign, like a dog rolling over on its back to bare its throat.

My first bullet came so close that the bottle nose went under. It bobbed up again.

"Your turn," I said.

"Nosuh, ain' no need. Yo' next shot take care of it."

"Shoot." I tossed the gun.

He shot and missed. I shot again. Over and over I sank that thing but it would not stay down, and with each bullet, the little wavelet washed it farther back under the mangroves. Henry, too, kept missing, barely. It was only after it drifted out of sight and he claimed I'd sunk it that it came to me how he'd missed each time in exactly the same place.

"Maybe your sight is out of line," I said. "You were always just two inches to the right."

"Yassuh, dass 'bout it. Two inches."

But a sharpshooter would compensate after a round or two, even if his rifle was out of line. If that spot two inches to the right had been a bull's-eye, Henry Short would have drilled it every time.

He had outshot me, and I knew he knew it. I made some excuse about too much whiskey, which made me even angrier.

"Who taught you to shoot?" I said real soft, after a while.

"Ol' Massuh Dan House now, he gib me his ol' rifle, and Mist' Bill, he slip me a few ca'tridges, let me use his mold. Taughts myself, y'know. Never learnt too good, don't look like. Here I gone and los' my wages on account I couldn't hit dat bottle—"

"*Henry!*"

That bellow made us peer about at the black trees, as if uncertain where its sound had come from. "Dammit!" I roared. "Don't you *ever* give me this runaround, boy. Don't try that. Don't you *ever* try to flimflam me with nigger talk!"

But when I turned to point my finger at his face, to warn him, Henry Short was gone. Wherever he was, he had me in his rifle sights, against the firelight. I turned back slowly toward the water, hands out to the side. "Unless you're fixing to shoot me, Henry, you might as well come out where I can see you."

Jungle darkness and blackness surrounding. Tree frogs and crickets, a huge chunking splash across the channel—tarpon or gator. The water was silver and dead still under the gray reflection of the mangroves.

"*Miss* Jane!" I burst out, in a real fury. "You want her, *Mister* Short? You *want* her?"

Here was his chance. That rifle was pointed, finger on the trigger, I could feel it. My breath forced hard against my chest to steel my heart against the fire of his burning bullet. "Finish it," my voice gasped. I waited. Not a whisper. The black shapes all around had fallen still. Jean Chevelier's skull, staring upward through the black-shell dirt on the mound behind me, seemed to listen as a witness for the dead.

In the morning he was there, making the fire. I would not speak either. We moved in that iron calm of profound anger. Setting him ashore on the narrow dock through the mangroves at House Hammock, I wondered what I had wanted of him, what I had waited for last night under the moon.

Near the dock, leaving no trace on the surface, a mangrove water snake crossed the sunlit amber of the dead leaves on the bottom. Heads of feeding mullet pushed the surface under red stilt roots blotched white where coons had pried off oysters. He touched his hat and I raised my hand halfway, but even now we remained silent, knowing we would not speak of this ever again.

*

In the spring rains, when the water level was unusually high, my friend Bembery's brother George accompanied some Yankees and their Indian guide on a three-week expedition, traveling by dugout from the headwaters of Shark River across the whole peninsula to the Miami River, lugging along a live two-thousand-pound manatee in a pine box. What they wanted with that huge and dismal creature and whatever became of it I never learned, but that trip would surely be the last expedition across Florida using the old Indian water trails through the tall grasses, because Napoleon Broward was now in office.

The new Governor's plan to conquer the Glades for the future of Florida agriculture and development got under way in April 1906 with the christening of two dredges for the New River Canal, which would dry out the lands south and east of Okeechobee and extend the Calusa Hatchee ship canal to the east coast. With the patriotic oratory, band music, and flags so dear to the simple hearts and minds of politicians, canal construction was begun on Independence Day, which was duly dedicated to the creation of rich farmland where only sawgrass swamp had lain before. There was also an auspicious planting of an Australian gum tree which would spread miraculously through the Glades, sucking up swamp water and transpiring it back into the air. The southwest coast would be next in line for the blessings of modern progress, and E. J. Watson was bound to be right up in front. My invitation to the statehouse in Tallahassee could show up in the mail almost any day.

With months to wait for income on the cane harvest, I was in debt again, with little left for stores and none for wages, and the house was in very poor repair. Out in the Glades, the drought of 1906 had crowded the gators into the last pools, and the slaughter had been terrible. "It ain't worth goin after 'em no more. We have killed out that whole country back in there." That's what Tant told Lucius at Caxambas.

Being dead broke, I fired all the help except Sip Linsey and the hog fancier Mr. G. Waller. I would have to work our white folks hard all spring and summer, until the harvest came around again in early fall. I told the hands to go get their stuff, get in the boat. With another loan from Hendrys at Fort Myers, I paid them half their wages, and gave 'em IOU's for the balance, which they would never dare come ask for and would never get.

That summer, we took Sundays off to give our folks some rest. I damned near went mad waiting for Monday, but kept myself busy with repairs, mended some tools. Lucius showed Kate and Laura how to fish for blue crabs off the dock, using a scoop net and old chicken necks rigged to a string. These spiky creatures with quick claws scared sweet little Ruth Ellen, who would turn to me, screeching *Da! Da!* in delighted terror. Sometimes Jane Straughter would join in, and those three young females spent hours at it. Each crab caused a great shrilling and commotion, and finally a man was summoned to toss a bushel basketful into the big caldron while they boiled the clothes.

Lucius was delighted to be living at the Bend and showing off its attractions to our new family. It thrilled him as much as it did them the first time he pointed out the giant crocodile. It tickled me to see him happy, this boy who had dearly loved our place since he came here first in 1896. Unlike Eddie, he had no use for Fort Myers and little interest in the Fort White farm. Lucius loved water, fresh and salt, river and sea.

My son was studying the Indian Wars and old Florida history, and knew all about the Calusa relics that Bill Collier had dug up at Caxambas. Inspired by my stories about the Frenchman, he was determined to hunt and dig in his own mound after exploring not only the forty acres of the Bend but every piece of high ground in these coastal islands. For the table, he would hunt and fish, but he refused to shoot the scattered plume birds or hunt gators or otter, no matter how often it was pointed out that others would shoot them if he didn't, and that we still had buyers and could use the money. In the October evenings when the cooler weather came, he would hunt and trap coons at night the way Tant had taught him, using his new Bullseye head-lamp for his torch.

Lucius was still dueling with Old Fighter, the giant snook his brother Rob had hooked long years ago but lost in an oxbow up toward Possum Key. Out of loyalty, Lucius claimed that Rob's fish was still waiting in the shadows, tending the current that swept along under the branches. One day his bait would come drifting past, turning and glistening in that underwater sun, and—*whop!*

Though he never questioned it, a side of Lucius had never been quite sat-isfied by my account of his brother's disappearance. He had decided that vanquishing Old Fighter would be Rob's vindication in some way.

*

Sometimes at evening, sitting in the dark watching the moonlight on the river, we sang those grand old songs that Mama used to play on the piano, especially "Old Folks at Home" and "Massa's in de Cold, Cold Ground." We also liked "Lorena," and "The Bonnie Blue Flag." Not until everyone had gone to bed would I sing "Streets of Laredo" in a kind of mourning tone, al-ways quietly and always alone. I had learned that old song in the Indian Na-tions, is what I told anybody who inquired, though the truth was I had picked it up in prison. Once it came into my head, I might be stuck with it for weeks, humming not only in the house but by myself out in the field under the sky.

Kate asked if that old Texas song reminded me of my "cowboy days" out West. Though unacquainted with his daddy until age seven, Lucius knew I had never been a cowboy. He would flush and look away, knowing his dad had told a few tall tales while courting this young woman. Even white lies made him uncomfortable, that's the way he was. Having a gentle nature, he did not judge me, but sometimes his discomfort made him hard to live with.

At last, my Kate seemed happy at the Bend, forever giggling with her dear Laura, and it was wonderful to watch those pretty creatures, heads bent to-gether over some discovery or other. Yet she was so raddled and exhausted by the little child that she had lost interest in our loving, she would fall asleep before I was half started—not that that stopped me. I would clamber on and toil away, feeling grotesque and lonely in my struggle. Sometimes her old fire got poked up and she came with me, but mostly not.

*

Nephew Julian had promised a year's work on the plantation, but after his experience at sea, he never really trusted me again. Perhaps he had heard some local stories, though I can't be sure, and perhaps he had alarmed his wife, for poor Laura miscarried her first baby three months into term. I sat up at the young mother's bedside the rest of that night, trying to console her, because Julian and Kate, worn out by their emotions, needed rest. There was high wind that night, the mangroves thrashed, the whole house sighed and rattled.

Not sure of my welcome, I asked Laura if she would prefer to be left alone. (I was quite aware of a weak need to be liked by this young woman who had ranted at me.) Too worn out to spit up anything but the plain truth, she shook her head. "Mr. Watson, I need your company because I'm always scared here on the Bend. Less on these windy nights," she whispered, "than the still ones, when you douse the lamps and sit on the dark porch with only your cigar tip glowing and dying. Not that you oblige your household to be quiet—you don't need to! Your silence overwhelms us, and everyone falls still. The river sounds seem suffocated in this quiet, even the owls and tree frogs and the crickets, even the mosquitos whining at the screens. There is something else out there, something that's listening." She twisted in bed in her fight for the right words. "Something which will come for us sooner or later."

"Well, my dear," I said cheerfully, to soothe her. "That is quite true."

"Is it only mortality I fear? Because of my baby?" She smiled but she was desperate. "I don't really know what I'm afraid of. I'm just scared."

"Not of *me*, I hope." I was doing my best to seem benign and reassuring.

Laura studied me, a little feverish. "Uncle Edgar, you make everyone feel lively, that's the ginger in you. You make me laugh, you are very kind and jolly, and I am ever so grateful for your company this evening. But when you laugh, are you laughing with us or at our expense?" She waited. "Does everything seem to you absurd?"

"Not everything."

Afraid she'd gone too far, she closed her eyes. I could think of nothing that might bring her back. I went to the window and peered out at the moon-beams scattered by small wind waves on the river. Soon her voice came in a rush, "I am frightened of a man who wears a gun under his coat in his own house way out here in the wilderness." Still I said nothing, nor did I turn. She continued bravely, "I come downstairs sometimes when I can't sleep, and there you are, still sitting on the porch, and it is daybreak. Who are you waiting for? Who could you be afraid of?"

I returned to the bedside, took her hand again. I could have said Rob Watson, the prodigal son, unheard from in six years. Or Wally Tucker's brother John, who had sworn vengeance in Key West saloons, or one of the Bass clan from De Soto County, or that damn bounty-hunting Brewer who came here with the Frenchman years ago. But of course it was none of these I feared. (Perhaps it was only darkness I awaited, like poor Laura, the darkness that rose around us in those silences of night when our tired minds could not distract us any longer.) I had no idea who I was waiting for, I only knew that one day he would come—"the Man from the North," as I had always thought of him. Since Chatham River was so far away in the wild south, in bitter scrub and brackish swamp and labyrinth of muddy rivers, on a peninsula at the farthest end of wild America, the one I awaited could scarcely come from another direction. But to Laura this would make no sense, and so I said, "Jack Watson, maybe," to end that conversation. "Long-lost brother," I added, when she looked confused. I kissed her hand and touched my fingers to her cheek and rose and said good night.

It was daybreak. Weeping, Kate brought Julian's son outside, wrapped in fresh muslin, and I took him to a pretty place upstream. I dug the grave and laid the bundle in and buried it, but just as I finished, an image of Lost Man's River and that unborn child alive in its mother's corpse under the current struck me to my knees in remorse. With my hands, carefully, I exhumed the bundle and parted the muslin and confronted the blind shrunken face of my great-nephew. Still on my knees, I lifted it toward the daybreak in the eastern sky over the Glades, then kissed the cold blue brow by way of parting.

*

In the winter of 1907, suddenly, Billy Collins died. To Kate's relief—she feared the thought of Chatham Bend without her Laura—we returned to Fort White to be with the family and stay on for the spring planting.

Laura dreaded moving in with Julian's family, and who could blame her? Granny Ellen was sharp-tongued as ever, and as for my sister, she had shut herself away long before her husband's death, drifting deeper and deeper into realms of shadow, leaving her younger children to Aunt Cindy's care. Offered a roof at my farmhouse, even that tight-wound nephew of mine appeared relieved, and dear Laura hugged me with fond gratitude. "Please try to forgive me for those awful things I said at Chatham, Uncle Edgar. You have been so hospitable and generous. I shall always respect and love you, no matter what." She pressed my hand. "Please be careful," she whispered then. "Watch out for that Jack Watson."

"Oh yes. My bogeyman." I tried to laugh at that idea, and she tried, too.

Kate Edna was near term with our second child. Knowing her Laura would be left behind, she was homesick and pining for right where she was even before the time came to leave for Chatham. Becoming ever more withdrawn, she barely put up with my attentions, silently attending to little Ruth Ellen. Sometimes we did not touch each other for a fortnight.

Addison Tilghman Watson came into the world in May at Fort White,

Florida. Mama assumed the name was "Tillman" in memory of Great-Uncle Tillman Watson at Clouds Creek, and I did not correct her, being unable to explain the impulse to name my new son for the Owl-Man. When Kate entreated me to let her stay a few months longer, I returned to Chatham River by myself. In November, Kate and her babies met me at Fort Myers, where we spent Thanksgiving with the Langfords. Walter and his railroad friend, Mr. John Roach, Carrie had written, were still discussing my participation at Deep Lake—there had even been casual mention of a partnership. So when my son-in-law said nothing about it, I was furious. Most humiliating was having stooped to getting ourselves invited in the hope of nailing down the Deep Lake job. Walter's family came to dinner but they still treated me coldly, like some drunken poor relation who might embarrass the household at any minute.

One evening Mr. Jim Cole told the table how he'd served on a grand jury in a case in which one black man killed another in cold blood in front of four eyewitnesses. The young defense lawyer assigned by the court worked hard for his first client, did his very best, but it was hopeless, an open-and-shut case. To his astonishment, the grand jury dismissed the case, set his client free. Congratulated by the Prosecutor and the jury foreman, he protested, Are you people crazy? It was cold-blooded murder! Four eyewitnesses! The defendant was guilty as all hell! And the jury foreman took him by the arm and said, Well, hell, Lee Roy, this bein your first case and all, we didn't want you to come up a loser, and anyway, it was only some ol' nigger, ain't that right?

Jim Cole told a story well, and everybody laughed except for Kate, who just looked baffled. Annoyed by her lack of sophistication and a little drunk, I spoiled the evening, picking stupid arguments with half the guests. That was all the excuse the partners needed to end all talk of my participation at Deep Lake, but the true cause was gossip, rumors, and false stories from Fort White. I could only suppose that the source of these within the family was my own son Eddie, who always had to be the first one with the news, bad news especially.

*

Carrie and Kate were still awkward with each other, very stiff. My daughter had generously invited us to stay on for "a family Christmas," but Kate told me she felt unwelcome, and would even go back to the Islands rather than stay here. Once at Chatham, however, she could not stop crying at the thought of Christmas far from home. "I hate this spooky river and these green walls all around," she cried. "I hate that awful crocodile. *I hate this place.*" The girl had to be near hysterical to speak in such a disrespectful way.

All she wanted for her Christmas present was my promise to kill that brute across the river (I had often tried, but it was much too wary) or take her north for a few months after the harvest in late winter. Since I wished to go there anyway for the spring planting, I agreed. Kate was delighted, all the more so because her dear Laura would still be living in our house.

When the time came, I had some misgivings. Young Walter Alderman, whom I'd sent to Fort White to help Eddie on the farm, had returned to Chokoloskee to spend Christmas with his family. The Tolens had been defaming me while I was gone, he said, especially the shifty James, who had moved in with Sam at Aunt Tabitha's house while the Myers nephews were challenging her will. I told Kate nothing about this. For her sake and for our future, I resolved to live peacefully and protect my new family from my past mistakes.

And so we went north, but after Christmas, leaving my family behind, I went back to Chatham Bend to oversee the harvest, returning to Fort White in April 1908 for the spring planting.

Chapter 7

Sam Tolen

In recent months, the fat widower Sam Tolen had taken bit and bridle off his drinking. He let his fields go, let his animals run wild through the woods, and vilified all of God's Creation which passed before his eyes. Up there in that big empty house with its bad smells of rat droppings and rotted food, old hogs snuffled down the hall and half-wild chickens squawked and fluttered through the windows, and the Lord of the Manor was in his liquor morning, noon, and night. The summer previous his Tolen Team had told Sam they would quit if he didn't stay the hell away from his own baseball diamond, that's what a mess he was. Young Brooks Kinard, who played catcher for Les Cox, said Sam's own team could not agree on whether their manager behaved worse when they won or when they lost.

These days Sam's way of keeping touch with his sharecroppers and neighbors was to accuse them in turn of rustling his cattle. He had eight hundred head or more roaming all over the woods, and never bothered to brand his calves, just ordered his tenants to pen up any strays and let the cows in at dusk to give them suckle. Being poor, Sam's croppers tried hard to oblige him, but he bullied them anyway, hollering a lot of stupid stuff about hanging rustlers from the nearest tree. Preacher Bethea and Josiah Burdett had both been threatened, also William Kinard, who was not even his tenant. There were days when Sam's only activity was to ride around on his big red horse and shout abuse, knowing that young Brother Mike would back him up.

Mike Tolen was a county commissioner now, working hard to get along with all and sundry. Mike did his politician's best to pretend that Sam was joking, he'd even wink at the victim over Sam's shoulder. Mike had tasted Sam's bile, too, but he was a Tolen and he backed his older brother no matter what. Any croppers who stood up to any Tolen were run off the land as soon as their lease ran out. They always hoped Sam had been too drunk to remember his own threats, but the one thing a ridge runner never forgot, dead drunk or sober, was retribution.

*

One day, Sam rode over to the Junction and cussed out my old friend Will Cox, just sat high up on his red horse and shot off his mouth across the yard. Will Cox was a good-looking man with a hank of black hair like horse mane across his forehead, lanky and clean-shaven, always calm and polite right up to the last moment. And here was this fat and filthy Tolen hollering for all to hear how he'd never liked the looks of this damned bastard.

Cornelia Cox came out and stood beside her man, her arms folded high up on her chest, hazel eyes like chisels. Mrs. Cox was a hard frontier woman of the old school. Years before, when Jim Tolen got her simple sister in a family way, she sent word to her big mean brothers in Ocala County. When they came hunting for him, Shifty Jim slunk back to Georgia and had never returned for more than a few days.

Next, Will's oldest, William Leslie, hearing Sam revile his pa, came out onto the stoop hoisting Will's rifle. And Leslie snarled, My daddy ain't no bastard! You get down off of that horse and get down on your knees, tell him you're sorry! Looking down the barrel of that rifle, Sam Tolen saw hell coming straight at him.

Will knew his oldest boy and knew he wasn't fooling. He told him, Boy, you cut out that damn cussin! He grabbed the gun barrel, turned it away, saying, "Mr. Tolen, y'all best get on down that road." Sam wheeled that bay horse and headed back the way he came, never said a word until he was out of range, then reined up, shouting threats over his shoulder. He purely hated being run off by a boy, especially a boy who was his star fireball pitcher on the Tolen Team. Folks heard about it and they laughed, and from that day, Sam was spoiling for a showdown.

Will Cox was proud of Leslie but uneasy about Sam. He knew this wasn't going to be forgotten. He said, Ed, it looks like next year our family will have to find another lease.

Sam wasn't waiting till next year. A few days after my return, he came along on his red horse and caught Leslie at the railroad crossing at the Junction. Les was talking to his cousin Oscar Sanford, they were setting on that pile of cross-ties that Old Man Calvin Banks cut for the railroad company. Sam was so drunk he could hardly ride, but he wasn't so drunk he didn't notice that the Cox boy was unarmed. Oscar Sanford went scrambling down behind the pile, shouting at Les to jump, but Les did not even stand up, just spat his chaw in Sam's general direction and otherwise ignored him. Sam was trying to haul his own shooting iron from the saddle scabbard, hollering how that young skunk had pulled a gun on him at Coxes, so he aimed to exterminate him here and now in a fair fight. Probably thought Les would grovel for his life like any normal feller. He would not do it. Just lay back on the cross-ties with a long grass in his mouth, hands behind his head, to watch the show. Sam was too drunk to hit the woods but not drunk enough to murder him in front of witnesses, Les figured. (At least that's the way I would have figured. How Leslie's mind worked I don't know to this day.)

Mike Tolen was nearby in the little commissary run by the turpentine concern, where the first order of business was to cheat their ignorant workers and recoup every last cent of the payroll by foul means. Hearing the yelling, Mike came out and ran over to Sam's horse, where his brother was all red in the face trying to free his gun from under his own leg. Not caring about baseball, Mike did not excuse Les Cox, not the way others did. He thought Les was a mean bully and conceited both, and he wasn't wrong. Nevertheless, he talked Sam down, reminding him that there might be talk if he was to go and shoot his own star pitcher. Finally Les stood up in no hurry and jumped down off the pile. He turned his back upon Sam Tolen and his rifle and walked away from all the shouting. Taking Oscar Sanford's mule, he rode across the woodlots to my barn, told me the story, asked what he should do.

I looked him over for a minute, trying to gauge him. Les was already a good-looking young man, unusually husky for his age, close to six foot one way or the other, maybe 180 in his weight. Dark hair like his pa, with that same hank of hair across his brow, and Cornelia's stone green eyes. His hoof scar had offset his cheekbone, giving his mouth a small twist, and on that side, the eyelid sagged a little in a kind of squint.

I liked Les well enough, I guess, because he was Will's boy and had some grit and stuck up for his daddy. Not only that, he held a very high opinion of a certain individual in the community at a time when most folks gossiped that this man was the killer of John Hayes and John Russ, both. So I sat him down like my own son, put my hand on his shoulder and looked him in the eye, saying he should not trust my advice because I was prejudiced against Sam Tolen. I meant that, too, I was trying to be honest, having noticed that honesty no longer came to me as naturally as it had before. "But I'll tell you this much, son," said I. "That fat feller is scared to death of you, so he might just shoot you when you are not looking, call that self-defense."

"So I better shoot him first. That what you're trying to tell me, Mister Ed?"

"I'm not trying to tell you one damned thing. I'm pointing out the facts. A man has to face the facts, make his own decisions."

Les nodded, saying, "Better to shoot a man who's threatening your life before he can shoot you. That's only natural, ain't it, Mister Ed? That's only justice."

"Every man has his own idea of justice, son. Every man does what he has to do."

Chewing on that one, we frowned and nodded. Leslie's brow was furrowed up from trying to work out what I might have meant in the hope of discovering my approval of a killing. When he asked what I'd seen fit to do in the Belle Starr case out there in Injun Country, I told him how the victim's son had been hidden along the road where his mother died. "Saw fit to shoot," I said.

Les wanted to know if I'd broken the frontier code by "naming my confederate" this way. I had *not* named my confederate, I retorted, and anyway my confederate was gunned down dead back in '97, so nothing I could do besides dig him up would disturb my confederate one little bit. Les nodded wisely. And besides, I snapped, the only genuine frontier code I ever noticed was dog-eat-dog and Devil-take-the-hindmost.

My sour rejoinder and the anger behind it wiped his frontier squint right off his face. I was merely tired of this boy and tired of this word game we were playing, but a person would have thought from his expression that I'd told him there was no Jesus Christ nor Jesse James. "You shoot Belle in the back?" he inquired after a little while—not to criticize, mind, but to pick up a few tricks of the bushwhacker's trade.

"I have said I was a witness to the killing of Belle Starr. I never told you I took part. But I do know this, Belle never saw it coming. That is a life lesson that will stand you in good stead: you don't play games with varmints, you exterminate 'em."

Having said that, I backed off, not wishing him to get the wrong idea. In fact, I repeated that he must take into account my own prejudices in this matter. I then went on to speak more philosophically, endorsing the principle of defending one's rights by dealing forcefully with injustice or insult, threat or humiliation, no matter the cost or consequence to life or limb—the right to defend one's honor by main force when force seemed appropriate and by cunning where open force would not prevail. According to old codes of Border skirmish, there was no honor in defeat, however gallant, and no dishonor in avenging that defeat, however cruelly. No matter what moralists might preach, bowing to defeat was the sole dishonor. Lying, craftiness, so-called betrayal—all these became acceptable and indeed honorable when they were the sole means to defend and maintain the honor of family or clan.

These noble lessons, faithfully learned at the knee of Ring-Eye Lige, were lost on Leslie, just too much thought for him to handle all at once. He cleared his head by closing one nostril with his fingertip and blowing out the other, then got straight to the point. "Tuesday mornings, on his way to Ichetuck-nee, he goes right past that fence jamb down yonder by our cabin, know the one? All thick with brambles? Just like the place you was tellin me about out there in Belle's case." He watched my expression. "Too close to Coxes?"

I sighed. "That's what's so remarkable about it. Only a crazy man would suspect that any man could be so stupid as to settle a famous feud that way in his own front yard." To ease his mind, I added quickly, "I mean, that's why some folks had to conclude that I was innocent in the Belle Starr case. *Hell no, Ed Watson never done it! We know Ed, and he ain't dumb enough to shoot her so close to his own house. Might be stupid hicks, but we ain't so stupid we don't know Ed Watson knows we know he ain't so stupid as all that.*"

At Leslie's stare, I had to laugh. However, not wishing to appear face-tious, I wiped that mirth off my own face quick as a snigger. "Mind you," I resumed, frowning in sincere respect for the serious nature of the situa-tion, "Sam Tolen is not popular, and nobody but Mike is going to miss him. And even if Mike accuses you, your daddy is good friends with Sheriff Purvis, so . . ."

"So . . . ? You are advisin me . . . ?"

I lifted both palms and withdrew from the discussion. "Son, don't put words into my mouth. I'm *not* advising you, because I am prejudiced in this case and I admit it. What I am talking about is the Wild West, where a man must do what in his heart of hearts he knows is right." Some way these words seemed to contradict the wisdom imparted earlier, but Les was too in-tent on his own plan to make distinctions.

"Well, what I mean—well hell, now, Mister Ed, what would you do? In your heart of hearts, is what I'm talkin about."

"Depends. Naming no names, but if I thought an enemy was out there gunning for me"—I pointed toward the shadows of the trees—"I reckon in my heart of hearts I would take care of him first, and do it quick."

Leslie fell quiet, flicking his jackknife at pinecones on the ground. He couldn't be dead certain where I stood. What he was really asking was, Would Mister Ed throw in with him, or at least advise him, because in my be-lief, he had already made up his mind to kill Sam Tolen. "I'm kind of new at this," he said, uneasy. Even his baseball cap was all askew, sticking out to one side over his ear. In that moment, Leslie looked like a young boy, probably for the last time in his life.

*

I took Reese with me. Black Frank was his own man except when he was my man, and in the end he would do what I told him. Not that he was glad to be there. He had no use for Sam Tolen—there wasn't a nigger for miles around who did—but he protested that Leslie's quarrel "ain't none of my nigger business, never will be." This was Frank's way of assuring us he'd never heard a word about this plan whether he took part in it or not. Anyway, he refused to be a shooter. Of course not, I told him, this was Leslie's quarrel. All Frank had to do was shoot the horse.

Frank wanted to burst out, *What about you?* This was not wise, so he burst out angrily, "Why shoot that horse? Tha's a good horse. I wish I'd of had that big red horse when we was ridin out of Arkansas."

I said, "If Eddie Reed had shot Belle's black stallion instead of figuring he might inherit him, there would have been time to scratch away some foot-prints."

Leslie looked drawn. "How come it ain't you doin the shootin, if you know so much? You think I'm some kind of a dumb kid? Think I don't know you want this worse'n I do?" But afraid I would walk away, he only muttered this and let it go, nervously checking the loads in my double-barrel.

At the last minute Leslie showed up with his mama, who hated the Tolen brothers worse than anybody. Frank groaned that women were bad luck, he was all set to back out. I persuaded Les that this was men's work, not fit for a lady, and offered his mother my respects along with my earnest wish that she go home. I never asked Will Cox if he knew about what his wife and son were up to.

We hid in that fence corner behind the jamb where the fence rails joined to make a barricade of thorn and vine. I was suffering mixed feelings, I admit it. First of all, I had vowed years before never to take part in another killing. Second, I had known Sam Tolen most of my life and we'd had some fun be-fore we had hard feelings. However, it was too late to turn back now.

Crouched in a kind of cave under the brambles, we waited near an hour before the squeak of buggy axles came down the road. It was a fine and bright May morning, and early sun streamed through the new small leaves, and a hermit thrush sang its wistful song—like a child's sweet ques-tion, as my Charlie once observed, not a quarter mile from where we skulked, hell-bent on mayhem. All around, the spring chorus resounded strangely loud and clear, and I wondered if Sam's hairy ears ever heard this song of his last morning—thick-bodied Sam, still belching on his burly breakfast of hog and hominy as he slapped his reins on the rump of his red horse and came rattling down the woodland track from Herlong Lane toward Ichetucknee Springs.

I doubt he heard anything at all. Stupefied by his long evening of drink, in the pounding rhythms of the big bay's hooves, the powerful workings of its dung-flecked haunches and its fly-switch tail, Fat Sam would be as deaf to birdsong as he was to the stillness of the woodland roadside where men hid in waiting. No, his dull gaze would never register the amorphous shapes obscured by rails and brambles. That is what I hoped. In Sam's name, on his behalf, I hoped that his Baptist Lord would show him mercy.

Hearing those hoof shots and the clicking of the wheels, Black Frank raised his barrel to the rotting rail under the vines. I kept my eye on the creased black finger on the trigger, and a moment later, I flinched before the *bang*. Frank Reese did not flinch. He knew his business.

At the crash of gunfire, the red horse shied and shrieked and fell, all within the echo of the shot. The buggy climbed the falling horse and overturned, pitching Sam Tolen out onto the road. At the blast, he must have grabbed his shotgun, because he came up with it as he rolled over and up onto his knees, mouth wide in a black hole. He saw us then and had time to curse because Les Cox had frozen on the trigger.

In the last moments of Sam's life, my old adversary and nemesis sought me and found me through the thorns and rails. His eyes were huge and his mouth, too, as he tried to holler, unable to believe his time had come. With a shrill yelp, he floundered sideways, trying to get behind the thrashing horse as he swung his gun up, but even before he got it to his shoulder, he flung it away like something hot and raised his hands.

"Shoot," Frank whispered, furious. Frank had been furious before he got there, wanting no part of this damned business in the first place, but no matter how often I explained that, Cox would never forgive him for the insolence and contempt in that harsh order, far less recognize that Frank's order did the trick. "I seed that sliver gleamin in his eye, and I reckon Mist' Sam Tolen seed it, too, cause right then is when he knowed he was a goner," Frank reflected later. "And that's when I shut my eyes. Ain't decent to watch a man as scairt as that, it were embarrassin."

Poor staring Sam, too scared to speak, had whimpered like a pup. That last sound burned a hole into my heart, and I cursed Cox for it, after the many times I'd warned him that these things must be done quick or not at all.

Sam's bug eyes were obliterated as his face ruffled up bright red. Struck hard, he was spun half around and down by that charge of buckshot at close range, and gave only a couple of quick short kicks as if trying to escape while lying face down. The body sprawled on the clay road, shivering and twitching, snuffling up blood-spattered dust like a slaughtered hog.

With a victory whoop like some wild Indian, Leslie jumped out on the road and gave the corpse a second barrel in the back of the head, almost beheading it. That second barrel made no sense, just made a mess, and Leslie backed away, unable to take his eyes off the bleeding body. Then his nose squinched in disgust. "He shit his pants!"

"You sure that isn't you?" I snarled, extremely angry. The dead man might never have messed his pants if Cox had done his part as he was told. Hearing Reese snicker, this fool kid swung his weapon toward the nigger. Reese saw it coming and he knocked the barrels up. "Wouldn't try that if I was you," Reese said, "till you reload."

All three of us were enraged, isn't that peculiar? Why I was so angry I don't know, but it was much more than annoyance at Les Cox, who was screeching at me now, fighting back tears, "You and your fuckin jokes! Got a dead man layin here in a mess of blood and shit, and you're still *jokin?* Wasn't you never taught no common decency?"

Well, I had to laugh out loud at that, to ease my nerves, and Frank did, too. Les Cox actually burst into tears—rage mixed with fear and relief that it was over. His feelings tumbled around together and got in one another's way like new blind puppies. But while he wept, this fool was jamming shells into the chambers. Reese wrenched the gun away, ignoring Leslie when he yelled, "Gimme that fuckin gun, you fuckin nigger!"

Reese was an outlaw and he knew his work. He emptied Leslie's gun and Sam's gun, too, then stripped Sam's wallet and good boots. When he slung the boots for Leslie to catch, our young killer went as pale as suet, as if these sweat-creased relics of the dead man's works and days had finally brought him some dim revelation that his life had taken a sharp turn and had changed forever, possibly not for the better. He looked on the point of passing out, also incensed that we could see that. He kicked the boots away and knocked Sam's yellow pigskin wallet from Frank's hand as he lost his balance.

"I ain't no fuckin vulture," Leslie snarled. He fell when he tried to rise.

"You don't take his stuff, then nobody gone be huntin for no robbers. They be huntin for his best-knowed enemy. Tha's you. Mos' likely they will do that anyways, but no sense makin it easy for 'em." He held the wallet out a second time, raising his voice a little. "Take the money, boy, then drop the wallet, you hearin me? We wastin time, standin round here on this road."

"*You* rob him, *boy*, if you're so smart! Don't go givin me no nigger orders!" But he snatched the wallet, picked the money out, then hurled the wallet at the body. Seeing Sam's wallet bounce onto the road, I had the thought—

more like a pang—that if his thick carcass would just grunt and sit up, I could probably make Fat Sammy laugh about the way his future as a rich plantation owner had panned out.

"Show some respect," I growled. "That's a man laying there."

"*Was,* you mean!" But Leslie's laugh was broken and his eyes looked close to tears. He couldn't believe that his partners had jeered at his dangerous deed, committed in the name of family honor.

That is how Mr. Samuel Tolen, very well-behaved, came to follow his loved ones into Oak Lawn Cemetery. To keep up appearances, I went, too, accompanied by Kate and Granny Ellen. Aunt Tabitha's imposing stone rose austerely between the lower, smaller markers, as befitted the person in charge of the money. Like a chaperone, the old lady was still guarding her fool daughter from the lowlife son-in-law so many years her junior.

*

Mr. Woodson Tolen of Andersonville, Georgia, the administrator of Sam's estate, gave power of attorney to Sam's brother James, who at least knew how to write down his own name. Apparently Woodson did not think that our County Commissioner was bright enough, or sly enough, to take over the looting of the plantation, and knowing Mike, I'd have to say he was correct.

Jim Tolen hustled down from Georgia and moved into the manor house like he was born to it. After the funeral, he stayed on for the court fight to keep the old Myers Plantation in the Tolen name, wearing his rented funeral suit in court. Of the three brothers, including the deceased, I liked this one least. I treated Jim Tolen like a hunk of slag, too worthless to be noticed, yet too mean and sharp-edged not to keep an eye on.

Being less greedy than his brothers, our County Commissioner had no illusions about the true worth of the Tolen claim on other people's property, but he was loyal to Sam and that was that. After the burial, I went up to Mike and offered my hand, saying I was sorry, which I was—sorry for Mike and Mike only. Tolen flushed under his beard and refused my hand with everybody watching. He said loud enough for folks to hear, "I know who killed my brother, Watson. They will pay."

He knew no such thing, not for a fact. But by spurning my hand for all to see, the dead man's brother had all but accused me publicly of murder with no evidence, flouting the very principle of American justice. I said to him in a low voice, "I'll make allowance for your grief, but you'd better be more careful whom you threaten."

Jim Tolen was a fox-eared feller, born to overhear. "You're takin Mike's words kind of personal, ain't you, Watson?" Indeed I was, and for good reason. Yet in showing my anger, I had made a bad mistake. Mike and I had set in motion something that could not be stopped, and this business could only finish badly.

*

Having no evidence against me, Mike Tolen had gone to Sheriff Dick Will Purvis in Lake City and filed a complaint against Leslie Cox, and also against his parents, Will and Cornelia. The evidence was entirely circumstantial— the public dispute at the Junction between Leslie and the deceased, and the faint boot prints of two men, also a woman's prints, that Mike had discovered in the fence jamb near Sam's body. However, those prints had already been rained away, and anyway, Will Cox had beaten Mike to his old friend Purvis. The Sheriff reminded Commissioner Tolen that he too had visited the scene and that he had found no evidence whatever against the Cox boy. No offense, he said, but from what he had been told, almost any man in the south county might have done it. So until more evidence turned up, Commissioner, the smart thing for you to do would be to go on home, get a bite to eat and a good night's sleep, and forget the whole damn business. From the look of him, Sheriff Dick Will Purvis had resorted to that remedy on numerous occasions, in the simple-hearted faith that food was a cure for anything.

The Commissioner objected, saying the whole county knew that Dick Will Purvis was a crony of Will Cox from old Lake City days, besides being a kiss-ass like most of those elected by the public. Dick Will said, Well, since you feel that way, Commissioner, I will get that Cox boy in here, ask a few questions. So Leslie came in and informed the Sheriff that he was otherwise engaged on the day in question. That being the case (as Purvis duly informed the plaintiff), he had let the Cox boy go.

Before leaving the Sheriff's office, Leslie mentioned that while in High Springs on the day following the shooting, he had heard that a nigger known as Frank was attempting to peddle the dead man's gun and boots. Whether he said that to revenge the way Frank Reese had spoken to him, or simply in some damnfool attempt to deflect suspicion from himself, Leslie must have known that any nigger implicated in the murder of a white might very well get lynched without a trial. Sure enough, Reese was arrested two weeks later—not a smart move on Leslie's part, since Reese could give plenty of firsthand testimony that might get him hung.

Mike Tolen knew that Reese was not the man he wanted. However, he went along with Purvis, hoping Reese might talk. I went up there and told Purvis earnestly that my hired man had worked all that day with me. "That make him innocent or guilty?" one deputy sang out, and the lawmen laughed, and I did, too, showing I knew a good joke when I heard one. Frank was jailed pending his June 12 trial, which was just as well for his own safety. I told him he was fortunate indeed to be alive.

Being a tough, jail-smart nigger, Frank kept his head when the deputies kicked him black and blue, or rather black and purple, in poor Frank's case. They pissed on him and spat on him, reviled him, told him they aimed to hang him slow but that if he confessed, they might not torch him first. And Frank just hunkered down and took it like he was too ignorant and scared to understand, rolled his eyes back like a minstrel darkie, hollered *yassuh, nosuh, nevuh knowed nuffin about nuffin, nosuh, yassuh*. He plain wore 'em out. When it came to nerve as well as brains, Black Frank was a good long way ahead of Leslie Cox.

Les was drinking too much and suffered from bad nerves, shooting his mouth off, but he always claimed he never knew why Frank had been arrested. He was too excited for his own damned good, not to mention ours. As if still unable to believe what he had done, he would come over to my place and act out what happened—not only that but hoot and crow in glee, somersaulting in the dirt behind the barn to remind me how that big bay came crashing down, and the red buggy humping up on top of that thrashing horse, pitching Sam out, and the iron shoes banging like shotgun fire against the buckboards, and fat Sam, up on his knees in that white dust, staring at us. "Looked like a woodchuck," Leslie whooped—one of the few times I ever heard that feller laugh out loud. That laugh sounded all wrong, like a dog whinnying.

Next day, drunk, Leslie acted out Sam's death for May Collins and her brothers and young Jim Delaney Lowe, telling them he got the story from "a nigger was mixed up in it." The Collins boys, though not mourning Sam Tolen, were horrified by the queer pleasure that Les took in the telling and knew at once that he must have been involved. It was their testimony which got Cox indicted a year later.

When sober, Leslie blamed me for his bad deed, claiming I had put him up to it. When it came to killing, he liked to say, Les Cox sure went to the right teacher. "Mister Ed, you damn near got me hung!" he'd shout, to make a joke. But Leslie wasn't good at jokes, and his eyes did not fit his smile. If a June bug flew into Cox's eye, you would hear the *smack* of it, because those eyes were hard as shiny stones.

Will and Cornelia worshiped their oldest boy because he had a hero's looks and stood up for his family, so he had gone unpunished as a child for his fits of meanness. The community overlooked his arrogance and spite because of his exploits on the baseball diamond. He was dead spoiled—killed by kindness, as my mother used to say—and maybe his friend Mister Ed had indulged him, too. True, he had wanted to kill Tolen before he talked with me—his own mother had been after him to do that. Also, the killing could be seen as self-defense, for he'd been threatened. But by agreeing to stand by him, I might have let him think that he was justified, and I knew better even if he didn't. Not that I was sorry about Sam, I won't pretend that. Fat Sam had pissed on everybody, but he had pissed on Watsons first and foremost, so he had it coming.

To Les I said, "Double-crossing Frank was pretty stupid. What if he decides to talk? Better tell the Sheriff it was a case of mistaken identity, being that your average niggers look so much alike."

I warned Frank, too, on a jail visit. "The trouble is, you can't implicate Leslie without implicating yourself. You will get lynched." He only grunted cynically, looking away. Frank thought he had no chance whatever. "Instead of being hung lawfully," I added, hating to see such bitterness in a Negro person. However, he was in no mood for my jokes.

Cox backed off his Reese story for his own good. Manfully, he told Sheriff Purvis, "I might could been mistook there, Shurf Dick. I surely would hate to see a innocent man hung, nor a nigger neither." Although the Sheriff had been quite content to make Frank Reese the scapegoat, he didn't have a single thing to show to a grand jury, and finally Mike Tolen notified Purvis that he would not testify against Reese either, admitting he had only hoped that "the nigger would crack" and implicate Cox or Watson. Certainly there was no lynch mob in the street demanding justice, since most folks figured that, with Sam's death, justice had been served about as well as anyone could hope. So the circuit court said to hell with it and sent Reese home. Probably assumed that the Tolens and the Russ boys would attend to that hard nigger, which was all right, too.

Frank and I sat back against my barn and celebrated his triumph over bigotry with a jug of whiskey. Impressed by how sensibly and well my old partner had behaved, I sent for Jane Straughter and reminded her how she owed me a big favor, having caused me so much aggravation over John Russ's death. And I winked and said that I would not hold it against her anymore if she let Frank Reese hold it there instead. She could marry this feller common-law or any way she wanted.

Jane Straughter did not smile. She liked Frank well enough, it wasn't personal, but marrying him was quite another matter. The Robarts clan were not going to like this either, she reminded me, and anyway I had no right to coerce her. By the end of it, Jane was spitting mad. "You all done with me, so you handin me along to your coal-black nigger!"

Meanwhile, Kate Edna startled me by asking my opinion on who killed Sam Tolen.

"People die, dear," I assured her. "It's not always someone's fault."

"That isn't the answer that I hoped to hear." My wife seemed scared by her own persistence.

"I did not kill Sam Tolen," I said, feeling the heat come. "How often will I have to tell you that?"

"Not often," she said, ambiguous. "Just reassure me once in a while." She crept over in the bed. "Tell me you love me."

"Love!" I exclaimed, pretending astonishment that she would speak of such a thing at such a time. "You suspect your husband of cold-blooded murder, and then you say, *'Tell me you love me'*?" Frightened, she burst into tears, and I relented and took her in my arms. I have never figured out how women work, I only know that skin color is the least of it. Black or white, they are all difficult, but every last one is pretty pink on the inside.

Afterwards, I whispered to her, "Kate, do you love *me*?" I had never thought to ask her such a question, nor imagined myself in so much need of the right answer.

"With all my might and main," Kate said, not smiling.

*

Jane Straughter still helped around the house but would scarcely look at me. Seeing Jane and Frank together, I wondered how much she thought about that brown boy Henry Short down in the Islands. One day, leaned back in my chair into the corner, I asked her for the fun of it if she still missed him. She came around on me so fast that I threw my hand up, thinking she might fly straight for my eyes. In her distress, she had gone so pale that the little freckles in that fine skin beneath her eyes stood out in points.

When I give in to that urge to drink and stir up trouble, there comes an even stronger urge to become drunker and behave still worse. Jane's fiery ways, so different from Kate Edna's, had hit me just as hard as in the past, smack in the trousers, and before I knew it, I had grasped her wrist and told her fervently how pretty she looked, and how much I needed her.

Jane was gazing out the window at my wife, sailing across the sun-shined yard, pinning up washing. "Supposin I was to tell Mis Kate what was done to a young girl one year, down Chatham River?" she whispered. "Supposin I told your man Frank what his boss was up to?"

Releasing her, I banged my chair down hard. "Missy, I dislike threats, remember? Nigger threats especially."

Jane retreated into nigger talk as quick as our little fence chameleon changes its color from leaf green to stick brown. "Yassuh, Mist' Edguh, nosuh, I ain't threatenin, nosuh." And she ran out, sobbing. After that, she stayed mostly out of sight until Black Frank had her good and married.

A few weeks later, I was cleaning up for supper when Kate Edna sent Jane

out to the well with fresh hot water and a towel. When I asked if she was enjoying married life, she splashed the hot water roughly into my blue basin.
"Long time ago, back yonder in the Islands, you ast me how a light-skinned
gal might feel, passin for white. You best ast me now how that same gal feels,
passin for nigger."

*

When our paths crossed, Mike Tolen looked right past me. Even when I
greeted him, he never spoke. Mike understood why others might have
wished to kill his brother, and perhaps by now he had lost some of his desire
for a showdown. But sooner or later, Cox's loose talk would force him to
avenge his brother out of cracker honor, a very dangerous situation. I went
to Leslie, warned him to shut up. Maybe he did, but it was much too late.

One day in Fort White, in Terry's Store, his neighbors cornered Mike with
some tough questions. Mike burst out, Yes, he knew who had killed his
brother, and no, he did not aim to let the matter die. Yet what could he do?
He knew better than to challenge either of us in a fair fight, and he could not
poke a shotgun through those high windows of my house even if he got past
my bad dogs. Mike had no choice but to waylay us, one at a time. And knowing how unlikely it was that Cox or Watson would stand by and wait for that
to happen, he would have to act soon, for his own safety, before we heard
what he had said in Terry's Store. But of course we had heard already, and
he knew that, too.

I went to him and told him he was talking dangerously. He said, No, I am
not, who gave you that idea? And I said, Just about everybody, Mike. You are
talking too much and you are painting yourself into a corner, and you better think about it, because you are cornering me, too. Is that a threat? he demanded. You know what it is, I told him. That's how we left it. We had
nothing more to say. I never wished Mike Tolen harm, but with that dangerous attitude he had, it was him or us.

I felt sorry for Mike because he had no way out. He had no experience or
skill with arms and little support from his brother or the Russ boys, and was
therefore no match for Cox and me, separately or together. His only solution
was to leave this district, but he was too angry and proud to cut and run.

I caught Mike coming out of church. I told him I had no quarrel with him
but because he had made threats, I had to warn him that any attempt upon
my life—I stopped right there. My brain stopped. What was there to say?
With so much fear and pride in him, any promise he made now would be
worthless, and because this was so, he was in danger, too. We were trapped.
"I'm sorry," I said. "You'd better leave here, Mike."

But he only struggled like a hooked fish, doing himself harm. "*You* leave!"

he protested. I shook my head. Even if I left, Cox would still be here. Finally he shook his head, too, and we turned away.

*

Frank Reese would not throw in with us. "No mo', Mist' Jack," he said. "I'se done retired." He flatly refused to work with Cox, who had nearly got him lynched, and anyway, he had his Jane in his own cabin, he wasn't a field hand anymore but a tenant farmer, as close as he had ever come in a hard life to being his own man and well looked after. Nosir, he didn't want to know one thing about this. He'd be out in the field tomorrow morning, same as always, turning over the Lord's good ground and getting set to plant his corn and cotton. "I finally come to rest in life, I found the little place where I belong, so I'se puttin all them bad ol' times behind me." Frank was grateful to me for his new life. I could have forced him but I didn't want to.

Leslie yelled, "We got to get that fuckin Reese mixed up in this, so's he won't talk!" I shook my head. "Unlike you," I told him, "Frank can be counted on to keep his mouth shut."

"Then it's your turn to shoot first," he challenged me, "unless you're fixin to hang back like you done last time." I shrugged. "All right," I said. But it was not all right. I had nothing against Mike and was mindful of my vow. I had assumed that Cox would be the shooter.

*

Mike Tolen had his mailbox at the Junction. There Herlong Lane met the old road which ran along the west side of the railroad tracks, the road that Sam had renamed Tolen Lane. In the past year, with all the slash pine lumbered off, the turpentine works had been closed down and the commissary, too, and Will Cox, with his lease canceled by Jim Tolen, had moved his family across the county line into Suwannee. The Junction was now a silent corner being taken back by woods. Near the huge live oak was a sagging shack bound up in vines and creepers. I hid inside while Leslie climbed into the oak and stretched along a heavy limb, ready to take Mike from another angle. Mike having brought this on himself, I was resigned to it, but I did not like it, and had to breathe down deep into my belly to stay calm.

Mike Tolen came down the road a little late, carrying his shotgun over his arm and a letter in the other hand. He slowed his step as he drew near the shack, and his eyes crisscrossed the lane, scanning the trees. I set myself, took a last deep breath, and drew a careful bead on Mike's broad forehead, to make sure he never knew what hit him. Leslie claimed later that I held my fire too long—God knows I never had my heart in it. But I believe that he shot first out of buck fever and greed, he could not restrain himself, because

Cox wanted the credit for this killing, too, wanted to take over from Ed Watson as the local desperado, maybe call himself the Ichetucknee Kid.

Even before Mike reached his mailbox, Cox threw a double-ought slug into his chest, whacked his shirt red, and the Sears order he was there to mail went flittering off as he spun backwards in the echo, which ricocheted away through the cold bare trees. To this day I hear that ringing in my ears and the ugly thump of that feller's head as it struck the ground. I stepped onto the road and that same second was knocked to one knee by concussion. I damn near had my head torn off, that's how close that second load rushed past. I hollered up at him in outrage, but there was no stopping him, he was already reloading. That fool put two more rounds into Mike's body before he sprang down from his limb, gun barrel smoking.

In the silence, the screams of Sally Tolen at the cabin flew down that road from a good quarter mile away, broken by the shriek of jays and the frightened cries of children.

Blood was welling in Mike Tolen's mouth, and morning light was reflected in those eyes staring past my boots. "That's *one* sonofabitch ain't goin to back-shoot us," said Leslie's heavy voice, thick with strong feelings. He was deeply flushed, very excited, though trying not to show it. "Shoots pretty good," he told me with his lip-curl grin, slapping the stock of his new gun. In a strange ceremony of death and triumph, he rose up and down on boot toes in a kind of slow dance, circling the body twice. "Well, shit," I exclaimed, turning away, unable to watch.

Beyond Mike's cabin, out toward the Banks place, light flashed and shimmered on the turning wheels of a farm wagon coming south down the white road. Under tall hardwoods of the forest edge, the flashing danced from sunlight into shade, sunlight again. Whoever drove that wagon—probably Calvin Banks—was not close enough to identify the killers, but he would be shortly, and Mills Winn, the mailman, might show up at any time.

Cox was still grinning. "Go home," I snapped, disgusted. "Keep your mouth shut this time." Slipping the unused revolver back into my coat, I ran for the woodlot where my horse was tethered and jammed my old shotgun back into its scabbard. Staying well clear of the roads, I galloped south through the pinewoods west of Collinses. On the thick needle bed, the horse left little trace. I mumbled something from the Baptist service, praying for Mike's soul, but to pray seemed sickenly insincere and I could not finish.

The trouble was, I felt very bad about Mike Tolen, I felt older than dirt, and knowing I had not pulled the trigger did not ease my remorse as it had the last time. I had taken aim and meant to fire, and to finish him off with the revolver, too, if that were necessary. There was no way to absolve me of my part in it, not if I lived for another hundred years.

The revolver. Feeling the absence of its weight, I grabbed at my belt and pockets. My heart dropped to my guts, and pins of fear raked at my temples. By now the postman would have come along and found Mike's body. It was too late to work back along the trail.

I left the woods and crossed Reese's field at a flat gallop. That morning Jane Straughter had sent Frank out with a fresh denim shirt, stone blue against the dark brown of the loam. I remember spring robins drawing worms from his new furrows, and the rich spring chirrups the birds made as they scattered across the furrowed field toward the woods.

Frank Reese must have heard those shots over by the Junction, and he knew whose horse was pounding down on him right now. He never slowed or looked around but gazed fixedly on his mule's rump as it shifted along between the traces. I'm not here, his closed face said. He refused to see me. Not until something thumped into the furrow right behind him did he stop the mule—*Whoa up dar!*

"Throw some dirt over that gun," I called, cantering past as he stared stonily ahead. "Mark the place some way and keep on going." Over my shoulder, I watched Reese kick clods of earth over the shotgun, using the backs of his boot heels, looking at the woods. Then he took up his reins and slapped the mule's rump hard—*Giddyap!*—and kept on coming, solitary on the bare March landscape, following at a greater and greater distance as he fell behind me.

*

At my sister's house, Julian and Willie and young Jim Delaney Lowe were butchering a hog out by the smokehouse. I rode right up on 'em, scattering the dogs. "Boys, if anyone comes asking questions, I was right here in this yard since early morning, showing you fellers the best way to dress that hog. Your Uncle Edgar left for home just a short while ago." I had been helping and counseling Billy Collins's family since he died in the previous winter, so this made sense.

"We heard guns over yonder," Julian blurted. My nephews looked scared and unhappy, knowing I had come from that direction. Julian was looking at the empty scabbard. I pointed sternly at his face. "You understand me, Julian? Uncle Edgar was here dressing that hog when you heard those shots. That is all you boys need to know or say to anybody." There was no need to remind them that their uncle was now head of the family, and they were expected to do what they were told.

Looking sullen and unhappy, my nephews said nothing. Jim Delaney Lowe stared at his boot toes. Granny Ellen came to the kitchen window, then the door. Minnie's pale face appeared over her shoulder. Then young May was in the window, waving. Seeing her brother talking with her sons, Minnie raised a weak arm and waved, too, but my bright-eyed little mother only watched me. "Tell them what I said," I told the boys. I rode toward home.

Carrying fresh bread in a basket, Julian's Laura was leaving my house as I rode up. Surprised to see me returning home at this time of day, she stopped short and her nervous glance in the direction of the Junction told me those shots had been heard here, too. Laura had the sense not to ask for explanations, to avoid embarrassment for all of us in case I had to lie. Scarcely waving, she kept right on going.

Chapter 8

The Trials

Sheriff Dick Will Purvis in Lake City was notified by telephone of the death sometime toward noon, and a local crowd had gathered at the Junction. When the law arrived that afternoon, bloodhounds were turned loose all around the mailbox. The early spring weather being cold and dry, the dogs lost my scent where I swung into the saddle, but Deputy R. T. Radford, fooling along a ways tracking the hoof prints, saw the glint on the woodland floor of what turned out to be a .38 revolver, fully loaded, not two hundred yards from the scene of the crime. Very few new Smith & Wessons had found their way into the back country, and it was known I had one. What Radford yelled back to the posse was, *I got Watson's gun!* So much for the presumption of innocence until found guilty: it was enough to shake a man's faith in American justice.

How about Watson's nigger and the Cox boy? another man said. Weren't them two supposed to been in on it the last time? So Purvis went to Sanfords' place at Ichetucknee, where the Coxes were now living with their kin, and Will Cox told him, My boy Les been plowin yonder by them woods all day. We heard some shootin over east, so Les reckoned he'd go investigate. Asked where Les might be right now, his father said he didn't rightly know. And his old crony Sheriff Purvis said, Don't make one damn bit of difference, Will, your word is good enough for me and always will be. That was all Les needed in the way of alibi. He was never charged and never indicted in the death of D. M. Tolen.

On the way over to my house, the posse saw Reese working in the field, and four of 'em rode over there to pick him up. This bunch was under Dr. Nance, who had always hung around the law and later took over Purvis's job as Sheriff. By pure bad luck, one of their horses stumbled in the furrows when its iron shoe struck on the barrel of the buried gun. The man dismounted and dug out the shotgun with its buckshot loads. Nance ordered Frank to let go of those reins and walk on over with his hands behind his head. Shown the shotgun, Frank said, Why yessuh, please suh, us'ns got us a buck deer been usin that old field edge yonder, browses out into the sun ever' day. The gun was kept handy in case it was needed.

"That why you buried it?" Nance snarled at him. "That's Watson's gun, ain't it? You was ready, all right, but not for no damn deer." They marched him over to the road, hands high. But I liked to think Frank Reese would never turn on me, not if they strung him up and burned his balls off.

At my place, "Mr. Watson met them in good humor," according to what I read in the next day's paper. If that meant I was calm and amiable, I guess I was. Not knowing they had my revolver, I was confident they had no cause for arrest. Kate and I stood on our porch, watching armed men line up along my fence down on the road. Everything would be all right, I told her before she could ask questions.

Soon Josiah Burdett came up the hill, the Kinard youngster behind him. Joe was a dogged little feller, looked like a Mormon, had a scraggy horse tail of a beard down to his belly. He took his time, and I met him at the gate. When I stuck my hand into my pocket, I could see him flinch.

Joe told me that my neighbors were down there to arrest me. His voice was mild but his tone tight. He looked embarrassed. Asked if the suspect could see the warrant, he shook his head. No warrant had been issued. I'm sorry, Joe, I said, but if you have no warrant, then I can't come with you.

Behind him, young Brooks Kinard was clutching a rifle so damn hard his knucklebones were white, but it was Joe Burdett who did all the talking, though not much. He said, "You best come anyway, Edgar." He waved his shotgun toward the line of men along the road. Warrant or no warrant, Joe was trying to tell me, you are coming with us, so please don't make us shoot you down in front of my boy Herkie's childhood sweetheart.

Seeing Herkie's daddy, Kate ran out crying, "Mr. Watson has done nothing, Uncle Joe!" Joe Burdett said, "Morning, Edna," but he never glanced her way, that's how close he watched me. "In that case," I said, "I'll have to go inside, change to clean clothes to go up to Lake City." He shook his head. "Let's go."

"You're barking up the wrong tree, Joe." I was trying to hold my temper. However, I saw that he meant business, he would shoot me if he had to, although he'd never shot a man in all his life. As for young Brooks, he was set to do whatever Joe did. The boy had enough spirit to come up the hill with Joe Burdett, and he had good instincts, too, because without being told, he moved back and to the side where he had a clear shot in case I tried something.

I whispered to poor Kate that they had no evidence, I would be home again before she knew it. About then, my son Eddie showed up. Putting his hands on his hips, he demanded to know what the heck these men thought they were doing on our property. I told him everything would be all right, and gave him some instructions for the farm before leaving.

They took me first to Fort White, Terry's Store. There I was set on a keg in the back room where the late Sam Tolen had invited me to meet so he could shoot me. Frank Reese was sitting on the floor against the wall. Frank was wearing handcuffs and a murderous expression that could get him lynched one day on general principles. "You look like some kind of a black-hearted murderer," I whispered. Frank would not look at me.

Terrys were among the few who had been friendly with Tolens, mostly because Tolens had been unfriendly with me, and I was hooted by that dogless family when the deputies stood me on my feet and handcuffed me to my nigger field hand for the train ride to Lake City. For the crowd's benefit, I spoke right up, declaring that our great republic was in mortal peril when our own lawmen became lawbreakers. By God, I would file a formal protest with the Governor himself, on the grounds that Jim Crow law had been Florida law for at least three years now and our trains were segregated, so how could they ride me handcuffed to a nigger?

"Principle of the damn thing. Nothing personal," I told my companion, who was still brooding over my role in his arrest. "Law of the land."

"Mus' be dat American justice you was speakin about."

"I'm sure you can understand," I told him. "A man in my position can't be seen riding around the countryside handcuffed to a black man. I have my good name to think about."

"Man can't be too careful," Frank agreed.

"Law's the law, you know."

"That's what she is, okay. Leastways for white folks." His sulk was easing by that time, he seemed more rueful. I sighed, philosophical. We had been arrested before and had come through it, I said, so why not again? What I didn't say was that the law worried me less than the cold attitudes of the neighbors. When men decide to burn and hang a man, they have trouble looking him in the eye—not women. The Fort White ladies who peered in at us through Terry's dirty windows, hat plumes bobbing, looked as hard-eyed, mean, and curious as broody hens, while the men scarcely looked at us at all—not a good sign.

By the time we were shoved onto the Lake City train, it was plain these local folks had their own plan. Even the deputies were irritable and nervous. Sure enough, a crowd of men awaited us at Herlong Junction, eager to take us off the train. The train window was opposite those mailboxes where Mike Tolen had been killed, and people were walking all around the dark blot on the Junction Road where he had lain. What my neighbors were shouting for was a good old-fashioned hanging from the limb of that live oak on which Leslie had lain when he shot Mike. To look out a train window at your own lynching party, especially when the mob is thronged with familiar faces, friendly only yesterday, now hideously transformed into red gargoyles, brandishing guns and hollering for your head—that is enough to sadden any man, and give him a bad case of indigestion, too. A metal taste coated my mouth, and my guts quaked and loosened. I was able to hide my fear from Frank as long as I didn't speak, but I didn't feel like joking anymore. He didn't, either. He had closed his eyes. Like me, he was praying every second that this train would lurch ahead and carry us safe away.

None too soon, Sheriff Dick Will Purvis was backing up the steps in a big hurry. We heard him hollering, *Now come on, boys, don't go makin a damn monkey out of your duly elected Sheriff by takin my prisoners here at the whistle stop! We'll see you fellers up the track a little ways!* Hearing that, I knew that we were finished, and fear seized me so violently that I felt sick. The train creaked and jolted, stopped again for no good reason. Finally it passed the crowd, which was streaming along the track, whooping and hollering. The train eased along a little ways to the wood rack there at Herlong, where the fireman piled split logs on the caboose for the wood-burning engine. That was the wood stacked up by Calvin Banks, the same stack Cox was perched upon that day when Sam Tolen came along and threatened to kill him—the place where this mess got started in the first place and was now about to end.

I glanced at Frank at the same moment he glanced at me. We didn't fool ourselves. "Goddamnit, Frank," I said, shaking my head, "I did you a bad turn and I am sorry."

The black man nodded. I said, "Good thing we had this bad luck, I guess, cause otherwise we would have had no luck at all." He grunted, saying quietly, "Yessuh, we got some bad luck dis time, no doubt 'bout dat." We shook hands.

Purvis was yelling at the engineer to build up a head of steam. With a long whistle and a lonesome wail like a falling angel, the train yanked and lurched forward. Dreadful howls arose, rocks whacked the cars, bullets burst the glass. A deputy yanked me down away from the train window.

Once the train was in the clear, I sat back with a smile, congratulating Sheriff Purvis on reestablishing law and order and safeguarding the rights of prisoners by thwarting illegitimate mob rule. And the Sheriff grinned right back at me and said, "Ed Watson, we don't need no mob, cause we got all the evidence we need to hang you legal." The Sheriff confessed that his sympathies were with the crowd, but he felt obliged to stick to his sworn duty because E. J. Watson was paid up in his taxes.

"Also, you heard he had a good friend in the statehouse."

"That could be." The Sheriff nodded wisely.

Not a word was mentioned then or later about Cox. They never even brought him in for questioning.

*

The train stopped at Columbia City to pick up two deputies and a third suspect, John L. Porter, arrested because of a dispute with the victim after Mike had been put on the County Commission the year before. Pushed aboard in handcuffs, John gasped and moaned, for he was scared to death. Over by the crossing stood John's weeping wife and their poor dim-witted Duzzie, blowing her nose while her mother dabbed her eyes.

John Porter and I were cuffed together on one bench, with Reese shackled to the bench leg opposite, to permit him to ride seated on the floor. The roadbed was rough and his spine was jolted hard, until finally he groaned in torment. To comfort him, I pointed out how fortunate he was to ride in the white man's car in defiance of Florida law. "Praise de Lawd," Frank said.

John Porter frowned at us. "Ed? What's this business all about?" Porter had his eye on the Sheriff, and his tone was both plaintive and pompous— his idea of what an outraged citizen's tone is supposed to be. Not being a stalwart sort of man, he saw no reason to be hung for being my friend. "I demand an answer!" he shouted into my face when I failed to comment.

John's breath was bad—no doubt a nervous stomach. "I have halitosis," he said miserably, seeing me wince.

"Halitosis is better than no breath at all," I reasoned, to remind him that death by hanging might be worse. I winked at Frank, but Frank's own mood had turned against me. As for John, he missed my point entirely.

"Ed, you have to tell 'em I had nothing to do with it! I wasn't even there!"

"Now I ask you, John, how in the heck would I know that you weren't there when I don't even know where 'there' might be?"

Reese's laugh sounded more like a short cough, so brief and unwilling was his pained amusement, but Porter, who was frantic now, yelled, "Is he laughing at me? You tell your damned nigger to keep his nigger mouth shut or he might get lynched!"

"You will never string up my damned nigger," I said with a stern frown, "because the indignant citizens of our fair county aim to beat you to it."

"Jesus, Ed!" By now, Porter was screeching. "How can you sit here cracking jokes when any minute they might drag us off this train? Hang an innocent man who never done no wrong!"

"There are no innocent men," I said. "Reflect upon that."

Frank Reese had a lot more cause to bitch than Porter did, but he was too busy trying to brace against the jolts and save his spine by hitching his ass up on top of his chained hands. Finally he gave up exhausted and sank into a daze of pain, gazing blindly at the toes of his torn boots, taking his punishment.

Now that danger from the mob was no longer imminent, I had time to wonder why a seasoned outlaw like Frank Reese had not taken the pains to hide that gun a whole lot deeper. Had it never occurred to him that they might come hunting the one suspect arrested in the death of the victim's brother? Or was he just too angry to think straight, having had my shotgun dropped into his furrow after Cox had tried to implicate him in the first case? Frank must have known he'd be in fatal trouble if that gun was found anywhere near him, yet all he did was kick a little dirt over it and keep on going. Never emptied the shells out of the chambers, never buried it deeper, never walked a hundred yards to hide it in the woods. He never touched that gun, he told me later. He didn't want anything to do with it.

"You reckoned I just dragged you into it, the same way Leslie did, so you wouldn't lift a hand to help, is that it, Frank? Not even if you got yourself hung?"

"It ain't *me* gettin me hung!" Frank Reese burst out, so violently that a deputy hollered at him to shut up. "I reckoned you knew what you was up to, droppin that gun." He nodded with just the shadow of a smile. "Don't have to go explainin nothin to no dumb-ass nigger."

"You're even dumber than you think!" I said, disgusted. I was still bothered. Frank Reese was a more complicated man than I had thought.

*

We arrived in Lake City that Monday evening of March 23 and lodged in the county jail. I would not have had much sleep anywhere else. Next morning the deputies passed the word that the south end of the county was forming a huge mob. By Tuesday afternoon, rumors were swirling—*The mob is on its way!* Sure enough, we heard wild yells and restless gunfire. Poor Porter was beside himself with the injustice of it all, howling his innocence from his cell window to all who passed the jail—*You men know me and know I am no murderer!* Those who did not know John before sure knew him by the time he finished. So did every flea-bit dog that trotted past, because he hollered out his tale every few minutes and for many hours, in case the mob had spies out in the street and might take pity on him, and spare him any rough stuff when the time came.

Frank Reese, who had no part in the killing, either, remained quiet. As a black man, he did not expect much from his life, knowing that all the protest in the world would never save him. So far as Frank Reese was concerned, life was right on schedule.

My attorney telegraphed word of my predicament to Governor Broward, and the Governor sent orders back to move the suspects out of town for their own safety. That same night Deputy Bill Sweat, who ran the jail, heard the train whistle at the crossing and quick-marched us out of there in a big hurry, right down the center of the main street to the railroad station.

To devil John Porter, I complained loudly as we went along that we didn't care to be marched down the main street in chains like common felons when we hadn't been found guilty of so much as loitering. Sure enough, Porter's nerves gave out—"For Christ sake, Ed! Have you gone crazy?"

Deputy Sweat, mopping his brow, explained that this well-lit thorough-fare made more sense than taking a back street and falling prey to unknown men who might be laying for us in the darkness. Sweat was the right name for ol' Bill that night, cold as it was. Sure enough, a passerby ran off into the side streets to spread word, and we heard hollers of frustration as we boarded. Armed escort was provided to Jasper, in Hamilton County, and to the Leon County jail at Tallahassee the next day. I sent word to Broward, inviting him to step downtown and visit his old friend in his roach-stained cell, but Governor Nap was a politician now. He stayed away. A few days later we were moved to the Duval County jail at Jacksonville.

*

By now I had learned that my Collins nephews had represented me so poorly that my own mother was persuaded of my guilt. In fact, Purvis informed me in his picturesque rural way that my so-called alibi had held up about as long as outhouse toilet paper. But on April 10, at the Sheriff's instigation, the coroner's jury charged my nephews with being accessories to the crime after the fact—a tactic designed to coerce them to confirm the sworn testimony of their friend Jim Delaney Lowe that E. J. Watson had solicited an alibi. Sure enough, Minnie's boys caved in after a day or so, having been persuaded that said solicitation was tantamount to a confession of cold-blooded murder. With the suspect's dropped revolver and his buried shotgun, the state was building a strong case, my attorneys warned me, preparing the ground for charging their new client a fat fee. Within the week, Frank Reese and I were indicted for the murder of that noted farmer, devoted family man, pious churchgoer, and dedicated county commissioner Mr. D. M. Tolen.

As for the real killer, he was now in trouble for carrying an unlicensed pistol and disturbing the peace. Will Cox and my son Eddie were also included in that "peace warrant," and the plaintiff was James Tolen, who told the judge that these three had threatened him with the same fate that had befallen his two brothers, making Watson's gang suspect in advance for any harm that might befall him. As it turned out, Les was already in custody, and he joined us the next day in the Duval County jail.

After almost a year, Cox had finally been charged with the murder of Sam Tolen. It seems that Julian and Willie Collins and their friend Jim Delaney Lowe, along with the Tolen stepbrother Will Russ, had implicated Leslie in that death on the evidence of his own boasting, overheard while he was showing off for Miss May Collins and other local damsels. This time, even Sheriff Purvis could not ease him out of it.

Thanks to Cox, Frank Reese had come close to being lynched over Sam Tolen. When Les joined us in the hoosegow, swearing vengeance on the Collins boys, Frank groaned dolefully and shook his woolly head, arm flung up in grief over his eyes. Lo'd, Lo'd, how pitiful to see, he cried, a nice young white gen'leman like Mist' Les Cox in de county *jail*! Broken-hearted, Frank actually commenced to cough and blubber.

When I laughed, Frank let go and whooped so hard that he had to lie down on the floor to get his breath back. Leslie said, "If they don't kill you, nigger, I damn well will." He meant that, too, and Frank knew he meant it, but that was not why Frank fell quiet, nor why the tears ran down those scarred black cheeks. Someone had to pay for the death of a county commissioner, and Reese had no doubt it was going to be him, and he wept because he suddenly realized he had nothing more to hope for, nothing left to lose. Facing death, Frank Reese was free at last, free to speak as he pleased to any white man, free to say anything he damn well wanted. And so he sat up and wiped his eyes and said in a cold calm tone, "Not if I reach you first, you fuckin redneck moron."

Les squinted at me in honest disbelief that I could grin at such an outrage. Before stomping off to the far side of the pen, he pointed his forefinger and spoke to Frank in that thick heavy voice, as if his throat was full of clotted blood—so choked, in fact, that we could not even agree on what he'd said.

"Maybe some kind of secret redneck curse," I suggested, watching Les go. Frank Reese looked me over coldly. "Redneck, whiteneck—don't make no difference to us blackneck niggers."

*

In early April, thanks to Walt Langford and his weighty friend Jim Cole, Senator Frederick P. Cone of Lake City had been retained as our defense attorney. It was Cone who had persuaded the Governor to order the prisoners removed from Columbia County. Cone was a silver-haired aristocrat who was friendly with Broward, and there wasn't a judge in all north Florida who would stand up to him. They knew that "Senator Fred" was certain to occupy the Governor's mansion in the future, and stay there long enough to settle up old scores with the judiciary.

In our first meeting, Fred Cone warned me that the state's attorneys were already claiming "an ironclad case"—just the kind, he said, that he most enjoyed "smelting down." It was true the deputies had found my shotgun and revolver, but he would oblige them to confirm the fact that neither of those weapons had been fired on that day, much less used in the killing.

Having been charged by the grand jury and indicted, the defendants appeared on Friday, May 1, in Columbia County Court in Lake City. There we were arraigned and pled not guilty before Judge R. M. Call. The Lake City *Citizen-Reporter* called Frank Reese "a very dark-colored negro, wearing overalls. Asked to plead, he was stopped by counsel." Lawyer Cone had told Frank to be quiet, which was all right with Frank, but Cone did this with a cold, impatient gesture, not looking at Reese but at me, as if requesting that I put a stop to my dog's barking. Back in jail, still brooding about this, Frank muttered something so bitter that I had to warn him. Talking to Les Cox the way he had, and now this cynicism toward the Senator—no good would come of it.

That day the Judge asked him to plead was Frank's last chance to speak out about his innocence, for he was never questioned nor even mentioned in the case again. Day after day, in courtroom after courtroom all that summer, he would sit like a dark knot on the oak bench. Even his own counsel never spoke to him. That lone figure might have been the Almighty's witness in our white man's courtroom, passing silent judgment. Once in a while, I caught his eye and winked, but he never winked back.

*

By returning us to Lake City, Senator Cone provoked the populace into raucous demonstrations in the streets. If we survived it, this was a smart tactic, demonstrating before the trial could begin the dire prejudice against the suspects in this county. With threats and abuse being shouted through the courtroom windows—for May had come, and the warm weather—Cone prepared a petition for a change of venue, waving a whole sheaf of affidavits for the benefit of the reporters and the court.

Even before the coroner's jury concluded we should be charged, Cone had heard dark rumors of a lynching. Since then he had discussed the case with two hundred local citizens without finding one not strongly prejudiced against his clients. "I am reliably informed," Cone told the court, "that practically the whole south end of this county was in attendance at the coroner's inquest, which was in session for nearly three weeks. I have been told by businessmen in Lake City and Fort White that it would be impossible to find a fair and impartial jury in this county. They declined to be witnesses for the defense, being afraid of personal violence or for business reasons."

Next (in case he lost his motion), Cone had his assistant Joseph Stripling make clear in court that, by offering these affidavits, the defense meant no reflection whatever on the worthy residents of Columbia County. "Honest men can be prejudiced as well as other men," Stripling told the court, "and some men mistake their prejudices for their principles."

With that mob out there, the defendants felt like rat cheese in a trap. Cone didn't deny there was a risk, but he saw the change of venue as our only hope—the key to our acquittal. Anyway, the Governor was following the case and meant to take "all appropriate measures to ensure the safety of the accused."

That morning the court was informed by Mr. Charlie Eaton, a special investigator appointed by Nap Broward, that he had heard about a lynch raid on the jail planned for 3:00 A.M. on Thursday night, in the week previous. The defendants, he testified, had been in such peril of mob violence that he rushed to the Elks Club to alert Lawyer Cone. These two concluded that the state militia should be called out to guard the prisoners. Cone told the court he had gone to Sheriff Purvis and demanded protection for his clients, and that Purvis responded that "those ol' boys" in the mob had given him their word that the accused were not in any danger, since the evidence against them was so strong that they would hang anyway. Purvis admitted he had ordered extra guards around the jail, but he had done so, he said, only as a courtesy to the defense attorneys.

If the truth be known, declared the Sheriff under oath, the real trouble was far more likely to be caused by Defendant Watson's friends in southwest Florida. Even as he spoke, crowds of these people were on their way north by sea and rail to rescue him. This mendacity was so astounding that my attorney smote his brow. He was finally reduced to asking Purvis if he really believed these parties could get a fair trial in Columbia County.

Why, I do.
And you haven't heard this case widely discussed?
Why, no, sir. I do know I have heard you say more about it than anybody else.

Cone invited the Sheriff to admit that as recently as the previous week, he had confided to Detective Eaton that he feared for his prisoners' lives. Purvis denied this, saying, "If I told you that, I told you a lie." Cone retorted, "Well,

Sheriff, I am not responsible for *that.*" Stripling told Purvis that he had no confidence whatever in his truthfulness, and even less in the intentions of his deputies, having heard that certain deputies also served as members of the lynch mob. Purvis cheerfully agreed that he had heard that, too.

Attorney Stripling now advised the Judge that when he had gone to Purvis and State's Attorney Cory Larabee to express concern about the prisoners, they had merely laughed at him. Hearing this complaint, the Sheriff and the Prosecutor laughed at him again, and their gall in a court of justice struck me as so funny that I had to clap my hand over my mouth to keep from laughing heartily along with them, as Fred Cone, beside me, irritably rattled his papers.

Next came Will Cox's brother Jasper, who testified he'd been solicited to join the lynch mob on Thursday, March 26, only three days after the alleged murder, by none other than Mr. Blumer Hunter, at a time when Mr. Hunter was a member of the coroner's jury which was holding impartial hearings on the case. Jasper said he had declined, explaining to Mr. Hunter that he "was not in that line of business." Next morning, according to the Lake City paper, Mr. Hunter came to town (in brown coveralls smeared with wet cow manure, if I know Blumer) and informed the court stenographer that the testimony of Jasper Cox was "an unqualified fabrication." Even John Porter cracked a smile at the idea of such fine words springing forth from the mush mouth and brown tobacco teeth of Blumer Hunter.

In the afternoon, Banker Langford arrived from Fort Myers with a note from Carrie—*Oh Daddy, we just know that you are innocent! Eddie has written us all about those dreadful Tolens!* On the witness stand, Langford allowed that "Yes, I am his son-in-law, but that don't mean I am a stranger to the truth! And the truth is that ever since my arrival, what I have heard over and over is, *That murdering skunk should be hung on general principles!*" Later I told Walt he was not obliged to quote that in court with such strong feeling, and the banker flashed me kind of a scared grin. Walt could never quite make out when his father-in-law was being serious and when he wasn't.

Meanwhile State's Attorney Larabee was implying that all these rumors of mob violence had been spread by the defense attorney's four assistants who, as was well-known, were out day and night bribing and coercing all potential witnesses. Larabee had his own batch of affidavits, which all agreed that there was no reason in the world why the defendants would not get a fair trial in Columbia County. This naked lie, set down under solemn oath, was signed by the Herlongs and most of that Methodist bunch down around Centerville—the selfsame neighbors who had howled for my head that afternoon at Herlong Station.

At the end of the day, Judge Call announced that he would need the entire weekend to inspect so many contradictory affidavits. He ordered the defendants returned to Duval County, but not before Defendants Reese and Watson, "having reason to believe that certain people are using all efforts to keep the minds of the people of Columbia County inflamed against them," signed affidavits stating that their lives were in danger and petitioning the Judge for a change of venue.

On Monday morning the Sheriff himself came to Jacksonville to fetch us to Lake City, and this time I rode handcuffed to Les Cox. For all his big talk, Leslie was pale and nervous. Fred Cone had made him get a haircut and put on his daddy's Sunday shirt, but the collar was tight and the new hairline gleamed on his sunburned neck, and for all his good looks, he appeared kind of young and green. When he bragged that some church lady had told him he looked like Billy the Kid, and I said, That is correct. Billy the Kid looked like weasel shit, and you do, too. Les decided he would laugh, in the mistaken belief that I was fooling.

Though it broke his heart not to get the credit for Mike Tolen, L. Cox promised to keep E. J. Watson out of the S. Tolen case, since his own name had gone unmentioned in *State of Florida v. E. J. Watson and Frank Reese*. Leslie said, "Well, somebody sure done a good deed on them sonsabitches, and I ain't sorry, how about you?" And I said, "You are not sorry, son, because you think Senator Fred P. Cone will get you off. You might repent of your black sins if you thought you might be hung by your dirty neck till you were dead." But my fatherly attempts to improve his attitude and awaken a sense of humor were wasted on this unfortunate young man.

On May 4, Attorney Cone won John Porter's release, establishing that he had been seized unlawfully without a warrant and held unlawfully without a formal charge. Next, he persuaded Judge Call that one Tolen case might prejudice the other. That way he got Leslie's case held over till the summer term, when the climate in the county might have cooled a little. Last but not least, he won a change of venue for Defendants E. J. Watson and F. Reese.

*

We were tried next in Jasper, in Hamilton County, where we traveled from Jacksonville on a warm Tuesday of late July. Kate and my son Eddie, and my sister Minnie with Julian and Willie, came there to testify, also Jim Delaney Lowe, old Calvin Banks, and a crowd of others.

Peering around for a place to spit his chaw, Deputy R. T. Radford related the heroic saga of how he had stumbled over the defendant's revolver in the woods. Next, Dr. Nance described with due pomposity how Watson's shotgun, "heavily" loaded with buckshot and "all primed for mayhem," was found a short distance away from that "hard-faced Negro." Here Nance pointed a bony finger at Defendant Reese, who sat at the farther end of the defense table, hunched into himself like some gnarled woodland growth. Finally, my Collins nephews and Jim Delaney Lowe revealed nervously how E. J. Watson, arriving not long after the victim's demise, had solicited their support of a false alibi right in their barnyard.

Neither Julian nor Willie cared to meet my eye. True, their dad had never taken to me nor me to him, but as a stern believer in old codes of clan loyalty and family honor, Billy Collins would have horsewhipped his two sons before permitting them to stand up in court and betray their own blood uncle in this manner.

Hearing her sons testify against her brother, my peculiar sister went to pieces with loud sniffles. (Since childhood days, when we fended off the blows of Ring-Eye Lige, I had never been sure whether those sniffles helped or hurt us.) Almost inaudible when called to the stand, Minnie testified in tremulous tones that her sons and their friend must be mistaken in their recollection that their kindly Uncle Edgar—"who had been so generous with his time and means since Mr. Collins passed away"—had shown up at the Collins house less than half an hour after the death of D. M. Tolen and stayed just long enough to plant his alibi. She recalled quite clearly that her brother had arrived well before eight to teach her fatherless sons how to dress a hog, and had not left until close to noon, when he went home to get his dinner.

State's Attorney Larabee wished to know why she was weeping—*Are you perjuring yourself, ma'am, by any chance? Objection, Your Honor! Sustained!* I feared that Ninny would be panicked into blurting something idiotic that would get me hung. Instead, she explained tearfully in soft murmurs that it broke her heart to see her family torn in two. Plainly the jury was affected—hurrah for Ninny! But when she shuffled back to her seat like a sick old woman, nobody in the Collins row could look at anybody.

Strangely, all of this upset me. My sister's lifelong low opinion of herself had been much worsened. Here she was, a good churchwoman, lying under oath, and furthermore making liars of her sons, though they spoke the truth. She had been frail even before her day in court, and this might finish her. Prosecutor Larabee did not call Kate or Young Eddie, who would be sure to back up Minnie's story, but the man made a serious mistake when he excused the former Ellen Addison for that same reason. If her only alternative was to contradict her precious grandsons, Mama would banish me to hell before she lied for me.

In the recess, the prisoners were taken to the outhouse. I stepped right up behind Jim Delaney Lowe and slapped his shoulder with my chains like some old dungeon ghost. That boy jumped a mile. I hope he wet himself. I whispered, "Jim, the day they turn me loose, I aim to take care of those who did me wrong. So you keep a real sharp eye out, boy, you hear?" Jim would pass that message to my nephews, give 'em something to pray about in church. I would never harm my sister's sons but they didn't know that, and there were nights in that hot cell, in that long summer, when their Uncle Edgar wasn't so sure, either.

Throughout our trials, Frank Reese sat inert. He was there as "Watson's nigger," nothing more. If I was guilty, he was, too, and if I was innocent, the same, and so he waited for these white folks to decide my fate. Sometimes after the court cleared, they had to prod him to stand up, like a sagging croker sack of turnips in a muddy field. The Prosecutor forgot him, so did the defense, and there were days when I forgot him, too. Reese didn't count—that is the fate of Injuns and niggers. But this man had ridden a long road with me, he had stood by me and it made me feel bad when I thought about him, so I mostly didn't.

Frank understood that I could never tell anyone, not even Cone, that Frank was innocent—how would I know such a thing if I had been at the Collins place, helping my nephews? However, I gave him my solemn promise that if we were found guilty and Cone lost on the appeal, I would make a confession, telling the court that Defendant Reese had been an accomplice neither before the fact nor after, and had no idea that shotgun would be brought to where he was plowing in the field. I couldn't confess any such thing while Cone had a chance to save my skin, but once it looked like I was finished, I'd say, *Listen, Judge, speaking of innocence, this black man here is as white as the driven snow*—something like that. Frank smiled a little. I guess he appreciated my jokes and good intentions, but he also knew—I knew it, too—that even if my confession was believed, no one would bother to throw out a nigger's conviction, far less go to the trouble and expense of a new trial. Defendant Reese was certain to be hung no matter what.

The one way Frank could save himself was to turn state's evidence, but what use was it to the Senator's career to get the nigger off and lose the white man? He never advised Frank Reese about that choice and forbade me to discuss it with him, either. I said, Well, I guess you're right, but I felt bad about that, too. I asked why Cone couldn't get Frank's case severed and dismissed, as he had with Porter. Because the Prosecutor had no evidence at all, Cone said, that Frank Reese knew anything about this killing, and getting his case dismissed at this late stage might leave an impression with the jury that the remaining suspect, against whom evidence was plentiful, must be the guilty one.

Trying to justify this reasoning to Reese got me all snarled up in my own words. Cone's arguments weren't as clear to me as I had thought, nor my own feelings, either. "Looks like you're fucked," I told Frank roughly, giving up. Frank shrugged that off. All these months of waiting to be hung had turned him sullen. "Black Frank don't count for nothin in this case," he whispered, "no more'n he did on that March morning when Mist' Jack dropped his shotgun in dat nigger's furrow, rode on by. The worstest thing Frank Reese ever done was foller Mist' Jack Watson to Florida."

As it turned out, Cone never asked me if I'd killed Mike Tolen. He didn't want to know. I could have said I had not done so, which in a way was true, but I did not care to read in his expression that he thought I was a liar, so I never bothered.

*

In the back country, field niggers in rough homespun have a way of vanishing into the land like earthen men. I noticed that as a boy in Carolina. They drift along against far woods in the slow turn of the earth, and after a time the shapes dissolve into the ground mist, browns sifting into the leaves and furrows, and you don't see them anymore, only a shift and shadow in the cornstalks. Or a figure straightens to listen to the distant whoop of others, half-hidden in the broomstraw on that red soil over yonder in the oldfields. Some white people will kill or even screw in front of niggers, knowing it won't be talked about, that's how easy it is to forget black folks are there. Not until the trial, when Calvin Banks was on the witness stand, did I remember the glint of sun on turning cart wheels, so far away that for a time the creak of wooden wheels could not be heard. Way down that long white road through the woods, in the fractured light of sun and morning shadows, I had seen that black man without ever seeing him.

When he heard the shots, Banks was on his way to Herlong Junction with a wagonload of cross-ties. Far ahead of him down the white lane, the postboxes by the Junction caught the morning light. The silhouette of a man on foot—Mist' Mike Tolen—was walking toward them. As the first shot echoed, he saw Mist' Tolen fall on his side, still kicking, as another man ran out onto the road. Though distracted by the shrieks from the Tolen cabin, he thought he heard a second shot and then another before a second man stepped out of the wood edge. Mis Sally Tolen flew outside barefoot and shrieking, started down that road toward the mailboxes, saw the two men and the still body, stopped, came back, both hands clutching her hair, as her little children, shrieking, too (Calvin said in court), "follered behin' dere mama like a line o' ducklins."

Calvin had pulled up at the shots, but when the two men went back into the woods, he kept on going, after begging Mis Tolen to shut her children in the cabin. She did so, he said, but after that she came running again, and ran right past him.

And did you get a look at those two men?
Yassuh.
And can you identify them for this court?
Yassuh. One them men was Mist' Edguh Watson—
Objection, Your Honor!
Sustained.

Approaching the body in the road, Calvin wondered why no one had come from the Cox cabin to investigate. (Fred Cone jumped up with another objection, which was sustained.) By the time the old man reached the Junction, the postman Mr. Winn was already approaching from the other direction. After Mr. Winn had coaxed and pried the hysterical young woman off his body, they had dragged the victim onto Calvin's tipped cart and brought him home.

"Well now, Calvin," said Attorney Cone in a hectoring and baited voice that was sign to the jury to pay close attention, "how can an old darkie with failing eyesight—you have acknowledged your poor eyesight, have you not?—how can that old darkie be so sure that the man he saw a quarter mile away was this defendant?" And Calvin said, "Cause I knowed Mist' Edguh since a boy, knowed the shape of him and knowed the size of him, knowed the way he walk. In the mornin sunlight I would know him from a quarter mile, maybe half a mile away, cause the sun shines up the rust in Mist' Edguh's hair, and nobody around dem woods exceptin only him had hair of that dark rust-red color like dried blood."

Frank Reese leaned around behind our attorneys' broadclothed backs. He whispered behind his hand, "Mist' Jack? Looks like you're fucked." There was no way to read Reese's expression, and no time, either, because Old Man Calvin Banks kept right on talking.

"I never seed no sign of no cullud man," Banks stated flatly, looking straight at Reese. He volunteered this of his own accord in the startled silence in the courtroom that followed his identification of Ed Watson, and I was glad, because Reese needed all the help that he could get. But neither Judge nor defense nor prosecution pursued this crucial point. Nobody queried the old man, not even Reese's defense attorney, Mr. Cone, who was busy scribbling notes for some new strategy.

A last-minute defense witness was Leslie Cox, whose indictment for the murder of Sam Tolen had already been dismissed by the circuit court without a trial. Attorney Cone had been much pleased, since Leslie's acquittal was a fine precedent for *The State of Florida v. E. J. Watson and Frank Reese*. He was happy to pay Leslie's railway fare to Jasper out of E. J. Watson's pocket, and his faith was justified, since after invoking the Almighty as his Witness,

Cox lifted his hand and swore to the complete innocence of Mr. Watson. Since he himself was D. M. Tolen's killer, he knew what he was talking about, and spoke with commendable conviction. The jury was very favorably impressed by the evident sincerity of this young man, and I understood much better now why Cone had cut off Calvin Banks before he could identify the second man he had seen with Mike Tolen's body.

Later Cone told us that seven of the Jasper jurors voted for conviction but could not dislodge the other five, who might have been bought off by Cone's assistants, for all I know. My attorneys never specified where all their client's money had been spent, but one thing was certain, his money was no object, and these paper rattlers spent every cent I had. Fred P. Cone had never lost a case, and he did not intend to lose one now for puny financial considerations, not at the outset of a brilliant career which would one day land him in the statehouse.

With a hung jury on his hands, Judge B. H. Palmer declared a mistrial and ordered the case held over until the next term of the circuit court. That same month, back in Lake City, he threw out the lawsuit of the Myers nephews against the executors of Tabitha Watson's will. Jim Tolen resumed his sales of our family property while I festered in the Jasper jail, unable to do a single thing about it.

Leslie got word to me that if I were convicted, he would assist in my escape. Les swore this on his honor and I believed him—not that I trusted him. The man whose honor I trusted was his father.

*

Outside my bars, on a fine morning in Jasper, a redbird chortled loud and clear, recalling a lost Carolina springtime. But instead of that redbird, I was doomed to listen to my fine-feathered son-in-law, who said things like, *I'm afraid your record is against you, Mr. Watson.* Walter Langford and his friend Jim Cole had twisted every arm in Tallahassee, but it was plain they didn't think I had a chance in hell. Cole was still eager for me to like him because it made him nervous that I didn't, but I would have respected him more if he'd told the truth, that he would have been very glad to see me hung.

When I first knew Walt Langford back in '95, he was a cow hunter out toward Immokalee, snot-flying drunk on rotgut moonshine from one day to the next. This morning he was dead sober in a three-piece suit. "Who the hell are you?" I said. "The undertaker? You come to take my measure for my coffin?" Walt mustered up a grin to be polite and passed me Carrie's note:

Oh Daddy, please! Walter says all the evidence is against you, and your record, too, and that you must throw yourself on the mercy of the court. Tell them you had to defend yourself against that man because he threatened you, tell them you regret it deeply but you had no choice. Walter and his business friends will gladly testify what a fine hard-working farmer and good businessman you are and always have been. And surely our side can convince the jury what a good provider and good husband—and wonderful kind jolly father!—our dear, dearest daddy has always been! If you'll just cooperate and plead guilty and accept a reduced sentence, Walter says, everything is bound to turn out fine!

"The family has decided I am guilty, is that correct?"

"Nosir, it's not that, exactly—"

Walter, I told him, it *is* that. It is exactly that, Walter. I sent a message back to Carrie that her dear, dearest Daddy had done no wrong, not even if he killed Mike Tolen, which he hadn't. For that reason, he would not plead guilty under any circumstances.

Walter told me I had better think that over because after the hanging it would be too late. Walt didn't even know he was being funny. Said he'd "heard on good authority that the State was ready to negotiate"—that's the constipated way Walt talks since he became a banker. And he had my son Eddie, who trailed in here after him, talking that same way, the pair of them sitting straight up on my bunk, nervous and mealymouthed, like they wouldn't mind a second helping of nice mashed potato. "I'm afraid your record is against you, Dad," my offspring said.

I knew right then that Walter's "good authority" was State's Attorney Cory Larabee. It looked like the Prosecutor and my son-in-law were in cahoots. And who should happen by an hour later to inquire if "Ed" was comfortable? The State's Attorney. Cory Larabee stepped into my cell already talking too much and too loudly, in the grand flatulence of politicians. He slapped my back and sat his ass down, made himself at home. *Now don't stand on your manners, Ed, just call me Cory!* Here I was, entirely at the mercy of any stupid sonofabitch who stepped up to the bars, and worst of all were this prosecutor and my kinfolks, who seemed to think they had some special dispensation to squeeze right into my small cell beside me.

"Spit it out," I growled.

Well, because Friend Ed had support from influential friends—Call-me-Cory meant the Governor—he might ensure parole in three years' time if I pled guilty. He raised his eyebrows way high up on that marble dome of his while his good news penetrated my warped criminal brain. Because *otherwise, Ed,* he said when I was silent, *we'll do our very best to hang you, boy!*

Damned if he didn't laugh at that and slap me on the knee, to show me no offense was meant by threatening my life. That was the politician in him. This public servant was out to please, no matter whom, no matter what, so

I damn well better take advantage—that's what he wanted me to think. That was the bait.

I jumped up with a sudden yell, protesting that my honor had been sullied. I backed him right up tight against the bars, squinting one eye. And knowing a dastard when he saw one, Call-me-Cory hollered *Guard!* Unfortunately, Big Earl had just stepped out to heed a call of nature, after locking up an innocent prosecutor with a dangerous killer.

I had him cornered, I was panting in his face. No *sir!* I shouted, backing the man around my cell, *No* sir, Mr. Cory sir! I am *not* pleading guilty, Cory sir, because I am as innocent as the Baby Jesus. All you have for motive, Cory, is hard feelings in the family, Cory, and if *that's* a motive, you will have to hang every defendant in the state of Florida. *No*sir! If the State intends to hang Ed Watson, Cory, it will have to hang him fair and hang him square!

All that stuff sounded pretty good, but mainly it plain tickled me to death to keep yelling his first name. Another thing, Cory—my voice was a whisper now, real quiet menace—you have mentioned my powerful friends in Tallahassee, Cory. Well sir, I am keeping them right up to the minute on every aspect of this case, including the behavior of the Prosecutor. So the next time you come in here and try to hornswoggle a poor prisoner in the absence of his legal counsel, those powerful friends will see to it that you are disbarred.

The Prosecutor was trying to chuckle, but all he made were little airy sounds, like a rooster with its throat cut. All right now, Ed, he whined, to calm me. All right now, Ed, if that's the way you want it. Shaking his head and looking sheepish, he told me I had a first-rate legal mind, I was much too sharp for him, that's all, no wonder the Governor thought so highly of me. He was shaking his head in honest admiration, laughing, too, the kind of laugh that might get away from him at any moment, go up way high like a fox yip, out of pure nerves. His hand came up as pale and slow as a dead thing to the surface, anxious to pat me on the shoulder, but when he saw my "crazy Watson eyes," he hesitated. That hand of his was hanging in the air not knowing where to go, and finally it turned to brushing his heavy dandruff off his shoulders. Cory's grin looked sickly, and he put out a rank body smell, that's how quick fear took him.

Where's that damned guard? he squawked, peering through my bars, as if we were in this damnable fix together. Next thing I knew, he was hollering at someone else. *Christamighty, you never heard me tell you to wait outside?* Damned if that ol' turd of a Jim Tolen hadn't snuck in here while Earl was in the privy. I only hoped he had arrived in time to hear Cory's philosophical observations on shiftless rednecks.

Jim was peering through the bars, looking us over, itching himself in his sharp-cornered black suit. "Mr. *Per*-secutor? Sposin I went informin to them newspapers how you was a-hobnobbin in here, crackin jokes and shakin the gory hand of the selfsame heenus killer you was swored to *per*-secute?"

The dignity of the Persecutor's office could not permit this sort of insolence, so Larabee climbed onto his high horse and rode all over that poor rube. "And prosecute him I shall," he boomed, "with all the might and main God gave me, sir! And the Lord willing, Mr. Tolen, sir, you shall see him hung! Because in my opinion he is red in tooth and claw! A man more guilty of a heinous crime never drew breath! Nevertheless—!"

"All I'm sayin, Mr. Persecutor—"

"*Yes* sir! And all *I'm* saying, *Mis*-ter Tolen, is the following: I have made the acquaintance of this man Ed Watson in halls of justice all over north Florida, and I can testify that he is a human being, made in the image of Almighty God! *Yes* sir! E. J. Watson is a *man*, sir, made from the same dull clay as yourself. He eats as you do, breathes as you do, and worships God as you do, Mr. Tolen! In point of fact, the sole and only and unique difference between you—"

"The Governor?" I suggested.

"Ed Watson is a *gentleman*, *Mis*-ter Tolen!" The Prosecutor glared, triumphant. "What's more, he is a lively man, piss and vinegar just don't describe it, and when he's up there swinging from that rope, I for one won't be ashamed to say I was proud to know him!"

When Cory paused to get a breath, he glanced sideways and gave me a sly wink which said, Well, Mr. Watson, how do you like *that*? Still want to make that not-guilty plea and go up against a ripsnorter like me in the public tri-*byoo*-nal?

"Now that don't mean Friend Ed deserves to live. Howsomever, may I remind you, *Mis*-ter Tolen, that no judgment has been pronounced, and that in this great democracy of ours, E. J. Watson is innocent until found guilty by a jury of his peers! So by all means, go tell the press whatever you damn well please, and I'll denounce you as a reckless liar and take you to court for obstruction of justice! *Jus*tice, *Mis*-ter Tolen!"

Larabee was having sport with this poor dolled-up redneck, but mainly he was sucking up to E. J. Watson, knowing that Napoleon Broward, with his sympathy for the accused, might return a favor to a smart young state's attorney with political ambitions who obliged him here with lenience and some discretion. Even were he to prosecute and lose, this trial's notoriety might lend some color to a gray feller like Larabee, which he would need when hustling votes on down the line.

Larabee was clever, yes, and I despised him for it. But maybe he did not realize that the defense attorney had him beat already. Fred P. Cone, according to Walt Langford, was already on the main track to the Governor's mansion.

Big Earl came galumphing back like a big woolly dog. "Dammit, Guard, where you been?" Call-me-Cory hollers. But Earl is wheezing and he merely grunts, fiddling his keys. Earl sees 'em come and sees 'em go on both sides of the bars, he's a philosopher. "Had me a bowel movement, Mr. Larabee," he confided, good-natured now that he felt comfortable again. But noticing Tolen, he frowned deeply and grasped the man's upper arm. "How'd *you* get in here?"

Cory signaled to Earl to let that weasel go. He was feeling magnanimous now that he was safe, and winked at Friend Ed through the bars after the door clanged. All the while, Jim Tolen had been eyeing him with that sliding look of the mean dog sneaking around behind with a plan to bite, and damned if he didn't spit his brown tobacco chaw on Cory's boots, in a loud wet squirt that would mean a fight for sure back where he came from.

Old Cory went stomping off after the guard, having had about enough of our rough company, and Tolen took advantage of this opportunity to ease up to the bars. Since the last time I'd seen him so close up, there was no improvement. Jim Tolen was the bitter end of centuries of inbreeding, with bad teeth and big bony ears and thick black brows that curved right down around those raccoon eyes. He gave off a dank chill of revenge and ancient deaths like the cold breath of an autumn wind down those dark ravines.

"Better not go spitting on the Persecutor, Jim," I whispered.

"Yeller Ed." His own whisper was hoarse, and we both nodded.

"For a little shit who's been looking up a mule's ass all his life, you're dressed up pretty smart there, Jim. Looks like you came by some stolen property."

"Maybe yer bein tried just for the one, Ed Watson, but you was in on both them hee-nus murders," Jim yelled for the Prosecutor's benefit, "and they ain't a man in the south part of the county as don't know that!" He turned back to me, nodding some more. "Yeller Ed. The Back-shooter. Ain't goin to parlay your way out of this one, you shitty bastard. Gone to string you up. And they's men waitin on you in Fort White as will take care of it in case they don't."

What kind of a jail was this, I wondered, where the prisoner had no legal protection—where some degenerate like this one could stroll right in and shoot an inmate through the bars? But of course any jail so easily entered might also be speedily departed. The Jasper jail would be a whole lot easier than Arkansas State Prison.

I put that idea aside for just a minute. The shoe slaps of Big Earl were pounding down on us, our interlude was coming to a close. I put my face close to the bars and fixed Jim's eye and murmured very fast and cold, "If I were you—and by that I mean a thieving white-trash Tolen—I would clear out of Fort White, because folks who have already had enough of your rat-fuck family might just want to finish up the job."

To talk that way once in a while does the heart good.

Tolen cocked his head back like a musket hammer, then snapped it forward, shooting his chaw into my face. My hand darted through the bars and grabbed his stripy shirt, and the cheap cloth tore as Earl spun him away, exposing a chicken chest so white under his red neck that a man might almost imagine he had bathed.

"Why, shit!" Jim screeched. He was clawing at that tear like he'd been scalded. "That's my new shirt!" he yelled, not knowing which man to revile. I cackled just to rub it in, I went reeling back against my cell wall, making the most of it. But life is peculiar, and somehow I felt a little sorry about Jim's cheap new shirt. I wanted to tear his rodent head off, but tearing a poor man's Sunday shirt was something else.

Again it hit me like a mule kick: Jim Tolen was not a poor man, not anymore. His dirty pockets were stuffed up with money that rightfully belonged to Watsons, and he was still selling off our land. The blood rush to my temples nearly felled me, as if I'd been stunned by a blow but had not fallen. I pressed my forehead hard to the cold steel. Somewhere back inside my brain, I was shouting at Jack Watson to stay out of it. It was too late.

You and your brothers stole our Watson land, and you will pay for that the same way—

—the same way they did? Those words had been following hard behind, they were right there in my mouth, ready to fly. Had I spoken them or not?

All color was gone out of the world. My foe stood dim and ghostly, making no sound. The Prosecutor's shadow neared, and the Guard behind, like Death's attendant, as if all listened to the echo of those words shouted out by someone else. Then time resumed, the morning fell back into place, the redbird sang tentatively outside my window.

My hasty laugh clattered away like an empty bean can dropped on this concrete floor. I watched the Prosecutor, who was watching me. The People of the State of Florida were watching this caged human being, that's how alone I felt—not lonely so much as separate, cut off from others, yearning for something beyond reach.

I winked at Call-me-Cory, who smiled thinly. "*The same way they did?* Guard? You heard what the prisoner just said, correct?"

"I ain't deaf." Earl gave me a reproachful look, shrugging his shoulders.

"Of course not, Guard. Please recollect carefully when I call on you to testify."

"Ain't goin to ask *me?*" Jim Tolen whined. "I ain't *never* gone to forget them devil's words!" Tolen vowed he would take the witness stand and testify, but

Larabee, intent on Earl, told him sharply to be quiet. "I'll come by later, get your deposition," he warned Earl, "before it slips your mind."

"Can't write nothin except only my *X*," Earl grumbled. Jim Tolen instantly produced a scrap of paper and a pencil stub and started scrawling, to prove that he suffered no such limitation.

To the Prisoner, the Prosecutor tipped his hat. "Three witnesses to an unsolicited admission of a deadly motive. I am confident, Ed, that the jury will see it that way, too. So I advise you, Ed, to reconsider and accept the State's generous offer."

"What generous offer?" Tolen shrilled as Earl dragged him away. "You ever turn that killer loose, he'll hunt me down! Shoot me in cold blood like he done my brothers!"

Thin Jim wasn't afraid of that, not really. When he turned and winked at me, he wore a twisty grin, hard as a quirt.

That evening, trying to clear my mind, I concluded that Ed Watson would come out all right. For all his cleverness, this State's Attorney was a stupid man. In his effort to suck up to me, he had shown his cards. His career was like the carrot rigged in front of the donkey. It was all he saw.

The Prosecutor was already in Cole's pocket, so despite his bluster, I was not going to hang. He was too scared of losing. A guilty plea would let everyone off easy, get the black sheep safely locked away. The only way I would make such a mistake was because I was so greedy for survival that I would suffer for the rest of my life being caged and fed and watered behind bars like a wild animal.

Over the years I have grown a nose for traps. I got a whiff from Carrie's note and another from Walter and Eddie: better a jailbird than a hanged man in our nice family. They were scared to death of such a scandal, and would not let it happen. If I kept my head, I was going to be acquitted, because none of my family had the guts to see me hung.

*

Ladies sometimes ask why such an amiable man has so often found himself in so much trouble. And I say, Ma'am, I don't go *looking* for trouble—here I let my voice go soft, lower my lids a little, tragic and mysterious—but when trouble comes to me, why, I take care of it. I guess I answered that way first to Mamie Smallwood.

Les Cox loves that kind of stuff as much as Kate fears and despises it. I have found it useful, and sometimes it's not entirely nonsense. But in that late summer of 1908, I faced the fact that I had not always taken care of trouble the right way. I had never admitted, for example, that a lot of it was really my own fault. Grandfather Artemas's gentleness and weakness had undermined our old plantation; the bad character of his ring-eyed son had completed that loss and driven the industrious grandson into exile. And of course, that ruinous start in life had forced me to desperate measures in my worthy determination to make something of myself and restore our Clouds Creek name.

All that was true. Yet here I was over fifty years of age, jailed and disgraced, with a mob outside howling to see me hung, and all my savings pissed away to pay the lawyers—the time had come to look the situation in the eye. "Well, dammit, Ed," as Bembery once said, "this ain't the first time and it ain't the second, neither, so you better think about changin your thinkin."

That is a whole lot easier said than done.

Some would say that Edgar Watson is a bad man by nature. I don't believe that men are born with a bad nature. I like to think there is forgiveness and some hope of Heaven for this feller yet. All my life I have struggled hard to mend my ways, done the best I could, and I always believe that next time I will make it.

I enjoy people, most of 'em, but I get much too angry much too fast, and by the time I come clear, trouble has caught up with me again. Maybe I learned too early in my life that if a man won't stand up for himself, stand fast and hard, some other man will put him six feet under. Most Americans these days don't have to think that way, but on the frontiers where there was no law, a man who did not think that way would be a goner.

I have taken life. For that, I will always be sorry. Generally, I have not done it for financial reasons. How many of these "robber barons" who are making America's great fortunes can say the same?

The Persecutor was right, I am Ed Watson. I am Ed Watson for better, Jack Watson for worse. Ed Watson is the man I was created. Those who think I was created wrong can go to church and take it up with God.

*

The new trial started on July 10, and testimony concluded on August 3, when the hung jury, unable to agree upon a verdict, was dismissed. In September, Cone petitioned for another change of venue, and in October Judge Palmer moved the trial to Madison County. If I lost at Madison, I decided, I would break out of its dinky jail, run for the Islands.

When I told Reese about my plan, Frank whispered gleefully, "We is fixin to ex-cape, just like old times!" Remembering how we crossed the Arkansas, a lilt came into Black Frank's voice, almost as if he hoped we would be convicted. (I did not mention the possibility of help from Cox.) Not once had this man reproached me for dumping that shotgun in his furrow, even though it might cost him his life. I had thanked him for this, assuring him he was a credit to his people whether the white folks strung him up or not.

By now our attorney had assembled a whole covey of well-paid young lawyers. I was already in debt to my son-in-law, and Kate Edna was warning me that we were broke. Finally I asked her to get word to Cox to visit me. Being afraid of him, Kate Edna was wary, but I hushed her protests.

Cox came in and looked over the jail. We got the details settled. Shaking hands, I squinted back at him man to man just for old times' sake—the Frontier Code. I owed him that much.

*

In Madison County, the trial took place in mid-December, and the defense got off to a fine start in the local paper: "The defendant Watson is a man of fine appearance, and his face betokens intelligence in an unusual degree. That a determined fight will be made to establish the innocence of the defendants is evidenced in the imposing array of lawyers employed in their behalf."

Strangely distressed, Kate paid me a visit in my cell. She had already arranged to sell some of our land to pay the legal bills, just as instructed. When I took her in my arms to comfort her, she confessed that she felt sick, then begged me to turn away while she tended to her person, modestly preparing, as I thought, to perform her wifely duty. Instead, she produced a thin packet of cloth bound tight around a small sheath knife in light deerskin, which Cox had told her I had ordered for the escape. She was to conceal it "on her person"—the skunk had winked at her—then bring it straight to me. When she did not understand, he had whispered slyly that she was to insert it "you-know-where, and kind of squeeze it, hold it snug there" when she visited the jail—

I roared with rage, I cursed him for such sly, vicious abuse. Mortified, Kate wept. She would not look at me. When the guard came running at the din, I bribed him to step out for a long smoke. Stiff and shy, Kate removed her undergarments and knelt astride me as I sat on the thin cot. I raised her skirts and settled her warm sweet hips onto my lap, gently rocking her, then not so gently. She murmured into my ear that she still hurt a little, but it was too late then, it had been too long, I had to have her. Afterwards I sat her beside me and took her hand and warned her I was not a man to tolerate a hanging or labor my life out on the chain gang. If I was convicted, I intended to escape that very night, back to the Islands, and I would send for her once I was sure that all was well.

"All will never be well, Mr. Watson," poor Kate mourned. "Not in the Islands." I had never seen her look so stricken. What had made Chatham Bend scarcely bearable for Kate had been her dear Laura, who was now estranged from us due to the bitter feelings in the Collins family. Kate said hurriedly that what she meant—well, she'd been thinking that, all year round, the Island climate might be bad for children. When I said she need not return permanently to the Islands but could spend more time at Fort White, she cried out, "How can I stay at Fort White? You can't imagine how those people look at me!" Around her eyes was a shadow like a bruise. "Our neighbors are saying you helped Leslie kill those men!"

"Kate?" I lifted my fingers to gently brush fallen hair out of her eyes, which were streaming tears. "What do you wish to know?"

She made a little squeak, like a caught mouse. "If you and Leslie didn't do it, then who did?" She jumped up and rushed to the cell door. I tried to soothe her while she waited for the guard, but she only put her hands over her ears and shook her head.

*

Ol' Jim Cole (that Merry Olde Soul) had bent the ear of everybody in the state capital, cajoling them to talk sense to the Judge. After that, he came on down to Madison, helped pick the jury. By trial time, Fred Cone had six assistants who kept themselves busy running up my bills in their efforts to suborn witnesses. In the end, the prosecution's "jailhouse confession by Defendant Watson" was not panning out as Larabee had hoped, because the defense had led the jury to mistrust Jim Tolen and the guard. In the end, the only witness left who might do harm was Calvin Banks, who was concentrating so hard on his duty as a citizen that he clean forgot that his Mist' Edguh might be hung. Cone and his staff had given up trying to bribe Calvin, they just wanted him off the stand as fast as possible.

Cox came to Madison to testify for the defense. Once again, he made a good impression, declaring earnestly that Mr. Watson had always liked and respected Commissioner Tolen, which was true. However, his real mission here, as Cone explained, was to "influence" Calvin Banks. At one point in Calvin's testimony, Leslie feigned outrage at Calvin's lies, jumping up to point a warning finger at the witness. Another time, he tried to spook him, rising up in the back row like a haunt until Calvin noticed him, then running his forefinger across his throat. Though Cox sank down quick before the Prosecutor could protest, that mule-headed old nigger stopped speaking and remained silent. Cone whispered, "He is finished." Calvin was frightened, all right, but he wasn't finished.

In that silence, the old man raised his arm, slow as a prophet, and pointed his old and crooked finger straight at Leslie. The courtroom saw that bony finger aimed straight at the young man in the back row, as if Cox and not

Watson were the man on trial. There was a stir as Cox stood up and left the room, scared that Old Calvin would identify him to the Judge as the second man near the victim's body on the Junction Road. Puzzled, the Judge struck his gavel, calling for order, and Calvin nodded, returning to his dogged testimony.

*

The jury was out less than an hour, enjoying Jim Cole's cigars. Mr. E. J. Watson was acquitted, and so was the Negro Reese. (Since no witness testified for Frank or against him, he would have been hung along with me had the verdict gone the other way.) When the verdict was read, Frank scarcely looked up. He showed no emotion.

The Judge discharged us there and then, he went so far as to bid me Merry Christmas—I'd clean forgotten it was Christmas the next day. Attorney Cone smiled and shook my hand and shuffled his papers back into his case. The life or death of E. J. Watson was all in the day's business. Fat Jim Cole, born to make noise, came forward with a hearty shout and slapped me on the back the way he might slap a heifer on the rump. He owned me now, that's what that slap informed me. Cole wheezed at me, "Now dammit, Ed, we sold our souls to get you off. You get back to the Islands while the getting's good and stay there. And try to stay out of trouble on the way!" His mouth was laughing but his eyes were not as he stood there ready to receive my gratitude. I felt none. Suppose I had pled guilty, the way he wanted? I opened my mouth, but not a word came out. I let him grab my hand and shake it. I looked past him at Frank Reese, by the wall. Frank seemed to have forgotten where he was.

Cole moved away without my thanks, red in the face. The Persecutor was congratulating Attorney Cone, winking and joking. "Why are you hanging around here, Ed?" Larabee called out, throwing his arm around Cone's shoulders. "You going to miss us?" There had been no real trial at all, only amateur theater, some light farce. All the lawyers on both sides that day had known in advance, perhaps from Tallahassee, how my trial for my life was going to come out.

Getting set three times for the same trial was like getting set three times for making love. Leaving that building, I was still nerved up and edgy. Old Calvin was across the street, saddling up his mule for the long ride home across north Florida to Ichetucknee. He would wear his white shirt and Sunday suit all the way there, sleep where night found him. Kate clutched at my arm but I shook her off and walked over to confront him. "I'se glad, Mist' Edguh"—that is what he said. That old slave kept right on hitching at his cinches. "I sho is mighty glad dey has set you free." Then why had he testified, goddamnit, against a white man he had known nearly forty years?

Calvin blinked and turned to look at me, surprised. "Tol' me tell the Judge the truth and nothin but the truth, so help me God, Mist' Edguh," he explained. I nodded, very grim, to throw a scare into him. "Tol' me to speak out," he continued. "Called dat de bounden duty of de Merican citizen, called dat de solemn duty of de Negro. Said black folks dat doan speak up for de truth, doan speak up like *mens,* dey best go back to bein slaves again. I never thought about it dat way, Mist' Edguh. So I done what Mist' Larabee instruct me, cause he promise me. Promise dat what dis ol' darkie say won't make no difference, Mist' Edguh gone to walk out of de courthouse a free man. And here you is!"

But Calvin's voice had diminished as he spoke. Like a creature slowing, sensing danger, he had intuited what I was thinking. He cleared his throat, then asked me shyly if I aimed to kill him. When I said my neighbors might take care of that, this ornery old feller gave me his sly smile. "Nosuh, Mist' Edguh, ain' Calvin they gwine take care of. I was you, I'd stay away from them home woods a *good* long while!" Despite his smile, he looked tired and sad, as if I were a likely youth who had gone wrong, and nothing to be done about it any longer. "I sho hated to tell whut I done seed, Mist' Edguh," he said. "I sho is thankful dem white folks paid me no mind."

"Watch out for Leslie," I said, and turned and walked away.

Frank Reese could not go home to Fort White, either. Even if Cox weren't running around loose, he was not safe there and probably never would be. Frank looked as weary as a man can look who is cold and hungry on a winter night at Christmas, without friends, family, future, or one dime in his pocket, and no place to sleep.

"Frank," I said, "you come on south with us."

Chapter 9

Modern Times

On the first day of 1909, on the new railway, Mr. E. J. Watson and his new family crossed the Alva Bridge over the Calusa Hatchee and rumbled downriver into Fort Myers Station. I sent Frank over to Niggertown—or Safety Hill, as it was called, because that was where those folks felt safe after evening curfew—to round up a few hands while the baggage was transferred to Ireland's Dock to be loaded aboard Captain Bill Collier's *Falcon*. Since the coming of the railroad, the WCTU had sent Miss Carrie Nation, and a circus had also paid a call, complete with elephant. The first stock-roaming ordinance, fought by the cattlemen for twenty years, now protected the public thoroughfares and trampled gardens, and Indian mounds up and down the river were being leveled for white shell for cement paving. When Henry Ford had visited Mr. Edison, Walter and Carrie had been invited there to dinner, and not long after that, the banker and his friend Jim Cole had bought Ford motorcars so they could go tooting north and south the entire quarter mile from one end of this metropolis to the other. Jim Cole was the kind of man whose self-esteem depended on the biggest and the best—in this case, the most expensive auto in town. Quick turnover of everything from real estate to cattle had always been the secret of his success, and he soon replaced his Ford with a bright red Reo. Meanwhile, Mr. Edison had leased Cole's steamer to bring royal palms from Cuba to Riverside Avenue, to ornament his Seminole Lodge and decorate Fort Myers for the tourists.

On Riverside Avenue, I rapped the banker's new brass knocker. In a moment little Faith tugged the lace back at the window. Carrie's daughters were only slightly older than Ruth Ellen and Addison, and I thought our girls might play and get acquainted while Kate washed up and rested for our voyage. When I waggled my fingers, Faith's pretty face flew open like a flower and then vanished; she was running to the door. I heard Eddie's voice and after that a silence—her face at the window was the last we were to see of my sweet granddaughter. No one else appeared. We stared stupidly at the closed door. Begrimed and hot and cranky from the train, my poor rumpled family waited dumbly in the street while Papa wrestled with his rage, as furious as Jacob with the Angel. I rapped again, three good hard knocks, and this time the door cracked and a black wench stared out as if the anti-Christ Himself had come to call.

"Tell your Missus," I growled, "that Mr. Watson—"

The girl disappeared and Carrie stood there instead. "Well, I do declare!" my daughter cried. Her smile was terrible. She did not come forward and did not invite us in. Plainly we had been preceded by my son and son-in-law, bearing word from north Florida that Mr. Watson had gotten away with murder. "Papa," she whispered. "Walter . . ." She didn't finish, and she didn't need to.

"Since when does Walter wear the pants around your house?" With those ice-hard, bitter words I turned to go before I uttered something worse, my heart dull and heavy in my chest.

"Papa? Please, Papa," she begged.

I whirled upon her. "If your husband and brother thought me guilty, why did they testify for the defense?"

"Oh Papa, what choice—"

"I'll have them indicted for perjury!" But my sour joke went right past my bewildered family, and Carrie was too overwrought to smile at anything. Perhaps she feared her neighbors might be watching. Kate Edna stared wide-eyed from father to daughter, discovering how these Watsons worked for the first time.

The servant girl came down the steps with a tray of milk and cookies, which she held out fearfully toward my children as if feeding wild creatures through the bars. I recognized Mandy's good rose tray, given to her by the Collins family as a wedding present and passed along to Carrie, whom she adored. Without my say-so, nobody would touch a cookie, and the darkie was so rattled by the children's hungry staring that she banged the tray down on the stoop before them like a plate of dog food and ran back inside.

Carrie sank down on one knee and picked up the rose tray. She offered it again, eyes brimmed with tears. Addison was the first to crack. He reached, but my eye stopped him. "We came as kinfolks, not as beggars. We'll be going along." I tried in vain to put more warmth into my voice, because Carrie was at least trying to be nice, unlike her brother Eddie. That righteous bastard who had eaten us out of house and home for the past eight years at Fort White had not even come out to greet us, a discourtesy I did not plan to forgive.

"Thank your kind sister for her hospitality," I told Ruth Ellen, who curtsied. Little Ad did, too. "No, Ad," I told him. "Gentlemen pay their respects like this." And I put one hand behind my back and with the other lifted my black hat. Holding her eye, I bowed to my beautiful Carrie, who burst into tears, knowing that her rejection of her father would be the last one, and that in all likelihood, we would never meet again. "Oh Papa!" she cried. But we went away with resolution, leaving that nice young Mrs. Langford in the public street with her rose tray of milk and cookies. Addison fretted, looking back, but he knew better than to say one word.

"I love you, Papa!" Carrie called, despite the neighbors. For that small courage, I almost forgave her. I lifted my hat a little but did not turn. "My daughter loves me," I told Kate, ironic. My unhappy wife struggled to smile, but her dry upper lip had hung up on her front teeth so she looked away.

Poor Kate had had a dismal year, with her husband penned in county jails, threatened with hanging, and her Fort White neighbors cold or downright hostile, all but her old family friend and faithful admirer Herkimer Burdett, who had come around often, it appeared, to see how his childhood sweetheart might be faring—a little more often (according to the leering Cox) than her husband might have cared for. When I mentioned this, poor Kate burst out that Herkie had been very kind, and that the only one who had hung around "in the wrong way" was Leslie himself.

"Were I to die, would you go straight to Herkie?" I demanded. Kate colored as if slapped. Shaking her head and refusing to answer, she busied herself over our little boy. At Dancy's Stand at the head of Ireland's Dock, I consoled my doleful tribe with candy, fruit, and peanuts I could not afford. The last of my money lined the pockets of my attorneys, and once again I was faced with gnawing debt.

Lucius turned up on the run before we sailed. He would soon turn twenty and was already taller than his daddy. He said he was coming with us, hefting his satchel to show me he meant business.

"How about your job?"

"I like boats better, Papa. I like Chatham. You'll find some worthwhile work for me, I know."

I nodded slowly. "This young feller is your brother Addison," I said. Lucius shook the hand of Little Ad, who was sitting on my shoulders. At Addison's age, living in Arkansas, Lucius had no memory of his father nor even an idea what he might look like. When Lucius said, "How do you do?" the little boy thrust out a peanut, which Lucius had the courtesy to eat straight from his sticky fingers. "An excellent peanut," Lucius assured Ad, wishing he hadn't when Ad unstuck another. I felt a great wave of affection for these younger sons, all the more poignant because Rob and Eddie were my sons no longer.

*

Old Man Waller emulated the habits of his pigs, which seemed to have the run of Chatham Bend. A sweet reek of hog manure lay everywhere, and the house was in rancid condition. Also, Green was a rough carpenter at best, even his hog shed creaked in the faintest breeze. In recent weeks two prime shoats had been lost to a marauding panther, and in great uneasiness Green demanded in the fierce tones of the drunkard that their worth be deducted from his salary. That offer meant nothing in my present straits, since he had gone more or less unpaid since his arrival. Green Waller saw the Bend as his last home, with all the hogs and moonshine a man could ask for. He had so little use for money that he had purposely lost count of what I owed him, in his fear that if I paid him off, I might get rid of him. This poor old reiver was younger than I was by five years but, due to a sadly misspent life, had overtaken me in our race for the grave and now appeared to be somewhat my elder.

We arrived on a winter norther and that wind was cold, with iron seas out in the Gulf and swift gray skies. Kate seemed stunned and the rest dispirited as if lost in strange low country. I put them right to work as the only cure. We patched mesh screens and painted them with oil to keep out sand flies, swept out spiders and scraped old crust, rust, and vermin from the stove. We burned off and harvested the half-wild crop and brewed a batch of our white lightning, to tide Green over into the next year.

With his growing family, Henry Thompson stayed mostly at Lost Man's with the Hamiltons, so Lucius took over the boats. On Sundays we fished or hunted for the pot while Kate went crabbing with the children, but without Laura Collins and her gales of sweet laughter, most of Kate's fun seemed to be gone. The poor thing felt banished to a purgatory of gray humid heat, unrelenting mosquitos, and the endless dull and raining greens of mangrove wilderness, with no end to her loneliness and nothing to look forward to, since we could never go back to Fort White. From her very first day back in the Islands, she felt imprisoned by the heavy rivers and dark walls and the alkali waste of salt prairie and hard scrub behind the cane fields, a fate made worse by nagging fears of the calamities that might befall her children—tropical disease, flood or hurricane and drowning, alligators, panthers, poisonous serpents, and wild Indians, to name only the ones which scared her most.

These Mikasuki or Cypress Indians, who called themselves *At-see-na-hufa*, often made camp at Possum Key on their way north from Shark River. When Lucius later came across a strong fresh-water spring right off that island, and tried to be helpful by telling them about it, they heard him out without expression, grunting once in a while to keep him going. When he was finished, they laughed for a long time, paying no attention to him anymore. We concluded that the At-see-na-hufa had always known about that spring, but having had almost everything stolen away from them, they never told the Frenchman while he lived there, preferring to watch that mean old man rig his rain gutter and barrels in the dry season.

Sometimes they stopped by the Bend, and we did our best to put something in their stomachs, if only our bad coffee and hard biscuits. One of the young Osceolas was a leader of their band, down around Shark River. He was some kind of cousin to Old Man Robert Harden's Maisie, who had been born an Osceola, too. I was careful to stay on the good side of these people, in case one day my luck ran out and I had to take refuge in the Glades.

By 1909, the Indians weren't wary anymore, they were coming in to the trading posts twelve dugouts at a time, and every dugout loaded down with gator hides and deerskins, coon and otter. What they wanted most was corn liquor and old-time Winchesters, the better to finish off what game was left. George Storter would be out on his dock morning, noon, and night measuring up hides—paid by the foot. Stacked 'em up on a long sawhorse table in front of the store and paid 'em off in cash. Then the Indians went through the store, paying for each article one after the other, stayed till they spent every last dime that George had given 'em. They returned into the Glades with their dugouts just as heavy-loaded as they were when they came in. One feller I knew who used to trade at Smallwood's was put to death by his own people. I guess those redskins knew what they were doing.

By the summer of 1909, times were hard for every settler on this coast. Fishing, hunting, and trapping had been poor for years, and what was left of the game and the furred animals were retreating deeper and deeper into the Glades. Needing guns where bow and arrows had sufficed before, those Cypress Indians, said to be so close to nature, must have concluded that nature was finished, and the red man's future, too, for they were shooting every deer and squirrel they could get a bead on. Stripped off the skins, left the carcasses to rot, and headed straight back to the trading posts to buy more liquor. In the end our deer became so scarce that even Tant Jenkins gave up hunting and went out to the clam flats off Pavilion, only to find that clams, too, were scarce due to Collier's dredging.

As for the plume hunters, the House boys and their Lopez cousins were traveling all the way south to Honduras to find egrets, but those foreign plumes were mostly confiscated by the customs. Gregorio Lopez came home deathly sick, and his boys lugged him off the boat on his chicken feather mattress, with the customs men trotting alongside asking hard questions. And Old Man Gregorio just rolled his eyes back, croaking, "This here is my deathbed, boys, so don't go harassin a poor old feller that is givin up the ghost before his time." But Gregorio could have died right there as far as those federals were concerned and it wouldn't have done him a single bit of good, because one of 'em spotted a white quill sticking out where the old stitching had unraveled. He drew forth a fine egret plume and twirled it in the sun, saying, "If this here is a chicken mattress, then what I got here in my hand must be the prettiest white leghorn feather in the U.S.A." Before they finished the dispute, Old Man Gregorio had made a full recovery and got up off that mattress and stalked away utterly disgusted, having given those pesky customs men a taste of a proud Spaniard's scorn.

*

Walter Alderman of Chokoloskee had married Marie Lopez back in 1906, and because there was no work to be had along the coast, I had taken him back north to Fort White to work for me. At the time of my trials, my lawyers tried to subpoena him to testify to my good character and generous nature, but suddenly this feller "was no longer to be found in the county of Columbia," Sheriff Purvis told the court, "having returned to his residence in the Ten Thousand Islands." My old nemesis Sheriff Knight, who was eager to assist the prosecution, had been unable to locate him, either, and I knew why; Walter was hiding at his father-in-law's place back in Lopez River.

It looked like Walt Alderman had slunk away as soon as my troubles started. My Kate and his Marie had become friends, but I could not promise Kate I would be nice to him. Walter's feeble excuse turned out to be that he had to go home to take care of his pregnant wife, the favorite of fierce old Gregorio, who had never abandoned his belief—which I now shared—that any daughter of Gregorio Lopez was much too good for the likes of this young cracker.

To the delight of her friend Kate, who rushed off to help tend her, Marie gave birth to Gregorio's grandson two months after our return, in late winter of 1909. Like my mother (who claimed that her "ancestral Addisons and Mountacues" were buried in Westminster Abbey), Walter's mother liked to say that the Aldermans were descended from the Emperor Charlemagne. That never meant much to Gregorio, whose peon forebears back in Spain had toiled their lives away beneath the iron heel of the same cruel Emperor Carlos. Even so, Marie would carry on as if her little Joe's squalls and smells were regal attributes.

I finally forgave Marie's husband, but I could not forgive the Walter Langfords. Carrie had explained in a long letter that as a banker—as "the civic leader" who had brought in the new railroad—her husband could not afford the breath of scandal. He had put his foot down, Carrie pleaded, though we both knew well whose foot carried the real heft in her household. (Like many women with weak husbands, my daughter pretended that her spouse was so domineering that his castle quaked in terror of his wrath.) "He has forbidden me to have you in our house," Carrie wrote in a fond tear-blotted missive to her "dearest Daddy," professing a daughter's heartbreak over her loss.

To mollify me, Kate made excuses for my daughter. Surely the idea of a younger stepmother would take getting used to for someone who so adored her daddy—

"You're talking nonsense, Kate." Poor Kate went soft as a crushed peach, and Lucius fixed me with that enigmatic look which was as far as he would go in criticism of his father. He had grown into a good-looking young man, tall and slim with brown-blond hair and greenish eyes. He did not smile falsely in order to please, as Eddie did, and in his gentle and soft-spoken way he let you know his mind. I said to Kate, "Come here, then, girl," and sat her comfy bottom on my knee to draw some of the sting from my harsh words. A moment later, it was all forgotten.

Our First Family Car

After that visit to the Langford house, I gave up all plans and ambitions for Deep Lake. Dead-tired after months in county jails, I could not muster the will to fight my way out of debt on this remote plantation when so much attracted me to modern enterprise in the great world. My cane fields were in ragged shape, sadly weeded up and overgrown, and I had no great hope for this year's harvest. Bill Collier's clam-dredge operation was still under way, and a small tannin acid factory had started up in the forests of huge mangroves at Shark River. But there were no good jobs at Shark River, either, only rough work for a few drunken Indians—crude manual labor quite unsuitable, Lucius teased me, for the great southwest coast entrepreneur whom Jean Chevelier had nicknamed Emperor Watson.

One day in Fort Myers, I ran into Cole and Langford in Edwards' Bar across from the courthouse. Both looked puffy from too much time indoors sitting on money. Walter's hair was disappearing, and neither man had a handle on his drinking. In fact, Big Jim had been forbidden by court order to set foot in this saloon, though his friend Sheriff Tippins did not enforce it. As for the banker, he looked seedy and unshaven, despite his slicked-down strands of hair and that three-piece suit.

When I came in, my son-in-law lurched to his feet and left without a greeting. "Don't let your customers smell that whiskey!" I shouted after him, intending to be heard in the whole saloon. Being trapped in his booth, Cole did not rise. With a poor smile, he waved me to a seat and asked me how my "cane patch" was progressing. I tried to ignore the sneer in that stupid question, but then, just to see the shock on that smug face, I told him coolly that I wished to buy his Ford automobile, which I understood he had replaced with that red Reo. I let him believe I had come to town expressly for that purpose.

"What with?" Cole jeered. His nose for money told him who was flat broke busted. But E. J. Watson had built a reputation as a man who made good on his debts, and Cole had no reason to doubt that I would restore my syrup operation in short order, and its profits, too.

"What's your collateral, Ed?" he said. I thought he was just meeting my bluff, but when he flagged the bartender and paid for two more whiskeys, I realized he was serious, and my heart thudded. I was not going to back down, not with Jim Cole.

"An up-and-coming truck farm in Columbia County."

"Who's on there now?"

"My mother and sister."

"Supposin you forfeit?" He cocked his head to peer at me, grinning again. "You fixin to shoot them ladies, Ed, or just run 'em off there?" I held his gaze, and he covered his nerves with that curly grin. "Where the hell you aim to *drive* the damn thing, Ed? Down to your dock and back?" When I said nothing, he asked for a business reference in town besides Walt Langford. I mentioned my friend Mr. Ben King, who had worked as a mechanic for Mr. Edison before opening this town's first garage. "Go on. Go talk to Ben. Right now," I said.

Ben King told Cole that Watson paid his debts and also paid his workers, never mind those rumors about "Watson Payday." A lot of those rumors had been spread, Ben told him, by a black man named Dave Smith, a former worker at the Bend. One day while this Dave was still around, little Ruth Ellen had wandered off while her mother was sewing out on the front porch, and got herself trapped in the red mangrove stilts along the riverbank. We found her all huddled up with fright, but otherwise all right. Well, this damn nigger told the Langfords' friend Frank Carson—he worked for Carsons in Fort Myers—that the frightened child wouldn't answer when I hollered, and that I had become so upset and angry that I shouted out, "If she is lost, I am going to kill her mother." Well, if I said that, I was drunk, and this damned

nigger knew that but talked anyway. Like everybody white or black in southwest Florida, Dave Smith was trying to make folks believe that he alone had
the inside story on Ed Watson.

I was fighting to stay in business and restore my good name. The last
thing I needed was more rumors. When I heard about it from Ben King, I
marched straight over to Frank Carson's place and demanded a word with
his damned big-mouth nigger. Carson refused me. Though I shouted, I did
not attack him, or even threaten further, knowing how urgent it was to behave circumspectly in Fort Myers. I said, "This isn't finished yet," just to un-
settle him. Well, Carson concocted a threat out of those words and
blackened my reputation even further. Trying to stop this erosion of my
name was like trying to stop Chatham River from eating at its edges in the
time of flood, with all the trees and mudbanks falling in.

Naturally Cole spread his tales, too, but my infamy didn't bother him one
bit when it came to extending credit. That same evening my Ford motorcar
rode south, lashed to the foredeck of the *Gladiator*. She was wrapped in tarps
against salt water, because with wind out of the south and that weight forward, my little schooner was shipping a hard spray over the bow. At
Chatham River, we worked upriver on the tide. Lucius fetched planks, and
we drove her off onto the bank hooting the horn—the first auto ever seen
in the Ten Thousand Islands. I had wanted that jalopy for a surprise, to lift
our spirits, and sure enough, the kids came whooping and piled right in and
jumped around the seats. There was no sign of Kate.

Frank Reese was standing in the kitchen doorway, wiping his hands on a
towel. The way that black man's head was cocked made clear that he questioned my good sense.

"Got her in a kind of swap," I told him, before he said something he might
regret.

"What you swap for her? Our pay?"

Reese's tone scared everyone, himself included. He stepped back inside,
and nobody said a word.

I stood waiting for him, getting my breath. If he didn't think better of it
and step outside again, there was going to be bad trouble.

He stepped out again. "My oh my," he said. Reese was still so angry that
his smile—his grimace—was fixed in a black death's-head.

Kate came outside slowly, in a daze. "What on earth can it be for?" she
whispered. "And how on earth are we to pay for it?" She burst into tears.
"What can you be thinking of, Mr. Watson?"

Annoyed because she had spoiled the children's fun, I told her that our
Fort White farm—her beloved "home upon the hill"—was the collateral.

She stared at me to make sure I was not teasing. "I have something on the stove," she gasped, and ran inside.

Intensely frustrated, I could not concentrate because thought was impossible in such a racket. Ruth Ellen had found the car horn—*toot-toot, toot-toot!* Cursing, I yanked her out of the front seat, making her cry. Addison scrambled out of the back seat, fleeing after his sister around the house. Only Lucius was left, observing me. I glared at him—*Well?* He shrugged and went inside. *"Damn!"* I yelled. I hurled my hat down on the ground, disgusted.

Alone with the new car, I was astonished at how fast the fun had ended. Then my folly struck me. It was true. I was losing hold.

From the doorway, Lucius's voice came gently, "Let's all go for a drive, then, Papa. I'll find the kids." Ruth Ellen and Ad ran out, miraculously cured. They sat on Lucius's lap and shrieked at the fireworks sputter as I cranked the motor, shrieked some more as we backed around the sugar works and rolled past the sheds and turned around in jerks and fits and starts, a drive of possibly one hundred yards before Ruth Ellen felt sick and vomited. I stopped the car, worn out and melancholy. The children ran inside, calling for Mama.

With the harvest finished, the cane crew was gone. Early next morning Sip and Lucius and Black Frank and I set to work hacking and clearing a half-mile road around the cane field edges. Having always been handy with boat engines, Lucius soon learned all there was to know about an auto motor—not tinkering so much as playing with every movable part, to see how it related to the rest. My son and I were never closer than we were that spring, laboring on our road to nowhere, laughing about it.

When the great day came—we waited until May Day—all but Kate piled into the jalopy and went for a memorial drive around the entire circumference of the Watson Plantation, chugging and honking, children screeching and dogs barking. All were good sports, though those little ones had not traveled far before turning greenish from the fumes and jolting. We only completed a single round before we had to stop.

Their mother watched us from the house, from an upper window. How pale her face looked, far away across the fields. In imposing this distraction, all I had done was to force that poor girl to face the truth that we could never return home to Fort White. The price of an acquittal rigged by powerful lawyers and politicians was banishment to this wilderness for life.

*

In damp cloudy weather—constant in most seasons—we were "in the mosquitos" all day long, but except at daybreak and in early evening, when the biting insects were at their worst, my new children, like the older ones before them, loved to play around the water edge and the dock and boats. They were never happy very far from water, and I was never quite at ease while they were there. The river current was so swift and strong, and I reminded them about those gators up to fifteen feet which came down out of the Glades with the spring rains. Whether or not that huge croc was still out there, I could not be sure.

I did my best to put a scare into the children, describing how those enormous reptiles cruised the riverbanks hunting unwary animals and wading birds, how these monsters would drift close in under the mangroves and hang there unseen, as motionless as submerged logs in that murky water. Eye ridges and snout tips might be glimpsed but usually not. Even those visible on the far bank could slip into the water without sound, crossing the current underneath the surface. Gators had snatched more than one dog off our bank, and could seize a small child fooling in the shallows in one lunge and thrash of that armored tail and then be gone, leaving only spreading circles in the water.

Sometimes sharks came nosing up the river with the tide. There were still cottonmouths around the swamp roots and rattlers back in the canebrake, and coral snakes still took the sun on the warm concrete around the sugar mill and cistern. But bear and panther tracks no longer crossed the Bend. Those shy and wary creatures were all gone.

When they weren't fooling in the boats, the children were sailing sea grape leaves or chucking sticks into the cistern, which was straight-sided and slippery with green slime. Lucius rigged a rope ladder, just in case, but knowing they would panic with the first mouthful of black water, I forbade them to go anywhere near.

One day, Ruth Ellen disobeyed me. I came up behind and grabbed her up and held her way out over that black tarn. *Any child who falls in there is a goner!* I was bellowing. My poor little girl screamed and screamed until she lost her breath and her face started to turn blue, for fear I might let her go. Kate got very upset with me for scaring the child so badly. Lucius nodded but said nothing. I said somberly, "Better scared than dead." We spoke no more about it. After that day, Ruth Ellen dreaded the cistern and would not go near it, and would not let Addison go near it, either. She would fly around him like a sheepdog, chivvying our little boy away from a sad death.

*

By mid-spring, all my fields were planted, and in the summer we rested before the harvest. Where a coco palm had fallen in the river, Lucius built an eddy pool walled in by brush where the kids were protected from the scaled marauders. Even so, he kept a sharp eye on the river, and he kept a rifle with him.

I had never seen Lucius so contented. He felt at home there on the Bend, he felt appreciated, being good at everything he did. My Kate loved him because he was so gentle—an antidote to her old brute of a husband, I suppose. (Comparing my own youth with his made me a little sad—not envious but sad, as if my life were somehow incomplete.) That young feller cheered her up and kept her company, and offered whatever time he had to spare to his new little half sister and brother, who adored him, too. Lucius spent hours teaching them about wild creatures by means of whimsical stories he made up.

One evening, he described to us the big panther scat with its cat twist at one end which he had found on the hot white sand mound of a croc nest, back behind the beach at Lost Man's. The scat had been dropped in the cat's spring away from the nest—Lucius had reconstructed the whole event from tracks—when what looked like a driftwood log back in the salt brush at the bay edge turned suddenly into a crocodile, risen on its quick short legs to drive the prowler from her nest. Lucius eventually dug out the cache of leathery white eggs, just for the feel of them, and made the children reimagine with him the warmth and firmness of those curious oblong shapes pulsing with ancient life.

On another day, east of Flamingo, he had traveled far up Taylor Slough to the hardwood hammocks, where in the airy stories of the huge mahoganies, he had seen a small swift flock of nine lime-colored parakeets—that beautiful bird so often spoken of by old-time plume hunters, especially Jean Chevelier, who had presided over parakeet extermination in all the upper rivers of this coast. That evening, as Lucius remembered, he had first seen the round pearly glow of the star spider, and caught a platter-sized green turtle for his dinner.

Though Lucius loved this remote region just as I did, it excited him in a quite different way. It pleased him greatly that the last wild Indians in America—"never defeated by the U.S. Army"—lived east of us on the far hammocks in "the grassy river" as they called the Glades, and that every attempt to open this water wilderness by dredging up some kind of road had foundered in the muck and broken limestone or been driven back by the rains and heat and the mosquitos. Lucius saw that hell back there as beautiful, describing the strange vast prospect that had opened when he, the intruder, had ventured up these inland creeks beyond the tidal reach. The mangrove walls diminished and thinned out, with glimpses of vast space and light beyond, and one emerged on the vast savanna grasslands, stretching away as far as the eye could see, all the way across to the east coast.

"Except that the sawgrass is taller than a man and sharp-edged as a razor," I would growl, "with nothing beneath but water, muck, and jagged limestone solution holes that will tear a man's boots to pieces in a day."

"And poisonous snakes and poison trees—all sorts of interesting things," he said, smiling, which was why the Everglades would endure when all the rest of the wild places in the country were overrun by roads bringing more people. But Lucius never criticized my ideas for development of this west coast, reserving his comments for the new canals being gouged through the sawgrass east of Okeechobee. The Governor's canal projects were encouraging more talk of a cross-Florida highway which would lay open "the hidden Everglades" once and for all. Tactful because Nap Broward was my friend, he said he hoped that all that dredging in the headwaters would not muddy up our "paradise" on this Lost Man's coast.

"*Paradise!*" cried Kate. "My goodness, Lucius!"

The Stowaway

Each Tuesday, running north to Everglade for mail and trade, I stopped over to eat lunch with Bembery Storter, who would take a consignment of my syrup on the *Bertie Lee* and bring back staples and supplies. Bembery had installed the first gas engine ever seen in a local schooner, a two-cylinder twelve-horsepower Globe, bright Christmas red. Once a month I would accompany him to Key West, staying the night and sometimes two with those jolly kindergarten teachers, the sisters Metz from Tampa, who now ran a boardinghouse on White Street.

Key West is and always was half-Yankee. Even way back in the old century, its attitudes were all mixed up when it came to niggers. Many people were upset by that, including my friend Gene Roberts and his brothers, who ran the old *Estelle* from Flamingo to Key West, carrying outbound mail and cargo, bringing back mail and supplies. Melch, Jim, and Gene were not brought up to tolerate coloreds mixing in with whites, they would not put up with it. They'd go over to Key West and have a drink, walk arm-in-arm down the sidewalk, and any black man who failed to get the hell out of their way, they'd knock him down. One time they went into a restaurant, sat down, ordered their breakfast, Gene was telling me, and the next thing they knew, a great big ol' buck nigger walked right in and sat down at the next table. Well, those boys rared back and glared at him, and when he didn't leave, ol' Melch got up without a word and took his chair and wrapped it over that man's head, and Jim hauled him off the floor, tearing his collar, and booted his black butt into the street.

Key Westers disliked Mainlanders—one reason Walt Smith was not indicted for Guy Bradley's murder. So the Sheriff would say on the way to jail,

Well, here ye are again! The Mainlanders! And they'd say, Yessir, we sure are, and proud to say so!

Sheriff Richard Knight, returned to office, was as truculent as ever about E. J. Watson. One day he accosted me at Duval and First, on my way out of W. D. Cash Groceries, Provisions, and Ship Chandlery. He had heard that a wanted murderer named Melville might be hiding out at Chatham Bend, in which case I was harboring a known criminal.

Young Herbie Melville, known as Dutchy, had been notorious at Key West for several years. Back in 1904, when my friend Deputy Till tried to arrest him and his gang for breaking into a coffee shop at White Street and Division, this young feller grabbed Clarence's pistol, beat him to the floor with it, then took out his knife, started to scalp him. Bleeding, Clarence broke away and ran to borrow another weapon at the Mayor's house. Poor Clarence hadn't learned much from that time in the nineties when he tried to arrest me single-handed at the Bend, because without waiting for reinforcement, he returned to that coffee shop, where Melville shot and killed him. Dutchy was convicted and sentenced to be hung, but because his family had influence, the charge was reduced to manslaughter and a one-year sentence. Next, the jail rented his labor to the fire station, during which time he committed several robberies, covering his tracks by burning these places down. In destroying the Cortez Cigar Factory, however, he went too far. Murdering a law officer was one thing, but damaging rich men's property was a lot more serious, and the indignant judge sentenced this bad actor to thirteen years' imprisonment at hard labor.

Just recently, said Sheriff Knight, Dutchy Melville had escaped from the chain gang, but not before confiding to another convict (who had the ear of the authorities) that if he made it, he would head straight for Watson's Place at Chatham Bend. And the reason for *that*, the Sheriff said, looking me straight in the eye, was because this man Watson was well-known for hiring fugitives and other undesirable individuals as field hands.

I sometimes recruited field hands at Key West, mostly blacks but some white drifters, too. These men were called Buck and Doc and Slim and Blackie and John Smith. I never asked if they were chain-gang fugitives— that was their own business. Except for Green Waller, who had served his time—"paid my dues to society," as he put it—they accepted whatever pay was offered with no back talk. Anyway, they never stayed long, because working in the cane was hard and dangerous. Kate was unhappy that I gave this work to nameless men, fearing that one of them might harm the children, but Watson Syrup Company needed cheap labor for the harvest and that was that. In return for this vacation from the law, they put in their time until the smoke cleared someplace else. This way everyone came out ahead—sound business practice.

I told Knight I had not laid eyes on any Dutchy, and no Herbie either. I also told him I did not care for his insinuation that E. J. Watson had no respect for law and order. The Sheriff said, Them words of yours sound all right, Watson, but a man gets knowed by the company he keeps, ain't that right, too? And I said, Well, in that case, Sheriff, we'd better part company right now, because I have my good name to think about. And I tipped my black hat to him and kept on going.

Eddie's Bar had a stylish sign, DINING AND DANCING, NINE TO ELEVEN, FIGHTING FROM ELEVEN TO TWO. The cost of a drink was all that was required to enjoy this lively social situation. With so many good fights to choose from, any man of healthy tastes could fit right in. Knives and pistols were frowned upon, but that very night I had to wrench a loaded six-gun from a client's hand. He was dead drunk but still dancing, waving it around, and being in the mood to make a speech, I soon tired of his noise and bragging and gave this fool a taste of his own medicine, making him dance Oklahoma style. The one time I tried this in Tampa, I got thrown in jail, but Key West was a more roisterous town—seamen and soldiers, big ships in the harbor from all over the world—and nobody paid barroom horseplay much attention.

"Let's see can I work this thing!" I hollered, pretending I had never fired a gun and waving his shooting iron around real wild, the same way he did. It kept going off, made one hell of a racket, and with each shot I yelled in fear, as if I had no idea how to control it. I had this young feller struggling to control his stagger so as not to step across the neat half circle his six-gun was punching through the floor around his toes.

But when the cartridges ran out, he came up quick with another gun he had under his coat and made me dance in that same ungodly fashion. I tried to smile, stay calm about it. "Not many men, let alone boys, would try this game on Ed Watson," I warned him. But he hooted and went right ahead, and when his gun was empty and his friends dragged him out of there, he was still laughing. It was only after he was gone that Dick Sawyer sidled up and said, "Ain't that boy a ripsnorter? That is Dutchy Melville."

I was disgusted. This young pistolero had killed Clarence Till, a fair and well-liked lawman, and also robbed the businessmen and committed arson, and here he was, a local hero whom fools like Sawyer talked about with shining eyes. I'd seen this same public foolishness out West, time after time, whenever the outlaw had some style to his wildness. To join his pals at Eddie's Bar and draw attention to himself, show off, at the risk of being sent back to the chain gang—that was pure drunken stupidity. But because he got away with it, he made it seem dashing and defiant—*I am laughing at you and your damned law! What will you do about it?* I was never that kind, not even in the early years. I have wanted to be an honest and upright citizen all my life, and respect the law as well as I am able.

*

The next morning, headed home, I was somewhere off Shark River when the sky turned black and the weather caught up with the *Gladiator* in a hard squall. When I stuck my head into the forward cuddy to dig out my oilskins, I found myself looking straight into the muzzle of a six-gun. "Hell," I growled. I backed out on my knees and raised my hands. "What's that damn cannon for? This some kind of piracy on the high seas?"

"If I was you, I wouldn't talk so smart." The man climbing out after me had another Colt stuck in his belt. He was green olive in his color because he felt seasick down in that hot cuddy, but he looked like a pirate all the same— big nose, pocked skin, and hard black wire hair, a real mean hombre. And I knew better than to fool with him, because when he came out into the light, I recognized the selfsame sonofabitch who had made me do that dance in Eddie's Bar.

These cocky greenhorn pistoleros out to prove themselves tend to shoot first and think afterwards, if they think at all. Ever since pimply Billy the Kid caught the public fancy, the country had been plagued by boys like this, aiming to play as fast and loose as Billy. "Keep them hands high," he scowled, waving his big gun.

"I can't steer this schooner with no hands," I explained. "You'd better follow me back aft before she yaws on a big sea, maybe capsizes."

A flicker of fear crossed that swart face as he waved me aft. With that black muzzle hole right at my back, I felt a little queasy, kind of hollow. Even my skin winced, twitching away from the burning bullet. But I knew his weakness. If this kid had spent even one day on the water, he'd have known there was small risk of yawing and capsizing, not in a light wind with a lashed helm.

I freed the tiller while he swayed in the fresh air. He was sallow and dizzy, but sleepy-eyed and confident nonetheless. Frowning a little to keep his attention, I swung her off the wind and let her jibe. In a rush of canvas, that boom swung back across the hull and knocked him flying right over the gunwale. He'd heard that creak of wood behind him, but not knowing he should duck, he spun right into it.

If my stowaway hadn't grabbed a shroud, he would have gone overboard and stayed that way. I had no plan to come about and go back after him. As it was, he'd got separated from his gun, which he'd had to drop to grab that line, and now he was dragging in the water, hanging on to a rope fender with both hands. From the way he clutched, it was plain he could not swim.

When he hauled himself halfway up the side, grasping the gunwale, I leaned over and yanked the second Colt out of his belt. "Ah shit," he said, as if he'd dropped something, and went back down again, dragging heavily in the wash along the hull. He was very pale and short of breath, he thought he was a goner. I emptied the chamber of the Colt and tossed it into the cockpit after the first one. Then I took the tiller and lit up a cigar, letting him drag while the *Gladiator* resumed her course toward home.

"Can't swim too good," he gasped when he got his breath back. He looked like he was crying, having no way to wipe the sea out of his eyes. "I reckon my arms ain't goin to last much longer." I blew some cigar smoke down into his face to make him cough. His eyes snapped with black anger over getting himself into this fix, and naturally I was angry, too, with my own heart still pounding. Yet I had to admit that this boy had some grit, considering his piss-poor situation. He had stated the bare facts, he had not begged, and even if he was sorry for himself, he had not whined.

Melville knew he had to save himself if he was going to be saved, because this man Watson wasn't going to help him, and he had to do it now while he still had strength, even if Watson planned to shoot him once he'd done it. One boot swung up onto the rail, which was all the purchase this sonofagun needed. The rest was cat strength, timing the boat's roll, and he was back aboard so fast that I grabbed for the first gun, which was still loaded. Seeing how he'd startled me, he dared a little grin as he eased down out of the wind in his wet clothes.

"You're the man who killed Belle Starr," he said, cool and conversational, wringing his shirt out.

I ignored this. I was emptying his cartridges into my pocket, and my expression told him he'd better start explaining. "Dutchy Melville is the name," he said. "You heard of me?" I shook my head.

"Don't want to know what I'm doing on your boat?"

"I *know* what you're doing on my boat."

He nodded. "Emperor Watson!" He grinned some more.

Even now, safely aboard, Dutchy Melville was hanging on for dear life, and I realized that after that bad scare in the water, he was no threat to me at all. Far offshore, with nowhere to drift but that wild coast or Cuba, maybe Mexico, he had more sense than to harm the man who ran the boat. "You strike me as a pretty kindly feller," Dutchy ventured. "If a man drew down on *me* on my own boat, I'd blow his head off."

"I have other plans."

"You aimin to kill me in cold blood?"

"After the harvest, maybe."

"You mean 'Watson Payday'?" He'd heard the bad stories, his grin said, but he kind of liked my style. "You know something, Mister Ed? You wasn't so sociable in Eddie's Bar, you couldn't take a joke, so I never got a chance to shake your hand. But the way you turned the tables on me here today? Heck, I'm proud to know you!" Still smiling, he stuck his hand out, but I did not take it because it was attached to such a strong young feller and an acrobat besides. My wariness caused him to laugh some more. "*Emperor Watson!* I bet you like that name!"

"One month, no pay. How comical is that?"

"Mister Ed," he repeated softly, shaking his head, as if this were his lucky day. He couldn't get over Mr. Watson, I was just wonderful. "We'll see," he promised cheerfully. " 'He who laughs last laughs best'—ever hear that one?" Next he said, "I'm thinkin I might change my name." He sighed, wiping the mirth out of his eyes. "John Smith, maybe."

"How about Little Herbie?"

I'd guessed correctly that he hated that name. On the other hand, he was quite flattered that I'd known from the start just who he was.

"You can call me Dutchy, okay, Mister Ed?"

"Okay, Herb," I said.

*

At Chatham Bend, Melville learned to take orders from a black foreman. Respecting Frank's toughness and his prison record, he got along with Reese about as well as could be expected. He liked me, too. He wanted to stay on, he announced, so he could take away the foreman's job. But when he realized that I'd meant just what I said—one month, no pay—he got to brooding, concluding finally that Watson had taken advantage of his generous nature. Criminals *always* feel angry and abused, which may partly account for why they become criminals. The other thing they always do is, they get even.

A fortnight later, returning from a trip with Bembery to Tampa Bay, I discovered that Dutchy had gone off on a fishing boat, but not before spoiling a thousand gallons of my syrup—about half of the stock I'd counted on for unpaid salaries, lawyers' fees, and enough supplies to see the plantation through until next harvest. Maybe two months later, a picture postcard came from New York City:

> While you was at Tampa drinking up my pay, I had some fun mixing terpentine into your sirup. Now I am up here seeing all the sites. Mery Chrismas Mister Ed and hello to all the family from Yr. Friend Dutchy.

To my friend Dutchy it was all a joke, but for Chatham Bend it was a serious crisis. For a fortnight or more, I forgot my vow that I would never again raise my hand in violence. Every time I thought about that grinning devil, my head split with that old pain of boyhood, so violent that I had to sit down or I would fall. If I'd had money, I would have headed straight for New York City on a steamer and paid off that young criminal once and for all.

I told my crew I was dead broke but would pay them when I could. Some bitched, of course, but most believed they would have had their wages if it had not been for that devil Dutchy Melville. Kate burst out at me, "Well, that's what comes of harboring these outlaws! Why can't we live like ordinary, decent people?" And I said, "Didn't you tell me just last week that you were fond of Dutchy?" Kate went off sniffling, having admitted that the children liked him, too. In fact, our kids followed Dutchy everywhere, and the Harden and Hamilton and Thompson kids rowed all the way north from Lost Man's to see Dutchy and his six-guns—they enjoyed him almost as much as my trained pig Betsey. Everybody liked that rascal, even Lucius, even Reese, even "Mister Ed," who had sworn to kill him.

*

The west coast was falling far behind the east as I stood by and watched. My grand ideas depended on the interest of Nap Broward, who had already committed most of the state's money to his steamboat canals east of Okeechobee. Meanwhile the east coast developer and railroad tycoon Mr. Henry Flagler had established his Model Land Company at Palm Beach and was finishing his hundred-mile spur of the Florida East Coast Railway, from Homestead south across the keys and channels to Key West. From his seaside headquarters at Palm Beach, Flagler called that railway "the hardest job I have ever undertaken," ignoring the brutal labor done by the hundreds of unknown men who labored in that humid heat to make his fortune. (One newspaper reported that railroad death tolls in Florida approached the numbers compiled by the Panama Railroad, where the company helped defray expenses by packing its workers' corpses into brine barrels for sale to medical schools in the U.S.A.)

Under the circumstances, these rumors about "Watson Payday" were infuriating. Our field hands on the Bend might be paid late, but they were much better housed and fed than those miserable Spanish and Italian immigrants and Caribbean niggers and po' white crackers who, despite all the hoopla and new locomotives and fine speeches, had perished on the job for the past ten years building Flagler's empire. Nobody wanted to investigate all that dying, least of all the U.S. Government, because Flagler was opening up south Florida for big investors and their commerce and development. "The kind of red-blooded American who made this country great"—that's what the papers called him. Those crews finally revolted, forcing his men to kidnap drunks and bums to break the strikes. There was red blood, all right, but it wasn't his.

Not that I opposed progress in this brave new century—on the contrary. But it seemed to me unjust—in fact, it enraged me—that a small cane planter on a remote frontier should be slandered for a few deaths among his workers when the powerful men building great empires were permitted to write off human life as simple overhead. The most basic of their damned Commandments against killing, stealing, and lying were routinely ignored in the name of progress, wherever profit was the least bit threatened.

Well, as they say, you can't make an omelette without breaking eggs—that's what successful businessmen will always tell you, and that's how I'd respond to Pitchfork Ben Tillman and his crazy populist ideas. Trying to make my cane farm work under hard, marginal conditions, I know what I am talking about, too. But my dear Mandy would only shake her head when I talked that way. "Those eggs don't belong to you," she once said quietly. "Those precious eggs are human beings whose small hope of happiness is being stolen from them in the name of profit, and all the more so if they are colored people, or illiterate people, or immigrant people who can't speak our language. The more defenseless they are, the more abominably they are treated, have you never noticed?"

"Human nature," I would say. I always felt false when I discussed these things with Mandy because she was so thoughtful and well-read. I could only argue hopelessly that it was no longer a question of right and wrong, there were larger questions of the nation's progress, of finance and economics, to which individual welfare had to give way. For example, the development of this wilderness, and a great cane industry for southern Florida—think of the jobs and livelihoods, the higher quality of life progress would bring.

Now Mandy was gone and my new wife was not interested, and so I argued with her son, who nodded politely at my earnest words, only to say something exasperating like, I've been thinking about progress, Papa. Shouldn't progress mean progress for everybody?

That man Tucker died for the common good, the future good, because he'd obstructed the progress of this region—that's what I told myself. Occasionally I came quite close to discussing the whole business with Lucius, who was sad that he'd never heard from Rob, but being too much in need of his good opinion, I did not quite dare. I was less afraid of my son's condemnation than of his silence.

Well, most of the men who have worked for me over the years have nothing bad to say about Ed Watson. They never saw one thing out of the way. And they knew Watson a whole lot better than those who speak behind my back on Chokoloskee Bay.

*

After my acquittal, I had written a long letter to Nap Broward, thanking him for his kind interest and help. In that letter I outlined some long-range proposals for what I called "the last American frontier" and requested an appointment at the statehouse. Unfortunately, I could not even afford the railway fare to Tallahassee, and anyway (on those days when I faced the facts), I recognized that real progress on this wild coast lay far in the future, even if Broward dared support a controversial figure who had been tried so recently for murder, and even if he was still interested in my proposals—for instance, the Broward Ship Canal, which would follow old Indian water trails across the southern Glades from Fort Dallas on the Miami River to the Lost Man's headwaters. To inspire him, I mentioned the far more difficult canal construction taking place in Panama, with locks to lift the ships over the mountains.

The answer to my letter was a typewritten copy of a letter from the archives of his predecessor in office. Though unaccompanied by any note, it could not have been sent without Broward's approval. Dated Chokoloskee, Florida, February 1896, it was addressed to Governor Henry Mitchell:

To his Excellency Gov. Mitchil. Sir, I wish to call your attention to a crime perpetrated against the Laws of the state with the following result.

I was in Key West on business some time ago when I met the perpetrator of the crime. He came up to me in a store and shook hands with me. We had a few civil words. He wound up by saying that he was not affraid of any man. I in reply said that neither was I, when he immediately slapped his knife, which I suppose from the quickness of his act he must have had open in his pocket, into my neck, coming very close to severing the jugular vein. I seized him by both wrists and held him until he was taken in charge by an officer who was nearby. He drew his pistol but could not make use of it as the lether case came with it. He was then lodged in jail, being unable to give bond. Some days after his lawyer procured a man who was willing to stand on his bond. The bond was accepted and the prisoner was released. When the time came for the trial to come off, the prisoner was not forthcoming but sent two negroes to swear that he was sick and not able to go to court. It is a proveable fact that but a short time before court he went to a store some twelve miles distant from home and purchased a quantity of ammunition. The prisoner not being present in the court there was no trial had. The court ordered the bond raised although the bond was declared a straw bond. The prisoner's lawyer raised the bond by using money belonging to the prisoner. No effort was made to bring the prisoner to justice, so he stands in the same position as he occupied before he made the attempt on my life.

Is it any wonder that there are so many lawless acts committed by linching offenders when the law is so loosely executed? Let the Law be administered in justice and without fear, favor, or affection. The Law need not allow itself to be overcome by the power that money possesses, and linch law will be done away with. But until that is done we must expect the people to take the execution of the law into their own hands.

Very Respectfully Yours
A. P. Santini

The "store some twelve miles distant" up the mangrove rivers could only have been McKinney's trading post at Chokoloskee.

Adolphus P. had gotten revenge and didn't even know it. That Broward permitted this letter to be sent anonymously to his friend Watson made it all too clear that he wished to avoid political risk, and that I would not be welcome at the statehouse until I had rebuilt my reputation—in other words, until I was prosperous again, which amounts to the same thing in this great land of ours. As for taking "the execution of the law into their own hands," Santini had moved away to the east coast more than ten years ago.

*

Our new cane crop came up better than expected in those rain-swept days of spring and early summer, when new shoots can grow six to eight inches in a day. But on the eleventh of September, just before harvest, the worst hurricane in living memory flattened my cane to a tangled mat of leaves and twisted stalks. Because the new cane was still green, it bent those stalks over without killing the plants, but the damp weight of that green mat threatened the harvest. I drove Green Waller off his hogs, worked Kate and Lucius in the field—worked 'em like niggers because, being broke, I had no real ones except Sip and Frank. Grabbing and chopping night and day, we salvaged what we could and burned the rest, but the new sugar in those stalks was watery, and the syrup so thin that I could not put my label on it. I sold off just one small consignment for the little it would bring at Tampa Bay.

While I was away, we lost another nigger feeding cane stalks to the mill. Caught his apron in the belt, got his hand caught trying to free the sacking, chewed up his whole arm right to the shoulder. They rushed the man into the house for some damned reason, and before he died, he bled all over a whole corner of the front room parlor. Though there was nothing to be done, people were running to fetch useless things like chickens with their heads chopped off, and by the time they thought to mop that blood with cold water, it was much too late.

We tried to paint that blood out over and over, but sooner or later, for some damnable reason, the shadow of it rises through the paint like a gator rising slowly through the muddy water. Tried to hide it under a straw mat but we all knew it was there. The-nigger-blood-that-would-not-wash-away spooked everybody on the Watson place, including me.

We sewed the body in a sheet and gave it to the river. Maybe that crocodile tore him up, or a big gator, because a few days later, one leg with chewed pinkish meat still on it came ashore downriver on an oyster bar, and that strange pink thing was spotted by some passing fishermen. The next time I went to Everglade, that same old bad story was going around—about "Watson Payday"—that when it came time to pay his help, Ed Watson knocked 'em on the head and dumped 'em in the river. I told Bembery the truth and I guess he took my word but it did no good. The story spread like a bad flu as far as Tampa, where my buyers were upset about "black blood in Watson's syrup." For six months or more, we hardly sold a quart of the best cane syrup in the U.S.A.

Jim Howell of Chokoloskee came that year and brought along his brother George's boy to help. Jim was the slowest-working man I ever saw, but something put the fear of God in him, because he was burning to finish up, get the hell out of there. Kept stalks coming to the mill from dawn to dusk, kept his nephew working that same way, which was why that fatal accident happened again. That boy got tired, got his apron caught, then his hand and arm. But this time there was some arm left above the elbow.

We bound a tourniquet as best we could, made him cough down moonshine to keep his heart going, put shine-soaked linen in his mouth to stop his screaming. Frank Reese's expression when we laid him in the boat needed no interpretation—*You let a black man bleed to death but try to save the white one.* There was no time to explain. "Frank," I warned him, "this is the way it's going to be, all right?" Black Frank said nothing. I ran young Howell straight to Marco Island, where a faster boat was found to take him north to the Fort Myers hospital. He had hardly enough blood left to keep a mosquito alive. They saved his life but perhaps he was meant to lose it. A few months later that boy perished with his daddy and the younger children, drowned in a sudden squall on Lake Okeechobee.

That September hurricane of 1909 tore off roofs and blew to pieces most of the Key West waterfront and the cigar factories. Here on the Bend, it washed away a boat shed and a skiff and half the dock, but the house stood fast up on its mound in the middle of a thick brown flood that was twice as broad as was usual at high tide. Kate was scared we would all be washed away, but thanks to Lucius, who made a great adventure of the ordeal, the kids felt more excited than scared and came through it fine.

Little Ad was proud of our strong house, which hardly creaked. Their mother had read them "The Three Little Pigs," and Ad boasted how our house stood up to all the huffing and the puffing to everybody who came through for the next year. It was only when he wouldn't stop that we saw how that little feller had been a lot more frightened than he let on. All through that storm, Ad had been certain that the Big Bad Wolf awaited him outside.

After the hurricane, the family lost all interest in my auto. I never once took the tarp off her after that storm, just winced about the waste when I walked past. Finally we loaded her onto the *Gladiator*, took her up to Tampa Bay, sold her cheap to a damn-Spaniard cigar king in Ybor City, which had already replaced Key West as the world center of the Cuban cigar industry. Despite the continuing prejudice against them, these rich Spaniards still looked down on all and sundry.

Speck

Christmas that year was a sad occasion, with no money to spend on our little children. I was in low spirits, and I drank too much of our own moonshine, which was cheap. It seemed to me I had made no progress in my life since that starved Christmas in the muddy snow out in the Nations.

A year had passed since our return, and Kate, who was pregnant, grew ever more remote, spending more and more time away at Chokoloskee. She always took the children with her, saying she feared for their safety in the rough company which came and went with the seasons on the Bend.

One day that autumn after a bad quarrel, I dropped Kate and the children at Smallwood's landing, from where they would walk over to Marie Alderman's. On the way home to the Bend, I stopped off at Pavilion Key with intent to trade a gallon of syrup for two bushels of fresh clams procured for me by Mrs. Josie Jenkins Harden Parks Johnson (to name but a few of her discarded and deceased). That little woman was a marrying fool, and her men had a way of dying on her, though one feller went back for a second try before he kicked the bucket. Josie remained a good friend and also "family," since she was the mother of young Pearl, whom everyone referred to as Pearl Watson, and also half sister to Netta Daniels, the mother of my fourteen-year-old Minnie.

Her brother Tant, who brought the clams, explained that they were growing scarce due to Collier's dredge. The contraption tore the living hell out of the bottom, broke the shells or exposed them to the drills and starfish, and generally put those clammy fellers off their feed. I was very thankful that Captain Bill was the man held responsible for the calamity—or the "clamanity," as Tant Jenkins called it—surely the only mortality in southwest Florida that nobody had tried to blame on E. J. Watson.

Mrs. Parks, as she was known that year, looked somewhat the worse for wear, but her spirit seemed lively as ever. She offered me a mug of rum to seal our dealings, and we nailed that mug down with another to celebrate the mystery of life. Before I knew it, this spry widow had grown so alluring in my eyes that I awoke next morning in her musky bedding for the first time since the turn of the old century. After that, as Tant Jenkins used to say, "things went from bed to worst," because I'd hardly snapped my galluses before I got Miss Josie in a family way. She told me the happy news in April (scarcely a fortnight before Kate presented me with our new baby girl). "A sign from Heaven!" Josie marveled. She called it "our love child." By any name, it promised to be the very last thing that I needed.

In the clam camp, my footsteps were dogged by a young feller named Crockett Daniels, who had some idea that I might be his daddy. His confusion was understandable, since nobody was sure which Daniels bunch he came from. Some seemed to recall that he had turned up here with Tant, who claimed he knew nothing, either. But he was a Daniels, no doubt about that. Like so many frontier people, the Daniels clan was what folks called "half full of Injun," and a good many of their offspring had black hair straight as a horse tail and a dark copper coloring to go with it. Some had the high cheekbones and the hawk nose, too, and young Crockett was one. Besides, Netta's brother John Henry Daniels had hooked up with an Injun-looking woman, and Old Man Henry Smith married the sister, and their kids were all mixed up together, big loose litters. Not only did this gang look Injun but the families had that Injun custom of raising up stray kids, this one included.

Young Crockett was publicly attributed to Phin Daniels's son Harvey, who stumbled drunk out of his boat in pursuit of a raccoon and jammed mangrove mud into his rifle muzzle. "Hell, that don't mean nothin!" Harvey hollered, waving off warnings. Anxious to get a shot off quick before that coon slipped away, he blew most of the mud out of the barrel, blew the gun up, too, and himself with it. The family agreed at Harvey's funeral that he was very likely Crockett's father, which made an orphan of the boy but kept things orderly. As for the mother, she was also a young Daniels. It was said she had gone away someplace to recover her health and reputation.

Young Crockett knew that Pearl and Minnie were the children of "Desperado Watson." Since nobody had really claimed him, he set his heart on me, calling and waving, tagging along like a kitten underfoot, running errands that I only gave him to get rid of him. On Pavilion Key, he was never out of sight, he was like a speck of hard grit in my eye. One day I called him Speck, and the men laughed when I explained why, and the name stuck.

Another day Josie Jenkins, drunk as usual, decided to pay me a visit on the Bend, and this boy rowed her to Chatham from Pavilion. I was just about to leave for Chokoloskee. Bothered by her presence in Kate's house, I told her to leave once they'd had a bite to eat. Next day I returned to find her gone, but she'd left Speck behind in the hope I would adopt him.

Speck was waiting on the dock, and jumped to take my lines. "You're trespassing," I told him, in no mood for games. Seeing my face, he backed onto the bank in case he had to make a run for it. "Mr. Watson," he said coolly, "I ain't doin you one bit of harm."

Trying to run him off, teach him a lesson, I chased him around the buildings. Unable to catch him, I fired past his ear to scare him, and this wild boy dove into the river and swam underwater—either that or he drowned quick, because he disappeared. I hunted up and down the bank, hollering and calling, fearing something might have grabbed him and knowing there would be hell to pay when Josie heard about it. Only later did I realize that I still had my revolver in my hand, which might have been one reason he would not answer. I put that gun away and shouted more, I even shouted that he could stay the night, that's how worried I was that the big crocodile might get him if he ducked along the riverbank too long. I drifted down the current in the skiff but found no sign of him.

When he never reappeared, I went to Pavilion Key with the bad news, and the first person I saw on shore was Crockett Daniels. It turned out he had splashed and clambered all the way downriver. The tide was with him, and he drifted on his back down current, crawling out every little ways to make sure that no shark or gator got a bead on him. Finally he swam and waded out to Mormon Key, where a fisherman spotted him waving, took him home.

This Speck had some spunk, he was pretty nervy. I wanted to say, "No hard feelings, son," and tell him I had only meant to scare him, not to kill him. But when I drew near to shake his hand and maybe rough his head, he backed away. When I stopped, Speck stopped, too, regarding me with an un-blinking gaze out of greenish eyes as bright and cold as broken glass, and nodding his head as if to say he knew what I was up to. Then he spat onto the sand between us and turned and walked away. He never followed me again. That year Speck Daniels was no more than ten years old, but I knew right then he was not the kind who would forget that Mr. Watson winged a bullet past his ear, much less forgive it.

As the clammers watched, Josie Jenkins shrilled how that crazy Watson had shot at a poor homeless boy with intent to kill him. She was not to be reasoned with, there was no changing her mind, though I followed her in frustration to her door. If Josie Jenkins would not listen to my side of the story, then who would?

Through the door she said, "You're dead, Jack Watson, and you don't even know it! Your heart has died like the heart of some old oak from your bitterness and emptiness of spirit." Astonished and moved by these words from her own mouth, Josie opened the door to gauge their effect on me. Black eyes filling up with moonshine tears, she raised her hand to touch my cheek and lips, then let it fall like an old leaf onto my trouser buttons. "Dead," she whispered. "Stop that," I growled, because young Pearl was watching, and this tempestuous bitch slammed her door right in my face. As poor Pearl backed away in fright, I kicked that rickety little slat right off its hinges.

The clammer families and their mutts fell back as I turned to leave. "Go fuck yourselves," I told them with as much vigor and good cheer as I could muster. I returned to my skiff and rowed home, feeling so lonely as I entered Chatham River that even the company of young Crockett Daniels might have proved welcome after all.

*

In the Fort Myers *Press* for April fourth of 1910 (beside a society item about Mrs. Carrie Langford entertaining the Thursday Afternoon Bridge Club at her gracious home), what should I find but an account of a visit on the new auto road to "Deep Lake Country" by a festive party which included Mrs. and Mr. Walter Langford, Mr. Frank Carson, and Sheriff Frank B. Tippins. Paradise, the writer gushed, was not to be compared with "one of the most magnificent citrus groves in Florida," producing oranges and grapefruits "fine as silk." Alas, this miraculous fruit was not yet on the market et cetera, et cetera, which told me that Walter's citrus was still rotting on the ground.

I swallowed my pride and wrote a letter entreating my son-in-law one last time to take me on as Deep Lake overseer. I didn't have to tell him I would work like hell—he knew that. If at the year's end, I said, I had not earned that job, I would cheerfully quit. Among other contributions, I would survey and stake out that small-gauge railway I had mentioned, to transport Deep Lake's produce south to Everglade for travel by fast coastal shipping to the markets.

As president of the new bank (and the Man Who Brought the Railroad to Fort Myers), Walter Langford could have hired his father-in-law at little risk, especially if he banished him some fifty miles southeast across scrub country to some hell-and-gone where even E. J. Watson could not cause embarrassment. But he had his reputation as a stuffed shirt to keep up, and in his view, my notorious murder trial in north Florida had already spilled egg all over that shirt, never mind that I had been acquitted.

Not having the guts to refuse me outright, Walter sent word that he would have to think about it. He was a slow thinker, I knew that much, and perhaps he is thinking about it still, for no word came. What I did hear, early in the summer, was news of Banker Langford's plans for his new "citrus express," a small-gauge rail line from Everglade to Deep Lake, to get the citrus out. Already his crew was pushing north through the coast mangroves toward Deep Lake, making a rail bed by digging that black muck with shovels and heaving it up in a broad bank. It seems that Langford had arranged with Sheriff Tippins to lease the county's chain-gang niggers for his labor, just as I had recommended years before. What the newspaper did not reveal (it came out later) was that the company had adopted those techniques of labor management so successful in railroad construction on the east coast. From what we heard, they used up chain-gang prisoners like goobers and covered the bodies in the spoil bank where they fell. Those road bosses were paid to get the job done, probably never told Langford one damned thing about it.

But these good citizens would not hire Ed Watson, pretending horror at the rumors of foul play whenever a worker died on Chatham Bend—that made me bitter. True, there had been deaths on my plantation, everything from cane mill accident to alcohol. And there were those two I had to deal with by myself. But for all the reasons I have mentioned, I believe I was justified in eliminating agitators who caused serious trouble when Watson Syrup was struggling to survive—what else could I have done under the circumstances? We had no law down here. I had no overseer or foreman to do my dirty work. The choice was between two nameless lives and the waste and loss of many years of hard and dedicated work to build a cane plantation and develop a new agriculture of great benefit to the future of the state of Florida. If you represent huge industry, you are a visionary, a man of progress, worthy of flags and commemorations from the nation's leaders. If you are small like E. J. Watson, you are a murderer.

On Chatham Bend, it had come down to a matter of survival. It was them or us. And nobody missed them, nobody would have ever known or cared about them, had I buried those graves deep enough not to be rooted up by my own hogs. That led to the episode with the Tuckers (which led to blackmail, which made it necessary to clean up that mess, too), which led to the flight of my son Rob and critical years of absence from the Bend. And now it looked like I would have to start all over.

Big Hannah

One day at Everglade, Green Waller introduced me to an enormous woman celebrated hereabouts as Miss Big Hannah, who wore a long black old-time dress right down to her big high brogans. Able to outwork most men, Green said, and thrash the rest to huckleberry jelly, this Hannah Smith had a fair start on a handlebar mustache and mighty shoulders that a man could yoke into a team of oxen, but she also had a generous heart and tender ways. That evening she told us all about her childhood on Cowhouse Island in the eastern Okefenokee, where she had three sisters as mighty as herself and three more of the common size for human females. Out of Green's hearing Miss Smith winked and said she recalled me from another year when I passed through on my way south from Carolina and stayed on Cowhouse Island with her family. "They called me Little Hannah then, remember? I knowed

350

you in the biblical way," she whispered, closing bashful eyes in a face of the dimensions and deep brown color of a large spiced ham.

A few years before, she had worked her way south, hunting some sign of one of her huge sisters, the Widow Sarah McClain, who had run off when her husband was hung by mistake in Waycross, Georgia. This sister was well-known throughout south Florida as the Ox-Woman, having been the first human to cross the Glades driving an ox team. That had been a few years earlier, in the dry season of 1906. Sarah McClain dwelled in a shack near Old Fort Denaud on the Calusa Hatchee.

Hannah called the Ox-Woman Big Sis and my name for Hannah was Big Six, for she was somewhat more than six foot tall. Hannah first showed up out in the Cypress, at Carson Gully, near Immokalee, and the Carsons remembered her distinctly. "My mother and me was all alone with our dog Cracker," one child told me, "and Cracker came from Key West, and he would bite ye. Cracker was barking, so we sung out, Hello. Who's there? And a voice says, A lady from the Okefenokee Swamp. So we tied up Cracker, lit the lamp, and went on out, and there she stood, had a little black dog tied to a big rope from her belt. I never forgot how that great big lady looked. I was scared to death of her!

"So then she said, Well, can I come in? Cause I've walked all day and ain't had nothin to eat. So Mama took her inside—she had to bend half over not to hit the lintel—and we give her some grub, and she ate and ate and *ate*! We thought she'd bust. Sat back and said, I sure do like to rest after I eat. So Mama laid her a bed of corn shucks in our shed. I was scared she'd break loose and get into my room, but she never did."

Hannah showed a wedding photo of her sister Lydia, who was every inch as big as Hannah and Sarah and was wearing a whole rosebush on her head. She was seated in a chair with the groom standing at her shoulder, and if she had stood up, Hannah said, one would have seen just why she called him Doll Baby. Doll Baby was later convicted of murder and sentenced to thirty years in prison, but Lydia, unable to tolerate her lover's absence, offered financial incentive to some high official to see to his release, then went to the penitentiary and paid up and lugged her Doll Baby off under her arm. The first thing she did when she got home was stop payment on her check, and all that high official could do short of going to jail was shake his head over Miss Lydia's financial acumen. "Ain't a man alive who can out-figger me," Miss Lydia liked to say. "I always said I could make five dollars out of every dollar I could get my hands on." She had already got her hands on plenty, Hannah told us.

Anyway, all of these big girls had known me as a youth, and I could only thank the Lord that I escaped alive.

These days Miss Smith was a farmhand for our former postmaster C. G. McKinney on the farm he called Needhelp up in Turner River. She was plowing and hoeing and building fences, too. Grew a lot of malangas and cabbages, which C.G. rowed down to the Bay and shipped to Key West with Bill House on the *Rosina*. In the field as well as at all other times, Hannah wore her high brogans and gray dress down to the ground and a sunbonnet big enough to hold a bushel of fresh cabbages. She removed her footgear to feel the good earth when she plowed, and in the evening she dearly loved to sing sad ballads about young women and their sweethearts.

Hannah was tired of working Needhelp all alone, she told us, and as soon as she got her crop in, she aimed to come down to Chatham Bend and try her hand at women's work, see how she liked it. Green brought her on a visit once or twice and finally installed her there for good. This was fine by Kate and fine by me, since Kate was away more and more frequently, visiting friends in Everglade or Chokoloskee.

Green Waller was unusually annoyed that his lady friend had been followed from Turner River by Charlie Tommie, the only Mikasuki in the Glades who had got himself snake-bit by rattlers and moccasins three different times. The first time he got "sick, sick, sick," the second time only "sick, sick," and the third time scarcely sick at all. That is the only interesting thing I ever heard about him. According to Green, this pesky Injun had spied on Miss Smith unstintingly at Needhelp, having fallen in love with this white damsel who laved her mountainous white body weekly in the river shallows. Sure enough, he showed up at the Bend, making some kind of camp across the river out of rifle range from where he could keep an eye on Hannah as she came and went, and make sure she was treated in the manner she deserved until such time as she realized his true worth and permitted him to lead her off into the swamps.

Green Waller never looked like much but he was certainly in love, you never saw such a damn fool in your life. And his adoration had poked up the primordial fires smoldering in Hannah, for she hadn't been in residence a week when she took that hog thief to her bed and clung to him for dear life ever after. Since she was ten times stronger, Green explained, he knew it was useless to attempt a struggle.

"Thought you always wanted to grow up to be a virgin, Green," I said. "Why, hell, no!" Green retorted with a dirty grin. "It's just I was savin it for Betsey!" Betsey was that brindle sow I'd trained up to do tricks for the children. Green Waller claimed that in his early years, all alone here on the Bend, he'd trained her, too, providing himself with some low fulfillment which no decent human being would ever care to think about.

Green and Hannah had washed up on the Bend after hard voyages, and they were tired, with nowhere else to go. They swept out the little Dyer cabin and made it "the first home I ever knew," as Green said weepily, having drunk somewhat more than he could handle. There they vowed to love each other the best way they knew how "until death do us part."

Poor as we were, we had plenty to eat, with Hannah's garden patch back of the cistern, also two milk cows, hogs and chickens, papaws, pears and guavas, coconuts, bananas—all in addition to the good fish in the river and wild fowl and game. Lucius and the rest believed it was only time before Watson Syrup came back strong and silver jingled in our pockets, and gradually my own faith was restored, and my hopes, too. These people trusted me to get back on my feet, and I aimed to do it. "Can't keep a good man down," Waller would snigger, jerking his thumb at Hannah, winking at me. Hearing those words, this unsuspecting creature would sigh enormously, gazing at her man with adoration as she scraped back her chair and rose like a genie from the table and hurried him to bed.

The Stranger

May 1910 was the month of the Great Comet, which was seen at first as the Star of Bethlehem but was later feared by the more pious as the Great Chastisement or Great Tribulation or even the Exterminating Angel of the Book of Exodus, who would spare only those earthly dwellings whose lintels were marked with the Blood of the Lamb. According to the newspapers, the ghostly white fire was Halley's Comet. A broad luminous streak across the heavens all that spring, it had caused suicides around the world, out of man's terror that this sinful world was coming to an end (though some found reason to believe that certain local sinners might be spared). I decided to take that mysterious comet as a good omen for the birth of our third child, which was delivered at the Key West hospital while that light was still flaring in the heavens.

Not long after Kate came home with Amy May, I made a business trip to Tampa. Passing through Chokoloskee on my return, I was warned by Ted Smallwood that a stranger was awaiting me at the Bend. "Calls himself John Smith," Mamie Smallwood said. "Looked like a preacher." Ted harumphed loudly. "Never seen a preacher yet with a big ol' half-moon scar across his cheekbone." At the mention of that scar, I had to wonder if the Great Comet had been a good omen after all.

Hearing the *Brave*'s motor coming upriver, Kate and her baby were waiting on the dock. I could see how jittery she was before I stepped ashore. "He's here," she whispered, close to tears. "He's been drinking since he got here." When I took her in my arms to comfort her and calm her, she wept desperately into my ear. "He murdered Old Calvin and Aunt Celia Banks, and another darkie, too! He *boasts* about it! He claims you wanted him to do it for revenge on Calvin! Claims you put him up to killing both those Tolens!"

What I was thinking about as my wife spoke was not poor Calvin and his Celia, not at all. I was thinking about the way this sonofabitch had humiliated this innocent young mother when he sent her with the knife into the jail. At that memory, I pushed Kate aside and strode up the mound toward the porch.

Lucius, Waller and Hannah, Sip, Frank Reese, and two young niggers were all out working in the field, but "John Smith" sat in my chair drinking my whiskey. His boots were sprawled on my pine table, a pistol beside them. I suspected he'd put both boots and pistol on the table when he heard me coming. In his cheap hard-cornered black suit—he was aping a riverboat gambler, not a preacher—Cox looked degenerate. He was long unshaven, with a growth of unkempt beard and long ducktails of greasy hair on his dirty neck. Deep creases like knife marks between his heavy brows were dark with dirt. He stank.

"You don't smell so good," I said.

"Howdy, partner," says this fool by way of greeting, putting on his best gunslinger squint and dangerous smile. I stood in the doorway considering the boots until he removed them. He was still smiling—more or less—as he stuck out his hand. Ignoring it, I sat down across the table.

"So," I said. "The Exterminating Angel."

Cox said, Yep, he'd shot them niggers, *had* to. Had to fix that fuckin Calvin for what he did in court to Mr. Watson. No nigger did that to no friend of Les Cox and lived to brag on it. Cox spoke in lean whispery tones out of his respect for his own drama. He had come to split Old Calvin's savings, help Unc pay off his legal, restore his good name in the community, "hold my head up proud."

Sickening as this horseshit was, it was horribly sincere, straight from the heart. This hayseed really thought he had saved my honor. The truth was, he had robbed and killed for money, but since then he had persuaded himself that he had acted in good ol' Unc's behalf, exacting the revenge he imagined I would have wanted.

Les Cox, drunk, succumbed easily to self-pity, as if being a dangerous liar and cold-blooded killer were not bad enough. He assured me that he wished no gratitude for his act of friendship, and saying this, he fought back manly tears. I could have fought back tears myself after hearing what he'd perpetrated on my account. Having been right there in the Madison courthouse, even Leslie must have known that Calvin Banks meant me no harm. He had only done what he was told to do, which was to speak the truth, so help him, God.

*

Leslie had found Calvin on his porch, pushing old half-blind Aunt Celia on the porch swing. Leslie told him to hand over his money, and Calvin said, "Nosuh, I can't do that." Although warned that Leslie didn't have all day, Calvin knew his rights and would not change his mind. Enraged, fed up with arguing, Cox shot him dead, then put two bullets into the old woman as she toppled off the swing and tried to crawl away. Rooted through everything they had to find a little money. He even got down on hands and knees and scratched around under the cabin for the chest of William Myers's missing gold.

Afraid that someone might come along, and spitting mad about the trouble and the risk that mulish old couple could have saved him, Cox took out that anger on their son-in-law, who was waiting for him down the road. "He was supposed to get a little money, but I never found near enough to share nothin." Anyway, the nigger moaned that he would fry in hell for getting his old folks killed without so much as one thin dime to show for it. That was a threat, Leslie decided, and for once he was probably right. "What I was lookin at was a damn whinin witness. I thought, Les, you better shut his mouth, so naturally I did."

"Naturally," I said, feeling kind of tired. "If a man has killed two niggers, no one will hang him from a higher limb for killing three." As usual, my little jokes were wasted on Les Cox. Those furrows between his eyes were pinched in a black scowl.

Les had let his cousin Oscar Sanford and their friend Tom Gay in on his plan. Wasn't much of a plan, of course, but knowing the planners, it probably took all three of 'em to think it up. Once he was indicted, Leslie named the other two as his accomplices, to teach 'em a lesson for running off when he started killing people, then failing to help out with his alibi. That instinct for revenge led to his downfall, because Tom Gay turned state's evidence against him. Young Luther Kinard gave some testimony, too.

Being a crony of Will Cox, Sheriff Purvis released Les to go to his own wedding and was astounded when he actually came back. Now that Jim Crow had come to Florida, few were detained for killing niggers, let alone indicted, but because of all the Tolen rumors, this boy had to be tried. Les was flabbergasted when he was convicted and sent to prison for the rest of his natural life. He complained to the Judge that a gently reared young man such as himself would never survive the ordeal of the chain gang, and the Judge said, Heck, son, you'll come out of it just fine.

That judge knew what he was talking about, too. In February, Will Cox went over to where the gang was laying rail near Silver Springs. The guards unshackled the gang chain so each man could work, and one guard told Will to pass word to his son to uncouple the last car while the guard's back was turned and hang on while it rolled back down the grade. None of the guards took any notice when Will's boy jumped off and lit out for the woods.

I recalled how Leslie bragged in jail how his daddy was such good friends with Sheriff Purvis that even if he got convicted for Sam Tolen, the guards would turn their backs and let him go. At the time that sounded like more of his big talk, but now it turned out to be true, at least when it came down to killing niggers. He went across country to his uncle John Fralick, who took him home in his wagon a few days later.

His friends Gay and Sanford were not prosecuted, Les told me, because the one witness who could implicate them had escaped. "It was a pitiful downright disgrace," he complained, "that I couldn't do my bounden duty and go over to the county court and testify on them yeller sonsabitches without getting arrested for escapin! If *that* ain't obstruction of justice, I don't know what!" Les could say these hilarious things and never crack a smile. He never even knew why I was laughing.

That first mention of splitting his loot with his friend Watson was the last I would ever hear. I don't believe he begrudged me Calvin's savings, it was more his reluctance to admit he had blown three people's heads off for next to nothing. As Black Frank remarked when I told him about it, "Three human lives for thirty-eight dollars is pretty doggone cheap even for niggers."

The girl Les married was my niece May Collins, which was why this idiot now called me Unc. May's father was dead and her mother was oblivious, but even so, the marriage caused an uproar in the family. Having defied her brothers by eloping, May had been living with my in-laws, but after Leslie's escape, she went over from Betheas to stay with Coxes. The Sheriff was still going through the motions of being on the lookout for the fugitive, and that spring the young couple had to hole up in a little cubby in Will Cox's attic. My virgin niece had been mad about him, Les confided, and hot as a firecracker, too, but their bower was airless and so hot and humid that his bride got "slippery as a greased pig. I couldn't hardly hang on to that nude, she went so crazy. Couldn't hardly tell which end was up." He was straightfaced, very serious about this problem. Offended by my smile, he demanded to know what manner of man would grin so dirty over his own niece.

When he wasn't getting a handle on his randy bride, Les helped his daddy with the crops, wearing one of his sisters' old dresses as a disguise. But in the end, he got tired of laying low in that hot attic, and women's dresses, too, so he came on south. "Breaks a man's heart to leave his darlin," Les informed me, looking far away downriver in the bittersweetness of it all. "But I knowed that li'l ol' gal o' mine would sleep a whole heap better onct her man had made good his ex-cape, and was safe under the roof of her Uncle Edgar."

He cocked his head. "Ever get that knife I sent into the jail? With your young wife?" With a sly grin, he kicked back in his chair, lifted his legs, and set his boots back on the table, clasping his hands behind his head.

Containing myself, I gazed at his dirty boots. "I'll find a way to thank you, boy, you can count on that. And I won't make you wear your dress at Chatham Bend, not unless you want to."

" 'Boy'?" Leslie squinted harder.

"What I meant was, boy, if you are planning to eat while you are here, you'll keep your damn boots off my table, boy, and go earn your keep like everybody else." I grabbed those boots and swung his legs so violently that he spun right off his chair onto the floor. "Meanwhile, stop snooping around my wife."

Cox picked himself up slowly and retrieved his shooting iron, dragging the metal on the wood—his way of warning me that killers don't care to hear abuse like that. Taking his time, he shoved his revolver in his coat and kicked his whiskey down. In the doorway he paused long enough to say, "You was fixin to shoot that ol' nigger yourself, ain't that what you told me? Fore you left Madison?" He nodded, smiling, as if he knew my secret, then went out.

Had I told him such a thing? I don't think so. He was lying, for whatever reason. Yet I had betrayed my jealousy over Kate, which Cox would find a way to use sooner or later. Lately, I mistrusted my good sense, not only my memory and good judgment but my explanations to myself for my disintegrating spirits. Out beyond all my anger and suspicion, wild spaces opened where my mind would go careening, and beyond all that, some far despair, ever nearing, coming ever closer.

*

To keep the peace while I got things straightened out, I notified Lucius that Cox would replace him as my foreman. Cox was big, strong, and rangy, and a real hard worker, if only because he needed to feel he was the best at everything he put his hand to. Also, he'd been a farm boy all his life and had more experience than anyone but Hannah. And Hannah, however tough and able, would be unacceptable as the crew leader unless I was right there to back her up.

Frank Reese had no use for Cox, who had nearly got him hung, but there was nothing he could say once Les was foreman. As for Lucius, he raised his brows and went on about his business. My son was surprised I would give his job to a boy of his own age—that's how he saw Les, never having known him, and not quite understanding yet what kind of "boy" we had here. On the other hand, he trusted me. He knew I knew something he didn't know, and was content to let it pass until I was ready to explain.

Leslie was older than Lucius by only a few months, but from appearances it might have been ten years. Both were tall and both were twenty, but that was about all they had in common. Lucius had started off in life kind of frail and timid, while Leslie was husky by the age of ten. (Will Cox claimed that his oldest boy got his baby teeth and dropped his balls on the same night.) When the census taker showed up on the mail boat, he took Leslie at his word that he was "John Smith, age thirty-seven." The census taker seemed uneasy on the Watson Place and did not linger.

Les missed his slippery bride in bed if nowhere else, and he had his hungry eye on Kate right from the start. Trusting Kate, I mostly let it go, though I remained watchful. Kate had thought Leslie handsome back in school days, and Les assumed that the Bethea girl had never got over him, to judge from the way that he behaved when he thought I wasn't looking and even sometimes when I was. He liked to talk dangerously in front of Kate, having no idea that his bloody deeds, far from exciting her as they had our foolish May, would truly horrify this good young woman, to the point where she flinched and went all stiff and even held her breath when he drew near.

I surprised Kate once by asking her if her husband horrified her, too. Startled, she gave a quick shake of her head and closed her eyes. Then she opened them and looked straight at me, as if trying to discern something behind my eyes—had I taken part in those killings, as Leslie claimed? As yet, she had not dared ask me that straight out, fearing the truth.

Kate said, "Why do you let him stay, a man like that? With your small children?" And I said, "Because he is family now, at least by marriage. He is my nephew. And because he spoke up for me in court." Without him, I reminded her, I might have been found guilty by a jury of my peers and hung by the neck until deceased.

Cox took out his restless lust in drink and troublemaking. One evening he announced to Green and Hannah that sexual activity between most couples was downright disgusting. "Older people," he sneered when Hannah asked if he had somebody in mind. "And ugly people."

"How about killers?" Hannah Smith, who did not like Cox and would not pretend otherwise, whooped and slapped her thigh at the expression on his face, and Green did, too, his own thigh and hers both. Cox shifted slowly in his chair to look at him.

Les was getting pretty good at these menacing pauses. When Green could not meet that cold-eyed squint, he gave me his most knowing wink, and I gave him one right back, to keep things lively. "Who you calling a killer?" he asked Hannah, speaking evenly as a real desperado should. Having made the acquaintance of plenty of hard men, she was not impressed by this hard boy who took "killer" as a compliment. Hannah did not know Les Cox, not the way we did. But right then, something made her wary, made her sit up stiff and beady-eyed as a squirrel perched on a stump. Though she met his gaze head-on, placid as pudding, she put her hand on Waller's arm, to keep him silent. Unfortunately, Cox saw this, too, and sneered at both of them for Kate's benefit. For a split second—I saw it in his eye—he was on the point of doing something stupid.

"Go slow," I said.

His eye wavered. He "let a little smile play on his lips," as dastards did in Kate's romantic novels, and maybe bastards, too, for all I know. Folding her knitting, my wife got up and left the room.

Old Fighter

Before he left home at the century's turn, my son Rob would take Lucius to a deep hole upriver where they fished for hours for that huge old snook that Rob had named Old Fighter. The boys could never hook Old Fighter, until finally I doubted that such a fish existed outside of Rob's somewhat feverish imagination. But Lucius kept on trying in the years after Rob left, and one Sunday he persuaded me to go along. That afternoon, he dared mention Rob, saying he wondered where his brother might be now. I said, "Your half brother ruined my good name," and changed the subject. Right then, Lucius hooked a fish which made a relentless run and broke his line—that was Old Fighter, Rob! he cried. He got away again!

Still trying to make friends, my son mentioned the huge fish to Leslie and invited him to go along sometime. The following Sunday, when Lucius was off setting nets downriver, Cox made Sip Linsey row him upriver to Old Fighter's lair. With sticks of dynamite left over from the construction of the cistern, Cox killed out every last fish in that hole. Sure enough, the biggest snook had white hook scars all around the mouth. Old Fighter, Leslie crowed when he came home.

I shook my head. No, Les, I growled, that one is Little Fighter. Old Fighter is still out there. Lucius will have to try for him again.

Lucius tried to smile. He was less upset that Leslie took their fish than by the means used to defeat a legendary creature of his boyhood that he and Rob had never really wished to catch, far less destroy.

*

With the fading of the comet, a cavernous kind of darkness gathered on hot summer afternoons behind gaunt running clouds on the Gulf horizon. Fishing offshore, Lucius saw something—a strange shadow rising from the depths, drawn to the silver sprays of frightened fish chopping the water.

Since the thing had never breached the surface, he could not honestly say just what it was. He stared all about him at the empty sea, then hauled his lines in and took off for home.

Over several days in the late summer of that year, the cane leaves stirred and twisted as if seeking to escape, very unusual in light variable wind, and hearing those small sad scraping sounds that I could not recall from other years, I felt an odd foreboding. Hurricane. After the bad hurricane of 1909, no one expected another quite so soon, but folks were still spooked by that great comet in the spring, and the weather had been undependable all year.

Restless, Hannah Smith informed me that after the harvest, she and Green aimed to move on, maybe find a small place up around Caxambas. They had a lot of back pay coming and wanted part payment in advance so they could invest it in a hog farm. Not that they were in a rush, they only thought they should let me know, give me fair warning.

Hannah was nervous, having dealt me a hard blow. Green had never nagged me before Hannah came, knowing it would not do one bit of good. I owed him so much in back pay that he couldn't leave me—an indentured servant indentured to himself. To pay him off would cripple this year's earnings, which I had counted on to get Watson Syrup back in business. Hannah would have ten months coming, too.

Leslie understood what I was thinking, he never missed much when trouble was afoot. While Hannah was talking, he raised his eyebrows, nodding for my benefit, a bad twist to his mouth. I would recall that cruel expression later. I would also recall having told my new foreman about the advantages of large enterprises over small when certain hard measures were required to get the job done. "Not," I had added, "that you need to be more harsh. You've got them terrified already." This was true. The cane crew were so fearful of him that they hurried their work dangerously when he came into the field and begged his forgiveness even before they had done anything wrong.

*

One day while I was away at Tampa, buying our supplies on credit and taking orders from our buyers, Cox gave a few gallons of our syrup to a passing trader for carrying a temporary crew back to Fort Myers. Those boys, he told me, were so anxious to go home that they never even waited for their pay. "If them ol' niggers was to come up to you someday in the street askin for their money—which I doubt—you can pay 'em then." Les was very proud of the whole deal. Wasn't it part of his job as foreman to keep my payroll just as low as possible?

That evening, my son let me know that this trader had turned up on a Sunday, when everybody but Leslie and those field hands was away upriver on a boat excursion to Possum Key. In fact, he said, in that astonished way of his, Cox was the only one who ever saw that trader, since the four hands were gone by the time the rest came back.

"Also," Lucius insisted when I seemed impatient, "that trader would have had to tack his ship upriver on a falling tide—" Irritable, I cut him off right there. I was distracted at that moment, and anyway I was relieved that we had saved hard money. To question my foreman's story was the last thing I wanted. I had to concentrate, I said, because unless I found just the right buyer for our syrup, this year's harvest would scarcely pay our debts, leaving nothing to tide us over in the year to come. Having just returned from Tampa, I had to head out for Key West that very day.

"There's more to tell," Lucius said quietly. "You can ask Frank Reese." I yelled at him, "Now dammit, Lucius, this man John Smith gets the job done, so don't you pester me about him!" And mild-mannered Lucius shouted back, "Why do you insist on calling him John Smith, when everyone knows that he is an escaped murderer named Leslie Cox!" That was the first time in his life Lucius ever spoke to me with disrespect. I said harshly, "Frank Reese tell you that? Or was it Kate? We will settle this when I get back from Key West. Tell Reese the same."

On the way south, having cooled off a little, I worried that I'd drunk too much and talked too freely. Telling Cox tall tales about outlaw life in the Old West was one thing, but confiding in a boy like that about my financial difficulties and growing desperation might have been a very bad mistake. In his zeal to prove himself as foreman, Cox might have terrorized those hands until they were happy to escape unpaid, which would only spread more rumors about "Watson Payday."

*

Lucius left the Bend for good on the same day I got back from Key West, throwing his stuff into his boat, disgusted. Everyone loved him, they were all out on the bank waving good-bye. I went out, too, but I did not wave. He was departing without explanation, just as Rob had done. This was not like him. I was angry because I was wounded, hurt, more than I would admit to anybody except Hannah. She was a woman in her way, and we enjoyed each other, she was my friend, the only person on the place who called me by my Christian name. But when I went to her, seeking some sort of explanation, I got abuse instead. "Your Lucius is a very good young feller and he loves you dearly and you wouldn't listen to him, Ed. You don't want to hear the truth, or see it, neither."

"What's the truth then, woman, since you know so much?"

Hannah burst out in a rush, "Your boy can't work with that foreman of yours, and me 'n' Green can't neither. We done our best to bide our time 'n' see things your way, Ed, but we sure don't like what's going on! Mr. Waller 'n' me don't care to live no more around that feller." She lowered her voice, looking over her shoulder, but could not stop blurting her fears. "You know me, Ed, I ain't what you'd call a scairdy-cat nor superstitious. But lately Green—well, both of us—been kind of hearin somethin." She looked more and more uneasy. "Hearin this kind of a *hummin*, like Green says, somethin like a hummin on the wind. It feels bad, too, it feels like somethin bad is comin down on us. We never aimed to let you down at harvest time, but we want to leave here!"

She was wringing her hands red on her dish towel, she was so upset. The thin ax mark of a mouth under that sparse mustache was sign of her determination to get away from Chatham Bend as soon as possible, and since she was a strong level-headed woman, I had to listen. "What happens here ain't no business of ours. We never seen nothin and never heard nothin, we ain't never goin to say a word to *nobody*, and that's the truth. But you got to let us go." She was close to tears. "Why don't you talk?" she cried. "You had the use of my man all these years and never no complaint. Since I come here, we have both stuck by you and worked hard. We want our wages and we want to go!"

I had to shout her down. "Now dammit, Hannah, you know the bad luck I have had. If I pay what I owe you and Green, on top of all our debts, there'll be nothing left for laying in supplies!"

"Whose fault is that? It sure ain't ours. *We* didn't need no lawyers." She backed away, afraid she'd gone too far. "You let my man go unpaid all these years, to tide you over your hard times." Hannah's red eyes had filled again, she mopped them with her apron. "You shouldn't ought to ask no more of him, Ed Watson."

Big Hannah shut up because Leslie Cox, drawn to the racket, had come to the corner of the house to watch. He lounged against the wall, picking his teeth, casual and cynical and unabashed. Not until I glared at him would he go away. Then I asked Hannah to think this over, urging her to stay just one more year. When she shook her head frantically, unable to consider such a thing, I said, "If you leave here, you will leave unpaid. That's the rule here."

"Ed, we ain't young no more. We ain't got nothin to take care of us except what we got comin." Hands clenched on her apron, she stood there on the porch steps for a long time. I waited for her out of courtesy. "I reckon we will have to wait," she murmured finally. Nodding to herself, she shuffled back inside in her home-hewn sandals. Except for the cutters working in the cane, Big Hannah Smith was the only person on the place other than me who did not go barefoot.

362

I found Frank Reese down by the boat sheds. "Talk," I said. His eyes flicked toward my hands. He got to his feet before he told me that the Sunday I was away in Tampa, he had gone fishing. Rowing back upriver at dead low water, he had seen something pinkish caught on the jagged oysters on the bar. What it turned out to be was bone and meat. It was so badly chewed by sharks or gators that he couldn't tell who it was.

"*What* it was, you mean."

"Nosuh. I mean *who*. I *knowed* what it was. Soon as I come close."

"Oh hell, a deer, maybe a manatee—"

"Rags wit' it, Mist' Jack. From de hide on it, I seen dat dis here pinkish meat come off a cullud man. Went back wid a shovel next low tide, fixin to bury it. Sump'm beat us to it. Gator, mos' likely."

"Us?"

"Me 'n Mist' Lucius. He seen it, too."

"Is that why he left? Why did you take Lucius?"

"Mist' Lucius, he was along de first time, too. Him and me went fishin, and dass what we found."

The strange "meat" was gone, Lucius was gone. No witness and no evidence, let alone proof. I could make what I liked of Cox's strut and foxy grin. Then something else fell into place that I was sorry I remembered. At Fort White, a few years before, when Leslie had worshiped me as Desperado Watson, I had drunk too much and talked too much, and one day I mentioned those two troublemakers I had taken care of down on Chatham Bend. That was something Leslie Cox would never have forgotten.

*

Kate and the children went along one day when I went to Chokoloskee, and they stayed behind with her friend Alice McKinney. From there Kate went to stay with Mamie Smallwood, then Marie Alderman, finding excuses not to return for weeks. She did not speak of Cox again, but only said that Chatham Bend was too hard on the small children—the rainy season, the mosquitos—and too dangerous with all of those rough men. I assumed she had heard rumors about Josie Jenkins, doubtless from her female friends on Chokoloskee, but she later confessed it had been Leslie who told her.

Chapter 10

Hurricane

In the hurricane season of late summer, the heat and humidity were something to fear. Even at midday, mosquitos hung outside the screens on a miasmal air so moist and sweet that it might have come on a south wind out of the tropics.

That summer we had a young Mikasuki squaw who'd been thrown out by the tribe for living in sin with that damned moonshiner, Ed Brewer. Discarded, she hung on awhile at the edges of Cory Osceola's band over on Onion Key before Brewer showed up and took her back. She was not for his own use, it seems, because he snuck in to the Bend one day, tried to peddle her to our coloreds for a small commission. Sip Linsey was a pious darkie of the old-time religion and Frank Reese was still pining for Jane Straughter, so these boys had no use for this beat-up aborigine with her advanced alcohol addiction and hygienic problems.

When Big Hannah got wind of what was going on, she grabbed Brewer by one arm and swung him off the dock into the current. "Flung that sumbitch off the Bend," Green boasted, "and cast his boat loose, too. Never knew and never cared if he could swim." Hannah led that squaw back to the house for a good wash. "First things first," she said. "I never give much thought to that moonshiner's future. Might not of had one, not if that croc got him." But somebody saw him grab hold of his gunwale, and probably he dragged his boat ashore downriver.

Hannah named the squaw girl Susie and gave her chores around the place to pay her feed, along with as much Baptist instruction as an Injun could get a handle on who could not speak one word of the language. But she'd scarcely started saving Susie's heathen soul when Cox showed up, and Les wasn't there a week before he saw this girl slip into the outhouse on a moonlit night. I guess that stirred his imagination, got him thinking about this and that, because he caught hold of her when she came out. The way he told it at the table—he thought it was comical—he had both her small wrists in one hand while he yanked her old rag of a mission shift up to her waist with the other. He held her there squirming against him until the mosquitos swarming her bare bottom made her weep. Pretty soon she gave up struggling and followed him into the bunkhouse and lay down for him. "Couldn't resist me," Leslie said. Hannah said, "Know somethin, boy? You ain't nothin but a raper. Hang your head in shame."

*

One day Earl Harden turned up in his new launch, which looked and sounded so much like my *Brave* that I thought someone had taken her without permission. Ever since 1901, when he went to Key West to accuse me in that Tucker business, Earl had been scared to look me in the eye, in case Watson decided to shoot him and be done with it. When he had to look at me, Earl smiled so hard that the smile got left behind when he turned away.

This day Earl never hailed the house, just swung up into the current and dropped his passenger without tying up. By the time I reached the porch, he was out of gun range in mid-river, idling his motor. He was not waiting for his passenger, as it turned out, but only curious to see what happened when Watson realized who that passenger was.

I forgot Earl at once, so intent was I on the figure on my dock. He stood dead still against the river shine, arms folded on his chest. Though his silhouette was black on the westering sun and that wild water, I knew him from the big gun butts jutting from his hips like horns against the quicksilver of the current.

Green Waller had come to the door behind me, napkin still tucked into his shirt, Big Hannah huffing behind. In the kitchen, Frank Reese got up from his beans and went out the back door and came around to the corner of the house. Seeing Dutchy Melville, he stepped back, respecting the line of fire. "Lo'd!" his voice said, half aloud. But Dutchy had the Devil's ears, and without looking at him, he raised one hand toward the black man in a kind of greeting. Only my foreman kept right on with his eating, to show his indifference to anything the help might do.

I could not imagine that this man would be so foolhardy, so brazen as to return to Chatham all alone in the broad daylight. Waller was still coughing on his food, unable to explain, while Hannah, who had never known the stranger, stared from one face to another for a clue.

I knew better than to draw my gun, but I worked it loose to have it ready. I had practiced that trick often enough to know how to do it undetected— so I thought. This pistolero drew down on me so quick that I had to jam that gun against my side, using my forearm.

"Drop it," he said.

Green Waller jumped at the dangerous clatter of a loaded weapon on the pinewood porch. Dutchy was grinning and I grinned right back at him, lest he imagine I was paralyzed by those big guns of his. I wasn't. I knew my man. He would never shoot me in cold blood, not without a dose of his palaver.

Out of bone craziness or love of life, Dutchy chose this moment to flip both six-guns high above his head and spring into the air in a backwards somersault, making a full revolution and landing right where he had stood before, catching his guns neatly on the spin, all set to shoot. One barrel was pointed at my heart, the other covered the dropped revolver on the porch. It had not even occurred to me to test him with a lunge for that revolver, and this pleased him, too. He dropped his guns loosely in their holsters and came forward. The others backed and filled like cattle in the doorway. Retrieving my weapon, he dumped the cartridges into his pocket and tossed it back to me.

"Glad to see me, Mister Ed?"

"Bet your sweet life," I said.

" 'Bet your sweet life.' Same ol' Mister Ed." He shook his head, grinning some more, entirely gratified that Desperado Watson hadn't changed a bit. "Damned if it don't feel dandy to be back. Home is where the heart is, ain't that right, Frank?"

That fool Reese had been grinning right along, and Green and Hannah, too. All these idiots were pleased to see this swarthy little criminal who had cost them a year's pay. Even his boss, who had sworn to take his life—even I was tickled to see this youth who had spoiled so much of our hard work in a bad year, causing me insomnia and a pounding rage which I could only stifle out of fear that it might burst my heart.

"There's no work for gunslingers around here. You aim to stay, you better change those fancy duds, start working off that thousand gallons of good syrup you still owe me."

Dutchy said, "Now Mister Ed, you best go easy on a sensitive young feller before he takes a mind to spoil another thousand." He flashed me a grin and ambled over to the bunkhouse, where he found his old coveralls on a bunkhouse nail, put them on, and reappeared, delighted. On purpose, he had given me all that time to reload and get the drop on him. I didn't do it, and a good thing, too. One of his guns was out of sight and the other was rigged butt to the front on his left side, with the gallus on that side hanging loose and the coveralls unbuttoned.

"There's a law against concealed weapons in this county," I informed him. "I'd sure hate to make a citizen's arrest."

"Well, I *know* that, Mister Ed, bless your kind heart!"

Standing there on his bandy legs in the hot swelter of September, young Dutchy Melville looked all set for anything that came his way. I had sworn an oath that he would die the next time he strayed across my path, yet it seemed a great waste to kill such a likely young man so full of ginger. Anyway I had to bide my time. This daredevil could snipe a birdsong entering a man's ear before he heard it.

Lifting his hat, Dutchy greeted Big Hannah with a dandy bow—the first bow she had ever received, without a doubt. Next, he saluted her old hog reiver, "How do there, Mr. Waller!" Green waved and grinned, nudging his Hannah, proud to be singled out by name. Dutchy waved to Frank with a warm grin, and that hard man raised both hands high and shook them in one fist like a black champion. Dutchy set his hat back on his head and looked about him. "Where's Lucius?" When I said, "Gone back north," he nodded, glancing around the place, wary of ambush. "Old place looks kind of run down since I left," he said, "but I reckon it's as close to a good home as a poor outlaw boy could ever hope for, so I sure am grateful for your hospitality."

"You abused my hospitality. Don't forget that. I won't."

"Mister Ed, I won't forget it and I don't regret it. You had it coming," he answered cheerfully. "Anyways, I'm here to take back my old job as foreman."

"You'll have to clear that with the foreman. Right this way."

I was dumbfounded. To feel so sure he would be welcomed back! And in a way, of course, he was quite right. By making me laugh, he had slipped past my guard. I need to laugh as I need salt, having been starved for merriment as a young boy.

Anyway, too much time had passed, I had no heart for killing Dutchy or anybody else. This situation would resolve itself of its own accord.

"You two young fellers have a lot in common," I said. Cox set his fork down.

Without moving a muscle, these two young killers sniffed and circled like mean dogs. From the start, each disdained the other and talked only to me. Melville understood at once why Cox had not deigned to come outside, and Cox saw Melville's dangerous glee and instinctively feared and disliked him. They never bothered to trade greetings, knowing their acquaintance would be too brief to waste breath on civilities.

Leslie belched when told the other's name. Then he stood up, stretching and yawning. To me he said, "Ain't this the little piece of shit who messed up all that syrup?"

And Dutchy said, "Ain't this the back-shooting sonofabitch whose sloppy mouth got you and Frank in so much trouble in north Florida?"

For a man of our back-country breed who loves his mama no less than he loves Jesus Christ, this mortal insult to his ancestry was beyond all hope of negotiation or forgiveness. Cox started nodding as if to say, I will take care of this, and the other mimicked him. With everything spelled out so quick, they nodded simultaneously in bird-like ritual, in philosophical acceptance of the duty to put the other one to death as soon as possible. At the same time, each man shifted his gaze slightly to one side, as dogs do, to avoid a tangle before everything was ready—before, that is, one had the other dead to rights.

Melville helped himself to a hearty repast and went out into the field. Knowing his job from the year before, he ignored the foreman's orders and worked as he pleased, whistling away all afternoon. That whistling was brassy and aggressive, and it got on the foreman's nerves just as intended. He wanted Les to blow up and draw a gun, giving him an excuse to cut him down.

The tension gathered like rolled-up barbed wire, and the next day was much the same. I was very glad that Kate and the children were at Chokoloskee, and relieved that Lucius was gone, too, although I missed him. He was the only son I ever missed.

I warned Les that Dutchy was after his job, that he never went anywhere without a gun and knew how to use it a lot faster than most. "Faster'n Desperado Watson?" Leslie said. He had sniffed out my wariness around Melville. "Hard to take that feller by surprise," I said.

"I noticed." Leslie yawned and stretched some more—not anxious exactly, just flexing his nerves, getting ready. "But I ain't noticed no eyes in the back of that boy's head. How about you?" He took my silence for approval.

From that first day, the enmity between Cox and Melville flickered silently and without cease, like the tongues of hunting snakes. It was only a matter of time before all hell broke loose. Not wanting a shoot-out before the crop was in, I forbade them to carry guns, I even frisked them, but neither went anywhere without his knife. "I need my foreman for the harvest," I told Dutchy. "Can't have you using him for target practice." And Dutchy said, "Mister Ed, I want my job back. The man is in the way. It's up to you." He was still living in a damned fool's paradise. Handing over his shooting irons, he held my eye by way of saying, I trust you, Mister Ed. His trust ate at me, I won't deny that, but it would not save him.

*

In the old days, I ran across outlaws in the Territories and a lot more in Arkansas State Prison. These men agreed they would not hesitate to kill when that seemed necessary. They never made too much of it, made no excuses, nor offered to explain—the less said the better. Belle's son Eddie Reed was one of these and Dutchy Melville was another—a young hellion and an arsonist and robber but not a killer, not unless somebody tampered with his tight-wound spring. Dutchy murdered a good man, Clarence Till, so I can't honestly say he was good-hearted, but he had lots of fun in him and enjoyed good talk, so our folks liked him.

Leslie was different. In my experience, very few have a real taste for killing, as if it were something they were born with. *Sometimes it gets so us ol' boys might feel like killin us a nigger.* Coulter had only been talking about niggers, but even so, I believe the Major was this same cold breed. Whatever the seed of it, they needed to take life the way an ordinary man might need a woman. They persuaded themselves and sometimes others that the man lynched or sprawled bloody on the ground was the guilty party, and if nobody could be called guilty, then "inferior" would do.

I never saw Les easy around anyone outside his clan. He was never sympathetic nor even curious, never humorous, had nothing of interest to tell, nothing to share. His interest in people all came down to how much deference they paid him, which would be demanded sooner or later even if he had to scare and bully them. Because of that, he felt left out and did not know how to find his way back in—a very bad feeling, as I know myself. Perhaps he dreaded his own isolation, not understanding it, and perhaps loneliness made him dangerous. Then he struck something or took something—even a life—to feel in touch again, to make sure he was seen by others and belonged someplace.

The habitual killer who is not a professional—not a lawman, say, or an outlaw or a soldier—must account for himself to his community and church and state. The fear that otherwise he might be banished was why Cox made excuses for his killings, why it was always someone's fault, why he could never accept responsibility for what he'd done. He had been banished long ago, of course, but did not know it yet.

Anyway, those men agreed that the first killing was the hard one. That was true even for Cox, and it was true for me. The next one comes easier, and after that there is nothing much to stop a man from the third and fourth and fifth. It is too late to go back so one may as well go forward, though the track goes nowhere, like a track into the Glades, dying out at last in the sea of grass. Out there, there is no destination, only a great emptiness, a great silence like the south wind in the grasses.

I wondered what Les might have become if circumstances had been different, if nothing had triggered him, laid bare that streak in him, if he had never killed that first time with Sam Tolen. Perhaps he would have gone on pitching, gone off to the major leagues and found the notoriety he needed, throwing beanballs when he felt an urge to hurt. Or perhaps that instinct toward murder would have sprouted anyway, like certain lunacies.

For most men of criminal persuasion, notoriety is crucial, with ill fame far better than no fame at all. Ill fame is a dark kind of honor that replaces traditional honor in certain circumstances. When we were in Duval County jail, a reference in the newspaper to "the handsome young murder suspect Leslie Cox" was the only detail Les gave a damn about. He would snatch that paper right out of your hand to see his name in type, read it over and over, as if that black ink in a public record restored his confidence in his own existence. That utter lack of knowledge of himself made him unpredictable in everything he did, like a rabid dog which has left behind the known traits of its kind to become a strange lone creature.

Back in Arkansas Prison, I knew a mountain murderer—scraggy feller with gat teeth and one long unbroken eyebrow. He was fond of observing that a man's first killing was a kind of initiation, like his first naked rassle with his mother or sister. (Had 'em both, he'd cackle in that rooster voice, so I guess he knew something.) Murder and incest are the worst of sins, because in the committing, a man cuts himself off from the natural order of Creation. So perhaps this man meant initiation into some realm where right and wrong have little meaning and where the sinner plays at being human, having become some unnatural damned thing howling alone in a wilderness where even God can't find him, let alone redeem him.

Sometimes the cold empty universe was how I imagined hell might be when I thought I was headed there myself. I have committed grievous sins and damned myself beyond redemption. William Leslie Cox, a vicious killer at the age of twenty, had done the same, yet he had never turned a hair nor lost a wink of sleep. He saw himself as Dead-Eye Dick—his eyes were dead, all right—but also as a bold-hearted young American.

*

In late summer we had a "family visit" when the mail boat brought a young feller named Joe Gunnin from Fort White whose sister Amelia was betrothed to my nephew Willie. With him was his friend Bill Langford of Suwannee County. Since I was unwelcome in a Langford house, and probably in any Collins house as well, I resented having to feed these two for a whole week until the mail boat came back, took 'em away.

Joe Gunnin mentioned that my mother had died. She was not yet eighty. Cox shrugged, indifferent. He'd neglected to tell me about my mother's death although he'd had carnal knowledge of her granddaughter all this past spring.

There had been no room for Ellen Addison in Auntie Tab's tight, iron-girded plot, and no money to pay for a headstone in the Collins ground at Tustenuggee, where at present she lay like an old hound in an unmarked grave. True, I had mostly disliked my little mother, but it galled me not to have contributed one cent toward funeral expenses. When I asked why my sister had sent no word, Gunnin explained nervously that Mrs. Collins had been feeling poorly.

The past went storming through my heart and mind, grief hard behind it. I said, "Well, that's because she's a damned morphine addict. She lost what poor wits she was born with a long time ago."

Hannah was bringing venison and sweet yams from the kitchen. Offended that I would speak harshly of my own sister, she banged the platter down in front of me, and I served the plates in a bad silence broken only by the knock and scrape of crockery. I regretted that I'd spoken caustically about poor Minnie, who had now moved in with Willie and his bride. When we were little, I could make her cry, saying, "Is your name Minnie? Or is it Ninny?" Those big dark lustrous eyes of hers would fill with tears, as they always did at the first whisper of an unkind word.

Tended by Aunt Cindy, my sister passed most of her time in the chimney corner, where she might breathe unnoticed, like a moth, until the great day when she crept safely to her death. Since our days of terror in the house of Ring-Eye Lige, that was all poor Ninny had ever asked of life—not to be noticed.

*

I questioned Joe Gunnin, checking Leslie's stories. In the long year after Attorney Cone had wangled the dismissal of charges in the Sam Tolen case, Leslie had returned to Fort White, where thanks to his bad reputation, his family had become outcasts and had finally moved away to Suwannee County. Even so, Les was offended that his neighbors had not welcomed him, that there was no baseball team to star for, and that the ball clubs at Live Oak and High Springs had not invited him to try out as their pitcher. All over the south county, folks shied from him as from a dangerous dog. At first he acted sulky, Gunnin said—that was Les all over—but before long he was drinking too much and making threats against those who had joined the lynch mob, until finally he was warned to leave, being in more danger from scared neighbors than he ever had been from the court of justice.

Leslie's plan had been to run off with May Collins, join a big-league baseball team. He needed a grubstake, that was all. Like everyone else, he had heard about Calvin Banks's hoarded-up money, and Calvin's son-in-law had mentioned to him where it might be found. Jim Sailor had been no-account from birth, he'd pulled a muscle in his brain or something. Probably never occurred to Jim that those old folks might be harmed, so he waited for Leslie back along the road, expecting a share of the proceeds—a bad mistake, since finding no proceeds worth sharing, Leslie killed Jim, too. He had not come to Chatham Bend to give me half of the Banks money but because he had no other place to go.

*

I was now so broke that I agreed to sell off my best Fort White farmland to Jim Delaney Lowe, even though he had testified against me. My lawyers had got wind of that sale and were threatening me with forcible arrest and extradition to Columbia County for non-payment of their fees, knowing full well how dangerous that might be.

After such a year, I had reason for my rages, yet it troubled me how violently these eruptions of black bile would split my head, yanking my heart around so hard I scarcely dared breathe for fear of stroke. Breaking out in a sudden chilling sweat, I could only sink down gasping. On those days it seemed that all that was left of Edgar Watson was the dry husk of a man out of the past, stiff and useless as a rot-hollowed tree.

Well, I thought, you'll have good company in Heaven. The newspapers which had come in on that mail boat brought news of Mark Twain's death—the death of the Old America, that was my thought. I could never abide that man's idea that common racism and manifest destiny—what Mandy called imperialism—came down to the same thing, yet that man was on to something that I thought important, for I returned to him over and over, like a panther to its scent. With her Twain books, Mandy had also left behind two volumes of Tolstoy, another high-principled do-gooder whom I could not abide and yet read furiously. In 1910, both Twain and Tolstoy went to meet their Maker and plague Him about the various shortcomings of mankind.

In the Twain writings, I ran across this famous saying: *I don't believe in hell but I am afraid of it.* When I read that out loud to Lucius, he asked me how I felt about it, no doubt wondering if his Papa, too, was afraid of hell. The question was so unlike him that I shrugged him off, saying I'd had no word from the higher-ups as yet as to whether I was bound for hell or not. He laughed politely but was disappointed. True, I could have answered him more honestly. I could have said that on Judgment Day, when one learns the true worth of one's life, the judge whom I feared most would be E. J. Watson.

*

I notified our unwelcome guests that at Chatham Bend nobody ate who did not earn his grub, and I gave 'em every dirty job that I could think of. This was because I did not believe that "kinfolks" was the real reason for their visit. What these two summer rovers really wanted was to take a gander at the famous killer in the family, then go home and boast that they had dined with Desperado Watson in his island lair and his henchman Les Cox, too.

Because Gunnin had recognized "John Smith" and was bound to reveal where he was hiding, Leslie was more riled up about our visitors than I was. When he was drunk, which was most of the time, he would hint in stage whispers that what made most sense was to knock these two greenhorns over the head and toss 'em in the river. Again and again, I reminded him that their kin probably knew where these boys were headed and would show up at the Watson Place with a large posse if they failed to come back.

One night after Green and Hannah had retired to their cabin, and the rest of us were finishing a jug, "John Smith" boiled over when Joe Gunnin slipped and called him Les. He snarled, "The name's John Smith, like you was told. That other feller that you thought you might of saw, you ain't seen hide nor hair of him, you understand me? You go forgettin that again, he will come gunnin for you, that is a promise." Les glared hard at one and then the other. "So don't go makin me regret I didn't shut your fuckin mouths right here this minute."

Dutchy guffawed at Cox's threat, and tried to mimic it. "How'd that one go again? *He's aimin to go gunnin for a Gunnin?*" Dutchy always said whatever popped into his head, I never met such a carefree feller in my life, but this hooting was only another attempt to bait Cox into a showdown. "You two boys ain't never seen that sonofabitch you thought you seen with your own eyes settin right here right now—*that* what he said?" And when Les, white around the mouth, pointed at Dutchy's eyes, Dutchy pointed right back at him and whooped some more. "Don't go squintin at me, Mr. Cox, I beg of you!" He laughed in delight, going on to say that if he were to practice up on his mean squint as long and hard as that dumb hayseed over there across the table, he would probably end up with the same kind of ugly face, all squinched up tight like a bat's asshole.

I thought Les might go for him bare-handed. But drunk though he was, Les knew what this boy was up to, and only squinted harder. And Dutchy yelled, "God have mercy, Mister Ed, please tell that boy to stop that dretful squintin, cause he is scarin a poor city feller half to death!" And he put his head back and laughed so hard that he toppled his chair right over backwards.

Cox's hand shot for his knife as he whisked around the table. But Dutchy had toppled that chair on purpose, and being an acrobat, he kept right on rolling in a backwards somersault and bounced back up onto his feet with something glinting in his hand. Those black eyes were glinting, too—even his teeth seemed to be shining. Nobody saw that knife fly to his hand, but likely he had it in the lining of his boot and had trained himself to slip it out as he was rolling.

Cox was no knife-fighter. He sobered quick and stopped his lunge by grabbing at the table, barging it noisily across the floor. He backed a little and then he quit, dropping his knife. Dutchy kicked it skittering through the doorway. Taking his time, he backed around toward the door to cut off Les's escape. He had Cox where he wanted him, with more excuse to finish him than he would ever need in court. He wrinkled his nose at the thin blade in his own hand, as if loath to defile its pristine edge with the blood of such a coward.

Les could not look at him. He was staring at me, expecting his old partner to step in. *Didn't you tell me you had sworn to kill him?*—that's what his expression said. His predicament was already my fault. When I folded my arms on my chest, he let out a small grunt of angry panic, and I let him twist. I already knew how all this had to end, which didn't mean that the best man would win.

Dutchy's cat eyes twitched in little shivers of the pupil. Possibly it crossed his mind that I might use a gun to stop him, but I don't think so. I poured a drink and lifted it to Dutchy. Understanding this as my sign to let Cox go, he put his knife away. This feller lacked philosophy and the hard heart which would let him kill Cox in cold blood.

Cox sank down slowly on his chair edge. His dark brown hide had a dead pallor in it. He looked relieved to be alive but also incensed by his humiliation and my toast to the victor. But in a moment his expression changed, and the pallor was replaced by a dark excited flush, while the whites of his eyes went kind of dirty watching Dutchy. I never saw eyes so dead in all my life. He had just seen what I had seen, that the mercy he had received was a fatal weakness, and he knew how this feud was going to end, another day. Anticipation of the killing—a metallic foretaste at the back corners of the tongue—put that edge to his mouth which Sam Tolen saw as he knelt in the road on that spring morning, that curled edge which comes with power over life and death.

Dutchy Melville would be missed at Chatham Bend. This rascal had done me a great harm, beyond forgiveness, but that was no longer why he had to go. Les was my friend Will's oldest boy. He had stood up at my trial and offered help in an escape, had that been necessary. Also, he had married my niece May. Like it or not, Les Cox was kinfolks.

As for our Fort White visitors, their summer adventure was all over. From that hour till the day the mail boat came, those boys fell all over themselves thinking up ways to win the favor of Desperado Watson and his outlaws, swearing to John Smith over and over that his presence here was no business of theirs, and never would they mention it to a single soul.

When the boat appeared, I did not quit work, nor walk over to the dock to say good-bye. Before leaving, Gunnin and young Langford confided to Hannah their great shock at my failure to express the slightest grief at the sad news of my poor old mother, and my cruel derision toward my poor ill sister—small wonder I had such a dreadful reputation! This was passed along to me by loose-mouthed Green the Hog Man, who had sense enough to wait until they had departed. According to him, Big Hannah bit their heads off. "Ain't that why you two come gawkin around here in the first place? To visit a real live bad man in his hideout, then run back home and brag about it?"

Like my dear Mandy, Hannah Smith had a pretty good idea of who Ed Watson was. She did not approve of all his little ways, but she would not hear him criticized by anybody who had not earned the right. I only had a few true friends and that woman was one. She saw my good side and she wished

*

Needing some income to pacify my creditors, I drove everybody hard to get the crop in early, get our syrup to market ahead of my main competition, which was Old Man House, upriver at House Hammock, and George Storter and Will Wiggins at Half Way Creek. With my large vats and boiler, I could turn out more syrup than all those three together, and the Cuba strain I had developed made better syrup, too. But to stay ahead, I would have to expand this operation, farm more land, and for that I needed some new capital investment.

In early October, Kate returned from Chokoloskee, where people were turning cold toward her, she said. By now it was common knowledge that E. J. Watson was harboring two killers and no doubt other criminals as well. According to another rumor, the Watson gang aimed to found an outlaw empire back in this wilderness. Even Ted Smallwood, who claimed to be my friend, was referring sardonically to "Emperor Watson" and taking credit for the nickname, which actually had been given to me by the old Frenchman.

"My trigger finger's itchin somethin pitiful," Les would whisper—his way of complaining that he wanted the suspense over and wouldn't mind a little help from his uncle Ed. Leslie's nerves were getting to him now, and everyone was looking drawn and tired. The tension was a lot more fatiguing than hard labor in the field, and it had gone on too long. I could no longer pretend to myself, far less to Kate, that our children were perfectly safe here on the Bend, and anyway, the time had come to confront those Bay folks and their stories before any more damage could be done. I ordered Kate not to unpack, since I was taking her right back there the next morning.

Dutchy came with us at his own request, saying he needed a change of air after "all them weeks cooped up with that yeller skunk you got for foreman." The knowledge that Cox was laying for him and would kill him at the first chance—and his doubts about where I stood in the matter—were wearing away at Dutchy's spirits. He wasn't so sunny anymore, and he had dark circles under his dark eyes from watching his back throughout the day and listening all night. As soon as the *Brave*'s lines were cast off, the poor feller said to Kate, "Excuse me, ma'am," and lay down in the stern. He fell asleep flat out on the bare boards while the children stared at him, and he never woke up till the launch nudged the dock at Chokoloskee.

Dutchy was proud to see his Wanted poster plastered all over Smallwood's post office. The whole community sidled down to have a look at this "armed and dangerous" killer wearing big six-guns. Folks were elbowing and grinning, making nervous jokes, wondering if those Wild West guns were real. Dutchy did his sudden back flip on the dock, coming up with six-guns blazing at the sky and scattering his delighted audience into the trees. But when he strutted up the dock and crossed the yard and banged his heels on the store porch, there arose a low and ugly mutter, that mix of fear and anger sensed by Kate. Folks felt humiliated by "Watson's hired gun," and they blamed me.

"Dammit, E.J.," Smallwood whispered, "folks don't want that kind of outlaw around here."

"How about my kind, Ted?"

"That Cox feller neither." Smallwood was in no mood to be teased.

"*Cox?*" I said. I gazed after Kate, who had gone to see Marie Alderman's new baby.

Ted looked alarmed. "Weren't your missus, E.J. She never told us nothin. It's just, some feller was mentionin John Smith—his scar and all—and another feller said, 'That so-called preacher you are talkin about sounds mighty like a killer name of Leslie Cox.'"

I nodded. "Walter Alderman," I said.

"No, no, I never said that. Can't rightly recall who might of mentioned it, E.J., but it sure weren't Walter." Just when I needed someone I could trust, Smallwood was lying to protect a neighbor. Ted's friendship with Ed Watson, which he had valued so much back in the early days, was now a burden.

Raising my voice to be heard by those crowding the door, I informed the postmaster that nobody should believe these scurrilous rumors about the Watson Place. I had never hired the two men in question, they had just turned up. I had to take who I could get, so I put 'em to work, but they would be sent away after the harvest. I was making a new life here in the Islands and establishing an up-and-coming industry, and I wished to remain on the best of terms with my friends and neighbors.

No one seemed to be reassured, and Dutchy didn't help a bit when he celebrated my speech by firing off his guns like firecrackers. Still, no man cared to challenge my sincerity, not with that drunk pistolero there beside me, flipping those six-guns every minute to scatter the kiddies, make them screech.

Kate rejoined me, very close to tears. Like Friend Smallwood, my wife was faltering just when I needed her. She dreaded going back to Chatham and she dreaded staying here, where doors were closing. She no longer felt welcome at Marie's house and she feared for our little children, who were crying. How about Mrs. Smallwood? I asked in a low voice. Oh no, I can't, we've imposed on them so often. Wigginses? McKinneys? She shook her head.

I went to Aldermans. "Walter, come on out!" He cracked his door. "You listen to me, boy," I said. "It's nearly two years since I came back to the Islands, and never once have I said a word about how you ran off from Columbia so you wouldn't have to help me out as a defense witness." I let that sink in. "For the moment, I won't tell 'John Smith' who revealed his real name to this community."

Alderman tried to talk. Nothing came out. He did not dare say that he'd abandoned me before my trials because he thought I was guilty and did not wish to testify, though Marie had hinted to Kate that this was true.

"By the way, I'd be much obliged," I finished pleasantly, "if you and Marie could take in Kate and the children while I finish up my harvest at the Bend."

Walter said he'd sure be happy to oblige me, and I said I'd be happy to pay their keep. That's the way we left it. I went back to the boat and told my wife and children that they could expect a warm welcome at Aldermans. She moaned, in tears, which was not like her, and I told her to get hold of herself and not upset the children. Dutchy helped me lug their stuff to Aldermans. Having no hand free to draw, he stepped along uneasily in a kind of zigzag, turning halfway around every few steps, thrashing his head from side to side like a stepped-on snake.

*

Dutchy was sodden by the time we left Chokoloskee, and I drank with him some more on the way home. Staring straight ahead, he looked bewildered. He sensed the darkness in my mood, and more than once he turned to look at me, as if to catch an expression on my face that would let him know where Mr. Watson stood. "Mister Ed," he sighed after a gasping snort. Not knowing what he wished to say, he was almost wistful. He knew I liked him despite the harm he'd done, and was probably counting on my presence to protect him.

I ran the boat down the autumn coast, parting the immense solitude of this empty coast, thinking of nothing. In the October afternoon, the cloud reflections appeared sunk beneath the surface of the sea, like submerged white mountains. The boat turned east and passed through the narrow mangrove channel into the delta. Toward dusk, she slowed, approaching Chatham Bend.

Splashing water on his face to sober quickly, Dutchy studied the lay of the land as we drew near, loosening his guns in their holsters. Hopping off onto the dock as the boat coasted in, he waited anxiously for the tossed line, at the same time peering about him like a deer. For all his big guns and sideburns and bravado, he looked pale and wide-eyed as a boy. He slapped a mosquito, rubbed his neck, touched his gun butts lightly over and over, not knowing where Cox might be. The river and its walls of silent mangrove, the oncoming night, ate at his nerve.

I let the *Brave* drift downstream to clear the dock before turning her bow offshore.

"Mister Ed?" he called. "Where are you going?" His voice was a notch higher than usual. I almost yelled at him, *Duck down!* because from the house in this late light he would be silhouetted on the river.

"Lost Man's." I felt all wrong about everything.

"At night? How come you never said nothin about it? Mister Ed?"

His questions stabbed me. I lifted my hand in a kind of blessing and gunned the boat into her turn as those questions wandered out over the river.

Dutchy knew that on that dock he was a dead man. In a sudden astonishing sideways spring, he leapt onto the bank, then bounded in swift zigzags toward the boat sheds, seeking cover and the time to appraise his situation. In short, he did exactly what I figured he would do. I never talked to Cox about it, never planned it, yet I knew Cox's instincts, knew he would be ready.

A voice from the house—Big Hannah—cried a warning. I fixed my gaze dead ahead, increasing speed. When the shot rang through the twilight, my heart jumped, because it hurt. A second shot, scattering the echo of the first, was broken by scared clamor from the house.

At dark the river turned a shining black beneath black walls of mangrove. In the west, the rigid stars burned all the way down the sky to the Gulf horizon. Escaping the delta, I anchored on the flats off Mormon Key. Bright phosphorous glimmered where the hook tore the water. I threw down what remained in Dutchy's jug, in a kind of toast to Herbie Melville. Stupid sonofabitch, I muttered, as tears came to my eyes. The hurled jug made a *smack* on the flat surface.

*

That was the tenth of October, a blue Monday. At first light, I went south to Key West. Entering by the back door of Eddie's, I remained three days—left for dead by unknown companions and rolled under the bar. Crawling out at last into the light, clothes caked with stale beer spill and rank sawdust and piss—my own, I hoped—I reeled over to White Street, where the kind sisters Metz put me to bed and took turns trying to cheer me. When I finally left the premises in new-washed clothes, it was a Friday. I returned to my boat and headed north without any clear idea where I was going.

My story was: I had dropped Dutchy at the Bend on my way south to Key West, which was quite true. If there was a shooting, I was not responsible, and if Green and Hannah doubted that, I could not help it. Frank Reese, he liked Dutchy fine, but Frank also knew that what Dutchy had done could never be forgiven. Anyway, he would keep his opinions to himself.

I stopped off at Lost Man's Beach to make sure I was seen by the Hamiltons and Thompsons on my return journey. Foolishly I waited until Mrs. Hamilton appeared before thinking up my poor excuse for coming. With her men away, up Lost Man's River, she seemed leery of me and behaved queerly, never asking if I wished something to eat. I was not welcome there and I left quickly.

I stayed that night with the Lee Hardens on Wood Key. More rumors had come from Chokoloskee. The Hardens were troubled by the weather, a heavy stillness in the atmosphere that made everybody irritable and restless. Concerned for my safety, they advised me to lay over a few days until this storm front had dispersed or passed on through.

*

At dawn, the Gulf sky looked blotched and peculiar. I went on north. Ascending Chatham River against the tide, the *Brave* throbbed hard against the whole force of the river. I dreaded seeing Dutchy's friends, but at the Bend no one came out onto the porch or walked down to the dock. The fields were empty and the house was silent. Perhaps they had learned of the oncoming storm and had gone off with the mail boat or some fisherman. Being a fugitive, Cox might not have gone with them. I called and shouted. There was no echo here, there never had been, yet I heard my own voice as if I had been answered by Jack Watson. I did not call again.

Taking the shotgun, I approached the house and peered in through the windows. Unwashed pots and mildewed food left on the table were less repellent than the strange thickened flyblown blackish pools on floor and stair. I kept on going.

In the boat shed, the old coveralls on their nails gave me a start. In a strange storm light, the wind whispered, cracking the coco palms, stirring dry leaves on the cane stacked at the boiler, feeling out the Watson Place for the coming storm. By now every helmsman on the coast would keep an eye on that weather off to westward, knowing the worst of it was gathering a day or two away in the Gulf of Mexico.

I mustered my nerve and called a final time. There was nobody here—or nobody, at least, who wished to answer. That silence seemed to creep around behind me, and I didn't linger. Dutchy might be closer than I wished to know. If Cox had dragged the body to the river, he might be caught under the dock or hung in a drowned tree under the hull, held fast by current.

Mister Ed?

*

At Pavilion Key, the clam boats were all gone. Instead of running to throw her arms around my neck, Pearl Watson fled me, flying across the bare and littered barren where the tents had been. From behind her mother's shack, she called in a frightened voice that everyone had left here in the hour before. As for Minnie, she had run off to Key West to get married—"to get away from you and your bad reputation!" Josie hollered without opening her door.

I rapped on the shack door, ordering Josie to pack up her stuff and come with me because a bad storm was on the way.

Tant wrenched her door open. We nodded at each other. Brother and Sister had had a drink or two, and Sister did the talking. "If I'd of wanted to leave here, Mister Jack, I would of left a while ago with all the rest of 'em." She had a fit of coughing. "But I don't aim to leave, and Tant don't neither, cause Pavilion Key ain't goin anywhere at all."

Tant gave a kind of rueful smile by way of saying that Josie was his sister and her kids were his sweet niece and baby nephew, and if his sister aimed to stay, he reckoned he'd stay, too. An old-fashioned feller like Tant Jenkins would have no choice about it, because this comical bachelor whom nobody took seriously had always been serious about his family. Tant Jenkins was thirty-some years old and tall and skinny, a handsome man behind that darned mustache, which jumped on his lip like a hairy frog whenever he spoke, made him look foolish. I believe he knew that but he wore it anyway and let folks laugh.

Tant stepped outside and we discussed the weather, concluding that this storm might be a hurricane. Feeling neglected, Josie hollered, "Mister Jack? This ol' chicken coop of mine come through last year's blow just fine, and no storm couldn't never be as bad as that ol' Hurricane of nineteen and oh-nine!" As I have related, this small woman was spry in the head and spry in bed, and she had grit and plenty of high spirits to go with it, but common sense was quite another matter. I hollered back, "Well, you and Tant can perish if you want, but if that little feller on your teat is mine, the way you're telling people, I am taking him along with me, and Pearl, too!"

Josie cackled. "You show up at Chokoloskee with your backdoor family, Mister Jack, that preacher's daughter will kick you out of bed!" She was right, of course. Kate was weepy enough without having this drag-ass bunch dumped on her household. I said, "My wife is not your business, Missus. And she knows how to hold her tongue, which is more than you do."

With my encouragement, Tant Jenkins tried to reason with his sister, who ignored him. "You can go to hell, Jack Watson, and take Pearl with you, if she's fool enough, and Stephen, too!" (When drunk, she called Tant by his real name, which was S. S. Jenkins.) "But I aim to stay right here where I'm at with your sweet baby boy!"

I was tempted to take her by the scruff of her neck and throw her into the *Brave* with the two children, towing Tant's small boat along behind. I considered this, looking around for Pearl. There was no sign of her. And Josie gave me a queer wry look, saying that poor little Pearl was scared to death of her own father, together with everybody else along this coast.

In the end, Tant decided he would stay there, too. I said angrily, "If you damned people are so drunk and shiftless you won't save yourselves, then you better start your praying. I am leaving."

Pearl slipped around from behind the shack and followed me toward the water, keeping her distance like a half-wild dog, never coming so close that she could not cut and run. At the skinny dock, gray wind waves slapped along the pilings. She watched me casting off the lines, frightened to leave and frightened to be left behind, frightened of the future altogether. Except for Tant's moored sailing skiff, rising and falling on the whitecaps, the anchorage was wind-dirtied and desolate. I said, "Are you sure, girl?" and the child nodded. I blurted out, "Your daddy loves you, Pearl." I'd never told her that before, not in so many words. That poor pale thing was leaned way back against the wind, thin and frail against that high wall of dark weather. She waved and waved until sea mist closed over her and she was gone.

This was Saturday, the fifteenth of October.

Off Rabbit Key, the *Brave* passed the last clam boats, on their way north along the coast toward Caxambas. No one on those boats returned my wave. When twilight came, I was headed east down Rabbit Key Pass. At dark, I moored in a lee cove on Chokoloskee and walked across to Aldermans and crawled in beside Kate. She pretended she had not awakened. Bereft, I had a need to hold her. She was trembling but made no sound. "Kate?" I whispered. "No," she murmured, "please, no, Mr. Watson!" She was staring straight up at the ceiling. I withdrew, feeling more alone than ever.

In fitful sleep, I dreamed that the great crocodile had come ashore on my side of the river. When I went to the boat, what looked at first like a dead tree left by flood lay stranded on the bank below the dock. I shuddered at the size of it, the long and heavy head set into the mud like a slab of iron, the smiling curl of jaw beneath the eye, rough jutting teeth. Between the pale claws and spread toes of the small forefeet, greening the ancient dorsal scutes and the stone eyes, grew a crust of algaes from lost ancient epochs, as if this hard-ridged armored brute had been here from the start of life on earth.

In one thrash of its heavy tail, the crocodile was gone. The muck exhaled the weight of it with a hard *thuck,* and the brown surface opened like a wound and slowly closed, leaving brown viscous bubbles. Where the thing had lain was a fossil excretion, a white sphere as smooth as clay or stone.

*

On Sunday, on the eve of the Great Hurricane, young Claude Storter came into Smallwood's store with his brother Hoad. Though disconcerted to see me in the corner, he went ahead and blurted out his story—that on Friday evening, "Watson's Negro" had made his way to Pavilion Key and reported the murder of three people at Chatham Bend.

"This nigra accused Leslie Cox," Claude Storter said. Then he said, "He claimed Mr. Watson put Cox up to it, but all them Danielses just hollered at him, made him back down."

The men in the store gazed my way, let their gaze slide. Two went out. I tried to find my voice. *"Three?"* The word came out in a low croak. I had betrayed myself with that reaction, but nobody noticed unless it was young Claude. "Three," he repeated. "Melville and Waller and the big Smith woman."

"The white people?"—again, that broken croak like a gigged bullfrog. I couldn't take this in. And what had happened to the field hands, at least seven—

The black man, escaping in a skiff, had come to Pavilion Key on Friday afternoon. Tant Jenkins had led a burial party up Chatham River early Saturday morning. Meanwhile, the clammers, knowing Cox was at large, and restless due to signs of coming storm, had broken camp on Pavilion Key and headed for Caxambas, taking the nigger. At first I had thought that nigger must be Sip, but Sip would never have had the nerve to go ashore at Pavilion Key with such a story.

Frank Reese. Why? Frank had watched the *Brave* passing those boats off Rabbit Key the day before.

Hannah and Green. Green was one of those men you'd never miss, he was such a fool, but after all these years those fool ways of his had got under my skin. He was part of the place and I would miss him, and my hogs would miss him worse. As for Hannah, she was strong-hearted and straightforward, a true friend, and the hardest worker on the place except for me.

I had gone ashore at Pavilion Key on Saturday at midday, after Tant had led that burial party up Chatham River. Tant and Josie had known the whole Reese story while they talked with me, yet not even drunken Josie had dared bring it up. Did they fear that Jack Watson had ordered the three killings, as Reese first claimed? Or taken part, perhaps? I sank down on a nail keg, greatly shaken. Frank must have assumed I was the man behind Dutchy's ambush, and that I'd had Green and Hannah taken care of, too, because I owed them so much money.

I stared at the floor, my head between my hands. I was thinking fast because my life depended on it. My obvious shock upon hearing this evil news, my pallor and speechlessness—and also the fact I had come here yesterday and put myself into their hands, which a guilty man would surely not have done—all that would argue for my innocence for long enough, at least, to let me leave. I was not safe here, I would sleep better in Everglade. Also, I had to catch Frank at Fort Myers before he told his tale to Sheriff Tippins.

I stood up abruptly, called good-bye, and was out the door before a group could organize to stop me. Knowing I was armed and desperate, no one challenged me or trailed me to the dock, but when I looked back, the whole crowd had come out onto the store porch, gazing after me as the *Brave* moved off-shore.

*

Gaunt twilight birds were stalking the bare flats. Even in the channel, the *Brave* churned a mud wake all the way across, grinding the bottom. Such dead low tide was another sign of storm.

Claude Storter had reached Everglade ahead of me. His father was anxious to believe in my innocence, and seemed to do so. Because my launch was too low on fuel to risk rounding Cape Romano in such weather, I asked Bembery to take me as far as Marco on the *Bertie Lee*, and toward dawn, after Mrs. Storter was in bed, he agreed to do it. To hell with it! said Captain Bembery, banging down the jug.

From behind her thin wall, Mrs. Storter cried out in anguish when young Claude volunteered to go as crew. In the morning, she would not acknowledge my thanks and good-byes, in fact refused to speak to me at all. Even Bembery seemed to regret his promise, as if I had tricked him.

We left at daybreak. Towing a skiff, we took the *Brave* up Storter River past the bridge and lashed her tight into a small cove in the mangroves. On this very dark and ominous Monday morning, there was no sunrise, only oppressive leaden light at all points of the compass, with the barometer falling and the wind gusting hard from variable directions.

Under way, I questioned Claude about "the Negro" and his story—how he had escaped from Cox and rowed out to Pavilion, how he had handled those hard questions from my friends. Claude related how close that man had come to being lynched when he admitted laying his black hands on a white woman's body, because this could never be forgiven, not even if his claim was true that Cox had ordered him at gunpoint to gut her out, fill her body with sash weights and God knows what so they could haul her off the bank into the river. At no point had this hard nigger lost his composure. He was steady and measured even when he contradicted his first version.

The *Bertie Lee* dropped me at Caxambas and cast off at once, so buffeted by wind out in the channel that the Storters had no time to turn to wave. Gale winds thickened by torn leaves and dust mixed with slashing fits of rain. Shielding my eyes, leaned against the wind, I trudged north across the island to Bill Collier's store in the Marco settlement, where I found Dick Sawyer. He did not dare refuse to row me across the swollen creeks to the mainland shore. All alone with me out in the storm, unnerved by the surly wind chop in the channels, the man babbled. By now the bilge water sloshing around our ankles threatened to tip seas in over the gunwales. I kept on bailing.

*

Walking north through the pinewoods, I arrived soaked through at Naples, as its inhabitants had named the litter of shacks huddled at the pier head. Captain Charlie Stewart, known as Pops, was the postmaster, and his house had a spare room for the circuit preacher. That's where I stayed that black and howling night, although I never took my boots off or got into bed. I could not sleep with that wind shaking the walls and a heart heavy with dread. I only hoped that Bembery and Claude had found safe anchorage, knowing that the *Bertie Lee* could never have reached Everglade before that storm hurled itself upon our coast.

Downstairs, the door was banging in the wind. Pops and wife lay like the dead, listening to the creaking of the killer's footfalls, back and forth all night. Over and over, I prayed for my family at Chokoloskee and also for those two children at Pavilion Key, fearful that with so many in peril, God might ignore the prayers of a deep-dyed sinner who had no true faith in Him, and had taken His name in vain throughout his life.

*

That Monday evening of October seventeenth, when the Great Hurricane descended—one week to the day after the murders at the Bend—Tant pushed Josie and her young as high as he could reach into the mangroves. He lashed them tight into the limbs, then got a grip on scrawny Pearl, while Josie clutched her infant boy under her slicker. But the few mangroves left unrazed by the clam colony were squat and meager, and storm seas soon began to break across the island. Hour after hour, the battering cold wind and water wore at Josie's strength, until at last, being slight and small, she could scarcely hang on to her limb. She was shifting her grip when a big sea loomed up through the rain. Tant yelled too late, and when it crashed, the baby was torn from her arms without a cry and borne away into that maelstrom.

On a previous visit, I had asked Josie his name. "What name do you fancy, Mister Jack?" his mother teased me. "Well, Josie, if he's really mine, the way you're telling people, then name him Artemas after his great-grandfather." Thinking I wished to bestow my family name (which poor Pearl had been given, not by me but out of local habit), Josie whispered happily, "Master Jack. Master Jack Artemas Watson." She lifted the baby and gazed into its eyes. "Oh, yes! He's yours, all right!"

"Jack Artemas Jenkins," I corrected her. Josie frowned but made no comment for the moment. All the while Jack Artemas observed me with my own blue eyes, shining over the round of her small breast.

After the hurricane, when the water had subsided, they hunted for that infant boy, picking around among the mangrove roots, heartbroken and bedraggled. If the Lord works in mysterious ways, few of them are merciful, and the last of my line was awaiting his mother when the seas receded, not one hundred yards from where she'd lost him. The tiny hands protruded like sponge polyps from the sand, as if the babe, his blue eyes wide, had stood upright just below the sea-smoothed surface, yearning to be lifted up even as he perished.

Up and down the coast, over that night, the hurricane blew the water from the bays, blew every last green leaf from the outer islands. It blew most of the shacks and cabins down and carried the boats out to sea or far inland. It blew that coast to ragged tatters, destroying last chances, scattering last hopes. It sucked the last turquoise and blue from the inshore waters, transmuting sea and sky and bay to the dead gray of the marl-caked mangrove. It blew the color right out of the world.

*

The road north was strewn with fallen trees. The horse had to pick and clamber its way through. Where not blown flat and pointing in the wind's direction, the woods were twisted in giant snarls of broken growth that oddly brought back Cousin Selden's descriptions of the blue lines of Union infantry at Fredericksburg, struck over backwards by barrage after barrage from our artillery.

On Tuesday evening I reached Punta Rassa, where I found a man to run me up the river to Fort Myers. Wanting nothing to do with my ungrateful children, I slept in the hayloft at the livery stable, unshaven, dirty, and in dangerous temper. Early next morning, I went to the courthouse, where the court clerk informed me that Sheriff Tippins had left the day before, bound for Chokoloskee, and had probably reached Marco not long after I left.

This court clerk in his tight high collar, stuffed to the gills with unearned self-importance, was none other than my own son E. E. Watson, who had shunned his father ever since returning to Fort Myers from north Florida. Seeing his parent standing before him red-eyed and disreputable, in filthy clothes, the new court clerk was as cold and haughty as he dared to be. "Sheriff Tippins has interviewed your nigger. Sheriff Tippins wishes to question you, as well." And he uttered that world-weary sigh which drove Carrie and Lucius to distraction.

"That what you call Frank now? *Your nigger?*" Disdaining the Lee County Court spittoon, I spat on the varnished floor. Frank Reese was a nigger, true enough, but all those years when this ingrate infested my house in Fort White, Frank had been kind to him, looked out for him, cleaned up after his carelessness and plain damned laziness out in the field. "Never mind," I barked. "I want to talk with him."

"The Sheriff has left strict instructions that nobody may see this prisoner under any circumstances." Eddie shuffled his little papers in my face, to show he was too busy to waste time with me. I could scarcely look at him, that's how repelled I was by my own flesh and blood, my own dark red hair, reborn in this pale and freckled carcass. I took a deep breath, trying to calm down. Unless he bent the rules right now, I told him, I would go down the street to my attorney and have him cut out of my will, but not before stripping off my belt and flaying him raw.

"Sir, this is a court of *law!*" he squawked, outraged. But my threat had taken the fight out of this feller—not that I took much satisfaction from it, wall-eyed as I was with worry and exhaustion. E. E. Watson, deputy court clerk, frowned in official disapproval, folding his arms high on his chest and glaring the other way as I went through the rear door marked NO ADMITTANCE.

At the holding cell, white drunks and drifters commented sardonically on my poor appearance, saying I looked like I belonged in there with them. In their own cramped pen next door, the blacks said nothing. I told these lowlifes I required a word with Nigger Reese, but the white boys only yelled that Sheriff Tippins had locked that dirty nigger in the cellar to keep them from cutting his throat the way they wanted.

I went out a side door into the jail yard and knelt beside a ventilation grate along the wall. My knee pushed a trickle of dry dirt down the hole. I whispered, "Frank?" No sound came, but I heard a listening. "Frank?" I repeated.

Still on my knees, I told Reese he must trust me. I gave my word that I never knew that Cox would go crazy, try to kill them all. I asked that man down in the darkness to recall how Jack Watson had helped his friend Frank go free back there in Arkansas and had given him employment ever since. I told him I had returned to Chatham Bend before the storm to take him and the others to a place of safety. How could he imagine that Cox had my approval in those killings?

"Frank? Answer me. What happened? How come you told those lies at Pavilion Key?" But nothing came up through the grate but a faint urine stink.

In the grate corner where moisture had collected in a crack grew the small white flower of a weed. I picked that flower, twiddled it to calm myself. "Frank? Goddamnit, Frank, what happened to the field hands? What did you tell Tippins?" On my knees this way, in the cement bits and limestone turds and broken glass, in the bare heat, my brain had started throbbing, on the point of hammering holes through at the temples, so suddenly incensed was I about Reese's clear intent to do me harm. A man I'd counted on. The only man I could still count on besides Lucius.

But no answer rose out of that grate. "Black bastard!" I called down the hole. "You damn well better tell the Sheriff you were lying, and the grand jury, too, or you're a dead man!" I jumped up and booted the jail wall like a loco drunk, bruising my foot.

Eddie was watching from the door, his arms still folded. He had heard everything. "Tell your sister her father expresses his regrets that he has no time to pay a call." I strode right past him, never looked at him.

*

The streets were empty under a dark and heavy sky that held no rain. Overhearing a conversation about the Governor's untimely death, I stopped dead in the street, trying to think clearly. My last hope of state funding for my visionary plans had been buried in Nap Broward's grave.

If I had any sense, I told myself, I would swallow my pride and borrow from the Langfords and head north on the train this very evening. Yet it was too late to start a new life somewhere else—starting dead broke when I was nearly fifty-five, a murder suspect and a fugitive, dishonored and discredited on every side.

I was too tired to think. I knew I must cool down here, keep my head. If I protested my innocence, talked my way through it, as I had done so many times before, I was going to be a free man one more time.

*

Over and over on the journey south, I wondered why Frank had done me so much harm with his damned lie. If Cox had threatened him, as he claimed, he had even less reason to blame me for those murders. Cox might lie out of perversity, but why would Reese do it? We had been through a lot together, fifteen years and more. The man knew Jack Watson for better or worse, knew we were friends.

I felt sure Frank would agree with this, though he knew better than to speak it aloud. Maybe he thought I had taken his loyalty for granted, maybe he thought I had abused it here and there. Perhaps I had. But even if he felt justified, would he have risked his neck by going to Pavilion and admitting participation in those crimes, just for revenge? I could not believe that.

Gradually I had calmed, come to my senses. Perhaps my fear of Reese's testimony was unfounded. As Calvin Banks had shown at Madison, a black man's testimony won small credence in the white man's court.

That evening I caught up with Sheriff Tippins at the Marco store. We talked privately in the cabin of the *Falcon*. I told him the best thing he could do was to deputize me to arrest Cox, who could neither swim nor run a boat and who was therefore trapped at Chatham Bend. Since Cox could not know where Reese had gone, far less that the murders had been reported, he would not be suspicious when I showed up. I was the only man, in fact, who could take Cox alive with no risk to the lawmen.

Tippins suggested that my real aim might be to eliminate a dangerous witness under the cover of the law. He would not deputize me. He said, "I consider myself a good friend of the family, Mr. Watson, and I'd sure like to oblige Miss Carrie's daddy, but the best favor I could do you now would be to take you into custody for your own protection." Sheriff Clem Jaycox, of Monroe County (who had beat out my old nemesis Dick Knight in the last election), was gratified that the Dutchy Melville case had been cleaned up. He promised that Sheriff Jaycox would waive jurisdiction over E. J. Watson in return for custody of the Negro, and that no jury in Lee County would convict Walt Langford's father-in-law for murders committed by another man, not while Frank B. Tippins had a say about it. "Not on your life, Mr. Watson," Tippins added. "If you take my meaning."

However, I could not trust Frank Tippins nor anybody else. I got the drop on him before he could arrest me and marched him back over to Bill Collier's store. Disgruntled, he warned me that he'd have to charge me with resisting arrest, not to mention suspicion of murder, but I had already backed out of the light into the darkness.

*

From Caxambas, Dick Sawyer ran me south to Everglade, where Captain Bembery described how in the hurricane, the *Bertie Lee* had abandoned the open water route for the inside channels and finally took refuge from the storm at Fakahatchee. Before the wind shifted and the Gulf rushed at the land just before midnight, the inner bays had emptied out entirely, the bare flats silver as a gleaming fish beneath the racing moon. With no water to float the boat, the Storters did not make it home to their terrified family until three days later.

Bembery helped me haul the *Brave* out of the mangroves. She had sucked marl sand into her engine when she crossed the Bay on the eve of the Great Hurricane, as the papers called it, and was making an ominous low grinding. Also, she had storm water in her fuel. Her motor skipped and missed, crossing the Bay.

Chokoloskee was a muddy ruin with windrows of dead fish, uncovered privy pits, storm debris and broken boats, and rags high up in the branches of the trees. Every cistern had been flooded out, with no rain since the storm and no fresh water to be found anywhere closer than the upper Turner River or on Marco Island. The low heavy sky was an impenetrable gray, and the island stank of putrefaction and perdition.

Jim Howell having lost his house entirely, was camped with his new son-in-law, Bill House. At Aldermans, the floor was a foot deep in bay mud, with the one window gone and their lantern broken. I found Kate shattered, imagining I was dead. "Why did you abandon us without a word?" she cried. "Where have you been?" Walter Alderman described the great tides which rose with the churning onshore wind, until finally folks had been driven from their shacks to take shelter in the little church up on the mound. When the water rose ten inches above the church floorboards, the men made a raft of the door and siding, but being so terrified of boats, Kate vowed she would perish in the church, hugging her little ones, rather than brave the chaos of that storm. Finally she fled with all the rest, retreating to the top of the highest mound, called Indian Hill, forty feet above sea level. Kate had plump Baby Amy on her arm, and a food packet and dry clothes, and Alderman had one hand free to lead Ruth Ellen. His brother Horace, here from Marco, kept an eye on Little Ad, who boasted that he had climbed that mountain unassisted.

Before the winds abated and the seas retreated, the Great Hurricane of October 1910 had submerged most of Chokoloskee Island. Huge storms had struck our coast for two years in a row, and this one had been worse than the year before—something terrible and primitive and wild, Kate whispered, like the Lord's Creation. Unable to find words to account for her deep fear, she began to tremble, and wept when I took her in my arms. Teasing her, Marie Alderman said that Kate would not be separated from a little wooden whatnot stand I had carved for her birthday back in our courting days, which reminded me that next Monday was Kate's birthday. To cheer her, I vowed that her husband would be here "if my life depended on it" to celebrate her twenty-first with his dear wife. Kate begged me not to make any more morbid jokes, because October 24 would follow two "black Mondays" of murder and hurricane, and bad luck and disasters came in threes.

I gathered from Alderman that his Island neighbors had been too stunned by the storm and too defeated by the whole ordeal to organize a posse, but everyone was suspicious of Ed Watson, and the killer Cox was still at large. Those who were not off hunting fresh water or lost boats were awaiting the Sheriff's arrival, and their mood was dangerous. Though he didn't dare say so, Walter wanted me out of his house.

*

In an endless day lost to engine repair, I stalked all over Chokoloskee, worried because Tippins might arrive before I could get away. Maintaining my innocence to anyone who would listen, I refused to hide, but the shotgun on my arm was a warning to my neighbors against any attempt to arrest me. I could walk that island for an hour and glimpse no one, for people stayed out of my way, but I felt their eyes observing me everywhere I went. That night, desperate for rest, I dared not sleep unless Kate watched and listened from the window.

I was somber and short-tempered, melancholy with the ache of life and a deep weariness. When I let my breath all the way out, I had trouble drawing it back in. I forgot what I was doing from one minute to the next, I mislaid things, dropped things, I was strangely clumsy.

Walter Alderman, who had taken so much pride in "E.J.'s" friendship, was morose and scared at the same time. I disliked lodging where we were unwelcome, but Will Wiggins had moved recently to Fort Myers, the McKinneys claimed their house was full, and the Smallwood store—the family inhabited the second story—was storm-damaged, with boards torn away on the ground floor and no escape from the sweet reek of a half hundred drowned chickens, caught by the storm in a wire pen under the house.

While Mrs. Smallwood rummaged through the heaps of piled-up goods for some double-ought loads for my gun, I slipped my boots off and stretched out on their old sofa. Ted promised to warn me if anybody came. Within moments, I was dead asleep, and was still unconscious when Old Man D. D. House barged through the door, shouting for Mamie. I sat up quick, grabbing my revolver, but D.D. had seen me and turned right around. "Well, Watson, you've come back." He did not approach to shake my hand but kept on going. Ted Smallwood said, "Darned if I know how that old feller got past me!" I decided that Ted could not be trusted either.

Sure enough, D. D. House returned with others—Charley Johnson, Isaac Yeomans, a young Demere. By this time I had my boots back on, and my shotgun handy where his little posse could see it. Old Man Dan told me I must wait right here, give some testimony to the Sheriff. And I said, Nosir, Mr. House—and I laid my hand over the trigger guard—I gave my testimony to the Sheriff at Marco. What I must do is proceed to Chatham Bend and tend to that bloody-handed Cox before he makes good his escape and evades justice.

Those men stepped outside to consult. D. D. House came back, saying, Well, we'll send men with you. And I said, Nosir, you will not. As I explained yesterday to Sheriff Tippins, Leslie Cox is a fair shot and will shoot to kill any man who tries to stop him, because he is a desperate criminal with nothing left to lose who will not hesitate to take a human life. If I go alone, he will suspect nothing. I can get the drop on him and bring him in. If he is uncooperative, I said, I'll bring his head in.

"His head?" Isaac Yeomans looked astounded. "You aim to bring him in dead or alive, that what you mean?"

"Might be a little more dead than alive."

"There is nothing to grin at, Mr. Watson," snapped Old Man House. He went stomping out.

Though they were unhappy about letting me go, they would have been unhappier had they tried to detain me. Mr. House would have told them about the revolver and they had seen the shotgun for themselves. They went outside to consult again, and probably concluded that once I was gone, they had seen the last of E. J. Watson. *Why hell, boys, unless that feller is crazy, he won't never dare come back here to the Bay, whether he kills that fuckin Cox or not.*

Meanwhile, Mamie brought me a few loads, explaining that they were storm-swept, pretty waterlogged. "I wouldn't count on 'em," Ted warned, "not for taking care of a skunk like that." I broke my gun to try them out.

The shells were too swollen to slide into the chambers, but I took a few anyway, saying the wind might dry them out on the way south.

The Smallwoods were alarmed to see that my shotgun had been empty all the while I talked those men out of detaining me. It was still empty, since I couldn't load these shells. But knowing I carried a revolver, they decided they would honor our old friendship. Oh yes, they glanced at each other— the revolver might be unloaded, too—but they never reported that empty shotgun to Mamie's daddy and the neighbors, who were still shifting and muttering out on the porch. Somebody hollered in an angry voice, "You know the *real* reason he don't want company? He don't want to leave no live witnesses, that's all!"

I rose to go. Ted harrumphed loudly toward the men outside, "Ed, if you don't come back with Cox, you better not come back at all." Then he winked at me and whispered behind his hand, "That ain't a threat, E.J., don't get me wrong."

His wife said for old times' sake, "You're such a nice man, Mr. Watson. How come you always get yourself in so much trouble?" This was a question she had asked me seriously some years before. And I responded as I had that day, in gruff slow voice, with a deep frown, "Ma'am, I don't go hunting trouble. But if trouble comes hunting me, why, I take care of it." Smiling and a little wistful, she recited that last part right along with me.

The Smallwoods did not come outside to see me on my way, which was unlike them. They no longer wished to seem so close to E. J. Watson. "Be careful, E.J.," my old friend said somberly, shaking my hand for what he thought was the last time. From the door, they watched me walk down to the boat landing, shotgun across my shoulder, lifting a hand in a parting wave to all my neighbors.

*

The channels between storm-battered islands were choked with twisted leafy limbs forced underwater, like the old-time fish traps of the Indians. An egret huddled in the mangrove roots with dragging wing, a drowned deer was upside down high in the branches. And still the Glades flowed in gray-brown raining rivers, washing westward through the mourning mangrove walls. I went west to the open water of the Gulf, then south toward Chatham River.

The forest along the coast was yellowed, the gray sea thick and dead. In these great storms, the roiling earth fought to rid itself of its old skin, its itch and mange. Now it lay inert, tongue-out exhausted, like a creature run to earth, flank shivering, ear weakly flicking at the passing sounds.

In Chatham River, banks had sagged away into a flood silted so thick that a man could come out here and hoe that water. At the Bend, my dock was gone, all but one leaned piling, and the boat shed leaned precarious over the current. Despite the loud *pop-pop* of the motor, no one appeared out of the house. My shout was met with silence. And yet . . . a waiting in the air. I scanned the banks for some strange tone or color, something out of place, like that dark mass, half hidden by the Deepwood vines.

On the far bank, three copper figures rose out of the reeds. Dressed in the old-time banded skirts and blouses and plumed turbans, they carried a long flintlock rifle and two muskets. The formal dress and ancient weapons— there was ceremony here, but what it signified I could not know. Slowly one man raised an arm and pointed at the house.

I eased the boat in, cut the motor, coasted up-current to the dock. Cox would be wary, and I might be covered. Leaving the shotgun in the boat, I stepped up on the bank, spread my hands wide, shouted his name.

Wind-tattered shingles, broken windows—the Watson Place on its small concrete posts looked old and gaunt. The lower walls, the steps and porch, even the Frenchman's poincianas, were caked with a brown marl cement of leaves and sedge washed down out of the Glades during the hurricane. The pall of dead matter coated the place in a heavy odor of earth rot and reek of carrion. Rattlesnakes stranded by high water had gathered in slow piles on the cistern concrete. Sliding and scraping in their heaps, the pit vipers kept watch through vertical gold slits. The horn tails whirred when I passed by, split tongues running in and out in their quick listenings.

I felt the yearning of his weapon, the black hole of the muzzle turning slowly as a snake's head turns to meet the oncoming intruder. One boot on the porch step, I stopped.

"Ho! Les! You in there, boy?"

Unable to swim, lacking a boat, Cox would be crazy to shoot the one person who might help him—that's what I told myself. He was a prisoner, waiting for the outside world to come and get him. He could not know that Reese had talked, far less that those three gas-blown bodies had dragged their weights back to the surface and been found. He would assume Watson had come to rescue him, help him escape from the Ten Thousand Islands.

Through the porch window came the light click of a spun chamber which he meant me to hear.

"Les?" I crossed the porch and rapped gently on the screen door.

For a long time the house held its breath. The lone small sound was the dry repetitions of an insistent birdsong from behind the house, the sound of the world turning, on and on. I could feel him, a few yards away, and my heart lurched with the sudden fear that after endless nights and days alone in this place of blood and death, he might be insane. The man on the far side of this door, pursued down lonely nights and days by shrieks and images of crimson slaughter, made more terrible by solitude in storm and flood, might have howled and shivered and cracked and come apart in fear of final judgment, and in madness shoot whoever came.

The voice was odd and guttural from long disuse. "Come slow," he said. "My nerves ain't so good." Entering quietly, I closed the screen door—uselessly, since the storm had warped and blown it full of holes. The house was filled with a bad iron smell, unfamiliar and also unmistakable.

*

Dutchy's big six-guns lay on the pine table pointed at the door. Between them sat my brown clay jug. Cox had sniffed out my last cache of moonshine.

Leaned back into the chair, he watched me set my black hat carefully on a peg. "Unc," he said. "Unc never come for me."

"I came back before the storm. I hailed the house."

"Never come back for me," he muttered, as if complaining to a third person in the room. There was no food left, he complained; he had not eaten in days. He looked crazed and jumpy and aggrieved. He picked up one gun. "Left me in hell." His eyes were darting. His demons were still here. "Alone in hell."

Alone because you killed everyone else, you goddamned maniac.

Leslie had been alone in hell for years, not knowing how to exist any other way. I pitied him a little but not much. Still gagging on the reek of blood, I took my jug and poured a drink into a dirty glass. "I figured some fisherman must have come by, took you people off." He would not meet my eye. "Where is everybody, Les?"

Cox looked down into his lap and shook his head, over and over. "All alone in hell," he muttered. "Days and days and days. All them long nights. You never come."

He had tried to escape overland, plunging hopelessly across the bitter salt country behind the mangrove—that's where he had been when I came the week before. He arrived nowhere. Soon his hope and water were exhausted, and he made his way back by retracing his own steps in the greasy marl. Relating this defeat, he nearly wept.

I banged my fist down on the table, making him sit up. "Where's Green and Hannah? Where's Sip? Where the hell's Frank Reese?"

Cox sat wide-eyed, still, like a rabbit listening. Then he said craftily, "How come you ain't askin after Dutchy?"

"You killed them, right?"

"You ain't got no call to go talkin to me in that hard voice, Unc." He was calm again, almost sleepy, reaching for the jug.

In a while, he said softly, "Them damn people got het up over Dutchy, is all it was. They got ugly with me, that's what it was." He looked up. "They knew you was behind it, Unc. It's better this way." He shrugged. "Them fools got on my nerves, is all. We was drinkin some, and next thing you know . . ." He shrugged again. "Good riddance, right? I mean, owin them all their pay."

Oh Jesus, Will. Your boy has finished me.

"No sense gettin hard with me for doin what you wanted done back in the first place." He drank and sighed. "You never took on this way about them niggers, Unc, back in September. Let the foreman take care of it, same way the railroads done, like you was tellin me one night when we was drinkin. I figured I might's well go ahead, clean up the mess for you—"

"Hannah was a friend of mine, goddamnit!"

"Should of told me that before, I reckon." Cox set down the six-gun. "Unc, I sure do hope you ain't goin to go blamin all your troubles on a young country feller as was only tryin to help out."

I sat silent, doing my best to think of nothing. Cox ranted on. He was glazed from days of drinking, muttering loosely in his need for speech. Monotonously, endlessly, he spun the heavy barrel chamber of the six-gun.

"One time up there to Silver Springs before I run off from the road gang, the road boss caught me lookin at the woods. Very hard man. Says, 'Don't you go runnin on me, boy. See this shootin iron I got here? Six rounds. And one of 'em has got your name on it.' While he's talkin, this man is pickin cartridges out of his revolver, one after the other, holdin each one up to the light before he drops it back into the chamber. 'Got it right here somewhere. Not this un—nope! Not this un—nope! This here's the one. Yep. Got your name writ right *on* there. C-O-X.'"

Cox gave his mirthless laugh. "C-O-X!" he yelled, to make sure I understood. "C-O-X spells *Cox*!"

I nodded, picking at my ear. "C-O-X. Spells Cox, all right."

"You funnin with me, Unc?" Cox hoisted the six-gun and pointed it between my eyes. "I'd surely hate to have to haul back on this trigger."

Gently I used my fingertips to reach and push that black muzzle hole aside. He would not fire unless startled, and anyway, I did not seem to care. Something had let go inside like a worn sinew. He saw that in my eyes and became afraid.

*

Cox was pursued by the slaughtered and their ghosts. One moment he whimpered like a child, blaming all that had befallen him on my bad influence. Next, he jibbered with relief that I had come. Though still articulate, he was staring drunk, in the way of a man who has drunk for many days, to the point where more alcohol slides off the brain like water off a turtle.

The first thing that went wrong, he said, was that damn Injun. The squaw girl hung herself from a crossbeam in the boat shed before Dutchy returned from Chokoloskee. Hearing the *Brave*'s motor, he went over to the shed, figuring that's where Dutchy had to head for, and there she was. Scared hell out of him, he said, because looming out of the shadows with her eyes bugged out, she looked almost alive, watching him come. Big deer eyes in a purple face—he shuddered and drank, coughing and muttering. There was no time to deal with her before getting set for Dutchy, which he had to do while she hung right there behind him—*It was like she watched me do it! Lookin right over my shoulder!* But afterwards, when he told Frank to cut her down, the body was gone.

He'd seen Injuns across the river. Maybe them Injuns come and took her. He was brooding. Maybe he'd been a little rough, but Hannah blamed him for the suicide. That was ridiculous. That was another reason he took care of that old manatee. What that squaw did with her own life was her own business.

"Her people are still over yonder." I yanked my thumb in the direction of the farther bank. "Looks like they have some business with you, Les."

"Why don't they do somethin, then? What do they want with me?"

"Injuns have nothing but time, boy." I poured more lightning. "How come you never shot Frank Reese?"

"You seen Frank?" Red-eyed, bristling, with sharp brown-coated teeth, Cox had a sideways look like a trapped coon. However, he lost interest when I didn't answer. "Know what I was thinkin, Unc, all them bad nights alone?"

"You thought, Now what is a nice country boy from a nice farm family inland doing way out here to hell and gone on a jungle river on some godforsaken coast in a damn hurricane?"

"Somethin like that," he acknowledged. "When you never come, I got to thinkin, Maybe ol' Unc never *wanted* me to kill that fuckin Dutchy. Maybe it was the other way around. Maybe he let on to that greaser where I might be at, maybe that little bastard was runnin over to the shed to murder me, the way you wanted." He was pointing the gun at me again, squinting one eye. I couldn't trust his trigger finger when he was this drunk, so his game made me mad. I told him not to point that thing unless he meant to use it. He gave his alligator grunt but laid it down.

"Why Green and Hannah? Harmless old alky drifter? And a woman?"

Cox said those two were troublemakers, better off dead. "Hell, I seen that when I first come here. Insulted me, that's what they done." Leslie shook his head, cruelly disillusioned. "Didn't trust my word, that's what it was. When they run out askin what the shootin was about, I told how Dutchy tried to jump me by the shed, and they seen he had his gun right in his hand. Might of doubted me some, but they went along with it. We went back inside, needin a drink. Then Frank Reese come in from the kitchen. Frank liked Dutchy for some damn nigger reason. Told Waller and the woman that he run outside when he heard the boat and he seen everything. Said I bushwhacked Dutchy. Then he said, real kind of bitter, that I had only done what the boss wanted. Told 'em you was layin for Dutchy for a long, long time but was too smart to go up against him by yourself. Then Old Man Green tells Reese to shut his mouth and mind his nigger business and don't go speakin bad no more about Mr. Watson."

Cox nodded and nodded. "Yep. You went and used the farm boy for your dirty work."

"That's how I do my dirty work, all right. My farm boy does the killing for me while I'm out relaxing on my yacht or something. Only you did a poor job, because I learned about it."

For no good reason, Leslie laughed, a sharp short squawk of near hysteria, shaking his head over ol' Unc's mirthful ways. But those words were not meant to make him laugh, they were only my own bitter musings. I was sickened by what had happened here, sickened by the thick dark smears tacky as pine sap on the floor and stair, sickened by all the fear and pain and lying.

"So them old warts was drinkin and they got excited. Got to hollerin that what I done weren't no such a thing as self-defense, it was cold-hearted murder. Old Man Green says, 'If Dutchy aimed to kill you, boy, he would of done it long ago. That feller could of blown the head off a dumb hick like you any time he wanted.' And Hannah laid the squaw girl on me, waggled her damn finger in my face. Says, 'You damn idjit! Weren't no call to go rapin her the way you done! And how about them four nigras you shot, back in September? You tryin to tell us Mr. Watson was behind that, too?' See what I mean, Unc? She was insultin me!"

"So you murdered her."

"I done Green first. We had words over what I said to Hannah."

"Words," I said.

"Unc, they was callin me a liar. My daddy always told me, Boy, don't you never let no man call you a liar."

"So you had no choice about those killings. Point of honor."

"Yessir! Point of honor!" He picked up Dutchy's six-gun and spun the chamber, which was loaded. "Green had that old pistol of his on his lap under the table, only I seen it before I set down. Then we had them words. Green surprised me, the rough way he talked. Dead scared, y'know, but tryin to show his woman that he weren't.

"I had one of these Colts stuck in my belt, under my shirt. Seein he would not shut up, I let him have it under the table, burned his belly out right where he sat. I can still recollect how the table salt jumped with the *boom*. Or maybe Green give the table leg a kick, that's what I been thinkin. I seen his mean old mouth fly open, heard his shootin iron hit the floor.

"When Green slid down off of his chair, Big Hannah run into the kitchen. When I run after her, she was ready with her two-blader ax, damn near took my head off. She had it hid behind the kitchen door. Then she run huffin up the stairs, probably huntin a weapon on the second floor, but I caught up with her before she reached the landin."

Leslie looked grim and tragic now, staring past my ear at his bleak future. "How come you never cleaned up all that blood?" I sighed, looking out the window.

"Didn't have no heart for it," he murmured. We sat silent awhile. "Looks like I ain't never goin home," he mourned. "Never goin to play ball again. I can hit good, too, you ask anybody, Unc. It ain't only my fastball I am knowed for."

"No, indeed."

"I want to go home," he moaned more loudly. "I got to see my pa."

*

Gradually the hours passed as I waited my chance to disarm him. Leslie brooded and drank more, mouth puffed in petulance. "Them damn people was right," he muttered suddenly, picking up the gun. "You put me up to it, makin me worry how this Dutchy might go killin me unless I got him first."

I thought about Eddie Reed in Oklahoma. I thought about Rob, who ran away for good—*Oh Papa, NO!*

"You had a taste for it. I never did." I had to finish this. "What happened to Sip Linsey and the field hands?"

"Sip? He run off. A fishing boat come by. Anyways, that ain't your business, that's the foreman's business. Cuttin down on overhead."

"Oh Christ," I said.

When I asked again about the field hands, Leslie slumped back in his chair, saying he would not answer that question. When I stood up, he sprang back from the table. I reached across and pulled the guns out of his reach.

Cox watched me do this, in some dim awareness of what must be coming down on him. He was retreating into helplessness, relieved to put his fate into his uncle's hands. Seconds passed before he sat up straight. Trying to conceal his instinct, he let his gaze wander past the guns.

"If you're so fuckin smart," he whispered, "how come you never even noticed what your pretty wife was doin behind your back?" For such a dullard, Cox had always been a mean liar and a troublemaker, and his tone was vicious. Unable to read my closed expression, he risked a leer, as if there were plenty more to tell about Kate Watson should he decide to.

My wife and I had scarcely touched in months. We had been apart most of this year. I was not the man I was—good enough for Josie, yes, but Josie scarcely needed help in rushing where she wanted. However, I trusted Kate and I knew that Cox was lying, and knew why. His game was much more intricate than common meanness. Like a child in tantrum, behaving worse and worse, he was fearful of losing my interest and attention, for that meant I might go away, leaving him alone again on Chatham Bend, a prospect which terrified him even more than capture.

Cox was waiting for his insinuation to work its rot. But this time I said nothing and showed no expression. I turned that rage to a task as dead and cold as that black mud around the mangrove roots.

"Just a joke, Unc," he whispered.

"You don't know how to joke." I watched him for a while, biding my time. "Frank Reese went to Pavilion Key and told what happened. Those bodies were found, Les. You are going to hang."

"Frank *helped,* goddamnit!"

"At gunpoint. That's what he told them at Pavilion Key, and that's what they believe. I believe that, too. He had no motive. Probably they'll lynch him anyway. That make you feel better?" I picked up one of the guns. "They want blood, Les." I felt spent, in a weak lassitude, like a man dying in a bath with the last heat in the water running out. "They aren't going to settle for Frank Reese."

"They aim to hang Les Cox? That what you're tellin me?" Cox was incredulous. "Supposin I told 'em you was the one behind it?"

"Doesn't matter. Cox, Watson, or both." I pointed the gun at Cox to see how he liked it. He shied back, almost toppling his chair, then shut his eyes and waved his hands to wish that hole away. I said, "Now you just tell me why Reese was so angry. Why he told 'em what he did at Pavilion Key. Did you tell Frank I ordered you to kill the help?"

"No! When we was weightin Hannah's body, Reese ast me, 'Was it Mist' Jack told you, Go kill them four niggers?' I reckon he was friendly with them field hands. So naturally I got hot with him. '*What* niggers?' I said. But he waited me out, the way he does. And when I told him, 'Boy, you better mind your fuckin business,' he likely come to his own nigger conclusions.

"Later he got to mutterin how Mist' Jack Watson explained to him way back in Arkansas that ever'thin in this ol' life come down to property. Said that's how come niggers don't count, cause they never had none. Then he said that since them four, he couldn't never trust you.

"I told that nigger he better just shut up. All the same, I reckoned he was right—now don't go lookin at me that way, Unc!" Cox yelled. "Don't point that thing! All I'm sayin is what he said. And I told him, 'Nigger, I sure hope you ain't lookin to get paid, not after my uncle hears how you been runnin off your mouth!' " Cox stared at me eagerly. "Ain't that right, Unc? Ain't that what you would of wanted me to say? Anyways, I was plannin to let him have it soon's we got done with them bodies, only he run off on me."

"You have finished me, boy," I whispered after a while, looking around the empty house. "You are my ruination."

"You fixin to turn me in? After all I done for you?"

"Dead or alive," I warned him.

Leslie shook his head. "I ain't *never* goin back, not on no chain gang." But he declaimed this without energy, eyes averted. After so many days of terror and hallucination, what fight was left in Leslie Cox had guttered right down to a stub. "I told the Judge first day in court," he muttered. "Told him straight out that William Leslie Cox were not the kind that could tolerate no chain gang. Told him—!"

I rose abruptly, kicking the chair back. "Let's go, Les."

Carefully he laid both hands flat on the table, crouching a little, backing a little, inch by slow inch, like a bobcat not yet sure it has been seen.

"You ain't listened. You will have to shoot your baby niece's darlin. Cause you sure ain't takin me to Chokoloskee."

I offered to take him up the rivers to the Glades, from where he could trek across the peninsula to the east coast, maybe get a job on the new rail-road. I explained what that meant—the razor-edged sawgrass and jagged limestone sinks, the heat and rain and greasy dragging muck, the no-see-ums and mosquitos, the deep sloughs where the silent gators sank away be-neath the surface, the thorny hammocks ringed with moats crawling with deadly moccasins. But until he was far out there, lost, beyond all hope, with retreat impossible and without destination, maybe his ignorance would spare him the worst part of his fate—

His hands were waving.

"All right, then, stay here. I'll let those Injuns have you."

Leslie's tears brought a shine to his eyes but the tears were not soft, they were more like the hard brine around two clams. Sure enough, when I waved him ahead of me, he lunged for the gun as he went past, so weak and dizzy from his days of drink that he fell down. "Gimme my gun!" he screeched. Then he rose and reeled toward the door and pitched and banged his way onto the porch and down the path toward the dock, so eager to es-cape that he scarcely looked where he was going. Then he stopped short. Though he spoke over his shoulder without turning, I could feel the smile.

"It's me they want the most, ain't that right, Unc? Les Cox? Outlaw number one?"

"You're number one, all right."

He turned and looked into my face, and his smile disappeared. "You promise to witness for me in court like I done for you?"

"I wasn't here, Les."

There was no way to hogtie him. If I took him north untied, he would try to jump me or escape along the way, and if I got him there, he would do his best to implicate me. What made most sense was to shoot him as he stepped into the boat, deliver the body.

Leslie's legs gave out. He sank to his knees at the foot of the dock. "Please, Unc," he begged.

My plan changed every moment. I had to decide whether to shoot him or hand him over to the Indians across the river or take him eastward up the creeks and abandon him in the Glades. More than any man I ever knew, this cruel, handsome boy deserved to die. Yet seeing him kneeling on the planks, shrunk up in fear like a hurt insect, my finger felt lifeless on the trigger.

Who would condemn me? Nobody except Will Cox and Cornelia. I was here as the chosen executioner. My own life was my fee. It was Cox or Watson. In one second it would all be over, a public service, with no risk and no reckoning. Like Quinn Bass, this man could be executed "on the house," for free.

That's what was wrong with it. I'd seen too much blood. It was not true that after the first one, taking life was easy. Since Mike Tolen's death, I could scarcely dress a deer or skin a gator without waves of nausea, I was sickened by the welling blood and the cold cave smell of raw meat. I had gone soft just when my last hope of life demanded that I be hard in every way.

For taking a life, one paid with one's own soul. I learned that long ago. To behold the light in another's eyes before extinguishing that light was self-destruction, because those eyes looking back at you became your own. I had left that fate to those who hadn't learned this—men like Eddie Reed, who could walk out in the echo of his shot and use his boot toe to turn his mother's body in the muddy road, and shoot her again and damn her soul to hell as the last dim glimmer faded from her mud-flecked eyes. *Damn ol' cunt. I hope you're satisfied*—that's what her boy told Maybelle Starr as her back arched in spasm and her jaws drew wide, baring her teeth.

Cold Eddie Reed had been hell-bent on taking his mother's life, with or without support from Edgar Watson. I myself was told by the postmaster at Whitefield that the day Belle horsewhipped him, her son promised he would kill her, and having a frontier reputation to keep up, he naturally felt honor bound to keep his word.

Well? Was that entirely true? Was I implying that Jack Watson had no part in it?

It was time to face the truth about Jack Watson. E. J. Watson was Jack Watson or had become Jack Watson long ago, and probably the two were never different. There was no Jack Watson anymore because Jack and E. Jack and E.J. and Edgar had grown into one. Jack Watson the Killer was Ed Watson.

*

Leslie was praying—whether truly or falsely God Himself might not be sure, since Leslie had never known the difference. My thought was incoherent. I knew nothing either. Moments passed. Seconds . . . a minute? The river licking, that dry birdsong in the thicket . . .

I never knew which choice was best because at that moment, Cox sprang from the dock toward the bank. I forced my nerve hard as for a jump into cold water, and even then, in what should have been a point-blank shot with that big six-gun, I faltered and my hand jumped with the explosion.

Cox's hat spun off into the shallows. He jerked as he twisted in the air, and his back thumped heavily on the steep bank. He bucked hard like a steer as if still trying to get away, his scuffed boots kicking in a heavy thrash that shifted his weight and rolled him over into the edges of the current.

He was not shot clean. He might be scalp-creased, more or less unhurt, and he might be drowning. All right, I thought, if that's how it is to be. Then I remembered it was not all right, I needed him. I leapt into the shallows, grabbing at his galluses, but the river had already taken hold. The galluses pulled off one shoulder, then tore away entirely. An arm broke the surface, then the head, mouth vomiting the swallowed water. The shocked wide eyes stared straight at mine before the surface closed over his head and he descended into deeper currents.

The one chance was to dive downstream of that place and grope for him and wrestle him ashore. I tossed the gun down, shucked my boots. My heart pounded. I was a poor swimmer, and I got no farther than knee-deep in the silted flood. I feared the touch of him, and the flailing strength of a man crazed by drowning, and deep down in my gut dreaded that huge crocodile, turning silently toward the thrash and the commotion.

*

Cox's hat was a little way down the bank, caught in the mangrove roots. In other days, this stained wet thing had been Will Cox's Sunday hat. It was pierced below the crown by a black-ringed bullet hole through the paler felt that was formerly encircled by a hatband. Well, Will, I am sorry. Eyes misted by queer emotions, I lifted his hat in both hands, in need of ceremony.

I squatted by the water, hunched into myself, arms wrapped tight around my legs. In humid light, the alluvial mud had caked on my pale feet—queer blunt appendages, yellow-clawed, so transformed from the tanned clear feet of boyhood. Under the blind windows of the house, blown out by storm, I crouched beside the water, old and timid. I dreaded my own house. With its muddied floors and walls and mildewed mattresses, old food odors, the reek of cigar ash and spilled moonshine, the smell of rotten blood, my house was no longer my house but only its own grim presence by the river.

Now something had shifted, making me restless. Though I saw no dugout, the three Indians had crossed to this north bank and were watching me from the wooded point upriver. One lifted his hand in a slow signal, then all three disappeared behind the branches. In a little while, the dugout crossed the river shine, bound eastward and inland.

*

The north wind bore the smell. I found the shovel. Out in the salt scrub northwest of the cane fields, those swollen bodies lay in a loose row, each shot in the back of the head or brained by a hammer. So careless in his power was my foreman that the cutters had stood there and submitted in a group—so desperate for his indifferent mercy that they were no longer men at all. Doubtless those poor devils would have touched their hats and jumped to dig their graves if he had thought their burial worthwhile.

Bandanna bandit-style over nose and mouth, I set to work in the thick heat, never resting. I had them in a shallow pit by afternoon. I mumbled *Amen* and stumbled off, drained by the heat. That afternoon I slept. In the evening, under a sentinel star as solitary as a spark flown off the point of the crescent moon, I wandered my torn, matted cane fields, overcome by a surge of feeling for poor Son Born. That lost boy twisted me. When I thought about his mother, still a young girl when she died, I was sick with yearning to be cleansed of life and born anew.

Days after the hurricane, Chatham River remained turgid under the steep, rainless heavens, in a pewter light. Where autumn gusts raked the broad waters, the dark tips of tree branches, revolving slowly in the current, parted the surface, disappeared again.

One day, watching the river circles, Lucius said, The earth is forever turning and returning.

From dawn till dark, I hunted up and down the tides, scanning the storm wrack for the shape of a drowned body. For three long nights, I sat in darkness, hearing the unknown cries from behind the black walls of the forest.

On that last day on Chatham Bend, under dark rain skies of this ominous dry weather, I shot a doe drawn in from the salt prairie by the cistern water. Thinking I must eat, I removed the gall, dressed out the carcass. Its fresh flesh smell seeped into my sinuses, and after that, I could not escape the taint of it, the thought of venison made me gag. The deer's life had been wasted. What would Lucius say to that? And where was he tonight, when his father needed him? I consigned her to the river. She did a slow turn in the current, and one neat hoof described a spiraled wake before she was drawn under.

*

From Key West, large ships sailed every day. The new railroad was no farther than Long Key. In the end, I put aside thoughts of escape and committed myself to a return to Chokoloskee.

Today was October twenty-fourth, Kate's birthday. I had promised her I would be with her and I had promised my Island friends I would return. These reasons seemed more urgent now than flight. Facing those men, I would declare that Cox was dead, offering his weapons and the hat as evidence. How could they doubt a wanted man who had returned because he said he would, returned of his own free will when he could have fled? Only a lunatic or one armed with the truth would put himself at their mercy under such circumstances.

In that last noon, I torched my fields, running like an escaped madman down the wind. The cane took fire quickly with a low thunderous booming, creating a column of thick oily smoke and the sweet odor of burnt caramel and leaving behind bare blackened stalks ready for harvest. This week or next, Lucius could bring a crew here to take care of it, unless he had turned his back now, like the others.

In the late afternoon—another Monday—I went away downriver. In my cane fields, flames rekindled by the wind still leapt and darted. In this somber weather, in the light of fire, I forsook my white house in the wilderness and the clear voices of the generous spirits who had lived here with me, all those lives damaged by my headlong passage on this earth, all changed and not one for the better. In the smoke shadow, the spirits danced and swooped and shrieked and vanished skyward and were gone as the house withdrew into the forest. Then the Bend was gone, and the Watson Place, the past and future. Ahead was the endless falling of the river to the sea, and the lonesome mangrove clumps of the salt estuary, and the horizon where dark high clouds of drought surveyed the battered coast and empty Gulf.

*

On the open water off Pavilion Key, I drifted for a time in the gray sea mist, listening for some last sign. Only faint fish slap and soft blow of porpoise. I could sell the *Brave* at Long Key for good money, board a train bound north and west, find a new frontier. "Hell, *yes!*" I yelled. What I had been setting out to do was crazy! I turned her helm back toward the south, full speed ahead.

Nothing felt right. I had to shout to keep my spirits up. For an interminable hour, the *Brave* plowed that leaden sea, stretching my heart like some rusty hard-coiled spring. Soon the pale strand of Lost Man's Beach rose from the mist. Off Lost Man's Key, I howled one last time over the racketing of the boat engine and wheeled the helm and headed north again, in the direction of Kate Edna and my children, certain now that however far I fled, there was no destination. "Might not be purty but it's true," Tant used to say. The common truth.

In the pearl mist, I took great drafts of cool October air, clearing my head. Off Wood Key, I longed to pay a final visit to the Harden clan, who would do their utmost to persuade me that I must never return to Chokoloskee. But when I slowed, a heavy fuel exhaust swept forward on the following wind, and sensible reflection was obliterated by hard bangs and clatter and metallic ringings, and the faltering *pop-pop* of the single cylinder, sharp as rifle fire. I speeded up, drove the boat onward, yelling at the hellish din, yelling for the sake of yelling, howling my wits out to clear space for my careening brain. To arrive half-mad with doubt at Chokoloskee would be fatal.

I roared at the winds all the way north along that coast—howlings which for all I knew arose from some more ancient woe, back in Clouds Creek. When the fit passed, blood pounded at my temples, I was cold-soaked in evil-smelling sweat. This time I stopped and splashed my face, trying to think through what awaited me, step by slow step.

Probably the Chokoloskee men did not expect me. However, they would hear the boat, they would be ready. Unless they shot me down at once when I came into range—and if one fired, all would—they would try to take me into custody, having failed the first time. I had weapons and I had Cox's weapons. Even so, a man alone could not shoot it out with twelve or twenty neighbors.

I might try to bully my way free. I would not kill for it. Would a bold bluff work? I had talked them down before. These men were truck farmers and fishermen, they would not challenge a well-armed desperado who did not care whether he lived or died. And even if he was overpowered and captured, would they lynch him in front of his young wife and children? Against the wishes of the Smallwoods and McKinneys? After he'd proved that Cox was dead?

Stuffed in my pocket was Will's old hat with the bullet hole burned through the crown. I also had Will's long-barreled .22 revolver, also the six-guns they had seen themselves at the time of Dutchy's visit to Chokoloskee. The only man who could have had these weapons was Leslie Cox, who would never have relinquished them of his own accord. Plainly I had executed my niece's husband and my old friend's son. I could not do more.

All this was true. Would the truth satisfy them? It would not. And the instinct that my word would be doubted, and the injustice of it, sent rage ricocheting to my temples, even though I knew that in a time of so much fear my evidence would not have satisfied me, either.

*

The *Brave* drew near the coast at Rabbit Key. The storm had stripped this barrier islet, leaving only a sand spit with one broken mangrove clump on the outer point. Where white terns dove on sprays of bait, I slowed the boat, skirting the breaking fish, trolling a pair of handlined spoons. Almost at once they were struck by a Spanish mackerel, then a large barracuda. I hauled the fish in hand over hand and knocked them off the hooks with a hard smack of the fish club, not on the crown (which makes a nice clean job) but on the gill covers, which would send blood flying as they slapped and skittered all over the stern.

Maybe they won't believe the truth but they will believe blood.

Charlie McKinney's fishing boat gave me a start, appearing in an open channel between islands. He might have seen me, busy with those fish. More and more uneasy, I loaded up the shotgun, peeling Smallwood's swollen shells from brass to tip and jamming them into both chambers, just in case. I checked the cartridges in the revolver, returned it to my coat pocket, then laid the loaded six-guns under a piece of tarp where they would be handy. If an arrest was attempted before I could get my family safe aboard, I could probably scatter the scared crowd, shoot my way out of there. No boat on the Bay could catch the *Brave*, and she carried two oil drums of spare fuel.

The silver fish stopped their wild slapping and lay still on the floorboards of the cockpit, gill covers lifting, falling. Slipping on fish slime and gurry, I went aft and dropped them overboard, then resumed my course eastward and inland down the Pass, which opened out on Chokoloskee Bay. The *Brave* wound through a wasteland of broken trees where the Great Hurricane had kicked itself into a spin. On both sides, giant mangroves, twisted by the storm, clawed at the sky.

The motor would be heard before she cleared the Pass. Men would be gathering at Smallwood's now. When I slowed the boat to steady my nerves and get my breath, the *Brave*'s wake, catching up, lifted her stern, and running wavelets slapped into the mangrove roots along the channel.

The late October night would soon be falling. In this somber twilight, with the sun setting unseen on the horizon off to westward, and the Glades stretching away behind the black walls to the east, all my days were gathering to bear witness. Nothing done or left undone would mend my life. There was no sanctuary.

The bow turned northward up the Bay toward Chokoloskee, which rose dead ahead like a black fortress. The light out of the west withdrew until the day was gone from the iron water. The engine gurgling at low speed along the oyster bars seemed much too loud. I strained to winnow out the slightest sound.

They would be waiting in the shadows of the trees at Smallwood's landing. As the boat moved closer to the island, the helmsman's outline would offer a bulky target that even farmers quaking with buck fever could not miss. The weapons in the shadows yonder might be pointed at my heart. I might see but never hear that burst of fire.

Rounding the last bar and taking a new bearing, the *Brave* slid remorselessly toward the shore. She was coming within rifle range, and my whole body longed to crouch down out of view. Instinct told me to stand straight and bold, but fear seeped in like a cold brine leaking through the seams of an old boat.

In the last light, the wind had backed around into the east. It carried the distant hooting of an owl out of the Glades, which bothered me for no damned earthly reason.

There it was, my darkling star, just off the point of the quarter moon. In the days past, I thought I had experienced the outermost and innermost and utmost loneliness, but I had not.

*

Smallwood's docks had been ripped out by the storm. The *Brave* would have to be beached next to the boat ways. It made more sense to idle her just off the shore while we negotiated, but that would appear nervous, therefore guilty. I slowed way down, to coast in light and easy, in case she had to be backed off in a hurry.

I saw the boats from Lost Man's now, here since the hurricane. Perhaps my neighbors were talking to the rest, calming them down. The darkened vegetation was one mass misshapen by the men.

I raised my arm in a slow wave, then took a deep breath and yanked the spark plug wire. That ringing silence when the engine died seemed even louder than the engine, crossing the water to the foreshore, breaking that mass into clusters, moving shapes. At the store, hurried figures crossed the yellow lamplight in the doorway. I stifled a frantic yell—*Don't shoot!*—scared that any sudden sound might break the spell and turn this hydra-headed thing into a lynch mob.

The *Brave* was within shotgun range, coasting toward shore. Casually I turned my back and, back still turned, picked up my shotgun and set it gently on the cabin roof, as if readying some gear to bring ashore. This caused a low moan, which suddenly increased when the boat struck the shelly bottom with a hard loud scrape, setting gnarled fingers twitching on the triggers.

Out in the channel, I had run a bow line aft so I could handle it from the helm. Slow and easy, I tossed its loops onto the shore for some boy to grab and hitch to a tree. I did that smiling to show that E. J. Watson had never doubted a warm welcome, and the stir and shift caused by that action was the distraction that I needed. I waved and called—"Happy Birthday, Kate!"—in the direction of the store, and at the same time took the shotgun, stepped up onto the bow, and jumped, my whole body braced for the explosion that must come right now or never. I struck firm ground and set my feet, gun cradled on my arm, facing the porch with a broad smile of sheer relief as the startled crowd milled back from the water edge. I felt dizzy, and for a moment, all went black. No one spoke at all as we got our breath.

"Evening, boys," I said, lifting my hat, still smiling hard, as if pleased to see such a fine company of friends out taking the night air. The worst was over. I was ashore. I was still alive.

Willie Brown's call came from way back by the store. "E.J.?" he screeched. "You hear me, Ed? Lay down that gun!"

That told me that this bunch had expected shooting. I grinned as if that fool Willie must be joking. With my free hand, casually, I picked up the bow line that no boy had run forward to take and threw a loose turn around a stump.

Old Man D. D. House was right up front, flanked by his older boys, Bill and Young Dan. Not counting Houses, there were no less than twelve men, and all of them had raised guns with fingers in the trigger guards. A few were even squinting at me over their barrels.

"Ed? Lay that gun down!"

"Looks like everybody's here"—I smiled—"except my own darn family."

"Where's Cox at?" snapped D. D. House.

"Shot and drowned, both. In Chatham River."

Bill House said, "You was supposed to bring him in, or bring his head."

The crowd backed up when I reached into my coat. It groaned when I drew forth Cox's hat and waggled my finger through the hole. "Got kind of ventilated," I said. A few men laughed, eager to ease the tension. I smelled moonshine. There were sheepish faces I was sad to see—Walter Alderman, for one, also Jim Howell, Andrew Wiggins. In the back my erstwhile admirer, young Speck Daniels, craned for a look.

Little Ad had escaped the women and was running toward me from the store as voices called him. Kate Edna was coming, too, with Mamie Smallwood. On the store porch Ted Smallwood stood, arms folded on his chest. Seeing me look his way, he stepped inside. The Lost Man's men were back there, too, and Willie Brown. None of these friends came forward to support me, only the two women. They stopped short when D. D. House raised up his hand.

"That hat ain't good enough," Old Man House growled. At those words, a bad silence fell, and a sudden shift of atmosphere, like the waft of cold air across open water that precedes a squall. Mamie turned Kate right around and tugged her back toward the store, calling to Addison, *Come quickly.* I longed to call out after them, *No, don't go! Wait!*

"Not good enough? I put a bullet through my nephew's head. Hell, look at my damn boat! Got blood all over it!"

Bill House came over and peered into the cockpit, Isaac Yeomans, too. Bill shrugged. "Mr. Watson? No offense, but maybe you better hand over your weapons. We'll go to the Bend first thing in the mornin, have a look."

"What in the hell do you think I've been doing for the last three days?" I bellowed, and again the line milled backwards.

Bill House said calmly, "We was wonderin. We thought you might of took off for the east coast." The men muttered, resentful that I had not done so.

Isaac Yeomans stuck his finger in the blood. He sniffed that finger. "Sure ain't three days old. Smells like fresh fish."

"You calling me a liar?"

"Nobody ain't callin you no liar," Bill House said. "All you got to do is put that gun down."

"We're takin you into custody," Old Man House said, stubborn.

"Dead or alive?"

"That's up to you."

A figure slipped forward from the line of trees. The better to see me, he waded out a little ways into the water, his rifle down along his leg on the far side. At first, in the fast-fading light, I could not make out the face under the hat, which was gazing down as if meditating on night water. Then he raised his eyes to mine and touched his finger to the brim of his straw hat, and dread stirred my gut.

"He has no damn business here," I growled.

Bill House growled back, "We told him to come."

"They'll lynch you, Henry, when they're done with you."

"He ain't none of your concern."

"GODDAMN FOOL! *WHO THE HELL ARE YOU TO TELL ME THAT?*"

Up and down the line, the weapons jumped. My head hurt, that's how fast that anger took me. I was tryng to think fast, knowing now that If I raised my gun, some would break and run but more would shoot. It was much too late to bluff them. I could take these House men to hell with me, but that would only make things harder for my family. Anyway, there was no sense in it.

I raised the hat again. "I told the truth. He's dead."

I looked past the House men, appealing to the crowd. I had not returned to Chokoloskee looking for trouble. I had come to notify them that Cox was dead. I had kept my promise. They knew it was Cox who killed those people, so they had no right to ask for a man's gun.

Also, I said today was my wife's birthday. I had made my wife a promise, too. But the more I talked, the more humiliated I felt, and the more enraged. "I am leaving the Islands for good. I came here for my family. You won't see me again." And I turned toward the store to call to Kate, *Come quickly.*

That old man said in his stiff voice, "Nosir, you ain't leavin."

"We're done talkin, Mr. Watson." Bill House hitched his gun. "Drop that weapon on the count of three or take the consequences."

"One," his daddy said.

The others shifted and backed up a little. I looked at Henry Short, holding his eye. "Finish it," I whispered, very tired now, and very calm.

"*Two,*" the old man said.

I took a deep breath, filling my chest, as a voice said, "You boys want Watson's gun? You will have to take it." And I swung it up in the face of D. D. House as if to fire.

*

finish it? that what he said?

      well, he sure is finished   shot to pieces   godamighty

    never got to three

       who shot first, then?

moon masks   mouths

eyes come   eyes go

                                        a star

    in starlight shadow

            how the world hurts

                                        a star